Man of the New Millennium

A Search for Us in an Age of Me

First published by O-Books, 2010
O Books is an imprint of John Hunt Publishing Ltd., The Bothy, Deershot Lodge, Park Lane, Ropley, Hants, SO24 0BE, UK
office1@o-books.net
www.o-books.net

Distribution in:

UK and Europe
Orca Book Services Ltd
tradeorders@orcabookservices.co.uk
directorders@orcabookservices.co.uk
Tel: 01235 465521 Fax: 01235 465555
Int. code (44)

USA and Canada
NBN
custserv@nbnbooks.com
Tel: 1 800 462 6420 Fax: 1 800 338 4550

Australia and New Zealand
Brumby Books
sales@brumbybooks.com.au
Tel: 61 3 9761 5535 Fax: 61 3 9761 7095

Far East (offices in Singapore, Thailand, Hong Kong, Taiwan)
Pansing Distribution Pte Ltd
kemal@pansing.com
Tel: 65 6319 9939 Fax: 65 6462 5761

South Africa
Stephan Phillips (pty) Ltd
Email: orders@stephanphillips.com
Tel: 27 21 4489839 Telefax: 27 21 4479879

Design: Stuart Davies

ISBN: 978 1 84694 339 3

A CIP catalogue record for this book is available from the British Library.

Printed by Digital Book Print

O Books operates a distinctive and ethical publishing philosophy in all areas of its business, from its global network of authors to production and worldwide distribution.

Man of the New Millennium

A Search for Us in an Age of Me

Gregory Dark

BOOKS

Winchester, UK
Washington, USA

Dedication

'Man of the New Millennium' is dedicated to **YOU**.
Without you there is no us;
And without us there is no hope.

Acknowledgements

Elsewhere in this book, one of the characters talks about the meaninglessness today of credits in films. Finally, she suggests, we cannot thank everyone who makes a movie possible. Well, likewise for a book.

There are those, for instance, *selling* books – like **Josephine Walsh** of The Wise Owl bookshop in Drogheda, and like **Sinéad McCory** of Waterstone's, whose kindness to a new writer was of a value I doubt they could imagine. Josephine and Sinéad, though, are only two names amongst the many thousands of people working in bookshops throughout the world. The vast majority of whom are the unknown soldiers in the battle for literacy. Their anonymity belies the importance of their work.

Before ever it gets to the shops, there is another not-so-small army working on this book: at 'O'-Books, for instance, and its subsidiaries; at the printers; those involved with marketing and distribution ... and so on. The identities of most of these colleagues will never be known to me either.

I should like them all to know, all these colleagues of mine, all of them indispensable, that my gratitude is no less intense for it being nameless. Indeed I see this inter-dependence as yet another example of how essential we all are to each other, and thus further evidence of the need we have to ditch the 'methos' of today and replace it with a 'wethos' which has to enhance our tomorrow.

Others who have helped me have asked to remain anonymous.

For all of these reasons, the following are (I recognise) only *some* of the people to whom public thanks are due.

Without the encouragement of **Dr Teresa Parrott** and **Miriam O'Gara** I doubt 'Man of the New Millennium' would ever have been finished; without the diligence of **Bruce Crowther** it would not only have been wordier, but many of the words that do remain would have been misspelt; and without the ongoing help of my brother, **Daniel**, the manuscript would probably have been lost when the computer (as it would have been) was hurled through the window!

My daughter, **Lyubov**, continues to help me in oh so many ways. All of them special because all of them hers. Nowadays so does her husband, **Keith**.

Were it not for **John Hunt** 'Man of the New Millennium' may well not have been published. I'm very glad I didn't have to find out! And were it not for **Nick Welch** it would have lacked a cover. If a mention here is being 'in the sun', the following of John's colleagues at 'O'-Books are also due their place in it: **Kate Rowlandson**, **Catherine Harris** and **Trevor Greenfield**.

Stuart Davies is 'O'-Books' Production Manager and **Maria Watson** works on its marketing. Both have supported me in a way their boss would probably have considered indulgent!

Finally, it is almost certainly because of **Anne Piper's** quite staggering commitment to my work that you are currently reading these words. The debt I owe her, however, is personal quite as much as it is professional. It is one which can never be discharged.

***

I suppose that my attitude towards the metaphysical is agnostic, best summed up by Hamlet's admonition to Horatio that there are more things in Heaven and Earth than are dreamed of in his philosophy – or indeed *most* philosophies. I know of those who believe in Earth Angels, for instance, and the like. I'm not one of them: not in that literal sense, anyway. But there have been people who have come into my life who have, for want of a better expression, served as *guardian* angels. These are two of them. I acknowledge them here because, I fear, I will have no other means to do so.

Martin, first of all. He is, I'm sure, dead by now. Martin wasn't quite a tramp: He'd bathe, for instance, once a fortnight or so – whether or not he needed to! He visited a pub I used in my drinking days. It was some distance from his 'home', wherever that was; but it was the nearest pub which hadn't banned him. Martin could be loud, cantankerous, foul-mouthed, intolerant. But he could also be incredibly kind and sensitive and funny. He was barely literate, but he was possessed of enormous wisdom. He couldn't *live* by that wisdom, but that did nothing to compromise its depth – nor even its practicality. Martin was a guru in my life, one of my teachers, one of those who helped me distinguish between thinking and thinking I was thinking. As an angel would, he entered my life suddenly one day; and on another, equally suddenly, he left it again. Except that, of course, he never did. There are many aspects in the character of Polly which are Martin's. I'm really not sure what Martin would think of me today. He was fairly scathing at the best of times. But if he lugs a Marley-like chain I do hope my ongoing fondness and respect for him lets loose a couple of links.

Was her name **Yvonne**? I was nine-years'-old. 1959 or so. Just outside London. On the 715 bus (I think – or was it the 718?) that used to take me from Kingston-upon-Thames to my school in Hammersmith. It was a long haul. And, had it not been for Yvonne, it would have been an intolerable one. It was a school rule that we had to offer our seats on busses were there adults standing – which inevitably there were. Yvonne used to let me sit on her lap. And she lent an ear to all my pre-pubescent angst with a patience that made Job look like a tobacco auctioneer. She was engaged to be married with, I think, a merchant seaman. She'd regale me with tales of his adventures; she allowed me to marvel over a shark's tooth he'd given her. She offered me unconditional love, in the purest of senses. Also in the purest of senses (well, mostly!) I loved her back. When a couple of years later we moved closer to my school, I lost touch with her. The move happened during a summer holiday, and I was never able to say good-bye. But, of course, the fact is (as with Martin) that I never have. I continue to remember her with the deepest of both affection and gratitude.

In a very real sense, in their dealings with me, both Yvonne and Martin exemplified the 'wethos' I seek to describe in the following pages.

We are creating a world where the actions of Yvonne and Martin would be viewed with suspicion. I sincerely hope we can start reversing that trend. By an enormous margin I have in my life been helped by strangers more than I have been hurt by them. I think my experience is normal. Eventually suspicion manacles us. A substantial jewel in the treasure-trove of 'us' is the freedom that 'we' gives us – one which 'I' never can.

Gregory Dark, Nérac, 2009

I want no revolution. I want ordered progress. I want
no disordered order. I want no chaos. I want real
order to be evolved out of this chaos which is
misrepresented to me as order. If it is order established
by the tyrant in order to get hold of the tyrannical
reins of Government, I say that it is no order for
me but it is disorder. I want to evolve justice out
of this injustice.

Mohandas Gandhi, 'The Hindu', 13th August 1920

And I sat there and thought: If the first tiny droplet of
truth has exploded like a psychological bomb, what
will happen in our country when whole waterfalls of
Truth burst forth?

And they will burst forth. It has to happen.

Aleksandr I. Solzhenitsyn, 'The Gulag Archipelago',
Chapter 7

Chapter 1

Giselle doesn't care that he's married.

There has just been a oneness between the two of them, almost a completeness – a completeness, though, that was less complete than it was one.

Still she squats on him, panting out a gentle smile. The freckles of sweat glisten in the candlelight like dew stippling the buds of autumn roses. And she can feel the oneness within her; and she feels one with the oneness.

And she can feel the oneness well within her; and she feels well and one with the welling oneness. She can feel the oneness embrace her from the inside out, laminate her from the inside out, caress and care for her from the inside out.

She remembers feeling this oneness before.

On her knees, usually shivering from the pre-dawn cold of the stone-flagged chapel. She remembers being on occasions infused with luminescence there, her insides an ingot of solid light, a tangible halo suffusing all the workings of her, basking her in wholeness and holiness and completeness and a sense of being that far transcended the carnal carapace which enclosed her in solid boundaries.

Her prayers had ceased to be separate from her at such times, they had become absorbed by her: the water which, because it has been drunk, is no longer water but part of the creature which has drunk it. And at such times she was praying not to a God Who was separate from her, but Who had both absorbed and been absorbed by her – the God Who was, at that moment, simultaneously drinker and drunk water and yet-to-be drunk water.

She can feel the unity within her spreading from an electron within some sub-atomic part of her to join the mini-universe which is that within the electron; she can feel that mini-universe uniting with the other mini-universes in her chest. And those then join the other universes of her body; and her brain; and those of *his* body, *his* brain;

the whole universe of universes encompassed by her bedroom, by her flat, by the street she lives in; by London as a whole, by England – finally to unite all the universes *of* the universe. Which itself could be but another electron in an even huger universe.

And with all of that she is one.

Always for her there has been something holy in sex. Always she has felt its holiness, its divinity. Never previously, not with sex, has she felt this oneness. And she wonders at this oneness, and she wonders with it.

When Rodolfo had turned up that evening, she hadn't been feeling romantic or sexy. But when he'd kissed her, her body had spumed into a million tingles of expectation and into a jeroboam of bubblied sensations. She had surrendered herself to him with such an absoluteness of the all of her that he could not have been but vanquished by her. The carnal had been uninhibited and wanton, the tactile a soufflé of libido and lasciviousness.

And yet never has she felt more overwhelmed by the divine than she is now. She has obeyed, it seems to her, not only Nature's imperative but has also heard and heeded destiny's tiny whisper. She will, and she knows it, never be more complete than she is at that moment, as complete as ever she's felt in the chapel, as total, as one.

There in the chapel the divine found the carnal before they fused into one; here it had been the physical stretching out its tentacles for the metaphysical and finding that it already contained that for which it was searching. It was the alchemist discovering that the metal he was trying to turn into gold already *was* gold.

She knows such moments *are* moments, and fleeting; knows that, almost by definition, they have to be. As a nun, she had been endowed only fleetingly with the Holy Spirit. Her faith, when she had it, had been sustained not by being permanently endowed with that Spirit, but by the knowledge that she had been so endowed and by the hope she would be again. She knows, as a woman, that only fleetingly will she be endowed with this oneness – and it will be a similar memory and hope that will have to palanquin her into the future.

She feels him kissing her palms, her wrists. And she smiles. Not at him. Though he is embraced by that smile. As he is also a part of that smile. That smile is both the Sahara desert and the grain of sand within it – as he is, as the universe is and universes are, as God is, as the oneness is, and as she is in that oneness and *as* that oneness. She knows this hasn't been sex, not just sex, not sex that is partly divine. This sex, the sex she's just had, that is God. It wasn't even coupling with a seraph, it was not even union with God, it was fusion with God, a fusion where coupling was not coupling but absorption.

She shudders and almost topples onto him. She kisses him slowly, languorously, hoping to keep her oneness one, sensing it drift away, sensing it melt – into another oneness. Like a kettle's steam, being absorbed by the atmosphere around it.

She doesn't care that he's married, because it doesn't matter that he is.

Chapter 2

"I am an idiot," says Rafaél. "I say that to my credit."

"Okay," Polly returns tentatively.

"One of the things that has brought mankind to the pretty pass at which it now finds itself," Rafaél continues, "is cleverness." Rafaél looks like the Limeñan he is: stocky and squat, slightly pigeon-toed, deep brown eyes, his olive-skin now leathered with age. "One has to say therefore that cleverness is not always a good thing. Being an idiot, I say 'hooray' to that."

"Okay," Polly returns again. Polly is an American. She has lived now in London for some years. Her accent, however, remains stubbornly Bostonian and much of her vocabulary too has yet to cross the Atlantic.

"I used to think I was clever. Exceedingly clever, *amiga mía*. It was when my wife died ... my world collapsed. So many of the things previously I had believed in I then saw to be false: either a fiction or a fraud. I looked into a mirror. I'd had the illusion I was Einstein. In the mirror I saw I was stupider than the village idiot."

He and Polly met barely an hour before. In a queue for tickets to a theatre called 'The Roundhouse'. Just two people, thirsty for beer and hungry for company. A casual queue chat developed into an invitation to a drink.

Polly looks considerably older than the early forties she is. She could be a good-looking woman, but almost wilfully she doesn't allow herself to be. The grey hair is, one senses, immaculately unkempt, the wardrobe carefully uncared-for. She wears wire-framed glasses which mask the blue of her eyes – mask their prettiness and brightness ... mask their pain.

They adjourned to a pretty pub, 'The Queen Victoria', on the corner of North London's Primrose Hill. Earnest conversation flowed as liquidly as the lunch. Already, and despite their age difference, they are firm friends.

"That's some village you're inhabiting there, Rafa: If you're the idiot, I'd be scared as hell to meet its wise man."

"Oh, we idiots, Polly, often we are wise. 'Out of the mouths of babes ...' and such like. Does Shakespeare not tell us this? Just as, so very often, the clever are so very rash. Also as Shakespeare tells us. Is it not usually the jester who is wise? And the savants who are Lear-like? We have clevered our way into this pretty pass, my friend. Mayhap is by idioting that we shall find our way out. Is, for instance, only the clever who tell lies. Lies require cleverness. Idiots have to tell the truth."

"Okay," says Polly yet again, still unsure whither this conversation is taking her, and whether she wants to be on the trip. They are now walking up the hill. It's a steep hill. Polly is beginning to pant.

"We are fighting a war today, Polly."

"Oh, Rafa, please! Not the War on Terror."

"The War on Terror, *amiga mía,* is a skirmish. The War on Terror is a diversion from the real war – merely one front, perhaps more accurately, on the real war. I don't mean to make light of the War on Terror. It has cost human life. Anything which costs human life is something which merits being taken extremely seriously. But the real war, Polly, the crucial war, that is a war exacting a death toll *daily* in excess of that on September 11th – each day, *amiga mía,* fifty-two weeks, three hundred and sixty-five days a year."

"And *that* war then would be?"

"Is in both senses, the Third World War, my friend, and is a war already costing millions *and millions* of lives – a Holocaust, what? Twice a year? Three times a year? That war, my friend, is the war between the Truth and the Untruth."

Rafaél speaks English too perfectly; it smacks almost of pedantry. Hard though it is to believe it, he learnt it in his native Peru, but now some years ago. The unkind, particularly those with a fondness for cliché, would describe it as past its sell-by date. It is closer to a Victorian sampler: belonging, yes, to another epoch, but beautifully embroidered. Because onto the dumpling stodge of English vowel-sounds the citrus of his native tongue twirls zests and flourishes that are Byzantine ... rococo.

"And whilst the truth, *amiga mía*, or anyway the *whole* truth, may be something which takes us outside the physical and into metaphysical realms, we can most of us recognise a lie when we see it.

"*When*, Polly, we see it," Rafaél repeats slowly. "Which is why is so very rarely that we do see lies today, that we are *allowed* to.

"The invisible foe is always the most dangerous. Gas is harder to fight than tanks. If we can diagnose an ill, we can treat it. Is hard to make such a diagnosis if the symptoms are hidden from us.

"The Untruth is propagating genocidal poverty, global warming, violence, intolerance, illiteracy, pollution, physical ill-health and mental and emotional ill-health ... virtually every problem and issue in the world. That we hear so little about this war is an indication only that, at the moment, the Untruth is winning.

"If the Untruth wins this war, mankind is doomed. Is that serious. Do I have to be gender-conscious with you? Do I have always to refer to 'he *or she*'? To *human*kind?"

"I'll take it as read," Polly replies.

"Is not a problem for me," Rafaél insists.

"It can be for me, to be frank. Sometimes it chimes so awkwardly I wonder whether it's not counterproductive."

"If it does win, Polly, the Untruth, we can say good-bye to even the vestige of civilisation, we can say good-bye to hundreds of species of wildlife, to vast tracts of the Earth ... and to numbers of the human population that will, quite literally, beggar belief.

"These lies – the lies of today's liars – these aren't the lies of children. These are sophisticated lies, and enormous lies.

"As all liars know, the best lies are those which aren't completely lies. The best way of killing the truth is by telling as much of the truth as you can, but failing to tell all the truth – disguising or veiling or ignoring that odd little detail, of itself so apparently innocuous, and yet within a theory so crucial." A portly Pembrokeshire corgi trots past with an obsessive shuffle. Its tongue lollops from its mouth, its docked tail appears to be wagging in the abstract. It seems interested neither in the smells which clearly surround it, nor in any of its fellow dogs. The two friends look around for its walker, but there is no-one in sight. The dog continues single-mindedly on what seems to be its pre-determined path. "Is true, for instance, that dogs have bad breath. That is not the truth about dogs."

"Okay," says Polly.

"Ours, Polly, is not the age of *information* technology. That is already part of the Untruth. Or rather ours is the age where, as never before, we are drowning in information we cannot rely on; one where the technology exists to swamp us both with *dis*information and *mis*information; one where there are entire industries dedicated to the task of manipulating information, or manipulating our reactions to that information. And we are *drowning* because that information is today deliberately torrential.

"One of the reasons Al-qaeda was, in its own terms, as 'successful' as it was on September 11th was that the FBI and CIA lacked the staff necessary to sift through the amount of intelligence received. If, that is, the CIA and FBI are to be believed. A big 'if', mayhap.

"These are government agencies with almost unlimited budgets. And *they* cannot digest the amount of information being thrown at them, cannot separate the wheat from the chaff. What chance do *we* have? We, I mean, as individuals? Wouldn't you imagine that such might be the job of a free press? To help us in that task? Sadly, so much of the press constitutes such an enormous segment of the world's liars.

"The responsibility of a newspaper does not begin and end with its sale; the responsibility of radio or TV news is not only to attract ratings. Indeed the press would be the first to insist as such.

"The press – particularly the tabloid press – sees its job as to champion 'morality'. And I would entirely endorse such an opinion. What a terrible tragedy, then, that is failing so badly in doing so. The press seeks to enjoin in others a sense of responsibility when, and so clearly, it abdicates from its own.

"The object of a free press should be, in the words of someone so famous I can't remember his name, 'to disturb the comfortable and to comfort the disturbed.' All it presently does is further to comfort the already comfortable, and to disturb more profoundly those already disturbed."

"They call this a *hill*!" exclaims Polly. "'Primrose ...' they call it '... *Hill*'. Now if that's not a lie ..." She musters a wan and unconvincing smile. She is perspiring quite freely.

"Your English writer, Chesterton ..."

"Whoa, there, Rafa. You hadn't noticed, I'm American?"

"I am so sorry," says Rafaél. "Sorry, I mean, for my mistake. Not sorry that you're an American. My English, I fear, is lamentable. My ear is not yet attuned to accents."

"You want to hear my Spanish, *señor*? In fact, you just have. '*Señor*', that's it, my Spanish! The grand total of it!"

"*The* English writer, Chesterton ... okay?"

"Better." She is still not sure whether or not he had been teasing her.

"Chesterton said that the best place to hide a leaf is in a forest. Today vast forests of distortion and obfuscation are being built merely to create hiding-places for leaves."

"You don't think both sides of the argument are guilty of that? Of any argument?" Polly pants.

"Of course. And so often, just by building those forests, those who normally tell the truth become liars. At that moment they too become part of the problem rather than part of the solution. And at that moment too, they impede – they have to impede – true debate and healthy debate: civilisation-saving debate.

"If we use the tactics of barbarians, we become barbarians. The means can never justify *any* end. Because the unscrupulousness of unscrupulous means just has to infect both the end and the person striving towards it. And both, therefore, (sometimes despite themselves) join the ranks of those fighting the Truth. So, the dilemma about the end *justifying* the means is almost irrelevant. Because the means *change* the ends. The process affects the solution. It has to. Bad means inevitably result in even the purest end being sullied. Is not possible that the end not be sullied by such means. And history has shown us that time and time again.

"I hate the way, for instance, that in London today charities have touts walking the streets, pouncing on shoppers like time-share salesmen. Charities (many of which are extremely important) have started thereby emulating the tactics of the ethos which made their charity necessary in the first place. They – thereby again – cede propriety to that ethos.

"As do the salaries some of those charities pay their executives. Thereby they too condone the lie. And to condone the lie *is* to lie."

"You ever heard, Rafaél, of the USAID'S Competitiveness Program?" asks Polly.

"Of course," Rafaél replies.

"Well, then you'll know, they received serious money for tsunami relief," Polly continues. "Of which serious money, a serious chunk was used by its director, Mr Varley, to further the cause of globalisation, to enforce the permanent removal of villagers from coastal regions the multi-nationals thought would make good tourist attractions. So very often the so-called 'aid' merely finished the job started by the hurricane. Fishermen whose homes had been wrecked found that their villages had now been confiscated.

"And this was all done, Rafa, with the money old age pensioners gave from their meagre income, or kids gave who had sold their Christmas presents in order to help ... from the dollars, Rafa, that most of those who gave could ill afford. What must they be thinking now? When their scrimpings have been used only partially to alleviate the desperation of the desperate and substantially to make the already super-wealthy even wealthier?

"Certainly, no question, it is a sensible use of charity money to, as the old adage has it, teach a man to fish. But that does not extend to it being a good idea to give a grant with charity monies to a multinational with which it can build a fish-processing plant, in the hope such plant will provide employment to erstwhile fishermen. Usually at below minimum wage salaries.

"How is this, in fact, not simply Sheriff of Nottingham economics? Where we rob from the poor to give to the rich? And how much more evidence do we need that there is something, not just rotten in the state of Denmark, but rancid?

"How would we feel if we saw a limousine slide to a halt, its Savile Row-suited occupant get out ... and for him to steal the meagre takings jumbled on the cardboard before a beggar and his dog? We would be appalled, Rafa. Appalled. And yet that is precisely what is happening with the world's economics today. The theft just happens behind closed doors – in boardrooms and Cabinet offices.

"How much poverty *does* it cost to create a billionaire? How much poverty are we prepared to allow it to? How much poverty are we prepared to allow? How much suffering and misery? How much duplicity? How much lying? The cynicism is quite staggering. Milton Friedman's likewise after Hurricane Katrina. And how is it that such has not been condemned as what it was?: looting. Looting quite as brazen and infinitely more damaging than the incidences of kids snatching DVD machines or iPods or whatever.

"It makes my blood run cold, Rafa. What's even worse is that such people and such policies are not condemned by statesmen and by the media, but *applauded* by them. We're supposed to honour them: these people and policies that have robbed from the desperate, that have caused *so* much misery – untold misery. Yes, 'untold' in both senses of the word."

"Mr Varley was, so I have read, helped in his task (abetted, I should more accurately say, in his crime) by the Maldives' President, Maumoon Gayoom, and Sri Lanka's President, Chandrika Kumaratunga. Political and economic cynicism is not exclusively, my friend, an occidental product."

"No," Polly agrees.

"If one buys stolen goods, one countenances theft," the Peruvian continues. "If a society depends economically on theft, that entire society is tainted by that theft. Is akin to a society which allows the death penalty. That society condones violence: It grants to the murderer the possibility of rectitude. If governors lie, those whom they govern will lie; if the prevailing climate is one of cynicism, the voiceless will also become cynical; if charities become opportunities not for giving but for taking, the charities eventually have to betray those they claim to be helping. *Have* to."

"Pragmatism, no? I mean, isn't that what the charities would say? I'm playing devil's advocate here. Wouldn't they argue, those charities, that pragmatism dictates, if you can't beat 'em, that you join 'em?"

The older Peruvian is breathing less deeply than his younger female friend. "There are plenty of things, my friend, pragmatism would seem to dictate. Might not pragmatism also have dictated that Miep Gies and their other friends handed the Frank family over to the Gestapo? That, instead of retiring people at 60 or 65, we merely execute them? Likewise that we demolish hospices and build gas chambers?

"What today is spun as *realpolitik* is not pragmatism at all: Is what vested interest would like us to believe were pragmatism. Finally is obedience to the dictates of that vested interest and obeisance to the lie.

"Is no longer a question in the political debate as to which side one believes. Politics themselves, and in their totality, are embroiled in one of the biggest lies of them all. Which is why those who enter politics with the most honourable intentions soon find those intentions so besmirched that they too become tainted with them."

"Rafa, Rafa ... 'twas ever thus, my friend. And, what's more, you *know* 'twas ever thus."

"That doesn't countenance it, Polly. Likewise murder has always been done, since time immemorial. Men for that long have gone bald. How much money have men spent trying to cure baldness? And the consequences, my friend, the consequences of allowing all these problems to fester, the consequences, Polly, 'twere *not* ever thus."

"Oh, yeah, real 'lamentable', your English!"

"Hitler was not the first anti-Semite."

"Nor, even more sadly, the last."

"As you say, Polly," agrees Rafaél. "There is very little 'new' in today's sins and vices and crimes. Other than their scale. And the scale of their consequences. The consequences today, my friend, could be literally earth-shattering. How many pogroms does it take to prove to us all that racism is bad for us? How many times must history dictate to us its lessons before we learn from it?"

Two joggers, both in grey track-suits, pound effortlessly past them. They talk fluently together as if swapping post-prandial anecdotes over cognac in winged armchairs. Polly glares after them, but her energy tank is running low, and her daggers therefore flop, limp and depleted, only a few yards into their voyage.

"There was a time indeed when I thought Man, he was now fighting for his very survival. As a species, I mean. But I realised the liars love such hyperbole. It helps them so easily to tar us with the same brush. We all become the man with the sandwich-board announcing that the End Of The World Is Nigh. We can all be dismissed as cranks, even those of us who warn of dire, but not apocalyptic, not eschatololigical consequences."

"Will you look, Rafa, at that view!" Polly eulogises expectantly. Her tongue is now lolloping quite as brazenly as had the corgi's. "I say to my entire embarrassment that I have no idea what that means."

"Eschatological?"

"Not a clue."

"Eschatology, my friend, is that branch of theology which deals with the end of the world."

"Right."

"And you have no need, no need at all, to feel embarrassed about not knowing the word. Is not one in common currency. I know it only from books I have read which deal with this rather esoteric subject.

They say the world's knowledge now doubles every five years, Polly. Doubles every five years," he repeats slowly. "Which would be an awesome thought. Except that we seem not to know what to *do* with all that knowledge.

"In the last fifty years there have been not even any significant inventions. Developments, yes: of the computer, of telephones and Internet; and discoveries – of DNA, for instance (though that discovery is almost fifty years old!). But not inventions. Not of a significance to match the hype: the microchip is all I can think of, and the contraceptive pill. Both enormously significant, but scarcely enough to define a generation – two generations.

"The Catholics maintain that faith without work is dead. Well, knowledge without application is even more dead, my friend. We seem to think that knowledge is there to help us win game-shows or general knowledge quizzes. There is no point – no point at all – in having knowledge unless one also has the knowledge how that knowledge might serve humanity. And to claim otherwise is just another nonsense perpetrated by today to demonstrate its superiority over yesterday. No, that's not quite true. I accept that the thirst for knowledge can have unexpected spin-offs. Was radar not the consequence of trying to make a tangible model of the abstract figure minus one?"

"Really?" Polly asks.

"Something like that. Muslims, almost from the inception of Islam, have prized the pursuit of knowledge. And its pursuit, of course, is a worthy aim. Even only at the level of, let's say, cerebral callisthenics. But one could be missing a trick. Is that which I am saying. If one doesn't have in the forefront of one's brain the benefit to humanity, one may not notice that one has discovered radar or penicillin or whatever else it might be. If today an energy source were found which we could all access for nothing, would we ever hear about it? Would we be allowed to?"

"Quite a climb," pants Polly. "Hooh!" she puffs. The hint is so heavy, being dropped it clangs. Rafael fails to hear the clang.

"There was also a time," he continues, "when I despaired. But despair, that really is in the interest of vested interest. Despair is famously debilitating. Despair means nothing can be done. And there are things, *amiga mía,* that can be done. Indeed, I am coming to the conclusion that the situation today facing Man and his planet is *so* serious, the actions which we will need to take are *so* radical, that they may indeed be the foundation-stones of what may be a civilisation in fact and not one only in fancy.

"I don't like to exalt in this – because there are far too many people in far too much pain for us to consider this time one of exaltation. But there is a charge around the world today, an excitement. There are terrible things happening, awful things, evil lies and lies being told in the name of evil. But there is also so much good. The evil you referred to earlier: that of politicians and industrialists funding their own projects with money designed for the desperate, that, my friend, however appalling, however disgraceful, is finally nowhere near as significant as the good of all those wonderful people who rallied to a common cause in a time of crisis.

"We are on the brink – the brink, my friend – of learning about the origins of life itself. Quantum physics is opening up universes of possibilities. Literally that: *universes* of possibility. And *this* is what is new.

"The 'new' vaunted by most of the world's political leaders is a system of economics and a system of repression which, for their bases, date back to the eighteenth and seventeenth century respectively: specifically to Adam Smith and Thomas Hobbes. (Though I also think both would blanch at the way their ideas were today being promulgated and 'developed'.)

"The *truly* modern sciences, though, as of quantum physics and mechanics (and particularly the implications these have for Man), these are being ignored by these modernist politicians, and by a press normally in love with the innovative. Apparently such are only interested in the 'new' when is in their interest to be so interested. These could so easily, my friend, be such exciting times."

"Not quite so exciting, though," says Polly, "if you're a child in a Bangkok brothel or a tiger in Siberia or an untried prisoner in Guantanemo. Nor if you're starving or being bombed or being abused."

"No," Rafaél agrees. "Is that what I mean. I notice you are panting, my friend. Me too. I think I should like to sit for a while." With which he sinks heavily onto one of the green-slatted benches that gaze winklessly at the magnificent patchwork spread out before them. It has, that patchwork, all the tones and liquid shapes of good abstract painting, all the opulence of texture of a coronation. Polly is quick to follow his lead. She breathes heavily for a little while.

It is summer.

The sun is shining with a commitment it usually lacks in England; the birds are cawing and cavorting; from the nearby zoo emanate roars from some fearsome, unidentified beast.

"Mind if I smoke?" Polly asks.

"Technically I'm a non-smoker. Technically I can therefore say to you, 'They're your lungs, Polly'."

She lights a cigarette, draws on it with relief. "I was brought up, Rafa, with the axiom that we don't inherit this Earth from our parents, we hold it in trust for our children. Whatever happened to that axiom? Was it confiscated or something when I wasn't looking? Who confiscated it? When? What the hell was I doing?"

"Then, Polly, let us reclaim it, you and I."

"Oh?" snorts Polly. "And how would you suggest we do that?"

"First of all, we do what we *are* doing, my friend: we talk together. That is so terribly important. Vested interest wants us to feel isolated, out of step with the rest of the world. More and more, though, and despite their very best endeavours, the truth is seeping out.

"And part of that truth is that we're *not* so alone, we're *not* so isolated. I read the other day that, in Europe and North America alone, there are some 140 million people seriously disabused by the ethos which informs their world and which is seeking to inform the entire world. 140 million: is a lot of people, Polly. Only in a small part of the world. Globally, then, the figure must be close to half-a-billion. Mayhap even more.

"One way that the truth is getting out is by our telling each other *of* each other, by telling each other we no longer believe either the lies of vested interest. Not any longer.

"Presently, Polly, one can divide the world into three groups: There is a very small, but fabulously wealthy and grotesquely powerful oligarchy which is lying to us: vested interest, by any other name.

"Then, there is the vast majority of the world which is being lied to.

"And finally, my friend, there is we: those like us – becoming more plentiful each day (as I say, presently mayhap half-a-billion) – who realise we are being lied to and are becoming increasingly resentful of the fact. And what we do, what we need to do, we make a commitment to the truth. We recognise that, if our civilisation is to become one in fact and not only in words, is a requirement that we make that commitment.

"And that, of course, means, I'm afraid, recognising that that which we *think* is the truth may *not* be. Is now so effectively hidden, the truth, that is almost impossible to recognise it even when we are confronted with it."

"That's real helpful!" Polly sarcastics.

"As a rule of thumb (no more than that), if is in the interest of vested interest, that which is being portrayed as being the truth is not the truth. Is, at least, dint of such fact worthy of further investigation – of detailed scrutiny. Of a scrutiny as detailed as is possible today. Because IT firewalls are also built around information vested interest would prefer were not in the public domain. Is, at the *very* least, a sensible premise from which to start."

They stretch out their legs, bask in the sumptuousness of both the weather and the view. Polly draws heavily on her cigarette. "You watch much tv?" she asks.

"Not so much, no," Rafaél replies.

"About a zillion cop shows on TV tell us, over and over again, how incorrigible the hoodlums are – the 'perps', as they call them. Tell us that the law is loaded far too much in favour of the defendant."

"This is also, Polly, part of the lie."

"Oh, absolutely. But let's not, just for the moment, get side-tracked onto that one, huh? That once a thief, these TV shows say, always a thief, once a liar always a liar.

"Why don't we, is all I was thinking, apply the same thinking to *corporate* criminals? *Corporate* thieves and *corporate* liars? *Political* ones? What I'm saying, why don't we apply such Napoleonic law to companies? Allow the burden of proof to fall on the accused, that it is they who have to prove their innocence? Assume all vested interest is Enron until it can prove, beyond a reasonable doubt, that it isn't?"

"Mayhap," says Rafaél. "Mayhap too we should always remember that, 'All that is necessary for evil to triumph…', Polly, '… is for good men to do nothing.'

"The lie is evil. And the lie is today as triumphant as it is because we, who are in the overwhelming majority, are good people who are doing nothing. Is not the only reason, but, yes, is a big one. Because the whole seems overwhelming, we fail to do the little we can. We don't need to seize power – 'seizing' in this context implies violence and once violence enters the picture, the lie has already won. All we need to do to realise our power is, in fact, to realise it."

"Nice play, Rafa, on words," Polly smiles at him. It is an engaging smile, one she would do well to use more often. "And sure you didn't know I was American! Sure you didn't!"

"I thought you were Irish."

This pleases Polly. "Well, almost I am. As it happens. The land," she says, "of my forefathers." And she glows.

"Apparently unlike the producers of your TV cop shows, my friend," Rafa continues, "I do believe that the misguided can be encouraged into more fulfilling lives. I do believe criminals can be coaxed out of criminality. And I believe corporate criminals can be reeducated so that they do benefit society indeed and don't merely con it into believing what they are doing is of benefit.

"Oil companies and car manufacturers (even insurance companies) are, for instance, today spending vast budgets trying to persuade us of their green credentials; supermarkets and washing-powder manufacturers boast of their eco-awareness; tea, coffee and chocolate companies sell their goods today on the basis that they are involved in 'fair' trading – though who defines such trading as 'fair' would also be something good to know.

"And if these companies are indeed doing what they maintain they are, and if the ecology is indeed thereby being protected where it previously wasn't, and if workers today are being treated with a dignity absent heretofore, that is all to be applauded. Even if all this is being done only in response to our pressure. We must applaud good work as much as we must condemn the bad – mayhap even more so. Indeed another reason why today we are in the pretty pass that we are is because historically we have allowed ourselves to be censured for the bad in us, and have censured ourselves for our badness, rather than applauding and thus encouraging that in us which is good and life-enhancing.

"But is also very important to remember that these companies are taking this stand because they are reacting to our pressure, not (as they will very shortly try to persuade us!) the other way around. We can make those much vaunted 'market forces' work in the interests of the planet, not against them. We can even *force* those market forces to do that. We can realise our power if we realise we have it. In ourselves as well.

"We simply cannot allow ourselves the luxury, Polly, of believing that the world is conveniently one of 'them' and 'us' – 'us' the good guys, and 'them' the baddies – that all who espouse capitalism, even who advocate it (even those who espouse or advocate globalisation) are bad people, and all who oppose it are good.

"Heavens, I was once very much the capitalist myself. Member of the Rotary Club, owner of a small factory, perfect capitalistic credentials. And the other members of that Rotary Club, they were – by and large – upright people, decent and kind people. Not mayhap the Bruce Waynes they, many of them, like to think they are – Bruce Wayne, it was he, no?, the human manifestation of Batman?"

"'Course he was," Polly nods. She, of course, knows who Bruce Wayne is. But he is not a character Polly expects Rafaél to know. And, just like meeting an acquaintance out of his normal context, she had been trying to remember where she knew Bruce Wayne from.

"No, not Bruce Waynes, not any of them. But good people. *Flawed* people, of course. Of course, flawed people. All people are flawed. But good people too. Indeed many of them are now as appalled as the most avid socialist by the situation in the world today. They make a cogent argument that is not capitalism *per se* which is at fault, but the *abuse* of capitalism – well, that abuse plus a pernicious increase in control being slithered silently from us, the individual, towards the state and industry. Which makes it all the more intolerable, statements from the French President Sarkozy and his like that we must try to make capitalism 'sexy again'. Is like saying of a prune, we must try to make it into a plum again. Raw capitalism can only be sexy if we accept that the base in us, the craven, is a sensible foundation stone for society. The base is a bad basis. A bad basis simply has to affect – badly – any structure built upon it."

"President Sarkozy, he's only covering his own back, Rafa. Like Mr Brown, the Prime Minister here." Rafa's expression leaves her in no doubt that this information was surplus to requirements. Polly grimaces a 'sorry' as she continues, "The two of them having been such vigorous proponents, effectively, of economic neo-liberalism."

"And what a misnomer *that* is: neo-liberalism," Rafa returns. "By the same semantic exercise, black is neo-white. There is nothing in the least 'liberal' about neo-liberalism. Neo-liberals maintain they are 'liberal' because liberals always advocate freedom and they advocate economics 'free' of state control. But no freedom is absolute. No liberal, however staunch, advocates the freedom to torture one's opponents, nor to starve one's fellow man into submission. Which is precisely what neo-liberals do and which is, considerably more clandestinely, also what they advocate. Neo-liberalism may not be quite the travesty of the Nazis calling themselves National 'Socialists', but it is in the pack cycling up behind them.

"We have no need to make capitalism more sexy or sexy again or whatever inappropriate phrase the French president used. We have, in fact, one need and one need only: to make the world a more civilised place. Capitalism is now not doing that. Evidently and *evidentially* is not doing that. Even most of us in the West are now suffering – directly – from its inability to do that, from capitalism's contempt of all but the most wealthy. Indirectly we have always suffered.

"Is not that we need to return to the communism/capitalism debate. Is, I think, clear that we have now gone beyond that point. I do not accept that communism was ever seriously tried, but I do accept that is now a spent force, a spent idea and/or ideal. I also think, even if it weren't, the situation facing the world today is so serious that should the debate still be raging, it would nevertheless still be redundant. We have to find not new political theories, not new economic paradigms, but inter-connected political and economic systems which also embrace a morality appropriate to the twenty-first century, a code of ethics and a spirituality also of our time. We have to start searching for approaches to life which do not divide life into component parts but which embrace life as a whole. Shall we walk a little more?" Rafaél suggests.

Polly hauls herself to her feet. "Not one of the world's great walkers, me," she admits. There is tacit in the admission a hope they might retrace their steps. Rafaél seems not to hear such hope. Polly grinds her cigarette butt with the heel of her shoe deep into the path's asphalt.

"Two more things we can do: We can dream, Polly, and we can look into a mirror. If we want to know about our future, far more than we need a crystal ball, we need a mirror. A sort of emotional X-ray mirror. We need to start understanding our faults – start understanding what in us *are* faults, which are very rarely the same things as government or industry or the Church has tried to insist are our faults.

"We need to start understanding those faults, and then we need to start addressing them. The world needs us to. Needs us all to. Needs us to encourage those who don't to do so. How can the smoker preach about the virtues of non-smoking?"

"You hear me preaching about the virtues of non-smoking?" asks Polly.

"I've been known to, and my non-smoking is on some days more technical than on others!" Rafaél confesses. "Was once a pretty savvy Saviour in history who talked about first removing motes from our own eyes.

"I was reminded of that when Catholic adoption societies in Britain threatened their government they would cease operating if they were not allowed to debar gay couples from becoming adoptive parents. Because, so they said, homosexuality is 'immoral'. This after their Church's titan cover-up of its paedophile priests and their activities, and after it had tried to discredit those victims who had had the extraordinary, the enormous courage to come forward.

"And is not only my former Church, Polly, which is hypocritical. Many other religions also indulge in their fair share of cant. And so do I. So, my friend, do I."

"The 'Queen Victoria'?" Polly gasps.

"Excuse me."

"The pub we were in earlier. It's beckoning again. All this exercise, you know. Or, if you'd prefer to try *another* pub, maybe we could find one on our way home. Where did you say you were living?"

"Clapham. Not far from the Common. With my son."

"Your son?"

"My son, Rodolfo. Did I not say?"

"My memory ..." Polly lets the sentence dangle.

"You?"

"Oh, I'm, kind of, temporarily *between* fixed abodes. A friend of mine went back to the States for a couple of months. I'm house-sitting for her. Well, apartment-sitting, to be accurate. A nice block. Just south of Tower Bridge."

"Sounds very pleasant."

"It's only a temporary solution. But, yes ...yes, it is. Very, as you say, 'pleasant'. Go on."

"We could talk of other things."

"And we will. The shoes, though, the ships and sealing wax, those can wait a while. Please, Rafa, go on. You said earlier, 'We don't dream'."

"Yes, I did. No, we do not. Not as a species. Not any more."

"I'd have thought exactly the opposite. So much of life today, of the economy, it seems to me, is *all* about dreams, is about dangling carrots. Isn't ... well, advertising, as a 'for instance', *all* about dreams?"

"Those are not dreams, Polly, but fantasies," he returns. "*Personal* fantasies, what's more. Most are variations on 'winning-the-lottery' theme. How rarely today do we hear talk, is what I'm saying, about *goals*. Of goals, I mean, for mankind.

"Oh, we hear about targets *all* the time: Sales-targets and achievement-targets and totally non-sensical professional targets – the amount of operations performed by a surgeon, the amount of arrests made by a policeman. These targets and the need for them are just more lies – and part, of course, of the overall lie.

"Is also part of the overall lie when politicians talk about their 'goals' of lowering taxes or making the streets safer. They're not talking about either. And most of their voters now know they're not talking about either. The voters know those politicians are lying. Which is one of the reasons why so many voters these days *fail* to vote. All they are talking about, those politicians – and this bluff too their voters have called –, is finding ways of massaging figures so that it will *appear* those things have happened. Almost never do politicians any longer talk about even a *national* ambition for even the next *year* (unless it be to win some sporting trophy), let alone a goal towards which all of mankind can agree to strive. Even 'the end of poverty' was one talked about only in some countries. And we've all seen what a real triumph that was!

"There is, Polly, a dearth of real goals, of big dreams. Unless you dream about your ideal house, how do you build it? Unless we have the courage to dream, how do we know what we want our future to be?"

"Can you impose in that way, do you think, on the future? Like it's a dream-house, I mean?"

"Of course not," agrees Rafaél. "Neither can you insist when you take out a pension fund that you will be alive later to benefit from it. (Nor, these days, that such won't be misappropriated!) There is also no guarantee that the apple tree you plant will not be struck by lightning. But there is a guarantee that it will not grow if you fail to plant it."

"Okay," Polly agrees uncertainly.

"Our future today, my friend, has become a sort of hazy and ill-defined next year when there will be a hazy and ill-defined improvement in material comfort, with mayhap a few less dying of starvation and with us gaping at yet another miraculous advance in technology because now a mobile phone exists that can relay to you halfway up Everest the latest episode of your favourite soap!

"We pay lip-service to improving safety, for instance, but our practical application is very limited. We build endless speed ramps but we shy away from installing microchips into cars which would disable them from breaking the speed limit. And we don't install such chips because such would upset the car manufacturers. We care less about children being killed on the road, than that the profits of the motor industry should not be dented. Or even that joy-riders be given a hard time. What advantage would that give the police if there were chips in all cars other than their own? How much faster could ambulances get to hospital? Or fire engines douse one's flaming home? Their speed would not be impaired by having to slow down for interminable speed bumps. Is just, all this, so entirely typical of what you, Polly, called a 'Sheriff of Nottingham economy'. A phrase incidentally which, as you may have noticed, I have every intention of claiming as my own!

"Our present today largely lacks any sort of communal purpose – and remarkably little private or personal purpose. And that is one of the reasons why today's today is as uncomfortable as it is – more uncomfortable in many ways than London in the Blitz. Physical comfort which comes at the cost of moral comfort is, finally, not very comfortable at all.

"We work best when we are working towards something, when we are striving," Rafaél continues. "Racial parity, Polly, in your country, or mine – or, for that matter, almost in any other country in the world –, is very far from absolute. How much further from absolute might it have been, however, had Martin Luther King not had his dream? A dream, incidentally, that wasn't his. Not his alone, I mean. Any more than the abolition of apartheid was Nelson Mandela's dream alone. They both shared their dreams with millions of people throughout the world, perhaps even billions. Dr King didn't invent that dream, he merely expressed it."

"And, Rafa, came to personify it."

"Of course. Probably, to his embarrassment. I am quite sure too that my dream is not mine alone, that is one shared by millions, perhaps billions throughout the world. Indeed I suspect vested interest will seek to starve that dream of publicity for precisely that reason.

"That dream is not a dream that needs an oration nor a thousand words to expound. That dream, *amiga mía,* needs but one word: 'wethos'."

"'Wethos?' You want to explain a little bit more?"

"I doubt anyone is any longer so foolish today as not to recognise that we – we, the species; we, the world; we, the planet – that we are in a serious, serious crisis."

"Well, I wouldn't fight you about it."

"We are in that crisis, my friend, mostly because since Man has been Man (maybe when he was still ape, I don't know), the ethos he has created around himself has been a '*me*thos' – has indeed been a '*me-me-me*thos'. He has taken so much and given so very little.

"The biggest single task Man has in the twenty-first century is to learn how to check his taking and expand his giving; to change the current 'methos' into a 'wethos'; or, if you prefer, to change an unprincipled ethos into an ethos of ethics.

"An ethos, I should say, of *genuine* ethics – not synthetic ethics or genetically modified or spun ethics, but ethics that actually do what ethics have always been designed to do: make the world a nicer place.

"The world, we have got to start realising, is never actually a nicer place unless it is a nicer place for everyone. We have to make today that famous swap of *ego*centricity for *eco*centricity."

A young mother passes them. She wears blue jeans and a light blue T-shirt. She is pushing a three-wheeled baby-buggy, from whose handles sprout four Waitrose carrier-bags of bulky and heavy shopping. She is also pulling an obdurate Dalmatian. She makes the climb with considerably more ease than either of the newfound friends. She has a pretty bottom, and both friends are, albeit barely consciously, for a few moments abstracted by the sight.

"*Babies*," Rafaél continues, "are great believers in methos. You might plausibly argue that that which defines human adulthood is an ability to think of 'us' and not exclusively of 'me'. Maybe then, it's time that we as a species started to grow up." He smiles at Polly, "Thirsty work, walking."

"Everything's thirsty work, Rafa." She has started to pant again.

"Everything. Now, there is also a plausible argument to be made," he continues, "that Man is altogether too clever for his own good, that we are not – that we have never been – ready morally for our technological precocity: that, in other words, technology has always preceded the ethics we need to be able to control it. And that as a consequence we will perish. We are bound, we are doomed to perish.

"This might very well be the case. But one of the things I so admire about you Americans ... and I do admire Americans; my countrymen, I always feel, make a mistake when they fail to distinguish between American ethos and the ethos of Americans. ... And one of the things I *most* admire about the ethos of Americans is your grit: You Americans seem the most able people of any to cope with disaster, seem never to accept death until the corpse has stopped twitching.

"Such American grit, unlike Big Macs or Coca-Cola, is an export the world will desperately need – if, that is, that world is to survive.

"If man's biggest task in the twenty-first century is to shift from methos to wethos, then the biggest question he needs to ask himself is: '*Can* we? Do we have what it takes to do what it takes?'

"Is not it something we owe to the future, Polly? To do everything we can, I mean, to ensure there is one?

"If we bring children into the world, if we allow children to be brought into the world, do we not commit to doing all we can to guarantee their future?

"We are hurtling, my friend, towards an abyss. Do we have what it takes to do what it takes to stop us from simply plunging into it?"

He and Polly have by now reached the hill's summit, and they gaze over the tongue-lolloping landscape beneath as if they were Sherpa Tensing having *carried* Hillary to the summit.

"It has been a spiritual axiom for centuries, Polly, for millennia, that All is One. Is a sentiment shared by Hindus, Buddhists, Taoists, Jains and tacitly by certain Muslims, Jews and Christians – probably, for all I know, by many other beliefs as well. Quantum physics, if I understand it correctly, seems, in a fascinating way, to be providing the scientific evidence to support that ancient spiritual axiom: Its best advice is that everything in the universe *is* indeed one. Well, if God is now so unfashionable we won't do it for His sake, then for our own sakes, why don't we start *treating* it as one?

"When I allow a child to die from malnutrition or a lack of healthcare anywhere in the world, is part of me I am hurting. When I attack the world's protective shell or her lungs or her refrigerator, is part of me I am damaging."

"I know that President Bush Junior bemoans the fact that the French have no word for 'entrepreneur'! – and that the French language is therefore deficient. Despite that deficiency, I am an admirer of the French language. I do, for instance, love the distinction the French make between globalisation and what they call '*mondialisation*'; '*monde*', I'm sure you know, is the French for 'world'."

"*Claro*. In Spanish is '*mundo*'. Is not too different."

"'*Mondialisation*' is a commitment to respect the whole world. Unlike globalisation which is to unify the world by *dis*respecting the whole world. '*Mondialisation*' is as life-affirming a concept as globalisation is destructive. The body, like the planet, *is* one unit. That does not mean our toes and our eyes are interchangeable, we do not brush our kneecaps or shave our teeth."

"Quite. Is not it time, my friend, we started to see that the ethos of methos is no way to protect me, any more than the best way for me to have peace at home is by fighting with my neighbours?

"'I' am best protected by the creation of a true 'us'. When 'I', as all the 'I's in today's world are being encouraged to do, start waging war on 'us', then 'I' simply has to lose. 'I', in fact, simply has to be *obliterated*.

"And that obliteration of 'I' is a tragedy. I am a gigantic fan of 'I'. Indeed the reason why I am not an *ego*-maniac is because 'ego' so often wounds or abuses 'I'. I am not an *ego*-maniac, but an '*I*'-maniac.

"I do have a dream, Polly," says Rafaél. "I dream, my friend, of a world where 'I' is allowed to be the most 'I' it can be. I have a dream that I live in a world of wethos. You know how that dream is realised?"

"I think I may have an idea."

"There is only one way."

"By allowing everyone else in the world also to be the most 'they' they can be?"

"Mayhap even insisting on that," says Rafaél. "Exactly. I cannot be the most 'I' I can be unless you are also being the most 'you' you can be – in fact, without everyone in the world being the most 'they' they can be. Is just not possible, my friend. Just as a world that isn't nicer for everyone is finally not nicer for anyone. Is so very simple."

"And yet so unbelievably hard."

"Oh, immensely hard. 'Simple', though, is not the antonym of 'hard', *amiga mía*. The antonym of 'simple' is 'complicated'. Methos loves keeping things complicated. Complication is an excellent place to hide the lie.

"Politics is complicated, international diplomacy – complicated. Decommissioning weapons, test ban treaties, sociology and penology, dealing with hurricanes and floods – all complicated. Personal liberties, computer surveillance, the right to privacy – complicated. So complicated. The gold standard, the interest rate, the international exchange rate – indeed the entire field of economics – all of those also, complicated. Hugely complicated. And so often *unnecessarily* complicated: mechanisms designed to veil the rapaciousness, the financial nymphomania of those manipulating those mechanisms. Mechanisms which, as mechanisms are wont to do, become considerably more important than their mechanics.

"Marx was never more wrong than when he wrote of capitalism that it contains within itself the seeds of its own destruction. Would that it did! Methos is not only capitalism, of course. But capitalism, particularly today's *unbridled* capitalism, is – yes – an important element in it.

"Karl Marx, Polly, contained within himself the seeds of his own destruction. *You* do. So do I. That dog does. So do all the animals over there in the zoo. All the trees and plants and shrubs around us. Is entirely natural for something to contain within itself the seeds of its own destruction. And is one of the proofs we have of the indispensability of death to life.

"But the pernicious thing about capitalism – and methos – is not that they contain within themselves the seeds of their own destruction, but that they contain the seeds of *ours*. Our destruction,

Polly, yours and mine, that of our families, our friends, our neighbours, all the people on the bus with us, all the people in the local pub. Our destruction, the destruction of civilisation and of civilised ambitions. Our destruction, the destruction of our environment, our species, possibly our planet.

"Capitalism and methos will see the destruction of all around them before they allow themselves to be destroyed. And the most powerful weapons they have in their entire arsenal are those seeds they have implanted in us, and which grow in all of us, and which endow methos with credibility. Which is yet another reason why is so important, so vital, we journey inside to examine ourselves."

They start to walk down the hill again. A light breeze is now taking the scorch out of the heat. The birds seem to be grateful for that, and sing with more warbles and sashay with more gusto.

"The Buddha famously declaimed that 'life is suffering'. Well, that suffering is becoming ever more acute each day for ever greater amounts of people.

"Methos, normally the most materialistic and anti-spiritual of credos would, ironically, agree with the Buddha – on that point, at least. But methos sees that struggle as being one of the lone 'me' versus the world.

"Just watch today's television commercials. You do not need to see much television to understand the intention of those commercials. Just like your cop TV shows, my friend, they contribute enormously to a pervading ethos – to today's ethos of methos.

"Never listen to the text of these commercials, never pay attention only to the plot of such shows, always – *always* – listen to the *sub*-text. And the sub-text of so many commercials today is that the product – the bank, the car, the perfume – will give you an enviable edge in the inevitable battle you, the individual, inevitably wage against life.

"The sub-text is less trying to sell you the product, that's a side-issue. Always a side-issue. Often is trying to sell globalisation. Often too, what it's trying to sell us is the idea that we're alone: fighting, alone, the dragon of life.

"Well, guess what? Is so rare to fight a dragon alone and survive that such matadors tend to become national patron saints!

"Wethos would also agree with the Buddha. But it advocates, rather than each one of us fighting *against* everyone else and the world, each one of us *allies* with everyone else and the world – and we fight *together* all the vagaries of life, all its vicissitudes and perversities.

"Methos is the bee fighting the Rottweiler. The Rottweiler is irked by the buzzing, but no more. Occasionally it will eat the bee. And sometimes, dying, the bee will sting it. But that doesn't actually help the individual bee too much. Wethos, though, is a swarm of bees tackling a Rottweiler. Suddenly the odds have changed dramatically.

"I have to steal a cigarette. Sorry. Technically I have given up. Just occasionally I have to remind myself that my giving up *is* merely technical."

"They're your lungs, my friend," says Polly and smiles. She proffers him a cigarette, and then offers him a light from her Bic lighter. It is orange and running low. Even in the slight breeze therefore she has trouble keeping it lit. It is now Rafaél's turn to inhale deeply.

She lights herself one. They walk a little further.

"It's deeply entrenched, Rafa, the ethos of methos you talk about. Its roots go very deep. And its branches are all over the place. It's crab-grass with the roots of oaks."

"Curiously, Polly, if we as a species can find the will, I think the practicalities might be easier than a first glance would have it seem.

"Despite a prevailing, an all-pervasive, a ubiquitous and all-penetrative methos, there is, I feel – I *sense* – already so much good in the world. I mean, Polly, *so* much good.

"Such an enormous part of the enormous lie told us by the press is that they hide so much of such goodness from us. Is not news, they will tell you. Which is yet another lie. Certainly, good news is news, inspiring news is news. Is not mayhap news that sells newspapers, that much may be true – and we need to look at ourselves about that as well – but that does not stop it from being news. Newsworthy is not the same as circulation-worthy and is a lie when the press seeks to suggest that it is. Sadly, the press is extremely adept at lying.

"Unless newspapers can be relied on, we're better off not reading them. No information is better than disinformation. Instead, look around you in the street.

"Look properly around you in the street, in *your* street, scratch just a few millimetres below the surface. You will be amazed at and astounded by the generosity of spirit there is in the average man-in-that-street, how he responds to need or in an emergency.

"Too many of those people do, I think, live lives of the famous 'quiet desperation'. But that desperation is born mostly of a frustration that they are unable to live the life of quiet decency which they yearn for. Quiet decency and quiet happiness. And we all of us, yes, yearn to be happy. Which is not an unreasonable yearning, nor a blasphemous one.

"We need unhappiness, of course, if for no other reason than to define happiness. But that should be the primary function of unhappiness. I do not believe, as some ascetics seem to, that happiness is sinful or unspiritual or anti-spiritual. Is indeed one area in which I take issue with Gandhi.

"My unhappiness with the world today consists of the fact that Man is short-changing himself. Even in the West, he's being conned into believing he's happy. At best, he is settling for a third- or fourth-rate happiness instead of the first-rate one which is his due.

"A happiness bought at the cost of someone else's unhappiness is already a tainted, a third- or fourth-rate happiness. And we in the West are today inevitably buying our fourth-rate happiness at the cost of others' first-rate misery.

"That doesn't mean that Man is some kind of two-legged Bambi. Of course not. We are all of us capable of doing the most devastating things, hideous and atrocious things. The Gestapo and the KGB were not staffed by 'them' but by 'us'. And it was 'us' who denounced our neighbours and acted as informers. Or used the secret police to settle private scores. Is also true that, albeit mostly through ignorance or thoughtlessness or neglect, however good and noble and selfless we may think ourselves, almost none of us does not wreak some actual harm on others. And that would remain the case, even in Utopia.

"The 'I's of none of us are plateau-like. Every 'I' in the world contains its highest 'I', its worthiest; just as they all contain their lowest and their least worthy. As a general rule, no more, the former wants to give and the latter to take. The world as a whole contains these two extremes. And everything in between! This is the yin and yang of Eastern philosophies; those with religion see it as a fight between God and whichever the devil is that counterpoints their God. But one needs no formalised spiritual belief – indeed any metaphysical belief at all – to know that truth about oneself. One's own experience will vouchsafe that one's own fight is only a microcosm of the cosmic fight. If one really studies oneself one will also discover that one's own happiness derives far more, and lasts far longer, when one obeys the strictures of one's higher 'I' than the quick-fix and fleeting high one gets from heeding the lower. Almost the single biggest problem with the lower is that it demeans us – and we know it demeans us, and knowing we have been demeaned that further demeans us.

"One of the biggest problems with the culture that predominates in today's world is that it demeans all of us. It seeks to reduce us all to the level of those who control us. Napoleon, with some justification, sneered that England was a nation of shop-keepers. The Internet makes us a *world* of shop-keepers – a world, rather, of hawkers and whores. The property market is a honey-trap which seeks to make entrepreneurs of us all, and thus trapped by that same ethos that so predominates in the world today, that profit forgives all.

"At every level that ethos demeans us, and it demeans those around us – whether by a contempt for local culture or for the feelings of either employees or customers. Advertising demeans us, so much television demeans us, so many newspapers and magazines and films.

"Indeed, Polly, one of today's miracles is that – despite this gargantuan, this overwhelming juggernaut which daily poisons and demeans us – still it is, with that average man-in-the-street – *still* it is that his higher 'I' eventually wins through.

"And that, Polly, confirms my belief – what is, in fact, my *passionate* belief – that the overwhelming characteristic of Man is not original sin, but original virtue. Was a disservice done by my Church to the world when she propagated St Augustine's' myth about 'original sin'. Such, in fact, was a *huge* disservice. One of her two great sins."

"And the other?" asks Polly.

"The other was calling God the 'King of kings'. What a difference there might have been to world history had she emulated the Brahmans and called God 'the Servant of servants'! What an *enormous* difference that might have made."

"Yeah," reflects Polly. "Yeah."

"An important, an essential, component, not only of wethos itself, but in our struggle to assume it, is to recognise our original virtue. Recognise it and cheer it and, above all, nurture it.

"Even so many politicians who behave so shamefully do so most not because they themselves are shameful but because they are representing shameful institutions – particularly the institution of politics. As people, at home, at the dinner-table, most would, I'm sure, be considered entertaining and loyal and kind. Almost all of them would risk their own lives to rescue a child from a burning building. Because it wouldn't then be the politician rescuing the child, but the person ... not the man-in-the-senate but the man-in-the-street. It astounds me how well, despite (as I say) the enormous juggernaut appealing to that which is most base in all of us, most men-in-the-street continue to behave.

"The New York firemen on September 11th were, were they not?, oh so special. But I do not believe they were unique. Indeed I think those firemen were also representative ... as representative indeed of the truth and love as politicians are representative of the lie and hatred.

"Those firemen were representative of the soul within each one of us. And those firemen certainly weren't two-legged Bambis. In other circumstances, as we have seen, some of those firemen were not even *nice* people. And yet when the going got tough …

"I believe those firemen personified that within each one of us which just yearns, which *aches*, to be used – the hankering we all cradle for wethos. And I think the fact that so often today our wethos is suppressed causes yet another frustration to gurgle within us.

"That frustration gets added to all the other frustrations – creative frustration, for example, career frustration, frustration with unaccountable institutions or recalcitrant machinery or impossible-to-assemble 'easy-to-assemble' flat-pack furniture, frustration with the gathering speed of life and the stop/start of traffic, of emotional frustration and/or sexual frustration ... oh, and a whole galaxy of them, of frustration and frustrations. This becomes a cocktail of frustrations – a cauldron, maybe more accurately, of them. That cauldron seethes and bubbles most of the time within most of us. And each year that cauldron becomes yet more volatile, yet more toxic. And each year it contributes even more – it *has* to contribute – to the increasingly violent environment in which we live.

"And so a vicious circle – a vicious, rather, *spiral* – is created. That too is an inevitable consequence of methos: It creates vicious spirals. More often than not, it creates vicious spirals which then create other vicious spirals.

"I sense … I believe, Polly, I believe *passionately* that we all have within us a basic wethos that is yearning to be let out. And I think the methos knows that too. And I think too, that is something of which methos and vested interest are both terrified.

"That terror is compounded by the fact, Polly, that ours is a time when scientific and technological advances could render ever more possible the *release* of that wethos – its release and realisation.

"At the moment, technology is basically being used to shore up the status quo, not to challenge it. But that is changing. And already, as I have said, you can sense that changing. And is changing because we are demanding it change. Change is happening because, very slowly, we are beginning to realise that we have power to realise and that we have to realise our power.

"You've heard the phrase: 'Seize the day'. Well, it is today, my friend, the day we need to seize. Such seizure is one where there is no violence, there is only resolve. We resolve to insist those who so loudly proclaim their commitment to democracy put their money (in some cases, literally) where their mouth is.

"Man, if he is to survive with dignity, does not need revolution. But he will need resolution. He will need enormous resolution.

"And that day, Polly, that seizable day today, that could be such an *exciting* day – *such,* Polly, an exciting day. Quantum physics is ... Sorry, I've said this before ... but literally, Polly, it is revealing *universes* of possibility. These could so easily, *amiga mía,* be such truly amazing times. Is indeed, our time today, the best of times and the worst of times. Was not a political revolutionary I heard say that, my friend, but an eminent natural scientist.

"*No* time, though, is an amazing one seen from the bottom of an abyss. And it is to that – as also I have said before – that we are currently heading.

"Pulling back from the rim of an abyss, that does not require the advanced science of quantum physics. Not even pulling back from this one: If you realise you are hurtling straight for an abyss, you do what? You stop. Even I, the village idiot, know that. You apply the brakes. It really does not need rocket science to understand that.

"That does not, of course, mean that stopping will be without effort. Plenty of people will give you plenty of reasons why it is we cannot stop. Economists, for instance, will tell you, economics will not allow us to stop, will tell us economics demand indeed we need to go even faster. Sadly, that could even be true. But if this *is* true, my friend, mankind has kamikaze economics. Any train without a dead-man's-handle is a very dangerous train indeed."

"You know I'm an assistant film director, right?" asks Polly. "I told you, right, I'm an assistant film director?"

"It sounds very glamorous."

"Believe me, Rafa, it's really not. The employees of the Disney Corporation best summed it up. They used to refer to their studio as Mouseschwitz."

"That is rather witty."

"Typically of their corporation, they were told to desist or face instant dismissal. So much for Disney's much vaunted sense of humour. All email traffic stopped for an hour. Before someone came up with the alternative soubriquet of Duckau." Rafa laughs. Polly had forgotten the comment was funny. Now she remembers it is. And laughs too. She lights another cigarette.

"The assistant director," she says, pulling the fumes deep within her, "is responsible for the minute-by-minute organisation of a film as it is being shot – on the actual set, in other words, where the director is and the camera and actors and stuff.

"There are times on a film floor when the dog starts chasing its own tail. You find yourselves running round in circles. It shouldn't happen, but it does. A momentum gathers of itself, starts feeding off of itself. Bad assistant directors are so scared of, quotes, 'wasting time' that they keep going – like so many headless chickens. Good ones call a halt. They stop hurtling towards, in their case, chaos. They gather together the key personnel and spend ten minutes devising a new agenda. A few minutes of this thinking time saves hours of doing time."

"But if an executive should wander onto – you say 'floor'? – onto the floor during such thinking time, his perception would be that there was no work being done," Rafaél suggests. "He would be angry that there was no work being done."

"These days, he'd probably fire the a.d.," Polly adds ruefully. "Executives don't any longer want people who are good at their jobs, just those who *appear* to be good at their jobs."

"Is a good analogy. You are right, Polly: Is that, I think, such a big problem with today's work-place. Not just work-place: one, Polly, of the central problems of today's *world*.

"Is all about appearances, and nothing about substance. Is about looking busy on a film-floor not organising yourself intelligently; is about burying problems, not confronting them; is about building a film-set of Metropolis and claiming thereby to have solved the housing crisis.

"The sculptor who never steps back to look at his work but who just keeps on chipping away at his block of marble may *look* like he is very industrious, but he will end up merely with a pebble. If bees never returned to their hives, they would pollinate without making honey.

"As never before have we needed to, today we need to stand back and look at the sculpture as a whole. And we don't. We're told – like, Polly, your bad assistant director – that would waste time. We cannot, economics tell us, afford that time.

"The hours employers today expect from their employees, the commitment, the loyalty and zealousness are all in my lifetime unparalleled. But not one of those aspects do I believe is the result of, or will result in, problems being tackled or work being done. Rather more is about *appearing* to be tackling problems, *seeming* to get work done. And the social consequences are going to be devastating. They are already starting to be. As a social policy, is both tragically and disastrously ill-advised.

"Confiscate time from children and you steal from them their sense of security. The planet's future demands that its next generations be the most emotionally robust of its history. The insecure can never be emotionally robust. Confiscating time from children is building fire-breaks by dousing trees in petrol.

"And is not even, children, the *only* aspect of life from which time is confiscated. No-one has the time either, not any longer, to question or to challenge – and this in an age when questions need to be asked more urgently than at any other in our history! We need to ask questions. We need to ask very many questions. We need time to do that.

"We also need time to anticipate consequences.

"And to scrutinise alternatives.

"One way in which schooling has for generations failed in its duty is that it has not instilled the impulsion to challenge into the breast of each of its scholars. Curiosity may have killed the cat, but civilisation was created by it. Just as is scepticism which stands guard over it.

"Today the need to question is not only vital for civilisation, is vital for survival. We have been lied to so often about so much that it is, yes, *vital* that we challenge everything we hear. *Everything,* Polly. And that includes even the opinions of friends, even the 'facts' proffered us by fellow-travellers, even those opinions, *amiga mía,* we have ourselves.

"And we need to *keep* challenging, as I said, Polly, even if we stumble on the truth. Always. And all of that, Polly, needs time.

"Speed, my friend, is not all that economics vaunts it to be. Gandhi said that there was more to life than making it go faster. Speed is addictive, and addiction is not healthy. We even talk about 'rushes' – of adrenalin, for instance; 'speed' is also a synonym for drugs.

"Is *runaway* trains which travel the fastest, far faster than those under control; bolting horses go faster than galloping ones. I don't yet know whether our train is still under control, but I do know, if is not yet runaway, is gathering such powerful momentum that soon it *will* be. We must, Polly, find a way to slow ourselves down. We cannot possibly see through the windows when we are travelling at the speed we are."

"It's what in movies we call a 'whip pan'," says Polly. "When the camera whips, as it were, from one image to another as quickly as it can. The image of the whip pan is always blurred. It has to be. The eye can't cope with receiving information at that speed, and most certainly the camera can't."

"'Whip pan', I will remember that. That too is a good analogy. So much of what occurs today, my friend, is like that, a whip pan. We need to slow down, enough anyway to see through the windows, to see the images as our camera pans.

"If one is hurtling towards an abyss, one stops. One puts on the brakes. Does one at that time listen to the train-company's accountant insisting the company cannot afford to brake? Or to the insurance company's loss-adjustor insisting that braking will inevitably incur a rise in premiums?

"Of course one does not. One brakes. Immediately. And hard. With everything at one's disposal. Every other situation is dealt with only after the catastrophe has been averted. The further one is from the abyss when one starts braking, the more evenly can those brakes be applied. A slow braking is painless; slamming on brakes nearly always ends in catastrophe.

"Is this not obvious? Most of the solution, Polly, far from being rocket science, is really simple. Like most things. Napoleon, for instance, said of war, 'The most difficult thing to discover is the enemy's plans, and to detect the truth in all reports one receives; the remainder requires only common sense.' The same is true in this war between the Truth and the Untruth. Most of it is so terribly, terribly simple. Grotesquely simple, in fact.

"I do not drive in London. I cannot cope with driving on what, for me, is the wrong side of the road. But I do drive in Lima. Probably too much. I was driving to ... coincidentally to the British consulate, to enquire about my visa to come here. Is in Miraflores, a busy, Greenwich Villagey part of town. The traffic is always awful. On that day was also raining. Torrentially, as sometimes it does in Lima.

"The windscreen wipers were working flat out but still what I was seeing was being diffused through a permanent gush of water. A pedestrian just marched into the road, blindly, perhaps a metre away from me. I slammed on the brakes, but, because the road was wet, I skidded. I must have missed him by a hair's breadth. He, of course, who had received a shock, screamed some obscenity at me before scuttling across the rest of the road.

"'*Malditos* pedestrians,' I said, probably aloud. 'Can they not see is raining?' '*Malditos*', I think you would translate this as 'bloody'.

"Probably because of the rain, I had to park even further away from the consulate than I'd feared I might. An umbrella, in those conditions ... well, is a pea-shooter against an Exocet. Within seconds I was drenched. I nipped across a road, causing a car to squeal to a skiddy halt. The car hooted furiously at me, and I gesticulated back.

"'*Malditos* drivers,' I said, probably aloud. 'Can they not see is raining?'

"Inevitably in the consulate there was a queue. I was still dripping, trying to dry my face – and with a pocket handkerchief, for God's sake. Feeling sodden and soggy. Suddenly it came to me. One of my biggest problems – one of mankind's: The very moment I step into a car I become a motorist, and the very moment I step out of it I become a pedestrian.

"How does mankind pull itself back from the abyss? How does methos become wethos? We invert that process. When driving we are pedestrians, and when walking motorists. Wethos actually needs no more rocket science than that.

"Some of the *details*, they will need rocket science brains, certainly that is true. But guess what? The world has rocket scientists available. Is not the brains which are lacking, not the skill, is the application. Is the realisation, globally, that we are facing not one catastrophe but an entire maelstrom of them, my friend, a blitzkrieg of them, and that they have to be tackled. Now. And together.

"And of course we won't act all the time as pedestrians when we're driving, nor as motorists when we're walking. Of course we won't. But ethics are not what we are but what we strive towards. Ethics are the highest 'I' pulling away from our lowest 'I', not because our highest 'I's are killjoys but because they know the difference between a fourth-rate happiness and a first-rate one. Ethics are our parents insisting we go to bed at a certain time because (contrary to our childlike beliefs at the time), if we sleep enough, our tomorrows will be happier ones.

"Because we fail to live up to our ethics does not mean that we shouldn't still have them. Nor that we are bad people. Only that we are *human* people.

"Life, let us say, is an archery lesson. The bow is ambition and we are the arrow. Ethics are the target. Occasionally we'll hit, more often we'll miss, sometimes we won't even get close. But ethics all the time give us something to aim for, an end against which we can judge our progress and our skill.

"And, in a curiously circular way, ethics supply us with the will which is what we have to supply in order to find ethics.

"Each *one* of us has to supply that will. And, of course, because not all of us will do so, those of us who do will have to supply the will of others with him.

"Many *cannot* supply that will: the poor, for instance, and the desperately poor; these are involved in such a daily struggle just to survive that they have no resources left to shoulder wider responsibilities.

"There are also the culturally impoverished, the mentally or emotionally inadequate who are involved too in a daily and similar, though less obvious, struggle. Which means that those of us with health and means have to assume more than we might believe to be 'our fair share' of responsibility.

"And part of that responsibility, *amiga mía,* a large part must involve us examining ourselves. That too is a spiritual axiom of intensely practical application. Without that examination, is less likely we will survive this crisis. And even if we were to survive it, it becomes even more likely that we will shortly find ourselves again in another.

"I doubt mankind will ever be able to manufacture for itself a lust for responsibility – responsibility is the roadie to power's rock star. But mayhap we need to start insisting that our rock stars also carry the amplifiers. Particularly those, like Sir Bonio, who describe *themselves* as rock stars."

"I think that's Bono, Rafa."

"Is not he, Sir Bonio, a dog's dinner?"

"Good point."

"We need to start seeing 'I', Polly, as being a part of 'we', not 'we' as a pluralisation of 'I's; and the 'I' we need to respect is the 'I'ness of others, more than that of ourselves. Paradoxically, is precisely thus that the 'I'ness of ourselves will be most effectively protected.

"Is such a simple yardstick to apply to the actions of those who would govern us: Is he driving a car as a pedestrian? And to those of ourselves: Am I walking as a motorist? Such an easy phenomenon both to recognise and to check.

"I am reminded," says Polly, "of when Mel Brooks was asked what was the difference between comedy and tragedy."

"Mel Brooks?"

"He's a movie director, Rafa. Usually of comedy films. I think, maybe exclusively of comedy films. Actually I was also told that Gene Wilder had said the same thing, so I've in fact got no idea who the real author is. Be that as it may, one of them, as I say, was asked what they thought was the difference between comedy and tragedy. 'Comedy,' said, say, Mr Brooks, 'is when you have an extremely painful illness and die a slow, lingering and painful death. Tragedy is when I have a hang-nail.'"

"Like most wit, there is – sadly – much truth in that. We are creatures overwhelmed by ego. Mayhap another tragedy of Man is, asleep, he always dreams in the first person."

"Following on with your traffic analogy here for a moment, Rafa: I remember asking my mother (who, for God only knows what reason, took it into her head to teach me to drive) ... I remember asking her what the hardest part was about driving: was it shifting the gears? Parallel parking? Hill-starts, what? She told me, it was manipulating through traffic. These days, as a driver, I *know* exactly what the answer is: the most difficult thing about driving is other drivers. Is the most difficult thing in life other people?"

"Isn't the thing that most irritates us drivers, in fact, ourselves? Don't we get irritated with ourselves because we take longer than we 'should' parallel parking? Or because we smash the brake light when we don't see the bollard behind us? Don't we get irritated with other drivers usually because it's easier to blame them than ourselves?"

"Other drivers don't help, Rafa."

"Particularly not when they behave as we do – and blame us for their mistakes. Oh, you're right, Polly. The most difficult thing in driving is other drivers. And ourselves!" Feigning astonishment, he then exclaims, "Well, who would have thought it? Here we are again at the 'Queen Victoria'."

Chapter 3

Saskja's still to put her clothes on. She knows he's trying to be attentive. It's not that, now he's 'had his way' with her, he's churlish or disinterested, he's just not yet experienced or clued up enough to know quite how to gift-wrap his attention.

She'd thought him a man. He's still a boy.

She recognises he is being courteous, even thoughtful. She's even grateful for his courtesy. But the gratitude does not allay the disappointment. It's not a catastrophe. It's a lazy disappointment, this – one bodiced by apathy. Nevertheless, yes, she does feel it waddle through her, does feel its disgruntled trudge.

She needs to talk to Giselle.

No, making a special call would be to make too much of it. She'll email her. Not even that, she'll include it, rather, in her next email, her regular one. It doesn't warrant its own missive. She'll make mention of it, no more. No point making mountains out of molehills. The sex was listless not ghastly, and its failures far less of commission than omission. The event is a bummer not a tragedy, a shame not a crime.

The room is dark, but the Orphalese sun rattles loudly on the shutters. Throughout their frolicless frolics, she has been aware of the life cascading beneath that window, of the bustle further sweltering the already sweating street: the belch and bellow of the thousand mopeds and scooters and motorbikes all with silencers either punctured or removed; the muted roar of so much human concourse; the pan-piped tweets of the ambulant knife-sharpener; the wail of an odd child forbidden some desire; the scream of one who'd just been hit; the smell of jasmine simmering and almonds roasting; the buzz and drone of a galaxy of flies; the oddly lop-sided 'woop-woop-woop' of the overhead fan as it fights vainly against a merciless heat.

Sex has before stopped the world for her. That this time it had continued on an unchecked orbit, yawning deeply as it did so, means (so Saskja feels) that an attraction she'd imagined to be there actually isn't. No big deal.

Oh, he's a nice enough man – even now solicitous close to the point of being cloying, closer to being annoying.

No, no, *not* a man. *Really,* still a boy. A boy *really*.

She has known a man's love. This was not it. Vigour cannot replace concern, nor energy sensuousness. She feels cheated. Not mugged but, yes, short-changed. Angry with herself because she suspected all along it was precisely thus that she would be feeling.

She's still to put her clothes on. Really she should do something about that. And soon. She's over the disappointment now. Mostly over it. Now mostly calm. She will include news of the folly in her email to Giselle. That's what it was a folly, a silly mistake, nothing more. She'll tell Giselle about it and that will be the end of it.

He kisses her eyelids, her nose. He nibbles at her mouth. He wants to kiss her full on the mouth.

It's just easier to let him.

Chapter 4

"*God*, I am so tired of it," says Polly. "So tired, I mean, of living in a world which claims to be one where the weak are protected against the strong. But which is actually one where the strong are protected against the weak."

"Always we have lived, Polly, in a world where the strong have been protected against the weak," Rafaél returns.

"Isn't that, though, the entire point of government? To protect the weak against the strong?"

"And when in history, Polly, has there been such a government?" They are standing in the queue for the London Eye, the huge Ferris-wheel on the South Bank of the Thames, from which to gaze on panoramic views of London. It is a long queue. "As with so very much of what is happening in the world today is not the situation which is new, but the scale. The weak have never been weaker, nor the strong stronger. Which is why the strong feel so vulnerable. And why government internationally feels the need to bully and suppress the weak on behalf of the strong.

"The scale of the world's problems is without precedent, my friend, as is the scale of their consequences – of both the probable consequences and the possible ones.

"The probable consequences are serious: species-threateningly certainly, possibly planet-threateningly serious; the possible ones either totally disastrous ... or, yes, they could be triumphant. But to triumph one has to overcome.

"And the first requirement of overcoming a serious problem is that that problem be *recognised* – both as being a problem and as being a serious one. Ignoring or trivialising problems is the road to disaster. And is that, the road we tread at the moment. If we are to be triumphant, we have to find another road. There is no choice. We have to. Is that simple."

"Sounds," says Polly, "like a Hope/Crosby movie: 'The Road to

Somewhere Else'."

"We certainly need hope, Polly," the Peruvian smiles. "Is a commodity today in too short supply. Maybe we also have a need of a Bob Hope. Is always valuable to laugh. In crisis, very valuable."

Polly has decided it is appalling how little of London Rafaél (in the six weeks he has spent there) has seen. She has, to Rafaél's great pleasure, taken it upon herself to correct this deficiency, and has nominated herself his guide to Britain's capital. Once the capital of an empire on which, famously, the sun never set.

"There is nothing new about any of it," he continues. "It has all been around for as long as Man. Is all, in fact, much the same thing: the protection of the strong against the weak, Man's abuse of the planet, Man's inability to give, they all are part of methos. What *is* new, as I said, is the scale of those phenomena today; the scale, their intensity and consequences.

"And, just as the world's financial polarisation becomes daily ever greater and the moral cost of money becomes daily ever higher, so philosophically we will soon have extremely stark – mayhap polar – choices to face.

"Either we can allow today's methos to continue unchecked, until we create a feudalism of the twenty-first century – as absolute as that a thousand years ago, perhaps even more so. A feudalism where all our actions will be controlled by a government working exclusively for the interests of the virtual lord of the manor.

"This turning back of the clock, this is not some distant and far-fetched nightmare. It was, we need to remember, when President Bush was still Governor of Texas that the first woman was executed there since the time, Polly, of your Civil War. How is that not an attempt to reverse history's tide?

"And the feudalism too, that has already been conceived. Is the consequence (I think, absolutely the desired consequence) of the economic theories propagated by neo-liberalism. And we need no ultra-sound to be aware that the embryo is daily gaining strength. Methos even has a name for it. It calls it 'meritocracy'. As if by calling your child Clement you will guarantee he be merciful. A rose by any other name may smell as sweet, but, by any other name, sulphur also smells as *foul*. You need look no further for evidence of the lack of merit involved in this so-called 'meritocracy' than at those today who today wield their power or who are endowed with money.

"And that look will tell you, far from 'meritocracy', this is (at best) '*meretricious*-ocracy'; is the triumph of the gaudy over the genuine, of the specious over the profound, the tacky over the truthful. Is the triumph, my friend, of both barbarism and barbarianism.

"To allow the world further to degenerate in this direction would be to negotiate for ourselves a rawer deal than even Esau managed. He, after all, sold his birthright for a mess of potage. We would be selling our birthright only for a mess.

"Perhaps, Polly, that mess won't be the annihilation of Man – not quite. But, whatever it is, it will almost certainly involve misery on a scale the like of which history has never seen: a Black Death of the soul.

"Alternatively, we can start working towards creating a wethos where we start to realise that, in actual fact, without 'we' there is no 'I'. And that, in actual fact, it is that simple.

"Well, in *actual* fact, all we need do, we need to start realising that wethos is a much more efficient form of methos than is a naked, an unrestrained methos – just as finally the self is much better protected by altruism than by selfishness.

"We claim to be oh so sophisticated, Man in the twenty-first century. Is it not time we started living up to that claim?"

The Eye queue shuffles forward.

"Methos developed, of course, from a belief we had (quite possibly, as I said, when we were animals) that putting 'me' first, last and always was the best way to protect me. Is ironic therefore that 'me' is in fact so *badly* protected by methos.

"All around us we see evidence that we are, all us 'me's, already being savaged by it. Soon we are likely to be destroyed by it.

"Methos, you see, is a Frankenstein's monster, my friend, one which eventually will destroy its creator. Is not 'me' which gets protected by methos, but 'them': 'them' the 'have-in-abundances', 'them' those the already űber-rich and űber-powerful, the tiny percentage of the world's population which owns colossally the largest slice of the world's wealth.

"According to his wife, Howard Hughes was a sociopath. She was also, at the stage she voiced that opinion, his *ex*-wife and so, we must accept, she was probably looking at him through jaundiced eyes. But I do think it begs the question whether great wealth – and particularly institutionalised wealth – *sires* sociopathy."

"Or whether sociopathy sires great wealth."

"Another good question. Is interesting in Eric Schlosser's (interesting) book, 'Fast Food Nation', how careful he is to insist that the CEOs he met of these awful companies were not themselves awful. I'm afraid I was slightly reminded of how charming legend had it that Gőring was, or Hőss, the Auschwitz commandant. No, no, that is a most unfortunate reminder. Those captains of industry that I too have met were not themselves monsters. Also, mostly, charming people. So, who is it then taking the decision at, say, ITT that it will support the tortures of Pinochet's regime? Or at Ford's or Mercedes-Benz to countenance the 'disappearance' of political dissidents in Argentina? Or at Coca-Cola to market tap water?

"The ethos of today's business world, they call it a 'climate', is one where not only has capitalism been allowed to run riot, but so has the accompanying sociopathy. If a system (economic, social, political, religious or any other) has no regard for its impact on society, then it is (by definition) acting sociopathically. The institution of wealth and/ or profit (and these are not the same) has been allowed to flourish with a flagrant and absolute disregard for anything but itself or itselves.

"And we, who are the well-to-do but not the super-rich, we are beginning to see this too, albeit (for the moment) in a far less stringent form. The recent credit squeeze in the West has, I think, brought home to us the entire absence of ethics in today's ethos. And it has brought it home to us in a way that no amount of proselytising could have done. Those who continue to believe that such was caused by forces outside of Man's control are those who still believe in the tooth-fairy. There are many (myself included) who think the last recession was but the rehearsal for the real thing – one that will make that of the 1930's seem like a mild inconvenience.

"Witness, in fact, *all* the recessions, the collapse and near-collapse of financial institutions ... and the lack of serious accountability enjoyed by their executives and their cronies. Witness too the cynical contempt with which today companies treat us, who are their clients and/or customers.

"Would the bank foreclose on me? I who have been a customer of theirs for years? Who have a personal friendship with the manager? Who has honoured all his overdraft commitments? Whose personal account has invariably been in credit?

"In a heartbeat, my friend. In a nanosecond, if it thought it to do so were in the slightest bit in its interests. Would it worry about the consequences to me? Not, my friend, *for* a nanosecond.

"Would a bank sell the house from underneath your mother, who'd been its client all her life? In that same nano-second. We have thought, we middle-classes, we would be somehow protected against the vagaries and vacillations of the world. And we're not. Not if we impede by one cent the profits of the multi-nationals. Ask those like us in Argentina. Our protection by government, our security within the banking system, they are all manifestations of a ubiquitous 'climate' today which is all about packaging and nothing about substance.

"Read the menu on an aeroplane. The fare sounds, almost, as if it could be served at 'Maxim's' in Paris. The reality when the food arrives is somewhat different. The glitz of today's market, particularly when it comes to its financial institutions, is that of aeroplane menus. Such institutions have no-one's benefit in mind but their own. The so-called 'trickle-down' economy has a stopper in its bottle. Is allowed to trickle exclusively when it is that the financial institutions and the multi-nationals (often one and the same) deem such to be in their interest. Nigeria is the twelfth biggest oil producer in the world. The *average* income in Nigeria is under a dollar a day. The average income, my friend. If there are oil-billionaires and ecological rapists at one end of the scale, how many Nigerians must be living on well under a dollar a day to make that an 'average'? Life expectancy is actually dropping. In the twenty-first century, my friend.

"Whether the economy is allowed to 'trickle down' has nothing to do with whether such is in *our* interest. Not even in the interest of those being employed by vested interest. Is exclusively allowed to trickle down when is in the perceived interest of the institution that it do so. These institutions are 'methos' writ large.

"Methos indeed is, in fact, not a methos at all, is an *'abuse-of-methos'*, is a *'theythos'*.

"Is not *even* a 'theythos', actually, because even the super-rich (at least, at the level of being people) are not protected either by methos. Is institutions – the institution of super-wealth, for instance, or of the strong being protected against the weak, the institution of government or of multi-nationals – the institution, Polly, of profit at any cost ... is institutions, and only institutions, my friend, which gain from methos."

"Is it then," asks Polly, "that it *is* power which corrupts? Or that when power becomes institutionalised, it is the process of institutionalising it which corrupts it?"

"I suspect both elements feed off each other. Certainly, though, the process of institutionalisation seems to have the effect on institutions that they thereby become almost the opposite of what they were designed to be. Mostly they were designed to be good. They merely got somewhat lost along the way. Man invented institutions, I think, because he thought they would lack the personal flaws of us individually. Unfortunately they have become not only infected with man's flaws, but have created more, entirely their own. They are now much more flawed than the Man who invented them looking for flawlessness. Kafka warned us of this, of the dangers of institutions, nigh on a hundred years ago. Again is nothing new. Again is an indication that we need to tackle the illness, and not the symptoms. The symptoms may change shape but, until the illness itself is tackled, always they will remain.

"The tragedy of man's past is that he infected his institutions with his own frailties; and the tragedy of his present is that he is allowing himself to be re-infected by the frailties of his institutions. And the tragedy of man's *future* is that his future *will* be tragedy unless both those situations are addressed.

"Cults, for instance, or sects (I'm never too sure of the distinction) are formed often to help or support the weak. But cults and sects soon develop into religions. And their prophets then become priests. The religions soon become institutions. And the priests start to become cardinals and ayatollahs, who then begin to rule the institution. And as rulers these clerics then start behaving almost identically to those lay rulers whose autocratic conduct caused the cult to be started in the first place. So many trades' unions evolved in a way that was remarkably similar.

"The Russian Revolution began as the dictatorship of the proletariat and within months became the dictatorship of the Politburo. Mao's permanent revolution evolved into the hideously misnamed 'cultural' revolution. The liberal intentions of both the American Declaration of Independence and the French Revolution were soon distorted, often into complete travesties of themselves.

"Recently – and not so recently –, the *campesinos* of my country were terrorised by the national army on the one hand and, on the other, by the guerrillas, the '*Sendero Luminoso*'. *Terrorised* by them. Neither of those institutions was designed to terrorise those peasants. Indeed, I think both were designed – originally and genuinely – to *protect* them. Did not stop them, between them, killing 70,000 people."

"Like the Republicans and Democrats at *my* home," says the North American. "Originally intended to protect the man-in-the-street. Both now only protecting the street the man is in – indeed usually only the institution *owning* the street."

"Of course," returns the South American. "Such is the demand of the institution of your politics.

"Ideals in remarkably short order have throughout history been curdled by the institutions set up to protect or advance those ideals. Institutions have no soul, no conscience. That is indeed largely the point of them. They answer to no-one, are accountable to no-one. They feel allegiance only to themselves and to the present moment – not to their past or their future, and certainly not those of anything else. And they feel allegiance only to their *own* present, not the present of anyone else, not even of any*thing* else.

"Far more crimes against humanity were perpetrated by the Gestapo than by Himmler, by the KGB than by Dzerzhinsky, by the Chilean secret police, the DINA, than by Friedman. Despots create institutions, indeed, for the very reason that institutions have no conscience. And whilst is true that monsters are able to hide in the skirts of institutions, is even more the case that institutions cultivate monsterness within their ranks of the inadequate or insecure.

"The reactions are on record of Kennedy's military advisers during the Cuban missile crisis. Certainly there was some Dr Strangelove thinking amongst the Chiefs-of-Staff. But more dangerous than they was the fact that Dr Strangeloveism had so clearly infected the entire military institution which was informing those Chiefs-of-Staff. There was a 'climate' of Strangeloveism. Once institutions have become infected they will, if you will forgive the pun, stick to their infected guns with remarkable obduracy, whatever the consequences to the rest of humanity, to the rest of the planet – occasionally even to the institution itself."

The queue again inches forward.

As sometimes it is, August in London is too hot. The South bank smells of body odour and congealing shirts and sunburnt tarmac. Children whine for ice-cream cones which, when bought for them, melt faster than they can eat them. Buried tissues are retrieved from the fathoms of handbags, ironed between index- and middle-fingers, spat on and then daubed at faces to scrape away vanilla beards; the sticky hands of infants seek the sweaty palms of adults and are held distastefully.

"Institutions," he says, "always create Hamelins. They have to.

"No Hamelin ever starts off being a Hamelin, of course. All Hamelins start off as pretty medieval German towns: muralled houses and beer steins and dirndl skirts ... just with a tiny little rat infestation.

"At which time, the Hamelin vermin controller starts urging the town council to spend a few pfennigs to zap the problem. Immediately. 'A stitch in time ...,' he reminds them. But he is supported only by a slightly wizened family doctor and a few 'neurotically over-anxious' parents. The town council decides that Hamelin has better things to spend its money on. It needs a new council chamber, for example. The mayor's coach could do with a refit. They're not spending precious public funds simply to appease a few hysterics.

"And so the rats breed ... and spread. The small infestation becomes a serious one. A few children get bitten. Now the vermin controller, the doctor and the first parents are joined in their concern by a lot more parents, by worried teachers, by more health and sanitation workers. But now the cost of extermination is not a few pfennigs, but several hundred marks. A price considered too high. It would require a rise in local taxes, and when there's an election due!

"Also, so the town council decides, Hamelin's tourist trade would suffer badly from the adverse publicity. Nature will find a way to rout the rats. Nature always finds a way.

"Thus what had been a small problem develops into a big one. And even more quickly, that big problem becomes a giant one.

"This is methos at work. President Reagan did not care for the two reports previously commissioned by the Oval Office on global warming. These warned that there were clear and present dangers thereof, but that to address such would require sacrifice by American industry. This was unsatisfactory to Reagonomics, and so a third report was commissioned. From a Professor Nierenberg. Who, to the delight of his president, opined that global warming was happening slowly enough for Man to devise means of coping with it. Imagine how much healthier the planet would be today if the late president had then confronted the problem head-on.

"Is also worth mentioning in parenthesis that, at this time, Mr Gorbachov in his Murmansk speech was already expressing concern about the Arctic environment and urging unilateral action be taken about it. The history of that period, as we are told it today, needs some drastic re-editing. End of parenthesis.

"Professor Nierenberg's optimism, that is only one example, my friend, of an epidemic of wishful thinking. An epidemic which insists that tomorrow will solve the problems created by today. Income tax was a 'temporary' measure. Do you see any evidence of income tax disappearing? Would we want to visit a house which for the last twenty years would be cleaned 'tomorrow'? Such accumulated grime is the inevitable cost of methos. And an indication too of how the super-rich, as people, are not protected by it. The Black Deaths of history were no great respecters of class or of bank-balances. The powerful and the wealthy were smitten almost as much as the downtrodden and the needy. And the quality of rich lives – those that survived – that quality, if anything, depreciated *more* than did that of the poor: the more you have the more you have to lose.

"How many Hamelins are there in the world today? And not Hamelins, as in the Middle Ages, isolated one from the other? But Hamelins that are now part of the same complex? Hamelins where the rats from one are visiting another, where they are cross-breeding with those of another. Climate change, for instance, that is one Hamelin and the AIDS epidemic is another, the inadequacy (globally) of schooling is a third. The lack of nurture for our children, that is a fourth. And, yes, the rats from one Hamelin are infecting the rats from another – infecting them, cross-breeding with them. We therefore not only have the problem of the original rats still to deal with, but we have now the additional problem of super-rats.

"We today have a planet teeming with Hamelins – every continent, country, town, every village, every hamlet, every street is a Hamelin in its own right, infested with a myriad of Hamelin-like problems. Virtually every *family* is a Hamelin. Everyone in the world, we are also Hamelins all by ourselves. I read somewhere is now estimated that ninety-two percent of American families suffer from *serious* dysfunction. And, of course, one needs to know in considerably more detail what was considered by the compiler to be 'serious dysfunction', how big was the sample taken and so forth. But even allowing for a hyped hyperbole, Polly, that is an enormous figure. And is not a statement about America, but about the world. I do not believe that American families contain more dysfunction than other families elsewhere. Indeed probably less. Most American families are not hungry, for example. You cannot 'function' if famished. Not in any sense.

"The plague we have of Hamelins is worldwide – and is indeed a plague – of problems that have been allowed to fester for so long that nuisances have become catastrophes, and outbreaks have become pandemics. Catastrophes, any one of which could be become a cataclysm; and pandemics, any one an apocalypse.

"No less a brain than that of Professor Stephen Hawking, Polly, has said that man's first responsibility in the twenty-first Century is, wait for it, ... to survive it.

"Ought we not, my friend, to weigh this in the balance when we talk of man's 'progress'? Of our 'civilisation'? That we have come to a pass where, in the opinion of one of the world's finest brains, Man's single greatest ambition in the forthcoming century is only to survive it?

"How many times in their millions of years on this Earth have crocodiles put themselves in a similar predicament? Or macaroni penguins? Or dragon-flies? Just how clever *are* we? Mayhap too clever. Mayhap is our cleverness which has brought us to this pretty pass.

"Is not as simple as that there is a global plutocracy. The evidence for *that* is tenuous and almost solely circumstantial. Is far more insidious than that. There *is* a plutocracy – of course there is a plutocracy –, but is not, that, a plutocracy of the *wealthy*. Is a plutocracy rather of *wealth*.

"The global plutocracy that certainly does exist is, in other words, one controlled by the institution of wealth far more than by people with obese cheque-books. The giant plutocracy that governs the world is, in yet other words, remarkably deficient in plutocrats. The distinction is crucial. If you want to cure a sickness, is important to identify the *actual* symptoms; if you want to win a war, is important to identify the *real* enemy.

"Only rarely are people our enemies. Only very rarely are institutions not.

"There are evil people in the world. Of course there are. And if they are hurting you, is almost impossible to remember that they are doing so because they have been hurt. (Is an old adage, but a true one: 'Hurt people hurt people.') Our first reaction is merely to want to hurt them back. I understand that. Even knowing such will only create another vicious circle, we want to hurt them back. We have now become the hurt people who hurt people.

"When those that harm us are still people, though, they are not our enemies. They are people who have been hurt and who have decided (or have somehow been taught to believe) that *we* are *their* enemy. Is part of the war between the Truth and the Untruth.

"That belief may have become entrenched, mayhap is impossible to budge. There will be instances when no amount of effort will be able to do so. It nevertheless represents the only chance we've got. *Never* will we shift that animosity by hating them back.

"Hate is easy. And is part of the easy way. The easy way is the way of Untruth. It always is. And is part of the lower 'I'. Truth, though, is love and is love, *amiga mía,* which requires courage, which requires commitment. There is nothing 'do-gooder' about loving such people. Is simply the way we best protect ourselves. Not many, but some we will love back to wholeness. The fact that most of the time we will be unsuccessful does not alter the fact that such is the only chance we have that those who presently hate us will stop doing so. The *only* chance, my friend.

"And there are people too who *are* our enemies. The latterday Milton Friedmans of this world: Jeffrey Sachs, for instance, and those of Professor Sachs's ilk. Most of the world's political rulers. But these are almost exclusively those who have, in fact, *stopped* being people: They have instead become figureheads – personifications, very often, of institutions: identifiable human faces embossed on abstract forces. These abstract forces would as such forces be unacceptable. The humanising of those forces is designed to make those forces human and acceptable. They themselves would probably compare it to the personification of thunder by Thor. But that too is a lie.

"Thor is a myth, and myths exist to demystify the incomprehensible and to humanise the ethereal. Today's personifications are not myths, they're just lies. They are designed to do precisely the opposite of a myth: to elevate the banal into the divine, and make a mystery of the perfectly comprehensible.

"One of our biggest problems today (and another vital organ in methos's anatomy) is not that the *lunatics* have taken over the asylum – who *better* to run one? Our problem is that the *institution* of the asylum has taken over the asylum.

"The institution itself has become more important than any of the asylum's component parts, or the sum of its parts – and *much* more important. More important than all the psychiatrists, patients, nurses, cooks, administrators, gardeners put together; more important than the sum of all the buildings or the fabric of the buildings, all the grounds, the computer terminals, all the cars parked outside or the bars of soap within.

"The institution will protect itself against all-comers. As far as the institution is concerned, any of the component parts is expendable if such expenditure protects the institution. In fact, if such expenditure protects the institution, *all* the component parts are expendable.

"Capitalists do contain within themselves the seeds of their own destruction. Is the institution of capitalism which lacks such seeds.

"And that is so much the reason, my friend, why it is that we live in a world where the strong continue to be protected against the weak – indeed are more protected against the weak than they ever have been. Because is not only at a human level that power corrupts. Organisations designed to help the weak, as we have already talked about, soon become institutions. And as such very soon become part of the strong which need to be protected against the weak."

On the concourse around them, three street performers, made-up with 'mime' white faces, are (as Shakespeare would have had it) tumbling. They do so with a giant, bendy plastic tube. Most of the queue's children are mesmerised and enchanted by these comedy acrobatics, but a five-year-old, maybe ten yards ahead of them, is terrified.

The toddler wears crimson shorts and a stripy polo-shirt, and is trying to hide behind his mother's legs – whence he peeks back at the tumblers, equally frightened and fascinated. This sight tugs uncomfortably at Polly's memory, but the tug seeks to take her to a place she cannot yet see.

"*If* there is a twenty-second century, my friend, those living in it will regard us living today as barbarians. And they will be right to. They will see that we allowed our entire species to come to a point where its highest ambition for a hundred years would be that such species survived; and they will see that we allowed a world to develop where (as I've heard) one percent of its population owned ninety-six percent of its wealth – or (even more importantly) where ninety-nine percent of its population – *ninety-nine,* Polly, percent – was expected to subsist on four percent of its wealth. This probably is also hyperbole. But I wonder by how much that figure has in fact been exaggerated.

"If we divided this queue into ninety-nine percent and one percent, what would those respective queues look like? If we pooled all the 'wealth' of that queue and gave ninety-six percent of it to the shorter queue and four percent to the longer, what would you imagine that reaction might be?

"This is a greater polarisation of assets even than existed in Warsaw during the Second World War, where thirty percent of its population was squeezed into two-and-a-half percent of the available space. The Warsaw ghetto is now regarded as one of history's abominations. Today's even more inequitable distribution of assets, indeed one almost twice as bad, is considered to be, apparently, 'just the way the cookie crumbles'. Indeed Friedman and his ilk would suggest such were, in fact, desirable, the consequences of a free economy, the road to Utopia.

"The 40s Warsaw affected hundreds of thousands of human beings. Already a staggering amount of human misery. But today, we are talking, Polly, not in hundreds of thousands, but – Polly – in *billions*."

"There's nothing to say," Polly says anyway.

"No," agrees Rafaél. They both stay silent for a solemn moment. "I'm also prepared to bet," eventually the Peruvian continues, "that within today's wealthy top one percent, is again close to one percent which owns a good, let's say, sixty percent of the ninety-six percent."

"It's a bet I wouldn't take," says Polly.

"I'm sure I belong to the first one percent. I most certainly do not, however, belong to the one percent *of* that one percent. But, equally certainly, I do know those who do. And these people – most of them, anyway – are not monsters. I've said this before. Not akin, let's say, to those caricatures of Jews that used to lour grotesquely from the front pages of the Nazi press. Most of the super-rich that I have met are, in fact, delightful – flawed, of course, because none of us is a two-legged Bambi, but kind, attentive, cultured ... excellent company ... and, as friends, invaluable.

"More than a few times in my life I would have been completely ruined were it not for the spontaneous generosity of wealthy friends. Many, if not most, would be horrified if they were ever to know the true cost of their wealth. But from that they are cocooned. As are we all. Just as we were cocooned from the true cost of slavery, or the true cost of the Raj, or of oil.

"We are all cocooned from the consequences of our national actions or economic decisions. Journalists say of Vietnam that it was the first televised war – and the last! The cocoon is one of the tools of the lie.

"The rich's cocooning is just a more sophisticated form ... of the packaging done by supermarkets, let's say, which cocoon the less affluent of us from the real cost of our meat.

"Our responsibility lies in the fact that we like to be so cocooned. We have created those institutions which cocoon us. Is yet another indication of how urgent it is, my friend, not only to look at that which surrounds us but also at that we surround. But is also an indication of the fundamental goodness in us. Why else would institutions seek to cocoon us from the truth? Why would Professor Sachs choose to encase his ... let us call them 'theories' ... with the highly seductive title, 'The End of Poverty'?

"Professor Sachs mayhap apart, I simply do not believe, Polly, that the world's moral and/or economic dynamo (except in a tiny, tiny amount of cases) is somehow a deliberate conspiracy of multi-billionaires.

"Most of the super-rich I know, I say again, are not that callous. Nor are they, frankly, that politically adroit. In my experience, they find it hard enough to agree about the menu for one of their charity dinners. The idea that they would be capable of organising a political global cartel – however much it might be in their perceived interest – well, is, at best, that idea, ingenuous.

"That, though, does not make the planet's present situation any *less* dangerous. To the contrary, indeed, it makes it considerably more so. If the ship you are sailing is in danger of sinking because her captain is a Bligh, then you mutiny. Is simple.

"How much more perilous is your situation if that ship is in danger because she is being controlled by a faulty compass or a faulty rudder – or even by being rudderless. Particularly when you are unaware that she is. Then you have a problem indeed.

"If methos is endemic, then we are doomed. If, though, it has been adapted from a now redundant survival instinct, surely we have a need, Polly, to rethink it. Is perhaps worth remembering that change is vital for survival. Evolution depended on it. Even plants, which we think of as being without brains, adapted so they could survive. The human body is completely replaced every seven years. Is this not a lesson we should learn about our thinking, our morals, our values, our sense of purpose? Change is endemic not only to the human condition, but to all life.

"Oh, I accept that, in the foreseeable future, wethos is almost certainly unobtainable. Mayhap the very idea of wethos is Utopian. Mayhap finally there can be no Promised Land. Mayhap because the promise of the Promised Land lies far more in the promise of promise than in its realisation.

"In other words, mayhap we cannot create Heaven on Earth.

"But we can, Polly, create Hell on Earth.

"And we are doing exactly that at the moment. And each day we stoke the flames of Hell's fires. Simply by wandering around at the crossroads, failing to take the path that promises to lead us to the Promised Land.

"And that path, for all its unattainability and idealism, does serve one very practical, indeed indispensable, function: It will require us to steer away from the rocks of the raging methos dominating the world today. Logic dictates that very soon those rocks just have to smash our fragile boat, smash it into tiny pieces – the fragile boat we ride of civilisation.

"What happened in Chile and Argentina were not aberrations, but situations created deliberately. Do you know the work of Naomi Klein?"

"'No Logo'?"

"And 'The Shock Doctrine'."

"Their reading should be made compulsory."

"I entirely agree with you. Mayhap not compulsory, but certainly heavily encouraged. So very ably does Ms Klein expose the hypocrisy and double-standards involved in Friedman's no-holds-barred capitalism, how its essence has to be kept secret from those it is purporting to serve, the unspeakable cruelty it inevitably trawls in its wake – and finally its incredible inefficiency.

"Already there is talk that even affluent countries cannot afford state-run medical services, nor can they afford social security for their disadvantaged. Feeding the hungry is still considered (and very largely is!) a job for charity. The work-place daily becomes a more competitive, more aggressive and thus more hostile place; as does the business world which houses that work-place. That has to mean that the home becomes (and therefore!) a more hostile place, and therefore the street. How many hundreds of Hamelins do just those few sentences contain?

"We have so many genera of Hamelins in the world – thousands of them, maybe tens of thousands. So many genera and gener*ations* of them. And examples of Hamelins? Then, my friend, we are literally talking of billions.

"We have that many for as many reasons. But a major contributor to most of them is the fact that for far too long we have considered, and government has considered – industry has considered, technology, bureaucracy, school, religion – that is better to lie their way out of problems, or try to spin the problems into non-problems, rather than *confront* the problems. That tomorrow, as I said before, will find a solution to the problems created by today.

"How many of today's advertisements are about debt? Borrowing or getting out of debt or managing a debt now out of control? The companies involved are charging, usually, usurious interest rates. Those in debt have little choice but to pay those rates. Usually they have got into such trouble by failing to confront their problems. Is the domestic version, no more, of the same syndrome that is being mimicked locally, nationally and internationally about the whole panoply we have of problems.

"One of the biggest lies of the Untruth is that today has to be better than yesterday. When it isn't, we have to be convinced that it is. This is, in fact, the meaning of spin.

"Methos is Dorian Gray who thinks, now his portrait has betrayed him, he'll simply commission a fresh portrait.

"You don't believe me? Look under your feet. London has the problem with water that it does (I understand over ninety percent is now wasted to seepage) because for decades its sewers have not been maintained. It has the problem with its underground railways that it does, because *they* have not been maintained; and it has the problem with rats that it has (in London you are never more than a metre away from a rat) because rats have now built up a resistance to the poisons that had previously killed them. They have become super-rats. Hamelin is not *just* an analogy, my friend.

"Always these have been jobs for the next generation or the next administration or the next executive. Well, the world, *amiga mía,* is rapidly running out of 'nexts'. Very, *very* rapidly running out of them.

"And these, Polly, these problems beneath our feet, these are *tiny* problems. Minuscule problems. Problems barely registering on the Richter scale of inconvenience. Are not the problems, for instance, of generations of substandard housing and health and schooling, of generations of racial or religious hatred and family dysfunction and illiteracy and innumeracy and substance abuse and physical and sexual abuse, are not the problems of feeding the world's hungry or treating the world's sick, of vanishing animal species and plant species and ice-caps and rain-forests and fish-stocks.

"But I do say again, Polly, it is *we* who have allowed this situation – this 'shituation', as I once wittily heard it described –, not them. We have allowed methos to be the most dominant force in the world today because of the weaknesses within us all. 'They' didn't do it, 'we' did: we *all* did. We simply cannot allow ourselves, my friend, to fall into the trap of believing that the problems of the world are somehow *their* problems. We are just as responsible as 'they' are. In Aleksandr Solzhenitsyn's 'Gulag Archipelago', his history of the Leninist prison camps, I suspect the phrase that is repeated most frequently is: 'And we are all responsible for this.' Solzhenitsyn was right. It is we who are often responsible.

"Nor will we solve the problems by insisting that 'they' solve them. Or that Superman does – whether Superman be God or the United Nations or G8 or globalisation or government or industry or the IMF or Clark Kent himself. The planet will not be saved until we all stop saying, 'Is *their* job' and start saying, 'Is *ours*.'

"We have to see that 'we' created this mess as much as, mayhap even more than, 'they' did, and that it behoves *us* therefore to try to clear it up.

"Finally because 'they' will not.

"Indeed 'they' may well be fighting every inch of the way to prevent us from doing it. Methos is eventually kamikaze in its obstinacy.

"President Kennedy, he was so very nearly a great man. He missed being a great man, my friend, only by one word. If only he had said, 'Ask not what the *world* can do for you, ask what you can do for the *world*.' And Tiny Tim, Bob Cratchet's invalid son in 'Christmas Carol', he was a greater man than the greatest president ever, whoever that was, of the United States. Because that president said, 'God bless America'. And Tiny Tim said, 'God bless us, everyone.'

"Is the difference you talked about previously, Polly, between globalisation and '*mondialisation*'. Which is itself the difference between philandering and philanthropy.

"There are – let us make no mistake about that – those people doing very nicely from the present situation in the world. (A tiny, *tiny* number doing very, *very* nicely.) Many of these *are* in positions of substantial power, either industrial power or governmental power or power in the media. And those individuals are not going to cede their privileges without a struggle. But is not that, I repeat, the greatest danger. Far, far more perilous is the fact that institutions have evolved around us that will not allow that privilege to be ceded without a struggle."

The queue again shuffles forward. A few feet in front of them, an auburn-haired woman, with a complexion to match, is asking of her balding husband whether he isn't *roasting* in the jersey he's wearing. Polly can sense the man knows his wife's words are travelling; can feel the man's embarrassment as he shakes his head and replies, very quietly, that he's fine.

"This age, my friend, of so-called 'plenty'," Rafaél continues, "is also an age of plenty of dearths. Plenty of the world has plenty of nothing. And plenty of the world-of-plenty has plenty of things which are *worth* nothing. And plenty too of *that* world has plenty of dearths – not least, a dearth of real happiness.

"This age, this age of plenty, it also claims to have plenty of expertise. Well, one of the areas in which that expertise appears to be at its zenith is in throwing out the baby with the bath-water.

"This era, it also calls itself an 'unsuperstitious' age, a 'scientific' age, an 'empirical' age, a 'materialist' age – in both senses of that word too. It believes only in things which are tangible (which science in fact now tells them are *not* so tangible!) or in theories or theses which can be 'proved'. Forgetting once again how many of science's 'proved' theories are later rebutted.

"Religions are manifestly corrupt, spiritualists charlatans, maharishis businessmen in nightgowns. Ergo nothing which appeals to the soul is of any importance.

"It gets forgotten that the singer is not the song.

"Because the singer cannot hold a note, in other words, that does not mean – not necessarily – that the song is a bad one. You laugh?"

"Only at myself, Rafa. As a child, I used to struggle with Chopin's preludes on the piano," Polly admits, with a self-deprecating chuckle. This brings dimples to her cheeks that are enormously endearing. "The tone-deaf, let me tell you, were the lucky ones! Anyone else listening to my murder of his music would have thought poor Frederick unlistenable-to. I do know what you mean. Now *you're* laughing."

"Also at myself. You make *me* remember, Polly, my singing of 'Jimmy Crack Corn' in the bath. I don't even know the words. Very many 'dum-di-dums'.

"The song-*writers*, though – the prophets, in other words, who were either the instigators of sects or the early disciples of cults before either became religions –, they did, despite the quality of the song's later singers, write some extremely good songs.

"In other words, despite the way that the institution of religion and institutionalised priests have distorted their words, the prophets did have extremely important things to say.

"Listen for the song. Try to ignore the singer and listen only to the song. We are in danger, in this secular world, whilst we rightly throw out the dirty water of the rotten singer, also of throwing out the baby of the song. 'Jimmy Crack Corn' is still a good ballad despite my bathtime singing."

"And despite the fact," says Polly, "that the actual lyric is: '*Gimme* Crack Corn' – crack-corn, Rafa, was like pre-popcorn popcorn. 'Gimme crack-corn and I don't care' makes sense. 'Jimmy ...', on the other hand ... "

"'Gimme'?"

"Yup."

"You're sure?"

"Sure, Rafa."

"Which also underlines how careful we have to be about advice we hear by word-of-mouth. Chinese whispers soon develop. Within a few such exchanges sense erodes into nonsense. Is also worth remembering how many spiritual texts were, for many generations, passed down that way, by word-of-mouth."

"Right," says Polly.

"Accurately reported or not, there is some extremely good advice lurking in religious texts, my friend. Advice and wisdom that are important to all men. And mayhap deep within the credo of religions are universal truths which were understood by particularly enlightened beings millennia before the science would be available that would confirm their theories: 'All is One', for example.

"Because so many religions today advocate and propagate war

and hatred, let us not forget what the prophets actually said. Most of those prophets, for instance, enjoined us to, '*Love* thine enemy'."

"You think that's possible? To 'love thine enemy'?" asks Polly.

"Yes," Rafaél returns firmly. "More. I think, if mankind is to survive, is essential. Certainly with the weapons now available to government. The only utterly inevitable consequence of one government building a weapon is that another government does."

"There are some real bad people in the world today, Rafa," says Polly. "*Really* bad people, yeah, and really bad administrations."

"The change from methos to wethos is, like grief, a process, Polly," Rafaél says. "I think we might *encourage* that process by insisting to ourselves that, if charity begins at home, so should scrutiny.

"There is no question that there are areas of the world governed by those whose bloodlust and megalomania exceed the power of words to describe them. Certainly that is true. But I do wish we would subject ourselves and our own governments and our own ethos – wherever we live – to the same inspection as we use to dissect the regimes and 'climates' of other lands. We need such scrutiny, of course, for our own well-being. But we need it too because is only thus that our criticism of these other regimes can carry any moral weight."

"True. After the Bush/Gore debacle, we lost any credibility monitoring the elections of other countries."

"Is an amazing thing about us humans, Polly. Practically everyone in the world knows what's wrong with the world; and practically no-one in the world knows what's wrong with them.

"And is, of course, *amiga mía,* sometimes extremely convenient to have an axe-murderer living next door. We can 'tut' to our heart's content and forget about the wife-beater living under our own roof.

"I have thrown so many babies out, Polly, with the bath-water. I have tutted so often at the axe-murderer next door and ignored the wife-beater under my roof. I do know whereof I speak."

"You want to tell me about it?" Polly asks nakedly. Not unkindly, but certainly there is an issue of trust suddenly involved.

He looks at her carefully for a moment or two. He's been open too many times in his life, had candour explode on him like an emotional grenade. He's wary. He wriggles deeper into those eyes. Comes to a cul-de-sac. You cannot, he understands, cross a chasm in two leaps. He makes a decision. And then vaults with the abandon of the suicide.

"My wife died," he says. "I told you. Inma. What I didn't tell you, she died in horrible pain. And the pain I was in, watching her die in horrible pain, that was horrible too. Truly horrible. When eventually Inma did die and I had time to think – about more, that is, than the horrible pain she was in – I realised that all my thinking up to that time had been unthought. My 'philosophies' I'd acquired pell-mell – bought, as it were, in job lots –, my faith was one I'd been born into and had never really challenged. I saw dotage sprinting towards me, whilst wisdom was still struggling out of its slippers. I needed, I saw that, a complete rethink, an intellectual and a moral spring-clean, needed to re-examine my values and my ethics from basement to attic.

"My belief-system for a time became almost the inversion of what it had been. I had been a trenchant capitalist, for instance, and became a dyed-in-the-wool socialist. Religion? Well, I'll come onto that in a bit. If I had believed in black, I started to believe in white."

"Or," Polly interjects, "*neo*white!" Rafa grins lightly. "Sorry. Couldn't resist it. Sorry."

"And then, Polly, my former business partner died. Paco. He was a lot younger than me. He died of a stroke induced by cocaine. I never even knew he took cocaine.

"Nor did his wife, Aurora. Not till he died. Aurora had over the last few years developed a serious medical condition. It wasn't terminal, but it was chronic. It was also extremely painful, inexorably degenerative and incurable. It wasn't MS, but it was similar: a slow erosion of the muscles. Probably because of his drug use, Paco left her virtually destitute.

"Aurora was so much worse off than I was. I don't know why it was her case that so disturbed me. In Lima sight of those worse off than you is ubiquitous. Well, these days everywhere. Mayhap it was the fact that she had seemed up till then so okay. She had seemed, if not contented, at least able to cope with what life had to throw at her. And then she couldn't cope any longer.

"Worst of all, she felt hatred for her lost partner. She grieved not for what was no more but for what had never been. Whereas for Inma I still felt only the love I had always felt. And still do.

"Aurora helped me to realise that my inverted philosophy had been *only* that. I hadn't actually *rethought*, I'd just stood my former beliefs on their heads. I'm still spring-cleaning. It's partly the reason why I decided to get away, to come to London. That and to visit my son, of course, and his family. I'd like to do some of that spring-cleaning with you. Do you mind?"

"I'll show you London," says Polly, "and you show me round your dusty brain. Sounds like a reasonable deal."

"My dusty, I think more accurately, *soul*, my friend. I'd believed in God. Inma died and I didn't believe in God any more. All the clichés came out to haunt me: How could this merciful God have allowed Inma to have died in such pain? All that sort of ... well, not nonsense, exactly, but over-simplification. On the other hand, when priests sought to reassure me that God moved in mysterious ways, all that *guff*, well, that – frankly – I thought was downright offensive.

"And then Paco died and Aurora didn't, and I began to see that it wasn't God I no longer believed in, it was God as interpreted by religion. Which was when I started to question whether religion were indeed a force for good.

"It was, of course, particularly of the Catholic Church that I asked this – 'particularly' and 'of course' because that had been mine, my religion. But as I started to find out more about other faiths and religions, to most of those I took a similar exception. Far too many of them, Polly, as mayhap I've said before, suppress potential rather than encourage it.

"That one act alone has to make them a force for evil rather than a force for good.

"Psychiatrists will tell you, say to someone often enough that they are worthless and that's what they'll feel. When any Church tells us – and tells us over and over again – that we are sinners, guess what? It's precisely that which we'll become. When they tell us, of ourselves we are nothing, we'll start to believe our worthlessness. Is not a stone's throw away, my friend, the distance between believing myself worthless to believing *you* worthless. No, is less than a stone's throw, that distance, is less than a *spit* away. And if *you* are worthless, that is only a spit away from your *life* being worthless, your *dignity*, your *freedom*.

"The emphasis, as so often it is, is being put on the wrong end of the seesaw. Rather than deploring man's wickedness – wallowing in a self-fulfilling concept of 'original sin' – we should be glorying in his indomitable goodness.

"Mother Teresa once said she would refuse to attend an anti-war rally. Invite her to a *peace* rally, though ... There is considerably more wisdom in that statement than might be inferred from its simplicity.

"The SS and the Stasi, the KGB and MVD, Pahlavi's Savak and Khomeini's Savama ... and Hussein's 'Department of Internal Security' and President Mugabe's Gukurahundi and Pinochet's DINA – even France's erstwhile' Committee of Public Safety', these were not recruited from those who felt good about themselves, but from those tired of feeling bad about themselves.

"Nevertheless, Polly, the singer is not the song. And it behoves me to remember that. In other words, because institutionalised spirituality has betrayed humanity, that does not mean either that spiritual values are not important, nor that spiritual exploration isn't. It may even make those values and that exploration *more* important. The question is not can we afford to, but can we afford *not* to.

"Even amongst the apparently comfortably off, even amongst the more affluent of us in the West *very* comfortably off, there is a growing disgruntlement with the world today. Half-a-billion of us, as I said. And much of that disgruntlement stems, I think, from our mistaking God for religion.

"You don't have to have God to have a soul. Indeed a man without a soul is not a man. Even the most entrenched atheist has no difficulty understanding concepts like team 'spirit', a 'spirited' story or horse, a 'spirit' of humanity or kindness – even a lack of 'spirit'. I do not believe that a man who has not explored his soul can be a whole man. It may be a cliché today, Polonius's admonition, 'To thine own self be true', but is a cliché at the core of very much psychotherapy – and too of very many spiritual beliefs. The book of Job, Polly: '... till I die I will not remove my integrity from me.'"

"Job, huh?"

"Chapter 27."

"Chapter 27, of course. Remind me of the verse."

"You jest with me, my friend. Is not possible to be true to an incomplete self, therefore you have to be untrue to it. And for as long as you are untrue to yourself, your conscience will continue to jab you in the withers. You cannot therefore be happy. You cannot even be peaceful.

"And we see evidence of that, Polly, every which way we turn. Whether the consequence be an increase in domestic violence or street violence or public jostling or shoving or noise-pollution from blaring music-centres or car radios, or teenage girls on alcohol binges, or the erosion of propriety in business, or the increased dishonesty of politicians, or the ever tackier tactics of advertisers, or the collapse of Enron ... or ... or ... or.

"In a thousand different ways, some small, some tiny, some not so small, some huge. From the snarl of a bus driver to the collapse of the Twin Towers. In ten thousand, a hundred thousand different ways."

They mount the steps that lead to the Eye's embarkation point.

"When Paco died and Aurora didn't, I realised that whether or not God existed was an affair entirely private to each one of us. But whether or not we believed there was a God made not a scrap of difference about whether we should behave well or badly. Whether we heeded the higher 'I' in us or the lower one.

"Let's assume – just for the moment – that they're right, the existentialists, the humanists, the atheists. Let's assume we're all there is, that this life is all there is.

"Is that the end of spirit?

"Or soul?

"Or wonder?

"Can we not still gaze in awe at the night sky? Or be enchanted by the smell of a rose? Is murder more acceptable if there is no God there to forbid it?

"We do not need God, my friend, we do not need *religious* faith to have faith. We do not need God either in order to reverence life, or to recognise the soul of another being.

"We don't need God to tell us to love our children, feed our pets, love the kindness and potential in our fellow-man. Or if we do need a God, that God, Polly, is contained within each one of us. Mayhap indeed that God is wethos.

"True morality is not about creating for yourself a better life in the hereafter, but in the here. Morality is not important because it makes the next life more pleasant, but because it makes *this* one more pleasant.

"But for morality to *be* morality, *your* morality has to be *that*: *your* morality. You have to take responsibility for it. You cannot hide behind the skirts of your profession or your government or your church. Is *yours* the morality, and therefore yours the responsibility."

The child with the stripy polo-shirt is hauled by his mother into the slow-moving gondola, the street performers (now below) still holding their scary hold on him. The auburn-haired woman and still-jerseyed man follow. They find themselves mounting the same gondola as the child. Polly and Rafaél are the last allowed on board.

"If you believe in God, for instance, you cannot allow murder simply because your Church decides to countenance it. Any God who tells you to go out and kill in His name is anyway not a God worth having. That's a lobster praying to a pan of boiling water. Nor does the fact of your faith excuse your hatred or your nurture of inequality, whether or not your religion propagates them. Nor can you allow yourself to countenance theft because your Church may condone it – may even indulge in it!: Theft is still theft whether it is committed by individuals or by institutions.

"Morals certainly have to do with the *spiritual* part of man. They have *nothing* to do with his religious part – and their presence or absence has absolutely nothing to do with the Church he belongs to, or doesn't. They have, rather, to do with being a part of *him*. As we discussed. An *essential* part of him. And an intriguing part of him.

"The safari to the soul is the most exciting odyssey of anyone's lifetime – and probably requires the greatest courage. If methos is to be replaced by wethos, is a trip, though, we would all do well to make. Infinitely, incalculably more important than gallivanting to the moon. Most of us will, I think, be extremely reluctant to embark on it. None will return from it the person that set out. All who do will be immeasurably the richer for the experience. And so will the world be. And the planet.

"There is nothing wrong in exploring the moon. Other than its achievement masked so many of the horrors then taking place. And it diverted expertise, if not funding, away from where it might have been usefully deployed: devising cars that don't use petrol, for instance."

"You think the oil industry would have allowed that?"

"Of course it would not," says Rafaél. "Is yet another instance of finally how kamikaze methos is. Is yet another indication how important is a pervading ethos. Landing rockets on the moon is sexier than not polluting a planet or feeding its inhabitants. 'They' didn't create that ethos either – oh, they certainly encouraged it, but they didn't create it. 'We' created that ethos, my friend. Defined what was sexy, what was important, where our priorities should lie. Mostly because it wasn't us doing the dying."

"Those, Rafa, are the Houses of Parliament."

"I see them."

"Outside of which – to the great displeasure of both me and most of my compatriates (even those of us, Rafa, resident in the States for generations still feel allegiance to the Emerald Isle!) – stands a statue of the unspeakable Cromwell."

"Warts and all?"

"Know what? I was too busy being displeased to look."

"Cromwell also started with good intentions."

"So they say. Me, I've never been convinced. How happy would you be with a statue of Pizarro outside the Cortes?"

"I discovered not so long ago, the population of Peru, before Pizarro arrived, was nine million. In 1620 (that's less than a hundred years later), it was six hundred thousand. Before he arrived, Peru was one of the richest countries in the world. Today? ... Well, today, let's say, it isn't! I wouldn't be too happy, no, with a statue commemorating him."

"I'm not sure Cromwell's Irish casualties were that much lighter. They all become numbers, don't they? I mean, don't you find it hard to think of all these people as human beings? The nine million Peruvians there used to be? The thousands of Irish massacred by Cromwell? Don't you find it difficult, you know, to think as each of them having their own funny little quirks? Their own personalities? Don't they, as I say, just become numbers? Too big to really grasp? A bit like light years and such?"

"And is that not one other of Man's tragedies?"

"Yes, probably, Rafa, it is. If we did try to see all these people as being that – people –, different versions of ourselves, how differently might history be taught."

"Mayhap even taught well enough that we actually learn from it!"

"Just over the top of Parliament, there, that's Westminster Abbey. Completed, if not built (I think I'm right in saying), by England's Henry II. The same one who killed Thomas Becket."

"And that, no?, is the famous clock, Big Ben."

Polly ignores the sarcasm. "And which, as any good guide would tell you, Rafa, is actually the name of the bell, not that of either the clock or the tower."

"Interesting," says Rafaél, without over much interest.

"It weighs 13 tons, and was named after Benjamin someone or other who worked at the Whitechapel Bell Foundry where it was made. Cast, rather. 'Cast', I think that's what you do to a bell: 'cast' it. I interrupted. Excuse me."

The child in the polo-shirt is disinterested in London. His focus is rapt on the hand-rail that circumnavigates the gondola. He is fascinated by it, runs his podgy hands along its slithery length like a cabinet-maker fondling a length of very special timber.

"I'm no mystic, Polly, anything like it. Not some kind of Jain ascetic," the Peruvian goes on. "I have great respect for Gandhi. But neither am I he, nor do I aspire to be he. I enjoy comfort, like my food. I like nice things. I love them, in fact. I understand materialism. However shallow that makes me, nice things make me feel good. I don't advocate Puritanism. Joy, I think, is an essential element of happiness. In fact, if I espouse any one philosophy it would be hedonism. But a real hedonism, a genuine hedonism, a hedonism where the happiness we are seeking is, as I said, first-class, and not some pale imitation of it, which is the pup they're trying to sell us today.

"I also understand the hankering for profit. But just as we should strive for first-class happiness so we should also strive for first-class profit. Any prosperity bought at the expense of impoverishing others is a third-class prosperity. In fact, a twenty-third class prosperity. Man deserves a first-class prosperity. That has to mean a prosperity that's universal.

"The profit I understand is an impulsion. And at that point is usually fine.

"In so much of today's world, though, impulsion has ceded to *com*pulsion. And compulsion is always dangerous ... is a form of insanity ... usually it gets out-of-hand ... is often dangerously out-of-hand. Compulsions require us to do things we would not do if we were sane.

"Would a sane man tear strips out of his lungs? When we hack at the rain-forests is precisely that we do.

"Would a sane man reach into a baby's pram and snatch away its bottle? Yet is that which global economics demand that we do.

"I understand impulsion. Even, quotes, 'unhealthy' impulsion. I understand the punter who puts a few pounds on the result of a horse-race. But I do not understand the compulsion of the gambler prepared to risk his family's future on the turn of a card. And I understand even less the family that is prepared to let him.

"Yes, that is where we are. Yes, the impulsion for profit has, yes, turned into compulsion. And, yes, we 'tut' at the way our gambler father is risking our entire future. But we are, it seems to me, doing remarkably little to restrain him. And that we do not see it in these terms is only further indication that the war against Truth is currently being won by Untruth.

"At a personal level, even more do I understand the appeal of money. Life, it is considerably more comfortable with money than without it. Is also, life, beset with catastrophes and uncertainties. Money is an insurance policy: is an umbrella for rainy days, a shield against fortune's slings and her arrows, it allows us to be sick in comfort and offers a greater chance of recovery, to pay for the best advocates in case of legal trouble, to keep us comfortable in our retirement, to pay for little luxuries – even, occasionally, for big luxuries. Nothing wrong with any of that. And the wealthy Jews in the Germany of 1932, they thought they had all that.

"Money in our world also buys respect and courtesy. There is nothing in the least wrong either with wanting, even insisting, that you are treated with both respect and courtesy. Is such a shame, though, that now money *buys* both, that both have now apparently become commodities – wares that are sold rather than conduct that is freely offered. How does that not make us whores?"

"We are all whores, Rafa, today."

"All of us," Rafa agrees.

The man in the jersey, now freely sweating, has clearly heard the word 'whore'. His face whips round to hear more. But his expression seeks to remain blank, and he tries to mask his curiosity by an exaggerated peering at the sights.

"Wealth also buys sycophancy and grandiosity," says the Peruvian, "has always bought it. It countenances self-aggrandisement. Most of all, wealth buys power.

"And those, *amiga mía,* are all drugs that should be classed *double-*'A' – far more dangerous and addictive than heroin. Responsible for considerably more deaths and infinitely more misery."

"That's the statue of Boadicea. Or Boudica as she's become recently. For I'm not too sure what reason. It's from there we'll get the boat down the river. On our next trip. And that's Old Scotland Yard. You've seen that on all sorts of old TV crime shows."

"*I*, Polly, have money. Even a lot of it. Not by comparison, that is true, with Mr Gates. Against a street child of Lima, though, I *am* Mr Gates. As indeed, Polly, are you."

"Not even, let me assure you, next to a Limeñan orphan. Oh God, I'm sorry. So sorry, Rafa. You're right. Of course you're right. I was being ... I don't know: flippant, I guess. I guess that stems from ... embarrassment. I find it so hard to imagine, that degree of poverty."

Rafaél waves the apology aside as being unnecessary. "We talk, Polly, you and I, of the Church's hypocrisy. What about *mine*? Me, I'm not prepared to give my money away. How is that not hypocritical? Certainly it could be argued that I, like methos, am avaricious. Even rapacious."

"I think that's *New* Scotland Yard there. It's such an anonymous building, it's hard to tell. It's by St James's Park tube station. Old Scotland Yard's now used as overflow offices for the Houses of Parliament."

"Others, though – even socialists –, they would argue that for me to give away all my money in today's world would be irresponsible to the point of foolhardiness. (Well, they wouldn't worry about me giving away *my* money. They would argue in that way in case it were ever suggested they should give away *theirs*!) And they're both right. Both sides of that argument. ... This, by the way, this view over

London, this is a pretty stunning vista, my friend. ... And some days I agree with one side more than another, and on other days I agree more with the opposing view.

"I like to think I do, mostly, what I can within the bounds of caution. But sometimes I also doubt that. I was embarrassed when I gave so little to the tsunami relief. When I discovered, though, how Mr Varley had misdirected the funds ... well, frankly, I felt almost relieved that I was at the time so strapped for cash."

"That tall thin bit of stone, there on the Embankment, that's called 'Cleopatra's Needle'. You notice I'm 'guiding' a lot. That's to cover my embarrassment: my remark about Limeñan orphans."

"It was a moment of thoughtlessness, Polly. A moment. Don't be so hard on yourself, my friend.

"In a world where everyone is the most 'they' they can be, we'll have less need for enormous reserves of money. We will need prudence, of course, but prudence is not avarice. And money will diminish in its importance as a commodity and will increasingly become again what it was designed to be, a simplified form of barter. Once our souls are nurtured, we will feel the need less to fill the emptiness with gewgaws outside of ourselves."

"Beyond Cleopatra's Needle, is the Savoy hotel. I'm not entirely sure which building it is, to be frank. It's one of them in that grey block there. It's where Monet stayed when he painted those famous views of the Thames. Come to think of it, I'm not sure he didn't paint them from one of its balconies."

"We will not, Polly, need to keep up with the Joneses, because the Joneses will not need to keep up with us. And we will no longer be dominated by a system of economics that demands this sort of commercial war of attrition, this envy between the Joneses and ourselves.

"We will not need retail as a therapy because we will be using our friends to help us through crises – maybe talking to those selfsame Joneses we used to have to keep up with! We won't need the sense of power given to us by fast cars because our own sense of power will be nurtured by its ambience and not diminished by it. And for that reason we will not feel the need to subjugate others."

"And there ... there St Paul's. Behind it – there – a new building, rapidly becoming a landmark, the famous 'Gherkin'."

"We *will* need good restaurants, of course, because good food is a pleasure and pleasure is a large part of what life is all about. *True* pleasure, at any rate. *Genuine* pleasure. It may indeed finally be what all life is about. And we will require that in such restaurants we are treated with respect. But we can stop being fawned over. That finally debases us."

"If you look closely, you can see the Old Bailey."

"What I am not saying, *amiga mía,* is that we will ever get there: to a world, I mean, where everyone is the most 'they' they can be. That too is Utopia: a place where the promise is the promise of promise not that of realisation. I will likewise not, not if I lived to be a million, write 'Hamlet' or paint 'Guernica'. That does not mean I cannot write a letter nor sketch a map explaining where I live.

"We do what we can.

"And once we all start doing that, we will be starting to do okay. 'From each according to his talents to each according to his needs', another good axiom supplied to us by history.

"Throughout history, history has supplied us with wise men saying pretty much what I'm saying today, my friend. There is nothing new in what I am saying. Because we treat history in an imbecilic way, those wise men have usually been derided as being ingenuous – or, worse, 'idealists, for God's sake': well-intentioned but hopelessly impractical. Well, the so-called 'practical' has brought us to the verge of catastrophe, my friend. Mayhap we should start redefining what is practical and what is merely convenient to the Untruth."

"The Old Bailey, that's the central criminal court."

"Is also a requirement, if I am to be the most 'me' I can be, that I do the most of what I can. We do, my friend, the most of what we can. Finally, the destination is always the grave. Is not only that the journey is more significant, is also that – when all is said and done – the journey *is* the achievement. We do what we can. And what we can do, Polly, what we can *all* do, we can look into a mirror.

"Remember last time we met I talked about a savvy Saviour who kept on about us removing motes from our own eyes?

"If we are to address the problems there are in the world, my friend, we must also address the problems there are in us. Because there are not only Hamelins outside of ourselves, but also we have them within. We do what we can, Polly. We remove the motes from our own eyes. We start disassembling the Hamelin we each of us house."

The auburn-haired woman tells her husband (and the rest of the gondola) that she's sweltering just looking at him. Would he *please* take off his "jumper". He sighs, passes her his glasses without comment, pulls off the diamond-patterned jersey, ties its arms around his waist and, commentlessly, holds out his hand for his glasses to be returned. "Isn't that better?" his wife asks him.

"I do not know what is the solution, Polly, nor what are the solutions. But if we truly want to save this beautiful planet, it must start, that saving – it, Polly, *must* start – with each one of us accepting responsibility. I know I have said this before. We cannot say it too much. It does not help to point the finger outwards. It works best, pointed inwards. 'How am *I* …' we need to ask ourselves '… responsible for what is happening today to the planet?' Until you first tidy up your garden, you cannot criticise others for not cleaning up theirs."

"It's a lot easier, Rafa, pointing outward fingers than inward ones."

"*Claro* – excuse me: 'Clearly', I should say. History, re-assessed with less gory eyes, is the chronicling of the easy way. And what that history unequivocally teaches us is that the easy way has led us to where we are today. And where we are today would seem to be the very brink of disaster."

"Back, Rafa, to: 'Do we have what it takes to do what it takes?'"

"Yes."

"Do we? Do you think?"

"I do not know, my friend."

"Maybe we should start finding out."

"We do, my friend, what we can. We remove the motes from our own eyes."

The Eye has almost gone full circle.

The child with the stripy polo-shirt looks around anxiously for the tumblers. And Polly remembers as a child being terrified by a clown at a circus her father had taken her to. And she remembers her father finding her terror considerably funnier than the antics of the carrot-haired harlequin.

"Thank you so much, my friend, for this trip. I cannot tell you how much I enjoyed it: A wonderful view, Polly, of a wonderful city."

"It's as wide a picture of the town as you get. Hall, by the way."

"Hall?"

"Benjamin *Hall*, the man after whom Big Ben is named."

"Always so valuable, wide pictures."

"There's one thing, though," says Polly, "about wide pictures."

"They need long drinks to accompany them?"

"Took the words, my dear Rafaél, right out of my mouth."

Chapter 5

Giselle doesn't care that he's married.

She's leaving the doctor's surgery. She hadn't needed this confirmation. She'd known since the night it happened: 'the' night. A home pregnancy test had already been the braces added to the belt. This visit was a *second* pair of braces.

She's used to floating now. She's been floating since 'the' night. She understands now why it was the ancient Romans attached wings to Mercury's sandals. She continues to be surprised that no goddess was also so endowed. She quadrilles on wingéd feet through all the pantheons of all the world, her dance-card marked by Venus and by Wodin, by Shiva and by Eros. She knows that all gods now want her as their confessor and as their confidante, that all gods are now her minions, her slaves. That they are also still her masters.

The gods, all gods, are her allies. They are her friends, her peers, her co-authors, co-creators ... co-conspirators; she knows she is blessed amongst women – and amongst men; she knows too that *all* women are blessed amongst women, and amongst men; knows that all men are as well.

She knows, as well as Rodolfo, the archangel Gabriel entered her that night, and that Gabriel had been entered by every angel and every god, every pixie and hob-goblin that had ever been – both those known and those still yet to be known.

She'd lain that night with ten billion souls as, ten billion times over, her virginity had been restored to her. This was the immaculate conception.

As all conceptions are.

Immaculate.

And because all conceptions are immaculate she doesn't care that he is married.

But he does.

Chapter 6

They meet at the ticket-office in Westminster underground station. They take the stairs up to the street which finds them opposite the side of the Houses of Parliament. From there they walk towards Westminster Bridge, across the Embankment, and take the steps to the river over which a petrified Boudica and her daughters ride defiantly in their chariot of axled knives.

"There is some irony in that," comments Polly of the statue.

"In?" asks Rafaél.

"The English celebrate Boudica's stand against Roman tyranny, and its villainy. And yet their institutions continue to be riddled with Roman influence. That influence continues to constitute a major problem."

"Rome's influence likewise on Christianity – *Imperial* Rome's, I mean," says Rafaél. "Imperial Rome, which should more correctly be called 'Tyrannical Rome' or 'Despotic Rome'. Mayhap 'Psychopathic Rome'. Is an interesting side-note in history that Mars, the God of war, was worshipped almost not at all in ancient Greece. In imperial Rome, however, he was almost on a par with Jove."

He thinks he can smell coffee. He looks around him to see whether or not there is some kind of al fresco coffee stand, but he can see nothing like it. Other than, just before the bridge, there is a man selling hot-dogs from a van. Curiously, Rafa can smell neither hot-dogs nor onions frying, but he can still smell the coffee. He decides he has to be imagining it.

"Amazing, isn't it?" Polly continues, "Rome is hailed as some kind of paragon. As if public baths somehow exonerated slavery, or straight roads nullified genocide. Those straight roads, Rafa, became roads of great danger for humanity – in both senses of 'humanity'. They still are. Not any longer because of what they *are*, those roads, but because of what they symbolise. And continue to symbolise. How avowedly redolent of ancient Rome in so very many ways was Nazi

Germany. How rarely do you hear that comparison made.

"Over and over (and, Rafa, over) when we trace back today's muddled thinking or addled thinking – that which has, to use your phrase, Rafa, brought us to this 'pretty pass' ..."

"We find the influence of Rome," Rafaél finishes the sentence for her.

Polly agrees with a smile. "So many roads still lead to Rome."

"That's less of a problem," Rafaél returns, "than that, still today, so many roads lead *from* Rome. Rome, for one thing, was for many years an oligarchy pretending to be a democracy. Sound familiar?"

"And espoused a dual system," Polly continues, "where there was one set of principles for the patrician, and another for the plebeian."

"And another yet again for the emperor," Rafaél adds. "Or rather, there was an acceptance that the emperor was somehow above all constraints in regard to morality – even legality. Again, sound familiar?

"At the other end of the scale, the slaves and the downtrodden, the 'untouchables'. Interestingly, the Hindus also divided their world into four remarkably similar castes.

"We have to consider, therefore, that there may be something appealing to us, at some level, of so organising society. I mean, even prison society (which is a very basic structure) also organises itself along similar lines.

"Basically, is that which we also have in the wider world today: a handful of emperors, those quite above the law and ethics and morality – those for whose glory the rest of humanity works; there are the patricians, those with wealth and power (subject always to the emperor's approval and his whim); the plebeians, who live okayly provided they toe a line (one drawn in the sand by the emperors and rubber-stamped by the patricians); and there are the slaves. Who are fed and clothed, but who have in reality no rights beyond that. There is also the fifth class – one, I think, deliberately created: the untouchables, the untermensch, the Jews of the Third Reich. They serve as a ghastly warning to the other four remaining classes of what awaits them should they incur the emperors' displeasure.

"The Romans (actually) did not invent this system either, just endowed it with the laurels of being 'civilised'. For two thousand years we have bought into that lie. Societally it would appear that we are still wearing togas."

"Often," says Polly, "societally we are still covered in fur. Roman emperors were mostly sadistic psychopaths and sociopaths, who executed friends, even their family members, on a paranoid whim, who subjugated all around them in a terror as absolute as the Nazis' – monsters who indulged plentifully in paedophilia, incest and rape. How many of Caligula's later outrages could be traced back to the fact that Tiberius outraged *him* as a child? Yet we continue to talk of Roman 'civilisation'.

"Is it any wonder we have a somewhat bizarre understanding of the word 'civilisation'? It's one of the Hamelins that has grown because, for so many centuries, history has been so appallingly taught.

"It's also one of the reasons for another Hamelin: the sort of bifurcate morality I was talking about – one for me and one for everyone else. 'Do as I say, not as I do'! This is another nonsense part of methos."

"It doesn't require rocket science," says Rafaél, "to recognise that most of the world's traffic-jams today continue to be caused by thoughtlessness, by a self-defeating selfishness. The driver, frustrated at being in a jam and therefore blocking a side-street, is usually in that jam because further along the road another frustrated driver has blocked another side-street. It may be human to want to block the side-street, but is still unnecessary and irritating. And is conduct we do well to change both at a personal and at a communal level. Is also worth remembering that, meeting another car in a narrow country lane, is impossible for either car to move forward unless one car gives way. How many of the world's problems today are two drivers confronting each other in a country road, both refusing to give way to the other?

"Infinitely more pernicious even than this, though, does it become, that same two-tone morality, this mutual stubbornness, when is indulged in (as it is throughout the world!) by institutions. So many of which would have us believe that a different set of principles need apply to them, to corporations generally, to their officers and share-holders, than do to the world at large."

"I've known a few movie-directors with the same idea!" Polly snorts, mostly to herself.

"At heart, this proposition has about it the same intelligence as the notion that commercial vehicles should drive on the opposite side of the road to private ones. But, insane as it is, that is what we *do* have. Worse: we also have a system where the limousines of the wealthy are allowed to flout the rules all other cars have to obey. And yet we wonder we're now in traffic chaos. Approaching grid-lock. It beggars belief, the crassness of it all.

"It may be completely unrealistic to suppose that our politicians or our clerics or our industrial magnates should be held to a *higher* moral standard. But that does not mean they are allowed to claim for themselves a *different* one.

"And precisely because institutions do not have souls or consciences, at corporate and bureaucratic levels, the need for institutions to be informed morally is not less urgent but more. Considerably more. And for precisely that same reason too, institutions – *of course* – have also to be held to more stringent, not looser, moral standards than do human beings.

"And to think anything else is simply to believe in a nonsense which the world inherited from the Romans.

"The problem with history is not that we don't learn from it, but that we learn the wrong things from it. We are the child who, having nearly drowned, resolves never to go near water again. Rather than learning how to swim.

"I do not agree with Marx's interpretation of history, but I do agree with him that history needs to be re-visited, re-chronicled, re-

assessed.

"I have heard history described, my dear Polly, as the biographies of great men. I hear it being described as that even today. This is a view of history started by ancient tyrants several millennia before Christ, propagated by Julius Caesar and Machiavelli. Plutarch as well. Why does our hankering for the new not extend also to the way history is taught? Is most assiduously, history, not 'the biographies of great men'. So few in the history books are great, in any sense of the word. Which political or military leader would you want to spend time with? Which historical figures could serve as positive, as opposed to negative, role models?

"There are exceptions, of course there are. Overwhelmingly, though, history is the biographies of bullies and moral degenerates and vandals – and of a few brave souls fighting against them. What that teaches those who aspire to be in history books is that they too need to be bullies and vandals and moral degenerates.

"Is not that is unfortunate we have today governing us those who do govern us. Or rather what *is* unfortunate about that is that, given the way history is taught, is virtually inevitable. The likes of President Mandela and the Mahatma Gandhi are as notable as they are precisely because they are so exceptional."

"Not forgetting Martin Luther King," Polly adds.

"Of course, Polly, not forgetting Martin Luther King. We must start calling historical spades spades. Peter the so-called Great's principal greatness was for killing. Was even Galileo a great man? He was a great scientist, but a great *man*? I have no idea, my friend. Edison and Newton were also both great scientists. Mayhap that forgives their unpleasantness as human-beings, I don't know that either. What is there in their lives which forgives the viciousness of Henry VIII, say, or Ferdinand and Isabella of Spain or most of the Chinese emperors? '*Veni, vidi, vici*' ... '*L'état, c'est moi*' ... these phrases, they may be endowed with pith, but they do not flow with humanity.

"Of course we must re-assess history. Of course we must. We need urgently to redefine our heroes, the whole notion and understanding of heroism.

"Roman heroes were demi-gods, objects of veneration. Today we still have demi-gods; we call them 'role-models'. They are almost always chosen for us. But they come to expect similar veneration to that afforded demi-gods. Which would be entirely their problem. Were it not for our problem: which is that we give it to them.

"Our heroes are exaggerations of that we aspire to. We therefore start emulating them. Often in whatever way we can. You don't become a concert pianist by practising the harp, and certainly not by playing bridge. When we venerate bullies, we venerate bullying. Which of the world's political leaders today is not a bully? If we venerate bullying, we will create more bullies. This, my friend, is not rocket science either.

"Certainly some soldiers are heroes. The lives lost in wars by soldiers are lives which are owed reverence – more reverence than they're presently given. Those soldiers thought they were making the ultimate sacrifice on *our* behalf. That, sadly, does not alter the fact that only very rarely have those lives been forfeit for any reason other than the self-aggrandisement of some tinpot despot.

"I'm not talking about *rewriting* history, '1984'-like. The '1984' approach to history I have, in fact, always found uncomfortably close to the way history has (if you will forgive the pun) historically been taught. Certainly to the way I was taught it. What I *am* talking about is going to the mirror to re-examine our reflection. Nationally, as well as personally. Is in very different ways that we look into mirrors if we are simply combing our hair, or if we have just been told we're going bald."

"That sounds like an analogy with its own history," says Polly.

"As you too, my friend, have, I think, your own history. 'The History ...' no? '...of Miss Polly'!"

"Yeah, very funny, Rafa."

"We can only re-chronicle, re-assess history," he continues, "by identifying what we want our future to be, and then seeing how history has helped or hindered that cause – or, more precisely, where it has done either. Finally we can also only judge our present in the same way. The past means nothing without the future."

A middle-aged woman sits behind a pane of thick glass in a wooden chalet. From her Rafaél buys two one-way tickets to Greenwich. Despite the heat, he can see she has an electric fire burning. All bars. She has a chalked face and wears a rubber and dimpled thimble on her middle-finger. She seems to pore over her roll of cloakroom tickets in the way he imagines Scrooge would have counted his guineas. He folds the tickets, puts them in his pocket.

"We'll have seen most of this from the Eye," Polly comments, almost apologetically.

"As we also saw much that we saw from the Eye from Primrose Hill," Rafaél reassures her. "And this view will be as magnificent as either of the other two. Is always good to have different perspectives. Is healthy to note how things change by a difference in our point-of-view. This does not make one view righter than another, more accurate, even prettier – the new view is just different. If there is only one side to an argument, whatever you think *is* an argument is not one. At that point it becomes a doctrine or dogma – and untouchable. That which is rigid is also very fragile. It snaps easily, it becomes worthless.

"I understand that Jesuits start their learning by proving that God doesn't exist. If I have heard that correctly, is one of the few things in their way of life of which I whole-heartedly approve. The 'Mishna' in Judaism teaches that the question is not how much knowledge has been acquired, but whether the process has even begun. The word 'sikh' means 'student'. I seem to remember reading in one of the Dalai Lama's books about the Nalada school of Buddhism. This, as its central purpose, exists to challenge all Buddhism's precepts. This seems to me an extremely healthy way of subscribing to a faith."

They join the small queue waiting patiently behind a light chain, manned by one of the boat's crew: a tallish man, leanish, in his early thirties. There is nothing '-ish', though, about his hair, which, along with his beard, is an unequivocal and unapologetic orange.

"When we blind ourselves to anything we deprive ourselves," says Rafaél. "When we do so to the virtues of those who disagree with us is an act of self-sabotage quite as great as that we commit when we fail to recognise the faults of those who agree with us. I am quite sure Professor Sachs and Mr Blair take the pain of their family very seriously, that both would be entertaining as dinner guests, that both would lend their friends money if times were lean.

"We like to think of things, my friend, as black-and-white. Is so much easier that way. But is very, *very* rarely the case.

"War, for instance, is very black-and-white. Is mayhap, I suspect, precisely that, one of the aspects that we find most seductive about it. We are the guys in the white hats and the Iraqis or the Argies or the Vietcong, they're the guys in the black hats. Is all very cut-and-dried. As the military is all very cut-and-dried – literally. Short hair: good; long hair: bad ... obeying orders: good; disobeying orders: bad. In a war, everything done by us: good; everything done by them: bad. The bombing of Dresden is acceptable because such is the Primrose Hill, my friend, against the Everest of Auschwitz.

"One of man's most besetting weaknesses – we touched on this, Polly, in an earlier conversation – is that we like to blame 'them'. We, in fact, *love* to blame them.

"Man's favourite pet is not the dog or the cat or the budgerigar or the tortoise. Is the scapegoat.

"We love our scapegoats, we're in fact *addicted* to them: No dysfunctional family is complete without one.

"With war the *national* dysfunctional family has ready-made scapegoats, permanent ones.

"Which is yet another reason why government loves war. Because so often, when not at war, the scapegoat becomes them.

"Government also loves war, because it debars too much scrutiny at home. Which is why today is a 'war' we have on terror. When the IRA was involved in similar acts, there was no 'war'. The government then went to extreme lengths *not* to call it a war. There was no 'war' against the Mau-Mau or the Malay insurgents or Baader-Meinhof or ETA or the Weathermen or the *Sendero Luminoso*. To have so called it would have been to give these groups a kudos governments were then anxious to deny them.

"We have a 'war' today because today, I suspect, government has a greater fear today of scrutiny.

"Listen to the rhetoric of today's politicians. Those of us protesting against the lies told us are 'giving succour to the terrorists'. Likewise those of us lamenting the erosion of human rights. Or complaining about other less than honourable actions executed by government – in Britain the devastating inefficiency of the management, for example, of the health service. Do not look so surprised, my friend. My son, Rodolfo, he is a surgeon here. He has told me all about this."

"Okay," says Polly, seizing her default position.

"By declaring a 'war' against terror, Polly, the politicians are allowed a rhetoric that would otherwise be debarred them.

"This is an enormously efficient way of veiling the Third World War: that between Truth and the Untruth. 'Too much information,' they are allowed to tell us ('allowed to' because we live in a time of 'war'), 'would surrender too much advantage to our enemy.' If the terrorists didn't exist, my friend, they'd have to be invented."

The Thames, like the Danube, is never actually blue except in the fantasy of artists. But, on days such as today, when the sun of late summer tambourines upon it, its grey does *include* blue – a deep metallic blue – and that causes the river's greyness to deepen, from that of a dolphin to that of a sperm-whale. The river is mill-pond calm. The tide is coming in.

"And who (it might be pertinent to ask as a side-issue) and what *created* those terrorists?

"Yet other questions we all too rarely ask ourselves. Why? Because looking into a mirror is such an extremely painful business. Is so much more pleasant just to indulge our fondness for scapegoats. To blame an ever-present 'them' and not look at ourselves.

"The reason why the press was as scathing as it was of the British royal family just after Princess Diana's death is exactly a case in point. I'm no monarchist, as you know. If anything, to the contrary. Which does not mean, of course, that I dislike the British royal family as people. I even admire some of them, even quite a lot. I know, I know ... that, I know, is a digression.

"The British press would insist that, unlike me, it *were* monarchist. And yet it spent a week mercilessly chastising the royal family for what it called their callousness. That same press had, as her brother emphatically announced, killed Diana. (Well, yes, that – of course – is contentious; less contentiously they contributed to her death.) As a matter of great urgency, you would have thought, the press consequently needed to examine itself and its methods. How very much easier, though, to point the finger outwards, to find a scapegoat and divert the public's anger from where it should have been, on Diana's murderers (and, whether or not MI5 planned the whole thing, and whether or not the chauffeur was drunk, the paparazzi – at the very least – abetted her death) ... to divert the public's anger away from them and onto a family in grief.

"Now, I don't think those advising the royal family at that time did a good job. And probably the family itself did not conduct itself with sufficient sensitivity to the surrounding distress. (And there were, admittedly, considerably more factors to that distress than simply her death.) But we do not always behave appropriately when we are in grief. We are not in full possession of our faculties. And the editors working at the time had, I presume, felt grief. Had known therefore that grief can do strange things to us – even the most level-headed of us. Would in almost any other circumstance have cut this family in grief considerably more slack. Except that the press had to divert attention away from where much of the real guilt was – with themselves.

"And for precisely that reason, *if* the royal family had behaved in the way the press criticised them for *not* behaving, I'm sure they would have been impugned for being 'populist', for trying to 'hide their guilt by currying favour'. If the royal family had behaved *impec-*

cably, they would have been criticised for *behaving* impeccably, for being automatons, for not allowing themselves to be human. And if the royal family had somehow managed to square all the circles and behave in a manner that was above reproach, the press would have found someone else to malign: the French traffic police, for example, or French doctors. Anything to stop them looking at themselves – or stop us from looking at them.

"Too often too many institutions behave in exactly the same way as did the press in that week after Diana's death. Too often we ourselves do!

"Institutions like war for similar reasons to governments: no-one in war has too much time to investigate them. It continues to amaze me that neither IBM nor Coca-Cola has been forced to make a public apology for their wartime profiteering, for their abetting of Nazi Germany – and, in IBM's case, for their direct assistance in the Holocaust. I mean, if it was right (and I think it was) that the citizens of Bergen were made after the war to file past its corpses, why was the same de-cocooning not held appropriate too for the CEOs of IBM and Coca-Cola? Surely no-one in the world would suggest that double-standards were being applied.

"When not at war, scapegoats are more thin on the ground. Immigrants, they're good ones. Immigrants have been good scape-goats for as long as there have been national boundaries. The histories of France, Spain and Italy are histories where immigrants from one in lean times have been criticised by the others in times of prosperity. French emigrant workers were 'stealing' the jobs of Spaniards and/or Italians; and vice versa. Likewise the Chinese at the end of the nineteenth century when they came to my country and to the United States.

"When not at war, life becomes more complicated, issues become more complicated. We cease dealing with simple, black-and-white arguments, and start having to fathom those of ever more subtle shades of grey.

"How many greys do you see in the Thames right now? Is not one colour there, but a hundred. Mayhap a thousand. And, as Monet will tell you, is all those colours together which make the colour of the Thames.

"And all that colour is, is *today's* colour of the Thames. Not even today's, but the colour of this moment. And that colour is not the same colour as it was the other day. Or as it was even a second ago. Nor is it the same colour boating on it as it is seen from the Eye. It takes a hundred, maybe a thousand greys to make the colour of a river.

"To make a tenable *morality, amiga mía,* takes yet more greys – a thousand greys, probably, mayhap *ten* thousand of them. And to make a *person* ... ten thousand times' ten thousand greys.

"When I was writing the eulogy for Inma's funeral, I realised it was she who was the mass. She was the mass because that which was holy about her still was. But she was also *a* mass ... sorry, Polly ... a mass of contradictions. Oh, at some level, of course I'd always been aware of that. But it was only as my pen was touching the paper that I was forced to recognise it.

"She was a kind woman, for instance, extraordinarily kind, Inma. She hated any form of cruelty, would find homes for stray dogs, take wounded animals she found to the vet. And yet, as soon as ever we landed in Mexico, the first thing she'd want to do would be to go to a bullfight. She hated the noise and bustle of town but insisted we live in the heart of it. She loved jazz, but almost never listened to it. Oh, and a thousand similar quirks.

"But as I was facing all these contradictions in her, so was I constrained to do so around myself. I hate football, for instance, and jingoism, yet cannot resist sneaking a closet look if Peru is ever playing. Even as a staunch capitalist, I was always a republican. Yet I watched Prince Charles's marriage to Diana with the tears running, *amiga mía,* with the tears *streaming* down my face.

"We are all, I think, a mass, Polly, of such contradictions. And mayhap we're all as interesting as we are largely for that reason. We're all, as I have often said, fallible and we're all contrary. Is not important that we are, that seems to be endemic. Is what we do with those contradictions, is that which matters. Is how we handle them. How we try to ensure we come down on the right side of any ethical problem."

Along the river's centre, chugging downstream is a tug towing two ... three ... *four* barges. Of rubbish probably. It is for centuries, for millennia, that people have been boarding boats at this point. Not one person in the lengthening queue is conscious of that. And yet the sense of history – and the sense of history's unity – penetrates the subconscious of each one of them.

"The lie, of course, incorporates so many lies. So very many. More lies even, Polly, than there are Hamelins.

"Mayhap, Polly, returning to our chat the last time we met, mayhap the very first lie we need to vanquish is that the strong are actually strong. Or that the weak are indeed weak. Because the fact of the matter is, of course, that the weak are not weak at all.

"The only thing we need to do to realise our strength," Polly recites from memory, "is to realise it."

"Which wise man said that?" Rafaél asks. Polly withers him a lopsided grin. "The so-called weak are, in fact, my friend, *enormously* powerful. And is for that reason the strong feel the need to protect themselves against them. Eventually is the weak who are Dr Frankentein. Is the weak who create the institutions, the monster. It has, yes, that monster started to control them, is threatening now to destroy them. But is still *their* monster. Once they become aware of what it is doing, they can start to disassemble it.

"Very often, Polly, we create those institutions – 'we': the weak – we create them to dilute our own responsibilities and to emolliate the urgency of looking into ourselves. Is easier to blame governments for health service cuts or disastrous schooling than ourselves for having voted for tax cuts.

"The tragedy of man's past, I repeat, Polly, is that he infected his institutions with his own frailties; and the tragedy of his present is that he is allowing himself to be re-infected by the frailties of his institutions. And the tragedy of man's future – I also say again – is that his future *will* be tragedy unless both those situations are addressed.

"We don't like to look inside – either institutionally or personally – for many reasons. Is, I think, indicative that more people have travelled to space than have ventured into the deep ocean.

"One reason at a personal level is, I feel sure, that we're so scared of what we may find there. And for how much of that nastiness we will ourselves be responsible. We're scared that, at a personal level, we too are Hamelins. Scared we have often acted in exactly the same way in connection with ourselves as Hamelin's town council did with its burgh.

"And the reason why the strong *are* strong is because often they do look inside. They therefore, unlike the weak, do comprehend the paradox: They realise not only how weak they actually are, but also how strong are the weak.

"Unlike the weak too, they have learnt the lesson of David and Goliath. And that lesson is that David did not win. Goliath lost. And Goliath lost because he thought David was weaker than he was. He had contempt for him. Contempt is not only contemptuous but also self-defeating. Is the ingredient in pride which guarantees the prideful's fall.

"From that day forth, the strong have only very rarely underestimated the strength of the weak. Indeed in other circumstances their vigilance would be admirable. And their vigilance today remains as rigorous. Which is why they continue to devise so many instruments to stop the weak realising their power – yes, Polly, again in both senses of the word 'realise'."

"You think it's a coincidence we're having this conversation in the shadow of the Houses of Parliament?"

Rafaél laughs lightly. "Psychiatrists will tell you there is no such thing as coincidence."

"I've known a few believers in God who say likewise. 'Godincidence,' they call it."

"God and psychiatry are not as diverse, my friend, as you might think. Jung was, if I remember aright, a firm believer in the spiritual hankering at the core of man, of too the coupling of spiritual health with psychological health. Many modern concepts of healing include elements of the spiritual. I think there are things being done today, my friend, to try and find the baby, and retrieve it from within the effluent.

"One of the ways that is happening," he goes on, "is that we're allowing ourselves a certain eclecticism in our beliefs. Is religions which create heretics, not God.

"Well, I suppose what I'm saying is that *I'm* allowing *myself* some eclecticism in mine. I have read things which I find appealing in most faiths. Indeed I think the greatest act of faith I have ever made is learning about other faiths. Probably too that is the single greatest act of devotion I have tendered to God.

"One aspect I find attractive about Buddhism, for instance, is that, as I understand it, Buddhism has no commandments. It has rather a series of suggestions. Which, of course, makes Buddhism much harder work."

The orange-haired man unhitches the chain and the, now not so small, queue starts to embark.

"Dealing not with black-and-white, my friend, only with shades of grey, that too is much harder work. Suggestions are harder to follow than dictates. Dictates save you the problem of questioning yourself. Another of our most besetting weaknesses as a species is that we are lazy."

"Busted!" admits Polly.

"Oh, me too," Rafaél returns. "I think of an afternoon couch-potatoing as a heavy work-out. But is a different kind of lazy, that which stops us all from taking responsibility for our moral selves.

"You cannot possibly frame laws to cover every future eventuality," Rafaél adds, tossing a casual hand at the Palace of Westminster. "Is just not possible, *amiga mía*. But you can develop principles which do."

"Right," Polly agrees.

"The seven deadly sins, for instance. Is a good place to start an examination. The problem with the seven deadly sins is not in themselves but in what has become their inviolability. We never return to examine them: their efficacy or efficiency or relevance."

"Didn't the pope do that a couple of years ago?"

"He tried. Mayhap it was a valiant try. At least it was a try. But substance was lacking, it was an old haircut with modern lacquer. The investigation needs to be far more radical. How would we feel about visiting a dentist who was using tools of even fifty years ago? And yet we feel it appropriate to examine our own consciences (which, if anything, are even more sensitive than teeth) with tools of over two thousand years ago! Our cars we send for servicing every year or so. And that which underpins our whole life? Every, so it seems, millennium."

"Good morning, ladies and gentlemen," announces the tannoy irksomely. *"Welcome aboard the ..."* The boat starts to pull away from the pier, its motors throbbing a sort of laryngitic gargle.

"Sin is a big word," says Rafaél.

"A religious word," suggests Polly.

"Even in a secular world, still big. Huge, in fact."

"... Our journey to Greenwich should take thirty-five minutes ..."

"The seven deadly sins, as described in the Bible, are only, in my opinion, seven vices. Usually, only shades of grey again. Indeed, often, they are virtues. Pride, for instance. What's wrong with pride? Nothing, that I can see, wrong with pride.

"*Arrogance* is dangerous and unattractive. Arrogance stops us listening, is one of the elements which persuades us we are always right. And when we stop listening, belief becomes dogma. And from dogma to the gulags is a very short hop indeed. Arrogance *does* threaten humanity. Arrogance *is* a sin. But arrogance is not pride.

"Being proud of our work makes us work better, being proud of our children nourishes their confidence, being proud of ourselves helps us to square up to those who seek to demean or abuse us. Being proud of the achievements of Man is appropriate – the slaves erecting the blocks at Stonehenge, those who died building the pyramids were all brush-strokes on the 'Mona Lisa'; the crews on the 'Santa Maria' or the 'Mayflower' or the 'Beagle', each man of them, they are each of them notes, the total of which is a symphony of what could be eternal beauty."

They pass through a small cabin with a bar (not yet open) and a few Teflon-topped tables. Most of the boat is open to the elements, its well-swabbed deck jigsawed with blocks of benches, slatted with wood which is varnished a dark brown.

"Oh, any one of the seven, quotes, 'deadly sins' *can* be sinful. And often are. But rarely in the way described by churchmen.

"Let me be clear before I go on about the distinction between a vice and a sin – or my understanding, anyway, of that distinction: A sin, to me, is something which *threatens* mankind. A vice is that which *demeans* mankind or *debases* it. And, yes, certainly, I can be both viceful *and* sinful. No doubt about that. But is no good my saying of myself, 'Oh, I'm full of pride', for instance, without analysing what aspects of that pride are viceful, and what sinful. And what, indeed, might be beneficial."

"You have to look into a mirror?"

"You mock me, my friend?"

"Maybe just a little."

"It always appals me how difficult I continue to find it to be mocked. Is, I'm afraid, *my* pride."

"Should I apologise?" asks Polly.

"No," replies Rafaél. "I fear it is I who should be. Apologising, I mean. Probably to myself."

Polly and Rafaél make their way to the boat's stern. They prefer to stand. Being England, they have brought jerseys and umbrellas just in case, but these have been stowed in the black leather shoulder-bag Rafaél has brought with him for just that purpose.

"Much of pride, you said, is beneficial."

"Hugely, *amiga mía*. I have often wondered how a Church which condemns pride can also have the arrogance to suggest that only she can interpret God's words; nor that a marriage not consecrated by her is no marriage at all and thus a sin. This is not even arrogance, this is hubris."

"Part too, isn't it," suggests Polly, "of 'Do as I say, not as I do'?"

"Part, yes, of that methos too. Is hubris, my friend, not pride which usually precedes a fall. Is hubris, not pride, which is both the vice and the sin. *Is* good for us, much of pride.

"Pride in our work, as I said, makes us work better and more happily. Artisans were considerably happier as people, by and large, than their relatively better paid heirs working on assembly lines.

"If we are happier, we are more pleasant to be around. If we are more pleasant to be around, we create a more pleasant atmosphere around us, which has to benefit those around us. Who – consequently – also become nicer people to be around. Thus a benign spiral. Instead of the vicious one we see all too prevalent today."

"Because the work-place is so hostile."

"Well, is one ingredient, my friend. Yet another Hamelin. Another is because so few people are allowed pride in their work. And yet another is that mostly is considered that wages are sufficient in terms of remuneration. Such very few workers (even today 'workers' in professions) as do receive any acknowledgement receive a recognition as token as an ansaphone thanking us for calling. It means precisely nothing."

"Tell me about it," Polly agrees.

"... On our left, ladies and gentlemen, Old Scotland Yard. This now houses offices ..."

"There is also a phony pride which is a sin, a pseudo-pride.

"Talk, for instance, to people who have served in the armed forces (women quite as much as men), particularly with those who have not seen combat. Most talk of their days so employed with great affection – and with a deal of so-called 'pride'. The forces instil pride. And there would be nothing wrong with that. Other than the pride the forces instil is a false pride and a fabricated, a phony pride. Is not endowing unconditional self-worth, is endowing worth which is very conditional indeed."

"Sounds like something else which might have been inherited from the Romans."

"Very possibly, my friend. The military process starts by *stripping* the new recruit of all pride. It usually starts with that recruit being physically stripped. That is no accident. He, or she, is so humiliated, so debased that he can have no self-worth left – except in relation to the worth ceded to him by those in, quotes, 'charge' of him. The process of basic training or boot camp is one designed to make you into a number, an automaton, amenable to the fact you are merely cannon-fodder because such, so your indoctrination tells you, *is* your only worth.

"But hand-in-glove with this spiritual denuding, you are given boots to sparkle and buckles to glint; you cut a dash in your uniform. (And, no, I don't know why that is, but it seems to be a fact.) You are told, of yourself you are nothing, but as a member of the regiment, or crew or squadron, you are indeed something – and your sparkling, glinting, dashing uniform seems to confirm that. Your previously worthless existence now does have worth – provided it's dedicated to King and Country ... or President and Country – or, of course, Führer and Country.

"The Nazis' genius (and 'genius' can be applied on the side of evil as well as on that of good) was that it took the basic tenets of military training, expanded them – and then applied them to the entire nation, with the consent (what's more) of the overwhelming majority of that nation.

"Industry is today adopting similar tactics. In that is following the lead, as I understand it, of Japanese industry: Self-worth is gained through one's loyalty to the company, by accepting one's position as a cog in a vast machine – a machine infinitely more important not only than oneself, but also than all the cogs together, indeed than the sum of all its parts. The institution of the asylum has again taken over the asylum.

"This is most assiduously *not* self-worth.

"Firstly, because this machine is another Frankenstein's monster, an institution that has (as all institutions do) now become more powerful than those the institution was designed to serve.

"And secondly, because this is worth granted one by an outside agency and is completely conditional. One is worth something *only* if one meets the company's ever increasing quotas or accepts without complaint a colleague's sexual harassment or forfeits one's weekend to attend the company's barbecue or accepts a pay-cut or a reduction in fringe benefits ... or ... or ... or. This is absolutely *not* the road which leads to everyone in the world being the most 'they' they can be. Indeed, is the road travelling in exactly the opposite direction.

"There is, and one can sense it, within the workforce a growing and a burning resentment at being so treated. I fear for the violence it could lead to. I also fear methos may, covertly, encourage that violence. Because that would justify it in 'retaliating'. But that is mayhap outside the ambit of our present discussion.

"This block, I remember, is the back of the Savoy."

"I pointed it out from the Eye?"

"You are a good guide, Polly. An excellent guide. And not just of the sights of London. The Savoy from the balcony of which Monet painted his London riverscapes."

"I only *think* that, Rafa. I suppose I could check," she adds without undue enthusiasm.

"*... On your left, Charing Cross Station, one of the main London terminuses. And coming up on your right, what is called the South Bank complex. Originally built for the Festival of Britain in the 1950s, it now comprises the Royal Festival Hall, the Purcell Room ...*"

"Is odd: I hear various priests and shamans talk about the evils of pride. Still, today. And yet never have I heard one condemning this abuse of pride by industry. You don't find that curious, Polly?"

"That too, Rafa, 'twas ever thus."

"But – and this too I say again, my friend – the consequences 'twere not ever thus."

"No," Polly agrees.

"A trip down the Thames, sun, good conversation – *great* company, Polly – what could be nicer?"

"*... The National Theatre comprises three stages: The Lyttelton, the Olivier and the smaller, more experimental Cottesloe ...*"

"The bar seems now to be open," says Polly without emotion.

"Drink?" suggests Rafa.

"Why not?" Polly concedes gracefully.

"Is good, no, to talk like this?"

"Is very good, my friend," Polly agrees softly, mildly mimicking him, the pain in her blue eyes melting into a glow of easiness and camaraderie.

They both wobble along the boat's length, and both trip over the upraised threshold that leads to the small wooden bar of the cabin.

"Let us return, Polly, to the hubris we talked about earlier. This hubris is the element of pride, my friend, which *is* a sin: and which is certainly deadly, even perhaps genocidal – certainly with the potential of being genocidal.

"Hubris has been around an awfully long time. The first dramatists were already warning of its dangers. (Though they did so more at the level of being a human failing – albeit sometimes with national consequences – rather than what it actually is: a failing in humanity.)

"How much misery has been inflicted on the world by the hubris of priests, by them insisting they talk the truth? And that *only* they do? Heretics, as I have said, are the creation of religions. And it is religions, not God, which are omniscient. To those who recognise their knowledge is limited, heresy is not possible. A 'heretic' is only someone whose ambit of knowledge is different from his own. Someone, my friend, looking at the Thames from a boat and not the Eye."

Seated on two benches, like so many toby-jugs on a shelf, is a group of Korean tourists, all men, most with glasses on, all toting cameras and in grey suits with white shirts. The bohemían of the group is its solitary member wearing an open-necked shirt, and not the tie worn by all his colleagues.

"Cheers, Rafa."

"*Salud.* One of the dictionaries sponsored a competition at the start of the millennium to find the one word which would best describe the previous century. I don't know which word eventually won, but for me there was only one possibility: 'genocide'.

"The development of the car or the computer, Man landing on the moon, the discovery of penicillin, even the population explosion were all small beer against the vastness of the slaughter which took place. Whether that genocide were militaristic as in Hiroshima and the First World War (and many more); medical as in the outbreak of avian flu which succeeded that World War or the AIDS pandemic in which still we live (and many more); political as in Mao's purges and Stalin's; ethnic as in the Holocaust and in many of the African and Balkan conflicts; climactic as in the Ethiopian famines and the Pacific tsunami; or economic as in the quite barbarous death-rate at the century's end, the only word to describe the century is, in my opinion, 'genocide'.

"What was the cause of this genocide? Nine times out of ten, my friend, was the certainty of being right. Ninety-nine times out of a hundred, Polly, was hubris.

"The great philosophical, the great ideological debate for most of the twentieth century was between capitalism and what was called communism. Incredible amounts of energy were consumed persuading us – and especially those of us whom they ruled – how appalling were the realities of the other system. How wonderful was the system governing us. Imagine what better state the world would today be in, if that same energy had been used not in vilifying our opponents, but in examining ourselves. You think we would now be standing on the brink of disaster? In no century of history have more opportunities been presented to us than there were in the twentieth century. Nearly all of them missed. And mostly courtesy of hubris.

"Pride of itself is not hubris. Pride in ourselves is not hubris. It makes us, as I said, more fulfilled, happier. Pride in those we love, as also I have said, gives them confidence, assurance, a permanent haven. Pride in our environment helps us to protect it.

"At home, one of my sadnesses is that so few Peruvians recognise just how beautiful their country is. For that reason (maybe not by itself, but certainly largely), we have a big problem with litter and with waste. Ancient mattresses are just tossed from trucks, rubbish-tips scar the most scenic hillsides. And these litter-bugs would describe themselves as patriots, would look askance in a bar at anyone failing to cheer the Peruvian football team. This too is inevitable with methos. Methos tells me that my convenience is more important than your landscape. What it forgets, that thinking, is that is not *your* landscape. Is also mine. I am also destroying my own landscape.

"Certainly there are laws prohibiting such fly-tipping. But we lack the policemen to be able to enforce them. Would not the problem be far more efficiently tackled by opening local eyes to the beauty around them? The incredible, immense beauty around them? Would that not be a far more efficient way of tackling the problem? Also of directing patriotism?"

"... And on your left, ladies and gentlemen, Blackfriars Station. Just beyond that, the Mermaid Theatre. The Mermaid Theatre was built by Lord Miles ..."

To a man, the group of Koreans stands and takes pictures of Blackfriars Station. Polly and Rafaél have decided to stay in the cabin. It is less cluttered than the deck outside.

"We had a problem for decades," says Polly, "of dogs 'fouling', as the euphemism has it, the footpaths. Bye-laws by the thousand. It only started to get tackled when there was a consensus about how unpleasant it was, when peer-pressure was brought on dog-owners to clear up after their pets."

"I did not know this, Polly. But, yes, exactly. Patriotism, famously, is the last refuge of the scoundrel. And patriotism is pride, no? In one's country? But even that ... even – let me say – a *guarded* patriotism ... even that is sometimes good. Every nation has things of which it should be proud, and it is right that we celebrate those:

French cuisine, Italian architecture, English literature ..."

"Most of which should more correctly be called 'Irish' literature."

"*Irish* literature, correct; indeed, Polly, *American* literature, American generosity as well; Japanese Noh theatre and Kabuki; German music – and Austrian; Dutch painting. It becomes a vice (something which demeans mankind) when patriotism becomes nationalism. And when that in turn becomes jingoism, it does indeed become a sin – something which *threatens* mankind. One of the greatest sins in the world today."

" ... *The bridge ahead is London Bridge. That's not* 'the' *London Bridge that the nursery rhyme tells us is falling down. Nor, obviously, that which was sold to an American businessman ...*"

"Is really also time we stopped thinking that there is our patriotism and theirs. Ours which is a virtue, and theirs (wherever 'theirs' is) which is delusional or flies in the face of the evidence or is unwarranted."

"I'm pretty sure," says Polly, "it was Mark Twain who wrote, 'Your country right or wrong is like saying your mother drunk or sober'."

"I never saw my mother drunk," says Rafa.

"You haven't lived, Rafa," says Polly, and chuckles. Unhappily. Momentarily the eyes are again glazed with pain. Rafaél notices.

"Nationalism starts dictating that your country's needs should come before those of any other nation. That is to debase your own citizens. Thus too do resentments start – both with your own citizens and with those belonging to other nations. Is a system which finally demeans all of us. And which can certainly slide very easily into being a sin – something which threatens all of us. Threatens us gravely. Wars can easily develop from such resentments.

"*Jingoism* dictates that your country's *wants* should come before the *needs* of any other nation. Thus do wars *inevitably* start. *Quite* inevitably. And is a system which *must* pose a threat, and which today imperils – and very greatly – not only your own country and that of your so-called enemy, but humanity in its entirety. And because it makes strife inevitable, far from protecting its own citizens, is a system which puts them in the most absolute of dangers – in *mortal* danger. As such, jingoism is certainly both a sin – and, quite literally – a deadly one. One of the greatest sins Man is capable of committing."

"But you've already accepted, Rafa, that Man – if he does not love war – at least has a soft spot for it."

"Let me tell you this, my friend, with the weapons that we have today, even if Man *glories* in war, even if he *luxuriates* in it, war is an indulgence he can no longer afford. That he likes it, or loves it, does not countenance him waging it. He is severely diabetic. War is the chocolate bar. However much he craves it, he cannot be allowed it. We really do, Polly, have to start learning from our mistakes. We don't have a lot of time left to learn. We are, as I've said before, rapidly running out of 'nexts', my friend."

Rafaél takes a sip from his drink and continues, "Man's fondness for war, it has very much also to do with self-worth and having a defined role to play, one acknowledged to be important. And that returns us to the need we have, ourselves to be contented and fulfilled in our lives: a need to be artisans, not cogs; recognised for our competence, not recognised only when we are *in*competent."

"*... We are now passing, ladies and gentlemen, under Tower Bridge.*"

"Right by the apartment I'm staying in," says Polly.

There is a quartet of French twenty-somethings, two couples. They seem to think that this landmark is worthy of a toast, and they touch each other's plastic bottles of water before laughing uproariously.

Polly finishes her drink. Points her finger questioningly at Rafaél's. Who puts his hand over the top of his glass. "Maybe I'll just have a half," says Polly. But she allows her pint glass to be refilled.

"Pride is not vanity," the Peruvian continues, "even less is it vaingloriousness. The vain are prepared to be abusive; and the vainglorious are *bound* to be abusive. But those with a pride in themselves or in their work do not, on the whole, abuse others. They have no need to. They do not need others to be humiliated in order that they can feel worthy."

" ... *There's now really nothing of particular interest between here and Greenwich. So we suggest you just sit back and enjoy the ride."* To a man, the Korean tourists sit back into their benches. *"May we remind you that on board we have a fully licensed bar ...?"*

"What about ambition?" asks Rafaél. Polly senses there's more rhetoric in the question than interrogation. "Is ambition pride? I don't know, to be honest," Rafaél confesses. "I think mayhap we have to start wondering whether that same urge that brought us out of the sea, made us stand on our hind-legs, which impelled us down from the trees, I think we need to ask ourselves how much of that imperative is responsible for bringing us to this pretty pass we now find ourselves in. Is it something innate? Or is it something we can correct? And if is innate, does that mean we are doomed? Even literally? Can we, again we need to ask ourselves, still pull ourselves back from the brink?"

"Do we have what it takes," Polly intones, "to do what it takes?"

"When they warned us of the dangers of pride, what, I think, the early prophets might have been trying to tell us is this: that which made us what we are today may well also be that which destroys us.

"Not 'will be', you note; just, 'may well be'. Is ambition part of pride? Well, at some level, I think it has to be. And I think too it has to contribute to hubris.

"Is it necessary? Ambition, I mean? It was certainly necessary for us, and so quickly in evolutionary terms, to get where we are today. But – just perhaps –, as I've said before, we are too clever for our own good. And too ambitious for our own survival."

A hydrofoil coming in the opposite direction sends up a spume of wash which wobbles the craft and has the two of them sipping hastily at their beer lest it spill.

"I've been thinking, Rafa, about what you said of our institutions."

"Oh?" he asks. The sip has made him realise his throat is dry. He is now less drinking his beer than glugging it.

"If pride, Rafa, is the first deadly sin ..."

"Well, it isn't, my friend. Is hubris the sin ..."

"Just hear me out. Then, I was going to say, is not the first deadly *lie* that Man is Man?"

"Go on," Rafa tells her.

"If we need to revisit the seven deadly sins, do we also not have a need to define for ourselves their equivalent in the twenty-first century? If, as you say, the war today is between the Truth and the Untruth, do we also not need to start identifying some of those lies?"

"Go on," Rafaél says again.

"And isn't one of those lies that Man is Man? That Man, by himself, is (in other words) sufficient to define Man?

"Doesn't that lie also contain other lies, albeit alternative lies: On the one hand, that Man is just a lump of meat and, on the other, that he is some kind of supreme being? Indeed so supreme a being that it is, in fact, Man who is God? Aren't those all lies? And part of 'the' Untruth?"

"I think," Rafaél says, "that I will have that other drink." He orders it.

"I wonder whether this age *is* such a secular age," Polly continues. "I wonder whether there hasn't merely been some kind of heavenly *coup d'état*, where we've ousted God from His throne and replaced Him with ourselves. Have we, in other words, made a God of Man? Maybe even *Almighty* God of Man?"

"Cheerio," Rafa toasts her and drinks. He is listening intently.

"We are so pleased with ourselves as a species, so smug and complacent, so evidently the most evolved and sophisticated creature to have inhabited our planet, that we glory in all our splendiforousness and bask in our cleverness.

"One of the things, you said, that most defines us all, as human beings, is our fallibility. And I doubt anyone in the world would give you much of a fight about that opinion. And yet we seem to believe that Man the species is the reverse, that man collectively is, like the pope, *in*fallible. Isn't that a bit like expecting the vegetarian deer as a flock to become carnivorous?"

The door to the cabin opens and the group of Korean tourists file in. It wouldn't have surprised Polly had they done so in some kind of order – from tallest to shortest, for instance, or vice versa. As it was, she had to assume it was from thirstiest to most assuaged. It needles her, and not a little, that not one of them trips on the lipped threshold as they enter.

"Over and over and over again," she continues, "I read about the technological miracles of the twentieth century. As if those miracles somehow nullified the genocide you talked about, the concentration camps to vanish and the gulags – back to the Roman legacy: of straight roads exonerating crucifixion. Over and over (and, Rafa, over) I hear Man patting himself on the back, crowing over how much he knows, how much he has learnt.

"The young, when they howl with laughter at the clothes their parents used to wear, fail to realise that their children will also howl in the future at what they are wearing today. Likewise with so much of science – and of life-styles.

"Throughout history, Man has swaggered in his belief that he is the brightest thing ever to have graced this planet. He has swaggered in his *knowledge* – in what he believed to be almost his omniscience – and has only rarely been awed by his ignorance. I'm told it's a myth that medieval Man believed the Earth flat, but certainly he believed it was the centre of the universe, and that all the other astrological phenomena orbited around it. Certainly he believed that the atom could not be split.

"And when we discover we have been wrong for millennia, do we then pause to think that perhaps some of our most cherished beliefs today are equally mistaken? Do we start talking about 'truth', even about 'facts', using the codicil 'as far as we know'? No. We swagger even more in our newfound knowledge. And believe as vehemently that such newfound knowledge is the truth as our ancestors believed their misconception to be. We swagger in our belief that we are by far the brightest generation ever to have graced the Earth, that today is as glorious as yesterday was inglorious.

"You talk about quantum physics, Rafa. Quantum physics is opening up new dimensions, ones of incalculable importance and value. But even that knowledge is only knowledge we have *so far* acquired. To most of us individually, the more we know the more we know how little we know. How many new species of life have been discovered in the last decade? Ask natural scientists how many more species they believe there are yet to be found. The greater our knowledge the greater should be the knowledge of our own ignorance. The freshman struts in his omniscience; it is the professor in touch with his ignorance.

"But not so, apparently, us collectively. Man collectively thinks himself both omniscient and infallible. It is an opinion both fed by and feeding off methos.

"Thalidomide, that was known to be safe. When radium was first discovered, they made toothpaste with it! Even condoms! You ever hear about eugenics?"

"Genetic control, no? Sterilising those not considered to be sane or healthy?"

"Sixty thousand of my fellow Americans, Rafa, were sterilised, courtesy of eugenics. Sixty thousand. Twenty September the 11ths. With, I might add, presidential approval.

"Doubtless, post-Victorian industrialists who fouled the air and poisoned the water didn't believe *they* were doing any harm – or if they were that such harm was outweighed by the benefits of the 'prosperity' such was bringing. Because Man knows everything, Man never bothered to question what 'prosperity' was.

"And because Man knows everything, each development means 'progress' – without anyone ever questioning what *that* means.

"No, that's not quite true. There are always those trying to do such questioning – heroes all, because they have always faced a barrage of derision for their pains.

"Anyone who seeks to question the efficacy of a 'development' is, these days by definition, a Luddite seeking to impair the improvement of the human lot. Because those who believe the nonsense that a development is *'per se'* progress have to denounce those who would ask us all to question that.

"Of course anyone dying from cancer has a right to try any new treatment put on the market. Of course they do. No-one is trying to deny them that right. Indeed, maybe laws should be relaxed so that they may be allowed to do so more quickly and more easily. But that doesn't mean that drugs generally should not be tested before they're made universally available.

"The absence of five words in our thinking and in our pronouncements has wrought untold danger. Those five words are: 'As far as we know'. Prefix all our statements with that, we'd avoid so much of the irreversible damage we're currently meting out to ourselves and our environment.

"For how many years did tobacco companies insist there was no health damage from smoking? Some of them are *still* trying to insist as much. In our discoveries today, how many times do we acknowledge that we may be just another Walter Raleigh?

"Maybe we do need nuclear power, maybe we need genetically modified agriculture. We have to consider how it is we're going to feed the nine billion plus people, and give them power, who will populate the globe halfway through this century. By which time the world's oceans could well have risen by 130 feet. But it is only – at best! – 'as far as we know' that nuclear power and genetic modification will provide the solutions – and their side-effects likewise are known only as much as we are *now* aware of them.

"In Sherlock Holmes's London there used to be fogs so dense they were called 'pea-soupers'. And, literally, in them you could barely see your hand, Rafa, in front of your face. If you fell in the Thames at that time, you'd be killed by its poison well before you drowned. Despite the multiple howls of protest from the then industry, the British government passed bills prohibiting certain discharges. Guess what? London no longer gets pea-soupers and salmon have again been seen swimming in the Thames.

"My point is this: If we prefixed each new so-called development with 'as far as I know', how much would be reduce the consequences of any side-effects, and how much more quickly would we address them when they started manifesting themselves?

"Man has already done enormously more damage to this planet than any other creature in the planet's history. So much so that geologists have designated man's occupancy of this planet as a period: 'anthropacy', to be precise. Anthropacy is not a healthy geological period. The rate of extinction suffered by other species during man's tenancy of this planet, this anthropacic age, has been anywhere between a hundred and a thousand times more intense than beforehand. Wow! We should feel so proud! That really is some achievement!

"And *is* it a tenancy that Man has? Or a stewardship?

"If tomorrow Man were obliterated – an ambition he certainly seems to be doing his best to achieve! –, the planet would heal Man's wounds within, in evolutionary terms, an infinitesimally short space of time. If, however, ants were obliterated (as he also seems to be doing his best to achieve), or bees, worms or beetles or insects in general, the eco-system of the planet in an even shorter space of time would totally collapse. It would not be able to sustain life – certainly as we today understand it. Should that, Rafa, not give us pause for thought?

"Should we not also give thought to the fact that the area depopulated around Chernobyl after the spill is now thriving naturally? That Man has become such a menace to Nature, even a nuclear accident (by comparison) is considered by her a blessing?

"Man has learnt almost nothing about giving *to* this planet. Even in exchange for the vast treasures he has taken *from* it.

"Should we not start getting right-sized about all this?

"I agree with you, Rafa, entirely: that whether or not there is a God is a decision personal to each one of us. But there seems to me one thing which is unequivocal about God: Man ain't He. Or She. Or It. Man is not God."

"'Job' again."

"Really?"

"'God is greater than man.'"

"'Job' is Iyyov, right?"

"Iyyov, if you're Jewish. Chapter 33, my friend. Verse twelve."

"Right. Quite impressive, your googling ability, there, Rafa, of matters biblical."

"One of the sad consequences of an unmisspent youth. I am also impressed that you should know about Iyyov."

"Don't be. I once had a Jewish girlfriend. It is a curious paradox of our times that the more fundamental (it seems to me) the quotes 'religious' belief, the greater the difficulty met by the believer in coming to terms with the fact that Man is not God.

"And surely – surely, yes, to God – surely, Rafa, the biggest lesson Man has to learn from history is not how clever he is, but how ignorant. Surely screaming at us today from every page of every history book ever written is the very simple truth: We do not know what we do not know.

"That is probably the one axiom in the world that has been true for all time and that will continue to be true for all time: We do not, Rafa, know what we do not know. Shouldn't every action we take – certainly every irreversible action – not always be tempered with that consideration? That we do not know what we do not know.

"If we'd known then what we know now, the American prairies would now be as rich in bio-diversity as the African savannahs; we'd never have killed the dodo nor built a machine to transport ourselves that was so dependent on fossil fuel; we'd never have evolved trench warfare or allowed sewage to seep into drinking water. Or slavery. Or ... or ... or ...

"If we are as clever as we think we are, how come it took us so long to think of putting wheels on suitcases, or having toothpaste tubes with big enough caps for them to be free-standing?"

"I have always thought it significant that we have developed silencers for guns, but not for vacuum cleaners or dentists' drills. You do not think this is indicative of an ethos with its priorities askew?"

"Ubquitously, Rafa, there are such indications. Stephen Hawking, Rafa, is no brighter than Newton and Newton was no brighter than Pythagoras; Hubble no brighter than Galileo. Human knowledge, Rafa, evolves.

"There can be no surer way of confiscating the future from our children than harbouring a hubris which dictates that Man is somehow divine. We need as a species to stop being so self-satisfied with our degree of knowledge and start feeling overawed by the enormity of our ignorance. The most urgent thing we need to know today is this: We do not know what we do not know."

"Talking of hubris, *amiga mía,* is not that the Dome?"

Chapter 7

Stupid. So stupid. Stupid, stupid, stupid.

She doesn't know why she's paid good money to see a doctor. She'd known. Stupid … the test she'd bought from the pharmacy, that had confirmed it ... stupid, stupid. Good money, stupid, after bad.

Drowning men, Saskja realises, don't just clutch at straws, they mirage straws to clutch at.

She's nineteen-years'-old, for God's sake. Nineteen. A woman. Allowed to marry, smoke, drink alcohol, watch 'x'-rated films, *vote*. How could she *possibly* have been so stupid? How *could* she … *possibly* …?

She needs to talk to Giselle. Really needs to talk to Giselle. Needs to talk to her. Right now.

It is evening, but the sun still scorches the crisp-bread streets of Orphalese with the gritty pitilessness of a midday desert. She wants to run but she forces herself to walk. The heat demands she walk – demands even that she stroll. But soon she cannot stroll, she cannot even just walk.

Tears well behind her eyes.

A Lilliputian cat-o'-nine-*hundred*-tails whips the back of her eyeballs with razor-sharp thongs.

The first tear she wipes away with the back of her hand. She knows, even as she does so, this first tear is only the herald of a flood so strong it will be unwipe-awayable. It will be a flood she cannot staunch, one she cannot check.

She starts to trot. Just a step or two. Now three steps trotting or four. Now strides. Canters. And now the tears have indeed started their flow, no less inexorable for being not the gushing of geysers but the slither of lava.

She starts now to run. Full tilt. Home. Running. Pell-mell. Running. She has to be home. She hopes her mother is still out … still out, still shopping … *prays* she is. She needs her bed, her privacy. She needs to *howl*. And to rant and scream and punch pillows and kick doors – and kick herself. Most of all, kick herself. Kick herself black and blue. And senseless. Kick, for Christ's sake, some sense *into* herself.

Misery can be contained in a snuff-box; but to release it needs the infinity of firmaments. She needs to cry until her pillow is wringing, and scream till her throat swells shut.

Mostly she needs to talk to Giselle.

People in the street stare after her. What's she running from, this young woman? Is she being stalked? Has she been robbed? Or is *she* the robber? Is she fleeing the police? Sweat now mingles with tears, a monsoon of grief flooding what has become the oiled olive of her face. And she remembers ... *stupid* ... she cannot phone Giselle. No. It's not that she remembers it, she *realises* it. Stupid, stupid, stupid.

Giselle is pregnant too.

But Giselle is basking in the bliss of pregnancy. It is not the right of anyone, Saskja feels, to rob a friend of bliss.

Chapter 8

"Avarice is greed, *amiga mía,* and greed is hatred. Is finally as simple as that. To want more than others may be but a human foible. But when that foible assumes the dimensions that you want so much more than others that you are prepared to let others starve, or that their potential be stifled at birth, that – my friend – is hatred. Is mayhap that the reason St Francis thought it the most deadly of the sins."

"Guru Nanak, likewise, I understand."

"Guru Nanak, the founder of the Sikh religion?"

"No, Rafa, the Guru Nanak who's a postman in Utah."

"Yes, alright," Rafaél concedes. "At my age, though … I do forget, Polly. Or I *mis*remember. Is one of the taxes demanded by dotage."

"And there are others of us," snorts Polly, "who never remember having *had* a memory."

"They were *both,* then, probably right – St Francis, I mean, and Guru Nanak. Avarice kills over four children a minute. I think I said it before. I think it cannot be said enough. Two hundred and forty children die an hour, Polly, ten thousand children a day – over three September 11ths, in other words: over three-and-a-half million children every year. A Holocaust every twenty months, just, Polly, of children. Which is also only how many we know about. Almost certainly there are more. All these children killed, Polly, by avarice. The amount of adults also killed by avarice … well, completely impossible to measure."

The summer has been hot. Rafaél has enjoyed it more than Polly, who is happier in today's climes: a coolish temperature, skies a satin grey, the odd sprinkle of rain. Both friends wear jackets, Rafaél has (of course!) an umbrella in his shoulder-bag. The rain is not yet heavy enough to warrant using it.

This doesn't stop a blue-and-white striped umbrella being jabbed at them. The umbrella is being wielded by a woman in her thirties with badly-permed blond hair. She also wears a white mackintosh in some need of revirginising. The woman bumps into a barrister hailing a cab – a lawyer, as so many lawyers, with a lean and hungry look. Polly knows this man's a barrister as he's carrying a blue cloth bag which she knows contains his wig and gown. She can't remember whether that makes him a silk (a senior English barrister), or whether such distinction is the red bag. The workings of the British bar are sometimes so arcane, so *befuddled* a sober-minded critic might imagine they were conceived *at* a bar. Polly tells herself it's not worth the explanation, and that she is loth to interrupt Rafaél, now in full flight.

"Is no accident, my friend, that in so many faiths God is synonymous with love. And love, incidentally, with truth.

"Just as is love, my dear Polly, which is the enabling force of this planet, the joy of its present and the promise of its future, so hatred is its antithesis: hatred is the *dis*abling force of this planet. It compromises the joy of the present, and confiscates future's promise. President Reagan and Mrs Thatcher made greed acceptable; President Bush and Mr Blair made it *desirable*. They urged us to be greedy, they tried to tell us greed is good. And look where it has got us. Even economically we are struggling. Spiritually …?

"Well, look around you. How much joy is there in today? How much hope do you hear about tomorrow? Why so little of either? Could it be because we live in a world controlled by greed? And greed, my friend, is hatred. And hatred is such a big part of the Untruth. And that is one reason why the theories of Professor Sachs about eradicating poverty are not working (despite the way he would seek to spin it), and why they will never work. Nor will President Sarkozy's or Mr Brown's. Their theories have at their core greed. Greed will always take. Greed, in fact, *has* to take. And it therefore has to appeal to the lower part of our 'I' and not the higher.

"To feed the world we do not need to shop until we drop, we need to drop shopping. Drop the glorification of shopping, at any rate; drop the economic dependency there is on our glorification. We need an ethos and an economy which is the inverse of what we have today, one where we stop taking and start giving. Giving till we drop. And not (as I fear is the case with too many so-called 'celebrity' charity binges) because giving is good PR, but because giving is good for us – for our health, our soul and for our world. We need to start giving until the giving hurts. Anything else is a fiction. And a dangerous one. Because it claims to be working to an end which it simply does not believe in. Witness what you told me about, Polly, of Mr Varley's ... 'diversion', let's call it, of funds due to tsunami victims. Mr Varley is not exclusively responsible for that situation, of course. Probably not even partially responsible. Indeed, probably only responsible insofar as he is carrying out orders. To further the cause of the Sheriff of Nottingham school of economics, where the poor are being robbed to give to the super-rich. How much did the companies associated with Mr Cheney gain during President Bush's administration? How much at the same time was the misery even of *American* minimum-wage existence exacerbated? And how does that not exacerbate the misery of the world?

"Even if – a gigantic 'if' – methos succeeds in eradicating starvation, it will only do so conditionally. When times are good. As soon as a disaster strikes, the starving will be starving once again. We will not solve the problem until we address the cause underlying the problem.

"In such joy and hope as do – very weakly – exist (I talk of today's joy and tomorrow's hope), I sense a growing desperateness – not a desperation, not quite. And not despair. In fact, I almost despair at the *lack* of despair: It smacks of the debtor who, unable to face the prospect of more bills, just doesn't open envelopes. If he doesn't know about the debt, it'll go away.

"We live today not even on credit, but on *tomorrow's* credit – and governments quite as much as their citizens.

"Is not only *financial* credit either that today we live on. Probably even greater is an *enormous* natural debt that we owe to our planet. We have robbed so much and given so very little. Nature will one day protest. She simply has to. Demand that debt be paid – or that, at the very least, terms be arranged. If not, like the bailiffs of the world's banks, she will exact her vengeance. Indeed presently it would seem that she is clearing her throat, preparatory to issuing her demands – maybe even getting the baseball bat out of the cupboard. She'll break a few fingers first, Nature: the odd tsunami, an earthquake or two, melt a few glaciers, whistle up a hurricane or two. Soon her debt-collectors will be kneeing the groin, slashing the face, shooting off the kneecaps ... Is she not already threatening our children?

"Then there is the debt too of what we owe to our souls, our spirits – our souls and spirits, of course, at an individual level. But also at a communal, at a national and *inter*national and *planetary* one – the conscience we have put on ice till tomorrow. The tomorrow when we can *afford* to listen to our conscience. What we have yet to understand, my dear Polly, is that *that* tomorrow, my friend, is not only one which does come, but one which already came. That tomorrow came yesterday, in fact. In fact, several yesterdays ago. We should have started to heed our consciences decades, centuries ago. What were Christ and the Buddha and Muhammad trying to say, for God's sake?"

"And Guru Nanak."

"All the world's shamans, Polly. Those consciences will also one day protest. The consciences of many of us are already rumbling. Rumbling badly. And we are trying to ignore those rumbles. Ask the people of Pompeii what happens when you ignore a rumble. Ask a *doctor*, even. One day, I suspect, like the ignored appendix, our consciences too will just rupture. And because the guiding force of the planet, that seems to be, as the English would say, 'Sod's law', they will probably all rupture at just the moment that the world needs all its able-bodied at their *most* able-bodied. Instead of that, the globe will be teeming with the carcasses of the emotionally destroyed – will be splattered with the shattered."

"Please tell me, Rafa, you didn't say that."

Rafa smiles a not quite sincere apology before he carries on, "The good news is that, contrary to Hamlet's opinion, conscience does not make cowards of us all. Is ignoring our conscience which makes us craven. Conscience, heeding it, is, for most of us, the impulsion of heroism. But conscience is a muscle like every other. It needs exercise. Too often today we are allowing it to wither.

"Too often today our search for happiness is a desperate grabbing for the *crumbs* of joy – whose loaf is not a real happiness, but an ersatz one. We can see this in a materialism gone berserk, and in the amount of substance abuse there is around today. Look at the sales internationally of tranquillisers. Prozac and heroin are finally being taken for the same reason – because a chemically adjusted reality is considered to be more appealing than actual reality."

They pass a homeless young man selling 'The Big Issue'. He is rubbing his change-blackened hands against the cold, but this is from habit, not for need of warmth. A hand-rolled cigarette dangles unlit over a stubbly chin.

"The biggest industry today in the Western world is not involved with computers or telecommunications or even travel, is lending money.

"Why should governments be encouraging their citizens to acquire that kind of debt? Why do they want their graduates, those just starting out on life, already to be burdened with debt? And why do they allow borrowing to be so hard for those who have no history of debt? Could it be that they want to *encourage* us to borrow money? Is not by accident, my friend, that a debt is also called a bond. A bondsman is not a freeman.

"These are, of course (so the politician will tell you, or the economist), complex issues.

"But not because they *are* complex. At their core, they are incredibly simple. They are complex because methos has woven complexity into them. Spin enough wheels *within* enough wheels and is quite impossible to distinguish one wheel from another. You can't even see which wheels are providing the dynamo and which are being driven."

"Car wheels in movies appear to rotate backwards."

"They do?"

"I thought – on another occasion, you know – it might help your analogy."

"Alas, my friend, my analogies, I fear, they do need all the help they can get."

"You know perfectly well that's not what I meant."

"Car wheels in films go backwards?"

"Now you know, just watch."

"It does help the analogy. Methos, I have said this too before, loves complication. Is such a wonderful hidey-hole for the lie. Never do you borrow money from the institution apparently lending it to you. Is a vast industry, finding the most lucrative Peter to rob from in order to pay Paul. A *vast* industry, my friend."

"This is the City of London," says Polly.

"Yes," Rafaél returns, as if replying to a stater of the obvious.

"No, Rafa, the *City* of London."

"Yes," Rafaél returns in the way of: 'Duh, I do know I'm in London. This is not the Manhattan skyline, not the pyramids or the Leaning Tower.'

"'The square mile,' as it's called. The 'City'. The financial heart of London. Sort of London's Wall Street." They have met at Temple Station, and have walked via the Aldwych to the law courts. "An anthill by day, by night a ghost-town. Over a million people work here, and less than a hundred thousand live here. It has its own bye-laws and its own police force – their helmets, if you happen to see one, you will notice are different than those elsewhere in London."

"And what *is* the elsewhere of London if this is the 'City'?"

"That, Rafa, is what is technically known as 'a very good question'. London 'town', maybe? You know, I have no idea. Metropolitan London? It *is* quite metropolitan, London. It would be a good word to describe it. Metropolitan and cosmopolitan. That is one of its great strengths. See that dragon on its plinth in the centre of the road?"

"I do."

"That marks the boundary. If you were the Queen you'd have to stop at that point."

"I would?"

"She needs permission to enter the City."

"She is not also queen of the City?"

"Without question. Nevertheless she still needs permission to enter it. From, I think, the Lord Mayor. Who, just to confuse things further, is not the same person as the Mayor."

"Of course not," smiles Rafa. "The curious thing is that it was of *Russia* that Churchill said it was a riddle wrapped up in a mystery within an enigma – something along those lines."

"Such a description, you're saying, may have been better applied to his own country?"

"Is hard too for nations to look into a mirror. Is so very much easier to notice the mote in the eyes of others."

"We did, Rafa, already talk about this," Polly gently reminds him. The sprinkle of rain stops. It had been so light neither of them notices. Nor do the umbrella-toters, who continue to lunge blindly forward. "When I first came to London," she continues, "this – Fleet Street – was where all the newspapers were: both their editorial offices and their printing-presses. You talk of greed! You have no idea how greedy the print unions were. The fathers of the chapel! (That's what they were called. Please don't ask me why.) They were like the shop stewards, the local headmen, if you like. They knew every single trick in the book – and then some. I shot an episode of a TV show in the printing presses of one of the then newspapers. I'm guessing the couple of days we spent there cost the company more money than for the rest of the series put together.

"And the unions got away it, with their greed, that was the amazing thing. No-one would stand up to them. It was largely as a consequence of this union power, in fact, that Mr Murdoch got his foot in ... was allowed, more likely, to get his foot in. Not too many would-be purchasers then of newspapers – at the level, I mean, of buying the publishing house. Why would anyone pay for the privilege of almost constant confrontation? They were enough, the print unions, to dent the beliefs of even the most ardent socialist."

"Almost all unions were greedy," says Rafaél. "Wherever in the world they were. Or are. They are bound to be. Is a world dominated by greed. Is a world which allows, even encourages, your worth to judged by the amount you are paid. We even say of people: He is 'worth' that many thousands ... that many millions. Everyone in the world, Polly, needs to feel worthy – which, I suppose, is a return to our conversation about pride. So – *of course* – unions were greedy.

"The much-vaunted 'third' way was supposed to be a middle-way. But that third way is only globalisation. All we need to say about globalisation at this point is that is an economic theory given some kind of, highly spurious, academic dignity merely to disguise what it actually is: an endorsement of greed. (Also of control, but that mayhap is not here pertinent.)

"We have talked before about Professor Sachs's book, 'The End of Poverty'. A careful read of which will tell you all you need to know about globalisation. Read not just the text, but the sub-text. And weigh the implications contained therein. It – 'it', the system, and 'it', the book – tells those working on the shop-floor to be moderate in their demands, to be acquiescent in their working-life. But the insatiable greed of both shareholders and executives, *that* apparently is not only permissible, but laudable.

"Since I have arrived here, there has been much criticism of the train-drivers in London wanting pay increases during the forth-coming Olympics. Maybe I've missed it, but I have heard no similar criticism of hoteliers or restaurateurs. And almost none at all of Lord Coe – whose estimates of the Games' cost to London were ... let's call them 'optimistic', and whose personal gain from their presence in London has never been made public. It's the patricians of Rome, all over again: the patricians and the plebeians. The plebeians' greed is 'holding the country to ransom'; that of the patricians is 'essential to the national and international economy' – and that of Lord Coe, apparently, like that of Roman emperors, outside the remit of accountability.

"The Olympic Games are in fact becoming too expensive at every conceivable level. Not least that it is beginning to take far too many losers to create a single winner. And that, it seems to me, is part of the marginalisation process.

"We live in a world which increasingly does not recognise talent or ability, commitment or diligence. It recognises only the handful of those lucky or ruthless enough to win gold medals. In sports the newspapers like to write about. We want, in our world, to concentrate all the wealth, all the kudos and prestige into the microscopic world of gold-medal winners in sports which are popular. Let the also-rans fend for themselves.

"The unions are largely now, certainly in Britain and (to a lesser extent) in the United States, a spent force. And perhaps we do need them to be. On the whole, I don't think unions – at least, their leaders – were working towards 'wethos'. But is also true, my friend, that employers are now often greatly abusing those who work for them because there are no teeth left in the unions to bite back.

"Many union leaders, true, became more interested in extending their power-bases than they were in promoting the interests of their members. And, also true, that was a betrayal of the principles which were supposed to guide those unions. Such leaders were political, no doubt about it. But what we need to learn from that is not that protecting the interests of the weak against the strong is a bad thing, but that the corruptability inherent in power crosses all political divides.

"As if to prove which, I find it indicative, Polly, that so much of what President Bush said, and Mr Blair, should so closely mimic the words of Lenin. Lenin, for instance, also thought (as they did) that a concern for human rights was a 'dated' concept." He looks at the sky, wonders whether the time has come to seek umbrella protection. He decides, not quite yet.

"Is the corruptability of all power which needs to be examined, my friend. Most people in politics, I think, start out (whatever their political colour) as being people who care, people who want to do good. What is it that turns these people into what they become? What apparently they *inevitably* become?

"Is not enough to condemn those who harm us – whether politically or socially or financially or criminally, whether they hurt our bodies, our souls, our dignity, our purse, our peace-of-mind. We have in those who harm us to look at what creates that which harms us. And we have to look behind that to the institutions which cause that harmful element: to politics, for instance, as an institution, or economics, to banks and social deprivation. To our own greed too, to our own hubris. To ... well, an entire gamut of different institutions both outside of us and inside.

"Certainly the weak of the unions – the average worker, the factory-floor, the membership, those the union was meant to protect –, far from being protected by their leaders, were often considered as nothing more than pawns: pieces expendable in the cause of power-hungry tsars. But those leaders were called that, 'tsars', because it was precisely from such people that they learnt their arrogance and their tactics.

"There is today a substantial propaganda campaign abroad to exonerate the Romanovs. The Romanovs were not wonderful human beings – and the fact that crimes were committed against them and, particularly, their children does not exonerate them. The Romanovs were responsible for an enormous amount of starvation, deprivation and misery. The secret police in Russia was not introduced by Lenin but by the tsar. The gulags were only developments of tsarist penal colonies.

"Julius Caesar was also a tsar, also a political being, substantially less interested in the welfare of those in his charge than in extending his power-base. We don't condemn Julius Caesar. We indeed still commemorate him in our calendar. If we condemn the union leaders, why do we not also condemn Julius Caesar? From whom did these politicised union leaders learn (as I say) both their ambition and their strategy?

"The press barons you talk about, they are tsars of industry. You talk about the greed of the print unions. From whom did those unions learn their greed? You think William Randolph Hearst was a 'giving' man? Or that Lord Beaverbrook was? Or Robert Maxwell?

"The press barons (my friend) – everywhere, apparently, in the world – are champions of the principle of supply-and-demand. Provided – *always* – that such principle is working in their favour. They are considerably more muted in their enthusiasm if the principle is working against them. And that ambivalence (without it ever being recognised as such) is reflected often – very often – in the editorials, if not the reportage, of the newspapers they own.

"And, of course, such ambivalence is an entirely human failing. We all change the goal-posts from time to time to suit our present purpose. And, yes, I am quite as guilty of that as anyone else. But is time, I think, to recognise that what is excusable at the level of personal behaviour, what is (at that level) a foible, is not also a foible, is not also excusable at an *institutional* level. The fact that there are bank-robbers does not excuse, let alone countenance, the profiteering of the banks.

"This view, *amiga mía,* is quite magnificent."

"Really," Polly agrees.

"That metal bridge. Victorian, I'd guess. The majesty of the buildings behind it, St Paul's looking down paternally and cyclopically on all of it, the 'Gherkin' behind it." He is still gazing at the sight as he starts to cross the road. The furious clanging of a bicycle bell hurls him back onto the pavement. A male figure of indeterminate years shakes his leather-mittened fist at him as his bicycle zooms past. On whose wake surfs a white taxi, its doors emblazoned with advertisements for Easy Jet. The driver shouts at Rafaél, but this latter is too shocked to hear him. They wait for the light of the pedestrian man to turn green.

"We're actually running parallel," says Polly, "with the course of the Thames. We're, as it were, one block away from the Embankment

– though 'block' in that sense is an Americanism, rather frowned on on this side of the pond."

"Yet another fresh perspective," says Rafaél, rather more shocked by his near-collision with the bicycle than he would care to acknowledge.

"On anything, Rafa, there is, isn't there, an infinite possibility of different perspectives?"

"An infinity, yes," the Peruvian agrees.

"And yet you can say categorically, 'Greed is hatred'?"

"I can often *understand* that greed," Rafaél says. "But that doesn't mean that is not hatred. Let us say this: I have yet to come across an angle from which greed is not hatred. You ask how we save the world, my friend? Where do we start? Is so simple: We stop allowing it to be hate which controls the world."

"So simple and so hard?" asks Polly.

"Quite."

"So where, Rafa, *do* we start?"

"We need to do many things, my friend. We start ... First, my friend, first we must all – all of us, Polly – recognise the need to do it. That's where we start. We need to stop the thought that is a good idea for hate to control the world.

"Then, we have to start using the titan public relations industry we have, the enormous multi-, Polly, -media propaganda machine, to stop propagating the philosophy of hatred and start propagating that of love."

"And how do you intend doing *that*?"

"We think laterally, my friend."

"Laterally?"

"We need to shift not only our thinking, but also the way we think. Not hugely, but a little."

"Elucidate, Rafaél."

"I was never, Polly, a big fan of Westerns, I'm afraid. Too much casual murder for me. Too much 'might is right'. One I did like, though, was 'Butch Cassidy and the Sundance Kid'."

"Great film," Polly agrees. "Written by one of the very few screen writers, in my opinion, who is indeed a master of both his craft and of his art. I'll think of his name in a minute."

"The railway owner has organised a posse to hunt down the two bandits because they keep robbing his trains. Butch is identifying the people in that posse. They are all highly-paid experts. He turns to Sundance, 'If only he'd …' – he, the railway owner – '… if only he'd pay me what he's paying them to stop me robbing him,' he tells his friend, 'I'd stop robbing him.' If only, Polly, likewise, we used the energy for a communal good that we use to pursue our individual good we could create that communal good *individually*."

"Ah," says Polly enigmatically.

"And, yes, that is Utopia; and, no, we can never realise it. But if our civilisation is not to crumble around us, we must start taking the path that leads in *that* direction, and not the path that leads in the opposite one."

"William Goldman," she says. "The writer of 'Butch Cassidy …': William Goldman."

Rafa ignores the interjection. "'Wethos', we have to start understanding, is finally in everyone's interest – even in the interest of those investing in vested interest. It will only be the institutions which suffer. Not the individuals. Not finally.

"You will, in a planet governed (as this one presently is) by hatred, *never* create a world where I can be the most me I can be, nor where you can. Even were I at the very top of the pile – even if I were Mr Gates or the president of America or the pope or the Dalai Lama or the Queen of England or Paul McCartney or bin Laden or anyone else; Tiger Woods, say, or Mr Murdoch or today's Godfather, whoever that is, or Mr Heffner – your being of you is compromised by living in a world governed by hatred. That already inhibits your youness.

"You are enjoined to play the role that hatred demands of you. The *hatred* is in control of your youness, not you. Oh, you may be extremely comfortable (at least, physically) in your non-youness, you may indeed persuade yourself that you would prefer to be as physically comfortable as you are *not* being you. But even those apparently atop the pile will, by not being them, feel uncomfortable. And unfulfilled. Which is, I suspect, one of the reasons that so many of the super-rich are as troubled and unhappy as they appear to be.

"In a world governed by greed, thus governed by hatred, we're in a lose:lose situation. Even the winners are losers. Because neither the dustman nor the duke are allowed to be themselves. They cannot be true to their own selves. And that is just craziness." Without even apparently noticing, they walk around the billowy, *pillowy* sumptuousness that is St Paul's cathedral.

"Wealth, for instance," continues Rafa, "is supposed to buy you freedom. Is one of the most glittering items in the shop-window of wealth, freedom. We have in Lima *ghettoes* of the super-rich, *amiga mía*. In so many ways, these ghettoes are as much a prison as *Lurigancho* – that, sorry, is, you might say, Peru's Alcatraz. Those ghettoes, they are as much a prison as ... well, Alcatraz. Just that the cells are bigger and better furnished. These rich ghettoes are, I think, similar to Beverley Hills. Just five-star, *twenty-five* star, prisons. This is not freedom, my friend. Is worth mayhap remembering that the most glittering palace of them all, Beijing's Forbidden City, was actually devised as a cage for a cicada. These luxury complexes, Beverley Hills and their like, these are just cages surrounded by gilt – by both gilts, in fact, that with the 'u' and that without it. Is madness."

"That with a 'u' too?"

"Sanity is the opposite of madness. If madness is white, sanity is black. If hatred is white, love is black. If what we're doing is white and mad, in order to become sane we need to do what is black. We need instead to create a world of love, where even the so-called losers are winners. No. Not even that: where, much better, we abandon the concept of winners and losers. This concept too is one of the crib. 'I'm the king of the castle' is a game for small children, not for mature adults."

"And you seriously believe that's possible? In *any* society? Even in

Utopia? That's Utopia, by the way, with a *capital* 'u'!"

"If we could possibly get to Utopia it wouldn't be Utopia, Polly. I think we said this before. But, as Oscar Wilde so wisely wrote – yet *another* Irishman of 'English' literature –, 'A map of the world,' he wrote, words to this effect, 'that does not include Utopia is incomplete.' The map we are given of our world today not only does not include Utopia, it tells us not to dare even thinking about Utopia. And that, my friend, is even more pernicious than the newspeak of Orwell's '1984', because, instead of changing the past, it changes the future.

"'Live in the Now' has even become the *spiritual* axiom of today. And is one onto which 'methos' has grabbed with both hands. Because it has been taken to mean that we need, in this moment, to have no regard for the next. That our regard for the next will corrupt that we are living at the moment.

"Certainly the larger arguments of those advocating that 'we live in the now' contain a good deal of soundness, and certainly this message is often distorted by methos into a travesty of itself – just as L'Oréal has distorted the vital concept of self-worth into a slogan to sell its less than vital message: that worth is instilled from external beauty. You pull a face, my friend?"

"It's just ... I think, Rafa, it's always worth remembering, when the concentration camps, the – Rafa – *extermination* camps were liberated, before the women wanted food, they wanted lipstick. They needed lipstick, Rafa, for their recovery."

"That is an entirely reasonable point, Polly. And is a suitable punishment for my ... diversion. However, to return to the main thrust of what I was saying, *as thus encapsulated*, 'to live in the now' is nonsense. One basically need only ask of those who advocate it, 'Do you go shopping?' or 'Do you check the road before you cross it?' Mayhap a rather unfortunate question given my recent history. Nevertheless ...

"If those you question say they don't, they're idiots and you can stop listening to them from that point on; if they concede that they do, they have already conceded that a part of the present *has* to be – not 'is', Polly, '*has to be*' – a concern for the future. The discussion from that point is only then about degree. And at *that* point, let me add, some of the advocates of living-in-the-now do, as I said just now, start talking much sense."

"This is the heart of the City," says Polly.

"And the City is the heart of London."

"The heartlessness, probably, of London," says Polly. "If greed is hatred and hatred is heartlessness."

"You do not think greed is hatred? Look at the way, *amiga mía,* we treat our planet. At the way industrialists treat those who work for them. Would we treat people or planet in such a way unless we hated them? Clearly not. But even the most trenchant advocate of globalisation – even Mr Sachs or President Sarkozy – would claim they love people and the planet, that their espousal of globalisation emanates from that love. So, the questions we now need to ask ourselves are these: *Is* it that vested interest does hate Man and planet? Or is it that it has so bought into the myth that greed is a good thing that it cannot bear to accept the truth: that greed is hatred? Are we just dealing with a problem of denial?

"Are we really prepared to let millions – maybe even billions – die or live in abject misery merely to further the greed of a kamikaze plutocracy? Are we really prepared to wreak unimaginable damage to our planet so we can buy gadgets? Gewgaws? To be ruled by a system of economics which demand that of us? This planet which, unlike those gadgets, has given us so much? Which *continues* to give us so much? Has Man in his evolution really not developed beyond the moral capability of a jackdaw?

"Are we going to continue paying lip-service to our love of Man or are we going to start doing something about it? By, in the first place, ousting hatred from being the Earth's dominant force and replacing it with love? By acknowledging that hatred manifests itself in greed? By condemning greed as being a sin – something which endangers mankind? ('*Endangers*' it? 'Endangers' it in the same way that it is 'pretty unsafe', playing with live cables on a pylon.) By recognising it as a *deadly* sin? A *genocidal* sin? One responsible already for numbers of murders each day, of which the death toll at the Twin Towers would be but a fraction? Three hundred, Polly, and sixty-five days each and every year? How is this not *economic* terrorism?

"And this is before the going gets really tough. You think such numbers will decrease when the going gets tougher? We can't apparently feed ourselves today – well, mayhap we could, but hatred will not allow us to. How do we think we're going to feed ourselves when our numbers double? Through, as Professor Sachs would have you believe, increasing the polarisation of the global community, feeding its hatred? I rather think not.

"Quantum physicists, quantum mechanics are calling today, and urgently, for a new paradigm which embraces the new knowledge of the inter-connectedness they have discovered. It behoves us to find a morality able to complement that paradigm. Else we'll allow today's moral vacuum to expand. And Nature also abhors a moral vacuum. And the unscrupulousness now prevalent will simply seize hold. You ask where we start: We discover, my friend, quantum *economics*. We strip economics down to its component parts and we start examining both those components and their assembly. The Nobel Laureate Professor Amartya Sen has, time and again, shown the benefits of attaching humanitarian principles to economics. Indeed of allowing humanitarian principles to pilot economics.

"When we challenge the super-greedy with these propositions, most of them will reply, as they smile their patronising smile at us, that economics is a tiny bit more complicated than we imagine. You know what then we tell them? We then tell them, Polly, 'Then simplify economics, my friends.'"

"What about the work, Rafa, of Muhammad Yunus?"

"Well, first thing I think, I think, Polly, is so sad that the Nobel Peace Prize has been awarded to the likes of Dr Kissinger and has therefore lost so much of its prestige.

"The second thing, I say to my shame, is I know little detail of

Professor Yunus's work. He founded, I think, or helped to found ... was it the 'Gameen' bank? The 'Bank of the Poor', as it's come to be known. It gives micro-loans, some under ten dollars, to the direly impoverished. The hope is to create micro-economies – presumably which then grow into somewhat larger ones. And certainly it sounds like a good idea ... like a great idea, in fact. But, without a re-adjustment to the ethics of the world, I fear for its long-term practicality. I certainly applaud the thinking behind it. But I applaud too some of the thinking behind Professor Sachs's work, and virtually all the thinking behind Sir Bonio's. The latter is – if I'm being serious for a moment – far more misguided, I feel, than ill intentioned.

"I wish Professor Yunus well, and his bank ... and, of course, his bank's clients. It would, though, be folly, I fear, to think their venture will do anything other than make a dent until methos internationally has been replaced with wethos.

"In general terms, economics is no longer, as historically, about the distribution of resources. Is only now about the distribution of money. And money now, far from being controlled by economics, controls it. Dictates to it, in fact. Yet again, the institution has taken over the asylum.

"Indeed we are now striving to build a system where the world's economics are dependent on überwealth. Hence places the like of Dubai – with all its excesses."

"Excesses," Polly says, "and excrescences."

"And an excess of excrescences, *amiga mia*. Economics is striving to make überwealth indispensable. So that it will simply not be economically possible to create greater parity, less polarity of income. 'It'll be the poor who will suffer,' they will tell you. The poor are the porters and laundry staff at the seven-star hotels, those who sweep the streets outside or park your limousine for you or ... or ... or."

A tall man, early forties perhaps, short mouse-brown hair, little goatee beard, no moustache, lopes ganglily between the on-coming cars and across the street. He shouts to his girlfriend in a language Polly thinks is probably Scandinavian. The girlfriend, to the apparent delight of her companion, is stuck on a traffic island in the middle. Her tan is too deep and her hair too white for both not to have come out of a bottle. As she glances, ever more frantically, for a gap in the traffic, he snaps away joyfully at her discomfort. Eventually, she just closes her eyes and runs. She arrives on the pavement. He lets his camera dangle and cuddles her. Safe again, she mock-punches him in mock-censure, before she too starts to giggle.

"Global warming today," Rafa continues, "is no more caused by carbon emission than Mata Hari was killed by bullets. Greed has caused global warming in the same way that Mata Hari was killed by the judges at her court-martial.

"And I accept that there are scientists of good faith who contend that global warming, whilst real, is not a *manmade* condition. This is very much part of the devastating war we spoke about when first we met, Polly: that between the Untruth, my friend, and the Truth. We no longer know whom to believe. And, within the shituation in which we find ourselves, that is terrifying. *Absolutely* terrifying. Is like being aboard the 'Titanic' with the captain saying 'We're sinking' and the chief engineer insisting, 'No, we're not.' Except we're not talking here about 2,000 terrified passengers running like headless chickens hither and thither, but six or seven, my friend, *billion*.

"I don't know any more than anyone else what is the truth about global warming – or indeed very many of the conditions which threaten to annihilate us. I don't know either whether Mr Varley did misappropriate the tsunami funds, whether IBM and Coca-Cola did have truck with the Nazis. I do not even know that Dr Kissinger did say he felt no obligation to abide by democracy of an electorate irresponsible enough to vote in a communist government. Nor do I know how it came to pass that the facts – not the Truth, that (yes) is an elusive beast – but the *facts* are now so difficult to discover. Is all part of the War between the Truth and the Untruth and is yet another manifestation of today's madness."

"'Tis the time's plague when mad men lead the blind ...'"

"'Hamlet'?"

"'King Lear'."

"Is a good epitaph for our times, my friend."

"Ain't it, though?"

"Is more than madness, whatever that is, the impossibility of discovering facts. Perhaps is the ultimate madness."

"I saw an interview once with Roman Polanski's lawyer. You know who Roman Polanski is?"

"Is, no?, a film director."

"Bravo, *amigo mío*. And you know, right?, he was charged with what in California is called 'statutory rape'."

"His wife, no?, was murdered by the Manson family."

"Same man. Well, in this interview I saw – this was a retrospective long after the event – his lawyer said ... Douglas Dalton, I believe his name was. 'Everyone is entitled to their opinions,' Mr Dalton said. 'But they are not entitled to alter the facts.' I thought at the time that statement had far wider implications than just to the immediate case. We all of us, Rafa, have the right to our opinions. We, none of us, have the right to alter the facts."

A despatch-rider skips out of the building just ahead of them. He holds a jiffy envelope clutched in one of his mock-leather gauntlets. He seeks to stomp his helmet onto his head, but the envelope makes it difficult. By trying to save the three seconds it would have taken him to have first put the envelope into the panniers, he wastes half-a-minute. He has left his powerful motorcycle on the pavement. Now desperate to make up lost time, he guns it alive and screams off down the road.

"Of course," says Rafa, "we all of us have greed within us. Of course we do. And, of course, we must start by recognising that and dealing with it – looking into an X-ray mirror, a mirror of the soul. A difficult task. A superhuman, a *Herculean* task; and one in fact and not in myth.

"And, of course, we do need to be pragmatic. The street is not going to have no cars on it by us willing them away. Before we cross it, we need to check that street is clear of them.

"But we can – and immediately – stop lionising those with too much wealth. I've even heard that Mr Branson is being held up as a role model. Well, mayhap he deserves to be. Mayhap he's a good man. But if he is, is his goodness which makes him commendable, not his wealth. Wealth is a measure only of what one has taken; worth is what one gives.

"Mr Gates is today often called the world's 'biggest' philanthropist. And I really hope he is. For his sake. He certainly didn't seem to me to be too philanthropic when Mr Negroponte was trying to manufacture a laptop for a hundred dollars and distribute many free to the poor. But, *claro*, I would concede, even philanthropists have to be allowed their bad days."

Polly stops to light a cigarette. "I have to be a bit careful when I am discussing Mr Gates," she admits almost urgently. She's clearly uncomfortable saying what it is she is saying and thus almost forcibly ejects it. "I saw a TV programme once centred on him, on Mr Gates. During which they interviewed his father. Who confessed to being chock- full of pride for his son. An arrow passed through me. Straight through me. A physical pain. My father's *never* been proud of me, Rafa, never been proud of anything I've done. So, yes, I am envious of Mr Gates. Not for his money. Who on Earth would want that much money? But, yes, because he has his father's love. No, not his love. I think I have my father's love. I do not have his pride."

"I am sad for you, Polly."

"Oh, I came to terms with it, Rafa. And some time ago. I'm just trying to let you know what I'm seeing in my mirror. Please go on."

"He should be proud of you. I would be proud of a daughter like you."

"Thank you, Rafa. This is the Mansion House, by the way. It's here the Lord Mayor lives. Well, it's his official residence, anyway."

"The Lord Mayor who is not the Mayor?" asks Rafaél.

"The Mayor is elected. The Lord Mayor is appointed. There's been a Mayor of London for about ten years, and a Lord Mayor for close to a thousand."

"Well, that's all very clear," says Rafaél. "Each day I live here it surprises me less that the British invented cricket!"

The rain resumes. This time in earnest. It splutters up off the pavement before splatting down again like a spatula'd fried egg. The streets start smelling – of dust and debris and (for God knows what reason) the feathers from plucked turkeys. Miss Havisham's guest room would have smelled like this. But it is not altogether, and this almost surprises them, an unpleasant smell.

"At his zenith, Mr Gates will only be the 'biggest' philanthropist in terms of actual money. His 'sacrifice' is certainly no 'bigger' than those of the firemen in New York on September 11th, nor than the pensioner giving away her week's money for earthquake relief – nor than any of the other ten billion totally selfless acts performed anonymously (probably each week) by good people throughout the world. By *us* good people, Polly. Because we are also good people, *amiga mía,* you and I.

"The wonderfulnesses of Mother Teresa and Gandhi are, of course, wonderful. But just as wonderful (mayhap even more so) is the wonderfulness of those like Malalai Joya, who was the only female candidate in the recent Afghan elections. Or like Gareth Mallone, who teaches whole communities to find their individual and communal voice through their individual and communal voices – and others like Mr Mallone, working in Soweto, say, or Luanda, teaching music on broken-down pianos. Or like Gary Foxcroft, fighting on behalf of children in Nigeria designated 'witches'. Or Azra Pasalic, a Bosniak paediatrician, more interested in her patients' welfare than her own safety. Or James Mawdsley, who deliberately got himself arrested in Burma to publicise the plight of the Burmese generally and of Aung San Suu Kyi particularly. The vast armies there are in the world of people like them. The, Polly, *vast* armies of such people. The selfless, the anonymously good … the anonymously *magnificent*. The *countless* numbers of such souls.

"Certainly is admirable that Mr Gates should be giving to charity the sums that he is, of course it is – other than (and is an important 'other than') ... other than the ethos behind his acquisition of the money he now gives to charity is that which makes the charity necessary in the first place. And, no, Mr Gates did not create that ethos. But neither does he do anything (at least, that I've heard) either to dissipate that ethos or dissolve it. And those who are not part of the solution are, yes, part of the problem.

"I sincerely hope for Mr Gates's sake that his gift is not, as I have heard suggested, a giant tax write-off; nor that his motives are not a PR exercise for Microsoft. I've also heard he wants to buy himself a Nobel Prize. Well, if that's his primary motive, he's certainly paying a high financial price for it. Mayhap even *such* a high price that he deserves it. Not, however, if he is using his billions merely to further the interests of globalisation.

"And I greatly fear that Mr Gates's action, and that of Mrs Gates, *will* serve the interests of globalisation. If not directly (in the manner of Mr Varley), then subliminally: as an endorsement, for instance, of the system which brought him that obscene fortune to begin with. (A fortune which would not be so obscene if the rest of the world were, at least, eating.) The philanthropy of Mr and Mrs Gates is *certainly* no endorsement of that system. With that economic system there will always be a *need* for such philanthropy."

They pass by the Bank of England on their left – the Old Lady, as she is known, of Threadneedle Street. Polly thinks about imparting this datum, but her articulation has already past that point – and some time previously.

Rafaél is in overdrive. "Any charity's first task is to make itself redundant. That is 'of course'. Mr and Mrs Gates's more than most. I hope that is being borne in mind. I would hope some of Mr Gates's foundation would be spent investigating economic systems where the need for philanthropy in the future will be restricted to restoring church steeples – or, Polly, the 'Cutty Sark' –, or caring for abandoned animals and is not required to supply the necessities of human life. I would include protecting children and animals against cruelty a necessity.

"Now, I'm sure Mr Gates is a worthy man. Sure of it. And not in the sense that Marc Antony thought Brutus an 'honourable man'. Genuinely I am sure he is a worthy man. But he is worthy, not because of his money, but despite it."

"'Wealth'," says Polly, "'is only a measure of what you have taken. Worth is a measure only of what you have given.' I like it, Rafa."

"We can stop thinking, Polly, that the world's poor are going to be fed via child sponsorship (however admirable that cause) or telethons or Band-Aid concerts (however admirable those causes). Because that is what precisely these measures are: band-aids. Band-aids used to treat multiple fractures and internal bleeding and God alone knows what else. They are – of course they are – an indication that there is an inherent goodness in us all, that we feel a need to help those less lucky than we are, of an inherent commitment we most of us have to the cause of 'wethos' – and, as such, they are great boons to our communal morale.

"But the only way that global poverty is going to be addressed globally is if we change the moral impulsion of the world, and it we expose the lie that 'greed is good'. We are, I think, entitled to ask how much of the money harvested by charity concerts and concerns (like Band-Aid) has just gone back, via Mr Varley and globalisation, to those same forces which cause the need for such charities in the first place.

"Hatred can never be good. Never. Which is the principal reason why globalisation has so utterly failed to help the world's poor. And will continue to fail to help them. Globalisation, devoid of spin, is only hatred in five syllables.

"If God is love, then greed has to be the devil. We live in a world therefore which worships the devil. And yet we appear surprised, indeed astonished, that its values are all satanic, all upside-down.

"We need to recognise hatred as being what it is: hatred. We need to stop venerating hatred and believing we need hatred to keep the global economy afloat. We need, Polly, to start making a commitment to love."

"Make love not war?" Polly asks. There is the hint of a smile stroking her words.

"Yes," says Rafaél emphatically. "Yes, my friend. Yes. It's fashionable today to sneer at that: It was part of all the hippy nonsense, flower power and marijuana and sandals. Babies and bath-water, Polly. Babies and bath-water. Is a *wonderful* slogan: 'Make love not war'. Beautiful. We should feel no need to apologise for it. We should ask those sneering at it why they choose to do so. Would you, Polly, rather make love or war? What would *they* rather be doing, those who sneer?"

Threadneedle Street would have been an alley even in the days of sedan-chairs. With its solid stone and the mathematical precision of its architecture, there is something prison-like about its feel. No, it's too expansive for that: too expansive, and too expensive! Being in it is like a lone sperm, rather, having been abandoned by his colleagues, immersed and lost in the vastness of a fallopian tube.

"We are too frightened of derision, my friend. Well, I am, certainly. It appals me (I've said this too before) how frightened I am of it. I like to think of myself as a grown man, sometimes – often – I mewl like a baby.

"Derision is one of the main weapons in the arsenal of the strong protecting themselves against the weak. And is hugely effective. Is very hard to be laughed at. No-one wants to appear ridiculous. But we owe it to the planet, and to our children – we owe it, Polly, to *ourselves* – to rise above it. Is part of the question: Do we have what it takes, Polly, to do what it takes?" He looks again at the sky, rummages in his shoulder-bag and removes the umbrella. He puts it up.

"Feel like visiting the Stock Exchange?" asks Polly.

"Why would I want to do that?" asks Rafa. "Or is the 'Stock Exchange' the name of a pub?"

"Much better idea," says Polly. They have now turned off Wormwood Street.

"Do you have a second deadly lie?" asks Rafaél. "To accompany,

I mean, the second deadly sin?"

"Yes," Polly replies. "The material is material."

"Oh! Nice play on words," says Rafaél, mimicking her words to him on Primrose Hill. "But you will have to explain."

"I'm playing with you, Rafa," Polly concedes. "But not completely. There are two major lies, and eight subsidiary ones. Sub-lies, if you like. Together they have to add up to a lie that is indeed deadly."

"Go on," says Rafa.

"Major lie number one: the material is material. Major lie number two," she continues, "is that the material is *im*material."

"Go on," Rafa tells her.

"Major lie one, that the material is material, comprises four sub-lies: (a) that the material is material, in the sense of being real; (b) that the real is material, in the sense of being important; (c) that the *important* is important; and (d) that the material meaning 'real' is material meaning 'relevant'."

"Okay," says Rafaél. "Just repeat that to me, will you?" Polly does so. "Okay," he says again, this time with more conviction.

"Major lie two, that the material is *im*material – and this, Rafa, is where it becomes *really* complicated – is also four lies: and those four lies are all the opposite of those I've just listed. It is a lie to say that the material is *not* real, or that the real is not important; that the important is not important, or that the real is not relevant.

"One of the mistakes we make about the Truth is in thinking that because the lie is white, what is black is the Truth. Oh, it usually is, but not invariably. The Truth might well be neither black nor white. Nor grey, for that matter. It may be all three. And simultaneously. Or it may not be a colour at all. The lie may be white and the Truth be a strawberry, for instance, or a Panama hat or the beach at Fort Lauderdale.

"Ask the wrong question, whatever the reply, it will be wrong. Part, as you would have it, Rafa, of the Untruth."

"All very straightforward, then," Rafaél comments. "Go on," he bids her.

"The Buddha, millennia ago," says Polly, "figured out that reality is an illusion. And so it is. Atomic, and sub-atomic, sciences have confirmed that. What we think is *solid*, for instance, isn't. A chair is not actually a solid object, but a mass of microscopic particles whizzing around themselves in what is essentially thin air. It is a lie, therefore – a misconception, if you'd prefer –, to maintain that the material *is* material. However, see how immaterial that chair is if I hit you over the head with it. A head, by the way, which is also not material, nothing *like* what it appears to be.

"There is, therefore, untruth in both statements. But there is also truth in both of them. The problem with so much thought today is that it embraces one lie – or one truth – to the exclusion of the other. At which point, the belief ceases to be cogent, and certainly not complete, and starts to become dogmatic. There is nothing wrong with faith, provided it doesn't flout the evidence. We even need faith today: a faith, for instance, in the inherent good of man; a faith in, if you like, 'wethos', Rafa. Either that or we give up the struggle."

"Go on," again he bids her.

"There is also now fashionable – particularly amidst the self-help best-sellers – a notion that we create our own reality. That all we need to improve our lives is to 'think' ourselves into a better space.

"And, there is, in fact, also an element of truth in this belief – and quantum physics would agree that our perception of reality can *impact* on that reality. But to suggest that 'all we need' is to rethink is vastly, and grossly, to oversimplify that influence. From that belief it is but a very short step indeed to believing we need do nothing to help the starving because they have 'thought' this situation onto themselves. This 'shituation', excuse me. And from there it is also only a short step to a belief we need have no sympathy for Hitler's victims or Mao's because they too 'thought' themselves into such misery.

"I read Anne Frank's diary. I can remember no particular indication of her being negative. In fact, given the dire conditions in which she and her family were living, I remember being amazed by her cheerfulness and optimism. I saw a TV film about Rutka Lasker. Who was a sort of Anne Frank of Poland. Same thing: She was also murdered horribly. She also seems to have been a remarkably positive person. I find it offensive, what is tacit in that belief, that a child in a Bangkok brothel or, Rafa, one of your Limeñan orphans, that Anne Frank and Rutka Lasker and six million other Jews, that the private in the First War trenches or the rating in Nelson's navy press-ganged into the service, that the slaves brought by the Romans from Africa or Gaul, that the millions killed by mosquitoes or by earthquakes have, or had, only themselves to blame for their situation because they were all thinking wrongly.

"Even before we get to those extremes, in fact, I find much of this attitude offensive. It's just too easy, too convenient. Did you 'think' Inma into dying? Did *she*?

"Now, I fully accept that one of the most eminent cancer specialists in the world, Bernie Siegel, believes that unresolved emotional issues can make a major contribution to the contracting of that awful illness. Thus that the perception of reality impacts on reality. And that clearly is a claim that needs to be taken seriously – very seriously indeed, in fact: considerably more seriously than it would seem to be taken by the majority of those doing research into possible cures. I also accept the potential of the power contained in the 'consciousness' quantum scientists talk about – what might be the quite staggering power of that 'consciousness' – but that is a few steps removed from the 'put-on-a-happy-face' blandishments of way too many in the self-help industry.

"And, sure, my own experience tells me that an essentially cheerful disposition makes life more pleasant than an essentially gloomy one. (Not that I *have* a cheerful disposition, as you may have noticed. But I do recognise that I make my life tougher by not having one.) A book I once read about anger also categorically states that the happy are slower to anger than the unhappy. My own experience also tells me that it is nicer to be around people who are enjoying life than those who are merely putting up with it. I could easily, even cheerfully, accept therefore that the cheerful are less likely to get sick than the gloomy.

"But that is an enormously long cry from insisting, as I have read, that the most 'successful' human beings on this planet, the richest and most powerful, are those who think most positively and who give most substantially. Now, like you, I don't know either Mr Gates or, let's say, Mr Murdoch. For all I know, Mr Gates whistles as he works, and Mr Murdoch has the milk of human kindness churning by the gallon through his veins. But I have seen precious little evidence to substantiate such claims. Is the Sultan of Brunei such an incredibly positive person? I really don't know. How much has the bin Laden family given?

"And yet, for all the apparent nonsense spouted by some of its apostles, there is at its core more than a germ of truth in the theory that reality is what you make of it. The City of London, for instance, would apparently hold the belief to be self-evident that there *is* no reality; that the only reality there is is the *perception* of reality. It doesn't matter to the City, not one iota, how a company – or a country – *is* doing; it matters only how the City *perceives* that company to be doing.

"Global currencies become strong or soft not because of their actual worth, but because of the value the City (and other 'Cities' throughout the world) is (and are) prepared to put on them. The City in making such an assessment has only one criterion: the likelihood of financial gain. And historically the most 'gain' has come from countries, and companies, with the most disregard for those in their charge, and not those seeking the way best to care for them. For those countries (thinking about it) where the strong are most effectively protected against the weak. Currencies become strong (apparently therefore) if it is seen by the City that governments under-educate their young, under-treat their sick, scorn their lame – torture and imprison their dissidents.

"Companies' shares are assessed using very similar criteria. The shares otherwise of a whole array of fast-food outlets would totally have collapsed – companies which treat their employees appallingly, their suppliers abysmally and who are contributing substantially to substantial social problems.

"There's a company, for instance, specialising in supplying ... let's call them 'robust investigators'. It has been quoted on the Stock Exchange as being worth sixty-six million dollars. Sixty-six million, Rafa. How sick do you need to be, in God's name, to invest in a company supplying torturers? Why is it that their share price continues to rise?"

They see a pub sign swinging soddenly in the ever-strengthening downpour. They scuttle towards it, buy drinks, sit themselves down in horse-shoe wooden chairs at a round table.

"Don't get me wrong," Polly continues. "There is, as I've said, a lot of truth in the belief that reality is the perception of reality. But equally Truth does finally remain Truth whoever believes it. Christ did not suddenly become *not* the Son of God just because of the inception of the Spanish Inquisition. The City likewise didn't invent the credo that reality is only the perception of reality.

"Let's take the weather ... To me, the weather today is, well, horrible. And that is my reality. To the farmer, though, to the maker of raincoats or umbrellas, to taxi-drivers, today's weather is superb. And their reality is just as real as mine is. We're back to the view from the Eye and that on the boat. The City looks at the same scene from the Eye as those living in a country – or working for a company – see from a boat. And those are the realities, if you like, of the two opposing factions in a court case. Usually both sides believe they are right. And the point of justice is supposed to be that it digs deeper to unearth the reality that underpins those two perceptions of reality. (It doesn't, of course. Because justice is oh so rarely justice, but that is the *intention* of justice.)

"In exactly the same way, the perception of reality is not the *only* reality. There is, at least, one other: the justice, if you like, that lies deeper than the realities of the two litigants.

"This is the reality that supersedes the subjective interpretation of it. This reality is that, irrespective of whether the weather is horrid or superb, it *is* raining. The starving man isn't perceiving his hunger; the drought-ridden farmer is not perceiving his crop as being withered. The amputee may feel pain in his legs, but the legs have still gone. Try controlling an attack of diarrhoea by perceiving it as unreal.

"Reality can be affected by perception, but it cannot be altered by it. And it is a downright lie, and a deadly one, to suggest that it can be. We do really have to do more for this Earth than think beautiful thoughts.

"Furthermore, we have to be extremely cautious that this doctrine (that reality is only our perception of it) is not used as yet another weapon in the already mighty arsenal of the strong protecting themselves against the weak. As, for instance, economics has become.

"You also touched on this, Rafa, I know. Indeed, most of the points I'm about to make are evident too at the end of the path you were taking. That of greed, I mean, being hatred."

The pub struggles hard to be minimalist and basic, a twenty-first century (and affluent) equivalent of the locals which, during the Second World War, were designated 'spit-and-sawdust'. Other than that, of course, today sawdust has been mightily eschewed and, as for spit ... Well, the only spit that would be allowed in this pub today would be that on which the suckling pig is currently roasting. Even the so-called 'naked' floorboards have been treated with some kind of lacquer, presumably to protect them against the tread of ten thousand upwardly mobile soles.

"If physics and biology are two of the natural sciences, I've never been quite sure why economics has not been called an 'unnatural' science. Even to call the subject a science is to flatter it outrageously."

"Professor Sen, apparently, excepted."

"Professor Sen, Rafa, of course excepted. Doubtless too there are many others. Is part of the lie how rarely we hear of those others, indeed even of Professor Sen. Noting such exceptions, economics, Polly, it seems to me, is a devil's brew of necromancy, political expedience, guesswork and self-fulfilling prophecies. As a science, it's probably right up there with alchemy and tealeaf-reading. As an aid to philosophy or politics ... well, at its absolute moral apogee (at least in the post-war twentieth century), it has been concerned overwhelmingly, not with creating *wealth*, but with shifting poverty from my doorstep to yours. Economics, in that period, has had nothing to do with the distribution of wealth (not in any real sense), and has had to do exclusively with a constant recycling of poverty.

"We talk today about the 'developing world' – a phrase quite as patronising as the '*third* world', indeed perhaps even more, in that it implies the wealthy countries are 'developed'. I should like to know on what basis such countries like to believe they are entitled to think of themselves in that way. Very much I should like to hear that.

"The IMF says of countries in the developing world that they are bankrupt. Well, so are most of the so-called 'developed' countries. They may be able to meet their monthly repayments (though not always easily) but if their debts were called in ... Well, Mr Micawber is the chief economist of just as many 'developed' countries as of developing ones.

"'Dot com' companies – the vast majority of them – have absolutely no integral worth. Their worth is only in their perceived worth. If tomorrow cyberselling went out of fashion, they'd have no farms that could be reclaimed, no livestock nor assets that could be sold or realised, nothing. And there is certainly a danger that the whole 'dot com' explosion is a South Sea Bubble waiting to burst – drowning what will now be millions when it does so.

"But it begs an extremely important question. If we can build an entire economics around an abstract commodity, why don't we choose *as* that abstract commodity one of considerably more communal welfare than 'dot com' companies? Or the City's perception of a company's worth or a country's? Perception too is an abstract. When there is a run on the Dow Jones or Nasdaq, millions – if not billions – can be lost. But the loss is, actually, as illusory as the gain. There are not suddenly less houses in the world, less cows or supermarkets ... or, even, cars or televisions. There are not billions of dollars less in the world. We have just created a system of economics where the abstract controls the reality. So – is my question – why not change the abstract?

"Why doesn't the abstract of economics become benefit to the planet, for instance? Or benefit to humanity? Or just kindness? Hey, what about love?

"Wouldn't that, in fact, be but an adaptation of an old, old idea: the idea of a *common* wealth? What about creating an economic system around the abstract idea of a real common wealth? What a great tribute that would also be to the twenty-first century: the hundred years when the idea of a common wealth became real!

"One of the biggest economic problems in the world today (at least, the rich world) is that its inhabitants are living ever longer. And yet there is a total resistance to raising the age of retirement. This will soon – *very* soon – lead to a situation (and there is almost no argument about this) where those without gainful employment will outnumber those with it.

"Simultaneously, one of the biggest *social* problems we have is that there is a desperate undermanning of those doing what in today's system of economics are draining jobs: those that take more money from the pot than they contribute to it: teachers, for instance, policemen, medical staff, counsellors, probation and prison officers and so on.

("This has also a lot to do with our balance-sheet economics. Balance-sheets economics are completely false economics. They don't show the true cost of things.

"You're looking blank, Rafa. Let me give you an example: A good assistant director today earns ... well, let's say, fifteen hundred pounds a week. Certainly, though, you will find so-called 'assistant directors' prepared to work for a fraction of that sum: half, a third. Some for two hundred pounds a week. And there will be producers and production managers idiotic enough to employ such monkeys for such peanuts. And many of those producers will be applauded by many executives and auditors for having done so. Because auditors can only read balance-sheets. And what will *not* show up on the balance-sheet is how much money the bad assistant director has *cost* the film – both directly and indirectly.

"Excluding all other factors, like the direct costs that will have been incurred by overtime or by additional meals the crew will have had to be given and so forth, the chances are that the bad a.d.'s incompetence will have meant longer working days, which will also mean an increasingly tired and cranky crew – and an increasingly inefficient one. Because of the domino effect, what could have been a good film, is now – at its very least – a less good one. Which will probably impact on the box-office. Which will impact on the desirability to investors of putting their money into films. And on, Rafa, and on. The saving on paper of ten thousand dollars, say, will actually – if invisibly – have cost millions. Our system of global economics is also a balance-sheet economy. And spends pounds to save pennies in a very similar way. And is thus – surprise, surprise! – failing in a way that is even more spectacular.

"It is, for instance, balance-sheets economics that have devised the creation of endless 'targets' [which you, Rafa, were talking about] for jobs where the very idea of 'targets' is palpably ludicrous: doctors, for instance, policemen, teachers. The creation of such 'targets', that has absolutely nothing to do with improving job efficiency. In many cases, totally to the contrary. It has to do with being able to spin that 'inefficiency is being tackled'. Babies have been battered to death in Britain, Rafa, as a consequence of these balance-sheet economics.

"Balance-sheet economics is in itself a form of spin, so it's maybe inevitable that it creates more of it. It is absolutely not about saving money or increasing efficiency. It's about *giving the impression* that money is being saved or efficiency improved.) ... Where was I?"

"You were talking, *amiga mía,* about retirement."

"Retirement, yes. ... Yes, now I remember. Yes. ... Now, I absolutely understand, Rafa, a sheet-metal worker, say, at sixty-five considering he's done his bit. Let someone younger, fitter do this back-breaking, dangerous job. But would that same sheet-metal worker be quite so hostile to the idea of driving the disabled? Or lending an ear to a teenager who feels the world is against him? Or helping young parents who are struggling? How much money, how many resources, would be *saved* in the economy if we pre-empted problems? More problems than are already being pre-empted, I mean? *Sensibly* pre-empted them? If there were professional good Samaritans to supplement the apparently invisible army there is already of the amateur variety? 'Apparently invisible' because it is so very rarely we ever get to hear of them. Good Samaritanism doesn't sell newspapers. Pre-empting problems doesn't sell newspapers. It's not sexy, intervening at the molehill stage.

"Whilst for sure paying such people would be a drain on the economy, their earnings would generate further the circulation of money – and such circulation, even most neo-liberal economists would agree, would create income. The savings such a system could make on *expensive* social medicine – prison and hospital, for example – could be enormous. Enormous.

"It's probably always been abstract, economics. But it is abstract today with a vengeance.

"Eventually what is being sold by the Internet is convenience. Well, granted, finally all retail is that. But, at least, shops have premises which are assets. Shopping around on-line is considered today less strenuous and cheaper (and more private!) than either phoning around or pounding the High Street pavement. Its economic substance has very little weight beyond that.

"So, why – is what I'm saying – why don't we convert the abstract economics of today based on convenience into an abstract economics of tomorrow based on *social* convenience? Which will enable us to start tackling mountainous problems whilst they are still molehills? Where we supply the infrastructure that will intercede *before* old women get mugged or housing estates become gang-controlled ghettoes or drunken fathers lay into their innocent children or the victims of such abuse feel they have nowhere to turn? Or warlords butcher thousands? Or famines or epidemics kill millions? Or ... or

... or?

"If, Rafa, tomorrow we do want to create your 'wethos', we have to start thinking about an economic system which will allow it, the 'quantum economics' you were talking about. Just maybe that process starts by accepting that the real is both not real and also *not* not real. That the chair is, agreed, not a solid object, but that it's also agreed, it's still not a good idea to hit people over the head with it.

"The biggest industry today in the Western world is, as you yourself pointed out, now lending money. The amount of debt just has to exceed the actual money there is in the world. This too is, of course, only another offshoot of the belief that reality is only the perception of reality. And it forgets the other reality, likely any moment to bite it on the ass: the reality of realism. We have already had a taste of this. And recently. Was that taste not bitter enough? Is not this all foolhardiness? And is it not a foolhardiness redolent of that which immediately preceded the Wall Street Crash? And yet economists will tell you, that ours is a situation from which we cannot escape. The world's economics require us to be in the debt we're in – indeed require us to *increase* that debt.

"If that were not all alarming enough, we've also now sold ourselves out to a reamarkably fragile technology: The world's computers. Which could crash and cause a *financial* crash: a crash *indeed*. On at least two occasions that I know about, IT systems have been so efficiently sabotaged that the world's banking has been brought to the very edge of collapse. (If I know about two, God alone knows how many more there have been that the public knows *nothing* about!) We don't think that one day a hacker will succeed? And what provisions have been made to cover such an eventuality?

"And how, if the entire system of global economics were not an abstract, would that situation be possible? Is this not evidence of an economic structure being founded on very sandy ground indeed?

"In one of our earlier talks, we talked about economics demanding that the world move faster and faster. How insane that is. Well, here's another insanity: Economics is also demanding that we spend more and more. And, Rafa, more.

"GNP – excuse me: Gross, Rafa, National Product – GNP has to out-distance population growth. And it has to keep growing. Today's economics demand that. So the inbuilt redundancy of consumer goods has now got little to do with the manufacturers being greedy (so those economists would have us believe). It is (so those economists would argue) an essential for economic solvency. Mobile phones and computers are now out-of-date before they even leave the factory. How much more quickly is it possible to build in obsolescence? And it leads too to the nonsense I've heard that *never*, for instance, will they be able to design a laptop where the keyboard is not in the ludicrous position it is today. You just know that's nonsense, that *of course* the design fault will eventually be overcome (even if such is by redesigning the laptop's hinges). I suspect, in fact, that it already has been and that all that is being waited for is what the companies deem to be the right time for such companies to announce their 'remarkable innovation'.

"The computer industry also 'sells' protection against problems which it has created!: identity theft, for example. And, amazingly, we're so inured to a permanent blather that we don't even recognise that for what it is. We've become so totally brain-washed that we fail even to register the speciousness, not just of such claims, but of a system where such claims need to be made.

"Plastic money is a license for the banks to print money. This is so well documented, no further comment is really necessary. It's also a method whereby they can control both money more and us more. If a bank is teetering, it's much easier to control our withdrawal of plastic money than it is that of cash. Plastic money is far more convenient to the banks than it is to their clients. Which is before we get onto the fact that those banks are also allowed – even encouraged – to keep records of our private life. There are now databases (in fact, several) which contain the names and personal details of each one of us. The British government is planning to have the personal details of every child logged onto one such central database 'so that no child falls through the cracks'.

"And we're allowing all this because we continue to believe that the institutions which can access such databases have at heart our individual or communal welfare. 'Data protection' is supposed to guarantee that such information is not leaked to sources that might benefit from it. There seems, though, to be a mountain of evidence which indicates this is simply not true. Why do we continue to believe them?

"The British Home Office also sought to reassure us of its beneficence when it was seeking to introduce identity cards. We all saw what such guarantees were worth – even less than politicians' promises.

"This, in fact, was quite encouraging. It was one of the very rare instances latterly of the media doing what the media should be doing – exposing chicanery and incompetence, protecting us (their consumers), protecting liberty. It told us that not even today's far too acquiescent media can be pushed too far.

"If Edwin Black can be believed (and he seems to present an extremely convincing argument), in its very early history, IBM was making, as I think I said before, considerable profits from aiding and abetting the Holocaust; the propriety of Mr Gates's business methods have been questioned – I think you, Rafa, mentioned this – by more than a handful of his disgruntled competitors; the British government declared war using as a premise one it knew to be deceitful. Now, am I mad? Are these institutions which we should consider have our best interests at heart?

"Even the housing market, that is just more economic prestidigitation. Certainly individuals gain from the property market. But when they do gain, they do so at the cost of subsequent generations. And those who *really* gain are the institutions. For two reasons.

"In the first place, it makes profiteers out of ordinary people. That too I think is deliberate: It's difficult for Stephen Spielberg to condemn the film industry. It exacts from ordinary, decent people the price that they start to adopt the rat-race 'morality' of businessmen. It is a modern day version of the 'Faust' legend – other than we are selling our souls not for insight or wisdom but for the bits of trinketry, Rafa, you were talking about. We are selling Manhattan for a few strings of beads.

"Secondly, institutions also gain directly from such prestidigitation. It allows them to create recessions, and, contrary to mythology, institutions *love* recessions. It's another means of keeping subjects subjected. Recessions do no harm to plutocratic wealth – such wealth even *benefits* from it: recessions foster the polarisation of wealth. The institutions and super-wealth are rich enough to survive a recession until the economic revival – one as artificially created as (almost certainly) was the initial recession. And, whilst the recession was raging, super-wealth was able substantially to increase its wealth by, for instance, buying from the dispossessed, from the over-stretched, from the financially vulnerable assets at bargain-basement prices.

"If you do not believe me, look at who history will tell you were the winners from the Wall Street Crash. From the subsequent Depression. Why, if I am lying, did the bastions of big business fight as vehemently as they did against the New Deal? Why did Friedman have such contempt for it?

"House prices are not allowed to 'spiral out of control'. Their 'spiralling out of control' is, I'm sure, entirely controlled. For those same reasons. And we protest as weakly as we do because we have forgotten about holding this planet in trust for our children. Governments love such spirals. There are (at least, on paper) more 'haves' around. And the 'haves' are considerably less likely to protest than the 'have-nots'. Why should a government today care about how our *children* might vote? They'll be forgotten, today's politicians, by the time our children are buying a house. (Or, in my case, when my *hypothetical* children are.) The first-time buyers then, in twenty years' time, oh, they'll be bitter all right, bitter at the fact that their mortgages will probably take a hundred years, a hundred and twenty-five years, to ammortise. But because kids are kids, they'll be much more likely to blame the greed of their parents for that situation than the government of their parents' day.

"Which history book do you know which has ever blamed a previous government for the problems and the difficulties and the ailments it bequeathed? And even if those future first-time buyers do seek to blame the government, today's Cabinet will not be around. The buyers' parents will be, though. 'Oh? And who voted them in?' the thwarted house-buyers will be likely to sneer.

"All of it, it's yet another example of the strong protecting themselves against the weak. Calamities generally, they are in the interests of big business: recession, foot-and-mouth. Well, if you've read Naomi Klein, you know. Big business has enormous resources. It can withstand with consummate ease what to most of us are catastrophes. Indeed big business thrives on such catastrophe. It's the individual who succumbs, or the *small* business. Which finally either has to close down or has to sell for whatever the bank is prepared to offer – often, well below its market value. And in the worst of all possible events, big business is infinitely more likely to be bailed out by the government than small ones are, and than individuals are. Who did the governments help during the recent credit squeeze? And such bailings out happen, I am certain, considerably more than we ever hear about.

"You remember those cop shows I talked about? I see show after show after show bemoaning the fact that bank-robbers are let out on parole. And yet we have those in control of our economy who, for their theft from the world's most destitute, are not only being given early parole, they're not even going to jail! And not just not going to jail, but are being given every material reward that this world has to offer!

"Surely – is what I'm saying – surely to God, this is as crazy as it is immoral as it is unjustifiable as it is inefficient ... as it finally has to be disastrous. It doesn't (as, Rafa, we've now said many times) finally serve the interests even of the überwealthy. It merely appears to.

"All of these, Rafa, are problems which are innate today in our economics. They are, each of them, lode-stones filled with dynamite. It's not that these economics will protect us. In fact, unless we're Nestlé or Unilever, quite the reverse. But they would, Rafa, and could – miraculously – be solved if we were to devise a system of economics that were centred around social, as opposed to monetary, value.

"I accept that the idea of money was inspired only by wanting to simplify barter – and that subsequently the idea got corrupted. I can see how the economics of hatred has been created – and that the sins in its creation have been far more of omission than commission, of not checking an impulsion before it became a compulsion. And, like you, I have no idea – none at all – how we create the system of quantum economics we're both talking about. But we *are*, Rafa, talking about the entire future of mankind. Isn't it worth spending a few bucks on some R&D? Research, Rafa, and Development? Examining how we can find a way of controlling the world that isn't a Sheriff of Nottingham economics? Getting some research done?

"Perhaps the alternative is not a Robin Hood economics either, I don't know. I'm not too fond of robbery as a form of government, however well intentioned. Perhaps we need to enter into a sphere of economics that we haven't even previously dreamed about.

"How much has been spent sending spacecraft into the unknown? Well, why don't we spend, let's say, ten percent of that sum – no, let's not be silly, let's say, not ten percent, but one percent; let's even say zero *point* one percent – sending our *economists* into the unknown, asking them to investigate the possibility of life, of civilisation on *this* planet? Of real life? Of a genuine civilisation?

"Wouldn't it be wonderful if the twenty-first century were remembered by future generations as that in which an economic theory was devised with, at its core, not hatred but love? Where it was the welfare of Man that was its impulsion, and no longer man's subjugation? Where its dynamo was a common wealth and not a common poverty?

"If economists were sincere in their efforts to support the weak, they would already have been addressing all these problems. But economics today is not there to fulfil that role. Yes, Rafa, Professor Sen aside. Economics in its entirety seems to have become a weapon of the strong to protect themselves against the weak, an academic so-called 'discipline' which has, as we said, given a spurious guise of intellectual credibility to greed. Economics today are there – yes, Rafa, as we've both said before – to supply the strong with 'moral' correctness. When England's Queen Mary burned at the stake those she considered heretics she too was supplied by her toadies with 'moral' correctness.

"Economics are not the dog. Not anywhere but in a world gone mad. Economics must start realising that. At best, they are, economics, the dog's tail. The dog is the welfare of Man. If economics demand that the welfare of Man is not paramount, then change the economics. We must start insisting, Rafa, that the tail stops wagging the dog. We must also insist (and, no, it's not quite the same thing) that the dog does indeed start wagging the tail.

"It will be thus, and only thus, that these two lies become two truths: the lie that the material *is* the real and the lie that it is not."

"Another?"

"Why not? I'll just nip to the rest-room, if you'll excuse me, whilst you're getting them."

Rafaél continues to be a good-looking man. It is not entirely accidental that the bosomy barmaid, whilst pouring the pints, contrives to wiggle an increase in her cleavage. Neither is the charm of that cleavage wasted on the South American. His deep brown eyes twinkle their appreciation. He pays for the drinks, wonders about returning to this pub on another occasion without Polly, takes the drinks backs to the table, and, as he's setting them on the table, sneaks a peek back at the bar. The barmaid flashes him a smile toothy with promise. Almost coyly he returns it. Polly takes a long swig.

"Sub-lie two," she says, finally, cleaning her froth-moustache with the back of her hand, "that the real is *important*. Well, that becomes more accepted every day. We don't need to be Muhammad or Mother

Teresa to know that it's a lie, to see that material comfort doesn't bring happiness. It's so entirely obvious, and has been sermonised about so many times, that it's not worth spending any time discussing it.

"But neither is it worth wasting time on the lie that material comfort is *not* important. That too is offensive. Let me say at this point that, like you, I find nothing wrong with pleasures that are ephemeral or superficial. A new PlayStation, for example, or a new microwave or a new electric blanket; and pleasure is pleasurable. The pleasure of eating is momentary, so is that of sex. A good joke is, often, superficial. Such pleasures have a place more significant than their apparent transitoriness or superficiality. And a greater legitimacy too than is apparent. They only become a problem when we think that such defines pleasure; that such momentary and superficial pleasure can substitute for, or obviate the need of, the long-term and profound variety.

"Which is, of course, exactly how misery is for the dispossessed: long-term and profound. Their lack of material comfort is desperately material. It is not to be sneered at or laughed away as being trivial or immaterial. Again like you, I have no problem with ascetics – the Gandhis of this world – renouncing all worldly possessions. Quite the contrary. I couldn't do it, but maybe that's why I have such respect for those who can. And neither am I, in case you hadn't noticed, a very spiritual nor, Rafa, a very enlightened being. Those that can rise above materialism I salute. Those *willing* to do it.

"But I do not salute an economic system which removes the choice, which imposes such dispossession. And I do have problems indeed when, as occasionally it is, it is insisted that the dispossessed are therefore, in point of fact, the lucky ones.

"Money is only unimportant to the very wealthy – and, then, only rarely. What I'm saying, it's as much a lie to say that money will bring you happiness as it is to say that poverty will not bring you grief.

"'Wethos' has to mean finding a middle path where money is respected but not adored, where it again becomes a means of exchange and not a commodity in its own right, and where, even if sometimes it does become a commodity, it's that which it is: a commodity and not a god.

"And we really do have to start recognising that we never, ever give to the poor. At our most charitable, we return to them a tiny part of what has been stolen from them. Whatever they subsequently did with their money, Al Capone's beneficiaries, however generationally removed, whatever they may subsequently have done with their money were – and are – rich thanks to theft.

"Sub-lie three," Polly continues. She drinks deeply from her beer.

"Is the barmaid flirting with me?" Rafa asks.

Polly watches the interplay for a moment or two. "Outrageously," she decides. "Want me to go?"

"No," he tells her. "But I may just say good-bye to you here."

"You know, right, there's, like, three tons of cosmetics between you and her skin?"

"Me, I like mutton," Rafaél admits.

"Okay." Polly smiles. She takes another sip from her drink.

"Sub-lie three?" Rafaél prompts her. "That, I think, the important is important."

"Wouldn't you rather ...?" Polly suspends her sentence with sky-hooks.

"That can wait," he tells her. "Is not important."

"I'm going to really hope that pun was accidental."

"Go on, please," he encourages her.

"Okey dokey," she says. "It's also a lie to say that the important is *not* important."

"Okey dokey," Rafaél acknowledges.

She wonders about this 'okey dokey' for a moment, decides just to press on. "At this point, I want to make it clear that I'm not a Buddhist either."

"Okey dokey," Rafaél says again.

"We done now with the 'okey-dokeys'?" she asks.

Rafa smiles, raises his glass a smidgen in acknowledgement,

drinks lightly. "Completely."

"Like you, I've read a bit about Buddhism, is what I'm saying, but I don't think of myself as an authority or anything. A lot less of one than you. I've *read* is all I've done. I could have easily gotten the wrong end of the stick. But *if* I understood it correctly: once the Buddha understood that what we think of as reality is an illusion, he also figured that so therefore was our attachment to anything real, or our aversion to it.

"There is a problem with that, I think. And that problem is pretty similar to the dichotomy we have over the chair's reality. Or the reality, come to that, of an Uzi and its bullets. At one level, even the *Uzi* isn't real, nor are its bullets. A neutron bomb, for Christ's sake, not even – at one level – is that real. But its effects sure are. The effects are real too of a fired Uzi, or a chair over the head.

"Many of the things we're *told* are important clearly aren't: money beyond our needs, expensive toys like sports cars and yachts, an inflated status ... and so on. And certainly most of the self-proclaimed 'important' people aren't: sportsmen and -women, film and pop stars and (God help us!) even their partners, people who are locked up in isolated TV studios as they bare their lack of souls. Sadly, politicians and industrial magnates (who could have some importance) today are important chiefly only negatively."

"Go on," Rafa tells her, and forces his eyes away from the *paso doble* they had been dancing with the barmaid's.

"What we have created in this century, what – rather – we have *developed* is another trick of enormous prestidigitational skill: To convince us that what is important is trivial and vice versa. And we simply *have* to start seeing through the conjuring trick.

"So much of what we have created in the world today reminds me of the episode in 'M.A.S.H.' when the army would give the unit a juke box without any problem, but not the incubator they needed to save lives.

"But, because much, for instance, of what we're told is important is trivial to the point of inconsequence, that does not mean that *nothing* is important.

"Loving children, let's start with that one ... loving children is important. Gigantically important. We don't have to like them – I don't like the little ... baskets – but we do have to love them. We need to provide children with an environment where they can grow safely and healthily, and learn to love safely and healthily, and learn to nurture (and to accept nurture) safely – and, yes, healthily. There is nothing more important than the importance of that.

"*Feeding* children, another thing maximumly important. Keeping kids healthy, discovering their potential, eking it out, encouraging it, helping them to discover their own, and eke it out and encourage it. You ever happened to see a TV sitcom called 'Frasier'?"

"Alas," confesses Rafaél, "my knowledge of television, is lamentable."

"Limited to, like, watching soccer when Peru's playing?"

"Almost."

"'Frasier', in my opinion, is one of the very best of the sitcom genre. One of its creators, David Angell, was killed on September 11th. It brought the tragedy home to me in a very personal way."

"You knew this man?"

"I was such a big fan of the show, I felt I did."

"I think I understand," says Rafaél.

"I grieved for David Angell in a very personal way. But then, a few days' on, I also started to grieve for the amount of David Angells there are in the world, Rafa, who will never become David Angell.

"Mark Twain – yeah, always trotted out, right, when you need an authority for an opinion? – Mark Twain, even in his day, lamented the amount of talent there was in the world, either unrealised or un*recognised*. How much more true is that of today? How much potential is there out in the world, Rafa, that we haven't tapped into? You think this is a world where talent will always out?

"When they were publicising 'Schindler's List', I saw an interview with one of its lead actors, Ben Kingsley. 'How much potential was killed in the gas-chambers?' he asked. 'Think of it, we could have murdered the person who might have cured AIDS.' Well, I've got to say, I think the immorality around the Holocaust was more general than that, but you never know what some bright spark TV editor has cut out of these interviews. And, even if that was recorded accurately, I do know what Mr Kingsley means. By the same token, Rafa, we could *today* be killing the person who has the cure for AIDS. By the *economic* holocaust we have allowed to grow up around us. By the holocaust not just of starving people of bread, but starving them of education and belief in themselves and dignity and hope.

"By the *domestic*, Rafa, stifling of potential. Even by the not nurturing of potential. You know how many people here and at home now have to work two jobs just to house and feed their family? Not just 'illegals'? Americans born and bred? Britishers likewise?"

"You do remember, do you, I come from Peru?" he asks.

"Hey, sorry, 'course, sorry," says Polly. "What I mean to say, Rafa, I mean to say, added to my tears for David Angell – and those tears, Rafa, were big tears and real tears – added to those tears, there were tears too – also big and real tears – for those hundred thousand potential David Angells who would – who *will* – never be one. And that *is* important, Rafaél."

"Oh, it is, my friend, it certainly is."

"It is important too to respect people, to treat them with respect and to respect their individuality. But it is really *not* important which striker from which town made the most contact on a ball with a bit of wood.

"We are, in today's world, Rafa – over and over – being distracted from that which is important to that which is, essentially, trivial. There was a famous soccer manager here who said something like, 'Football isn't a matter of life and death: It's much more important than that.' Now, if that had been intended as an epigram, or something, a witticism, I'd have laughed at it, and enjoyed it. What really scares me is that I don't think it was. And I don't think it was understood as being.

"One of the biggest soccer teams here in Britain – and those teams, let me tell you, are *big* – is today owned by a Russian. Not Denisovich, that's the Solzhenitsyn character, but something like that. Donovich or Bromovich or Obromovich or something. Who cares, right? Apart, I mean, from his mother? Whatever his name, he's one of the billionaires whose fortunes can be traced back, basically, to President Yeltsin's fondness for vodka. There are rumours that some of the business practises of this billionaire are not ... well, let's say, don't follow the Queensbury Rules to the letter. What is for sure is that there is a whole batch of very wealthy Russians who owe their fortunes to all manner of nefarious and really nasty goings-on.

"A lot of it comes from human trafficking, from the prostitution of the extremely young and totally terrified, from the sale of nuclear components to the highest bidder (often in Iran and North Korea), from the wholesale theft from the Russian people of their natural resources. Yeltsin's booze problem (coupled, as I learnt, from 'The Shock Doctrine' with more of Friedman's and Professor Sachs's economic 'advice') led to the bestowment of vast, incalculable treasures on some Russians who, let's say, are unlikely to be contenders for 'Nice Guy of the Year'.

"I saw interviews with fans of this football club, the one owned by the Russian. To a man – there were no women interviewed – they said they didn't care *what* was the source of the billionaire's income. What was, yes, 'important' was that their club had stopped struggling at the bottom of the league, and was now at its top.

"Sure, with TV today, I already said this, you never know which smart-ass editor isn't trying to make a name for himself, and you can never be sure therefore how accurate these 'vox pops' are (which itself is an indictment of another situation we need to address), but if the editor in this case *was* true to the report, how can it possibly not be claimed that such football fans are not aggrandising the trivial at the cost of trivialising the important? And how can they get as irate as they do about child abuse when others of the billionaire's ilk are contributing enormously to their coffers from selling the sexual services of children?

"I'm not for a second suggesting this Denisovich's own money does come from illegal activities, I really don't know. But I do care that the supporters of this football club *don't* care. Do we seriously, as a culture, believe that the fate of our local soccer team – or even of our *national* side – is worth the cost of this much misery? If so, then, Rafa – to quote you once again – we are doomed, my friend. And how can we then serve on juries? Or imprison pimps or paedophiles? Or arms-dealers or slave-traders?

"There's today one heck of a lot wrong with sport. Less and less do I buy into the idea that competition is good for us. Maybe, at one stage, when we were trying to outrun ferocious beasts and stuff. But not today, not any longer. Not indeed for some time. Anything, it seems to me, which helped to get us to where we're at today, that is something the worth of which needs careful scrutiny.

"There is no ethic any longer in sport that 'it matters not who wins or loses but how you play the game'. There is only the desire – no, the *need* – to win. To win at any cost. Will we soon be poisoning the food of our competitors? Coating their pillows in bacteria? The professional foul is being transferred across to all life, the need to win at all costs, the perception of life that it is a sporting event where there are winners and there are losers.

"Essentially the ethos – the *ethicless* ethos – of both Enron and John McEnroe is exactly the same: No-one remembers who was in second place, so it's entirely appropriate to use whatever methods are available to you in order to win. Once we start accepting that as a premise, then we have espoused the causes of bondage and barbarianism. It's, I think, significant of our culture that Mr McEnroe has not been censured for his conduct, but – to the contrary – is now a major pundit for several large television companies.

"I really do think the time has come that we should be desiring from our leisure, activities which promote the cause of co-operation, rather than those of competition. It is perhaps worth mentioning that, without the co-operation of one molecule with another, life itself would not be possible. But, as ever, Man seems to have to want to know better than Nature, to 'out-sophisticate' Nature.

"Team sports no longer promote co-operation. Why else would we create a 'man of the match'? ... But, hey, the demise of sport, that's not going to happen. Leastwise, not for a bit. So, why am I bothering even to think about it? ... No ... No, for God's sake. We're talking about creating a new 'climate' for the world. So, alongside economists searching for new systems to control our finances, I think there's a good argument to be made that other experts should be encouraged to find alternative amusements, alternative to today's 'sport' ... alternative ways of taking exercise, ones that encourage love not hate, that extol the virtues not of competition but co-operation. Sure, that's *way* down the line, but I doubt the Wright Brothers would have believed that, within a century of their having mastered flight, Man would land on the moon. Sometimes the domino effect can have consequences that are on the side of good. Meantime, let's (at the very least) get right-sized again about sport. Unless, I guess, you're a Spanish bull, it really is not a matter of life and death."

"Or an English fox," says Rafaél, "or a Scottish grouse or an American deer."

"Or fish throughout the world, Rafa. What the present sport-mania does do, it stops us looking at what really is important. Importance is only ever prioritising. We even allow those more 'important' than we are to precede us physically. Hence the insistence at doors of 'after you'. If we deem the trivial important and vice versa we prioritise *wrongly*. And this you can see not only with the tabloid press (where it's literally staring you in the face) but, more subtly and iniquitously, also with whatever it's called the 'untabloid' press.

"Again we allow institutions to do what we are appalled by in human beings.

"What would we call the mother who got her priorities so wrong she bought herself a designer-label dress instead of food for her children? And yet we make no comment that our Press talks far more about, let's say, about a football player's broken foot than violations of human rights in Guantanemo Bay. We allow that wrong-prioritisation (which is, in fact, more accurately deliberately engineered wrongly *directed* polarisation) on the basis of free speech. And, of course, on that basis we must allow it. That does not mean, however, we need to condone or applaud it.

"There are now hours of television time devoted to so-called 'celebrity news'. And this comes in time the broadcasters have told governments they will use for 'news' and is therefore at the expense of breadth of news or depth of news that is important. We censor also by what we don't have time to say.

"Sure, such 'celebrity' coverage is cheaper, and that's one reason for its prevalence. You've also got these so-called celebrities in line to have their latest amour broadcast to a panting world. (Oh, they may bitch, and most never stop doing so!, about the never-ending intrusion into their lives, but most – including Princess Diana – also bask in it.) It's also a lot easier. You can do most of the reporting over the phone, don't need to fly reluctant reporters to far-flung corners of the globe."

"Can you have corners of a globe?" asks Rafaél.

"Oh, you are still listening then?"

"Is it not today called 'multi-tasking', *amiga mía*? I can listen, you know, as I flirt."

"How well do you listen, though?"

"Probably better than I do without flirting. Please, Polly, go on."

"And sure too, it's what the public wants – or thinks it wants. It's real life 'soap' – vicarious sadnesses, vicarious triumphs. But it – inexorably, Rafa – educates us to misprioritise. It's, of course, incredibly important to the pop singer concerned that his marriage is in trouble. But it is no-one's concern but his and his partner's. And it is not, Rafaél, it just is not something which has any significance in the least beyond that to their own family.

"There was a TV producer here, Julia Smith, now dead."

"Is there no-one in show-business you do not know, my friend?"

"Oh, I didn't know her. I've heard of her, that's all. I hear she was quite demanding. But, hey, I've heard that about a lot of people who just didn't suffer fools gladly. Be that as it may, Julia Smith was dubbed by the tabloid press here 'the Queen of soap'. She was one of the co-creators of a big show they have here, 'EastEnders'."

"I've heard of 'EastEnders'."

"Well, that qualifies you to have landed in England, *amigo mío.* You seem to be writing a soap opera right here of your very own, my friend."

"Please," says Rafaél, meaning 'continue'.

"Julia Smith contended that the success of soaps, as a genre, lay in the fact that they were surrogate families. Safer to worry about than real families. Where the emotional investment is not so intense.

"Well, I think Smith may well have been right. And if she was, then we need to do things very quickly to address that problem. Because that *is* a problem. Think about it. A humungous problem, Rafa. Because such would be a devastating consequence of swapping the important for the trivial. I also think, as a by-the-by, that the consequence of the proximity of news and soap operas leads to a confusion between the boundaries of each. That we start thinking the news is some kind of spontaneous, less disciplined soap. Which is another little problem all of itself. But the need for surrogate families is a bigger one. I think sports teams are also, at some level, surrogate families.

"One of the most painful realities we have to accept about the human condition is that our power, that of each one of us individually, is *incredibly* limited. I suspect that's why politics and big business may have the allure for some people that they do. Probably why film-directing has too, come to think about it.

"Anyone – like you, Rafa – who has had to watch someone die from a terminal illness has been confronted by the hugeness of their powerlessness. (I'm not going to call that 'impotence', because my experience is that men get all jittery around that word and stop listening as a consequence.)"

"Around me, Polly, you may call it impotence."

"Just don't say the word too loudly, right?"

"Mayhap."

"That's not the only area of our powerlessness, by any stretch of the imagination. And let's too put to one side 'acts of God', as they're called. Loads of parents want different careers for their children than their children want for themselves. Many of us want our partners to be more adventurous in bed, or more imaginative in the kitchen, more attentive or appreciative, to drink less or eat better ... whatever. Usually we can want till the cows go out again having gotten home the night before, and they're not going to change. Oh, maybe for a day or two – or a week or two – after a fight. But usually that change is very short-lived, and pretty superficial. We can want the bank-teller to smile more or the cop who stopped us for speeding to give us a break or the repairman to turn up at the time he said he would. And we can want for all we're worth but we can't *make* any of that happen.

"And that is – for all us normal folks without haloes round our heads – very painful. *Very*, Rafa, painful.

"It's also painful (let's make no mistake about that) if a soap character chooses to elope with the bad guy rather than stay with the guy with the really cute dimples who dotes on her, but who's satisfied with just running the local grocery store. But that pain, that's not an *overwhelming* pain. And by concentrating on that pain, we can put to the back of our brain the agony we're in because our niece is shooting up or because our only son has had to move to Abu Dhabi to find work or our granddaughter hates the school she's at. And, of course, because such problems are pushed to the back of the brain, they don't get addressed.

"We mistake powerlessness for an absence of power. We cannot dictate the outcome of any situation, but we can (and do) influence most – for good or bad. Quantum physics has opened up a whole shelf of cans of beans around what is called 'consciousness', and how such impacts on the world. We touched on this a whiles back. I was somewhat disparaging. 'We really have to do more for this world,' I said, something like that, 'than think beautiful thoughts.' Well, however harshly expressed, I think that's true. However, it's also probably true to say that, unless we start thinking beautiful thoughts about this world, we will not change it. I understand that there is a growing body of scientific evidence which suggests that, just as the Sahara desert is finally an agglomeration of individual grains of sand, the thoughts of each of us impact on a mass, and thus finally dictate the form of that mass. It seems to me that, even if this theory is later proven to be mistaken, unlike so much of what we hear, we have little to lose by assuming it to be correct. Correction: we have *nothing* to lose. And possibly, literally, the world to gain."

"*Claro*," Rafa agrees.

"Now, undoubtedly it is true that globalisation has built machinery which does not tackle problems but blocks complaint about them. Government and industry have both built machines with entirely that intention in mind. Anyone who has had dealings with the British Home Office, or with a telephone company – or virtually any other commercial venture – will have had that experience. Those on the other end of a phone supposedly 'dealing with' complaints are not there to redress a wrong or repair a fault, they are there to block the complaint and the complainant from getting any further. These 'customer liaison officers' (or whatever other similar grandiloquent, meaningless title) are reading from a script, denying you access to those who might be responsible for that wrong or who might be expected to authorise actions that could cost the company money. A friend of mine, who lived in Spain, has horror stories of dealing with the phone company there, Telefónica. It got so bad, he eventually moved countries."

"Only to find in the country he moved to, things were just as bad."

"Pretty much. 'Cept Telefónica was still worse."

"I have another problem with all of that," says Rafaél. "And that is that such people bludgeon you to the point where you have to be discourteous. You have to put the phone down on a telesales person, or you end up shouting at the check-out girl – because there is no-one else to shout at! Never on Internet sites does there seem to be the possibility to complain. Even on those rare occasions when you can complain, you can do so only by filling in their questionnaire.

"Read the questions carefully. More often than not, they include a premise which is completely false. Often they are phrased in the equivalent of that old chestnut: 'Answer this question "yes" or "no": "Have you stopped beating your wife?"' This is not registering a complaint. This is, in fact, providing datum to the company to whom you are protesting which they will use as evidence of the *worth* of their product!

"Should you decline to fill in this questionnaire (because it so clearly contains a premise which to any right-thinking person has to be unacceptable), the computer will register one as a 'don't know'. No protest would be registered, nor any disaffection. Companies are today not in the least interested in improving services. They're interested only in convincing us that their services have been improved. They change the wrapping-paper, but not what lies within it. 'Lies': *le mot juste*.

"We should, all of us, decline to fill in these questionnaires. All of the time. Is a way companies fabricate approval for their often inadequate product. They are able thereby to claim an acceptability for such product. Mark Twain claimed there were lies, damned lies and statistics. Well, this synthetic truth is in fact lower yet into the nefarious slime than statistics.

"They are designed, at best, these questionnaires, to gull us into believing we are of our importance to the companies sponsoring them and that such companies have only the best of intentions in regard to us. But in terms of future conduct they mean ... precisely nothing. They are as significant as one's computer wishing one a 'good morning'.

"If by any miracle you do find a way through all this morass and manage to register a complaint, what do those companies do? They simply ignore it. Complaining is today a complete waste of effort. This all impacts on the quality of our life, *amiga mía*.

"Just as worrying, the attitude of the questionnaire has entered our psychology – our 'mind-set', as today's vocabulary would have it. We say of something which pleases us that it 'ticks all the boxes'. It scares me that we are starting to think of life as multi-choice questionnaires, where we only have to tick the relevant box, and where the questions themselves are defined by others than ourselves – indeed, apparently *anyone* other, rather than ourselves."

"It's all part, as you say, Rafa, of the Untruth. It's part too of creating a hostile world. A world where you are the lone bee fighting the Rottweiller of life. And is yet something else which would be addressed by an economic system based on love not hatred. Someone you love you don't treat in this way; you don't even treat in this way someone whose dignity you respect. And, of course we do, we end up yelling at those tele-operatives, whatever they're called. They don't have a problem with that. I'm prepared to bet they're told to expect it. They don't mind because at that point you cede them the moral high-ground. And that 'legitimises' the scorn their company has for you. 'We don't need to listen to her complaint,' that company can now say, 'she's an hysterical old harridan who shouted at us.'

"I accept absolutely that it is the right of these tele-operators to be treated with respect – also, it might be added, by those who employ them. But that respect has to work both ways. Always respect has to work both ways. These tele-operatives use language which, on paper, is 'polite' – sometimes even ultra-polite; they never raise their voices. But the ethos that informs the writing of the script is enormously disrespectful. It's not even passive/aggressive. It's just plain aggressive.

"Bureaucracies are designed to act in the same way. I'm sure part of a bureaucrat's training is to be unpleasant. That way, less people want to avail themselves of anything that might cost the Exchequer money.

"Most school principals – they call them 'head teachers' here – I think do a good job, usually against staggering odds. Most, I'm sure, would take claims of a child being bullied very seriously indeed. But the bureaucracy which underpins that head teacher is much more likely to be programmed to respond to any complaint of such with,

'Nothing we can do about it. No, your grandchild can't change schools. Deal with it.'

"Nevertheless we are not entirely powerless ...

"Let's say for a moment that we live in a world where the bureaucratic, as well as the economic, tail wags the dog. (Got a lot of tails, this dog!) Let's assume, just for a moment, that we have created a world so totally upside-down in its values, that a bullied child does have to stay in a school which allows that child to be bullied, that still doesn't mean we are without power. There is still action that we can take, that parents and grandparents can take. A lot of action. Important action.

"We can, first of all, create an ethos which encourages the bullied child to talk, not simply to suffer his torture in a tortured silence. This already would be an enormous change for more children than we'd care to imagine. Grandma could also, for instance, *talk* to the bullied child, talk to the parents too of the bully. At the very least, grandma could thereby validate the bullied's pain, his sense of grievance, the burning resentment he has against injustice. The bullied's *parents* could, of course, also do that. But all of this takes ... guess what? ... time. And many parents don't have ... guess what? ... time. Because they're already working ten, twelve hours a day in their regular job, or even working two jobs. And then have to spend hours commuting. And then are expected to do other tasks at home. Sometimes on behalf of their employers, sometimes on the government's behalf. Guess what else? They're exhausted, these parents. They've had it. They're just plumb worn out.

"So much simpler, worry about whether Jo in 'EastEnders' should declare himself bankrupt or not or whether Aunt Ellie in 'Dallas' should go to rehab ... or Rafa in 'Coronation Street' should go to jail."

"There's a Rafa in 'Coronation Street'?"

"It was a hypothesis, Rafa."

"Maybe you should suggest to your friend, Judy Smith ..."

"Julia."

"Julia Smith that they include a Rafa in 'Coronation Street'.

Maybe that would help Anglo-Peruvian relations."

"You think there's a problem there?"

"We suggested a way to avoid war in the *Malvinas*. It was ignored."

"'Cos it was never going to happen, Rafa. Get real. Mrs Thatcher and General Galtieri were both gagging for that war. And for very similar reasons: to divert attention from what was happening at home. Political prestidigitation, Rafa, all over again: direct the eye away from where you don't want it to be, from where the actual trick is happening, to where the audience *thinks* it's happening.

"People were killed in the Falklands. A lot of them. I'm not going to make light of it. Like you, never do I want to make light of a situation where lives have been lost. But I'm afraid it was precisely with such cynicism that the two leaders entered that conflict.

"General Galtieri was already on his way out. At the very least he bought himself a little more time in the presidential palace. What, next to that, are the lives of a few thousand peasants? To Mrs Thatcher it gave an entire other term, plus – sadly – an international credibility she'd lacked up to that point. And probably otherwise would never have had.

"Even more sadly, I think that was a large part of the political bequest that Mr Blair inherited from her.

"It's not, Rafa, that the important is not important, it's that we have to be extremely careful that what we consider to be important – that that which we are *told* is important – actually is.

"What is important, if you like, is the import of what we give importance to. And what is not important is that whose main benefit is to enrich others."

"And the last lie?" asks Rafaél. "That the material meaning 'real' is not material meaning 'relevant'?"

"We could discuss that another day," Polly suggests.

"Polly, please."

"Fun's also important, Rafa."

"*Claro,* fun is also important. But the import of this, this I need to hear about."

"It's also a lie," says Polly, "to say that the real is *not* not relevant. Or, rather, it is true that the real is not relevant and that it is. Mostly for all the reasons we have already discussed.

"Finally, all that's relevant to us is the way we're feeling. And the way we're feeling, that's obviously an abstract. So, in that sense, the only material (or relevant) is abstract.

"But it is also true that, for most of us, the material is very relevant to the way we feel. Certainly there are beings who are more enlightened than most of us, and can to a certain extent rise above material considerations. But even Messiahs get crucified. And it's maybe also interesting to note that we call ourselves human '*beings*', not human 'thinkings' or human 'feelings' but human '*beings*'.

"For most of us it's real hard to feel good if we're hungry or very cold – or very hot – or sick or in pain. It's real hard to be present if you don't know how you're going to eat tomorrow, whether your kids will, or if you're going to have a roof over your head.

"If material bullets are fired into us, that's going to impact on how we feel. If the body dies, the abstract (at least in this world) dies with it. The soul, even if it stays here in the memories of others, at that moment (at the very least) stops growing. And that soul is, in fact, not your soul, but your soul as interpreted by another soul. Even Beethoven's soul is not Beethoven's soul. Not to me. To me it is his soul as heard by me. And the way I hear it, that can also vary from day to day.

"Which brings us to another point: that, of course, the abstract is also relevant to the real. And not relevant.

"It's not relevant in that when I fall in love, 'everything,' as they say, 'is all right with the world'. But, in point of fact, the 'world' has remained exactly the same. No fewer people are dying of starvation in the world, there are just as many children in brothels or working in sweat-shops, just as many tigers and gorillas being shot. So the impact on the world of my being in love is, pretty nearly, zilch.

"But the impact on the ozone layer of one cow burping would

also be, pretty nearly, zilch. It is because we have as many cows in the world as we do that the impact is so enormous of their eructations."

"'Eructations', I do not know this word."

"Aha! Revenge for 'eschatology'. It's just a long word, Rafa, for belch. Like 'sternutation' is a long word for sneeze. It's almost onomatoepeic, isn't it? You can hear the burp throttling."

"*Claro*. Is a Spanish word also. I was being stupid."

"The impact, Rafa, could also be enormous if we set up enough *benign* spirals. Sadly, we can't invent a way where the whole world falls in love again every week. But we can create a world where we see part of our responsibility to be to respect everyone's dignity. If that doesn't make everyone feel good about themselves, at least it will stop them feeling bad about themselves. We can see that it is a part of our responsibility actively to make people feel good about themselves. That too is possible.

"What we do about bureaucracies and institutions ... well, for the moment, I have no idea. But if we accept that it's a good idea to treat one another well, and not badly, then good ideas will occur to us about how to change both.

"And this is where the perception of reality can be used on humanity's behalf, and not as a club to beat it. We may think that, because we feel better, the hyacinth smells sweeter or the sun shines brighter. But this is, in fact, only one benign abstract feeding another, thereby creating a benign spiral of abstracts.

"Finally, Rafa, for want of a better expression, the 'grace of God' does not manifest itself in the beauty of a rose, but in our appreciation of the rose as being beautiful. And now," she says, "I'm going to love you and leave you."

"You don't want another drink?"

"I've been a gooseberry for too long. Gooseberries left for too long get so squishy they become gooseberry-fool. I'm working, I think I said, till the end of the week. I'll call you Sunday."

"*Hasta la vista*," says Rafaél.

Polly gathers her things together. "Enjoy," she says.

Chapter 9

He's gone now. She's numb. She'd expected no different. She's not angry. But numb ... yes, she's numb.

He hadn't been angry either. Nor recriminatory. These things happened, he understood that. He understood less that she wouldn't consider termination, but that he understood less should not be taken to mean that he didn't understand at all. And to show how much he understood, Rodolfo, he held her. And the holding was to show her that: to show her he understood. And his kissing her too, that was also to show her he understood. And that his feelings for her had not changed, and that he would continue to care for her and to protect her. And her child. Which was, she had noted, her child not theirs.

And the kissing, to begin with, that had been mixed with the holding – of the crown of her head, of her forehead, above her ears. And, betrayed as she felt, she also felt relieved and safer than she'd feared; and she'd nestled into his holding like a puddle seeping into all the cracks and indentations which contain it. Nestled thus, Giselle had started to stroke his thigh. Slowly, holding ceded to caressing and the kisses of comfort puckered into those of desire.

There had been desire also in her. But her desire, she now realises, had been confirmation of his desire. And it wasn't therefore that she had seduced him, but she had seduced him into seducing her. And the resultant sex had been many things, but making love had not been one of them.

They had made anger: individually when he would less thrust into her than bayonet her, or when she had moved, apparently in further surrender, actually to twist him within her; or together when, in the guise of uncontrollable passion, they had bitten into each other merely to hurt. Or scratched.

They had made reassurance: where both had sought via their bodies to communicate a commitment the articulation of which their ears would not hear.

They had made solace: in which both had gently pressed against each other in recognition of the other's pain, his trauma, her terror, and both had sought with their skin to rub away that pain – like chalk from a blackboard.

They had made fondness: tender kisses of 'let's-always-be-there-one-for-the-other', palms spread twiddling lobes and stroking cheeks, fingertips pollinating the other's specialness, raising the plinth of the other's splendour.

They had made sex: glorying in the sights and smells, the touch and feel of the other's arousal, glorying in both the delicacy and firmness of the other's body, enjoying being enjoyed, their own sensuousness engorged by the sensuousness of the other, by all the contrasts of liquid and solid, smooth and rough, sweet and bitter, tender and abrasive, lazy and frantic ... intimate and so very distant.

And the sex they had made had been some of the most glorious they had ever made. But it had been made not out of love.

Upstairs, prospective tenants are clearly being shown around the vacant flat. Their hollow footsteps grind on her, assault her almost, assault the quiet of her space.

Now she sits up, naked, in the bed, its other side still indented with his tousled shape. She thinks now maybe she is numb because she is emotioned out. And knows, even as the thought comes, that she's trying to kid herself. Even as they were lying in languid post-coital tangle, she knows that far from being emotioned out, her emotions were merely djinnis freshly released from their bottles, testing their sinews, sampling their various capabilities.

He'd told her then he couldn't marry her. He'd told her then he loved her, would – he had no doubt – love her child, but that he also loved his present wife, their children. He would do whatever he could. He was sorry, but there it was. He didn't want her clinging to any false hope. And she had become numb at that moment.

She remembers, numbly, reassuring him, numbly, that of course he could still visit her, that of course they could – and she hoped would – remain lovers, that she had never expected any commitment from him beyond that he had always made. This commitment, the one he'd just made, that was essentially only a reinforcement of that he'd made when the affair first started, all those years ago in Orphalese. And she remembers him leaning on his right arm, as he tucked a curl behind her ear and tried to fill his face with love and gratitude, gravity and solicitousness, selflessness and relief – and managed only to find an expression that was goofy.

She remembers, numbly, his kissing her, wearing that goofy expression, remembers him trampolining from the bed, picking out his expensive clothes from the jumble of *déshabillage* littered on the Moroccan hearth-rugs blotching the parquet floor, remembers him seeking jollity in his sallied words to her, remembers him suggesting the following Thursday they go out on the town together, celebrate this "joyous news". She remembers him telling her that he's glad she's a nurse, that he's no need therefore to tell her how important it is that she take care of herself.

For him too, she remembers him saying, it's very important she take care of herself. She does know, doesn't she, how very special she is to him? And, even numb, she remembers wincing. As in the dentist's, less from the pain of the drill than from its whine. She remembers him saying his list the next day was crazy, but that he'd try to find a gap when he could phone her. And she remembers his last kiss, and the bedroom door closing, and the pause before the front door closed.

She's numb. But in her numbness she knows there will be a time – perhaps even shortly a time – when she will be numb no more. And she has no idea whether that time will be a blessing or a curse.

Chapter 10

"I told you, right," says Polly, "I'm an assistant film director?"

"You keep insisting such is not glamorous."

"Trust me, Rafa, it's really not. The industry's going through one of its lean times," she continues. "And my own time, that's even leaner than the industry's. I thought it might be an idea – I hope you don't mind – I thought it might be an idea to, as the Brits would say, 'show the "boat race" around' a bit. 'Boat race', that's Cockney rhyming slang for 'face'."

The weather is prematurely grey. Still only September, the sky has already cocooned itself within a December poncho. There is a winter nip to accompany the winter light and only those unaware that the besetting quality of English climate is its vagary are not clothed against it. They have stepped over the homeless and their dogs begging outside the London Palladium, and have picked a jostled way past the Carnaby Street still trying to recapture a lustre lost with the 60s. They are walking along Great Marlborough Street.

"Soho! It used to be, Soho, the centre of the British film industry. Anyone looking for a film crew would often simply drop into a couple of the pubs here and, an hour or so later, would emerge 'job done'. It's not that simple these days, not as centralised. But it's still sometimes useful, 'put,' as I said, 'the old boat race about a bit', 'jog the old memory'. This way," she indicates a side-street choked with the barrows of a street-market: Berwick Street.

The barrows are covered in a rough plastic of blue-and-white stripes or green-and-white stripes. Mostly they are selling fruit. The brightness of whose colour only accentuates the surrounding grey, and the sweetness of whose smell blends uncomfortably with those drifting from exhaust pipes or extractor fans.

"I won't be drinking, by the way. Not liquor, I mean. It used to be, hooch, the oil that lubricated the cogs of the movie industry. Now that industry has become (publicly) almost dry. And, like any good convert, it now frowns on that which it used to … let's say 'revere'. It's still perfectly okay, by the way, to ram metric tonnes of white powder up your nose – that apparently is not the same thing."

"This," says Rafaél, "could give lust a bad name."

They are passing between two clubs advertising live sex shows. To the left of one is a pornography shop and to the right of the other is one selling 'marital aids'.

"Doesn't lust already have a bad name?" asks Polly. "My Church told me even to *think* of sex was sinful."

"Is a good place, no, to talk about lust? As a deadly sin?"

"Also, Rafa, to talk about the mortal lie that accompanies it: that, quotes, 'morality' is morality."

"Four a pound!" yells one of the costermongers, practically thrusting four oranges into their faces. "Four a pound!" A surprisingly young meter maid wanders past. Almost to his surprise, the costermonger finds himself aiming a mild flirt in her direction. Then he catches Polly noticing this, and returns her a half-grin of half-apology. "Luvverly oranges," he yells again. "Four for a pound. Four, luv? There you go. That'll be a pound to you, my darlin' …"

Polly asks, "You know the biggest landlord hereabouts?"

"The Queen?"

"I think the Queen – you're right – I think she's the biggest landlord in London …"

"Land*lady*, no?"

"Landlady, right. Though that makes her sound a bit like a publican. Either her or the Duke of Westminster. But, hereabouts, I mean. Locally, in Soho, the biggest landlord of property rented out to sex shops and live sex shows and the like?"

"If not then the Queen …?"

"The Church of England, my friend."

"Truly?"

"Truly. Leastways, so I've been told. And if not the biggest, then one of the biggest. If that *is* true and (as I say) I don't *know* that it is, then, my friend, if there are lies, damned lies and statistics, then there is also hypocrisy, damned hypocrisy and the Church."

"This is truly vice, *amiga mía*."

"You don't think that level of hypocrisy is a sin? You don't think that endangers mankind? It's not akin to those Western politicians censuring sex tourism – in Thailand, say – without condemning the (Western) profiteering which created that sex tourism?"

"This, I mean," says Rafaél, indicating the garish emporia around him. "This is truly vice. But is only vice. It cheapens something priceless, debases something noble. That is viceful. But is only viceful, is not sinful. Certainly they are sins, when people are forced into this way of life, those things doing the forcing: poverty, addiction, kidnapping. Those are nearly always sinful. Is also sinful that we seek to condemn the whores and not the pimps – or the landlords of the pimps. If an economic system, Polly, reduces people to a choice of prostitution or abject poverty, that economic system, my dear friend, is a pimp.

"If what you say about the Church of England is true, *amiga mía*, that too is certainly a sin. How is the Church of England not living off immoral earnings? She would do well, at least, to acknowledge this double-standard within herself.

"The Church – the *world's* churches, the world's *religions* – already commit a sin (they endanger humanity) when they consider they are morally superior to Man. That institutionally they lack the flaws that each of us has personally.

"Don't misunderstand me: is entirely acceptable for any philosophy or theosophy to set unattainable goals. Provided it recognises that such goals *are* that: unattainable. Such is a recognition – a very significant recognition – that what is important is the journey and not the destination.

"No, let me rephrase that ... Is acceptable with two provisos: Firstly that, in building that philosophy, one *accepts* that one will not be able to live by its aspirations, not, at least, fully; and, secondly, that neither will anyone else. If the goals are unattainable, the adherents to that belief must (by definition) fall short of them. This 'falling short' does not make *sinners* of those adherents, nor does it make renegades of them. Indeed to the contrary. Dint of their seeking an admirable goal they are striving towards goodness, seeking to subjugate their lower 'I' to their higher. And that is already a worthy aim. A very worthy aim, my friend. Instead of chastising the strivers after good for failing to attain unattainable goals, we should be saluting the fact that they are striving towards goodness. Saluting such adherents and encouraging them. The Church should be. We should all be."

"Vickis, thirty bob a pound," cries another stall-holder, a woman whose aging face is also rivuletted with those Stilton slithers of puce-red which testify to a life lived in the outdoors of inhospitable climes. "Oh so terribly sorry," she affects a genteel accent. "Victoria plums, one pound fifty per demi-kilo."

"I remember reading somewhere: 'Sex is God's thank you for putting up with life.' I can't think where," Rafaél continues. "But I thought it was rather nice. I think, though, is more than that. I think sex is touched with the divine. Not just when is concerned with procreation. And not just lightly touched with it either.

"And that is the trouble with most of this. Is blasphemous because it strips the body, not of its clothes, but of its divinity. By the way, I stand in no place of judgement when I say that. Just as all of us with mahogany tables have compromised our rights to condemn deforestation, just as the smoker cedes his right to tut at the over-eater, so I ... Well, let us say, after Inma died, I have (on the odd occasion) been part of the client base on which this industry depends. And that was an act of blasphemy, I do not seek to dispute that, a vice. But not, I think, a sin.

"If there is any 'sin' involved in sexual lust, I think the 'sin' – the element which is a threat to mankind – is in designating something sinful which not only isn't but which is positively beneficial. That, anyway, is *one* of the sins around sex."

"I'd be willing to bet," says Polly, "that, particularly in long-term relationships, a lack of lust causes just as much unhappiness, if not downright misery, as an excess of it; that often mankind is endangered far more by such lack of lust than by its abundance."

"Is not unreasonable as a premise. Unproveable but certainly not unreasonable," Rafaél returns.

"Like most of my gender, as a young man I sowed a few wild oats. Sometimes, yes, I even paid for the privilege. Sex was not as available in my youth as it is today. (And that is a better thing about today.) Was it wrong that I paid for sex? Probably. Certainly I still feel guilty about it. But I feel guilty a lot less about the sex than that I was further lining already tainted pockets.

"The day after sowing those oats – this is the point – whether that sowing was courtesy of professionals or inamoratas, I was a much nicer person to be around than I had been the day before. I repeat, Polly, the obvious: a world full of happy people is an infinitely nicer place to be than one populated by unhappy people. So already lust, even at that primitive level, is globally of benefit. This is only a variation, my friend, on the theme you have already talked about. I think I told you, my son, he is a doctor ..."

"A surgeon, I thought you said."

"A surgeon, yes." Rafa looks abashed. This Polly will discover is his way of disguising his pride. "He tells me that, among the chaste, prostate and gynaecological problems are significantly more prevalent than amongst the sexually active. Bonobos, as another example, are the most highly sexed of all the primates. They are also the least aggressive."

"You didn't, I notice, call them 'Boniobos'!"

"Why should I? Bonobos, my friend, *enhance* the quality of the planet. Boniobos, they are a different matter!" They share a gentle laugh.

Rafaél continues, "It has not, we must concede, chastity, enjoyed a past which would seem to champion its triumph. And religion's attitude towards it – particularly in the West – has exemplified so much of its teaching: 'Do as I say, not as I do'.

"Popes have historically had wives or mistresses or both.

Chaucer's work and Boccaccio's are littered with lusty friars and libidinous abbots. Even Luther, released from his monastic vows, was quick to wed. In the last decade senior Catholic clergy have been discovered to have fathered children. And then, of course, ... well, then there was the scandal of ecclesiastic paedophilia ... well, this too we have said before ... the even greater scandal of the utterly disgraceful – the utterly *sinful* – way in which the Vatican sought to discredit the victims ... yes, yes, that too said before. Sorry.

"As for the Pope's recent apology ... Well, the phrase 'far too little far too late' comes to mind. But, in fairness too, it *was* an apology. And that certainly is a step in the right direction. I'd like to believe that apology was inspired by the conscience of the Vatican – I was, after all, for many years a scion of its Church – but my cynical head tells me, I'm afraid, was far more likely to have emanated from some PR agency responding to the almost universal public reprobation. Another instance, perhaps, of 'them' realising our power more than 'we' realise it.

"You have told me, Polly – in your most able way – of the working practises of the British House of Commons. They are ... well, let us say 'whimsical' ... a trifle eccentric, mayhap. And mayhap too they were designed to be that way to facilitate the right honourable members in their extra-marital dalliances."

"Well, if that wasn't their intention," Polly chimes in, "it's most certainly historically been their result. The House of Commons has been (forgive the pun!) a hotbed of adultery. And yet, although perhaps less so today than heretofore, the Establishment continues to condemn in public that which not only does it *condone* for itself, but encourages. That kind of hypocrisy is also certainly a sin, I think. In your sense. That certainly endangers mankind. Because it further perpetrates a world of them-and-us."

"I have – I have also said this before – an enormous respect for Mohandas Gandhi. I will say it many times again. I also have an enormous respect for the Dalai Lama. Also which I will say again. But I do take issue with their espousal (and in Gandhi's case advocacy) of chastity.

"Unlike that of other clerics, I don't – not for a fraction of a second – *doubt* their celibacy. I'm not trying to imply they cannot practise what they preach. Nor (equally not for a second) do I seek to diminish their insight or their compassion. But I am not convinced that the latter is the consequence of the former. Almost to the contrary. Is also unproveable, of course, but my suspicion is that the latter may even be *despite* the former."

They turn into an alley which, Polly knows but Rafaél doesn't, leads to Wardour Street.

"Monogamy likewise," Rafaél continues, "has not historically attracted too many adherents. Even Zeus was not averse to a dalliance or two away from Juno. In fact, I've never been entirely convinced that monogamy wasn't an institution developed by man the gender in order further to subjugate women. I think is interesting to note that when there was felt to be a need to discredit female leaders (particularly in Europe), their promiscuity was cited as evidence of their moral inadequacy: one has only to think of the censure aimed at Cleopatra or Marie-Antoinette in France or Princess Charlotte in England or, in Spain, Maria Luisa and Isabella II. As for the nonsense about the Tsarina Catherine and her horse ... That the gossip was salacious and completely without foundation is less important than that it was thought enough to discredit her.

"It has several central flaws, monogamy. Not least, that death inevitably leaves half of the relationship lonely. Is also not as innate as we are told to believe it is. Sir David Attenborough insists that most of the so-called monogamous birds are so mostly because pragmatism dictates that they be so. In laboratory conditions, where their basic needs are supplied, the eye of both goose and gander is wont to wander.

"Does man, in his espousal of monogamy, already set up a conflict within himself?

"For as long as we were married, I *was* sexually faithful to Inma. Mostly I wanted to be. Mostly, frankly, because it would have hurt me too much to have hurt her. In another incarnation, with a different set of sexual standards – in my incarnation, for example, as a Chinese emperor, even with another incarnation of Inma alongside me – I suspect all Inma was was the leading concubine in a harem (as with all Chinese emperors) of several thousand. I use that as an example, my friend. I amn't saying I believe in such reincarnation." Polly's look seeks to remind him she's not *that* stupid.

Feeling now stupid himself, Rafaél continues, "In *this* incarnation, however, I swore to myself on our wedding day that I would remain faithful to her. I turned around at the end of the ceremony to walk down the aisle with my new bride and my first thought? What great breasts her bridesmaid had! For years I burned with shame for that – literally, burned up in a blush –, considered that thought sinful. Only much later did I see that thought for what it truly was: and that is, masculine!

"Lust, I can't help feeling, is less the problem than the problems there are surrounding man's ambivalence to monogamy. And the confusion we men get into over it."

"I think women also get confused over it, Rafa. I know this woman does."

They are now walking along Old Compton Street: the mix is curious of sex shops oozing a dusty tastelessness and small delicatessens and wine-shops catering to a gourmet taste. They pass by doorways the dark-blue paint on whose panels is chipped by the kicks of a thousand raunchy shoes. To the side of the door is a sort of inebriated mezuzah of door bells whose names are illuminated by a weak orange glow: 'Lola. Ring twice and Come Up.'

"One of the aspects of the world in which latterly there has been substantial improvement is in frankness about sex. We *need* to be more frank, frankly – That was a joke, Polly!" Polly over-smiles to confirm she understood as much. "I think too there has been a shift in the attitudes of both genders in its regard. But I still think (talking in enormous generalisations) that most women are monogamous – even if serially; and most men (if only in fantasy) are polygamous.

Mayhap that's part of our DNA footprint. It has now been discovered that men and women have cerebral grey and white matter in different proportions. You have read 'Men Are From Mars ...'?"

"Dipped into it."

"Is thought likely soon will be discovered the physiological distinctions to accompany the emotional ones."

"As far as they know."

"As far, Polly, as they know. Is it also part of the same phenomenon why in so many species the male is the more flamboyant? Because *his* survival finally is a lot less important to that species than that of the considerably better camouflaged female? And has that evolutionary imperative followed us into today? The Dr Strangelove principle was not, I think, an invention of the twentieth century.

"All of which, Polly, would be a deal less of a problem were it not that men are considerably more insistent than women that women are indeed monogamous.

"Already thereby man, the gender, has created conflict for himself. He wants, quotes, 'his' woman to remain monogamous, and all other women in the world (with the exception of his chaste mother and virginal daughters!) to wallow in promiscuity. How is that not already making for an unhappier world? Sadly too, I think both sides of man's inner battle are selfish, indicative of his fundamental insecurity. The real conflict, I suspect, lies between the pull he has in two contrary directions: his desire of other women and his desire not to be cuckolded. Both, you note, '*his* desires'.

"Which itself begs another question: how much of the sin of lust is really the sin of the possessive pronoun? That we think of our partners as our possessions? And that their bodies symbolise the whole of them? We even, in the act of love, talk about 'possessing' our lovers.

"Further to add to the misery of all of which, man then creates another conflict for himself: Those prepared to sleep with him have fallen off the pedestal he's erected for 'his' women. Thus he can only have polygamous sex with someone whom he now sees (at some level) as seriously flawed.

"That then gets further compounded. Because at some other level man *does* believe in monogamy, does believe (that is) that he should also be monogamous, cannot cope with the duplicity of different mores for goose and gander. And quite often he does love the woman he is now being unfaithful to. So his dalliance causes him to feel guilty. Guilt is pain. So, this woman he doesn't respect is also now causing him pain. How can he possibly like her? But she's also affording him great pleasure. Result: confusion and misery. ... Oh, I know, this is all over-simplified to the point where it becomes almost ridiculous, but I trust you follow my meaning.

"Man's contempt for the prostitute is often, I suspect, actually contempt for himself *manifested* in his contempt for the prostitute. In his youth as a junior officer in Paris, Napoleon came across an emaciated prostitute. He delivered her a severe polemic on the error of her ways ... right before bedding her. In 'Hunchback of Notre Dame', the archdeacon Frollo subjects Esmeralda to torture because he cannot control his desire of her. She is punished for his weakness. How true are all these examples of a double-standard operating worldwide?

"Napoleon Bonioparte, would that be, Rafa?"

"Oh yes, Polly, most amusing. Whores used to be sent to prison. They still are in some countries. By men who were not infrequently their clients. And who claimed (and claim!) to be 'appalled' by the 'sexual lassitude' of these women. Those prostitutes in England were sent to jails where the turnkeys were legally permitted to charge, I think, a shilling for their sexual services – whether or not the women agreed! (Such shilling going in its entirety to the turnkey.) No, *amiga mía,* is not only the churches (and I) capable of gross hypocrisy.

"I hate the causes for prostitution – now principally, as I say, poverty, drugs, violence or the threat of violence. ..."

"Or globalisation," Polly adds.

"Or, as you say, Polly, globalisation – which is, when you think about it, also poverty, drugs, violence and the threat of violence. I *really* hate them. But I accept that, even in Utopia, there is going to be some form – and forms – of it."

"You're singing to the choir on that one. I remember reading that one of the old-time Hollywood moguls – I can't remember which one – he kept an hour free every afternoon (from five, I think, to six) in order to avail himself of his casting-couch privileges."

"Of itself, only another form of prostitution."

"That's what I'm saying. Even in Utopia, is what I'm saying, there will still be those Norma Jeans desperate enough to become Marilyn Monroes that they are prepared to sleep their way up the ladder."

"I suspect the reason more countries do not have legal and licensed brothels is that government prefers to ignore the unpleasant. So it tries to hide it. It know it's there, right enough, but just so long as it's not seen to condone it, it can 'tut' till its heart's content. And so, my friend, can we. Is another example of government (and us!) hoping that, if it ignores a problem for long enough, that problem will simply evaporate. Is not called the 'oldest profession' for nothing. How long before we all recognise this is not a situation which is just going to go away? Problems *never* disappear by ignoring them. All that happens to ignored problems is that they grow bigger and become more entrenched.

"Isn't it one of the key jobs of government to keep its citizens safe?"

"Alongside, you mean, protecting the weak against the strong?"

"Alongside that, yes, Polly. Given the fact that prostitution *is* a fact, aren't those citizens better protected if is restricted to such licensed premises? Doesn't that make it considerably harder for thugs to kidnap teenage girls and smuggle them to foreign climes? Wouldn't that make it considerably more difficult for child pimps to ply their wicked trade? Isn't the health of both whore and client better protected? Isn't society as a whole?"

"Still singing to the choir there, Rafa."

The smell of freshly ground coffee hurtles down the street and peps the street's pedestrians with a whispy vibrancy. Rafaél wonders whether he might again (as he had on Westminster Bridge) be *imagining* the smell. But, no, they are now passing the Algerian Coffee Shop, an array of exotic coffees winking through its window, a smell percolating through its doors as seductive as any of history's scarlet ladies.

"Which man in history, Polly, has been monogamous from choice? Which man in history who has been able to get away with it, which man with any power (not only popes) has not had mistresses as well as wives? Harems, by any other name?

"Oh, there have been instances, certainly there have of royal monogamy (George III of Britain, for instance, or Prince Albert), but they are remarkably few and far between. The Church of England was *founded* on a king's 'lust' for adultery. Women in the French court, or of Jane Austen's epoch (particularly those of what they would have called 'status') may very well have been virgins at the altar, but used marriage often largely as a license for subsequent promiscuity. In Victoria's piano-leg-encased days it wasn't that proportionately there were more prostitutes plying their trade in London than there are now, was in *actual* numbers. At a time when London's population was a third of what it is today. Mayhap a quarter. Mayhap even less."

"Don't look at me," says Polly. "I have no idea."

"And you are my guide?"

"Fire me, why don't you?"

"Is not important. I think the point is clear."

They turn into Dean Street. As befits a thoroughfare apparently named after either a senior cleric or academic, there is a sobriety to Dean Street lacking in Old Compton Street. Oh, it's had a drink or two, Dean Street, no question about that. Its cheeks are florid, its tie is loosened. But it's not slurring its words, its arm flopping over our shoulder, insisting we're its best friend ever.

"There's also John Dean's account," says Polly. "Mr Dean was the White House legal counsel during Mr Nixon's presidency."

"This, I think, I knew. Is also, no?, who this street is named after."

"Oh, very good, Rafa! Plenty of anxious faces in the West Wing when the self-proclaimed 'happy hooker', Xaviera Hollander, was about to publish."

"In any administration, my friend, since the beginning of time. I find it quite extraordinary that those same Republicans keel-hauling President Clinton for his fling with Ms Lewinsky should have kept so quiet about the long-standing affair the first President Bush was allowed to enjoy (if Kitty Kelley is to be believed) with Jennifer Fitzgerald – and with almost total impunity. This isn't politics, this is simply duplicity.

"And, no, of course, President Clinton should not have lied. And I think presidents should be keel-hauled when they do lie. When*ever* they lie. (With most presidents today we should then see a weekly keel-hauling, likewise with the vast majority of today's prime ministers. Doesn't that tell us something about the world we live in?) But the liaison with Ms Lewinsky was not the only lie President Clinton told when he was in office. And evading the question, as his predecessor had done, is in fact also lying – merely lying by omission.

"Now, having said all that, I do believe, Polly, that anybody's sex life is their *private* life. I don't care for the tittle-tattle of history any more than I care for it in the newspaper today.

"Who is the sexual partner of anyone else, what activities they get up to together, are both areas which (provided they are consensual and the parties are adult) are exclusively the business *of* those partners. I suspect that is a failing suffered by most of us, particularly in puberty, that we like to speculate on such matters. But when we do we should recognise that we are obeying the hankerings of our lower 'I'. And it ill becomes a press (particularly one which claims for itself the role of moral bastion) to encourage and titillate that lower part. The sex lives of our elected representatives, or our *un*elected ones (the episcopacy, for example, the Royal family or our industrialists), or even those foisted on us as demi-gods, the movie- and the pop stars ..."

"And the chefs," Polly regrets.

"And the chefs, Polly. The sex lives of all of them are, as I say, their private lives. They have nothing to do with any one of us. And is an abuse of press freedom when they intrude there. With one proviso – I always seem to have provisos – but this one ... well, is nearly the same as the previous ones. This proviso is that such person allows others the privacy of *their* sex lives. And I mention Ms Fitzgerald only in that context.

"When I say that we do not have the right to open the bedroom door, that means *none* of us has that right. Not the individual Peeping Tom or the press or the state or the church. But we do have the right – we indeed have the obligation – to expose hypocrisy and cant. To expose those who enjoin us to do as they say, not as they do.

"Neither press nor ginger group, for example, has the right to 'out' a gay bishop. Unless that bishop is preaching against what he claims to be the 'evils' or the 'sin' of homosexuality."

"You know I'm one, right?"

"I know you are ...?"

"Homosexual."

"I *didn't* know. I suspected you might be, to tell you the truth. You said you'd had a Jewish girlfriend. I wasn't sure what you meant. I didn't *know*."

"I'm not too closet about it."

"Thank God, *amiga mía*, these days there is so much less reason to be."

"I think you might see that in a different light if you were gay yourself."

"I accept that totally," Rafaél nods. "Excuse me."

"No apology necessary, Rafa."

"I talk of driving like a pedestrian and yet ..."

"No apology, Rafa, necessary," she elongates her words. "Please," she further encourages him. "Go on."

"Is not the real sin of lust, Polly – as I said before –, less that of lust itself and more of designating lust a sin? Lust, after all, is not sexual gluttony but sexual hunger. And many things which are blamed on lust have nothing to do with lust at all.

"Pre-marital sex, thank God, is ceasing to be considered even an issue, let alone a 'sin'. Adolescent sex, though, *is* an issue. 'Just say "no"' is as inane a slogan used in connection with adolescent sex as it is with drugs. Sex amongst the young is not an issue of itself – such yearnings exist in us all. But succumbing prematurely to such yearnings is less the issue than the issues which caused such sexual precocity – often other issues entirely. A desperation for love often transfers into a lack of discrimination in sex. A girl, starved of love by her parents, is likely to become promiscuous.

"And how often do we as parents act as the emperor Augustus? His daughter, Julia, was found to be dallying with rather more patrician Romans than was deemed princessly appropriate. She was so obviously *so* desperate for love. Probably her father's. Was the emperor overcome by remorse about his negligence? No. He had done nothing to recriminate himself for. Julia had simply been extremely naughty. Nothing to do with him. Naughty children have to be punished. And so ... he punished her: banished her, in fact. And to some god-forsaken rock. Because she had embarrassed him. Because *she* had embarrassed *him*. Yet another example of the magnificence we continue to call Roman 'civilisation'.

"Sexual partners can be (and often are) chosen by the young (and some not so young) for a whole host of misguided reasons: to anger parents or to substitute for parents ... even to please parents. And parents have *enormous* issues around their children's sex lives, also for a host of reasons – few of them having to do with what's best for the actual child. About the only thing all of which have in common is that lust has got nothing to do with any of them.

"So-called morality, of course, weaves its web *through* those reasons, and those manifestations, that much is clear. (And I suspect, Polly, you will have things also to say on this.) Morality weaves its web through all aspects of our lives. But that web has nothing to do with the sex *per se*; it has to do with issues not being addressed which need to be addressed. *Urgently* need to be addressed. We're talking about human misery. And we choose to misidentify the enemy.

"Sexually transmitted diseases or infections likewise have little to do with lust. Is a basic lack in fundamental instruction – an instruction as basic as if you decide to go deep-sea diving, don't forget your scuba gear.

"As Man evolves, of course he must shed his bestial ancestry. But if there is a choice between shedding aggression (also a bestial legacy) and lust, would aggression not be a better place to start? If between lust and possessiveness is not possessiveness a better place to start?

"Make love, Polly, not war."

"Yeah. You said!"

"My detractors would like simply to dismiss all this as so much hippy nonsense. Which it isn't, of course. But that won't stop the accusation being levelled. I am reminded of the global warming 'sceptics', as they were politely called – those who considered global warming either not to exist or, if it did, a phenomenon which had nothing to do with Man's polluting the atmosphere. (How many of these *eminences grises* were, in fact, in receipt of grants or salaries from vested interest?) They were, of course, finally conclusively disproved. At which point they turned their attack from spurious science to wholesale abuse of those who had proved them mistaken. We have to be prepared for this also to happen to us, Polly. The institution of wealth makes not nice people out of the nicest of us."

"Choir here," says Polly. "Still hearing your singing, Rafa."

"Today in the UK, of course, one has an additional problem of teenagers deliberately opting for pregnancy as a sort of ill-defined career choice. They can thereby get subsidised accommodation, are thereby entitled to government grants. And I understand the disgruntlement of tax-payers believing such people are scrounging, and believing these teenage mothers should just be left to fend for themselves. Other than, of course, this scrounging too is a symptom, not the disease; and other than, of course, those who will suffer most in such situations are the children arising from such pregnancies. Indeed many such mothers were themselves such children. And, as such, they already did suffer the most. We are now enmeshed in a generational vicious spiral – a Hamelin – which will be enormously demanding (and painful) first to check and then to unscrew. *Enormously* demanding and painful ... and difficult.

"Is allegoric of the world today. We identify the wrong enemy. We attack the wrong targets. We set ourselves the wrong goals. Certainly, a fair proportion of the teenage pregnancies are not the 'accidents' they're claimed to be. And the consequences of such pregnancies to us as a society are just as dire as those to the individuals themselves. But, again, is not lust the culprit here. Is just so very much easier for those who should know better (like clerics and statesmen) to hide these problems in lust's skirts.

"This situation actually has absolutely nothing to do with either it or, even, sex. Is indicative of a titan social problem. Of course it is. But is, I say again, the symptoms not the malaise itself.

"Which is rarely one malaise, but several.

"Sexual gluttony also has precious little to do with lust. Sexual gluttony – sexual obsession, if you prefer – is also an illness: this one, of addiction. An illness fed, it has to be said (as so many illnesses are fed), by a world which allows the advertising industry to be quite as unscrupulous as it is, and the media to concern themselves with profit at the expense of principles.

"Rape, paedophilia, sexual harassment or impropriety – rarely are these offences lust-driven. They are crimes, not of sex, but of violence, and their dynamo overwhelmingly is less libido than a craving for power and/or control. Often itself propagated by a sense of powerlessness and/or *lack* of control.

"One reason why AIDS will always be so hard to contain amongst the impoverished is because, when all other control is gone, the only power man, the gender, perceives that he has is that over his penis. It starts to represent the sceptre it so resembles. And, at that point, sex is the only nurture woman can supply. Is one of the few pleasures available to either. And to suggest – as I have heard it suggested – that the starving should refrain from sex ... well ... I find, sometimes, is really not easy to love my fellow man."

"Hardest thing in the world, love," says Polly. "Hardest thing in the world. Welcome to the 'Crown and Two Chairmen'." Polly pushes open the door and invites him in.

"I presume all pub names have a history."

"Please don't ask me, Rafa, the history of this one. My guiding is strictly amateur."

"Would you like me also not to drink?" he asks her.

"I don't think things have quite gotten that bad," she returns.

"Would you, in that case, allow me to *buy* the drinks?"

"I don't think," she assures him, "things have quite gotten that bad." And she squeezes his arm, both to confirm that and to indicate that she has taken no offence.

'The Crown and Two Chairmen' is surrounded by expensive bistros, trattorias and sushi bars and one cheap strip club – which dates back to about the time Salome was originally divesting herself of seven veils. It is a robustly English pub, whose staff are thus robustly Antipodean. The cheap wood has all been varnished dark brown, as if such of itself would give it solidity and elegance. A tomb-like table sepulchres its centre; a few lonely stools peer forlornly at it, like resentful sentinels. Sitters take up more space than standers and sitting is thus not encouraged.

Polly gives her order to the barman, and then is scrutinising the throng, looking for a familiar face – preferably belonging to someone who can secure her employment. She likes this pub for its lack of juxeboxed music. But today the rumble of the surrounding chatter is quite as noisy – and as noisome. There is a cutting-room crew whom she knows slightly. Nods are exchanged, a brief smile. But they are clearly embroiled in some kind of work-related discussion. There is a good-looking blonde of forty or so, seated on one of the rare stools, gazing absently at her long purple fingernails. Before even the idea of approaching her can come to Polly's mind she's joined by a man, maybe a bit older, his bald spot appearing almost as if he'd been tonsured. The barman returns with the drinks. Polly pays, and jostles her way back through the crowd to her friend.

She hands him his drink. They "cheers" one another. Polly pecks disgruntledly at her tomato juice, and seeks to talk 'smally'. Any time the door squeaks open, her eyes swivel to it lest it herald the entrance of an acquaintance. Their talk eventually meanders back to their earlier discussion.

"Lust is a biological imperative," says Rafaél. "To designate it a sin is like saying eating is a sin, or bathing. Is not even a vice, is almost invariably a virtue. And both the harbinger and creator of many other virtues. 'Libido', let us remember, in its original Greek means 'life-force'. Even when is not provoked by the desire to create life, is endowed, is indeed overflowing with the life-force, with *'ch'i'*. And with a commitment to *'ch'i'*, and a commitment to life itself and to life being both crucial and pleasurable.

"If there is a sin in lust, is not that sin, as I said before, the sin of designating lust a sin? Or, even worse, of hiding other lusts behind sexual lust? Or, as I also said before, in the skirts of lust? Or vice versa? Do we concentrate so much on sexual lust that we ignore other, and far more dangerous, lusts?

"It would be a foolish person, Polly, who sought definitive answers to these questions. And yet their impact is all around us all the time.

"Physics had to be thousands of years old before it discovered the quark. Psychiatry, by comparison with physics, is a science in its infancy, barely even teething, just over a hundred. I doubt it has yet discovered its own, as it were, atom. At the end of his (brilliant and occasionally understandable) 'Brief History of Time', Professor Hawking suggests that in the extremely near future we will know about the origins of the universe. But he also expresses the view that our understanding of the brain is negligible. I suspect he means its chemistry and neurology, but I think we would be safe to include psychiatry and psychology also in that opinion.

"We do not know, Polly, what we do not know. Was a very wise American who told me that. We *guess* at what impels us, and we are starting to get some very basic knowledge about some of it. But, just as we apparently find it sexier to explore the outer reaches of space than the depths of our own oceans, so too much psychology (and much psychiatry) is also directed outwards not inwards – is a science we still consider will teach us what is wrong with them rather than teaching us what is wrong with us.

"There is a tendency, for example, particularly in psychology (but also, as I say, in far too much psychiatry), to define 'normality'. Normality simply does not exist. 'Normal' is families with 2.3 children or 0.7 dogs or some such. But in seeking to define the normal, that tendency also starts to define the 'abnormal' and the 'subnormal' – conveniently ignoring the fact that all of us are, in fact, abnormal (and probably, in our different ways, all subnormal). Indeed the thing that most unites everything in the universe is that there are no two things the same. Even so-called 'identical' twins can vary enormously in their psychological and/or emotional make-ups.

"The tendency to define morality can be extremely dangerous. It can help to create a psychological caste system. Which can so easily be diverted to provide scapegoats in times of crisis. And is sadly often used for precisely that purpose. Is another form of control.

"That 'caste system' already exists in advertising, for example. (So much of today's advertising is a development of the abuse inflicted on Freud's work by his nephew.) Already advertisers – and you, Polly, probably know this better than I – divide their targets into classes: from, I think, 'A' to 'E'. The same myths thus get disseminated to the whole world, merely via different routes. Which is yet another form of control. And of wresting control."

Polly's eyes have not been still since she and Rafaél had arrived. She spots a couple about to leave their stools – she's a rather too skinny forty-something in an expensive beige trouser-suit; her brash and acned apparent assistant is probably ten years younger. He keeps pushing his glasses back on his nose. It's either an affectation or he urgently needs to consult an optician. As coats are donned, Polly and Rafa hover ... and then they pounce. Grabbing stools at

'The Crown and Two Chairmen' is, some consider, an extreme sport. It is not one for the faint-hearted.

"All these resources, heh, Polly?," Rafa continues, "all this expertise and hard work and commitment and imagination. And all being frittered away on such entirely frivolous ends. To the end, exclusively, of making the überwealthy überwealthier. And when humanity (*all* of us, including those überwealthy) teeters on the brink of self-destruction.

"Which would – you would think – be bad enough. But in its wake are trawled so many further cruelties: from minor slights to genocides."

A tall man, stooping slightly because of his height, wanders myopically into the bar. His hair is striving for Elvis, but its owner is about twice Elvis's age. Polly recognises him. She pointedly raises her glass of tomato juice at him by way of salutation. The tall man clearly does not see the salute, and squints his way towards the bar.

"I have, for instance, no idea whether the colour I see as blue you see as the same blue," says Rafa. "For all I know what I see as blue you might see as yellow. There is no objective way of describing colour so we will never know. At which level, its interest is only academic. (And probably not very interesting even at that level!)

"It becomes considerably more than academic, however, if we start talking about pain. Just as you are the only person seeing your colour blue, so you are the only person experiencing your pain.

"If you hit your thumbnail with a hammer, I have no idea whether the pain you're experiencing is the equivalent of what I would suffer, or whether (by comparison) you are suffering a pin-prick or the rack. No idea at all. And yet we talk about pain-thresholds as if they were universal, we formulate our medicines and our sympathy on pain being a constant throughout humanity. And if such is true (as it is) for physical pain, then how much more true is it of invisible pain: of psychological pain or emotional or spiritual pain.

"Psychiatry, I say again, is in its infancy. This has many other dimensions, and in many fields. Certainly one of them (it seems to me) is when churchmen talk of lust, and laymen talk of sexuality.

"Is that which is called 'lust' (the biological imperative), is that, for instance, a hankering for the act of sex itself? Or for, let's call it, genetic immortality? Or for our own immortality?

"Let's take me as an example. Me, I am extremely anxious to preserve the family name. Preserving the family name, that has nothing to do with genetic immortality. Hyenas don't have family names, nor do hyacinths, not amoebas or algae. Genes pass just as well to the next generation via women as they do via men – in fact, more accurately. Maternal DNA is, I understand, inherited intact. Is the paternal DNA which fluctuates. Does that imply my impulsion is not for an immortality that is genetic, but one that is personal?"

"I must be very odd," says Polly. "I have absolutely no desire for children. Never have done. Never been in the least bit broody. The immortality thing is not an issue for me. But sex? Oh yes, I do want sex. These days, it seems, ever more so. I offer this information in the cause of your research. And that – yes, I do know, Rafa, before you state the obvious – is only me."

"And what about all the other 'lusts' there are, Polly? How many of these are allowed to develop, and go rancid, because somehow they are more acceptable than the sexual lust they are veiling?

"What about the 'lust' for power? Do those who hanker for power actually hanker to be sexually desirable? Is it not curious the preponderance in politics of the physically less attractive? Is it possible that politics attracts such people because power, as Dr Kissinger was once quick to point out, is such a powerful aphrodisiac? And would the world not be better off if such people concentrated on their sexual lust rather than their political lust? And (believe it or not!) those politicians who are attracted to their profession for sexual reasons, they're amongst the healthier ones!

"How many others seek power as a sex *substitute*? And how dangerous is *that*?

"How many business magnates could trace their stop-at-nothing determination back to a sexual rejection in their adolescence?

"How many of history's atrocities and today's ills are the consequence of sexual slights or sexual inadequacy – or perceived slights or inadequacy?

"The lust for power is, of course, always dangerous because power itself is so enormously corrupting, but it also hides another string of lusts: for revenge, as an example, or for self-esteem.

"Then there is the 'lust' for money – which too is enormously dangerous to us all, because to *need* its acquisition to that extreme has to involve others being deprived of it. How often is that the cause of sexual lust being repressed?

"The 'lust' also for prestige, how much part of the alpha male syndrome? At the level of wanting your picture in the newspaper that lust is even perfectly acceptable; considerably less acceptable when you start to believe that, because your picture *is* in the newspaper, you are somehow more important as a person than someone who hasn't.

"Anyone who enters a VIP lounge does not vouchsafe his importance, but (often) gainsays it. Is not that the meek *shall* inherit the Earth, is rather more that they actually have. Meekness is not about self-abasement, but about being right-sized. Those who are right-sized know without a shadow of a doubt that they are indispensable: because today's reality would not be the same without them. But they also know therefore about the indispensability of all those around them.

"Someone who needs to be reassured that he is a Very Important Person is almost certainly one who doesn't feel himself to be that important. His importance comes from outside not within, and we're not therefore talking about importance but grandeur, not self-esteem but pomp – the pomp indeed of pomposity."

"The pomp of pomposity?" Polly asks, her eyes still waltzing over the pub's interior, trying to find someone prepared to recognise *her*.

"I make no apology, my friend. VIP designations do not exist for the benefit of important people. Who in the world is *not* a 'very important person'? No, such designations exist to persuade those who aren't so designated that they are *unimportant* people. To persuade anyone that he isn't important, that (my friend) is one of the biggest sins available to Man.

"There are also a number of other vice-like (as opposed to sin-like) lusts, *very* many of them: a lust, for instance, for the salacious or sybaritic (particularly when we have to pay for these things with our health or our children's health or our planet's health), or for adrenalin (what the young today, I think, call a 'buzz'), or indolence – which we will no doubt consider when we talk of sloth. But that is not all of them.

"There is indeed often a 'lust' for love. Which, also very often, hides itself in a lust for sex. And this lust is, I feel, more frequent (at least in adults) than that for sex masquerading as a lust for love. I'm willing to bet that the parts of her anatomy most used by prostitutes are her ears.

"All these 'lusts', *amiga mía,* these all contain the potential of growing from vices into sins. But they can also all travel in the opposite direction: become peccadilloes, even simply character traits. We are more often than not dealing so completely with degree.

"Finally, though, there is one vice attached to lust which is *species*-threatening: the 'lust', I talked about earlier, for immortality. How much misery has that ambition occasioned? How seismic, my friend, is what I shudder to call the 'immorality of immortality'?"

"As shudder, Rafa, you should!"

"The first Roman emperor, Augustus (the father of the Julia we were just talking about), sought deification. And to date he has enjoyed, if not exactly that deification, certainly immortality. And isn't so-called immortality the nearest Man is ever going to approach to deification? (Though, of course, if mankind dies so will the attendant immortality.) If we had simply let memory of Augustus disappear, would others have followed his ruthlessness? Was such lust for immortality also part of the impulsion behind Genghis Khan and Pol Pot? Ivan the Terrible and General Franco? Would we rather be remembered as Ceausescu or as Sweeney Todd than not remembered at all? (And is Hitler really more acceptable a human being because he was sexually faithful to Eva Braun?)

"Again we cannot be rigid in our condemnation of what appears to be this trait of ours, this hankering for immortality. (Indeed we should strive *never* to be rigid. Democracy should be a synonym for fluidity. Is despotisms which are rigid.)

"I mean, sometimes that trait might have produced remarkable results. Remarkable. Was too *Bach's* impulsion immortality? Was Racine's? Or Whistler's? Or was immortality simply a by-product of their work? And if immortality *was* their impulsion does that render their work any less beautiful?"

Polly intervenes, "Woody Allen famously said, 'I don't want to be immortal through my work; I want to be immortal through not dying.'"

"I think he might have been joking."

"You think?" Polly returns drily.

"The majority of senior politicians," says the South American, "certainly hanker for immortality. My guess is that, on their death-beds, most would assess the success of their lives by the amount of words they predict will be dedicated to them in the history books. And here history's historians have done mankind an enormous disservice – because overwhelmingly the statesmen most mentioned in history are those involved in war.

"War has been seen thus as sad but inevitable, gory but glorious. Those that win wars are national heroes forever. Even some of those who lose wars. Visit Paris. See the reminders there are there of Napoleon. And that, of course, has helped to make war as prevalent as it has been."

The Elvis-coiffeured man is bustling out. He suddenly sees Polly, does a classic double-take, squints more determinedly in her direction, clearly recognises her. He does a quick wave, points at his watch with a 'got-to-dash' gesture – and dashes. This by-play occurs as Rafaél continues talking.

"And this 'lust' for immortality, I think its tentacles are more than just those of the political. So are its implications and consequences. Do we want children, for instance, to protect not only our genes, not only our family name, but *our* immortality? Our *personal* immortality? And, if so, do we seek to mould our children into our likeness rather than encourage them to find their own mould? And if that's part of it, but *only* part of it, how big *is* that part? Are we procreating on behalf of the species? Or on our own behalf? Or on behalf of the consequent child? Who will then, of course, become the consequent adult.

"If we are procreating on behalf of the species, do we need to? Is today our species not better protected by *not* procreating? By severely limiting procreation? But if we do that, who will pay for the aged generation? Already that is a giant problem. If we limit births to the extent that the planet needs human births to be limited, how will we cope with the jobless hugely outnumbering the jobbed?

"At a quark-level, *are* all these 'lusts' hiding sexual lusts? I have not got a clue. I doubt anyone has. I also doubt that there are universal answers. What may be true for you might well not be so for me. Again it might be all a matter of degree. We do not know what we do not know. Psychiatry has yet to discover its own atoms. But we do know Man has billions of years of pre-Man history, all of it somewhere in his DNA. I think is a reasonable assumption that underlying all the sins of lust, and most of its vices, are one of these three elements: sex itself, I mean, genetic or personal immortality. Probably, as I said before, a mixture of all three, as different in all of us as are our fingerprints.

"And all the questions I posed have implications to our species as a whole. And they are questions we almost never ask ourselves. Mostly because there are no general answers ... no *pat* answers, no quick solutions, no universal placebos. And that is yet another reason why we need to develop a twenty-first century morality. We need to ask such questions of ourselves. Laws could never be framed to cope with this divergence of application.

"Is by asking ourselves such questions, Polly, that we will develop a morality that will cohere whatever the circumstances. Those circumstances are clearly unknown. What else is the future but the great unknown? But is, I think, a fair assumption that without a morality the future's circumstances have to be such that not only will morality not cohere, but nor will society. At any level.

"It would seem to me that there is absolutely no point in having children, nor lusting after immortality, if there is no future in which to house them."

"I think, if you don't mind, Rafa, I'll have (as they say) the other half just up the road. See if that isn't a better hunting-ground for cronies than it is around here."

"I don't mind at all," says Rafaél. He drinks the last of his beer. "I do like it, English beer. I was warned about it back in my country, also when I got here by Rodolfo – my son who lives here. I was told it was, I quote, 'undrinkable'. But I do not agree. I do, yes, like it."

Polly opens the pub door for him. The chilly blast that greets them is one to be expected only considerably closer to Christmas.

"Lust *is* abused, though, Rafa." She huddles deep into her jacket. "There's no denying that."

"Oh, enormously abused. By advertisers, and by pimps."

"Pornographers?"

"Pornography, I feel, that is a much more vexed question. Is the pin-up pornography?

"The nude is an entirely acceptable, often remarkably chaste, discipline of fine art. Why should that not also be true of photography? Is not the central problem – at least with 'soft-core' pornography – that of fashion photography? That it perpetrates a myth of womanhood? That it provides some kind of paradigm designed to make other women feel 'less than'? Is a pin-up any more an incitement to lust than printing a recipe is an incitement to gluttony? Men are, I think, going to look at naked women. The real problem, I also think, is less the lust, than the secretiveness about it."

They pass the 'Quo Vadis' restaurant. A cursory glance through the windows indicates there is no more than a smattering of clients lunching there. Above it, there's some building work going on. Scaffolding has been erected – carefully to leave the restaurant's access unencumbered. A swathe of blue plastic has been attached to its 'first floor', as it were, presumably to catch any accidentally dropped bricks or tools or chippings.

"Pornography as a word, it did not even exist until the nineteenth century – presumably therefore as a concept not much before that. Erotica and overtly sexual depiction has been present … well, that I know of since the Greeks. Most wealthy men in Renaissance Europe had hand-painted works detailing the full gamut of sexual practise – some that I have seen quite beautiful. In my country, the Moche civilisation – which pre-dated the Incan – made artefacts (oil amphorae, wine carafes) depicting many forms of sexual congress. Also very beautiful. In Pompeii it wasn't only the brothel which had what today we'd call 'pornographic' murals, was also the living rooms of the villas belonging to the wealthy, and very staid, middle-class. Mayhap, like beauty, pornography is in the eye of the beholder.

"Provided that those taking part are doing so consensually, I think the most that those who dislike it can say of it is that 'it's one of the prices of press freedom'."

"I'm quite into porn," says Polly. "I'm not embarrassed about that. Or, rather, with the right partner and in the right mood, I *can* be quite into it. As for it being degrading … well, frankly, I find TV shows like 'Big Brother' or ones presented by the … presented by 'Mr' Springer, let's call him, to be far more demeaning than any pornography. These are pornography of the spirit, of the soul."

"I have not seen these shows."

"Trust me, you have missed absolutely nothing. Except the joy of demeaning yourself by witnessing the demeaning of others. This is another price we pay for press freedom. In my opinion, it's a lot higher than that of honest-to-goodness – or even honest-to-badness – pornography. My strongest objection to pornography is not ethical but aesthetic: To me it never captures the love involved in sex. (I was going to say 'never captures the rapture' but I thought better of it!)"

"'Captures the rapture' would have been good," returns Rafaél with a smile.

"It reduces an act of love (or, at the very least, an act of tenderness) to a mechanical experience. Even the famous, and famously explicit, Japanese film, 'Realm of the Senses', I thought captured the obsessiveness of its central relationship, far more than that relationship's tenderness. I think maybe Nicolas Roeg got closest to 'capturing that rapture' in 'Don't Look Now'. Some people also consider that scene pornographic."

"As they do the Venus de Milo. Is always, Polly, about the aesthetic. Indeed a very great deal of morality has to do with aesthetics. Today, though, even the word 'aesthetics' is considered as rather effete, something which has to do with the privileged few rather than something with universal application. Beauty is, though, very much part of happiness. If we want to increase our happiness, and the happiness in the world, is also helpful to hunt down beauty – first-rate beauty, not the ersatz and fourth-rate variety of so much today which is *called* 'beautiful'.

"We all do know pornography, Polly, when we see it. And, of course, it has to do with aesthetics. With beauty. There is a clear difference between pornography and either art or artefact. And pornography *is* an abuse of sex – though, mayhap, not one that is so serious. Is, I think, the single biggest traffic on the Internet. So mayhap there is a need for it."

"Always in cop shows, if they find a serial killer, a serial rapist," says Polly, "*always* they're quick to say that he had a stack of pornography. They don't mention anything else. They don't mention that they also found Corn Flakes or aspirin or instant coffee – or copies of 'Time'. Certainly the thing most common to serial rapists is their use of steroids. How often do we get to hear about that? Is that more evidence, do you think, Rafa, of the war you talk about between the Truth and the Untruth?"

"Any quick fix diagnosis, any sound-byte solution is very much part of that war. Likewise that we do not see that when clerics and politicians rant against 'lust', that too is a form of sexual abuse. Is an abuse of sex. These people abuse sex by such ranting quite as much as the pornographers, even (if they support an economic system which fosters prostitution) as the pimps. They merely do so more speciously. Is evil to call sex evil. And is sinful to encourage young people to infer that their sexuality is 'sinful'. Or that other people's sexuality is 'sinful'. That is, in fact, *gravely* sinful."

"Whoa there, Rafa, we're getting pretty close to what I'm going to be talking about. In fact, this whole conversation, there's a lot of cross-over between it and the mortal lie that, quotes, 'morality' is morality."

"Suffice it to say, then, my friend, that we're nowhere near discovering the quarks of psychiatry. Is a science still in its pram. I think it would be foolish to be too determined about impulsions, even compulsions, and their causes. All those elements may contain the potential to be sinful, they are not so of themselves.

"Which is not to say that wethos is a code of ethics in which 'anything goes', or which encourages anything to go. Far from it. Is certainly the case that ethics (in whatever form those ethics take), in appealing to our higher 'I', require sacrifice of us: Often that we, for instance, 'sacrifice' the pleasure of the transient for the greater pleasure of the durable, that often we delay or deny ourselves gratification, or foreswear a pleasure because such will cause pain to others. And self-restraint is callisthenics for our higher 'I': It helps it to grow in both depth and width. Is as healthy for us as imposed restraint is unhealthy and causes our higher 'I' to shrivel.

"Part of the duty of care enjoyed by parents and teachers (and we are all of us, Polly, teachers) is less to forbid the child to do wrong things (important though that is). Is much more to encourage the child to do what's right. The fledgling requires little forbidding to topple from the nest. It needs much more time being taught how to fly.

"In asking us to restrict our sex lives to the act of reproduction – which was, I presume, the intention of designating lust a 'deadly sin' and certainly formed part of Gandhi's philosophy of ... *'brahma -'* something, I seem to remember he called it ... *'Brahma-'* ... No, gone, sorry. Well, I can't help wondering whether, as I said earlier, that would not be curbing the wrong instinct. Would we not be better off trying to curb our greed, for instance? Or our need for self-aggrandisement? Or, as I also said earlier, our possessiveness?"

Dean Street at lunchtime usually buzzes with activity. But the unseasonal cold acts like smoke on the hive. There is a postman pulling his yellow cart, there are a couple of Girl Fridays huddled into coats bearing cardboard beakers of take-away soup and paper-bags of sandwiches, and there is a youth of about eighteen straggling a would-be beard and pushing a trolley loaded with silver film-cans.

Of which Rafaél says to Polly, "I thought was all tape these days."

"Still celluloid for the big ones," Polly replies. "Screw looking for work. Let's go somewhere where I can have a real drink." And she turns on her heel.

"So, *amiga mía*, the third mortal lie?"

"That 'morality' is morality," ruminates Polly. "Or, rather, what is called morality is morality, that so-called *sexual* morality is morality, that our sexual conduct defines whether or not we are moral."

"Go on," Rafa tells her.

"I agree with you, there is some openness today about sex," says Polly, "and that's healthy. In most metropolitan areas, being gay, I no longer feel threatened. And I say that just round the corner from a gay pub, the 'Admiral Duncan', that was bombed some ten years ago. A little incident which, incidentally, I have yet to hear condemned by the very many factions which claim the centre of their lives to be the love of Jesus. You think Jesus would have countenanced bombing a gay pub?"

"Not a gay pub, nor a mosque, nor the headquarters, if there is one, of the Atheists Society. But nor do I think Muhammad would have countenanced flying aeroplanes into skyscrapers."

"Right, Rafa. We're not, us gays, not as safe as you like to imagine. But we're certainly a lot safer than we used to be. And that has to be good. Sex (gay or straight), now by a whole heap of the community, is accepted as being a vital part of life, both healthy and fun. And this, if it started with the millennium (which it didn't; it pre-dated the millennium) was less than ten years after the then-President Reagan had condemned a TV show because its heroine had a baby out of wedlock. (Wed*lock*, you notice, another linguistic accident?)

"One of the quirks of history seems to be that each generation believes it has invented sex. This one is no exception. And this one, like all its forerunners, is wrong: The 1920s, World War Two, the 60s, these were all times of great sexual freedom. The *fin-de-siècle* in Paris ... outrageous by anyone's standards. Even the redoubtable Queen Victoria herself, even whose name is synonymous with sexual repression and a joyless 'morality', was at variance in her own private life with the 'close-your-eyes-and-think-of-England' image of her portrayal."

"Indeed, my friend," says Rafaél, "the political map of Europe might have been very different if it *had* been true. What truly enormous oaks were born of her tiny acorns: the First and Second World Wars, the Russian Revolution – in fact, the whole history of the world would have been changed but for the libido and fecundity of a diminutive queen of a tiny nation. Is this a good way of organising a world?"

"Albert, when he oversaw the Great Exhibition at the Crystal Palace – my turn, Rafa, to side-track – Albert also started to propagate another example of not great ways to organise a world. In his case, the belief that anything recently invented is, dint of that fact alone, a benefice. We today continue to believe that garbage. Today, of course, that belief further feeds the coffers of the überwealthy, so we are *heavily* encouraged to believe it. But for all the spin and the hype, it remains what it was in Albert's day: nonsense. By which I'm not, of course, trying to say that there are *no* advances, that anything which is a new development or a new invention is '*per se*' valueless. Nothing so crass. Only that not everything invented or developed is '*per se*' of value. That each new development needs to be examined in considerably more detail than is happening at the moment.

"There's now so much evidence to show that what we used to think of as 'progress' is, in fact, a ... well, let's say, mixed blessing. But we'd rather ignore that inconvenient truth. The car, the television, even the humble aerosol, they're all now seen (at least, by anyone with eyes) as, at their very *best*, a mixed blessing.

"The computer is an entirely mixed blessing. But we have created a climate where even to question the magnificence of that invention is tantamount to blasphemy. Ignoring for a moment the small matter of civil liberties and the right to privacy, I know of very few people who do not fairly regularly complain about either their computers, or those of companies that they're dealing with. Surely, one definition of 'autocracy' is that it demands of you that you behave as that autocracy wishes. How is the computer, therefore, not an autocrat? It is a tool which is in control of its wielder. I have heard this age described as the 'I-Tyranny'. It seems to me a wholly justified description. Never before has a machine exercised such enormous power. Only very rarely has the exerciser of such power been quite so unchallenged, quite so unquestioned. How many times on TV do you hear characters doing any complaining – at all, I mean – about their desktops or laptops – or those of the corporate world?

"A cynical friend of mine believes that's because the TV companies are scared that the computer companies will exact their vengeance by infecting their technology with incurable viruses. I don't share her cynicism, not to that degree. It would mean that Mr Gates and his colleagues were guilty of the most enormous crime against free speech, democracy and thus humanity. Michaels both Dobbs and Crichton do paint, that's true, the most alarming pictures of future wars and conflicts, but I do not think the computer companies themselves would be capable of quite such heinousness.

"So, why, then? I mean, surrounded as we are by people complaining so frequently about computers and the whole technology, why then do we hear on television so few characters moaning about this I-Tyranny?

"Why? Well, partially because it's 'progress'. (Though quite who defines 'progress' is another interesting question.) It's what C.S. Lewis called 'chronological snobbery': anything which post-dates something else *has* to be better, if only because of the fact that it's newer. It's a snobbery which our insane world, of course, *loves*. But it's not a new phenomenon. It's just – as, Rafa, you were saying in a different context – the degree that is new and the possible consequences.

"Manufacturers see that snobbery as a permanent bonanza (thereby contributing substantially to global warming) and it makes advertising products so very much easier. Of course it is championed by those economists who eulogise the benefits of consumerism (thereby contributing substantially to the acceptance of globalisation). And it is just as much nonsense as any other snobbery is nonsense.

"It's a dangerous nonsense, what's more (over and above the dangers I've just spoken of), because we don't fully think through the consequences of these 'developments'. And also because it is thus, albeit through the back door, that enormously toxic concepts (yes, like globalisation) come to be accepted.

"But the silence on the part of script-writers is, I fear, more sinister even than that. And I'm not now talking about computers, but about the entire ethos which pervades today's planet.

"It can, in fact, that silence, mean only one of four things: The first is that television's script-writers are blessed with having computers and utility companies considerably more efficient than us less literate human beings. We have to concede that is a possibility, albeit a rather unlikely one.

"The other three possibilities are considerably more menacing.

"The first is that the writers are walking around with their eyes and ears shut. That would be *real* worrying. Writers are supposed to be society's eyes, their ears – and, most importantly, their mouths. If our writers today are so blind and deaf that they are not noticing a daily phenomenon, what use are their voices?

"The second possibility is that the TV companies are telling them not to write such gags. Now, frankly, I just don't believe that. There are just too many wannabe whistle-blowers around. And most TV shows are now 'resourced', as the current buzz-word has it: made, in other words, by so-called 'independent' companies, rather than in-house.

"Now, I do think there may be a tendency for these independent companies to be chosen for their sympathy towards corporate strategy. But that's not quite the same thing. And, hey, what are friends for if not to be awarded contracts? How many contracts were awarded to friends of the administration whilst Messers Bush, Cheney and Rumsfeld held sway? We think TV companies work any differently?

"The fourth possibility is the most frightening one of all: And that is that the writers *believe* that writing such observations or criticisms would somehow be contravening company policy – and that they fear such contravention would jeopardise their employment. They are determined, in other words, not to rock the technocratic and/or corporate boat.

"And that's frightening – that's terrifying – at two levels. First of all, that there is being created an ethos of terror – maybe not as overt as that McCarthy instigated, but in fact more threatening yet for its stealth. We've created, in other words, a McCarthy who does not need to exist. It's quite enough to suggest that there might be (lurking somewhere in very shadowy wings) a McCarthy, ready to strip insubordinate scribes or subversive hacks (or 'terrorist sympathisers') of their livelihood.

"The second reason that the possibility is so frightening is because it therefore also means that today's writers are fundamentally cowards. And cowards are the last ally anyone needs in a war.

"I entirely agree with you, Rafa, that today we are fighting a war – that between the Truth and the Untruth. Just as Solzhenitsyn was doing in communist Russia – he and a few incredibly brave souls with him. I started reading a book written by a Moscow correspondent for a US newspaper during the Cold War. I didn't finish it, to be honest, mostly because he was writing about a Russia that no longer exists. It alarmed me, though, and not a little, how many similarities there are between what the book described and the way we are living today in our famously 'developed' world.

"Now, it may need a Shakespeare to expose Truth, or expound on it, but it does not require genius to see a lie. Or to expose that lie. It just needs eyes and ears. Which are, I say again, the foremost tools of any writer. They are, those tools, *our* ears, Rafa, and *our* eyes. *And* our mouths. If writers decide to become like the three monkeys – except that rather than evil they choose to ignore the lies – then what good are they to us?

"We cannot afford the luxury of writers just sitting in their ivory towers, tutting about global warming or deforestation or whatever else it might be if they are not also in the vanguard of exposing both the Untruth and the multiple lies which constitute that Untruth.

"And, no, no-one's talking about abolishing sitcoms or soap operas, not even game-shows. We're just talking here about allowing some kind of balance into the medium. How much air-time is now devoted to programmes of Oprah Winfrey-like sincerity? Of genuine integrity? And how much to spurious and salacious spin-offs from that genre, so-called (and totally miscalled) 'reality' television, the like of Mr Springer's? How much air-time has been allowed to the hawks in the Middle Eastern crisis? And how much to the likes of Noam Chomsky struggling to find middle-grounds of peace?

"The present *im*balance (an imbalance you'd have to be blinkered not to see) has, in its turn, to beg questions about another extremely dangerous trend ...

"No-one with half a brain cell any longer doubts that we are at a crisis point in Man's history. I saw a TV show a while back in which an eminent professor from New York university said of this generation that it was the most important of man's history – because it would be the one which determined whether or not Man *has* a future. This was not Che Guevara, but a scientist. Of course I don't know whether he had a vested interest in making that comment (beyond the vested interest of all of us, that is, to keep our species going). We don't know that of any so-called expert invited to comment on a situation. That is hugely a part of the War between the Truth and the Untruth. But it certainly didn't seem as though his words were being bought.

"At the same time as we are facing such a crisis, it is also quite unequivocal that schooling is being 'dumbed down'. Oh, the brightest are still being pushed, but those not the brightest (and by that I certainly do not mean the most stupid) are not being encouraged – not even in the way they used to be. (That was also a travesty, but that's not the point just right at the moment.)

"We need to ask ourselves why.

"I mean, why would you do that? At a moment of global crisis when you're going to need every brain cell available to tackle the myriad of crises we've created over the millennia, at the time of man's defining generation, why would we dumb our schooling down? And its surrounding culture? Why would we not seek rather to push our children (and ourselves) to the very limits of their abilities – and ours?

"Unless, that is, we're being dumbed down for a purpose. Unless they want to dumb us down to the point of our own acquiescence in our own subjugation? The dumber, after all, have always been less likely to protest than the brighter. They're more likely to shrug and say that's just the way life is, less likely to be aware of what's happening to them.

"Is this what's occurring in our schools and in our culture today? And if it's not, why are we not addressing – and urgently, not with absurd ideas like 'league tables' and endless exams (and, God help us, 'Oscars' for teachers!) – the whole problem of schooling? Not only nationally but internationally?

"Is what is happening on our television screens an extension of that dumbing down process, compounded with a desensitising process?

"We have to accept that, even in Utopia, there are problems inherent with the entire medium of television. The machine is, for example, part of the furniture, and many of TVs regulars consequently are considered to be one of the family. Fact and fiction start, not even to coalesce, but to become enmeshed. News therefore, as we've said before, often gets relegated to being received as a kind of permanent soap opera. (There are other problems too, about whether the presence of TV cameras *occasions* news, about the erosion the medium wreaks on health and family life, and a whole panoply of similar contentious issues – and they are *difficult* issues and genuinely vexed questions. But again outside our present sphere.)

"*Inside* that sphere, though, is the worry that there is now a deliberate policy of encouraging the tendency to desensitise us. Oh, everywhere we turn we are being desensitised. Everywhere we go we come across 'have-a-nice-day' courtesy, the courtesy that comes from a script, which is wafer-thin and equally as vacuous, and which masks a growing Etna of anger and resentment. Television is a great contributor to that desensitising process, probably the single largest.

"Why else would we have so many programmes on the tube which demean our fellow human beings? Which are designed to make people appear at their ugliest and most selfish? From game shows to makeover shows to so-called chat shows, from 'Big Brother' via extraordinarily spurious 'talent' shows to totally pornographic shows like those, as I said earlier, hosted by … we'll continue to call him 'Mr' Springer.

"And, whilst I'd like to agree with you, Rafa, that the super-rich that I have come across don't have the 'nous' to organise themselves into some kind of demonic coterie, I think the evidence becomes daily more persuasive that it is precisely that shituation which they are seeking to create. Maybe you're right, maybe it's the institution of wealth creating that shituation more than the actual people. Sadly, for those of us the victims of their rapaciousness, it doesn't make a lot of difference. If someone's coming at you with a bayonet, does it make a lot of difference to your plight if this is a madman or a soldier working on behalf of an institution?"

"Sexual morality is not morality?"

"No. No, Rafa, it isn't.

"You know, when I first came to London, I was told that London is really a whole bunch of villages lumped together. These days, so I've been told by cab-drivers, that view is out-of-date. But I'm really not too sure. I mean, this pub – 'The Blue Posts', it's called, 'case you were wondering – well, you saw for yourself, it's just the other side of Shaftesbury Avenue from Soho, right on the fringes of China Town, and yet you'll see a film technician here about as often as a kangaroo in Kenya."

The pub is full. They manage to find two low stools on which, overhangingly, to perch. There remains that about many British hostelries which begs the question: Is it coincidence that there is more assonance between hostelry and hostility than between hostelry and hospitality? It is, you sense, almost Cromwell's legacy: We may not be able to curb the fun you have drinking, but we're going to ensure that you do so in the most austere of surroundings. Many such pubs still have upright wooden chairs, often without cushions and, *if* cushioned, then those of the same thinness as the slices of processed cheese with which the pubs likewise fill their sandwiches. The stools over which their bottoms presently lollop were clearly designed rather more for the patronage of Sneezy and Doc than they were for the normal adult human.

"Which obliges me, I feel, to ask the question: What then *is* morality?"

Polly swallows some of her beer. "Morality, surely, is a self-imposed set of self-defined ethics adherence to which will make your world a happier place. Impose the set, or define the ethics for someone else, and you are no longer dealing with morality, but stricture.

"And, of course, both set and ethics have to be reviewed constantly, because both you and the world are changing constantly. For one thing, the 'your world' of anyone today is very much bigger than it used to be. A hundred years ago, 'your world' was your country, a hundred years before that your city, before that your village ... your clan, tribe and so on.

"Morality is there, it seems to me, to afford the individual the maximum freedom concomitant with the welfare of those around him (and 'around him' is today a much bigger 'around' than even twenty years ago); to afford the maximum happiness to each of us individually which occasions the least unhappiness to others. As a by-the-by, apply that description to globalisation and almost immediately you see how impoverished that concept is.

"As such, morality has absolutely nothing to do with my sexual behaviour – unless that behaviour intrudes into areas where others are somehow endangered or debased. And how often does the sexual conduct of *any* of us do that? Oh, we usually – if not invariably – end up hurting those with whom we have a sexual relationship. Sometimes quite severely, sometimes (in fact) very severely. And the hurting may or may not be immoral. It's just not possible to generalise that enormously. But I think you can say that morality usually has less to do with such pain than those who deem morality to be sexual morality would have us believe.

"How is society protected by insisting I (a single woman) don't have sex? Or that I, a gay woman, have sex with men? With, in fact, *one* man? If anything society would be *threatened* by that insistence. Because it would then be asking me to behave in a way at variance with what I am. And so totally that I am liable – I am almost *obliged* – to become *anti*-social. Even more anti-social than I am anyway!

"I entirely agree with you, Rafa: Historically, the Church designated lust such a sin because we are, almost all of us, so obviously and unambiguously guilty of it. And by making us all into sinners, we are so very much easier to control. That designation is beginning with most of us not to work any longer. I suspect that, just as 'wicked' has come to be a compliment, to designate something 'sinful' endows it with that frisson of 'naughty-but-nice'.

"So today those who seek to control us have changed the vocabulary. Instead of sinners, today they designate us 'losers'. And that is, of course, sad. What changes the sadness into a tragedy is the fact that we buy into this wholesale garbage. That *we* do, Rafa. Us. Those they are seeking to control. And that is a tragedy on a grand scale, my friend. A tragedy building to a cataclysm.

"Presidents and prime ministers are considered – quotes - 'winners', the bus driver (who may well be an exemplary father and citizen) a – quotes – 'loser'; pop stars, film stars, the stars of certain, highly selective sports (not, for instance, archery or squash or boules), these are all winners, the kindergarten teacher racking her brains how to reach an evasive pupil is a loser.

"Who on earth defines them as such? And why do we allow such to be defined for us?

"Even the most benign political leader has had to indulge in so much contrivance and duplicity to acquire his status – or hers – that such a one can never be a creditable human being. How is someone who is not creditable a 'winner'?

"There is certainly nothing wrong with entertaining people, not even anything wrong for paying people handsomely (but not ludicrously) when they entertain us well. But that does not turn these human beings into gods. Or even demi-gods. And when we imbue our entertainers with demi-god status we do not in fact love them. We sprinkle them, not with stardust, but spiritual anthrax.

"I'm leery about believing too many things I read or hear about entertainers. Such gossip has so often in my experience been belied ... well, *by* my experience. I've worked with way too many actors, supposedly difficult but actually charming, any longer to believe without question what is said about them. Sure, those actors could be exigent, particularly that those around them should be as professional as they are, but that's no bad thing. Encouraging the best out of people is, finally, helping them to be the most 'they' they can be. And those who are thus exigent don't, courtesy of that, become ogres.

"I don't *know* therefore whether the less than endearing anecdotes I've heard and read about concerning, say, Frank Sinatra or Sir Mick

Jagger are true or are fabricated in order to make a good story. But, let's just suppose for a moment that they *are* true: were these two entertainers born the monsters such stories tell us they became? I really don't think so. Not anyway any more than Dick Turpin was born the way he became. Or Al Capone was. Or, let's say, Paul Wolfowitz was born the monster he became, at least politically and fiscally. Personally, of course, he might be delightful. I have no way of knowing.

"It's we who create both the celebrities and their can-do-no-wrongness. And most of these celebrities (becoming less and less celebrity-worthy also, I suspect, in an effort to desensitise us), maybe precisely because in themselves they know themselves to be so *un*important, they quite naturally seize the proffered validity. It's almost what you were saying, Rafa, about VIP lounges.

"Oh, don't get me wrong: In the extremely unlikely event such adulation were ever offered to me I'd leap at it. Grab it with both hands. And that's why we should be so very careful on whom we bestow such adulation. In fact I think history shows us that we should not ever bestow it on *anyone*. I think it's little short of a modern miracle, not how badly some of these deified human beings behave, but how well most do.

"In my experience, in fact, it's almost a rule of thumb that, amongst the stars, you can count on how well an actor behaves by how *big* a star he or she is. It's usually those who are *wannabe* stars or starlets (or those, like Monroe, abused en route) who are difficult; those who know their stardom is manufactured and is likely therefore to be taken back at any moment. They're absolutely right to be worried, by the way. That's no unjustified paranoia. It's enormously fragile, such so-called stardom. Subject to public whim and executive caprice.

"Having said which, there are certain notable exceptions, of course. Stars, I mean, who *are* marquee names, but who are also incredibly unpleasant. We don't, as the Brits would say, have to 'sully our lips' by repeating their unfortunate names. Please don't misunderstand me, Rafa, what I'm not trying to say is that actors in general are difficult. Or unpleasant. If anything, to the contrary. Maybe because they spend so much time being other people, on the whole I think actors know themselves better than most of us. And they're the better people for doing so. And when stars want to behave badly, usually the first people they behave badly to are their fellow-actors.

"Actors aren't stars, though. And a lot of stars are actors only in the broadest sense. And a lot of those stars today … Well, they aren't *even* stars. Not any more. Not in Hollywood leastways. Not in any real sense. Stars are merely a means to an end. And the end is that they enable studio executives to justify their enormous, and ridiculous, salaries. (Salaries, at least, that would be ridiculous anywhere but within a culture where money equals worth, and both prestige and power.)

"As Lord Puttnam discovered to his chagrin, the whole studio machinery – including the equally absurd costs of some movies – the whole cosy (only *apparently* uncosy) relationship between executive and agent, is geared to hype the stars so that, less limelightly, both agent and executive can amass vast fortunes. That is also the reason they are both trying to muscle out the independent producers (Hollywood doesn't care for the entrepreneur any more than Wal-Mart cares for the local corner shop); why there are relatively so few movies made; and why too the quality today of such films as are made is so entirely … adequate. I don't use the word 'adequate' as a compliment."

"And why do they need such vast salaries, Polly? You must ask yourself that. Often, very often, is so that they can be endowed with a 'success' which they don't feel. Oh, mayhap that's not true of all of them. I have no way of knowing. I am not in their heads. But if they did not feel themselves so inadequate mayhap they would not need this constant reinforcement of their worth. And as such they are to be pitied.

"Just as, almost inevitably, monster egos are veiling extremely fragile egos, those with a need to be considered successful are those who believe themselves unworthy of success.

"If we are going to exchange a world of hate for a world of love we also have to love, Polly, those we do not like."

"There are some actors, Rafa, some directors and executives, who – trust me – are eminently unlovable."

"And is precisely those, *amiga mía,* we need to love most. We do not need to adulate them, nor revere them – indeed, as you said earlier, we do not love them when we over-glorify them – but love them, that, yes, we do need to do. Even Sir Bonio. Well, perhaps not Sir Bonio, but everyone else! The actors that you find unlovable, Polly, the directors and executives, they are all finally human beings. As flawed and incomplete as any of us."

"Infinitely more."

"Then infinitely more in need of love."

"'Course you're right. Of course you are. I'd like to say I was only kidding you. And I was, at one level. Well, *mostly* kidding you. It's sometimes hard, though ... It's sometimes hard ... Put it this way: In the production office of pretty nearly every damn movie made ever is a placard which reads: 'When you're up to your ass in alligators it's sometimes difficult to remember you're only there to clear the swamp.' I don't think that's true only of movie-making."

"Excuse me, my friend. I do not see the connection."

"Know what? I'm not sure that I do either," says Polly. "You ever heard of 'Columbo'?" she asks.

"Is, no?, a detective show? On television? He is very scruffy?"

"A *big* show, Rafa, in the States. It starred an actor called Peter Falk, apparently a heavy smoker. I remember seeing another actor interviewed. For the life of me I can't remember who. And it's worth bearing that in mind: In my experience, one actor talking about another is not a scenario designed to encourage accuracy. The interview had gotten onto the subject somehow of smoking. The interviewee was saying how difficult it was in LA to find a restaurant which allowed it. He'd been dining with Mr Falk, however. Who, after he'd finished his meal, promptly lit up. The interviewee, so he maintained, reminded Mr Falk that they were in a non-smoking restaurant. 'I'm Peter Falk,' the interviewee quoted the actor as saying. 'You want to put money on the fact that they're not going to ask me to put it out?' As I saw it I remember thinking, 'Oh God, I do hope that's not true. How desperately, *desperately* sad for Mr Falk if that were true.'"

"Sad, yes, for Mr Falk."

"If true," Polly repeats.

"If, yes, true. Our culture today tells us, Polly, that it defines success. (Just as the Church defined – and defines – sinners.) It also allows that the 'winners' behave in a different way from the rest of us who are, dint of not being winners, losers."

"Like Roman emperors."

"Exactly. Is what I also said in a different context about limousines obeying different traffic laws to normal cars.

"But is actually not 'them' doing this 'allowing', Polly, is us. And we have to stop doing it. If we allow either the Church or our culture so to define us, then we are already unsuccessful. The only person who can, possibly, define success is one one's self. And even then one has to be extremely cautious.

"Our culture is not about creating winners. Is *all*, Polly, about creating losers. One person wins a gold medal. How many losers does that gold medal cost? Is even more pernicious than that. Because each time the gold medal winner does not win a gold medal, that 'winner' immediately becomes a 'loser'. Is, in fact, a lose: lose situation *par excellence*. For that reason. Because even those who are apparently its 'winners' are at times its 'losers'."

"Incredible, isn't it? You know how badly treated they are, the nominees who don't win Oscars? You'd have thought, wouldn't you?, getting nominated for an Oscar, that was something pretty good. But five nominees turn up for the ceremony, my friend, and four leave as losers. And that's how they're treated: like losers. The studio seems to think they didn't win the Oscar on purpose. Arriving they are fêted. Going home they're lucky if they don't have to catch a cab."

"And that, Polly, penetrates every sphere of human activity today. Every businessman who is not the world's richest person is a 'loser', every politician that is not premier or president, every rock star without a platinum disc, every athlete without a cup. Why? Does this make the world a happier place? Clearly not.

"It continues, and is propagated, *amiga mía,* precisely as we have said, Polly, because losers are so very much easier to manipulate than winners. And when we accept this nonsense, we actually forge our own shackles. The more we allow our culture to designate who are the 'winners' and 'losers' the more power we surrender to it.

"The more, Polly, we create a culture where it becomes an essential to be seen to win, the more we create a no-holds-barred set of principles which lack principles. As we also said before, eventually the ethicless ethics of Enron and John McEnroe are exactly the same."

"I'm told, Rafa, Mr McEnroe's a real nice guy."

"Is quite possible Sir Bonio also is a nice guy. Is a penalty you have to pay for becoming iconic, that is *that* which you become: iconic. You are no longer you, you *represent*. In Sir Bonio's case, he represents Professor Sachs's (in my opinion) fraudulent claim to be tackling world poverty; in Mr McEnroe's case he represents the, as I say, ethicless ethos that winning is all that matters.

"If no-one remembers who came second, Polly, if winning is all that counts, if winner takes all (and that's really okay with all of us), then (I'm afraid) we have to stop complaining if our old people's homes starve our parents, or our mental hospitals use the torture of so-called electro-convulsive therapy rather than psycho-therapy, or our insurance companies small-print their way out of our claims – or banks abuse us or governments lie to us. Because is all, all of it, entirely the same syndrome.

"But what do I know? I don't even agree with myself half the time. I change my mind as often as I change my underwear."

"'Confusion is chess for the uncompetitive.'"

"Excuse me?"

"I read it somewhere. I rather liked it."

"'Confusion ...'?"

"' ... is chess for the uncompetitive.'"

"Say 'hello' to a grandmaster, then. Is, of course, very much easier being a slave than a free man. Is also a lot easier to heed the promptings of our lower 'I' than of our higher one. But we are thereby spitting in our own eye, in the eye of our forebears, in the eye of billions of years of evolution – spitting, I would say, in the eye of God."

"Feel like another?"

"Always, Polly, I feel like another."

Chapter 11

The sheet is soft to the touch, starched but still lissom. The blanket at the foot of the bed is scratchy to the touch, lissom and yet starchy. But she feels reassured that it is there. Through what in winter are the central-heating radiators now purrs a gentle stream of cold. Perhaps it is too cool. Saskja feels cold. She even shivers.

She pulls the sheets up to her chin, almost like a shroud. She knows she's pale. "Deathly pale," her mother would say. A corpse-like face of deathly pallor. Her lips are deathlike blue. She will not think of death. She wills herself not to think of death.

She'd reach for the blanket only she fears the cold as she does so. She wears a very pale-blue hospital gown – essentially a sheet drawn together only by a tie around the neck. It has ridden up in bed. She still lacks the energy to pull it back down. Her hands fall to her thighs. She shivers again. Her fingertips feel like ice-cubes. And then they feel comforting. And she shivers again. Two skins pressed against each other, defining the other by such touch, plying into the other, a consummation of separateness and unity. The rough, well-used, well-kneaded, well-lotioned, the trollop skin of her fingertips; and the chaste and pristine, smooth-as-silk, pliant, pliable, the virgin skin of her thighs. Absurdly, surreally sensuous. And sexual. Almost sexual.

No. She wills herself also not to think of sex. Not sex nor death. Nor life. Nor love.

She thinks about her trip to London. She thinks about her stop-over in Rome. She thinks about the dinner party her parents are having on the following Friday. She thinks about how she will have to bubble at that party with vivacity and bonhomie.

She has a future. But it has cost the future of someone else.

Her teeth now chatter. She grabs for the grainy blanket and drapes it around her shoulders.

She would like to cry. But knows she can't. The tears are not yet ready. Their legions are still massing.

A twig scratches at her window. A bird settles on it and sings to the sun. But its warmth seems only to add another block to the igloo.

She knows she should talk to him. She has a moral something or other to talk to him. He is the father. Would be. But even as she recognises she should talk to him she knows she's not going to. Indeed she knows that this duty she's imposed on herself is only going to serve as a further transgression for which she can later chastise herself.

She's wicked. She knows she's wicked. She deserves to be punished. Oh, not for the sex. The sex was a mistake, but only a silly one. No harm really done. And if religion, if religious so-called morals thought real harm had been done, that was religion's problem, the problem of their so-called morals not hers.

As a young girl she had heard the Prophet's words. Many of them she now disagreed with, but nearly all of them had stayed that she might disagree with them. And from them she had realised that our private life is all those three things: life and private and ours. Not the subject of other people's dictates. Not even of their opinions – least of all if those opinions can somehow be imposed.

Giselle had also heard the Prophet. And she would like to talk to Giselle, but she knows she can't. She knows too she can't talk to her parents. Not about this. Again, not because she's had sex. She's nineteen-years-old, for God's sake. If her parents had a problem with her at nineteen having sex, then that is what it is: her parents have a problem. She does not.

It's not, she thinks, even her stupidity. She's done plenty of stupid things in her life. Her parents have witnessed many of them, have punished her for some, consoled or reassured her about others.

She doesn't want them to become accomplices, that's it. That's what the noble part of her thinks. The less noble wonders whether she might thereby be handing them a club that they have access to forever, whenever they think it in their interests to wield it.

What she has yet to know, Saskja, what will take some time for her to know, is that she fears diluting her guilt. She fears, far more than their censure, their forgiveness. Because she fears if they forgive her she will be forced to start forgiving herself.

And she fears her guilt is a cup of water, of finite dimensions. By telling them, they will drink of her cup and what is left for her will be reduced. And she needs to make reparation in the most absolute of ways. And she's not yet aware of any of these fears.

She sits quietly on the edge of her bed, stoically, the prisoner in his cell, waiting for guilt to overcome her and loneliness to overwhelm her. And she knows her wait will be a short one.

Chapter 12

"Not really my taste in art," confesses Rafaél.

"Paintings more than art," Polly suggests, "souvenirs. I presume they sell. I can't imagine to whom."

"This is, again?"

"Bayswater Road. Just up there is Lancaster Gate," she continues. "We can walk across Hyde Park that way through to Kensington. Feel like a walk?"

"Is always a pleasure to walk in London. What I do feel like, my friend, I feel one evening I should like to invite you to dinner."

There is a pause, which Rafaél senses is awkward, but is not sure why it should be.

"Sorry, Rafa," eventually Polly says, "but I never go out to dinner."

"Never?"

"Never."

"May I ask why not?"

"I don't like my friends to see me soulless," Polly replies matter-of-factly. A 94 bus rumbles past as they turn into the exaggerated, the almost mouthwashy green of the park. It is a summer's day halfway through October. And London, in all its diversity, is going as mad as October hares.

"Explain." Rafaél parries blandness with blandness.

"I drink too much, Rafa. By the evening I can't trust myself to be sober. An acquaintance of mine once told me (curiously, also in a pub), 'When a man is drunk, his soul leaves his body in disgust.' I'd prefer my friends not to see me soulless."

"Is, I think, a sickness, Polly. Are, I think, things that can be done."

"Right, it's a sickness," Polly returns wearily and dryly. "No, I'm sorry. I shouldn't be that … I don't know … 'ill-humoured', I guess, about it all. I do know it's a sickness, Rafa. I've even done stuff about it, all the, you know, 'usual' stuff: AA for a while, other what they call

'12 Step' programmes. My trouble was, I found the cure more painful than the sickness. I don't want to play the tortured poet here. But ... well, I *am* in pain, Rafa. Oh, emotional stuff, I mean, all of it. It's nothing physical. Would, in fact, sometimes that it were. I'm often in quite a *lot* of that emotional pain. Steeped in the, quotes, 'illness' I get, at least, *some* respite. When I was, quotes, 'recovering' I got no relief at all."

"But if, my friend, your sickness debars you from in the evening seeing your friends ..."

"In the evening, I see my *drinking* friends." Two barely adolescent boys hurtle by on mountain-bikes. "There is a camaraderie, Rafa, in the soulless: a ken and a *kin* of Fausts. It's an easy-going ken, undemanding. I suppose because it has to be. There is a truth, even a soul, to its soullessness. In AA I found a desperation to be 'souled'. It smacked to me a little of Aladdin's lamp-seller: 'new souls for old'. There was a prissiness in their lack of pissedness and a do-good condescension that I found both grating and unjustified. A lot of spiritual barnacles clinging to the first piece of driftwood they come across in the ocean.

"I also agree with Dean Martin. 'The trouble with not drinking,' he once said, 'is that when you wake up in the morning, that's as good as you're going to feel all day.' Oh, I know, Rafa, the pain that probably awaits me, the misery that will probably be my death, but to quote again, again a Hollywood lush, this time Errol Flynn, 'Who wants to die healthy?'"

"It saddens me, Polly."

"Don't be sad. Please. I know partners of people who've died from cancer. ... Wow, that was insensitive. Rafa, I'm sorry."

"No need to apologise, my friend."

"I'm so sorry, Rafa."

"Please continue."

"Still sorry. ... Well, quite a few of those – do stop me, right?, if this gets too painful ....

"*Por favor*, Polly."

"Quite a few believe it was not the illness which killed their loved ones, but the chemo. A number of cancer victims are now opting out of chemotherapy. Some are getting involved with alternative therapies, others are simply allowing Nature to take her course. I'm grateful to AA. As even those who decline chemo are grateful to the oncologists who suggest it and to the army of anonymous chemists who have developed it. AA, oncologists, chemists afford us a choice. Pity should be saved for those who have none – no choice."

"Okay," says Rafaél. "Is your life."

"You think that's going to be the case for much longer?"

"That it is *our* life?"

"Yes."

"All the information, you mean, that is being gathered about us? Without our knowing?"

"We've talked about this before, Rafa. Without the computer the Holocaust could not have happened. Likewise most of the civil rights' abuses today.

"The Holocaust would have happened, Polly. Just less what they would have liked to think of as 'efficiently'."

"And why, we need to ask ourselves, has that been kept so quiet? the computer's part in the Holocaust? Could it possibly be that if there were a wider knowledge of that, we'd be a sight more anxious about the information that is *now* being kept on *us*? Who in the Germany of 1923 could possibly have predicted what was going to happen in the Germany of 1933? Who in 1934 what would happen in 1935? Isn't the price of freedom eternal vigilance? Don't we need to be eternally vigilant that the apparatus is never put in place that *can* deprive us of our freedom?

"How many times in history has it proved to be disastrously wrong, the adage toted out by generation after generation of police, that 'if you've done nothing wrong, you've got nothing to fear'? Six million Jews had done nothing wrong, nor the *fifteen* million Soviets also murdered by the Nazis, nor the gypsies and socialists and gays, the autistic children and Slavs and prisoners-of-war, nor the untold millions purged by Stalin. Timothy Evans had done nothing wrong, nor Steve Biko, nor Solzhenitsyn or the Romanov children, nor the children of Louis XVI. When in history has an active policeman protested anywhere about a violation of human rights? Or an excessive use of force? When in history has institutional data on the individual been used for that individual's benefit? Even medical records, which you would have thought might be an exception, these days are used by insurance companies as a means to control you."

"You are getting angry, my friend."

"Know what, Rafa? I do get angry. Know what else? Suppression of anger, that is also not healthy. Never before in the history of Man, Rafa, has so much information been covertly kept on the individual. And never before in peacetime history has government been able to act with more secrecy. It is entirely the wrong way round. The individual's privacy needs to be as absolute as the openness and accountability of government.

"Never has there been a time when those with a vested interest in so doing have greater access to information on us – information that we would have every right to deem to be confidential. Our choice of restaurants or literature or sexual partner, the frequency with which we dine out or drive our car or go to the cinema. Our medical records, our tax returns, our credit rating – all are on databases over which we have absolutely no control, and to which access is considerably more difficult for the individual concerned than for the vested interest wanting to access it.

"This bonanza of private information aggravates another central problem of our globe – a virulent, and suicidal, consumerism. If the data had no more sinister an intention than to propagate that, that would already be several bridges too far.

"The use, though, that could be made of it by unscrupulous governments or by bastions of vested interest ... well, it causes shivers to run up and down my spine just thinking about it. What use would Stalin have made of it? Or Nero? Or Amin? What use *is* today being made of it by unscrupulous governments? Or by unscrupulous arms of scrupulous governments?"

"You are *so* angry, my dear friend. Oh, do not misunderstand, I sympathise – even empathise – with your anger. There is very much around which should anger us, all of us."

"But ...?"

"But, Polly, *amiga mía*, there are problems with anger."

"It's not a deadly sin for nothing?"

"Quite. Today," Rafaél continues, "in today's world with all today's problems, anger is almost self-indulgence. See, I see in your face, already you are angry with me. And that is already one problem with anger: It hides our friends. Our friends seem to us our enemies, the help they offer, it becomes a hindrance – and the truth they speak, that becomes a lie. Or, worse, a criticism."

"If someone stamps on your foot," Polly pouts, "it's very hard, Rafa, not to get angry."

"Very hard," Rafaél agrees.

"If the entire population of London files past stamping on your foot, extremely hard not to get angry."

"You cannot unlearn knowledge, Polly."

"Meaning?"

"For as long as there are nuclear weapons, there is a danger of nuclear war. I would love to see the dismantling of every nuclear weapon in the world. I'd *love* to see that. But should for once the nuclear powers all act both honestly and honourably and dismantle these atrocities, that is by no means the end of the threat posed by nuclear weaponry. You will not be able, Polly, to destroy the knowledge behind it. Likewise with computers. The databases that exist on all of us, you will not be able to destroy those either. And we waste energy seeking to do so.

"We would do better to wrench from that knowledge as much power as we can. We need to criminalise the abuse of that knowledge, inflict enormous fines, *hugely* punitive fines, on database companies who sell their information to inappropriate or dangerous clients, the imprisonment of those in authority, including bank CEOs and senior politicians, who access such information to serve their own personal or corporate interest. And if government declines to enact such legislation, well, yet again, we will be left to draw our own conclusions.

"I'm no IT expert. I don't even know what the technology is capable of doing. But it can be checked, its power. Just as you can eventually build nothing that is burglar-proof, so you can devise no system that cannot be checked. If we genuinely value freedom as much as we are told we do (and should – what else is democracy?), then we must start insisting that new laws be drawn up (and internationally) that will severely punish those seeking to hurt us. Laws, I should add, that would be considerably less necessary if there were internationally a set of ethics or morals or principles to inform us.

"Oh, don't misunderstand me, I continue to contend that laws are absurdly inaccurate methods of controlling human conduct. Is akin to trying to explain the 'Mona Lisa' to a blind man. Pass a law about anger, for instance, and there would have to be no difference between the raging tantrum and the fit of tetchiness, because the edges of all the intervening phases would be too blurred. But the principle of not getting angry allows that, even though is not a good idea, sometimes you will do so – but that, because you sometimes do, that does not stop it from being a good idea that you do not.

"As a principle, is sound that you avoid too much cream. What would a birthday be, though, without a squidgy cake? But the essentialness of cakes to birthdays – and of squidginess to cakes – does not dent the soundness of the principle to avoid too much cream."

"I think, Rafa, you would say '*claro*'."

"Governments, of course, will insist that we should trust them. We were supposed to trust the British government about the sanctity of the information it was collating to issue identity cards. That farrago spoke for itself. But was so grotesque, it almost served government interest. The press simply could not afford to ignore it. And their breaking of the story allowed the government to glory in the 'free speech' still available in the country. Curiously, though, that same 'free speech' has been remarkably quiet about the farrago which was the Home Office installing IT equipment desgined to control immigration. Billions of pounds, so I've been told, have been wasted on the project, and years of supreme inefficiency were the result.

"But still governments will insist that we need to trust them. Despite all the massaging of the truth effected by Mr Bush and Mr Blair ... effected these days, in fact, by virtually every political and business so-called 'leader' ... by enormously the majority of national, even local, politicians. The time surely has come to ask them, when we have to ask them, 'How can we trust you?' To ask of all governments internationally, 'Why should we? What shred of evidence can you supply which would lead us to suppose that you have our best interests at heart?'

"It doesn't matter what political colour or complexion the government, government has only ever concerned itself about the needs and trappings of government. And latterly, not less so, but (incredibly!) even more so.

"When industry insists we trust them, we need only ask the same questions. Look at the way governments and industry treat those they employ. Look at the way McDonald's treats its abattoir workers or the British government treats its hospital cleaners or the American government and American industry treated the victims of Hurricane Katrina. These are people within, as it were, an extended family. If they are prepared to treat in that fashion their own nationals, their own employees – even their own clients –, people with whom they have daily traffic, how do you imagine are they prepared to treat those who are totally anonymous to them, statistics (no more) on balance sheets?"

"You were getting pretty angry yourself there, Rafa."

"As you say, if all of London is marching past, stamping on your foot ... Of course I get angry. That does not counter what I said about anger. Why do people complain about the weather in London?"

"Because this, Rafa, is not London weather."

"I find it glorious."

The phenomenon *is* one, entering Hyde Park. Even though through it cars continue their combusted ways, almost as soon as the grass borders the footpath, engines are subsumed by birdsong. Both notice this, though neither comments on it. There is mustiness too in the misty, mellow fruitfulness. The smell of freshly cut grass nuzzles and sizzles in their nostrils.

"Do we have a choice in anger?" Polly continues.

"You remember how many lusts we talked about? A few, I think. If there are a hundred lusts, Polly, there are a thousand angers: from blind rage to mild pique, from anger that is ours to anger that is general, from anger that is inherited to anger that has been adopted, from personal anger to political anger, from anger with God to anger with the dog, from anger which is unjustified to that which is necessary, from that which we can control to that we cannot ... some – to answer your question, Polly – over which we do have choice, and some over which we most certainly do not. And some of these manifestations of anger are indeed sins. They do threaten mankind. And some are not only not sins, but are necessary for Man to survive.

"Let's mayhap begin by agreeing that some anger is sinful. Anger, for instance, that leads to murder. I take it that we would agree that, whether or not he can control it, the psychopath committing a murder is committing a sin. The sociopath likewise."

"Well, yes and no," says Polly.

"Oh?"

"Well, of course, killing's wrong. Who could possibly give you an argument there? But ... well, you said yourself, Rafa, psychiatry's a science in its infancy. 'Psychopath', 'sociopath', they're often very subjective assessments. In both the Soviet Union *and* the affluent West, many have been branded 'mentally sick' who were just non-compliant, or going through a temporary crisis. The abused wife who's finally had enough and snaps, killing her abuser with the carving knife, is that the action of a psychopath? The man deranged by grief at the death of his daughter and who then kills the drunk driver who skidded into her, is that the action of a sociopath?

"No killing is right, of course. Of course, no killing is right. Including that by the state. ..."

"Especially that by the state."

"*Especially*, as you say, Rafa, that by the state. But a deranged murderer is to me considerably more acceptable than the cynical and calculated murder committed by politicians or generals."

"Or bankers."

"Right. I can cope with a crime of passion, of raw anger, Rafa, more easily than I can cope with a crime of political expedience – or economic expedience – or one just born either out of calculation or cynicism. Maybe because I rage myself. Maybe because I therefore recognise that I too could kill in the heat of the moment. I don't think, though, I could commit murder in the dispassionate way that President Bush committed murder, or that Mr Blair did."

"Likewise, Polly. I have tasted such anger. The anger that could kill. I can even taste again its taste. Is a taste which lurks always: a bitter taste, with much salt and a hint of liquorice. Mostly I tasted that in the car. I *had* somehow to check it. I would else have ended up indeed killing someone. Was a habit I found very difficult, and painful, to break. What am I talking about? I am still breaking it.

"When I raged thus I was being sinful. And when I do rage thus I am still sinning. Because, just as I am as a non-smoker, *amiga mía*, so is only *technically* that I'm a non-rager. Such rage *is* a sin, it does threaten mankind. It threatens all those around me when I am in such rages. And is something which I can check. However clumsily, however inadequately, I *can* check it. One of the sins of anger, Polly, is not that we feel it, but how we choose to express it. This is another delightful part of London, my friend. Delightful." Polly acknowledges the comment without feeling the need to comment back. "You talked about spousal abuse, *amiga mía*. There is child abuse too. And not just the completely horrifying cases described in Mr Pelzer's 'A Child Called "It"' nor in Jenny Tomlin's 'Behind Closed Doors'. These are so terrifying that they mask the problems faced by an enormous amount of children, mayhap even the majority – that of being consistently demeaned and undervalued and of never achieving enough. All these emanate from anger. And, of course, create anger. All also wrong, no?"

"Of course, Rafa, they're wrong. How often, though, are these merely the manifestations of other angers?"

"And that, *amiga mía,* is so much of another sin of today allied to anger. That we direct our anger at mistaken targets or inappropriate targets. Anger is innate in all of us. Testosterone, apparently, intensifies that presence. Man, as a gender, is naturally angrier than woman."

"Like, that's news?"

"As you would say, Polly, 'Fair point'," agrees Rafaél.

"And," Polly adds with perhaps a whiff too much of demureness, "with certain notable exceptions."

The park is stippled with sun-bathers anxious to grasp the year's last tanning rays. A portable radio mauls the surrounding still like a lion with a wounded zebra.

"We only have to watch the conduct of other primates, Polly, to see that anger is innate to us: gorillas, for example."

"Yeah, I saw a TV programme saying much the same thing."

"Is not that it's something *man*made, therefore, is something simian. Mayhap it even predates that. Oh, I know the present thinking is that we're not directly descended from primates. But we did plough a parallel furrow. Anger is our pre-human response if we are hurt, if we are threatened, or our territory or food is threatened, if our mates our threatened or our offspring, if there is a threat we may lose our mate to a rival. Instinctive reactions. Probably outside our control. But we *can* control how violently we react to such stimuli.

"The process of birth, the shocks and hurts of early infancy all create anger. I'm not convinced that birth itself, its acknowledged pain and trauma, does not leave a residue of anger. Certainly there is anger involved in early infancy. As babies we see our fathers and siblings as threats to our food supply. As I just said, when we are threatened – and we would certainly perceive a threat to our food supply as a threat to us – we get angry. Is inevitable. And is probably for that reason, more than sexual jealousy, that we want to kill our fathers."

"Or in my case," says Polly, "one of the *many* reasons I wanted to kill my father."

"As your wanting to kill him, my friend, was only one of the many reasons why he wanted to kill you!"

"Yeah, okay, that too is a 'fair point'," Polly concedes.

"What I'm saying, I'm saying we trawl anger from a very early age. And some of it is innate, it stems merely from the process of living. Add to that the completely inevitable rebukes and disappointments of childhood and you've already created a powder keg. Add to that the equally unavoidable slings and arrows of a fortune which is, yes, outrageous; add to it further the (yes, equally unavoidable) stabs and sabre-slashes of an uncle's snide sarcasm or a teacher's put-down or a bus-driver's impatience and you've lit the fuse running to the powder keg. And we're talking here about the children of the prosperous and well-adjusted and sensitive.

"If statistics are to be believed – and that, yes, Polly, is an enormous 'if' (more problems with the war between Truth and Untruth) – then now dysfunction is very much more the norm, certainly in Western families, than whatever it is the opposite of dysfunction: 'function', presumably."

"Presumably."

"I read the figure ninety-two percent."

"Yeah, you said."

"Mayhap, at one level, is one hundred percent of families that are dysfunctional. Very nearly, anyway, one hundred percent. Freud, you know, was intrigued by the tie that usually exists between grandparents and their grandchildren. He came to the conclusion such was courtesy of the fact that they have a common enemy. I think that problem lies at the core of every family. I think is probably a global problem, and a problem which has global impact. And is not dissimilar to what I said earlier about drivers and pedestrians. As parents, Polly, we remember mostly how much we did for our children; and, as children, we remember mostly how *little* our parents did for us. I say this to my shame. Is a crime of which I am myself very much guilty."

"I think it's pretty common, Rafa."

"The cold too, that is called 'common', no? Does that mean we should not seek a cure for it? If, *amiga mía,* if the chaos theory is correct (and evidence would seem to indicate that there is more than a little truth attached to it) and the flapping of a butterfly's wings on the Amazon can cause a tornado in Toronto, then what are the repercussions, my friend, of each of us not dealing with his anger?"

"Or hers?"

"Or, of course, hers? And this, this dichotomy, Polly, between the way we regard our parents and our children, that, my friend, would seem to me a good place that we might start. All of us. We could start recognising how much was done for us by our parents, and how little we did for our children. A great many of the world's ills would be eradicated, a great amount of the world's anger checked, just by such a tiny shift in our thinking."

"Tiny, you think?"

"*Enormous* shift, Polly, in our thinking.

"As we do about so many things, when we talk of anger, we start from a false premise. We start from the premise that we're okay, that it's *them* who have got the problem, that all's okay with *us*. And it isn't. That doesn't mean we're *sinful.* But all of us, at some level, are damaged goods, bruised fruit. If we were really as okay, psychologically and spiritually, as we like to believe, how could we possibly have allowed ourselves to get into the global mess we're in? Just as we infect our institutions with our inadequacies, so do we also infect our children.

"Now, at one level, that may even be desirable. Our flaws and foibles are part of that which hallmarks the individuality of all of us. And anger at that level is a form of self-preservation, and probably an *essential* part of self-preservation. It stops us from becoming the clones of obedience and subservience, which is precisely, I think, that which vested interest is seeking to make of us. Yes, I do know I said that before. There are aspects, in other words, of this 'sin' of anger which are, not only innate, but beneficial to us. The trick is knowing which aspect of anger is helping us all to be the most 'I' we can all be, and which aspects are blockading that process. There are no universal answers, nor universal panaceas for the aspects of anger which are sins. Is an enormously difficult task we should all be facing. And we need help and support from those around us when we do face it. For this too we need to be schooled from our earliest days.

"The 'sin' of much of our anger – or one aspect, anyway, of its sinfulness – derives from our denial of how *un*okay we actually are, most of us: how inadequate most of us feel – at least from time to time; how bereft of power or control; how overwhelmed and insignificant.

"Certainly, a part of any code of ethics, and a part of the *function* of any code of ethics, is to overcome our infantile and our bestial selves, to urge that we mature away from the monomania of our toddlerdom. (You know 'mono' is Spanish for 'monkey'? Is that too, you think, linguistic coincidence?) When we rage we become again our primate selves or our teething selves."

"And as *I* said before, there are a few directors I can think of who should be told that."

"Sadly, of course, such puerility also is ingrained in the work of too many such directors. And such also becomes then part of the dumbing-down process and the desensitising process that we talked of in another context." On a lurid, 'Superman' beach-towel nearby, a young man with serious sideboards is kissing a blonde with an almost prim black skirt and a pink bikini top. "Is also not true, as I used to think when I raged, that such rage is a victimless crime. Being raged at, even witnessing rage that is not directed at you, has a severely detrimental effect.

"Was an experiment, Polly, done on water. This sounds crazy, but please hear me out."

"Strangely enough, I think I have an idea of what you're going to say."

"They divided a pool of water into drops, shouted at some of those drops, said kind words, validating words to others ..."

"Then froze them, right?"

"Right."

"Yeah. I saw it in a film: 'What the Bleep!?', it was called. The scientist was Japanese. Dr ... Emoto, was it? I think so. Something like that. And the drops that were talked to kindly, when frozen, crystallised into these immaculate, lace-like patterns ..."

"And the structure of those shouted at was radically different. Our bodies mostly comprise water – yes, I know, like, that's news too! What I mean is, this experiment, is not just of academic interest, is extremely significant. To all of us. Sadly, I think I have been responsible for making ugly many immaculate, lace-like patterns."

"Sadly too, me too. Like you, Rafa, I don't get angry, I rage."

"Is one of the things about me of which I am deeply ashamed."

"So much for 'sticks and stones ...', hey?"

"Excuse me?"

"You never heard that? It was an ... adage, I suppose ... a whatever when I was growing up: 'Sticks and stones may break my bones, but harsh words never hurt me.'"

"This was considered intelligent?"

"People who got hurt by words were wimps, Rafa, were Caspar Milquetoast."

"Presumably was a whatever, Polly, penned by the same author who believed that children should be seen and not heard."

"And probably the same one too who thought that to spare the rod was to spoil the child."

"Is not only in our times, my friend, in which toxic claptrap has been spoken."

"There's just never been a time when it has been more prevalent, nor when the consequences are likely to be so dire?"

"Quite. Actually, if I had thought about it, my own body could have told me a similar story. To Dr Emoto's experiment, I mean. As a child, when people shouted at me my legs felt like they were running water inside them. Like a tap, you know? Still today, if I think someone is upset with me, I find it hard to hold a pen."

"I don't think that's uncommon either. I don't suffer the same thing, but you're not the only person who's described similar sensations to me."

"There is, and I understand this, now (another clichéd phrase) 'zero tolerance' towards the manifestations of anger. In the underground stations here you see signs warning us, its customers, that its staff have the right not to be abused. As if papering such posters all over the place executes the employers' duty of care.

"I read somewhere that now one in three health workers are assaulted. One in three, Polly, one ...," he articulates slowly, "... in three. This is a totally appalling statistic. And likewise have I seen in hospitals (when I have met Rodolfo at his work) signs saying that patients who abuse hospital staff will not be treated. And I understand that too.

"Of course people need to feel safe at work. Of course they do. But, Polly, the lack of abuse has to work both ways. We also talked about this before. Passive aggression can sometimes be considerably more aggressive than its active cousin.

"The subway system in London is very expensive. In the days when Concorde was flying, mile for mile, it was more expensive to travel by London underground than to fly supersonically. Is also inefficient. Passengers, even in optimum conditions, are kept waiting for long periods. And in a society which (particularly in the workplace) has 'zero tolerance' for unpunctuality, and where the time of certain professionals (lawyers, for example) is hideously dear. Parents are admonished for being late at school to pick up their children, hideously dear appointments are forfeit; in the workplace, employees are severely chastised for tardiness, sometimes even fined. When the trains do finally arrive, they are (because of the delay) often extremely crowded. Is staggeringly uncomfortable for us all. For you women ... well, you must wonder in these situations whether you are being jostled or groped ..."

"Oh, you can tell, Rafa. Trust me."

"In summer, there is no air-conditioning (so there are further signs, advising you to carry water!), and these trains can become furnaces. Is no new development that leaves fall off the trees in autumn. And yet, still in the twenty-first century, trains are delayed by this phenomenon. The service provided by London Transport, as I say, is expensive and inefficient. And their customers have no effective, and easy, means of complaint. Is therefore quite inevitable (however regrettable) that it will be on the visible personification of the management (in other words the station staff) on whom the displeasure will be taken out. And London Transport clearly gives little more attention to the welfare of their staff than distributing a lot of posters.

"If London Transport were truly interested in its employees' welfare, there are four things it could do immediately:

"The first, obviously, is to improve its service. To be fair, it says is trying to do that, and (again as we said in a previous talk) it now faces a myriad of mountains because previous executives did not tackle the problems when they were still molehills.

"The second is to provide their customers with a simple, and palpably effective way of registering their complaint, protest or whatever else ... their dissatisfaction.

"The third would be to train their staff how to diffuse anger. Which is an important skill for us all to learn in this anger-inducing age.

"And the fourth, perhaps the most essential of all, is to stop abusing the staff themselves. Their abuse may not be yelling-at-them abuse, but is certainly often treating-them-as-less-than-human abuse: endless and senseless 'targets', for instance. I say again, passive aggression is often more aggressive than its active counterpart."

"You've reminded me of something there, Rafa: A few years back, during one of the endless disputes that exist between London Transport and its workers, the management flooded its stations again with placards. A bit, Rafa, like the ones you were talking about, 'cept that these explained why the management considered the union's actions to be unjustified. That I saw, it accorded the union no space at all to explain its counter-argument. I remember thinking at the time, 'And you seriously wonder why there are bad relations between the two of you?!'"

"Is just so representative of the way in which all the world's ills, Polly, are treated. Is all, almost all of it, like treating the lesions of AIDS without treating the illness.

"And is not dissimilar in hospitals. As many times I have said to Rodolfo, if you don't work in a hospital, when you visit it, nine times out of ten, you are in one of two states: pain or anxiety (whether for yourself or someone else). Now, of course, a certain amount of professional objectivity is inevitable in the staff. Is probably even quite desirable. But is also a fine line between that and appearing to the anxious person or the person in pain that you don't care. If is the *perception* of the person suffering either pain or anxiety that such is not being taken seriously, then that sufferer will start getting angry ... very angry. That too is quite inevitable.

"And how is that simple truism indicative of a worldwide malaise!

"How much anger is there in the world today because an initial grievance isn't taken seriously? An initial molehill tackled? An initial hurt treated? How much anger is anger that has festered? Because it has not been addressed at the time it was a small grievance? How big a part of the 'sin' of anger is that anger not being taken seriously?

"How do the poor feel that no-one cares about them? The malnourished, the abused, the deliberately under-educated? You think they also don't feel anger?

"Princess Diana, long before her untimely death, was always to me a tragedy more than a paragon. She was undoubtedly manipulative and self-absorbed. But she did touch something in the heart of nearly all of us. And what, I think, she touched amongst so many of the desperate is that finally they thought *someone* cared. Is a measure of contempt that government internationally has for those whom they rule that they have chosen to learn nothing from the lessons bequeathed them by Princess Diana. And for all her manipulativeness and self-absorption, there were things to be learnt from the princess. And are.

"This, yes, – this I have been discussing – this is political anger. And that is both a different anger from personal anger, and yet one and the same. Because we simply shy away from discussing the issue of anger, all its various (and variable) manifestations get melted into the same pot. And because all anger is taboo, the various untreated elements of anger all start feeding off each other, start nurturing and reinforcing one another."

They snake their way to the aptly named Serpentine. Two uniformed nannies have clearly escaped from the nineteenth century and are walking what they would doubtless call their 'perambulators' as if about to wave the gallant troops off to the Crimea. They seem not the slightest fazed by the quizicalness of the overt stares aimed in their direction. They exchange expansive smiles with Polly and Rafaél as they pass one another.

"We are being desensitised," says Rafa. "We are learning to care less. And this has to deepen our anger also. Whilst from the pulpit and from the hustings we are admonished for so doing – for caring less, I mean –, support is being given only to those who are doing the desensitising. Our 'parents' are criticising us for eating too many sweets. Yet we are banished from the dining room whilst those parents lay on banquets for sweet manufacturers, sweet wholesalers, fizzy-drinks makers, those who design the wrappers for the sweets ... ad infinitum. Ad nauseam.

"A friend of mine, with her boyfriend, was in the back of a taxi. A car went into the side of it, at the back, just where the couple was sitting. They were both hurt. Not life-threateningly, but quite severely. Her whiplash took her months to recover from, his cheekbone was broken. It was this boyfriend who phoned for the ambulance. Whilst the cabby and the other driver fixated on the damage to their *vehicles*. I don't think that situation any longer is unusual."

"Even, Rafa, at an instinctive level. Was the time, they tell me, that a woman, even before she *knew* she was pregnant, if she fell down the stairs would instinctively protect, not her head (as all humans normally do), but her womb. That is no longer the case. We have so warped instinct, Rafa, that such is no longer the case. I'm being a bit careful about this because so often urban myths are cited as evidence. And, to be quite honest, I can't remember now where I heard that. But it must have had the ring to it of authenticity or I'd by now have forgotten it."

"Is why is so important, *amiga mía*, why is the truth which starts winning the war between the Truth and the Untruth. We are being forced to decide debates on evidence which is flawed or insufficient or tainted. Is not my fault, not any longer, that I don't *know* that what I have read about IBM or Coca-Cola or McDonald's is true. Or about the high street banks or ITT or Ford's ... or ... or ... or. Is virtually impossible these days to be certain of anything. But that is a situation which has been created far more by 'vested interest' than by those seeking to expose it. And thus, if occasionally such business gets blamed for events or situations which are not their fault, it is nevertheless themselves whom they need to blame. It is the biter bit. 'Those who live by the sword ...'

"Those, Polly, who propagate the lie cannot be indignant if they themselves become victims of the lie.

"We also have to reverse a situation where Truth is a commodity that can be bought. In civil cases, for instance, both sides should only be allowed to pay the same amount for legal costs."

"Great idea, Rafa. You think the lawyers would agree?"

He laughs. "I think we might have a small fight on our hands," he agrees. "Let's get back, though, to your pregnant women."

They move past the restaurant and cafeteria which look likes the remains of a giant Rubik's cube hurled against a concrete well in vexation, and which adheres to the Serpentine's bank like fingers of quartz plucking at a liquid guitar.

On the lake itself floats a regatta of ineptitude that had been re-enacted for centuries – there the traditional family: daddy puffing in his shirt-sleeves, wallowing in the machismo of being the conveyor, mummy and daughter seeking acceptance of being conveyed, son desperate to assume the conveying mantle; and there the young buck trying to impress his first-time date, a gazelle-like young woman – big-eyed and anxious – and whose streaked hair had been cut like a Dauphin's. He feathers his blades, as if auditioning for the Oxford crew, rows efficiently, energetically – and is concentrating far too much on that and far too little on her. And there ... there is the aquatic farce, the latterday 'Three Men in a Boat' repeated in twenty-first century clobber, other than the boat contains four men, all of them already reeking of the pomposity that will assail their grand-children, all avowing an expertise in seamanship – or, at least, tiny-lakemanship – to which they are manifestly not entitled.

"If is true, the situation you describe of non-maternal mothers, that just has to increase the baby's natural sense of defencelessness and thus anger. And this just has to follow him into adulthood, and has therefore to affect his entire environment.

"As with lust, my friend, I fear one of the biggest sins attached to anger is in designating anger a 'sin', something which we just should not possess. By so designating it, we don't address the problems of it. Is a bit like saying: Sex is wrong. You got AIDS from sex. Therefore not only are we not treating AIDS, we're not even going to acknowledge it exists."

"Sounds like President Mbeki."

"Sadly, it does," Rafa agrees. "Anger is not wrong," he continues. "Anger is an entirely natural reaction to danger, or perceived danger. Anger is certainly wrong when it manifests itself in either violence or in rage. But to stop that manifestation for many of us requires skill and application. We should be teaching that skill.

"Because the other danger with anger (is it another semantic coincidence that danger is only anger with a 'd' at the front?) is that it *doesn't* develop into rage. That is allowed to fester. And to bubble away like a pressure cooker. You talked about suppressing anger, Polly. And, as you are so often, you are right.

"Of which there are a further two dangerous consequences: You get sick, that's one of them. I have read Dr Siegel's book, Polly, since you talked of him: Dr Siegel, the cancer specialist. He believes that the illness is frequently induced by suppressed anger, suppressed rage. Those like us, Polly, who do rage may detrimentally affect the health of others around us, but we're probably acting healthily towards ourselves."

"Apart from the strain on the heart."

"Even that too is probably less than would be the cardiac strain of unreleased tension. I should ask Rodolfo. But he tends to pooh-pooh all such suggestions. The war between the Truth and the Untruth is not exclusively one fought by politicians, Polly, and by industry.

"The other consequence is that, like any cartoon pressure cooker, suppressed rage explodes. Sometimes in a volcano-like way. Much comedy, I think, emanates from such explosions. But sometimes, Polly, it manifests itself in tragic ways, in ways too tragic even to contemplate: like the massacres at Dunblane or Columbine.

"As I said a moment ago, and as a matter of some urgency – I think this can be said without too much controversy – we need to teach ourselves and our children how to release whatever anger is inside us without such adversely affecting those around us."

A string of well-groomed horses, a little way in the distance, trot their clomping way to the start of Rotten Row. It's all very formal riding, mostly for children: tweed jackets and jodhpurs. Polly, in her American youth, had also ridden. Quite a bit, surprisingly. But her riding was T-shirts and jeans. She is suddenly spluttering within the white-water of memories not often remembered.

"There is another sinful aspect too to anger ... to anger today. And that is that we create vast swathes, Polly, of *unnecessary* anger. Everywhere we turn, Polly, in every avenue of life, we are creating more anger. We are in fact creating each and every day vicious circles of anger ... vicious circles of an ever more vicious anger ... vicious circles of viciousness.

"The child naturally is born angry for all the reasons we've talked about. We're now finding new ways not to reduce anger (which you might think was sensible) but to increase it.

"Bernard Shaw famously opined that youth is wasted on the young ..."

"And Bette Davis, equally wittily, insisted that growing old was not for children."

"And how right, Polly, they both were. But the wit hides the most salient fact: That children do not know what it means to be young. They know they are young, but they don't understand what that means. To quote again a dear friend of mine: We do not know what we do not know. Children, *amiga mía,* least of all. One thing that requires learning is the comprehension of alternatives.

"I doubt there is a parent in the world who hasn't threatened a child refusing to eat that he'll send the uneaten food to children who really need it. (And we *should* send our uneaten food to the famished, but that is not the issue we are currently addressing.) It's a ruse which didn't work on us as children, and yet we perpetuate it. It's not that children are cruel. There is often a certain callousness to them – the, excuse me, Polly, callousness of callowness – but such callousness emanates usually from ignorance rather than vindictiveness. This ruse rarely works with children because they cannot conceive of the idea. They can imagine that there are children whose reality is worse than theirs, but that imagination lacks conviction. It's part of the central monomania of infancy. *If* there is original sin in us, it manifests itself in such monomania.

"Do latchkey children understand they're happier thus than they would be if the absent parent were not working? How much anger is developed by being solitary? And nurtured by being lonely? How much by the fact that their parents are too tired to nurture them?

"A large source today of photographers' income – those who used to do wedding photographs and the like – derives from escorting families on days out. Their task? To provide photographic evidence of a 'happy' childhood. Is so Orwellian, the concept, I shudder to think of it: Do not worry about the reality. Create an illusion in the hope that such will be *perceived* as reality.

"I hear tell that Mr Blair once announced his intention to change a 'yob society into a *job* society.' There is so much to say about that epithet, the pith of that epithet, that we could walk through all of London's parks, Polly, before we reached the end of it. We'll avoid obvious remarks ... pots calling igloos black and the like ... does his phrase also embrace the 'yobs' of industry? Many of them sponsoring his political party? And who are inflicting untold misery on Mr Blair's compatriates? ... No, we will avoid such obvious detours and concentrate just on his remark."

"We wouldn't want to get ourselves side-tracked, Rafa! Perish even the thought!"

"This is simply sound-byte politics. This is trying to score cheap points at the expense of genuinely tackling problems. And this is also oratory that is so crass and so pandering that it has to exacerbate the problem it claims to be tackling.

"Did Mr Blair seriously imagine that these vandals minded his censure? They *bask* in such censure. They *welcome* such abuse. It merely serves to underscore their sense of isolation and of anger. It underscores it and *justifies* it.

"Oh God, Polly, I'm not trying to say that if you called all these young people 'young gentlemen' they'd all turn into so many Mr D'Arcys. But if you treat people with contempt (at any level, but particularly publicly), then in a very short space of time they will start returning that contempt. And for evidence of that, most of us (if we were honest) need look no further than at how we ourselves respond to contempt.

"Certainly children and young people have to learn barriers, boundaries. Of course they do. One of the most vital aspects of his education is that the child should learn the parameters within which he can operate – in the family, at school, with his friends, in the world at large. And the more clearly those parameters are defined, (on the whole) the happier and 'safer' the child feels. And, at some kind of instinctive level, if the parameters are defined by those who love him, the child intuits that they are being defined for his benefit. Smacking the wrist of a toddler investigating electrical sockets with gooey fingers is not abusing the child. He may not like the slap, but he is (as I say, at some level) aware that this pain is somehow for his benefit.

"Feeling safe here is the key. Too often we use children, even babies, as the outlets for our anger. How much further anger must that create in the child?

"Of course children overstep parameters. We even want them to. We don't want to create a world of yes-men and those complicit. The world has been changed (and for the better) far more by rebels than by the acquiescent."

"I've often thought," says Polly, "the real rebel in 'The Simpsons' is not Bart, but Lisa."

"As you say, Polly."

"You haven't got the first idea, have you, what I'm talking about?"

"Not the first idea, my friend. I can go on?"

"Please," says Polly.

"As with any discipline, you have to know what the rules are in order effectively to break them. I firmly believe that we fail in our duty of care to children if we do not establish those 'laws', those parameters clearly and consistently, nor when we do not let children know – clearly and consistently – when those parameters have been breached. But to be consistent, you yourself need to be without anger.

"Before leaping to designating our young people 'yobs' – those who *frequently* breach the parameters and those who overstep the mark by a long way – before insisting such be birched or subjected to a 'short, sharp shock', let us look at what is wrong with *us*, with how we have failed them.

"Have such 'yobs' been crying for help and we have not heard them? Can we now respond to such a cry? What domestic problems are these transgressions veiling? What part is being played in this delinquency by abuse at home? Or simply a lack of love at home? By addiction? Bullying at school? Inadequate nourishment? An excess of junk food? A lack of social facilities? A lack of adequate schooling? An entire absence of adequate education? Lack of appropriate role models? Inappropriate heroes? Junk television? A lack of hope? A lack of self-respect? And on and on and on.

"I read a book once. ..."

"Excuse me, Rafa. You did *what*?"

"I read a ... Oh, I see. You jest with me. Yes, most humorous, Polly, most droll. Not a well-known book, I fear. It was gathering dust at Rodolfo's. 'A Boy In The Gulag', it was called. Was, put crudely, a sort of '... Ivan Denisovich'. By which I do not mean to denigrate it, quite the contrary. Any such horror story is one which we would all do well to read and from which we would all do well to learn.

"At one stage the autobiographer, he talks about the prison's lowest rung of society, those barely now able to survive. '*Dokhodyagi*', they were called. They comprised prisoners who, for one reason or another (usually sickness), had failed one day to accomplish their given workload. So their anyway miserable rations were cut in half. But they were still expected to do the same amount of work. Which they now even more clearly could not accomplish. So their rations were cut still further. Eventually the *dokhodyagi* would die – usually of malnutrition or exhaustion, but of course some were also so emaciated that they lacked immunity to fight any virus that came along. Almost all of them also went mad.

"Now, whilst I was tutting about this situation, thinking to myself 'how awful', another thought also came into my head. How often in our enlightened, affluent ... in our 'developed' West do we apply the same solutions to our problems? Isn't the way, for instance, that we punish our 'yobs' using exactly the same principle as the gulags used for their *dokhodyagi*, merely transferring bread to love?"

"You know, right, 'bread' is a synonym for 'money'?"

"No, I did not know this."

"Also Cockney rhyming slang, matter of fact: 'bread and honey'. Do excuse me, Rafa. Please go on."

"That there are others who are reared in the most appalling of circumstances and yet who do not fall foul of the law is absolutely no reason to believe that therefore those who transgress are entirely, and single-handedly, responsible for their transgression. Is not everyone who has unprotected sex who gets AIDS. Because there were those who survived Auschwitz does not mean that the prisoners' diet was sufficient. We do not know the pain someone else is feeling. It is, we think, *easier* if we do not know the agglomeration of all these problems, and mayhap is in that way too that *sloth* becomes a deadly sin.

"And mayhap too the most serious of such problems is that, by the time these young people come to the attention of the police, they are already in so much pain that the pain is now too deep to be treatable.

"Is extremely rarely such pain responds well to concepts like a 'short, sharp shock'. That is a solution, not for them, not even for us, simply for the politicians. It doesn't work. Think about it, Polly. If prison in general worked, why would we be building more of them? If they don't work for adults, why on Earth do we think they would work for young people?

"One of the reasons why today anger is so prevalent, and growing, is that for generations we've been asking it to respond to short, sharp shock-like treatments. Which, rather than mollifying the problem – or the anger –, has only exacerbated it.

"Sometimes, I concede, there is no choice to prison. And the whole subject of penology, that too we could walk around every park in London to discuss (and also has much to do with anger). But that mayhap is not pertinent to a general discussion. That is the Albert Memorial, no?"

"That is the Albert Memorial, yes."

"Built by Queen Victoria in remembrance of her husband?"

"Correct."

"And the Albert Hall, that is the building opposite?"

"It is."

"Concert Hall?"

"All-sorts Hall. Concerts, yes. Tennis matches. All sorts."

"Also built by Queen Victoria in remembrance?"

"I have no idea."

"You think so?"

"I doubt it. I suspect it was named the Albert Hall only because it was built opposite the Albert Memorial. I suspect too its constructors thought there was some cachet to be derived from the name. Thus more profit. Something, let me tell you, of which the royal consort would have mightily approved. It's not new, the idea that profit is unequivocally good. Nor that it is not in the nature of the world that it should be divided into 'haves' and 'have-nots'."

"Is it not true that Albert discovered his eldest son, whilst at university, was enjoying an affair with an actress?"

"So I understand."

"The son was in his twenties?"

"Yes."

"Albert travelled all the way to Cambridge to reprimand him?"

"In the middle of winter."

"He caught a chill. Which developed into pneumonia. From which he died?"

"I think the advice today is that, before he left for Cambridge, he was already infected by the virus that killed him."

"Nevertheless the Queen believed it was as a consequence of the chill, which was a consequence of his journey?"

"Which was a consequence of her son's affair, yes."

"And she never forgave her son?"

"True."

"And these people were considered paragons of parenthood?"

"Albert, you know, is a pretty maligned figure in history. I say 'pretty' maligned because presumably it was largely his tutelage which led to the conduct of the tsars and the kaisers who were to cost so many millions of lives. But I do think that he himself did want to see a better life for everyone – at least of those countries in Europe over which he held sway.

"Did he care about the Indian untouchables or the Zulus in South Africa? Well, certainly not that I've heard. But I believe he wanted the worker's lot in Britain improved, and that in Saxe-Coburg – probably in Hanover as well."

"Albert, see," she continues, "was ... well, a bit like Melbourne, Victoria's first prime minister. Melbourne, so they claim, was never really happy in politics. He'd far rather have been running his vast estates. He felt politics was a duty, that was all. It's simply not true that these men (as it was exclusively in those days) were monsters or oligarchs who entered politics to protect their privilege. They were human, these men, fallible because they were human, full too of the curd of human parochialism and narrow self-interest, but not ogres. They believed in the status quo, of course they did, but I think their belief was sincere that the status quo was the system most likely to benefit the whole of humanity, as they then defined humanity.

"It's actually more pernicious, more insidious than if they *had* been bad men or evil men. And the legacy of their we-know-what's-bestness still pervades. We still allow it to pervade. Oh, today we, of course, have 'democracy' so it pervades more covertly today. But its covertness does not diminish its pervasion. The drunk now hides his tipple in his coffee; but the same amount of brandy still gets drunk. Even conceptually we don't make decisions: we vote rather for those whom we would most like to make our decisions for us. This was very much the patricians' position in ancient Rome, and is yet another instance of how the lauding of that unhappy state has infected the entire of our history for ill. And has cost, Rafa, literally millions of lives.

"I entirely agree," returns the Peruvian. He is tempted to remind her (inaccurately!) that it was he who had first criticised Rome, but he decides, on this occasion, his own counsel is the one to keep.

"Sir Thomas ... Bertrand, was it? ... the owner of Jane Austen's

Mansfield Park, ... no, not Bertrand ... no matter, Sir Thomas never seeks to justify his use of slaves in the West Indies. But he does insist that without 'order' (presumably as defined by Sir Thomas) there is merely chaos. The Duke of Wellington believed the same thing and became therefore a major force for reaction. And that in a world which was demanding reform, radical reform.

"Just as we are. And just as we need to. We think today's status quo is the devil we know and therefore to be preferred to the devil we don't. But today's devil is not the devil we know. That's just another lie. It doesn't represent the order which is the opposite of chaos, but the order which is creating chaos. Today's devil is an entirely new species of devil. Oh, he's blemished, that devil, with many of history's stains, and ridden with much of history's pox, but his satanism is of an entirely different shape – and scale. And he's being allowed to grow ever larger, because he is being hidden by Untruth behind the screen of Untruth's own construction. Yet another reason, Rafa, why it's so important that the Untruth starts to be exposed.

"A known devil may be more desirable than an unknown one. But there are angels also in the firmament. Why are we buying into the lie that the choice is between one devil and another? The choice is more likely to be between the fiend we now nourish and the host of angels there are out there flapping their wings, just frantic to be seized – and to dominate the world.

"Almost as great a tragedy as that we have lauded Rome is that we continue to do so. That we continue not to learn from that mistake. Even Republican Rome was in fact *oligarchical* Rome. Just as, I so fear, that which was once the republic of the U.S. is becoming oligarchical America. Sadly, it is already plutocratic America."

"And Albert?" asks Rafa. "We were, I think, talking of Albert."

"Albert wanted the working class to avoid drink because he saw the misery that drink caused them. He wanted them not to gamble for the same reason. And he's perceived therefore as a Calvinist killjoy. And there was that about him too. But I don't think that was the essence of him. Oh, I think he believed in ... let's call it 'decorum'. But

I think he believed in it because he believed decorum eventually leads to a happier and more fulfilled life. Or, rather, perhaps, its inversion: That their absence caused so much unhappiness that happiness had to be negated. And, know what? He could have had a point.

"It smacked, though – and here's the rub – with the same kind of sanctimonious patronising as those who suggest that the way to defeat the AIDS pandemic in Africa is for Africans to abstain from sex.

"If your only joy is sex – or, in the case of the Victorian working class, drinking or gambling – all that you hear when someone suggests you renounce such activities is that someone is trying to snatch away from you the last crumbs available to you of happiness in your crumby, unhappy life."

"Could that be another reason, Polly, why today we stand at the rim of an abyss?" asks Rafa "Because we choose our paragons so unwisely?"

"He did also, Albert, also introduce Christmas trees to Britain."

"Well, why did you not say, *amiga mía*? That, of course, forgives all."

"Our paragons today are chosen for us."

"They have always been chosen for us."

"Perhaps not quite so flagrantly."

"That is a sin."

"The vacuous, mostly, today's paragons, Rafa. The crass."

"They have to be crass. Methos doesn't want to lionise anyone who might threaten it. Methos is not going to make celebrities or stars out of dangerous people. President Mandela slipped through their net. Mostly today, the today of methos, it wants its paragons to be compliant and thus malleable: the less substantial they are, the more compliant they are likely to be. You think is an accident that today's politicians are as inadequate as they are?"

"That's not an angry comment?"

"Of course it is. I've said it before: I get angry. I try not to, but I do not succeed. I also try to drive as a pedestrian and do not succeed. Is such an enormous problem, anger. We have in our discussion as yet merely scratched the surface of anger at work, on the roads, anger with life, politics, economics – with all those forces you are told over and over again are on your side and yet, in practise, seem to exist only to fight you or frustrate you or debase you or hurt you.

"Environmentally, for instance, we are being crammed ever more into smaller and smaller spaces. Every psychological experiment (probably ever) has told us that overcrowding breeds aggression. Our own experiences – travelling, for instance, in rush-hour trains, or being jostled coming out of football matches – simply has to confirm that. There is, as I have said before, no point in having knowledge unless we apply it.

"We are never *quiet* these days. Is another cause of anger, another way chronic anger is manufactured. Tube trains are noisy places anyway, with the rattle as they move and the loud conversations. Now there are announcements on the train, on the platform (never in synch!), voices tell you in tunnels that you are stuck in a tunnel, on platforms that the Cockfosters train (or whatever) is delayed due to signal failure. Now this is no bad thing, not of itself. Is a mark of respect to explain to customers where they are, why an expected service is faulty. But soon the announcements start to constitute a barrage of noise. Compounded if you are close to someone whose personal music-player is tchching at you its metallic percussion. How soon before some marketing genius decides to pipe commercials through the PA systems? Interspersed with 'soothing' muzak? As they do, for instance, in supermarkets. How soon before department stores follow suit? Oh, we're oblivious, nine times out of ten, to the barrage. But the smoker too is oblivious of the harm he's doing his lungs. That we don't notice harm being done is no indicator that harm is *not* being done.

"We are *bombarded* by noise in cities today. Motorcycles roar, pneumatic drills throb, radios blare through open car windows, traffic gets impacted to create a permanent tidal drone of noise;

people now talk ubiquitously on mobile-phones, computer games bleep incessantly, telephones ring, and people chat more loudly to be heard above the surrounding cacophony.

"And a by-product of that is that it stops us thinking. You cannot think when you are being deafened. Indeed playing loud music to prisoners is recognised as a form of torture. Is designed to disorientate those bombarded with it. Clearly the noise is not (yet!) at the level of torture. But is equally clear that aurally we today virtually never have still. This is not only not conducive to thought, is also conducive of anger.

"And being frustrated in a desire to think, to cogitate, to figure things out, just how much anger is contained too in *that* frustration?

"How often today do we breathe in fresh air? There is a huge campaign – as we both know, Polly – against smoking. What about the pollution, though, from car emissions? What about the ubiquitous chemical 'air-fresheners'? Is another bombardment, my friend: this of chemical smells – whether pleasant or foul, often in cities synthetic. Most, I imagine, toxic. How often do we smell, as we are now, freshly- mown grass, for instance?

"Our space and our air, both causing us to get angry. Our diet? Yes, that too. Particularly what most of our schoolchildren are fed: an excess of junk food creates anger and diminishes concentration. So teachers get frustrated at pupils who get frustrated with themselves, and (of course) with their teachers. We're back, my friend, to the vicious circle of the *dokhodyagi*.

"How do we deal with that situation? I have absolutely no idea. But because we don't know the answers does not absolve us from identifying the problem.

"I hear American politicians – and some British ones – railing against the inadequacy of today's parents. As if those parents have decided, yes, we're going to be inadequate parents. As if there is no-one else responsible for that situation but themselves. There are inadequate parents. Of course there are. To a very real extent, as I've said before, all of us parents are inadequate as parents. Many of those parents woefully inadequate were themselves parented by inadequately parented parents. And so on, probably since the beginning of Man.

"And, like anger (of which, of course, this is yet only another manifestation), rather than bewailing the fact that there are inadequate parents, rather than admonishing them for their inadequacy – in way too many cases, akin to railing against those with freckles for burning in the sun – we should be looking at ways of addressing the problem.

"Often the inadequacy of our forebears' parenting manifested itself in not being there for their children. How much better would the world today be faring if the phrase: 'I wanted my children to have what I never had' had been taken to be, not iPods and PlayStations, but love and time. (Not that there's anything wrong '*per se*' with iPods or PlayStations. But they cannot substitute for love and time.) There is sometimes nothing less ethical than the work ethic. Because very soon such ethic becomes the *over*work ethic. Mayhap we'll return to this as well when we talk of sloth.

"When such politicians rail I wonder which planet they inhabit. An English journalist, Polly Toynbee, spent some months in London working at minimum wage jobs. Her book, 'Hard Work: Life in Low-paid Britain', should be read by those politicians. It conveys the fundamental cheerlessness of all such people's everyday activities, from getting up to going to bed: how your convenience is not the slightest blip on anyone's radar screen, how invisible you are, how your screams of pain and frustration are allowed simply to melt into the ethos until they are silent. One of Chesterton's 'Father Brown' mysteries was predicated on the fact that the postman did not get noticed going in or out of the building. How much anger do postmen feel that they are not noticed? Or porters in hospitals? Or ticket-collectors at stations? Or … or … or …

"What, I felt, Ms Toynbee's book did not convey (mayhap because no book *could* convey it) was the accompanying senses of desperation and hopelessness – a life stretching ahead of such people of being invisible and unheard and totally at the mercy of government whim, industrial fashion or economic caprice. Whence do such politicians think such parents can dredge up the energy to devote time to their children? As ever, we are conned into concentrating on the wrong issue.

"What we should be doing is saluting those parents who do manage to find such energy. These parents are heroes. And we hear nothing about them. Small wonder, then, that the apparently law-abiding, the famous 'silent majority' is becoming more disgruntled almost daily. Is of such heroes that the silent majority is constituted. We hear nothing about them because politicians and self-proclaimed moralists are more interested in their own ambitions, and in using society's problems as tools of their ambition, than they are in addressing those problems. Their ambition is better served by the continuation of such problems than their solution. In today's world for any parent to bring up children so that they become even moderately well adjusted is a triumph on a considerably greater scale than those at Tewkesbury or Marathon or Gettysburg.

"What anger is doing to the world is *incredibly* toxic and devastating to an incalculable degree: from child battery to the Twin Towers, from graffiti to globalisation. But one of the most efficient tools in our chest is one we almost never use: saluting the quiet achievers. Not the Olympic gold medallists, not the Oscar winners, but the quite enormous achievement of living a more or less decent life, bringing up children to live decently. If ninety-two percent – or even *eighty*-two percent or seventy-seven percent – of families are dysfunctional, to say of someone on their death-bed he or she lived as decently as they could is to acknowledge a major achievement. As they could and as they were allowed to.

"'As they were allowed to', what a key phrase, Polly. Is very hard today to think of a job the pursuit of which does not compromise ethics. (Unless you have no ethics, of course. In which case the world today is your career oyster: plenty of jobs available for conmen, thieves, usurers – and torturers!) There is no country which immediately comes to my mind whose conduct in a civilised world would not cause the rest of the world to boycott its products. (I'm sure there is one. But none immediately comes to mind.) We don't consider this an indictment of today's ethos? We don't think this situation has to lead to anger? *Has*, Polly, to lead to anger?

"If we stifle a part of us, we cannot (by definition) be the most 'we' we can be. And of not any part of us is that more true than of our conscience. If globalisation is indeed so good for us, why is it that its proponents are so economical with the truth about it? Why, we need to ask him, is Sir Bonio advocating the subjugation and torture of people in Chile and Argentina? The further impoverishment of those in Bolivia and Sri Lanka? Does he not recognise that the syndrome is, as Ms Klein points out, exactly the same whether imposed on the natives of Poland or Paraguay, Russia or Rwanda, East Asia or South Africa? Why is all this repression and cruelty still being camouflaged as 'help'?

"And how is it possible that this situation, and these situations, do not make us angry?

"When funds raised by charities are diverted to schemers further to enrich the already überwealthy and further to impoverish those for whom the charity was started, how do we *not* get angry?

"And yet we must. We must not, I mean, get angry. Well, we will get angry. Of course we will. And must. Anger eventually is necessary to right injustice. But anger quickly turns to rage. And rage is always counter-productive. Rage was probably the single biggest factor in creating what was very quickly the nightmare of the Russian Revolution – or the Iranian Revolution.

"I no longer watch the news. I find myself raging at the lies and the liars. I know I am not hearing all the news. Without all the news, I am better informed hearing none of it. Is better, I feel, to be uninformed than *dis*informed. (Is also indicative that the word 'disinformed' is not recognised by Microsoft's Spell Check. Why is that, we should wonder. Does Microsoft not care for the idea of disinformation? A word which, curiously, *is* recognised by it!) Is perfectly acceptable to say, 'We believe that Man began with Adam in the Garden of Eden. There is, however, another school of thought which believes Man emerged from the sea and evolved over billions of years via a primate stage to being what he is today.' Is, however, *not* acceptable to say, as so many news programmes do – and so many religions, 'Man began with Adam. Those who tell you differently are lying.'

"We must start seeing those things we manufacture which enrage us as yet other forms of pollution. Noise pollution is recognised up to a point. Though little is being done to correct it. Overcrowding, smell pollution, the vicious circles of anger, anger *pollution*, these are all problems that need to be addressed."

"There are now shows on tv," says Polly, "whose purpose is to incite anger, to propagate violence. I've mentioned them before. Daytime, quotes, 'talk' shows, those travesties I talked about of the genre Oprah Winfrey tried to create. Those hosted by 'Mr' Springer and his ilk. I feel desperately sorry for Ms Winfrey that her name should in any way be associated with these malignities. Talk about anger pollution, Rafa. This is anger pollution which is radio-active. It's also truth pollution. Because most of these shows which pretend to be spontaneous are actually as contrived and rehearsed as wrestling bouts.

"And they lead to violence because they are choreographed to lead to violence. And they want the violence, the show's producers, presumably their advertisers. The credit sequences of such shows feature the violence. And that, of course, is an indication to the audience that violence is an appropriate means of tackling differences. As if there weren't enough violence anyway in the world."

"And enough anger! Anger so *often* does lead to violence, my friend. Of course it does. The TV you describe is appalling. We should be learning how to control, still and release sensibly the anger within us. We need desperately to be encouraged not to rage. We need to help each other in this new skill. And support each other. And, rather than endless cookery programmes or gardening programmes, there needs to be programmes telling us how to acquire these skills, and how to nurture their development both in ourselves and in those around us.

"Violence, my dear Polly, that is such a large part of the reason why today we are where we are. President Mandela and his companions," the Peruvian continues, "saved South Africa from untold bloodshed. How? Because within their revolution they controlled their anger. And because, my friend, they insisted that both their anger and that of their supporters (righteous though it undoubtedly was) be controlled."

"Shame, really, that his successor President Mbeki (before even he was president) should have used that goodwill so totally to have sold his people down the river."

"Still you are angry, Polly. And, yes, right to be angry: President Mbeki in selling his country off sold his country out; in denying AIDS, Mr Mbeki propagated AIDS – so, certainly, right to be angry. Nevertheless anger will not help.

"If you are serious, if *we* are (as we have to be), about saving this planet, then we must rid ourselves of the anger we feel – however justified, however much is a spontaneous reaction."

"You'd agree, that's a lot easier said than done?"

"And yet," says Rafaél, "it must be both said *and* done. The Buddhists would have you believe that he who angers you conquers you. Many psychiatrists will tell you that he who angers you is being given a compliment by you. And both are right. But neither one is enough to define anger a sin. What *is* sinful about it, *another* sinful thing about anger, is that it distorts. It also diverts. And we can afford neither of those two luxuries."

Paris is a capital of boulevards. Berlin is that of thoroughfares and Bogotá of lanes. London is a capital, on the one hand, of alleys and, on the other, concourses. Exhibition Road, though, down which they are presently walking, is that rare phenomenon: a London boulevard. It's a bold sweep of a road – a Miró brush-stroke, not one of Constable's – and which is not as tree-lined as it suggests it should be.

It runs from the exhaust-pipey haze of the Cromwell Road, one of the town's main arteries, to the amazingly idyllic, albeit rumbling peace of Hyde Park. At its South Kensington base stands a trio of internationally significant museums: the Science, the Natural History and the Victoria and Albert.

"I fear for the poor's anger, Polly. I fear greatly for it." There is a deep sadness suddenly apparent in Rafaél's eyes. The chocolate of their brown is suddenly encrusted with an unpleasant chilli, snide rather than spicy, of pique more than piquancy. "However much I may disown violence, I do understand it. How much cruelty do the tyrants today believe they can unloose on the poor before those poor start to resort to reciprocating the violence meted out to them? How is depriving someone of their livelihood not an act of violence? How is overcharging the poor for their water not an act of violence? Selling the poor contaminated goods, how is that not an act of violence?

"There used to be a slogan in your country, Polly, during the Cold War. 'Better Dead,' it went, 'Than Red.' Your citizens were (and probably are) prepared to die in order to protect their culture. Wasn't that also a factor in your Civil War? Do they seriously imagine, your compatriates, that they are the only ones? How soon before there are similar banners proclaiming: 'Better Dead Than *In* The Red'? 'Better Dead Than The Bread-line'? 'Better a Death of Honour Than a Life of Dishonour'?"

"By its own admission," Polly chips in, "the Los Angeles Police Department could not cope with an insurrection if the city's gangs unified and fought them. I do hear what you're saying, Rafa. How long before those gangs realise that? How long before they realise that they don't hate each other, the Sharks and the Jets? That such is an artificial war? That, like grandparents and their grandchildren, they have a common enemy: in this case, the East side? An East side protected by Sergeant Krupke and his colleagues?"

"We talked previously about the ghettoes there are in Lima and Los Angeles of the very wealthy. ..."

"Oh, and here, Rafa."

"Now, I think, throughout the world. We spoke how they were gilded prisons. Well, as they learnt in South Africa, there is another disadvantage too to such fortresses: It makes the prosecution of a guerrilla war logistically so much easier. Anyone inside those ghettoes is your enemy. Certainly (and mayhap regrettably) you may kill a few innocents – servants, for instance, the odd delivery man. These, though, become the 'regrettable but inevitable' casualties of any war. Allow anger to fester for long enough and violence becomes as inevitable as such casualties become 'acceptable'. Allow anger to fester and the question starts getting posed, 'Why should I worry about killing someone who's trying to kill me?'"

"You know who Eldridge Cleaver is?"

"*Claro*. Was a Black Panther, no? Very active in the early 70s?"

"Mr Cleaver said, 'The hardest enemy to fight is the dead man. If the fear of death is not there, the most powerful weapon in your arsenal has been confiscated.' That's not an exact quote. But that was its gist. Doesn't the advent of the suicide bomber just underline his words? Prove them in a horrifyingly chickens-coming-home-to-roost sort-of way? It's not just dead men, Rafa, with nothing to lose. It's that I'm saying."

"And is what I'm saying as well, *amiga mía*. Those who believe that their security guards, their private armies will protect them forget one thing: mercenaries are mercenary. Emotionally and instinctively those 'soldiers' will have much more in common with those attacking such ghettoes than those fighting last ditch stands within them. If such troops are prepared to kill their own kind, just think (if, as they say, they get 'a better offer') with how much more readiness will they be prepared to kill those whose life-style they can only drool over.

"Let us even suppose, however, that such troops *do* remain loyal, would those employers believe that loyalty? Why should they? Business ethics today have taught them not to believe *anyone,* that all that motivates anyone is money. Would the ghetto-dwellers not spend a great deal of their time looking over their shoulders, wondering whether their security guards will turn on them? Wondering *when*? Is this seriously considered to be a life?

"The much vaunted 'War on Terror' should more accurately be called the 'War of Terrifying' – of government (oh, internationally) terrifying their citizens into a submission of their rights and aspirations; of industry terrifying their clients into buying, not only unnecessary (and often shoddy) goods, but also – much more sinisterly – buying into their even more shoddy ethics.

"Ms Klein demonstrates very clearly how this War of Terrifying helps the economy – at least, helps those within the economy who are unscrupulous enough to make their money by such means. I am not convinced that, like the economy, anger is not being quite carefully controlled. And monitored.

"I'd be willing to bet a substantial amount that any demonstration anywhere in the world is infiltrated by government *agents provocateurs*, and it is they responsible for a substantial amount of the wanton vandalism, so often what the Press chooses to focus on in such protests. And designed to compromise the integrity of that protest, to divide opposition to government policy ... and to ferment anger on both sides. By which I'm not trying to suggest that there is no vandalism also caused by non-government 'yobs' (as Mr Blair would doubtless call them). Because certainly there is. Some people are just so angry that they simply want to destroy – like a baby hurling toys from its pram. But I say again, we then need to ask ourselves, what has caused them to get so angry? How have we contributed to that anger? Government should be asking itself the same question.

"It's all well and good, us all saying, 'These thugs, these yobs, they've got to take responsibility for themselves'. But it forgets, that piece of advice, that mostly they don't know *how* to. And finally we have to beg the question, do we seriously want to tackle the problem of crime and delinquency? Or do we just want to appear to be doing so?

"The government's not going to tackle the problem. Not seriously. Government *loves* lawlessness. Violence enables government to pass legislation that lawful assembly would debar. And government by decree is infinitely easier than government by consensus.

"If we are angry, and this is another sinful aspect of anger, we don't see clearly. Government loves it for that reason too. Angry, we attack the puppet, not the puppet-master. Is rarely your wife who has angered you, is the insulting way you are treated at your job or the income tax bill (to pay for a war of which you do not approve) or your child being taught badly in school – and you being able to do *nothing* about any of those things. We are angry with the car and not the government, with our partner and not our boss, with the dog and not the economic system which controls us, with our mother and not the schooling which failed us et cetera, et cetera.

"If we are angry, Polly, anger diverts us from the solution to the problem.

"And that today is a luxury we most avowedly cannot afford – in the same way that vengeance was a luxury South Africa could not afford. Oh, we are right to be angry, Polly. There *is* rightness, even (as I said) *righteousness* in our anger. But it also suits methos very well. Anger can keep us in the problem. It can immobilise us. It blinds us to the way forward.

"I do not know what is the solution, Polly – to this or any other problem –, nor what are these solutions. Clearly we need to spend time in analysing the problems to discover what truly those problems are. But we must resist the temptation to stick in the problems, and not move always towards the solutions. Even if some of the routes prove to be mistaken and we need to retrace our steps and start again. We can – you are right, Polly – use anger positively. Is a fine tightrope we all walk, and we all walk a different tight-rope.

"Hitler and Mao were both angry men. Herod and Ian Brady and Charles Manson. But Mother Teresa too was not without anger."

"Neither, Rafa, was Christ."

"We talk too about the 'wrath' of God."

"The Dalai Lama got angry. When he was accused of inciting violence in Tibet. Why are you smiling?"

"Excuse me, Polly. I ... Just a side-thought ..."

"Go on."

"Appalled though I was by the tirade of the Chinese senior politician – Mr Hu, was it? – when he was so accusing the Dalai Lama, I could not fail but also be amused by it. I mean, who did Mr Hu expect we were we going to believe? We: those of us with half-a-brain cell who live outside his controlled and censored country. One of the rulers of a hugely repressive regime which continues to imprison and torture political dissidents, and to supply President al-Bashir with munitions? Which continues to endorse the actions of its border guards at the Nangpa la Pass and to pretend Tiananmen Square never happened? Which continues its illegal occupation of Tibet? Or someone who has dedicated his life to the causes of peace and truth?

"And that too is analogous to the further problem I have with IBM.

"IBM has enormous PR resources, part of which (it would be reasonable to presume) has been used to keep out of the public domain its wartime profiteering. Why then should we believe it and not Andrei Kasparov? Who insists that he *wasn't* beaten in the famous match between him and an IBM computer programme. That IBM had secreted a human grandmaster able to supply what the programme couldn't: the unpredictable move, the surprise gambit – the move, not of mathematical precision, but that designed to discombobulate an opponent.

"If IBM (and other companies) won't come clean about the murk in their history, why should we not believe that such murk continues to proliferate today? And to dominate that company's ethic, its 'climate'? And do we seriously want a company to have immediate access to all our most private details if it is one besmirched with murk?

"And this too is analogous ... The parole board's first requirement from an applicant is that he accepts responsibility for his crime. Far too many people have withered away in jails, denied parole because they will not confess to crimes they maintain they did not commit. (Tragically, sometimes that they even didn't!) Without his admitting his crime, his application will, if considered at all, not be considered seriously.

"How come we demand this of individual criminals and not corporate ones? Why is it not that we're demanding higher standards from institutions than individuals? And thus inflicting greater penalties on corporations than on people?

"Mr Hu's problem (and IBM's – oh, and Coca-Cola's, Barclay's, ITT's, HSBC's, Ford's and a thousand more, maybe ten thousand more) is, as so often, the problem of all liars – and of all bullies: that he has become so accustomed to believing his own claptrap, and of having lackeys signify they believe it too (and of violently silencing dissenting voices), that he cannot understand why there should be any. Dissenting voices, I mean. Is all yet another part, Polly, of the war between the Truth and the Untruth. And another part of that war is that the 'War of Terror' is considerably less significant than the 'War of Terrifying'."

"Me, I'm pretty sure, from what I've seen of him, if the Dalai Lama stubs his toe he's been known to 'ouch' pretty loudly – maybe even profanely. You think the Dalai Lama proves your point?"

"*Por favor*, my dear, dear Polly ... The search for Truth, Polly, that is not a battle, not a competition where there are somehow winners and losers. And when we think it is, we are contaminated by the ethos with which we are surrounded. We can only arrive at the Truth as a communal effort. Not even geniuses can do without their predecessors. Beethoven needed Bach just as much as Bartok needed Beethoven. Usually if we come across the truth, we stumble on it, by accident. And that accident occurs because of all that went before it, all the terrible ideas and, yes, the lies and obfuscations. Is one of the clues to the Truth, that is inclusive of all. Whereas the Untruth is exclusive – of all but itself. (A bit like the überwealthy shivering with fright in their ghettoes.) Is also why finally the Truth will triumph over the Untruth. Because the Truth can comprise (indeed must comprise) the Untruth, whereas the Untruth *cannot* encompass the Truth."

"See, my biggest problem of all about anger continues to be that nothing in the world ever got changed without it. Anger, it seems to me, has always been the impulsion to change things."

"But is also, my dear Polly, the impulsion *not* to change things. Which is not to say you are wrong. Is, as we have now said many times, a gigantic onion of a problem. Mayhap, though, the greatest sin (as I think also I have said) is in belittling or mocking or ignoring the anger of others.

"How many of today's murderers had their anger ignored in their childhood – including, I might add, Hitler and Mao? Would the French Revolution have happened if the anger of the poor had been heard? Would the Iranian, or Cuban revolutions? The recent Intifadas?

"Anger is a howl of pain. Is an instinctive reaction to a perceived threat. We allow our country to get angry, but not our children. How bizarre is that?

"A foreign sabre rattles gently in its scabbard and we allow our government to prepare for war. But our child returns home from school complaining he has been unjustly treated and we tell him to deal with it, that such is life, that the sooner he understands that, the better he's going to survive.

"Throughout history, Man has got his priorities wrong. And throughout history, Man has not been okay with himself. There is nothing new about either phenomenon. The sin came only in the denial.

"Perhaps never before has Man got his priorities so totally wrong, and perhaps never has he been less okay with himself. And maybe too there's an element there of cause and effect. But is *certainly* true that never before have the consequences been so grave. And if we are to avoid revisiting the abyss at the edge of which we currently stand, I say again, my friend, these are problems which we need to address. Which we *have* to address. And we have to address them however unpleasant they may be. We cannot – we simply cannot – afford to revisit this abyss again. If we survive this time, such will constitute Man's single greatest triumph to date."

"There is no Take Two."

"Excuse me?"

"A friend of mine, Rafa, he organised one of those real heavy-duty stunts, you know, that they have often at the front of action movies, the Bond films and such. This was a particularly dangerous one. They agreed the (enormous) price with the stuntman. 'And, just in case there's a camera jam or something, some kind of technical foul-up,' my friend asked, 'how much for Take Two?'

"The stuntman replied, 'Claude …' That's my friend's name. … 'Claude, you get away with a stunt like this once in your life. There is no Take Two.'"

"Exactly. Very good. There is, Polly, no Take Two. Mayhap the world's politicians and industrialists and economists and bankers should wake up to that: There is no Take Two. A very good analogy, Polly. The film industry seems a gold-mine of such good analogies."

"It's got to be good for something, Rafa."

"Apart, you mean, from providing you with a living?"

Polly laughs. "Apart, yes, from that."

"Anger is certainly one of the components which has brought us to where we are. Anger waits in the tall grass of even the most placid of us, the most together and self-assured and easy-going – those who have had apparently ideal childhoods. What then must be the anger of those who are abused in their childhood – either sexually or by negligent parents or by violent parents or by other violent carers? And how much greater would such anger be if it were ignored? Or dismissed as being exaggerated or untruthful? Or demeaned as being inconsequential?

"And how much greater would that anger be if childhood were confiscated? By poverty, for example? Or a parent's sickness?

"Our problem is that we see these people as separate from us. And one element of that separation is that we believe that we're okay and they're not. We are *not* okay, Polly. Not one single one of us. We are all not okay. It's only that some are less okay than others. And it would be okay that we were not okay. Except we're also not okay with *that*. So we pretend we *are* okay. And that pretence is absolutely not okay. Because it's at that point that we start insisting, if I'm okay, I can't be the problem. Ergo it's them the problem – it's *them* being *not okay, that's* the problem. Their unokayness is causing my unokayness. And that really is not okay."

"Okay," says Polly seriously. And then chuckles.

"Yes," Rafa returns. "Okay." He takes her arm.

Polly is gently surprised, but not hugely. The gesture is one of friendship not romance. "Most of the buildings hereabouts," she says, "they're all part of Imperial College." Rafaél fails to respond. "Imperial College is probably the most prestigious British university, of those specialising in science. Just back there, for instance, is the Department of Metallurgy. I happen to know that, as one of the first dates I had when I arrived in London was with a brunette doing a post-graduate degree at the Department of Metallurgy. She once explained to me in detail of what her thesis comprised. It might as well have been in Lithuanian. She was a nice woman. I've dated some nice people in my life. Even a nice man or two."

"This gladdens me. Really, Polly. You are a person who deserves happiness. We are all, all of us, Polly, people who deserve happiness."

"This all dovetails quite neatly with my fourth mortal lie," says Polly.

"Which is?"

"That the happy ending is the happy ending. There is nothing more guaranteed to provoke anger in me," she goes on, "than the concept, and now the insistence, on the happy ending. It is quite extraordinary to me that movies and books are allowed to indulge in it as much as they do. Presumably it's because so few people live a happy ending, that they have to escape into the fantasy that such exists. I guess it's similar to the way that movies were never better attended than during the worst years of the Depression.

"That people want it doesn't stop it being a lie. It's now, so my buddies tell me, impossible to pitch an idea to Hollywood with an unhappy ending, and almost impossible to sell such an idea to a book publisher. These days (just, of course, in the very nick of time) Antony wins the battle of Philippi, marries Cleopatra and they honeymoon in Hawaii; in 'West Side Story' the bullet only grazes Tony. He recovers in hospital. Krupke officiates at his wedding to Maria whilst the Sharks and Jets form a triumphal arch of flick-knives.

"Myth and fairy-story are both there, so I once read, to explain life to us, to give shape and substance to life's mystery, to supply reassurance in the face of so much uncertainty, to explain the purpose of life. I've got to say, I'm damned if I know one myth or fairy-story that does that for me, but I would accept that such might be my deficiency, not theirs. I'm perfectly prepared to accept that 'Little Red Riding Hood' is, in fact, an allegory about our repressed sexuality, inspired (probably unconsciously) by the repressed sexuality of generations of story-tellers. Of those who first coined the story, and of later tellers who then embellished it. Does this interpretation of the fable, though, *explain* ourselves to ourselves? Or does it merely ask us to ask of ourselves more about ourselves?

"However much life is a struggle, and however much we may actually welcome that life is a struggle, we continue to want it only to be a struggle so that we can conquer it. Perhaps, as you said, Rafa, about Nature, if we stopped thinking in terms of 'conquering' life and sought rather to co-operate with it, the happy ending would occur rather more often, and to more of us.

"In fact, I think both myth and fairy-story can be incredibly damaging. They propagate stereotypes, for one thing: the distressed damsel waiting for her white-stallioned prince, the intercession into human affairs of 'fairy godmothers', the equations that beautiful equals good and ugly equals bad, even the wickedness of stepmothers and on and on ... But in nothing is there more danger than in the enforced happy ending. Almost the six most dangerous words in literature: 'And they lived happily ever after.' Like hell they did.

"And *if* they did, such was the courtesy of a lot of hard work – of *very* hard work –, and not the consequence of their marriage being made in Heaven or any other such saccharine nonsense.

"Even Victoria and Albert ... the museum by the way, one of the ones at the end of the road, that's named after them. Well, I guess that's pretty obvious, huh? ... even, as I say, Victoria and Albert, a fairytale romance if ever there was one, even that marriage was one of titan arguments, rows that shook the royal establishments to their foundations – and the royal establishment.

"And even that 'happily ever after' ended in tragedy. With the surviving partner unable to cope, mostly because she was completely untutored how to. And this was a widow with unlimited wealth, position, children by the trainful, a fulfilling job, status, even (at least in the beginning) the love of her subjects. I wonder what answer you'd have gotten if you asked Queen Victoria – particularly before she met John Brown – whether she were living 'happily ever after'."

"I think I told you, when Inma died, I was in a kind of pain, the intensity of which I had never been close to experiencing before. I will not allow myself to imagine what it must have been like, the pain of being burnt alive, but it was, I imagine, the emotional equivalent of that. In the midst of that pain, I thought about the pain. I thought about it a lot. I was in pain, I decided, because something so precious had been snatched away from me.

"But what is life, I also wondered, what distinguishes human from purely animal life, if it is not that we have the faculty to recognise the precious? Surely then one of the purposes of life must be to *seek* the precious. Mayhap even, the search for the precious, that is *the* point of life. The pain of the loss is therefore irrelevant. Those of us who have sampled the precious have sampled life. Mayhap pain is the price of that admission.

"We talk of anger, my friend! I was so angry with myself that it took me so much time to come to that realisation that I had to stop myself from doing harm to myself.

"Now, though, I do know that the search for the precious is one of the major purposes of human life – if not, as I say, its *ultimate* purpose. The Dalai Lama maintains that our first responsibility in life should be to alleviate suffering. But if we are searching for the precious, how can the alleviation of suffering not be part of that search? Which then embraces much as well which is enjoyable – which is indeed first-class joy, as opposed to the third-class joy in which today we indulge."

"According to 'The Life of Brian', the meaning of life is forty-two."

"*Como*?"

"Nothing, Rafa. Bad joke. Really, I am so sorry. So sorry, please go on." Rafaél casts her an uncertain glance. "No, really, nothing more than a bad joke."

"Because," the Peruvian starts almost tentatively, "I now know that the point of life is the search for the precious – not 'know' in the sense of insisting that is the only truth or the absolute truth, but 'know' in the sense of being comfortable with a belief – I also know that I would not have exchanged one second of that grief. Nor one second of the grief I still have. Not exchange one second. What I had with Inma was too precious. Far too precious. Is not just that she supplied me, Inma, with so much joy, is also that she helped shape me to what I am today. Both for good and, it has to be said, for ill. I am not entirely her creation – of course I amn't. But she is a part of me, indelibly. A part, let us say, of my spiritual DNA."

"Neat expression," says Polly.

"I'm guessing Victoria would have had much the same opinion about her grief around Albert."

"That's not the same thing, Rafa, as kow-towing to the happy ending. And you know that's not the same thing. The insistence on the happy ending, that, Rafa, is also a battle in the War between the Truth and the Untruth. I'm a big fan of John Grisham's work. You know Mr Grisham, Rafa?"

"His work, some of it."

"Apart from anything else, he's a master craftsman. I always enjoy the witness of master craftsmen at their work, be they bricklayers, pastry chefs ..."

"Or writers."

"As you say. But there is also a danger in Grisham. He reassures us that the good, but lonely David can stand up to Goliath and can win. 'Erin Brokowitch' was a film with the same tale. And that too was a good piece of work. Nothing the slightest wrong with either Mr Grisham's canon or 'Erin Brokowitch' – except when we start seeing them as analogies for what is happening in the world generally, and not (as they are) anomalies. It is so rare to find examples of David beating Goliath that when we grope for an analogy we have to return to a battle of over two thousand years ago. There's nothing the least bit wrong with Grisham. But it *is* wrong to insist that life is Grisham-like.

"You want to visit the Science Museum?"

"Is it worth the visit?"

"It is spectacularly worth the visit."

"In which case I will return. For the present, is necessary that my feet not be walked on."

"Ah!"

"You just happen to know of a pub nearby?"

"The 'Hoop and Toy'. Right by the station."

"And there we can sit down?"

"It's 2.30, Rafa. What can I say? We've got a good chance. We are fed such a diet of happy endings that we think they are the norm. Thus that if we aren't living 'happily ever after', there is something wrong with *us*. And the fact is that absolutely no-one is living happily ever after. Some, of course, are happier than others. *Of course*. But the world's perception of anyone's success or value has very little to do with their own. Van Gogh, Hemingway, Tony Hancock, Kurt Cobain – all, in their vastly different ways, considered by the world at large to be enormously successful, they all committed suicide. You think Henry VIII was a happy man? Or Cardinal Richelieu? Nero? Howard Hughes? Henry Ford?

"But because our media propagate the lie, we further increase our own disgruntlement. It further adds to our insecurity that there is something fundamentally wrong with *us*. And there *is* stuff *flawed* with us, that's what makes us human. But that is not what leads to us not living happily ever after. We start to think, if we weren't more flawed than most people, then, like most people, we'd be in the happy marriage or the happy job or enjoying our happy retirement or ... or ... or.

"It holds out, this myth of 'happily ever after', an absurd and completely fraudulent carrot. 'Work hard,' that carrot tells you, 'don't make waves, pay your taxes, raise your children also to be complicit tax-payers and you too will enter the kingdom of Heaven, you too will live "happily ever after". We'll make sure of that. We *promise* you'. And, of course, they absolutely do not.

"Mr Major, when prime minister, spoke of a social contract. The main problem with such concept, though, is that it seems to work only one way. Citizens are supposed to make life as simple as possible for government whilst government condones, and nurtures, a system which makes life as hard as possible (at least, so it appears) for its citizens.

"Even the most rudimentary brush with business will tell you that, any contract, for it to be durable, has to be *mutually* beneficial. Even if both sides benefit, if one side *believes* the other is benefiting more, even that situation will cause acrimony. Usually to the point that the contract disintegrates."

They enter the 'Hoop and Toy'. Its bar wriggles like a snake digesting an egg. It is mostly empty. Rafa sprawls expansively on the red plush banquette whilst Polly fetches the Kensingtonly-priced beers. They toast each other, they drink. There is a lull. They drink again, feel fresh energy paddle lazily through their veins. They small-talk their way once again to the nub of their conversation.

"We are returning – you're absolutely right, Rafa – to a medieval feudalism where (at its best) the baron supplies protection to his serfs in exchange for the unquestioned loyalty of those serfs. It's that today what is meant by 'social contracts'. And today apparently the baron is expecting the loyalty without even supplying such protection.

"How many homeless in the States are veterans of wars? The vast majority of those suffering from inadequate medical care here in the UK have worked hard, paid their taxes and their National Insurance. And? To live 'happily ever after'? Scarcely.

"And, of course, the disgruntlement of this silent majority needs then to find targets. No point in targeting the government. The government responsible for their predicament today, they've moved on, its members are either dead, retired or have been booted upstairs. The government anyway is un-get-at-able. Voters aren't fools. They know that. The choice they have today is essentially no choice. The voters know whatever government they vote for that government is not going to *give* them anything, so they tend to vote for those who maintain they will take the least. And of course that doesn't work either. You extremely quickly create the Sheriff of Nottingham economy.

"Thus scapegoats are created. And thus the disgruntled attack immigrants (let's say), legal or illegal, and asylum seekers. And government says that it takes the problem of immigration very seriously. And, of course, it doesn't. It loves asylum seekers and immigrants, and particularly *illegal* immigrants. Today's present immigration débacle was caused by the colossal problems confronted by the Home Office as it was installing the computer programme to deal with it – a fact, as I know I've already said, kept very hush-hush indeed. Presumably there was an anxiety that too much publicity of this would adversely affect computer sales. But such a foul-up also, of course, did the government a big favour too. Governments love scapegoats even more than we humans do. Anger is directed towards the scapegoats and away from them.

"These immigrants are, we are told, 'stealing' facilities away from natives, those who have been paying taxes all their lives. And the government tuts in sympathy and assures Mr Speaker that the problem is being addressed with the utmost urgency. And effectively nothing is done. Because their presence is way too convenient. No mention is ever made of how much has been stolen from the silent majority by the greed of űberwealth, or by globalisation, or by the voraciousness of incompetence. Nor is any mention made of what has been stolen from these immigrants or asylum seekers ... by exactly the same thieves: the greed of überwealth ... et cetera; scant mention is made of the despair which must impel such people to leave friends and family and set up a new life in a strange culture.

"All the time, Rafa, every which way we turn, we return (as you say) to the need of addressing problems and not using all our energies designing ways of disguising problems.

"We do not live happily ever after, Rafa. Almost none of us lives happily ever after. And we need to treat with scorn all those infinite suggestions that we can, and that if we are unhappy or unfulfilled, then we have only ourselves to blame. We do indeed have to accept – however painful that may be – that we have *contributed* to our present disgruntlement. But only in the most extraordinary of circumstances are we *solely* responsible for it. We do not need to aggravate our disgruntlement by buying into the nonsense that it is *entirely* of our making. And whilst I applaud the efforts of those who will not allow themselves to be victims, that should not blind us to the facts, firstly, that there *are* victims; and, secondly, that in an incredibly tangible way we are all victims.

"The fact that we all suffer is something else which should unite us. The lie of the happy ending is finally just another weapon ..."

"... Used by the strong to protect themselves against the weak?"

"And by Untruth hoping to vanquish the Truth. I read somewhere, if you spent ten seconds examining each exhibit in the Victoria and Albert Museum, it would take you four hundred years to visit."

"Is that on the basis of it being open the entire time?"

"Know what? I forgot to ask. Fancy embarking on a four-hundred-year-visit?"

"I find I have nothing better to do with the next four hundred years," says Rafa. "Why on earth not?"

Chapter 13

The only sensation that pierces her numbness is a disgruntlement with feeling numb. This, though, is not the numbness of disappointment; not, more accurately, the numbness of an anticipated numbness being realised: this is the numbness of surprise. Of astonishment.

The surprise had started with the doorbell ringing. It is Tuesday. It couldn't therefore be Rodolfo. Not unless there were some kind of crisis. No-one else rang her doorbell. Not in the evening. Maybe it was prospective tenants, wanting the flat upstairs, and ringing the wrong bell. Maybe it was actual tenants coming to introduce themselves.

She'd been surprised when she'd opened the door to an elderly Latin, and amazed when the man had introduced himself as Rafaél, Rodolfo's father. It's now cold in the evening, and dark. She'd shivered on the doorstep. Still amazed, she'd invited him in.

She'd fixed drinks, small-talked, found herself wanting him to find her pretty. That too had surprised her. He's an amíable man, still with creased good looks, with excellent English and a smile constantly on the point of breaking agape. He'd clearly been nervous. And his nervousness had added to her own, inherent in the surprise meeting of, as it were, her father-in-law.

But all her surprises, her amazement combined had been but the earthworm to the python of astonishment that hits her now: He proposes marriage to her.

His son, he tells her, has told him she is pregnant, that he's the father. Rodolfo has also told him that, love Giselle as he might, he also loves his wife, their children, that he cannot leave them to marry her. Rafaél tells her he understands his son. He's not too happy with his recent conduct, but then (he concedes) nothing that Rodolfo might have done in this situation would have pleased him.

He, Rafaél, is a widower now. Not without means. He's proposing not a marriage, not in the accepted sense of the word, certainly he doesn't expect Giselle to sleep with him – indeed not even to live with him, not unless she wants (or wanted) to. But she would have a companion and some security and, from Rafaél's point-of-view, would also have the family name which is his grandchild's ... well, right, he supposes. He asks her not to just say "no", but to think about it. He knows this will have come as something of a surprise, as something of a shock. Just, please, think about it.

She promises she will.

He finishes his drink. She takes him to the front door. Thanks him for his offer. Promises she will consider it. Hard.

He tells her the flat above is no longer vacant. He's rented it. Even if she won't marry him, they'll still be friends. Neighbours. She smiles wanly at this news too. Closes the door. And hits a wall of numbness.

Which is actually only the watering-hole at which all her other emotions have gathered: astonishment, of course. She'd known Rodolfo's father was in England, but that was all. Riding shotgun, though, were indignation and resentment, mild vexation and consummate rage.

And yet there was also relief. A certain tenderness. A gentle sense of compliment. Even of well-being. Even of being looked after. And she finds herself not approving of herself for feeling these sorts of feeling. But she also finds the feelings themselves surmounting that disapproval.

Chapter 14

"Is not complicated, Polly," Rafaél is saying. "I have found a new place to live: You stay with me."

"It's kind, Rafa, but ..."

"But me, Polly, no buts."

"That 'but' with one 't' or two?"

"I have a bedroom busy doing nothing. Is settled."

"It's incredibly generous of you, Rafa."

"Generous? Not at all. You, my friend, are paying for tea." They are 'teaing' at Fortnum and Mason's, in a restaurant on the ground-and-a-half floor.

The *cognoscenti* will tell you that the Food Hall in Selfridge's is of a considerably higher quality than that more famously in Harrod's. Selfridge's Food Hall is a panoply of luscious and alluring bouquets: of cheese principally, and breads and highly scented flowers. The amphitheatre which is the Food Hall at Fortnum and Mason's, on the other hand, would consider it vulgar to smell. It would, one senses, not demean itself to do anything quite so prosaic, so quotidian, so ... *pas je ne sais quoi*. There is, just maybe, the merest wisp in the air of some delicately spiced tea from the Orient, the odd whiff of orange as you pass the preserves.

Fortnum and Mason's is known by the same *cognoscenti* as Fred's. It seeks, not always successfully, to be state-of-the-artly passé, contemporarily anachronistic, and bourgeoisly upper-crust. At its best, it is the Jeeves of retailers, apparently deferential to us Bertie Woosters, its customers, but sometimes too so fawning as to become self-mocking. But it can become (Jeeves on a bad day) merely supercilious and arrogant, a pastiche of a past that never was, as it smirks brazenly at both our follies and our folly.

Polly takes out her credit card to pay the bill. Fred's, like most of London, prefers to exercise its usury in whispers. "*We* don't care about the money," those whispers are supposed to tell you Lady

Bracknelly, "so neither should you. To check the bill, or to pull a face at the total ... well, my dear, it simply is not done." It is in the same hushed tones that vultures discuss their carrion. They cross the concourse, booming with the tip-toed reverence of a British Museum Reading Room, and emerge on Piccadilly at precisely four o'clock – just in time for Fred's clock to perform its hourly horological ballet. However, the clockwork struttings of the time-piece are surplus to Polly's knowledge. Both she and Rafa are mildly curious about the presence of a small crowd, but not sufficiently so that they feel impelled to follow the direction of its gaze.

It is November 5th and already it is almost dark.

"November 5th," Polly explains, "is when the Brits celebrate what they call 'Guy Fawkes' Night'." Rafa looks entirely blank. "Guy Fawkes was the man who very nearly blew up the Houses of Parliament. During the time of the Catholic persecution. I think maybe during the reign of James I, but don't quote me on that. Yeah, somewhere early on, I think, in the eighteenth century."

"The British celebrate this man's *failure*?"

They walk past Hatchards, the bow-windowed olde-worlde bookshop, and peer in through its quaintly domestic windows. They look at each other: Should they go in? Tacitly, both decide, better not. Both of them, like Wilde, are extremely good at resisting anything except temptation. And, when it comes to buying books, both feel temptation to be scorching.

"All nations, I guess, as well as their heroes need their anti-heroes. We need both Abraham Lincoln and John Wilkes Booth. You, I guess, need both Simon Bolivar and Francisco Pizarro. At the time of the gunpowder plot, as it's called, the British Parliament had precious little to do with democracy. At that level, Fawkes was even a freedom-fighter in its cause. Certainly in the cause of religious freedom."

"Violence is always self-destructive. But I repeat, my friend, that such does not mean that I do not understand it."

"It's not, today, anything to do with democracy: November 5th, I mean. It's just an excuse to let off a bunch of pyrotechnics. Just like our July 4th. It seems we all need an excuse to light up the sky, spend hundreds of thousands of pounds or dollars for a few seconds of sparkles and bangs."

"In my country, not once a year, but many times."

"It's a real shame, I think. I mean, I think, Thanksgiving, that's a great idea. Truly, a great idea. And a truly great idea! I think it's so healthy, once a year, to take stock of all the good things in your life, so many things in most of our lives that we should be grateful for. It's also a great idea, a kind of *national* birthday – maybe even the same day – when we all applaud what great things we've done for ourselves, what great things our nation's done for the world. But it'd also be a great idea, I think, if once a year – maybe on Guy Fawkes' Night, or on Independence Day back home – if we took stock of the not so great things nationally we've done to ourselves and to the world. You know, right, the Oscars are awarded by the American Academy of Motion Pictures?"

"Yes," Rafa replies uncertainly, uncertain whither this somewhat violent tack in their conversation is taking them.

"Well, this is the headquarters of the UK equivalent. BAFTA, it's called. The British Academy of Film and something Arts. TV, I guess. Yeah, that sounds right: the British Academy of Film and Television Arts."

"Right," Rafa returns, in order to make a noise.

"Can you imagine how much healthier the world would be if each country in the world had a day like that? A day of atonement or something, a day when we looked *critically* at ourselves – an anti-Oscar ceremony or something, an *un*-Oscar ceremony. You imagine how healthy it would be for them here to use November 5th to examine how well they're doing today with democracy. It's the next mortal lie, Rafa, that democracy is democracy."

"Is the *fifth*," says Rafa. "The fifth mortal lie."

"Not the fifth amendment, then?"

"And the fifth deadly sin, Polly, is gluttony."

"Right."

"Mayhap we do not talk about gluttony. Is a little uncomfortable for me. Gluttony too is drink. I know I drink too much."

"I think, Rafa, you mean that *I* drink too much. I know I have a problem, okay? I told you I knew I had a problem, remember? It's okay. Really, Rafa. You can't possibly say anything I haven't heard before. Can't in fact possibly say anything I haven't said to myself many times before."

"I *also, amiga mía,* drink too much."

"Okay." The smile they exchange echoes through all the fathoms that the depth of their friendship has now become.

It's not exactly cold, but there is a breeze gusting, in the midst of whose gentle breaths is a stalactited icicle. Rafaél brrs lightly to himself, and buries his shoulders deeper within his coat. "Is so entirely obvious," he continues, "the obscenity that, for a huge part of the world, malnutrition and sub-nutrition is a titan problem, and for another part of the world a big problem is obesity ... and, of course, mal-nourishment; that whilst our brothers and sisters starve, we need to eat less ... and more healthily. But is so grotesque, that gulf, so obvious, so flagrant in its obscenity that we do not need to spend time discussing it.

"Is in fact so appalling that even the appalling globalisation, with its lack of humanitarian principles, is being forced to address it. Forced to, not courtesy of its own ethos, but in order to protect itself. Is another instance of changing the world by creating an atmosphere where the world *has* to change. And the atmosphere is created by the revulsion felt by most of us who are well-fed that in the twenty-first century we should continue to see our less fortunate siblings scavenging for food or living lives that make those of the Oakies in 'The Grapes of Wrath' look like that of the Great Gatsby. There seems to be many passing down this alley. We could mayhap tarry here a while, smoke a cigarette jointly together."

"My cigarettes, I presume."

"*Claro,* my friend. You will recall, technically I am a non-smoker."

"A lot cheaper, this technical non-smoking."

"Thus better for one's health. Obesity in the Western world today is a big problem. I do not (mayhap for once!) make a pun, my friend. Fifteen percent of British schoolchildren are now obese. Not podgy, not plump, but medically obese."

"In the States, I think the percentage is even higher."

"Alcohol abuse in that world is the third biggest killer, after cancer and heart disease. And that figure does not, I think, include the contributory factor played in those health problems by excessive drinking. You're all right, really, if I continue?"

"Let me ask you this, Rafa: You're okay, really, saying all this to me whilst you're puffing at a cigarette?"

"I will also be really okay talking about it, Polly, whilst I am buying you a drink."

"Just checking."

"We have said many times before, my dear Polly, that there is in all of us the element of, 'Do as I say not as I do.'"

"'Just checking,' I said." Polly stomps her feet, but more out of a November habit than to vanquish the evening's chill. She wants to be broad-shouldered and grown-up enough to weather any criticism, actual or inferred. But her corns are feeling very exposed. She can hear the tread of hob-nailed boots as they march towards those corns. Soon, and she knows it, the exposed corns will be trampled on. Heavily. She is already steeling herself to suppress the yells which will be screeching for release.

And Rafaél sort of knows this, and sort of doesn't. Polly has told him to plough on regardless, so he thinks. So he thinks he should plough on regardless!

"There is a new thing now on bottles of alcohol, warnings – and on advertisements – exhortations to the drink's purchasers to 'Drink responsibly'. If one needed an example of how today's governments do not want actually to tackle problems, but want to be *seen* to be tackling problems, one need look no further than that. Is a nonsense. In fact, an insult. Like putting up signs outside rural villages saying, 'Please Drive Carefully'. Most drivers already do drive carefully.

They need no absurd exhortation to do so.

"The overwhelming majority of drinkers already do imbibe responsibly. Most motorists drive carefully. Careful drivers and responsible drinkers are, by this wanton crassness, being insulted. Those who drive carelessly or drink irresponsibly fall, both of them, into two categories: either they think that they do drive carefully (or drink responsibly) and that therefore such admonitions do not apply to them, or they don't *care* that they are thought to drive carelessly (or drink irresponsibly). Some of those are indeed even deliberately making a point by driving carelessly. Yet others are addicted – to alcohol or speed or adrenalin or mischief. In all of which cases, such exhortations are not only not of any point, but may indeed be fuelling the fire.

"Is part of the lie, such inanity. Do governments, does the liquor industry seriously believe that with such nonsense they absolve themselves of responsibility? Do they seriously think they can turn around to their electorate, to their clients and share-holders and talk of 'the giant strides' they have made to protect society against the consequences of alchohol? I wonder what would be the reaction of the Chiefs of Staff if they were told by the government, 'We will protect this country against the threat of nuclear attack. Please find herewith several bows and arrows. Go defend the country.' Is, this strategy, quite as crass.

"Chemical abuse and dependency, as an issue, is far more dangerous than anything which al-Qaeda has devised. The fatalities caused cannot fall far short *daily* of the September 11th death toll; the cost to industry only of absenteeism due to alcohol abuse is that of the GNP of several, albeit smaller, countries. The impact on society is incalculable: the disruption to family unity, the traumatisation of those within the family, the erosion of self-esteem in children, the need it generates in second-hand victims for control et cetera et cetera. ..."

"Et cetera," Polly repeats. She is hoping for dispassion, but what is heard is an acrid sarcasm. What both conceal is a simmering anger.

"What percentage of the ninety-two percent dysfunctional figure we talked about when we talked of anger is the direct result of alcohol and/or chemical abuse? Alcohol or drugs were factors in the crimes of over eighty percent of the prison population."

"Yeah," Polly agrees. She twists her cigarette-end into the kerb-stones. They start heading for Piccadilly Circus Underground Station.

"You think the 'Drink responsibly' label had any effect on them?" Rafa knows he has to continue. If he falters now, there will always be a no-go area in their conversations together. "Alcohol abuse," he therefore 'obliviously' expostulates, "obesity, bulimia, anorexia, they're all problems the symptoms of which are to do with 'gluttony', but the illness of which is fundamentally to do with reality. Reality becomes too uncomfortable a place, so one moves out of it. They are all devices so to change the chemical structure of our bodies that reality does become acceptable – or, rather, that the perception of reality becomes acceptable. The problem is, of course, that – in a similar way, Polly, to that you were talking about with economics – the real reality remains as uncomfortable as it ever was. Indeed when we return to that reality, that reality has got worse as a consequence of our flight from it and is, more often than not, even more uncomfortable than the reality from which we first escaped. We are back again, *amiga mía*, to the vicious spiral of the '*dokhodyagi*'."

"It's more than just that," mutters Polly. Rafaél is about to descend the Underground's stairs. Polly stops him. "They could be throwing fire-crackers in the station. It all gets a bit crazy, Guy Fawkes' night. Let's keep walking along the outside." They weave between the throng, and make their way across Lower Regent Street.

"Of course is more than that, Polly. *Claro*. I do not wish to mimic the mistake of pretending mountains are molehills. Alcohol has been abused for as long as there has been alcohol. Bacchus (or Dionysos in ancient Greece) was celebrated, perhaps appropriately, by *getting* drunk. There are many festivals of ancient religions, and still today amongst indigenous nations, which involve getting (literally) out of your mind one way or another. Hogarth in the eighteenth century was painting about the problems of alcohol; around the time of your Civil War, Polly, was estimated that over twenty percent of the country drank too much, was even a pre-AA AA called, I think, the Washingtonians. It had a membership of over half-a-million. At the start of the twentieth century alcohol abuse was considered by politicians in Britain to be the country's single biggest health hazard and social problem. Your country even sampled Prohibition. Is now generally accepted there are genetic proclivities in the contraction of alcoholism. Heavy drinking is part of the cultural DNA of many countries: Britain certainly, Russia, Finland, Ireland, some parts of your country, Polly, also by some sections of mine.

"Inappropriate eating or binge feasting, these have been along too since before the birth of history. These are problems which are not going to be sound-byted away, or magic-wanded away. These are all problems which have been compounded by millennia of not being addressed, or of simply being tutted at. Is going to take a long, long time just to control these problems. Not only these, but all addictions, all escapes from reality: drugs (most famously – but drugs that are prescribed are a more frequent problem than those which are *pro*scribed!), sex, exercise, spending, shopping, gambling, computer games, tv, soap operas, working …"

"Smoking?"

"Not a problem for us technical non-smokers."

"Of course not, Rafa. How dumb of me!"

"When people stop dying of hunger these problems – oh, and a whole vast array of others – are waiting in the undergrowth to claim a billion fresh victims. Who knows? Mayhap even more. And yet we still allow governments to get away with sticking labels on bottles: 'Drink responsibly'! Pontius Pilate has been reviled by history for washing his hands of responsibility. How do we not revile those today who likewise so completely wash *their* hands?"

"You're not, are you, suggesting we return to Prohibition?"

"On the contrary. I would welcome intelligent debate, not just about legalising what are called 'soft' drugs, but all drugs. It seems to me that the chief victor in their 'War Against Drugs' ... (Do you notice how many times it suits government to designate a problem a 'war'?) ... it seems virtually the *only* victor are the dealers. Not always, by the way, a bad thing. Sometimes those dealers, particularly in Colombia and Brazil, are doing things for the *campesinos* in their charge that their governments are failing to do: funding schools, for instance, or building clinics et cetera. How come the market economy is not allowed to work for drugs? For the drugs' *companies, claro*. But not for the *campesinos* dependent on growing them.

"A large part of the problem with drugs at the moment is, in fact, their very illegality (in a way not, in fact, dissimilar to Prohibition): thus both their enormous cost and the fact that their purchase requires entering the *demi-monde*. Is so often those factors rather than addiction to the substances which sets the victim down a vicious spiral from which is so hard to escape.

"There are enormous problems also attendant on drugs that are legal: tranquillisers, anti-depressants, sleeping pills and the like – the Prozacs and Valiums of the world. But these problems are not compounded by the fact that their users have to steal to feed their habit, nor do they have to enter into concourse with the criminal in order to obtain their supply. You know the biggest object of addiction in the Western world?"

"Go on," says Polly, meaning 'go on, tell me'.

"Trousers."

"Excuse me?" Polly asks.

"Deprive men of their trousers, they'll suffer all the symptoms of someone withdrawing from heroin. But more acutely. In the Second World War the Japanese used it as a form of torture. We don't talk about criminalising trousers.

"As I say, I do not advocate the decriminalisation of narcotics – this word, does it not, exists? – I do not, my friend, advocate it. But I do advocate serious debate on the subject. But serious debate, this seems a concept as antiquated today as wearing periwigs. We have instead spin, we have instead the insulting of opponents, we have instead the clash of the sound-byte. And that, as methods of tackling problems, is of the same use as a fly-swat in a shark attack. We argue about detail not substance, we accept unproven premises, we address the effect and not the cause. We argue about whether or not the lights on the Christmas tree should flicker, not whether or not Christmas any longer serves a function as a festival. I use Christmas, by the way, as an example. I have nothing against Christmas. In fact, I greatly enjoy it."

"Fear not, Rafa, I'll Scrooge for the two of us."

"I am relying on you to do so."

It is now almost dark. The street lights are on. Buses and taxis slouch their despondent routes. There is a smell in the evening air: freezing soot, is it?

"This exercise, my friend, this whole business of looking at the world via the deadly sins, there is much virtue in this. There is much – a surprising amount of – wisdom in *ancient* wisdom. Mayhap because wisdom does not have the obsolescence of knowledge. Is also, I think, interesting, Polly, that Sikhism has a remarkably similar list of traits to be avoided. And maybe prescient that one of Nanak Dev's first remarks was: 'Falsehood reigns over the land as a veil of darkness.' I enjoy this exercise with you, Polly. But it seems to me, almost the clearest thing that it tells me, is that, although these are *big* problems, they will not respond to *big* solutions. Or rather the only big solution to all these enormous problems has to be a commitment to address the problems and not seek to sound-byte them away.

"There is no one solution to the problem, let's say, of addiction or family dysfunction – not even one solution to problems like world starvation or global warming. And that too is, in fact, part of the problem today. We all of us seem to like the grand gesture, the bold stroke by which everything will come all right. Sydney Carson at the end of 'Tale of Two Cities': the selfless martyrdom that magically expunges all previous ills. Is mayhap a consequence of your fourth mortal lie, Polly, that the happy ending is the happy ending. We expect the cavalry, just before the end, to come galloping over the hill. And, in the nick of time, the distressed damsel will be saved."

"I think, Rafa, that's Sydney Carton."

"Sydney Carton, of course. Excuse me. Is mayhap our fondness for the bold gesture which is another element in our apparent fondness for war. We seem to think of war as a sort of extreme make-over – this is the word, no?, today. We want the fix-it pill, or the 'short, sharp shock' that is magically going to undo all the harm which has been impacted on each delinquent over generations. Problems – real problems – don't respond to that kind of dramatic gesture. Real problems are not solved at a stroke. They're chipped away at, ameliorated *slightly*, trawled with less intensity to the next generation. Ironically, a lot of that chipping away is now happening, but in very unspectacular ways. Another of Man's tragedies is that he seems so unwilling to acknowledge the small improvements. We do need, all of us, to address this tendency in ourselves. Just as the polio victim needs encouragement to walk – very much, one pace at a time – so those chipping away at these mountainous social problems also need their encouragement.

"Let's return to the '*dokhodyagi*', or to the victims of the Nazis' extermination camps ... When we've been deprived for too long, we cannot deal even with what in other circumstances would be considered enough. When the Allies liberated Belsen, they found themselves, to their chagrin, killing off yet more of its inmates. The prisoners had been so badly deprived of nourishment for so long that their stomachs could not accept normal food. And they died thus from *over*-nourishment. The Allies had to introduce, as it were, training diets – devised, appallingly enough, for the problem of starvation in India. It took quite some time to educate the prisoners' stomachs back to a normal diet.

"The same applies to social deprivation and political deprivation. Very many problems today associated with the former Iron Curtain stem from the fact that President Reagan and Mrs Thatcher were so gung-ho to see the end of a regime they loathed that they used their muscle to go helter-skelter for the abolition, rather than allowing it, as Mr Gorbachev had wanted, to be dismantled piecemeal.

"The alcoholic, true, can stop drinking at one stroke. But that does not, as I understand it, mean his alcoholism is *cured*. Is merely checked. The abstinence from alcohol is not the end. Is the means which allow him to start addressing the illness."

"You been to AA as well?"

Rafa laughs awkwardly. "I sometimes feel I should. I do not wish, *amiga mía*, to pre-empt anything you might have to say about democracy. But one of its problems is that politicians have inculcated into us the idea that they will solve our problems – very often problems created by their forebears. Is a nonsense. In a free society, at best politicians can encourage an ethos in which *we* can address those problems. Politicians it is who encourage the big gesture, the bold initiative … these, their 'advisers' will tell them, are vote-winners. But they are not solutions. One does not run a marathon the day one's hip has been replaced.

"But none of this is very exciting, very dramatic … very sexy. Where do we start, Polly? Mayhap we have to look inside ourselves, each one of us, and start redefining, as I've said before, what we find sexy.

"We have, for instance, got to start using our energy also to *pre-empt* problems. Good policing is not about solving crime, but preventing it; good parenting is not pulling kids back from brinks, but avoiding them getting close to brinks; good schooling is not about imposing disicipline, but about instilling self-discipline. How many whodunits would sell, though, if Miss Marple were discovering the *would-be* murderer? How many would sit glued to their soap-operas if its characters were spending hours reading to their children or helping them with homework or schlepping them across town for football practise or guitar lessons or dance classes. Perhaps, yet again, our love of drama is impeding the humanisation of our humanity."

"Humanisation?"

"Is this not a word?"

"I really hope not. It smacks to me of some kind of 'speak': sociology-speak or anthropology-speak or some such. And if it's not, it sounds like it should be."

"I shall therefore expunge it from my vocabulary."

"I'd be grateful."

"You're welcome. Back to Twain again. I think it was he who said of writing that it was ten percent inspiration and ninety percent *per*spiration. Well, likewise the solutions to most of today's humungous problems: ten percent inspiration and ninety percent perspiration, ten percent the surgery and ninety percent the convalescence, ten percent the performance and ninety percent the rehearsal. Indeed, closer probably, to one and ninety-nine percent.

"For humanity, *amiga mía*, to become more of what it is, for it to start realising its full potential, then all of humanity needs to be celebrated. Not just the sexy bits and the appealing bits, but also the nasty little private bits of it: the ear wax and the hair nose. The body also needs them. It behoves us to remember that cockroaches have inhabited the Earth a lot longer than pandas or peacocks. That too is an allegory, my friend. Of what I amn't too sure. But I do know is an allegory!"

They cross the Haymarket, past the Angus Steak House on the corner. It is a peculiar time of day to be eating a full meal, and yet the restaurant looks remarkably busy. To the extent even that Polly checks her watch. No, she's right: it's just after 4.15.

"Greed and gluttony," Rafa continues, "are different, and yet very similar. Both comprise wanting more than we need. And such is the kamikaze nature of our economics today that those economics rely not only on us being greedy and gluttonous, but greatly so. Which is why so much advice tendered us by government to look after ourselves better has such a hollow ring to it.

"There is, though, one fundamental difference between the two of them, between gluttony (I mean) and greed: gluttony is not exclusive in the way that greed is. Gluttony welcomes company, it does not shun it. At Christmas we even revel in a communal, a societal, a national gluttony. We want everyone to be over-feasting as we are. We enjoy the community of it. Is part of the fun of Christmas, part of its spirit."

"Yeah," Scrooges Polly. "Amateurs blocking up the bar, ordering all sorts of weird concoctions: 'snowballs' and the like, blackcurrant and Babycham!"

"Greed, though, is more selfish. Is wanting more than those around one, lusting after that more, craving that more, having to have that more. And when one does have that more, wanting *yet* more. Not for yourself. Just to have yet more than one's neighbours. Is a way of proving to ourselves we are more worthy than our neighbours. We are worth more. *We* are never greedy. Is always 'they' who are greedy. We are ambitious or successful or conscientious. 'They' are always the greedy: whether 'they' be unions or industrialists, our neighbours or our children. 'We' have always worked for our money. And it's always 'they' – the greedy – trying to wrest our rewards away from us.

"What impels a billionaire to seek a second billion? And then a tenth? A fiftieth? And just before we get too self-righteous, you and I, too morally high-and-mighty, let's just for a second play 'we've-won-the-lottery'. Let's play it honestly.

"If, Polly, you are as I am, you imagine winning a million whatevers – pounds, dollars. One imagines that would be great. All one's troubles would be at an end. Immediately, one would give twenty percent to charity. Of course. In the world which has become perfect for you, there are still plenty of problems. One recognises that. Then one would pay off the children's mortgages. At least then they would be housed for the rest of their lives. ... Well, no, come to think of it, there wouldn't be enough to cover that. No, what I'll do: I'll give *ten percent* to charity. Better, I'll win *two* million, then I could still pay twenty percent to charity, pay off the kids' mortgages, help this friend who's now in trouble, buy myself a bigger house, perhaps take a cruise ... Really, three million would be more comfortable. And then I could ... et cetera, et cetera. Soon, winning ten millions is barely going to make ends meet.

"Is because we all of us have greed within us that we need around us an ethos which checks it. A worldwide Greed Anonymous, if you like, supporting one another when a greedy impulse strikes. Instead we have exactly the opposite: an ethos pushing us towards both greed and gluttony. And then admonishing us for being greedy and gluttonous."

"And adding labels to bottles telling us to 'drink responsibly'."

"Exactly. Now, not for a second am I trying to suggest that, even with the most enlightened and humanitarian economic system possible, such would be the eradication of either gluttony or greed. Addiction too – certainly for the foreseeable, even the envisageable, future – is here to stay. There are certainly tens of millions, probably hundreds of millions of addicts in this world. And as many causes for those addictions as there are addicts.

"Even in Utopia reality will be there to stay, and for some the existence of that reality will remain too painful to bear.

"But mayhap we will have correctly identified in Utopia which of our weaknesses are in fact vices, which sins, which foibles and peccadilloes – and which indeed are positive virtues. We will therefore be channelling our energies correctly, in other words to the suppression of those elements within ourselves which are destructive, and to the encouragement of those which are beneficial.

"We will in Utopia have learnt to listen more, and to talk very much less. We'd be teaching children at school the two most valuable lessons anyone can learn: the way to love themselves, and the path to tread in order to be the most 'they' they can become.

"We'd recognise that we do not even begin to tackle extremely serious problems like alcohol abuse by attaching vacuous labels to bottles: 'Drink responsibly', nor by devising 'drink responsibly' websites. Like any self-respecting teenage drinker is going to log onto that before a night out! 'Drink responsibly'! Really one does not know whether one should laugh or cry!"

"It's enough almost to drive you to drink!"

"Now, that sounds like a sensible idea."

"Not too crazy, Rafa, tell you the truth, about any of the watering-holes hereabouts: sightseer saloons, most of them. Venues to assuage thirst, not haunts dedicated to the serious business of serious drinking."

"Between us we might be able to change that lamentable situation," laughs Rafaél. He is floating towards that state of over-buoyancy enjoyed by those who have successfully negotiated a minefield.

And if minefields can feel anything, then Polly too is expanding with relief that a path has been picked through her and she hasn't blown up. Mostly she tries to be frivolous about her drinking, but she rarely deludes herself that frivolity is what she is actually feeling. "Let's wait till we get to Covent Garden," she suggests.

"'Democracy,' you said, 'is not democracy.' 'The fifth mortal lie,' you said."

"Yeah, I did say that, didn't I? Yeah, it's a real problem that, democracy not being democracy. It's one of the reasons, I think, that most of our politicians (yeah, as you say, Rafa, anywhere in the world) are venal or corrupt or incompetent. The American public did not vote for President Bush in his first term, the Supreme Court appointed him. Mr Gore actually had more people voting for him than the man who became president. How is that democracy? At his last election as prime minister, Mr Blair received less votes winning than his predecessor, Neil Kinnock, had gotten *losing* – in his case to John Major. How is *that* democracy?

"Not that the choice presently between Republican and Democrat is any kind of real choice at all, nor between Conservative and Labour here. The choice between a rock and a hard place is also not democracy. Nor is the lesser of two evils.

"Nor is it a democracy where it is the most money which secures the most power. Power should not be a commodity in that way. It cannot be. Not in a democracy. Wealth buying power is, by definition, a *pluto*cracy. And how anyone can claim that back home is not now a plutocracy is something which ... well, it just bewilders me. Oh, certainly President Obama's campaign dented that plutocracy. But the car's dynamo, its engine, remains just the same. Not only do we have plutocratic government Stateside, we have a plutocratic justice system, plutocratic healthcare and education."

"Throughout the world, my friend."

"Many of today's Russians nickname democracy 'diemocracy'. 'Diem' in Russian apparently means shit. Mr Putin is not the only prime minister today of a 'shitocracy'. In fact, there are considerably more shitocracies in today's world than even those governments *striving* to be democratic. And I have no problem with those governments who admit that they are still striving towards democracy. That shows a commitment both to Truth and to the future. But I do have a problem with those countries which claim for themselves such an enlightened democracy that it feels it can lecture the rest of the world on the subject.

"Democracy is certainly *not* what exists in much of the Western world: is the choice, rather, between Tweedle-dee and Tweedle-dum, both of whom insist that they are much better placed than the electorate (or *demos*) to decide what constraints are necessary. Society is not protected thereby. It is the Tweedles who are protected – they and their pals – Tweedle-dum's chums! President Bush's administration was not the only one devoted to the welfare exclusively of Tweedle-dum's chums. It's even possible it wasn't the most flagrant.

"Where does *democracy* come into all this? Or *any* of it? In what field of human endeavour is it not money, and not *only* money, which talks? It is not the *democratic* principle that is causing globalisation to be extended to the rest of the world, but the *plutocratic* principle. Which is, of course, great news for the plutocrats – or, Rafa, as you would say, the institution of wealth. But not for humanity. 'Globalisation' is, of course, only a euphemism for 'Americanisation'. Where is the democracy here?

"There's a rather good book around, 'The Best Democracy Money Can Buy'. It's written by a journalist called Greg Palast. Well, the title says it all, of course. But he does exhaustively quote chapter and verse. Most worryingly of all, it was written even before we arrived at today's excesses.

"Like you, I'm not anti-American, Rafa. Far from it. There's a whole bunch of stuff about America that I'm real crazy about. Again like you, I continue to think its Constitution is one of the finest documents proclaiming civilisation yet to have been written. I really like American culture as well. Yeah, all the stuff I'm not supposed to like: the hamburgers and the hot dogs, the popcorn and doughnuts and all that. Even Disneyworld. Particularly when all of that is in America. And, sure, we have the right to export all that, but we do not have the right to impose it.

"It's yet another reason why it's so critical that we start defining concepts like 'civilisation', and like 'progress'. It's important we're clear what we all mean by them. For me, both are very simple: It is about freeing Man so that he can be the most 'he' he can be, it is about freeing him, in your wonderful phrase, Rafa, to look for the precious in life. Anything that goes towards those ends is good, and anything that impedes those ends is bad. If either concept is not about benefiting the whole of the planet, then it's not progress at all. It's not even maturity. It's regression … and to the kindergarten.

"I'm not saying, Rafa – believe me – that these people are monsters. Not the prime ministers, or presidents, not the CEOs either. They're not, Rafa. Certainly not all of them. They're just not. Inadequate, most of them, sad, but not monsters. They've just been given the wrong brief, or taken a wrong turn, or listened to the wrong people.

"I don't think either that Mr Blair when he entered politics was a monster. And we really need to examine whether the change that came over him arose out of an inherent deficiency in his personality or one in the political process. I'd put money on the fact that the answer, of course, is that it was a combination of the two. And that is uncomfortable because it raises a lot more questions than it answers.

"We talked about this before, about how we are appalled when we read of an old people's home where they are under-nourishing their patients, or a private school which hushes up the sexual abuse of their pupils by their staff. This isn't done either out of hatred for the old or young, not out of malevolence. But if profit becomes the be-all and end-all, it is given a higher priority than humanity. And those situations (and many, *many*, many similar ones of equal appallingness) become ... simply inevitable.

"Those situations are being emulated on a gigantic scale both by our elected representatives and by the multi-nationals. They are operating, Rafa, exactly the same principle – the same principle, I mean, of starving the old and condoning the abuse of the young. Except that the misguidance of the priorities is, in their case, so humungous that we can't take it in. It's like the size of the universe or the time since Big Bang: the figures are so large as to be meaningless. I also think *that's* quite deliberate, by the way. I think such huge figures are easier to massage. In fact, I am increasingly beginning to believe that – akin to what you were just saying, Rafa – the entire system, the entire so-called 'science' of economics has been developed just so that the robbed cannot fully comprehend how much has been stolen from them."

"Go on, Polly," Rafa gently insists.

"CEOs would maintain, they don't answer to humanity, nor to ecology, nor to civilisation, they answer to their shareholders. And the shareholders demand profit at whatever cost. Which neatly sidesteps the fact that most shareholders are institutional share-holders, run by companies who also have only one object ever in their mind: profit. It helps the managing directors of such misnamed 'trust' companies to justify their otherwise completely unjustifiable salaries. Apart from that, it merely seeks to keep money circulating – within a very small pool indeed. It's not that people benefit from such a situation, mostly it's – as you, Rafa, were saying a week or so back – it's only the institutions which do, those within that inner pool. If the world's people is the Atlantic Ocean, that pool is not the Mediterranean, it's not even Lake Michigan. It's, Rafa, the size of the Serpentine, the pond inside Hyde Park. Greenpeace encapsulated the history of the world into the time-frame of a day, remember? And Man has been around for fifteen minutes, or so. Well, the size of this small pool, that's maybe an even smaller percentage of mankind than the time in Earth's history that Man has been around.

"There are unspeakable CEOs, of course there are, the industrial equivalents of Papa Doc or President Suharto. But most of them are doing, so they would maintain, a job of work. And those who show sentimentality this week in business are next week *out* of business. And that's what they are: they're businessmen, they're not Messiahs. And businessmen, so they will insist (usually very quietly, usually in very measured tones) create … wait for it … 'PROSPERITY' … and for everyone.

"Well, if this is true – as they keep maintaining – then I should like to see the evidence of that. It is now accepted that, back home (in one of the world's richest countries; a land of millionaires and billionaires), one in five children – one, Rafa, in five – is born into abject poverty. *Abject* poverty, Rafa. Not 'not-two-cars' poverty: gut-wrenching, infant killing poverty. One in five is not an aberration. That means there are twice as many people born poor as are gay. In Michael Moore's film, 'Sicko', he claims that 18,000 Americans die each year as a direct result of inadequate medical care. 18,000, Rafa. That's four and a half September 11ths, every single year. In the United States, one of the world's richest countries. We have to start seeing that selective prosperity is no prosperity at all. Either we all benefit – which presently it is completely obvious that we do not – or there is no benefit. As you would say, Rafa, it's that simple.

"This attitude, this 'profit-conquers-all' attitude that the responsibility of business ends with the share-holders' dividends, these are all as a consequence of the fact that democracy as practised today is not democracy. And that situation will continue until … guess what?"

"Democracy *is* democracy?"

"Right. Until, Rafa, we have exchanged an ersatz democracy for the real thing. Till we, the '*demos*', start bankrupting companies that do not abide by … well, let's say moral and ecological standards, to begin with.

"Know what, Rafa? There could be civil rights in China within a year. Within one year, Rafa. All we have to do, we have to boycott all Chinese goods. Within one year, there would be some real semblance of free speech – probably as much of a semblance as we enjoy – and dissidents, Buddhists and Christians would all be freed from their jails. Perhaps, who knows?, even the tank man from Tiananmen Square."

"Today, *amiga mía*, the boot is on the other foot. Many Western banks are dependent on Chinese loans. And ironically Chinese banks are as rich as they are because its people lack the social security we have been used to in the West. The Chinese therefore save for their old age, for the calamities in life. We have talked about government protecting the weak against the strong. Now we have the poor bankrolling the rich, effectively the poor saving the rich from bankruptcy. And why? So that when the rich are rich again, they can further subjugate the poor. And we sneer at dogs which bite the hand that feeds them!"

The Odeon cinema glares blackly before them, an architectural Kafka; the Warners West End is showing half-a-dozen films that are a waste of celluloid. There's a burger stand, salmonella guaranteed!, a souvenir shop and a distinctly unprepossessing sex shop. Around them, a diverse and discombobulated bustle: a charabanc-load of Japanese tourists taking an album-full of group photos; a small party of 20-something lads rubbing their necks with Manchester City scarves; a tiny Malay nun in a dark blue habit with a surprisingly short skirt listening intently as, in order to expostulate, an earnest, gangly priest giraffes intensely towards her. There is a sense of the Orientally disorientated puzzling over the Occidentally insistent. Not an analogy at all. Almost in fact an 'antanalogy', whatever the word is.

"It's all part, Rafa, of the lie that today's democracy is democracy. You think the *demos* would be happy with that situation? President Bush declares a war to protect a democracy which, if it had been one, would never have allowed him in the White House. Mr Blair shouts back at a heckler, 'At least you live in a democracy where you can make your voice heard.' He then has the heckler evicted. He bans protests during the visit of Mr Hu, hides the protests during that of President Bush. How is any of this 'democracy'? Perhaps I'm just dumb, but to me the actions of President Bush and Mr Blair both, during their terms of office, would seem to indicate the same level of commitment to democracy as Henry VIII had to monogamy ... or WC Fields showed to temperance. Their barbarism is their shame.

"Democracy? Even at its conception, democracy was not democracy. Those who could vote in ancient Athens were exclusively free men. Slaves and women were excluded. *Any* society which incorporates slavery *cannot* be a democracy – indeed cannot be anything other than a state of barbarism. Likewise any state which countenances a political difference between men and women."

"Strange," Rafaél interjects, "what good friends are President Bush and his father with the rulers of Saudi Arabia, scarcely a haven of democracy, scarcely a place where women are afforded equal rights – indeed where very many are afforded such rights, outside of the central oligarchy. Ah, now I know where I am: Charing Cross Road. I very much like the bookshops in Charing Cross Road."

"You want to go browse?"

"I have not seen Covent Garden, my friend. That was the purpose, was it not, of our trip today?"

"This way." They pass the tiny Arts Theatre. It was here that 'Waiting for Godot' was first introduced to a largely bewildered London audience. It was directed by a recently graduated Peter Hall. It may have been his finest hour.

"There is an argument that democracy, however it is organised, can never be democracy – not truly –, that it contains two fatal flaws which make it untenable. The first is that anyone who seeks power should be the very last person ever to be awarded it. That much is almost obvious. Nothing too contentious about that, nothing too much to be said about it. Except that we do nothing about it: we recognise the problem, but just let it be. If we had woodworm in our house, and we just let that be, can we really be surprised if the whole house finally collapses? This is not a little philosophical nicety we're discussing here. It's yet another reason why mankind today stands on the abyss of self-destruction.

"Power is, of course, both incredibly seductive and incredibly addictive. Apparently, Rafa, a much harder habit to break than heroin.

"The people to whom we are currently granting power are those who seek it. And they are the last people to whom, as I say, it should be tendered. Because its influence, power, is already corrupting enough. Give it to those who want it, who may even crave it, may even be addicted to it, and you cede it to people who, once they get it, consequently don't know what to do with it. Oh, they orate nobly. But the oration means nothing. It is just another telesalesperson's pitch, a script, a pitch designed to sell you a bill of goods you don't want at a price you can't afford. And this means that methos or vested interest or call it what you will can so easily bribe them or cajole them, persuade them or inveigle them ... or, yes, seduce them ... and they have nothing inherent within them to protect themselves (or us!) against such invasions.

"There is therefore, at the very core of our system of government (even if it were honourably applied), a self-destructive flaw. One of the consequences of which is that it is of *necessity* that our politicians are of poor quality. For evidence of which all that is required is a reasonable pair of eyes.

"The second central flaw of even an ideal democracy is that politicians have to lurch from one election to the next. They're given a four-year term or a five-year term (or whatever) and the voters assess them – this again in an *ideal* world – on what they have achieved or have failed to achieve in that time. This presupposes that we are able to disregard the influence of spin or vested interest or personal prejudice and so on.

"The problem with such election-hopping is, again, twofold. First of all, it means that politicians need to court popularity. Instead of, as they sometimes need to, having the courage to accept opprobrium. And thus it is they start to lie. Once the first lie has been allowed … well …"

"'Oh what a tangled web we weave …'"

"Quite. The second flaw is that problems often take much more time than a five-year period even to be discovered, let alone addressed. Also, as you yourself just said, Rafa, most problems, for them to be tackled efficiently, need to be attacked not with the demolition ball but with the chisel. Good government needs to be thinking not five years, but twenty-five years into the future, fifty years. Government urges teenagers to contribute to pension funds whilst it won't see beyond next month's opinion polls.

"What consequently happens is that administration after administration (even the more honourable ones) just sweep the difficult problems under the carpet for the next administration to deal with: generations of inadequate schooling, deficient parenting, addiction. And that is precisely what we have seen happen. Over and over. And it's in that way that the Hamelins you talked about, Rafa, get created.

"Now Winston Churchill may well have been right when he said that democracy is the worst type of government imaginable – apart from all the alternatives.

"To young movie-directors who think the route to success is to emulate Mussolini I have been known to mutter: 'Making movies is hard enough as a process. There is really no need to make it even harder.' My philosophy of life is remarkably similar: why make the experience any rougher than it inherently is? Democracy is flawed. It may be the least inequitable system we have *yet* devised, but that does not stop it from being badly flawed. During the American Civil War, biting on a bullet might have been the best anaesthetic available. That does not make biting on the bullet an effective anaesthetic. How civilised would we consider ourselves today if we still handed out bottles of whisky as pain-killers?

"There are these two central – and devastating – flaws in

democracy even at a conceptual level. It's *already* flawed, we don't need to introduce yet more flaws into it. And yet it is precisely that which we're doing. Consequently, today we do not even *have* a democracy; we have an ersatz democracy, a shamocracy.

"I told you I read John Dean's book, 'Blind Ambition', about his involvement in Watergate. You are, Rafa, so right when you talk about the need there is for principles. Reading Mr Dean's book, you realise that within that administration crimes like the Watergate break-in were not regrettable but inevitable. There was an ethos – a climate – which considered that it (the ethos and/or the administration) was above ethics.

"And what frightens me as much as anything is that I think that ethos is today more prevalent than it was during Mr Nixon's administration, and I think further that ethos is part of the globalisation-slash-Americanisation of today's world."

"And what frightens *me*, Polly, is that I am no longer convinced that the press would break the story of Watergate. There is now just too much vested interest in vested interest.

"It frightens me as well that, so I have been told, had the Watergate break-in happened in Britain, news of it would never have been *allowed* to be published. These are worrying possibilities indeed, my friend."

"The world's problems today, Rafa – well, I don't need to tell you – they're huge problems, humungous problems. And one humungous problem of those humungous problems is that today's *is* an ersatz democracy, and that it is one without ethics. It will finally only be ethics which will solve what, finally, are ethical problems.

"We can 'logic' our way into anything. Me, I don't feel it's any coincidence that some of the most ruthless prosecutors of Hitler's 'final solution' were academically very gifted men, some of them with two PhDs. The more I think about it, Rafa, the more I think you could be right, what you said to me on one of the first occasions that we met: That cleverness could have gotten us into 'this pretty pass'.

"No point, though, too much in decrying brains. They may have been the kayak that got us into the creek, but we'll need the same kayak to get us out again. It is incredibly brainy scientists who have discovered (and understood) quantum physics and mechanics, incredibly brainy philosophers who see their application to the world at large. It's not only brains, of course, that we'll need, that much is true. Nevertheless we *will* need brains. And in abundance. The best brains available. All of them. Pulling for a common welfare. Because finally all welfare, for it to be welfare, *has* to be a common welfare. Which means we will need commodities too which have nothing to do with the brain. Courage, for example. More courage than Man has ever shown communally before. Courage by the truck-loads. Courage as well as brains, Rafa. Courage and hearts and souls.

"The good news is, I sense around me a real growth *in* that courage. I sense a swell around me of wanting, not an ersatz democracy, but a democracy indeed. Oh, just right at the moment, that growth may be no more than a ripple on the water. And yet it is becoming a very tangible ripple. It's not an accident, or a puff of wind. It is a definite stirring. Our job now, it seems to me, Rafa, is to keep on feeding that ripple and to keep allowing it to grow. We no longer need a wind of change – we're way past needing winds of change. We need a hurricane of change, my friend. We need to blow away all the cobwebs of our past, all our previous preconceptions which were misconceptions, and start afresh – all the shoddiness of this ersatz democracy, this ersatz civilisation, this ersatz economy, which is 'caring' only insofar as it cares for itself and its plutocratic doyens.

"But there's a problem with any hurricane. It is indiscriminate in its targets. We need to make sure, like chemotherapy, that we only destroy permanently those elements in the world which are killing the world, those elements our so-called 'civilisation' contains which are killing civilisation. We need to be more careful than we have been of throwing the baby out with the bath-water.

"There is so much good around us, Rafa. I mean *so* much.

"Forget the image of a wind: what we need is a thorough spring-clean. You don't spring-clean also by indiscriminately throwing away the antique furniture. You throw out only those bits of it riddled with termites. We junk the junk and keep what is valuable. The right of free speech, of lawful protest, of peaceful assembly ... these aren't passé concepts, these are Ming vases, or Titian's paintings, these are all antiques of infinite and quite incalculable value. As is the basic goodness of man, the kindness there is in mankind.

"This groundswell, this is ... let's call it, a 'burgeoning' democracy. And it starts with an ever greater distrust, not of politicians as people, but of what politicians have come to represent, and the interests that those politicians have come to represent. Having said which, it also behoves us, I think, to ask of ourselves whether we don't empower our politicians in order that they 'do' our hypocrisy for us. That we don't, in other words, cede power to, vote for those prepared to do the moral dirty work on our behalf. Is the price of power, inevitably, the exorcism of principles? Do we employ politicians to sacrifice their souls that our own may be kept ... well, if not intact exactly, more intact than they would have been without those politicians?

"We cannot simply blame the politicos. If they are internationally of the third-rate quality they are, we do need to ask ourselves how we are ourselves responsible for that. We know that violence never works. But violence daily becomes more likely. It becomes more likely yet if we continue to lambaste the senators, without also lambasting ourselves. It is fuelling the fire of what I sense is a growing disdain for the much vaunted 'political process'. This has always been something of a fallacy, but it's a fallacy rapidly becoming more and more fallacious, one which excludes ever more people. The danger is quite enormous that this swell will indeed become a hurricane, even a tsunami. It is no longer only the physically starving who are becoming so disillusioned, so desperate, so angry, so *disenfranchised*. There are also now the politically deprived, the culturally pillaged, the emotionally disregarded, the economically tossed aside, those from whom daily are being eroded their rights to life, liberty and the pursuit of happiness.

"You think the middle-classes no longer fall into that category? Ask those whose houses were repossessed during the latest recession. Or whose life-savings were decimated at a Stock Exchange stroke. The institution of wealth does not care about people at all. Whatever their creed, colour, creed, moral or social or financial commitment. The institution of wealth cares for absolutely nothing except the institution of wealth.

"Likewise, politics equally finally does not care about protecting anything other than the institution of politics. You ever heard of Scott Peck?"

"*Claro.*"

"He was a psychiatrist, you will remember. Would you think it a fair description that his work sought to propagate health by combining the spiritual with the psychological?"

"Is a bit back-of-book-like, but is okay."

"You will remember, Rafa, his exhortation – the lodestone of his entire opus, I'd say – that we need to sell the world on love. Well, here is a very real political application of that. And also of just how tough and unsentimental a concept love is.

"Because, just like South Africa's Truth and Reconciliation Committee, we're going to have some tough forgiving to do and some very tough days to survive if we are *going* to survive. 'Suicide,' like the 'M.A.S.H.' song says, 'is painless.' It's also easy. And at a personal level, I have no ethical problem with suicide whatever. It is an option I always keep open. But I do have a problem with suicides taking others with them – suicide bombers, kamikaze pilots and their like. Wasn't it the Reverend Jones or someone who instigated a mass suicide somewhere in the Caribbean? Some name like that. Hundreds dead. If we find we don't have what it takes to do what it takes, know what? We're just the Reverend Jones in sheep's clothing. And the suicide we're talking about is not of a few hundreds in the Caribbean, but, Rafa, of billions. *Bill-i-ons*. Possibly of our entire species.

"There was a good movie, directed by one of my favourite

directors, Sidney Lumet, and with one of Al Pacino's best performances. 'Serpico', it was called. It was based on the true story of a New York cop, Frank Serpico, who tried to fight the corruption inherent in the police force then. And probably now, I don't know. Anyhow, testifying to a grand jury at the end of the film, Serpico asserts that there cannot be corruption in the ranks without the complicity or tacit approval of those at the top. But that also works the other way round. Corruption in the police force, or in government, also requires that we, the men-in-the-street, look the other way. For too long we have tutted and thought to ourselves 'how awful' and have done nothing about it. 'All that is required for evil to triumph ...', Rafa."

"Sad, but true," the Peruvian agrees.

"Democracy also means that our leaders are accountable. Accountable in a way that means something. Our new emperors furthermore have got to *know* they're accountable. And *we* have to know it. And we also have to know that *they* know it. And they have to know we do. I guess you've never heard of an American comedian called Jackie Mason?"

"Alas."

"No, I didn't expect you to have. Comedy rarely travels across the language divide. He's a very funny man, Mr Mason. He said of President Nixon, for example – well, I'm paraphrasing, probably badly, but something like: 'Who says Nixon is stupid? Me, I think Nixon's a genius. A *genius*. I mean, every week they find out about some other crime he's committed, and every week someone *else* goes to jail.' And that is witty, I think, precisely because it's so true.

"I understand that presently a third of us Americans believe that President Bush had a hand in September 11th. (Of which number, as a matter of fact, I'm not one.) I really don't know how he governed at all if a percentage that high thinks he could possibly have had anything to do with a crime that large. But I also wonder whether, had President Nixon indeed stood trial, there would today be the depth of suspicion around him which clearly there is. I wonder if the

Warren Commission had not been the whitewash it so manifestly was, would there be such a degree of scepticism?

"It's for that reason that I should like to see President Bush indicted for war crimes. And Mr Blair. That there is also a General Kim Jong Il in this world or a Mr Milosevic – or possibly a Mr Putin – does not mean that these two have not committed crimes. We do not stop prosecuting shop-lifters even if there is a spate of bank robberies.

"Indeed there is so much wild and rampant speculation about the depths of their crimes that I should have thought these two statesmen would have welcomed their day in court. It would afford them an opportunity to clear their names. It'll never happen, of course. And that is sad. There will be many people in the world who will infer therefrom that, for these statesmen, such opportunity would not, in fact, be welcome. It is to be hoped that historians will record this inference.

"We have a system, Rafa, conceptually flawed. How do we check its decline, reverse it from the ersatz democracy we have today? By one incredibly simple measure, and at a stroke. Laws are passed in every land in the world equating political lying to perjury and enacting a similar penalty.

"Until governments throughout the globe pass such legislation they can have little surprise that we continue not to believe them, and that the countries over which they presently hold sway may shortly become ungovernable. Professor Sachs professes (appropriately) admiration for President Walesa. Well, I hope he remains an admirer of his. Because I see the founding of Solidarity-like movements everywhere on this planet. Maybe we need the short-term chaos that would cause in order to ensure a future we're in extreme danger of losing. Professor Sachs and I have at least one thing in common. When he was representing Solidarity, I, like Mr Sachs, was a big admirer of Mr Walesa's. Unlike Mr Sachs, my enthusiasm started waning when he started 'representing' Poland.

"In this war you talked about, Rafa, that between the Untruth and the Truth, we have to start insisting the playing-field be levelled. We have to start giving Truth a chance. Why won't vested interest give Truth that chance?

"Because, my friend, we, the 'demos' do have power. And vested interest knows that. Now is the time for us both to realise that power and to realise it. I believe that's a concept you're familiar with, my friend.

Rafaél acknowledges the compliment, and the mimicry, with a shy smile. "Long Acre?"

"Yes."

"That is the name of the street?"

"Yes, Rafa. Why?"

"Is not a curious name for a street?"

"I'd never thought about it, to be frank. It leads to Covent Garden."

"And your road, Polly, whither does that lead? I sense so much danger. The world's issues, they are – as you say – titan problems. Many, like addiction or like restoring natural habitats (rain forests and polar caps, for example) extremely complicated and inter-related, even inter-dependent. Are we, the '*demos*', are we *qualified* to come to sensible decisions about such matters? Are we not in grave danger of creating another Russian Revolution where the cure was even worse than the sickness? Where one appalling regime ceded to another which was even more appalling?"

"Well, it's a danger. Certainly it is. And it's a danger we have to be cautious about. Your thing, Rafa, about babies and bath-water. Of course we have to listen to experts, Rafa. Of course we have to. Anything else would just be insanity. And experts, Rafa, – even in Utopia – are always going to be divided in almost all opinions. And that's as it should be. There is rarely one categorical wrong and one right. But we do need to know, Rafa, that an expert is bringing nothing else to the table than his expertise. And that is demonstrably no longer the case. We're not listening any longer to experts, but to lobbyists. And it is the lobby with the most gold in its coffers whose opinion and 'expertise' we hear most often. That too is suicide. That's suicidal debate, suicidal journalism, suicidal research ... whatever. Everything screams at us, Rafa, how important it is in the war between Truth and Untruth that the Truth be given a chance to express itself.

"You talk about the Russian Revolution, about how it turned into a nightmare. It was spawned by hatred. Too much Marxist thinking is the politics of hatred. Philosophically, it's one of its fundamental weaknesses.

"And it's yet another reason why it is we have to sell the world on love. True democracy depends on love. True democracy concerns itself with voting for, not what is best for me, but what is best for us. It's the political difference between methos and wethos. And, like wethos, voting for what is best for us, finally has to be voting for what is best for me.

"This is not the phony, Southern evangelical love of 'We love you so much that, if you're gay or using drugs, we would really love to throw you in jail', nor of 'We love you so much, we really do want to see the end of the world', not that kind of love. I'm talking about genuine love. My understanding of the love Christ was talking about. And indeed that Judaism talks about. A love that wants what's best for your neighbour, a love which defines 'neighbour' as being any other sentient being you share the planet with. You don't have to *like* the neighbour. You can even be quite a miserable old curmudgeon like me, Rafa, a misanthrope, a misery-guts and love your neighbour. You do not have to like him, as I say, but you do have to respect him. And you have to respect the man's dignity. Whoever he might be.

"And, *of course*, Rafa, there's danger in all of this. Mankind has never faced such danger. If you jump out of a burning building, that has to involve danger too. But our choice is becoming that: risk jumping or do nothing and be burnt alive. Your house doesn't stop being on fire just because everyone's walking past telling you it's not. If you are choking on smoke, if you can see flames licking at the skirting-board, guess what?

"You used the analogy before, Rafa, of a train wreck. If it's headed for a ravine, you've got to stop the train. Period. Whatever happens after you've stopped it, then those are the circumstances you have to deal with. 'Least you're alive to be *able* to deal with them. And if you're not, at least you did what you could to ensure there were survivors.

"If we, the '*demos*', do not now take charge of the train, it will crash into the ravine. And, sure, there'll be survivors too from that wreck. We are all Nature's children and Nature is remarkably resilient. And when it comes to looking after her children, she is a tigress.

"But she also loves irony. Or God does. And irony would demand that many of those who do survive would be those responsible in the first place for the train crashing. And one thing that we should certainly have learnt from history is that such people do not learn from history. And it's therefore likely that, in another hundred or five hundred years' time, there will be another train hurtling towards another abyss.

"There's no 'Take Two' sometimes, remember? If a miracle happens, and this time we do pull ourselves back from the brink, it is our responsibility to ensure that never again do we get that close to it.

"If, though, we derail the train *before* it crashes, well, then there's a chance of completely rethinking our agenda. We may even start to question whether the best way to travel is by rail. Without doubt, we would need to wonder whether we are using the right fuel, whether we chose our engineers wisely, or our designers, or our signalmen. We need, in short order but in very precise detail, to scrutinise every aspect of the train and of train travel and … and … and.

"And, of course, any process of change suffers set-backs. It has to. That doesn't mean that the change isn't necessary. Your voice, Rafa, didn't just break. It went through a period when it was wobbling between *mezzo soprano* and *basso profondo*. And I'll bet you didn't have too much idea when you opened your mouth which of those would come out.

"I tried teaching myself the flute. Know what? It was all very much two steps forward and one step back. Sometimes even one forward and two back. Change, progress, improvement, they're none of them easy and straightforward marches. We get lost, we trip, we make all kinds of mistakes. In the march of civilisation, in the last decade or so we have not taken a step backwards, we have taken vast strides backwards. Which is okay. It might even be fine. Because it might – as again irony would insist – be just the thing which impels democracy to its next phase of evolution: one where it ceases to be a shamocracy and starts becoming a system of government indeed of the people for the people. One thing I did learn from AA is that often you have to hit a rock-bottom before you are prepared to change. Well, bottoms don't come a lot 'rocker' than that we've hit at the moment.

"Maybe we need that rock bottom in order for the '*demos*' to realise both their power and their destiny.

"And, of course, we'll certainly consequently throw babies out with bath water. Certainly we will. That has to happen. That's why we need to develop not the collective stupidity we seem to be striving for today, but a collective wisdom. It needs wisdom to see the baby within the bath water, and it needs courage both to acknowledge that and to retrieve the baby. The need for collective wisdom is yet another urgent one. But, however urgent, it cannot be imposed. It has to come from within us. And it will – just as soon as we have imbued each other with the self-love necessary to acquire it.

"Also in AA, I heard the adage that you can only keep it by giving it away. As applied to AA, the 'it' means sobriety. But doesn't that same adage have a far wider application? And in that wider application shouldn't that 'it' be taken to mean, I don't know, civilisation or security? Peace, perhaps, or happiness?

"Dr Peck was right. He was right about a lot of things, Rafa – and not so right too about some things. (But, hey, that's okay. That's *perfectly* okay, matter of fact. If we agree with everything anyone says we've just stopped listening.) He was never righter, though, Dr Peck than when he insisted that we need to sell the world on love.

"If we are sincere in that desire, we have to start by selling the world on *self*-love. This is not the monomania of egoism or egotism, not the vanity of vanity – real self-love, in fact, is almost the opposite of all of those: 'ego' (I remember a wise Peruvian telling me) so often gets in the way of self-interest.

"Those who love themselves will not for much longer tolerate the contempt with which they are treated by politicians, by the bureaucrats, by the industrialists and the bankers. They will not for much longer tolerate their duplicity and obfuscations, their 'being economical with the truth', with their spin or downright lies. Those who love themselves (healthily and without vanity) will start insisting that – maybe for the first time in history – it needs also to be democratically that it is the dog who wags the tail. The tail wagging the dog is a travesty of both dog and tail, in democracy as much as in economics.

"Self-love is where it all begins, my friend.

"I'm not too good at loving myself, to be frank. But I do know enough about it to know how important it is. We can't love anyone else properly unless we love ourselves. And that covers all kinds of love: passionate love, parental love, love for our neighbour, for our fellow man. Without self-love all we can offer is an ersatz love. And if we offer an ersatz love then we will have to have an ersatz democracy.

"It's finally, this self-love thing, the whole kit-and-caboodle. And it's maybe where those who have a God in their lives are so lucky. Not a religion. Too many religions have told them they are originally sinful. (And how has that, I am forced to wonder, contributed to Man so not loving himself.)

"If you have a God in your life you have there a force – and maybe too an intelligence – considerably more powerful than you are. Those with a God are able to believe God loves them. And if the Supreme Being thinks them loveable, who are they to question their loveability? But those of us who have no God in our lives, or a less defined God ... we may have a rougher time of it, but we can still find a genuine self-love. There are those (and I have met them) who have found self-love and through it have been able to find love – proper, unsentimental love – for their fellow man. There are even those, like Gandhi, able to love war criminals. They can hate the crimes whilst loving the criminal. I'm afraid I don't even aspire to be that advanced. Oh, I can understand the theory, but I just cannot apply the practice. I'd like the disgrace of war criminals to redound around the world and in the history books. It's one lesson of history that mankind simply has to learn: that it is not possible to advance civilisation by regressing.

"Not even the likes of Giscard d'Estaing's friend, Bokassa, or the much forgotten Greek colonels do I want to see them *killed*. Not even Eichmann or Mengele. Love them, though? That's a bit too hard. Sure, I accept (sort of) that these are hurt people who are hurting people. But their crimes ... well, they are *so* grotesque, *so* barbaric. Why make martyrs of them? Why make martyrs of tyrants? One of the quite staggering achievements of President Bush's administration is that he succeeded in ceding the moral high ground, of all people, to Donald Rumsfeld's friend, Sadam Hussein!

"Democracy, like grief, is not an event but a process. It burgeons. It is burgeoning. And it is relative. Today's democracy even in the UK is considerably greater than it was two hundred years ago – where registered voters represented about the same percentage as those today living in abject poverty in the States. Even a hundred years ago, suffrage here excluded women. In some countries – yes, some too in Europe – women didn't have the vote till well after the Second World War. And, as we have said before, there are still countries in the world where women are *still* not allowed to vote. Provided we recognise faults, we recognise flaws and short-falls and deficiencies, provided we are vigilantly addressing all of them, we are moving forward. And if we're moving forward we're moving away from the abyss. We stop moving forward, though, if self-examination is replaced by complacency – or, Rafa, the hubris we talked about."

"We could start, as you say, Polly," suggests Rafa "by demanding that laws be passed which would exact criminal penalties for political lies. And then that CEO's accept responsibility for the lies propagated by those acting for their company."

"And just as soon as those laws are enacted," agrees Polly, "we could pass another demanding the end of living statues!"

They have arrived in Covent Garden.

Chapter 15

Since she left Orphalese she's been in a dream world. Her thoughts are in clouds way above the clouds she's in.

She's flying.

In the last century of the second millennium after Christ, Man finally achieved the impossible: He learnt to fly.

Flying today is commonplace. We have forgotten its miracle. "Man," Saskja remembers Arkona saying, "seeks spectacle not sight." For most of us, the computer is either a convenience or a toy; the walk on the moon merely a development. It is flight which is the achievement, flight which was the major technological break-through of the twentieth century. And Saskja, only on her second flight, still revels in it.

Her first flight had taken her from Orphalese to Rome: A modern miracle zooming her to a place of so many ancient marvels – and medieval marvels. Her budget had allowed her only two nights there. She had queued from dawn to see the Sistine Chapel, she had gloried in St Peter's and gaped at the Coliseum. It is a city where history's soles have trampled into souls, and where no-one *with* a soul leaves as they arrive. A loaf of Roman bread has three thousand years of history kneaded into it; the pasta, olive oil, the wine, all of it flavoured with the sweat and failed experiments and benign mistakes of ancestors forgotten way before Jesus was born; a technology claimed to be Roman, but mostly developments from the Greek and Egyptian, the Babylonian and Etruscan, and, especially, the Punic. The Punic which the Romans had annihilated; the Carthaginians whom the Romans had butchered, but who for centuries previously had lived harmoniously and traded amicably with the residents of what today is Spain.

The song plays scratched-recordly in her head, 'Arrivederci, Roma'. She knows she will see it again. Most visitors to Rome instantly become addicts. They need their fix.

It's not over, the shame and the trauma of the abortion, but she now knows that, whilst never will either be completely removed, both will, in time, be livable with.

She drinks the little plastic bottle of white wine they have supplied with her cellophane-wrapped 'allday brunch' and she gazes at the cloud dunes out of the window. How could anyone tire of such views? These are views which even the most famous of history could only imagine gazing on. Aristotle had no such views nor Michelangelo, not Erasmus nor Thomas More. No king or pope had ever seen such sights – nor Luther or Confucius. Not even Jesus Himself, nor the Buddha, nor Muhammad.

She remembers reading somewhere that air-travel is the single biggest contributor to global warming. Surely there must be a way to protect both this miracle *and* the planet. Flight must help the planet consider itself as one. When it does so consider itself, its diversity will be encouraged, not eroded – and *Roman* bread will be kneaded by three thousand years of *Roman* sweat, not by multinational bread manufacturers (one of which had manufactured her 'brunch'), and the Orphalese bread will be that kneaded by three thousand years of Orphalese sweat. What was English bread like? What was England like? What would it be like, living with Giselle?

She imagines Giselle.

She imagines her at Heathrow, imagines how she'd be waiting for her. She knew from Rome's 'da Vinci' airport that the arrivals' board of up-to-date airports glides effortlessly from one set of announcements to another, but the board at home still clacked when it changed its bulletin. She doesn't know why, but it is at a *clacking* arrivals' board that she envisages Giselle checking her flight's arrival time – and re-checking it ... and then checking it again. And Saskja imagines her, as she checks, enfolding her arms around her girth, shielding her embryo, encasing it in love, already lullabying it on a tree-top. Doing all those things she has forced herself *not* to do. All those things, anyway, she has *tried* to force herself not to do, usually without success.

Giselle'd be nervous, Saskja figures. She'd have to be nervous. They scarcely know each other. As anything more than pen-pals, anyway. Many moons previously, when Lakshmi had still been alive, Giselle had offered to teach her Italian. There'd been a rapport then between them, sharing the grief of Lakshmi's illness, then her death. But shortly afterwards Giselle had left for London. Here they were, effectively strangers, about to share their lives for several months; here Saskja was, about to accompany her friend though the most life-changing experience of her friend's life – as Giselle, albeit not yet aware of it – was about to accompany Saskja through one of her life's biggest traumas, and certainly the biggest she'd had to confront to date.

And she'd have to do all that with a smile on her face, whilst her heart was breaking.

Chapter 16

"You sure I haven't shown you this before?" asks Polly.

"I am sure," Rafa returns. It's a cold, sleety day. The sky is grey, the more cheerless (paradoxically) for being quite light in its greyness; the drizzle as from a vapouriser, the more penetrating (paradoxically) for being so light. They are walking up the recently constructed steps from the gulch of Trafalgar Square to the base of the National Gallery. It's all rather pompous, and distinctly grandiose, but – for all that – there is a rectilinear, but also a plum pudding splendour to it all.

"Well, that over there, that slightly odd looking building, bowing over the red tarmac, that's Admiralty Arch. It marks the start of the Mall, at the other end of which is Buckingham Palace." Still Polly pronounces the 'ham' as if it were meat, and not in the English fashion of a truncated 'um'.

"Is the London residence of the Queen."

"Known recently as Bickering 'em Palace."

"What I think you might describe, my friend, as a neat driveway."

"You *sure* I haven't told you this before?"

"Mayhap a good place to discuss envy."

"Oh? Why? Why, I mean, a good place?"

"Do not most people envy the Queen?"

"You're asking *me*? I, Rafa, envy *everyone*."

"Anyone who isn't you?"

"Pretty much. Sure, I envy the Queen. Well, I sort of envy her."

"It occurs to me, one of the most sinful aspects about all the, quotes, 'deadly sins' is their ability to blind. Worse, to distort. Because, as we have said before, disinformation is more harmful than ignorance. At the level of distorting, these traits become weapons fighting on behalf of the Untruth. Greed, pride, anger, lust, gluttony ... and now envy. All of them are filters through which our perception of reality is altered. You are not, *amiga mía*, not by a long way, the only person who is envious of the Queen. The Queen has what is perceived to be a, quotes, 'enviable' life-style. I wonder, though, whether she believes herself to enjoy one. I wonder too whether you would continue to envy her if you changed places with her for a day."

"'Do not judge a man until you have walked ten leagues in his moccasins'?"

"Well, mayhap something along those lines."

They continue now walking up the front stoop which leads to the entrance of the National Gallery. It is, in its apparent horridness, a perfect day to be looking at pictures.

Polly is wearing a light blue puffer jacket. She seems quite comfortable in the insidious deluge. "I'm envious," she says, "of her sense of purpose: that she's never had to look for it, that it's always been there. Well, point of fact, in this queen's case, that's not true. She was destined to be some fringe member of the Court ... an 'attendant princess', to misquote Eliot. It was her uncle who was due to be king, not her father. I'm envious more of Charles that he inherited a sense of purpose."

"And this, you think, is a blessing?"

"To those of us, Rafa, riddled with sloth, sure it is."

"It seems to me, one of the problems with politics is that politicians are so desperate to get themselves into history books; paradoxically, it seems to me that one of the greatest problems with monarchy (as a system of government or even of social cohesion) is that monarchs aren't. They're *guaranteed* their place in history whatever they do or don't do. Doesn't that demean them as human beings? And if it doesn't, *per se*, do you not think that their own perception is that they are undervalued as human beings? That their function is iconic and titular and ceremonial, that their importance is as a figurehead and not as a person? That it is not them being curtseyed to or reverenced but their rank? Which, of itself, is nothing but an accident of their birth?

"Isn't depriving the royal family of choice an affront to the dignity due them as human beings? I am not, Polly, as you know, a monarchist. But that is not because I feel antipathy towards the members of the royal family, not *per se*: neither this one nor any other. For some I even have great respect. As I also have respect for the Dalai Lama. Indeed the utmost respect for him. His position too was one without choice, was what many would consider an 'accident of birth'. And I would most avowedly *hate* either his job or the job of being king of England – or Norway ... or Transylvania or Lilliput."

"King of Utopia?"

"In Utopia, my friend, the king, having a choice, would abdicate."

"Yeah, right," says Polly. "We have to check our umbrellas."

"Of course," he replies. They are attended by a remarkably ruddy Cockney, greying hair, almost white toothbrush moustache, and a manner as beguiling as it is unexpected.

"I love this gallery," exclaims Polly. "You ever read the Hannibal Lecter books, Rafa?"

"I fear not."

"Do yourself a favour and read them. You know he was this cannibalistic killer, right?"

"Yes, that I do know."

"But a man too of ... sophistication, let's call it, and of aesthetic appreciation."

"This has to do with envy?"

"Getting there, Rafa. It was Hannibal Lecter's ambition to see every Vermeer in the world."

"There are not too many, no? I think?"

"Such as there are, though, they're pretty scattered. My ambition is a bit more general: I just want to visit every major art gallery in the world – with or without a Vermeer. I've barely as yet made a dent in the list, I'm afraid. But, know what? Even if eventually I do fulfil my ambition, I'm willing to lay odds that this – the British National Gallery – would still be one of my favourites. You like Canaletto?"

"That anything like cannelloni?"

"Yes, very funny, Rafa."

"I think, mayhap I have a greater admiration for him than I have a fondness. Does that make sense?"

"They've got some great Canalettos here."

"In that case, I shall admire his work again. Take me to your Canaletto."

"Envy? The sixth deadly sin, envy, no?"

"Envy, yes."

"I walk around galleries like this," Polly announces on the stairs, "I feel envious. Incredibly envious. I'm, in fact, eaten away by envy. Do we need to be clear about our understanding of the difference between jealousy and envy?"

"To me," says Rafaél, taking his time, breathing heavily as he ascends the imposing treads, "jealousy is the fear of losing something you have: a lover, a reputation et cetera."

"And envy is wanting something which someone else has ..."

"Like a lover, a reputation et cetera. Mayhap obsessively also needs to be applied to both words."

"Obsessively, yes, 'mayhap'." Rafael again fails to hear the mimicry, or again chooses not to. "There are also, it seems to me, two types of envy."

"Oh, several, I think, my friend."

"I'm envious of the painters in this world like the Canalettos ... the Botticellis, the Gainsboroughs, the ... yes ... Vermeers. That's one kind of envy. But that, it's almost a kind of fantasy envy. My envy is an unrealistic envy. There is no way, not in this incarnation, that I could ever *hope* to approach their talent. Me, I can't even sharpen a pencil. Which can mean I'm also envious (another kind of envy) of those people who are certainly not major artists but who can squiggle three lines onto a scrap of paper and there it is: the identifiable depiction of that which they want to draw: the flower they don't know the name of, the umbrella ... whatever.

"I'm not expressing this too well. Let me try another tack. I've always wanted to direct, Rafa. My own movie, I mean. I think I told you that."

"No," he says simply. "No, you didn't."

"You sure? I'm amazed. Well, there you go. I always have. What can I say? Did we just use the word 'obsessively'? It sure applies here. *Obsessively*, Rafa, I've wanted to direct my own movie. Oh, it's never going to happen: I'm too old, drink too much ... but reality rarely inhibits obsession.

"Now, I'm envious of, say, Rouben Mamoulian. ... You've never heard of him ... Today, let's say of Baz Lehrman. Or Costa-Gavras. Of Woody Allen or Billy Wilder or Sidney Lumet or William Friedkin or Norman Jewison, at his best. Or Elia Kazan. Or, come to think of it, Chabrol or Truffaut ... or Berri, Bunuel, Fellini ... or Eisenstein or Kurosawa ... or ... or ... or. Not of them as people. I don't know them. But I am envious of their talent and their work. But that envy, that's a kind of respect. And it enhances, that respect, both my appreciation of that work and my whole life. It so enhances it, in fact, that such respect starts to *inform* my life – and would inform my work if I were ever allowed to execute it. All great art informs our lives positively, Rafa. I firmly believe that the paintings here, great music or drama or architecture, they all help to validate us, help to make us more whole, with greater integrity. I also think art has the power to change us. You ever heard, Rafa, of a Czech writer, Milan Kundra?"

"A vague bell tinkles."

"Amongst other things, he wrote 'The Incredible Lightness of Being'."

"I know the name. I fear, not the work."

"It's his opinion that the Prague Spring of '68 started eight years previously – with a production of Ionesco's plays at a small theatre there."

"Is not the only function of art, to inform us *politically*," says Rafa, "Indeed, is almost rarely such is its function. I think also we get informed by not great art. By third- and fourth-rate art. And is that, I think, which is happening today – and causing much of what is happening today. Ionesco asks us to rebel, to think radically. So much art today urges our compliance, enjoins us not to ponder, not to question. Or, if to ponder, then to ponder the wrong questions. We live on the San Andreas fault. We are more and more being asked to ponder whether we should build a bungalow or a two-storied house. Almost never do we ask ourselves whether it's sensible to build *anything* on a geological fault line. Never have all films, Polly, been great works of art. Very few even when he was working were directed by your friend Mr Mamoulian ..."

"Scarcely a friend."

"Of course a friend. These ... all these painters ... these are all my friends. Anyone who brings you joy is a friend. Why are actors so revered? Even anyone who seeks to bring you joy. There is nothing wrong with films that aren't works of art (or any other art that purists don't consider 'art') ... provided they are not enjoining you to participate in your own subjugation. Anyone who causes you to examine your soul or your conscience, anyone who urges you to rebel, these are all friends. Just as those who want you to comply are not your friends. The blacksmith who forges the manacles that chain you, he is not a friend. I do not think, Polly, we can be *not* informed by the 'art' or the 'arts' with which we are surrounded. One of the most influential figures today of the behind-the-arts-scene is an advertiser. He is, it seems to me, infecting the rest of the world with the same 'methos' which is the quintessence of his trade. The world of fine art is therefore suffocating. What art, what artist today is threatening? Or shocking, in anything other than the schlocking? Or challenging or demanding? Ironically, I think Mr Hirst might have been. Or Ms Emin. But ... well, it would seem they have chosen less ambitious paths.

"I said a moment ago that is not the only function of art to inform us politically. But, paradoxically, all art finally is political, if only circuitously. Which is why dictatorships always seek to crush or control it. Because all art is searching for Truth, at some level – and if the first casualty in any war is the truth, so is it the first casualty of any putsch. Great art is part of the precious, the quest for which is the point of life. If our precious is puny, if the Truth represented is a cheap truth or a fortune-cookie Truth, then we allow the precious generally to be puny, the truth generally to become cheap and specious. Which allows politics to become sound-byte politics.

"The place of truth has been usurped by glitz and by tinsel – sometimes, as with Damien Hirst's diamond-encrusted skull, literally. Gaudi has ceded to the gaudy. Is yet another part of the overwhelming Untruth. And its consequences are extremely grave. Precisely because our lives *are* informed by such images and imagery."

"What might be called 'graven imagery'."

"Or mayhap indeed 'craven' imagery."

"And 'mayhap' too we have strayed a fraction from the point."

"Do forgive me, Polly. I am so sorry."

"What I'm saying, Rafa – trying to – I'm saying that envy of a few great directors, that enhances my life. And my life being enhanced, that has to enhance the lives of those I come into contact with. Benign spirals again. And, were I ever to direct in fact, my work too would be enhanced by my envy of such talent. It would urge me to delve deeper to find my own. Just as Michelangelo, say, was driven to dig deeper out of envy of da Vinci. And thus again benign spirals start to grow.

"But I am also envious of those, Rafa, who call themselves directors (and who have 'director' stamped inside their passports) and who shouldn't be allowed to direct traffic in a one-way street. And that envy *detracts* from the quality of my life: It is corrosive and (as you said a bit back) it distorts. I don't actually *see* the films made by such directors. I see the inept or the meretricious or unwatchable films they make – and I have made that judgement before I have even sat down. There are just too many good technicians employed on even the worst film today for there not to be some quality in that film. But I can never see it. Even in 'Titanic', Rafa, the sets were good."

"I have been told so."

"There could be an interesting piece of lighting, or an innovative camera move, a clever make-up ... a good performance or two. But none of that matters. The film stinks just because of who directed it. What I'm saying, Rafa, this division of envy, I think that's got a wider application. I think envy can exert us to a greater effort, but I think too it can blind us to the good that there is in other people. It can be used positively, as a spur; but I think it can also be used negatively, to impede us. It can be used to enhance the quality of our life and of life generally, but it can also be used to debase it. It can be invigorating, but, misused, it can be toxic."

"This too seems something common to all deadly sins: that they are not necessarily sinful, or even viceful. Properly applied, they can be beneficial."

"Right. My point exactly. It's akin to competitiveness. A certain amount of envy *can* be healthy. My worry is that we left the point some time ago when our level of competitiveness was still healthy. And maybe that's also true today of envy."

They pass by Goya's portrait of the Duke of Wellington. But they are kids in a candy-store, so set on getting to the humbugs they miss the toffee-apples en route.

"All we bleeding-hearts and lily-livered liberals, Rafa, we've all, for the last hundred and fifty years, been warning that Man needs to evolve beyond the 'survival of the "fittest"', because anything else will lead to control by the barbarians and by the most violent. A danger Darwin himself foresaw and against which he warned us. Evolution does not require us humans, Darwin insisted, to treat each other with cruelty or a lack of compassion. Those warnings today seem to have an awesome prescience about them. Our need today is absolutely not for more aggression, but for *considerably* less, not for greater greed and selfishness, but for *considerably* considerably less."

"Professor Dawkins would agree with you, Polly. Professor Dawkins is mayhap most famous as an atheist. But is also a Natural scientist of international status. He contends that we choose our mates today, not for their aggressive qualities but for their qualities of gentleness and sympathy."

"I think I heard that. Canaletto, Rafa!"

"Canaletto, plural."

"Yes, indeedy."

"I amn't too sure I've previously seen plural Canalettos."

"One of the jobs of an assistant director is to organise what's called the background action: you know, choreographing when the passers-by pass by, that sort of thing. Consequently I'm overly conscious of it. One of the ways I can tell if it's a good movie is if I remain unaware of the background action. Good background directing, like all good directing, should be invisible. There are a few masters of the craft of background direction: David Tomblin was one, God rest his soul. Terry Needham today. Most a.d.'s, though, are – frankly – woeful in this regard. (Well, in most regards, point of fact. But particularly noticeable in that one.) Background action, it's sometimes also called 'atmosphere', and really that's what it is: you create the atmosphere of ... I don't know, a city street, perhaps, a busy train station ..."

"... An art gallery?"

"Or, Rafa, an art gallery. Maybe that's what I like so much about Canaletto, is what I'm thinking: the atmosphere he creates through his attention to detail. It's not only the intricate draughtsmanship of the detail, it's also the wit and the minor dramas of the vignettes he depicts, the sub-plots, as it were. Look at how busy it is on the far side of the river. You don't notice it. And yet it's there. The sense of bustle, all around you. Canal, I suppose it is. Canal, I mean, rather than river. I take it the Stonemason's Yard is in Venice."

"Are those not gondolas?"

"'Course they are. What am I thinking? ... You know what '*schadenfreude*' is, Rafa?"

"It sounds like *sachertorte*: Austrian chocolate cake. Am I close?"

"Only insofar as both are German-speaking. '*Schadenfreude*' is glee at the woe of others."

"I think I prefer *sachertorte*."

"Some would say that *schadenfreude* tastes much sweeter. Is that part of envy too, do you think?"

"Mayhap. Mayhap too is part of European culture. There is, I think, an element in that culture which inflates people only to prick the bubble of its own creation. Sometimes that's even healthy. Just as we need to know that no-one is above the law, so we also need to know that no-one is above satire. Or mockery. Or rebuke."

"I remember reading somewhere that Man's problem is not that he doesn't love his neighbour as himself, but that he does. Sadly, he hates himself. So he therefore hates his neighbour. Is that hatred of him compounded by his envy of him?"

"These things so often feed off one another. You have, I think I remember correctly, also read President Mandela's book, 'The Long Walk to Freedom'."

"Like Naomi Klein's books, its reading should be compulsory."

"In it, you will mayhap remember, President Mandela opines that what we are really frightened of, the single thing which most frightens us, is the potential within us.

"Well, I think, yes and no. Is true, I think, that we are very scared of journeying within, we are scared of what we may find. We call those with talents 'gifted' ... they have received a 'gift'. And they *have*. Of course they have. But is a gift with an obligation. And at some level we know that also. The artists exhibited here, how much choice did they have? Was there not a compulsion in them to paint? And does that not compulsion – like an accident of birth – confiscate choice?

"There is that within each of us, I suspect, which knows there is an Ali Baba's cave inside us of treasure. Which we call our potential. But we see this not as a treasure-chest but as Pandora's Box. God only knows the consequence of opening it. God knows what obligations it might contain, whither it might impel us we must go. We could become Gauguin, or someone, obliged to quit our comfortable lives because the muse of our potential is a dominatrix without mercy. Have to live rough, know hunger and want, die alone of syphilis in a deserted beach hut. We are in awe of it. Is a sleeping dragon. Better, more *prudent*, to let it sleep.

"Someone once wrote that the saddest epitaph for anyone is: 'potential still intact'. But is that not the epitaph of most of us? And might it well not be the epitaph for mankind as a whole?

"I wonder whether we also *know* this: at some level deep within us, I mean. And I wonder whether we are therefore disgruntled by our own cowardice. And we seek our heroism (therefore again) in other, more public, less scary ways – like waging war, for instance, or training for hours to perfect our kicking of a ball.

"Such creates problems for us. At some level, as I say, we *know* we have left this treasure-trove undisturbed. And at some level too that lack of disturbance disturbs us. We may not be able to put our finger on it (though we grope around and find catch-all phrases, like 'mid-life crisis' and their like), but we sense we have not made of ourselves all that we might. And this breeds a world of unfulfilment and discontent, Polly, and of frustration. Often, if we are frustrated with ourselves, is those around us, and nearest to us, who suffer most. Which returns us again to the vicious spiral of anger.

"At that level I entirely agree with President Mandela, and I think his apparently innocuous little sentence, or paragraph or whatever it was, if pondered, has serious implications for the entire of mankind, of enormous weight, incalculable weight. But so do I think there are equally serious implications in the 'no' I also have to his contention.

"The 'no': that is, that I suspect even more than we are scared by our own potential, are we *terrified* by that of our neighbour – and neighbours. We are *so* terrified of that potential, I think, that we are prepared to stifle our own potential in order to stifle his. Mayhap that's all part of the alpha male syndrome, I don't know. That provided we stifle our neighbour's potential, he won't be as alpha as he otherwise might be, and that therefore our territory and/or our sexual success is less likely to be threatened. As I say, I have no idea. Amateur psychiatry is a dangerous hobby. But that this fear – this *terror* – exists, for that one does not need expertise but eyes. We have, I think, to start recognising that such proclivity is common to us all – or almost us all. And that the only way to overcome it is for us all to urge, and continue to urge, one another that we do overcome it. Presently we laugh gently at it: is a foible, like a maiden aunt's fondness for canasta. Not a trait of much significance. It has *enormous* significance. It too has literally *earth-shattering* significance.

"We need to start thinking of our neighbour's potential as food. When we are starving. We have a window-box; the neighbour has a kitchen-garden. We need to recognise that is in our interest that we encourage him to grow his vegetables. It will be his vegetables which also feed us."

"That too, Rafa, requires methos to change to wethos."

"Mankind's entire future, Polly, requires that we change methos to wethos. Without wethos there is no future. Is that simple. And without change there will be no wethos. We cannot change the world until we change ourselves. And we cannot change ourselves until we start knowing ourselves. *Truly* knowing ourselves, warts and all. I love this picture, this 'Stonemason's Yard'. I feel warm just looking at it. The darkness of the shadow, the *starkness* of the shadow. I understand somewhere in this gallery there are also some Rembrandts."

"Sure there are."

"I'm rather an admirer of Rembrandt's. Would you mind?"

"That, Rafa, is a bit like asking Winnie the Pooh if he minds visiting a honey factory."

"You know the way?"

"That's what the attendants are here for."

"Oh? I thought it was for security."

"'Course it is, Rafa. Sadly. There was talk, you know, all these works, they'd all have to be put behind glass. Some years ago, now. After ... was it a paint attack? I'm thinking ... Amsterdam?"

"A schizophrenic, amn't I right?"

"Was that envy too, do you think?"

"Mayhap. In a demented way. Finally I do not think we can protect ourselves against that kind of attack. The suffragettes, no?, made a similar attack at the start of the twentieth century. Whatever world you create, however apparently 'perfect', there will always be the odd lunatic, the odd misguided zealot (or pawn) who will spray-paint a Rembrandt or who will set fire to a vivisection laboratory or will maim a Larry Flynt or kill a John Lennon.

"Some cultures *continue* to promote the idea that violence is an acceptable way of settling differences. Even today. Even with so much history showing so clearly such is not the case. And I think within such cultures, the deranged or the fanatical are more inclined to express their disturbance in a violent fashion. European statesmen have considerably fewer bodyguards than their American equivalents. Even in *South* America, even our fascistic dictators, even the likes of Galtieri or Lady Thatcher's friend, Pinochet, even they had less protection than we see surrounding American politicians. Is not – I am sure of this – that the average American citizen is more violent, more psychotic than the average Paraguyan or Venezuelan, is that there is underlying so very much of American culture the concept that might is right. Also that such concept is a morally acceptable one."

"American culture also extols *envy*, my friend. ..."

"Oh, yes."

"I hate the word 'star' today. Like 'genius', it's so over-used as to be meaningless. But because they have been dubbed 'stars', many of these so-called stars seek to be treated in the manner in which they think stars such as they *should* be treated. (Which is – ironically enough – not treatment expected by most of those who are genuinely stars.) Some of these so-called stars from Britain, for very obvious reasons, emigrate to the States. Which is fine – perfectly fine, in fact. I have no problem with that. But it does entice from me the odd chuckle when such 'stars' claim, as their reason for emigrating, the fact that in the States people are not envious of success. All I can say is, they must have moved to a different country than I grew up in.

"There's a great line in Mel Brooks's 'The Producers'. Zero Mostel is looking from his garrett at a bejewelled and ermined sex-kitten stepping from a stretch-limo followed by her elderly sugar daddy. 'That's it,' he expostulates to the timid Gene Wilder, 'if you've got it, *flaunt* it.' Well, I suspect that what the British stars mean when they say that America is a country not envious of success, they mean that: whereas flaunting is considered in Europe vulgar and *nouveau riche*, in the New World to flaunt what you have means that you have enough to flaunt.

"Everyone is, of course – in the Voltaire tradition –, entitled to their opinion. But to claim of the United States that it is a country without envy is like saying that Greenland is a country without snow: it flies in the face of the evidence. Like the snow in Greenland, envy is the very foundation of American life.

"Monetarism, globalisation, consumerism: they all depend on envy for their very existence. It's the utterly fictitious carrot which works in tandem with the all-too-real stick: that if you try to buck the system we'll make you suffer for it.

"And they do, my friend.

"And, my friend, they do.

"The carrot is that if you work – for *us* – that little bit harder, if you support the system that mite more diligently, it will be the Joneses who will need to keep up with you. You will be the subject of envy. It's the fundamental fantasy of the much vaunted 'American dream': Americans are loth to tax the überwealthy because they live in the dream – the fantasy – that one day they may *be* the überwealthy. The problem with the American dream is that it costs too many American nightmares ... and God only knows how many nightmares outside of America.

"Because it is the fundamental tenet also of American foreign policy: that the rest of the world is envious of her. Americans are taught to believe that the rest of the world (at least the 'civilised' world) has only one ambition: to be American. And that's why so many Americans cannot conceive why they are not universally popular, why they consider demonstrations outside their embassies as acts of treachery – worse, of ingratitude. Here they are, helping these people to become that which (so they have been taught) above all other things they crave: to be American. And now their pupils have the unbelievable presumption to *complain* about that!

"Oh, the majority of people back home live – at any rate, materially – pretty comfortable lives. The cost of that comfort, though, to their own physical, moral, emotional, spiritual well-being ... well, that too, Rafa, is probably so well documented that we don't really need to revisit it.

"But that cost to the rest of the world is ... well, as appalling as it is immoral as it is indefensible. And because another of America's prevailing problems is with the arrogance we spoke about earlier that is hubris, this evil trait is being exported throughout the world. As the lie too is being exported.

"I think it is great news that the Indian economy and the Chinese economy are starting to thrive. Why, though, does such have to come at a cost of selling their national and regional identities, their own ethos? Their own culture? (Though I do, I confess, get nervous about using that word 'culture'. It has been used far too often to excuse, even to seek to condone, blatant sexism, and blatant sexist violence: female circumcision, for example.) Why also does America feel it has the need to export envy? And the politics of envy? And envy as a tool of suppression?

"I understand the argument that the hungry have no culture beyond hunger. And, of course, the priority has always got to be that everyone be fed. But not everyone is fed back home either. And the price of being fed should not be your own soul. Nor should those who feed you expropriate your soul. Because he who extorts someone else's soul as the price for feeding that person has to lose his own. *Has* to. And certainly the cost of feeding the hungry should not be the abandoning of aeons of your own evolution. Because the world is thereby a poorer place: the world of the feeder as much as the world of the being fed."

"You do not think, Polly, there is also arrogance attached to what you are saying? Are we not in danger of becoming like politically appointed executives of television stations? Scheduling hours of what we think audiences should want to watch, rather than feeding them what they do want to watch?"

"That's the Rupert Murdoch argument, pretty much. It's a similar answer, I mean, to that I saw Mr Murdoch give once on a TV interview. And it's not an unfair argument. But is it not the place of art, however loosely you define that word, to be in the vanguard? To lead fashion rather than reflect it? In fact, whether or not it *wants* to be there is irrelevant. *De facto*, that's where it is. And it just cannot opt out of that responsibility. It'd be a similar sleight-of-logic to that which allows the NRA to deny any responsibility for gun deaths. That's the National Rifle Association, Rafa.

"And then we need to ask ourselves, do we have the right to put health warnings on packs of cigarettes?"

"Or on bottles of alcohol?"

"Right," she chuckles. "It seems to be one of our besetting weaknesses – one again common to us all – that we love giving advice ... and just hate receiving it."

"What Man certainly does not need, Polly, is anyone else today lecturing at him" suggests Rafa. "What he does need – and desperately – is people empathising with him."

"No question about that," Polly agrees. "I can't remember what the odds are, but they are quite – and literally – astronomical (several billions to one), the odds against life ever happening. The odds of any one sperm being the one to fertilise an egg, whilst somewhat less than those against life ever happening, are still so large as to be unimaginable. For the overwhelming majority of the planet's creatures, and for us until recently, it is rare – even very rare – to reach maturity. And even for those who do, death is likely to come in the form of being eaten, probably alive. One of the privileges afforded Man is that we are unlikely to die from having been hunted.

"But I think it is fair to say that life in its generality is tough. It is not an experience for the wimpish. Perhaps that's what the Buddha was trying to say when he opined that, 'Life is suffering.'

"So it's maybe one of the ways I can help you be the most 'you' you can be: acknowledging you're having a tough time. Maybe one of the ways you can best help me is by acknowledging that so am I. As you say, encouraging a climate of mutual empathy. It's not only when those we love die that we are in pain. Most of us, I venture to suggest, are in pain most of the time.

"Indeed I believe when Princess Diana was killed, the reason for the extent and depth of public lamentation was that finally the stiff English upper lip (as well as the rather less starched lips of those of us abroad) was allowed to slacken. Oh, I think there was a *genuine* sadness at her death, don't misunderstand me: She was the stuff of grand opera – a beautiful princess fated to live unhappily and to die tragically. And, of course, that genuine sadness was also massaged into a more contrived one. But that doesn't alter the fact that there was a genuine and profound grief. The outpouring, though, was one more than just of sadness. Just as that around the Kennedy assassination had been.

"I think they both gave us all the opportunity to wail.

"And we need to wail – not just for the obvious losses of our life, the deaths and divorces and failed exams – but also just for the fact that life is so terribly tough.

"Life for most here in the affluent West is, *of course,* not so obviously hard as it is for those in Ethiopian refugee camps or in Chinese prisons or Bangkok brothels or in the favelas of Rio or the refuse tips of Lima - but that doesn't mean it *isn't* tough. Indeed, more and more it is not the degree of toughness that is so different but the form that toughness takes. Is this progress?

"Read Dickens or Gaskell. Oh, we may not have workhouses, *per se*. At least, not in the West. The underlying misery of existence for most, though, has not diminished, it's just changed shape. Is this a sane way of developing a world? And if toughness is a requirement in life, why not tackle the toughness that already exists? Rather than inventing *new* forms of making life tough? Why not tackle the *really* tough job of changing the world's dynamo from hatred to love? Of changing methos to wethos?

"A world governed by love would be seeking to make life easier.

The world, as it is, governed by hatred is making it ever tougher. For most people in the world, their basic requirements become daily more expensive – particularly shelter. But food too, water, electricity, transport, telephones ... taxes. Making ends meet is becoming tougher and tougher. The energy left to seek the precious more and more depleted.

"Absolutely and unequivocally at the insistence of vested interest, the work-place daily becomes an increasingly less pleasant place to be. Daily those who should be serving us – our politicians – ever more dictate to us; daily our channels and chances to complain about corruption or price-fixing or poor service are being eroded; daily our value as human-beings is being further undermined, our dignity impugned. We are becoming inured to being spat on.

"Even if it weren't now essential to change tack, why wouldn't we *want* to? What on Earth is there about this situation which induces pleasure? Personally – as you may have gathered! – I want to change the ethos in which we live today. But my wanting it is not in the least important. Even if we lived in the most pleasurable world possible, today it is our very *survival* which would continue to insist we change that world.

"One of the things we can most effectively do to start changing is to start saying to our acquaintances, 'Know what? You're doing okay. It's so tough out there – *so* tough. If you've managed to leave your workplace today with your persona intact, you've already done well. *Incredibly* well. If you've managed to be kind to someone along the way, Jesus, well, that is the stuff of heroes.'

"To protect what they call 'liberty' methos is perfectly prepared to sacrifice the lives of legions of young men (rarely their own sons) and to spend many, many millions buying political influence: these, so methos will tell you, are the 'regrettable but inevitable' prices we have to pay in order to call ourselves 'civilised'. But as soon as we start wanting 'liberty' from hunger or under-education or sickness or cruelty or abuse or exploitation or pain or disenfranchisement, methos accuses us of fostering a 'nanny state'.

"Well, guess what, Rafa? If children don't have any other nannies in their lives, maybe it has to be the state (however inadequately) which assumes responsibilities which would, in Utopia, be the purview of the individual.

"Do we have the right to demand that people wear seat-belts or crash helmets? No, we don't. Not in Utopia. But that's not where we live. We don't live in an ideal world. And they – they: the advocates of methos – they *know* we don't. In fact, just as often as they can, they seek to remind us of how imperfect our world is, how imperfect *we* are, Man is, how imperfect are concepts like justice and parity and so on ... for just so long as it suits their purposes.

"If the weak banded together to become the strong, the end of government remains the same. Its primary function would still be to protect the weak, the new weak, those who have recently become weak. The identity of the weak doesn't matter. They are always they whom government needs to protect. It is that which defines us as a civilisation. Anything else is mere political cotton-candy. And that is why today's governments, internationally, are such an abnegation of government. And why the governments of history have so totally failed those in their charge, and humanity in general.

"Today cultures need to be protected in a similar way. There's a Canadian singer/song-writer, Rafa ... I'm sure you won't have heard of her."

"Joni Mitchell?"

"I stand humbled and corrected."

"As you should."

"Well, you'll know, then ... she once sang, 'You don't know what you've got till it's gone.' Once it's gone you're never going to get it back.

"The same thing is happening to the cultural world as is happening to the animal world. Each year we are losing irreplaceable species, treasures of incalculable worth. It takes not years but generations to train a Kabuki actor or a Noh one. If these traditions are allowed to stagnate or atrophy or merely waste away, we will never get them back.

"What about ballet as a discipline? It's no good just going to see the vastly over-rated 'Billy Elliot' and crying at the happy ending. If we fail to pay those dancers and their accompanying musicians at a rate which at least has some parity with their skill and commitment, we'll stop enjoying them.

"Now, I'm not too crazy, personally, about Morris dancing, nor about lute-playing, nor medieval canticles, but, know what? I'm real glad that there are those around who *are*. And I admire their valour, all those guys'. They're not stupid. They know they're being laughed at, that they're seen as ridiculous, as figures of scorn, and yet they keep going. More power, I say, to their jingle-belled elbows.

"When we lose species of animals we have lost them forever. And that is, at its very least, a tragedy equal to the loss of a great work of art. So is losing an element in the living arts.

"In my opinion, film and television have wreaked terrible harm on live theatre. At best, they have simply imposed on the theatre a direction it might otherwise not have taken. But that's okay. As long as it remains, it can change – in whatever direction it chooses. Inevitably with change, sometimes it is for the worse. And sometimes that 'worse' leads to a better better than the better would have been without the worse. As long as the whatever it is remains living.

"We don't have the dodo today because too often Man does not recognise the special. But we still today have the 'Mona Lisa' because he does. Traditionally I suspect Man has venerated the arts more than animal species because art is one of Man's triumphs whereas the panda or the tiger are God's. (As, incidentally, are scorpions and rattlesnakes and wood-lice God's triumphs. We'll just skip over mosquitoes for a bit!) That is not a new phenomenon either, that Man's veneration tends to be indicated by a price tag. But the case has never been endowed with more ferocity than, in the art world, it is today. In my opinion, that's thanks largely to the advertiser, and his pollution of that world. A work of art is today's status symbol. It's not even that possession of a particular piece of art is important. The kudos derives from having the money necessary to own that work of art, it's that which is important. And it's that, the ethos propagated by the advertiser.

"As if, Rafa, we *could* own a work of art. Even the concept of owning art is a travesty. At best, like our planet, we hold it in trust for humanity and for the future.

"I *understand* those in Brazil saying that, if we want to keep the Amazon intact, then Brazil should be paid to do so. In a world where money is the only currency, that strikes me as being an entirely reasonable request. How is the Amazon (and its oxygen) not a natural resource in the same way as oil is in Saudi Arabia? The world's governments unearthed a bonanza when they sold airwaves to mobile phone companies. Why should air-*waves* be a commodity and air not? Why should we *not* pay Brazil?"

"And all the *other* indigenous nations of the river? The Ashininka, for example? The Cashinahua, and all the others?"

"You know, right?, not all the inhabitants of that river are good guys. Some of the ranchers there are just as plutocratic as any JR in 'Dallas', some of the loggers still effectively use slave labour."

"But not, I think, the Ashininka. 'Ashininka', you know, means 'a brother to all'. Is rather lovely, no? Is it beyond the ken of civilised Man to create a world which could call itself 'Ashininka'?"

"Well, I'd certainly drink to that."

"If only you had a drink!"

"Patience, my dear Rafa ... What is so unreasonable, I should like to know, about Brazil's request? It'd be a good idea, I think, to stop allowing methos to talk of 'communal' good or 'communal' resources for just so long as (again) such designation suits its purpose or purposes. The commercial value of oil cannot be greater than that of oxygen. You don't need to be Einstein to understand that, before anything else, we have to continue the supply of what gives us life itself.

"'The point of life is the quest for the precious.' God, that's such a great maxim – at the very least, a very good kick-off point. Because it means we have to define what is precious. And surely one of the things most precious in the world are the world's cultures and animals. If we're serious – as another example – if we're serious about stopping the poaching of endangered species in impoverished countries, let's give those poachers alternative sources of income.

"As for cultures ... Well, I am, as I said, very envious that I cannot paint like these guys exhibited here. But I'm also envious of India, say, for the richness, not only of its culture, but of its cultures. Hundreds of different cultures, religions, languages, traditions, cuisines, music, dance ... hundreds, possibly thousands. And certainly Bollywood is doing to that culture exactly what Hollywood did to ours. It had the possibility of enriching it, and is choosing instead to diminish and to weaken it. But Bollywood is being abetted in that massacre by globalisation. In fact, Bollywood is *part* of globalisation.

"Which is, in fact, not new either. It's merely a development from the concept of conquest which started even prior to Alexander, in my opinion misnamed 'the Great'. From which has developed an insane myth that bigger is somehow better. Bigger is only better for emperors.

"More and more archaeologists and anthropologists are discovering that sophisticated societies existed before the Romans, after the Romans and despite the Romans.

"France was not properly France and Germany and Italy certainly not nations until the nineteenth century. When Napoleon seized power there were, in 'France', more non-French speakers than there were French speakers. The allegiance of these 'Frenchmen' to France very much took second place to the allegiance they felt to their immediate locality. There is no evidence that the lives of these people were improved by greater control from Paris, and a considerable body of evidence which suggests to the contrary."

"Picasso, you know, Polly, claimed that his adult work was his search to return to the skill he had as a child. I wonder sometimes whether mankind might not seek to emulate him. It seems to me so many indigenous nations continue to have attributes and values which our so-called 'civilisation' or 'development' has lost. I was thinking the same thing when I was talking about the Ashininka."

"It is an interesting phenomenon," says Polly, "that, as the globe gets smaller, so the demands for regional recognition get more clamorous. How many cultures and languages and cuisines have already been lost? How much of our identities been consequently threatened? Or frustrated? How many more treasures do we want to lose?

"I'm envious of the many thousands of cultures there are in the East. I'm terrified that America is envious of that history, that tradition and that its envy will seek to destroy both. You only need to remember the way in which Mr Rumsfeld, when President Bush's Defense Secretary, dismissed the thousands of years of European history as being without significance, or see how his troops desecrated the priceless artefacts and works of art in Baghdad – the *utterly* priceless pieces, pieces historically and culturally of incalculable value. Or hear American magnates when they drawl that Europe's future will be as the world's theme park, its culture, its art and traditions (presumably also its cuisines), of interest only academically and as a source of entertainment. And also when you hear the lies that accompany all these actions.

"That's when envy becomes unquestionably a sin. When it leads to a lack of respect. This has to lead to contempt. And contempt is only a polite way of saying 'hatred'. Hatred always destroys."

"But love is not always what makes us create."

"Explain."

"These ... these splendid paintings, my friend, these were not painted by angels, but by people. Often not only flawed people but very flawed ones. Fine painters, *amiga mía,* were often possessed as much by their own demons as by their own angels. Beautiful art was not always created by beautiful people. We must, in all of our thinking (especially as we are talking about ambitions), be careful that we don't paint with Disneyish brushes. Beauty and Truth are sometimes discovered or expounded or broadcast by very unbeautiful people. Many of the painters whose work here we admire so readily had serious emotional problems."

"Van Gogh?"

"For one. Caravaggio. Rossetti, for God's sake. Michelangelo was not a model of stability. Toulouse-Lautrec. Nor was Mozart or Beethoven. Schubert, seriously disturbed. Rimbaud, well ... Even the English children's writer, Enid Blyton, a model of propriety as she would have liked to think herself, even she, Polly, was a woman cancered by her devils. Rilke once wondered whether, if he exorcised his demons, his angels would also perish."

"The work is always more important than the artist. No? Always. Which is one of the reasons why, for instance, I don't think it is anything more than of academic interest whether or not it was actually Shakespeare who wrote the plays attributed to him.

"Does this not return us, Rafa, to the weakness we have, too many of us, the need to be immortal? That aspect of lust which we decided was sinful indeed.

"I've worked, credited, on a number of projects. It now means nothing. It's like being given a credit on a bus ticket: 'Bus driven by Polly Downer'. (In fact, I would have no problem with such bus tickets. Credit where it's due.) But how infinitely I would have preferred to have worked uncredited – as a gopher, even, as a floor-sweeper – on, say, 'Moulin Rouge'. What a privilege it would have been, in however small a way, to have contributed to bringing such a film to the world."

"One which was, I think, financed by Mr Murdoch."

"That's only because God loves irony," suggests Polly. "You've got your argument neatly tied up, just about to put the ribbon around it, when along comes a particularly uncomfortable fact which totally louses it all up. And you up! It's also 'cause God loves irony that Fox distributed two of the best, and most important, TV shows ever: 'M.A.S.H.' and 'The Simpsons'. My only consolation is that that fact is just as uncomfortable for the Fox board as it is for me.

"The Rembrandts, I think, are right through here.

"You talked, Rafa, on one of the first times we met about today's so-called 'meritocracy'."

"Today's 'meretricious-ocracy'."

"Quite. Credits – TV credits, particularly, are such a good illustration of what you're talking about. There was this great doco – *great*, Rafa, documentary – about a group of doctors who so wanted to find out more about the consequences physiologically of a lack of oxygen that they trained for two years – for two years, my friend, over and above their anyway arduous medical duties – to climb Mount Everest. And when they did so, they climbed it with all the equipment they'd need for the experiments, as well as their climbing gear. They then (suffering from altitude sickness and almost at the summit of Everest) performed these experiments on one another. This was a glorious endeavour. As selfless and as valiant as any act I've ever heard about, an act which all of us should salute and acclaim. Was there at the end of the programme a roll of these glorious men and women? There was no mention of them. Instead we learnt who the on-line editor was. The on-line editor *was* credited, but not these extraordinary, these quite outstanding philanthropists. Nothing that Mr Gates has done, in my opinion, even gets close to the philanthropy involved in that experiment. This, Rafa, is a measure of the meretricious-ocracy which today pervades. It's got absolutely nothing to do with merit. And only has to do with what's spun as merit."

"They sound, these doctors, like remarkable people."

"No political recognition either, that I've heard of. No medals from the Queen or anything. Nor the Spanish king nor French president. Watch too any ballet on the tube. You'll see the same thing: the musicians of the orchestra, the corps de ballet, all totally anonymous. These people who have sacrificed years – years, Rafa, of their lives – to become masters of their art. Again, the on-line editor, or the floor runner – the gopher – are considered more worthy of receiving public acknowledgement or recognition. We are perfectly prepared to cheer Billy Elliot the character, but not the Billy Elliots of real life. Even 'meretricious-ocracy' doesn't quite convey the contempt we should feel for such a system.

"Yes, there you go, the Rembrandts, as I said. Quite excellent. Quite exquisite too."

"Nothing meretricious about his work, Rembrandt's. Great integrity, I always thought, in his work. I can't see Rembrandt crediting the gopher and not the cellist. A delving for the truth beneath the eyes. If the sixth deadly sin, *amiga mía,* is envy, I think the sixth mortal lie is that self-love is self-love."

"Okay," says Polly uncertainly.

"I've been thinking about it since we last talked, en route to Covent Garden. You said of self-love that it was 'the whole kit-and-caboodle'. You made me think. I've also been thinking as you've been discussing envy. I become convinced of it: the sixth mortal lie is that self-love is self-love. I can go on?" Polly nods, indicating that not only *can* he but that she would welcome his doing so.

"Narcissus did not love himself. Narcissus fell in love with a distorted image of himself. Narcissism is no more *self*-love than love-at-first-sight is real love. Is, mayhap, instant attraction; is not instant love. And our generations have meted out so much harm on future generations by believing the nonsense that love-at-first-sight is possible. Is certainly true that such instant attraction can develop into love. My attraction to Inma developed into love. As (coincidentally) did her *dis*like of me. There have been many marriages or relationships in history, as happy as any, which have developed from Platonic friendships or which have started off antagonistically – or even happy marriages which have been arranged. When I say 'happy', I don't mean 'blissful', I mean as happy as the best marriages can be. Me, I care not one jot for the idea of arranged marriages, but to claim that such are of themselves doomed to failure is simply to refute the evidence. Quite as many such marriages work, as work via the extension of an attraction at first sight.

"Is such an all-embracing word, love. I love this painting, I love talking to you, Polly – I love *you* –, I love my children, my grandchildren, London, Lima. I still, my friend, love Inma. Not in the past tense, very much still in the present." Polly registers the comment, but doesn't feel able to react to it. "I love humanity. I love this planet, Polly. I love Nature and all her beauty and miracles. And I try, my friend – try very hard – to love myself. Is hard. I find this very hard. Mayhap because I was brought up to believe that loving yourself was akin to masturbation – something dirty and undesirable, a sin."

"Woody Allen once said that the great thing about masturbation is that it's having sex with someone you truly love."

"And like so very much of what you have told me of Mr Allen's work, this is most droll. But mostly is also not true. Most of us spend a lot of our time (as you yourself were saying, Polly) *hating* ourselves. And/or disliking ourselves. And/or disapproving of ourselves. And/or being disappointed ... oh, and/or very many other negative feelings we feel. And which, if exercised in moderation and with discretion, would not necessarily be a bad thing.

"They say love is blind. But I say, Polly, a love that is blind is no love. Is perhaps many things, love, but is not blind. We were talking about Oliver Cromwell. How he wanted his portrait painted, famously, 'warts and all'. And what I like about Rembrandt, he painted himself 'warts and all'. More than that even, I think. I think he delved for the inner warts, for the spiritual and emotional warts. What you see on the canvas is both Dorian Gray *and* the portrait in the attic. I think the art of great portraiture is to release the soul. You look at this self-portrait and you can see the soul of the man. You look at that portrait there, 'Portrait of Margaretha de Geer' and you know that woman better than your own mother.

"Those who love themselves accept their warts. And when one does, one finds it so much easier to accept the warts of others. Rembrandt could not have painted others as well as he did, if he did not paint himself as he did. Look at that self-portrait, there, at the age of 34. Do you not know a Falstaff-full of him just by that one depiction?

"One does not, Polly, have to *love* one's warts, one may even want to remove them, but nothing will happen to them for as long as one does not recognise the warts that are there.

"Is a journey of discovery, an odyssey. And it can be very scary. So scary in fact that only few people ever embark on it. If my own journey is a thousand steps, alas, I have barely trodden ten. I think we fear that the destination of this safari is ... well, the Woody Allen *persona*: neurotic, introspective, unhappy, self-obsessed et cetera – the Pandora's box to which you, Polly, alluded. But most of those who make the journey become, in fact, incredibly un-neurotic, and mostly very giving.

"I imagine that President Mandela, for instance, loves himself. Certainly 'The Long Walk to Freedom' would give you that impression. I suspect Dr Schweitzer did. And what happens to us personally happens to us socially, happens to us as well nationally and internationally.

"We should learn to love ourselves wisely. We rarely take the time to applaud ourselves or our bravery or our diligence or our kindness or ... well, our et cetera. And we should. We really should. Who was it who said, 'We, most of us, live lives of quiet desperation'? I cannot recall. But within those quietly desperate lives, most of us do amazing things. We struggle on through hailstorms of slings and arrows, we raise families, help those who need our help, forgive those who hurt us, survive tragedy. We do, yes, amazing things. And only very rarely do we give ourselves the credit, the applause that we deserve.

"You were talking in Piccadilly, Polly, about the Oscars. The Oscars are fine. No, *mostly* they're fine. We should have our own private Oscar ceremony each night when we clean our teeth. 'And the Oscar for the kindest thing I did today goes to ...', 'The winner for our most laudable achievement today is ...'

"The Oscars at their best are a method of doing professionally what we should be doing personally: complimenting ourselves on a job well done. At the level of theory, the Oscars are a sound exercise and a healthy one."

"A lot less so in practice."

"You know much more about such things, my friend, than I do. But such ceremonies need, I feel, also to be balanced with: 'What did we do wrong?' The un-Oscars you talked about. And *we* need the un-Oscars too. Cleaning our teeth, we also need to present ourselves with: 'The *un*-Oscar for the most unpleasant thing I did today goes to ... shouting at the meter maid ...,' let us say, '... for giving me a ticket' or 'for not phoning Mother' or 'for buying shares in a company manufacturing weapons ... or supplying torturers' ... or 'investing in an *insurance* company' ... or et cetera.

"The benefits of such an exercise to the world are, I think, incalculable. I wonder how many people could do such an exercise and admit to their reflection: 'My un-Oscar goes to mugging that old lady'; or '... to molesting that young child'; or '... to torturing a prisoner in Abu Ghraid'; or '... to ordering the invasion of Iraq'? How much anti-social, anti-*global* activity would be curtailed by this one device alone?

"Oscars without un-Oscars become a manifestation of narcissism. Not only narcissism either, but the narcissism of the child whistling in the dark. People, though, who truly love themselves want also to know their own faults. They know this lovable person is worth the effort of becoming more lovable yet.

"The most sophisticated civilisations encourage criticism and satire. These are two vital tools in the permanent task of self-improvement. Is a measure of how uncivilised we today are that there is such a shortage of both.

"For all his many faults, Marcus Aurelius is probably the lone Roman emperor to whom any respect is due at all. And one of the main reasons that he does deserve such respect is that he was perspicacious enough to welcome criticism. On paper, at least!

"In comedies we laugh at the business bully surrounded by yes-men and whose company therefore goes bankrupt. In life, however, we allow this situation to become more entrenched with each passing day.

"And that manifests itself in a world which spends its time

pointing fingers outwards. This also we have talked about before. Is worth repeating. And, yes, likewise neither is this a new phenomenon. 'It's *your* fault,' we spend so much of our time saying. The Israelis blame the Arabs, and the Palestinians blame the Zionists; al-Qaeda blames American imperialism and America blames Islamic extremism; North Korea and South Korea blame each other; Protestant and Catholic; Shi'as and Sunnis; management and the unions; parents and children; contractors and contractees ... *ad infinitum* ... *ad nauseam* ... and *ad* a huge amount of aggression. Throughout history nothing has ever been 'our' fault, always it has been either 'your' fault or 'their' fault.

"If we are serious about giving peace a chance, we need first to examine where we – personally, regionally, professionally and nationally – are at fault. And we need to recognise that.

"My daughter, Inma, she was robbed. (We call our children in my country often after their parents. Before you ask, Rodolfo's elder brother died.)"

"I'm so sorry, Rafa."

"Me too. Was a long time ago, but ... Me too. ... Inma was mugged. In Lima. She reported it to the police. As angry as she was at the robber, she became more angry yet with the police. Because they were so casual in their dealings with her, so cavalier. In Lima, of course, there are hundreds of such muggings per day, possibly thousands. This for the police was not a serious incident. They probably thought my daughter a nuisance for having reported it. And I can understand that. Is human, is normal. But also I understand Inma's anger.

"The point of this story is that when we are in pain we want that pain acknowledged. And in a world which debases or ridicules self-love, is very rarely that such pain *is* acknowledged. And this has national, and international, dimensions quite as much as it does personal ones.

"A large part of the reason behind Hitler's election in 1932 was that the German people didn't think anyone internationally was taking their pain seriously. (And, to be fair, I don't think many people were.) A combination of gargantuan First World War reparations and an international Depression had led to an inflation where weekly wages were counted in millions of marks and had to be transported in wheelbarrows. When along came this funny little man who did take their pain seriously. And he also told the Germans it was not the Germans' fault. The Germans weren't responsible for their calamities. "We aren't responsible," he told them. It was 'their' fault, the Jews' fault.

"Would a day of national soul-searching have displaced Hitler? Well, leaving aside for the moment that in no conceivable circumstances would he have allowed it, who – as you would say, Polly – knows? Probably not. But if such days had been instituted in the nineteenth century, just mayhap the First World War would never have occurred. Without the First World War there could not have been the Second.

"If Florence Nightingale's virulent criticisms had been heeded and published of the generalship in the Crimea War, would the appalling casualties have occurred in that First World War? Would it even have happened? If, during the Raj, the British had had a day of conscience, would it have been able to continue its pillage of India? Well, probably 'yes' to that as well, it saddens me to say. There was then about the British an arrogance that she was somehow divinely chosen to 'civilise' the 'barbarian' world. She had become the Rome of the nineteenth century.

"Most of us have now progressed a little since that point. We see that anyone trying to enforce what it deems to be a civilisation on what it deems to be the uncivilised is, dint only of that wish alone, far less civilised than the community which it is seeking to 'civilise'. Indeed, as I was saying a moment ago, many indigenous nations have developed a common wealth and a common purpose which we sophisticates would do well to envy.

"At the time of the Raj, your country, Polly, was fighting a civil war, largely on the issue of slavery. Well, things *have* progressed since then. Sadly, there is still slavery in the world – far, far more than is acknowledged in official figures. But that lack of acknowledgement is indicative that methos knows that such is no longer acceptable.

"Self-love is not the narcissism methos insists it is. Quite the contrary. Indeed those who seek to belittle it as such expose only how little is the love they have for themselves – or for their fellow man.

"People who love themselves do not aerosol pictures or mug young women, or *old* women, in the street or tell lies to justify their invasion of foreign soil.

"People who love themselves walk away from potentially violent scenes, and sort out their differences calmly and with respect for the opposing point-of-view.

"People who love themselves do not carry weapons, because they don't want *themselves* hurt. People who love themselves do not harm their children or other people or animals, they do not drink too much or gamble too much or use drugs inappropriately, they do not drive too fast or shout at their juniors or countenance the nefarious trading of the likes of Halliburton or Enron, or the concealed history of the likes of IBM and Coca-Cola.

"Those who love themselves do not blame 'them' but look at their own contributions to a given situation, they accept their own inner and outer warts and thus the fact that everyone in the world has warts, inside and out. In accepting their own fragility and fallibility, they acknowledge the fragility and fallibility of everyone else. It starts to create a win:win situation. Whereas narcissism (evidence of which is all around us) creates only a lose:lose situation. 'Wethos', paradoxically, emanates from self-love – an enlightened self-love, but no less loving for being enlightened. It is 'methos' (and particularly today's virulent 'methos') which is the manifestation of narcissism."

"And that's why self-love continues to receive such a bad press?"

"Is another weapon the strong have to protect themselves against the weak."

"A conspiracy, then?"

"No. I really do not think, Polly – as I've said before – they're that able. The strong, I mean. Nor that organised. Not that capable of organising themselves. I think it has occurred by allowing a soul-sickness to rage unchecked. But, whilst it may have happened by accident, it continues – believe me, *amiga mía* – it continues by design."

"It continues surely, Rafa, mostly because we want it to."

"Oh no. It continues, Polly, *exclusively* because we want it to. Is no longer the case only that responsibility has been wrested from us, is that we have – almost gratefully – handed it over. And we have done that why?"

"Because, I guess you're going to say, we don't love ourselves."

"You guess absolutely correctly, my friend."

"Masturbation is revolution."

"Worse slogans have been written."

"Not too many, though."

"Revolution, Polly, is toothbrushing Oscar ceremonies which we do alone, and days of national remorse which we do together. Revolution is looking for blame first inside yourself and not outside. Revolution is loving yourself so much you just have to be full of love for everyone else."

"Know what I think?"

"Tell me."

"I think looking at Rembrandts is good for your health."

"I entirely agree."

"There's another great room of more recent work, got a couple of van Goghs in it – one of his famous sunflowers, I seem to remember, his equally famous chair – some other pretty good work. Want to see if it's also healthy looking at van Goghs?"

"You know me, Polly: a real sucker for anything that is healthy!"

Chapter 17

Polly is an instinctual nomad. In days of yore she would have strapped a couple of panniers to an ass and would thus contentedly have moved onto grazing new. These days she throws half-a-dozen hold-alls into the back of her Volkswagen Golf. There are a few treasured books, some DVDs and CDs, her laptop, a framed photograph of her parents. Most of her baggage, though, is clothes she needs for work: wet-weather gear and cold-weather gear; anoraks and pacamacs; safari suits and climbing boots and Wellington boots and waders. Working *al fresco* in Britain is to be exposed to climates ranging from Siberian to Sri Lankan, and from Saharan to Amazonian.

She notices as she unpacks the car that there is a pub almost opposite. She suspects before the day is done she will have sampled its hospitality. She isn't wrong.

Within twenty minutes of parking outside Rafa's flat, she is ensconced in what has already become 'their' flat, drinking a celebratory gin-and-tonic.

She is already more at home than Saskja, who has now spent a month (almost) with Giselle. Giselle, of course, still has a living to make. She has now become a theatre sister – though at a different hospital from Rodolfo's. Since Orphalese, professionally their paths have never crossed. They have been careful that those paths should not cross. That would just be one complication too far. Saskja has spent great swathes of time alone in Giselle's flat. Rafaél has tried to invite her out, but she has resisted. She doesn't like to think of herself as shy but occasionally her innate timidity, like an unbroken stallion, gnaws through its halter and lunges defiant hooves at a world seeking to break it.

When Giselle is at home Saskja chats voraciously. But she cannot talk. She feels she cannot talk. And Giselle is too tired to listen. She hears the melodic line, but lacks the energy for the descant to penetrate.

And still Saskja cannot talk.

She cannot talk.

She cannot.

And the chatter after a few days becomes to Giselle clatter: a noise, no more. And the clatter soon passes her by, becomes absorbed by the ambience, the drone of long-haul aircraft engines, the clackety-clack of intercity trains.

Saskja doesn't see this, but she senses it. Then will not allow herself to sense it. Because if she becomes aware of what she's sensing, she will no longer be sensing it but seeing it. And if she sees it, she will have to see it as rejection.

She also knows that what she might see as rejection isn't. It's rejection of the chatter, of the clatter of chatter, of the vacuity of noise, but it is not rejection of *her*. The most efficient way of countering rejection, the most efficient and efficacious way ... and of *rejecting* rejection, would be to talk. And she needs to talk. She needs to talk so much. And she knows Giselle too needs her to talk. And each night without talking that she goes to bed, she recognises the need she has *to* talk. Tomorrow she will surely talk. Tomorrow and tomorrow and tomorrow.

Giselle loves her being there. Saskja may yammer nineteen to the dozen but that, isn't it?, is teenagers for you. That's what teenagers do. The flat is spotless now when she returns to it, there's a meal waiting. It's in a way like a sexless marriage.

She realises since her pregnancy she's felt no loneliness, Giselle. But neither has she enjoyed solitude. In recognising how much she has missed the latter she also recognises that, oddly enough, she had also missed the former. Maybe, like pain and pleasure, solitude and loneliness have to co-exist because finally they are defined by each other.

She gets now whiffs of both in Saskja's yammering, in the hammering of that yammering. Because reply is robotic; it's auto-talk. The responses are almost as liturgical as those in the Mass. And she is thus able to travel – not as far as either loneliness or solitude but at least to the zone where both can be sniffed. Like the opposite side of the street to a baker's making its bread on the premises. And, in like fashion to such distant hints of smell, there is their own lusciousness contained within these whiffs, their own teaspoonfuls of Paradise. Within which – or beneath which, she's not quite sure which – is a certain winsomeness: that for the foreseeable future she would not be lonely again, or solitary, that within her was developing her constant companion – one who would be constant and a companion for as long as the child chose, one whose constancy and companionship was outside of her, Giselle's, control, a relationship that was all give.

It is a shock to her to realise, in such musings, however much she aches to give – and she does ache to give – she also hankers after taking. She'd always held that the famous prayer of Francis of Assissi was redundant, that *of course* it was more blessed to love than to be loved. And she's always felt her only need was to do that loving. How ridiculous she'd been. How absurd, how self-delusional. She had a need – of course she did – a *desperate* need also to be loved.

And Saskja too needs to be loved.

And so does Rafaél.

And Polly? ...

Polly needs *not* to be loved.

Chapter 18

According to Shakespeare, clouds had loured upon the house of Richard III. Well, of course they had! Richard's house had been in England. In England clouds lour. It's what they do. They are louring today. They will lour in a similar fashion now until the end of April. And then will make a number of guest appearances throughout what Britain, in her naïveté, continues to call 'summer'.

Polly and Rafaél have Richard III rather on their mind. They are en route to the National Theatre to view its latest production of the piece. It is the last day in November. They had been talking about the date.

"How did that ever happen?" asks Polly. "This really weird thing about June, September, all that? The thirty day thing? Or maybe it should be the thirty-one day thing? I mean, I know that three hundred and sixty five *and a quarter* is not exactly divisible by twelve. But who decided that January should have thirty-one days and poor old February only twenty-eight?"

"Is the Gregorian calendar, no? Presumably therefore Pope Gregory."

"You reckon?"

"I have absolutely no idea, my friend."

"Not curious?"

"If I am honest, not very."

"Ain't it always the way with knowledge? We've agreed that we do not know what we do not know. But it's also true that we don't know how fascinating a piece of knowledge is until we've got it. Me, I entirely understand why people thought the sun revolved around the Earth. But now we know more about it, don't you think that's really interesting?"

They are dressed against the louring clouds. Polly is used to such climes, and has the clothes to protect herself against their ravages. Rafaél less so. But curiosity and courtesy combine, if not to stave off the cold, then at least to cloister it.

Polly has just returned from a week's filming in Scotland. She's made enough money to see her comfortable for the rest of the year. She's treated them to the theatre. She's feeling relaxed, able to saunter. Rafaél seeks infection from her mood. He's not there yet, but he's on the way. He is able to saunter alongside of her.

"Do you think of yourself as lazy?" asks Rafaél.

"God, no."

"Me, I am extremely lazy."

"No, no, I don't *think* of myself, Rafa, as lazy. I know damn well I am. I hate working. I hate getting up off my butt for practically anything."

"Are we sinful, you and I, being lazy?"

"Oh God, wouldn't that be nice?"

Two skateboarders, one behind the other, rumble noisily, and too closely, past them. The closeness is part of the game. The follower is armadilloed in all the protective gear available. His leader has none. Not even an anorak to knee-pad him against the cold.

"Sloth, right?" asks Polly. She's going to ignore the skateboarders. She knows that's the most efficient way of responding to them. "The seventh deadly sin?"

"Also a rather beguiling animal."

"You think? I find them rather creepy."

"We work very hard today."

"I'm hard work, huh?" Polly retorts in mock indignation.

"No," Rafa starts to stammer. "No, Polly, please ... My English ..."

"Rafa, I'm kidding. ... I'm kidding, right?" she repeats, uncertain whether to be appalled by her own clumsiness or Rafaél's failure to understand her humour.

"It is I, Polly, who am kidding," eventually he acknowledges. And a broad smile sweeps across his dark lips, exposing the gold edging of some of his back teeth. "We work hard. Very hard. Too hard, I think. And very often we work hard on absurd things.

"A little while ago, on a rare evening watching television, I saw a documentary on, of all things, shaving. Apparently there are now effectively only two companies making razors. Millions are spent each year by both researching and developing razors that will out-razor their competitor. They now have four- or five-blade razors, I can't remember which. But I do remember thinking, how close a shave does anyone want? Meantime, by how much has the cost of buying a razor soared? Well above the rate of inflation, that's certain. Even more sharply, I imagine, than the cost of housing."

"'Sharply? That was, right?, a pun."

"Not guilty: an innocent accident, my friend. Is a lot of work and is idiotic work. Even if they invent the twenty-six, the *fifty*-six blade razor which shaves you beneath the level of your skin, one will still have to shave each day. The customer is not protected because, of course, such nonsensical research-and-development costs are passed onto him – as are the equally absurd advertising costs. It just becomes a self-perpetuating idiocy. Oh, I don't blame either company. I blame the ethos which dictates the conduct of both companies.

"Whilst all this money, all this intellectual and imaginative energy is being frittered away addressing total non-problems, the real problems – and God, there is more than enough of *them* – remain unaddressed. I repeat, I do not say this emanates all the time from corruption or, even, self-deception. I think it comes usually from a misguided perception of what is important."

"Mostly," says Polly, "I think it's just corruption."

"I do not yet have your cynicism, Polly."

"Keep studying, Rafa. You'll get there."

"We use our imagination to create the fifty-six blade razor and not the petrol-less engine – or even a supermarket trolley that is pushable, or one for luggage; we create mobile phones that are cameras, but not cameras in our cars to record those tail-gating us; we put labels on bottles instead of tackling alcohol abuse; we ban smoking on aeroplanes so that we can now really pollute the cabin's atmosphere; we beam phone conversations via space but cannot invent a jet engine which can cope with driving snow; we look not for cures for AIDS or cancer but for *expensive* cures for AIDS and cancer; we invent the fifty-six blade razor but not a cure for the common cold. And on and on and on.

"And is in this way – in the way of investing our energy into absurd ends – that working hard is indeed sloth, and sloth (in this way) is both a vice and a sin. It inhibits us from tackling the difficult work, the never-ending work, the skin-of-an-onion work. Is a similar dissipation of our resources as it is burning all our carbon fuels."

When the clouds lour on London the Thames murks. Not Wordsworth's pen nor Monet's brush can alchemise such silt into silver. It has all the aesthetic charm and pictorial allure of a puddle curdling in a scrapyard, a squelch cobwebbed with the greasy rainbows of toxic effluent. It does not flow, a murky Thames. It skulks, it slivers. There is no ode to be found in its depths, no serenity, nor muse nor mantra. The Seine smirks; the Thames just murks. The Danube at Vienna oompapas and dividing Budapest hosannahs. The Thames at Henley slithers and at Fulham withers and, lapping the shores of Westminster, ... it murks.

But, for all its lack of obvious appeal, it is London's river and it is the river appropriate for London. It may lack the beauty of the Rhone or the sparkle of the Tiber, but it does have a dignity that is all its own. It is not the theme park to which Neptune takes his children. But it is, one senses, one of the places to which he might retire to ponder serious matters.

"We are becoming expert, *amiga mía*, in hiding our vices from ourselves. Our vices and our sins. And we do that best when we camouflage them. We are doing to ourselves what the absurd computer questionnaires are seeking to do for us: we are reassuring ourselves we are okay by asking ourselves questions founded on false premises. How many times, in how many ways, do we (for instance) hide sloth behind hard work?

"And how many times, in how many ways, is the hardness of work imposed by vested interest to confiscate from us the energy we need to challenge what is happening to us, what is happening to the world? How much time is spent inventing the fifty-six blade razor and not inventing a system of, for example, our old friend 'quantum economics'? Or just developing the work of those, say, like Professor Sen?

"And do we ourselves secretly like the idea of hard work? How much hard work does hard work save us from?"

"You've lost me."

"I'm talking, for instance, about the raising of children. Believe me, I throw no stones. My glass house is very glassy indeed. That does not mean I did not love my children. I did, and do, love them very much. But also I used to love those Saturdays when I had to work. No-one could criticise me. I was working, wasn't I? Putting bread on the table of my family? In fact, the family used to feel sorry for me, having to work on Saturday, sometimes even Sunday. 'Poor *papi*, poor Rafa.' But the work I had to do, that was somehow far more satisfying, far easier, far more fulfilling than taking the children to parties or going shopping or taking the dog to the vet's – all those thousand and one things that fathers and husbands have to do.

"From the moment, Polly, there were kings there were subjects. Mayhap even before. And from the moment there was money there were those who had it and those who didn't. From that moment too it was perceived not only that it was better to be a king, but that being a king was somehow a 'higher' calling, was a calling for the greater benefit of mankind, and thus kings were entitled to be pampered in ways that non-kings weren't. Like ivy this belief soon billowed across the whole of society. Kings sired mini-kings or lords, and they sired knights who sired squires and so on. A hierarchy was born. We're not going to change that overnight.

"One perk of being a king is that one doesn't have to do the boring, the humdrum jobs: make the beds, do the washing-up, play with the children. One is too *important* for that. One had other people to do those unimportant, undemanding jobs for one. And so it is we equate sloth, for such it is, with importance. And we continue to do that. Important people, we continue to think, employ nannies. When it is, of course, nannies doing the important work. Good nannies benefit humanity; good business magnates, good brokers, good estate agents and good advertisers merely propagate a system that is harmful to humanity."

"We've got millennia of brain-washing to get rid of, Rafa, before we'll understand all that."

"We have, Polly, millennia of brain-washing to get rid of in most regards."

"In English," Polly continues, "there's an entire vocabulary designed (if not devoted) to uphold the monarchy, the feudal tradition. I always found it curious that we – Americans, that is, and therefore constitutionally republicans – who have innovated or renovated so much never sought to change that situation. Words like 'regal', 'royal', 'majestic', oh and a whole batch more, all lauding monarchs. Counts count, nobles are noble – those who aren't nobles are '*ig*noble'. The animal *kingdom,* the 'king' of the jungle, the 'king' of the beasts. The 'Lord' *God,* for heaven's sake, the 'King of kings'.

"This then gets compounded by the phrases: 'right-' and 'left-wing' – the etymology of which, I think, is an accident of the British parliament. The Tories used to sit on the right of the Speaker, and the Whigs on the left. But 'right' in English is not only the opposite of 'left'; far more often it is used as the opposite of 'wrong'. 'Right-thinking' is correct thinking. We even talk of a civil 'right'. 'Left', though, is usually associated with bad things. He 'left' in a huff, the bride was 'left' at the altar, our business partner 'left' us with a mountain of debt. 'Sinister' was the Latin for left. And I think the sub-text of this vocabulary over time forms part of some kind of spiritual or intellectual or philosophical DNA. To be left-handed was to be kack-handed, and we all know what 'kack' means. You think there might have been a difference in our political climate if the Whigs and Tories had been allocated different seating arrangements? Or that they were called North- and South-wing, for instance? What if right- and left-wing had instead been called profit-wing and people-wing?

"'Rich' too and 'poor' are not words used exclusively in financial terms. We talk of a 'rich' fabric or a 'poor' piece of work, a 'rich' sauce or a 'poor' meal, a 'rich' baritone or a 'poor' tenor. At a subliminal level, this perception just has to enter the psyche. Poor people, in that psyche, are poor *as* people: they are not only those without money but those too without merit. And are treated accordingly. 'Villain' stems directly, and obviously, from 'villein', which was nothing more sinister than a feudal underling. (See, I used the word 'sinister' again. And quite unconsciously. You don't think such intrudes on our psyche?) It's also made me very nervous, personally, the assonance between Eve and evil, or between dam and damage. That worries me much more than expressions like 'manmade'. Because the connection is far more subtle, it is far more subversive."

"Phallus and fallacy?" asks Rafaél, with apparent innocence. "What about the assonance of that?" His eyes twinkle in appreciation of his teasing.

"Well, it has to get some things, right, Rafa, whatever it is: semantic serendipity, I suppose."

"Semantic serendipity?"

"Good point, Rafa. Let's leave it like that. In fact, *excellent* point. African Americans too, I think, have a legitimate point when they complain about phrases like 'blackmail' or 'black magic' – words, in other words, which associate 'black' with 'bad'. But I also think that to try to pc around it is only to add insult to injury. It's patronising and 'there, there'ing and ... well, awful. You asked me at the start of our friendship whether you had to be 'gender conscious'. Well, I am a bit, to be honest. But when 'manhole covers' gets changed to 'people-hole covers', the very banality belittles what should be a genuine concern. It provides easy ammunition for those trying to maintain an unacceptable status quo. So much so, in fact, that I'm not sure that's not what it's intended to do.

"I think we need to know what passes through our psyche when we use the word 'poor' to mean, as doubtless Blairspeak would have it, the 'financially challenged'. I also think we need to recognise we countenance a 'them' and 'us' world any time we use words like 'noble' or 'majestic' as synonyms for excellence. Of course we can't change them – 'wicked' is an exception that only proves a rule. But we should be aware. That's all I'm saying."

"And, to return to the core of our discussion, we should also, Polly, be aware that often what appears to be hard work is, in fact, sloth. With our kamikaze economics today, that too is a situation that cannot overnight be changed. But is one of which overnight we can become aware. We are aware, of course, most of us. But we need such awareness to shift from the subconscious to the conscious. And this, my dear friend, is only one way in which we are slothful.

"What is sloth, first of all? Let us try to define it."

"Another good question, Rafa."

"Is mayhap not doing something that needs doing because one is more comfortable not doing it. Is this a fair description?"

"Let's go with it for the moment."

"The key words, I think, are 'more comfortable not doing it'."

"Okay."

"What is the thing that most stops us looking at ourselves?"

"We're not comfortable doing it?"

"More, we're *uncomfortable, amiga mía,* doing it. And one is not misguided to find that uncomfortable. One is not aboard a private jet complaining about the meagreness of the comfort supplied. *Is* uncomfortable, that journey. Certainly at the start. Like anything which needs practice: like piano-playing or aerobics or meditation, is always most difficult at the beginning. And, also like such disciplines, this one takes *time* for any benefit to become obvious. Also some will be more proficient more quickly than others. So it can lead again to envy.

"All our destinations are the grave. Let us stop worrying so much about the destination. Start thinking about the journey. A journey that can only be an individual journey – and an individual's journey ... that will be as unique to each one of us, finally, as our DNA. But also a scary journey. A journey the view from which is another Pandora's box – likely to lead us into dark and frightening places. Better not to look at the view. To be 'too busy' to look at the view."

They enter through the glass doors, straight into a coffee bar. "I hate this building," says Polly. "Architecturally, I mean. 'Terminal 5', I always used to call it. I guess now I need to change that to 'Terminal 6'."

"I rather like it," comments Rafa, casting a look over it that suggests he might be returning, and to a place that holds some attraction for him. They pass through glass doors which lead from one coffee bar to another. "To a surprising degree it feels to me like it supplies both size and intimacy."

"Are you saying these things just to be contrary?"

"Surely you wouldn't like us to agree on everything?"

"We could agree we both needed a drink."

"No argument there."

It's still early. Most of their fellow audience, and those of the other two auditoria, have yet to arrive. They are served their drinks swiftly and go to the big brown leather couches to enjoy them. Opposite them are armchairs in the same leather. A cleaner darts about the place cleaning the charcoal grey carpet with an old-fashioned carpet-sweeper.

"Is also, my friend, very convenient to us, all this hard work, as we have no energy left either to join in the political process. We *are* being excluded from the process. Of that there is no question. But, very often, we also exclude ourselves. 'There's no point in my doing this because no-one will listen', 'Why bother protesting? No-one will pay any attention.' I say such things to myself *all* the time. I justify my own lethargy to myself. I get very steamed up about things and do nothing about it.

"In my country, voting is mandatory. For me, this is also a part of the lie. It provides government with an apparent mandate which it does not have. An enforced 'democracy' is as much an oxymoron as a republican monarchy.

"In all truly democratic countries protest votes should be counted as such. They're not. Protest votes are considered just as spoilt ballots and are simply discarded. Such votes, of course, will never be counted. Because, if ever they were, every election thereafter would be won, and massively, by such protest votes. No government ever would be seen to have a mandate from us, the '*demos*'. But until they start counting such votes as such, is a perfectly legitimate political statement not to vote. How many times, though, do we hide behind this to veil our laziness that we cannot be bothered to go to the polling station? How many times are we too tired to write to our politicians? Or to the newspapers?"

There is a short, tubby man, with longish hair and a goatee beard: a Porthos-like figure in the twenty-first century. No, a Geppetto, Rafaél decides in his head. And he's with a young man in his awkward teens. It would appear this were his son. Geppetto's admonishing his son over some misdemeanour obviously the son has committed. But he's doing so with patience and with understanding.

"The situation, the *shituation,* will not be changed. Not straightaway. Mayhap not for many years to come. But is in this way – and only in this way – that new atmospheres are created, new ethoses. If you like, that this methos changes to a wethos. It does not matter that politicians and civil servants acknowledge our letters – if at all – only from routine, that the press does not publish them. The previous situation, however little it may have appeared to, *has* changed. Is no longer a situation, for instance, which no-one has complained about. Someone now *has* complained about it. And your situation too has changed – from being one over which you have taken no action to one over which you have, yes, taken action. You ordered drinks for the interval?"

"What do you think, Rafa?"

"Feel like a browse round the bookshop?"

"Why not? Might even get some Christmas shopping done."

They return their empty glasses to the bar, stroll past the space-age box office, and into the den of well-displayed bookshelves.

"Today, my friend, we chat but rarely do we talk. We never stop chatting, in fact. Most of it, the inane blather of mobile phone conversations – noise to fill a silence. Politically we row but we do not debate. And when we do debate such is used politically not for clarity but for greater obfuscation. Likewise we work hard to veil our sloth. We work very hard to veil it. In fact, and ironically, the work we do to veil our sloth is much harder than the work we would be doing if we weren't slothful!

"So often we work (and so hard) on the irrelevant or on the trivial – not the importantly trivial either, the trivial that are the sprinkles on top of the ice-cream, the … I don't know … the aftershaves and HD TVs, the petits fours and cocktail umbrellas. Is like the line I quoted from 'Butch Cassidy …'."

"'If only he'd pay me what he's paying them to stop me robbing him, I'd stop robbing him'."

"If only, Polly, we would work as hard on the important things as we do on inanely trivial ones, we'd have the energy left to work on the inanely trivial."

"This is such a dangerous place, this bookshop, for me," says Polly. "I could blow what I earned last week in one splurge."

"I am also, in bookshops, very much, Polly, the child in the sweet shop."

"So much wisdom here, so much … fun."

"The works here of Anouilh, of Ayckbourne, of Edward Bond."

"Of Wesker here and Wilde."

"Of Caryl Churchill and Samuel Beckett. You like '…Godot'?"

"'*Waiting* for Godot'?" Rafaél nods, maybe with just a tinge of 'What other Godots, Polly, do you know?' "I *love* 'Waiting for Godot', Rafa. And that despite the fact that, in today's world, a theatre of the absurd is almost tautologous. Like 'frozen ice-cream', or something. A theatre of cruelty likewise. It's not, any longer, a portrait of the artist, but a portrait of the portrait. It's almost like laughing at your own joke."

"Do you think Godot is God?"

"Does it matter? Isn't Godot, more importantly, what they're waiting for? The waitee, if you like? Isn't that his significance?"

"This is a word: 'waitee'?"

"I was trying to be funny. I don't agree with his essential pessimism, oddly enough, Beckett's. But – yes –, mostly, I do enjoy his work. I enjoy the 'misery is fun' aspect of it all."

A school party suddenly emerges as if through a trap-door. No crocodile this, already several different handbags and pairs of shoes – even a rather nice belt. There is around them the over-exuberance engendered by 'treats', but (as both Polly senses and Rafa) this has almost certainly got considerably more to do with licitly bunking off school than from the prospect of a few hours in the company of the Bard.

"Rafa, I got to get out of this place. These books are demanding that I buy them."

"Mayhap ... Richard III is not a short play. Mayhap we'd be more comfortable not drinking another beer. A whisky, perhaps?"

"Strictly to keep out the cold, Rafaél."

Drink in hand, they wander around the foyer.

"See, I think so much of that French existentialist angst, Beckett's, Sartre's, is just ... well, so misdirected.

"Let me start this again ... If sloth is the seventh deadly sin, the seventh mortal lie, Rafa, is that God is God."

The crocodile's teacher is trying to hand out tickets. A boy with a blond crew-cut fiddles with the stud in his ear, his other hand is extravagantly clasping the hand of a bob-haired brunette wearing a red v-neck jersey, tights of the same colour, a kilt-like tartanned skirt, a forest-fire of acne and a grin seeking to be demure and finding only soppiness. Their hand-holding likewise is seeking to appear natural and casual. But it is enforced and marinated in recalcitrance.

"God is not God?" Rafaél asks.

"Not at the moment," Polly suggests. "As with all mortal lies, this isn't one lie. There are lies within lies."

There is a solitary girl standing slightly apart from the group. She has long, dark hair – 'tresses' they would once have been called.

Rapunzel tresses, even. She's no oil painting, the girl, but she's also a lot less of a plain Jane than she imagines herself to be. Her dark eyes are wide open, are unable to settle, travel hither and yon, explore, explore. She wears a full-length black skirt and an almost Victorian blouse of a coral pink with a cameo brooch central on its collar. There is no sense of hostility between her and the crocodile, it's just that water has been allowed to open up between two boats. In their own individual ways, sight of this young woman hurls both Polly and Rafaél back to their individual childhoods. But this is a journey that travels parallel with their present discussion.

The bells ring. They are summoned to the auditorium. They agree to differ about the Lyttelton as well, about its merits as an auditorium. Polly thinks it a concrete barn, soulless and deodorised of any whiff of grease-paint; Rafaél thinks it similar to the building as a whole: an ingenious concept that manages to give the simultaneous impression of both size and intimacy. The house-lights dim, there is the tremor of expectation ... and the winter of Richard's discontent becomes glorious summer.

Polly is now nursing her interval drink. They are talking about the play. "Just goes to show:" she says, "If you start off murdering the Duke of Clarence, it just has to end up with you killing a couple of princes in the Tower. The lie always spins more lies, the crime more crimes. I use the word 'spin' advisedly. 'Oh, what a tangled web ...', all that. The web today of politics and economics, of family dysfunction and social dysfunction, they're all today as enormously complicated as they are because, now for generations – for aeons, in some cases –, webs have been spun upon webs upon webs. 'Big-fleas-have-little-fleas ...'-like."

"No argument there." They notice the tressed schoolgirl. She is still alone. She walks the length of the foyer, backwards and forwards. But there is no tension in her walk, no sense that her aloneness is any kind of struggle for her. She could be looking for the loo, or she could just be looking for a brief sojourn in her own space.

"So much of the West, Rafa, has thrown out the Church. Even

those televangelists – making untold millions by exploiting the terror and confusion of their fellow human-beings – even they who purport to be Christian have no allegiance to any other church, except their own."

"And their own pockets, Polly, *por favor*!" Rafaél adds sardonically.

"And where, Rafa, did they learn that from? A guy I know, an assistant dubbing editor (as a matter of fact), sort of contemporary to Frank McCourt, he grew up in Ireland amidst a poverty that was abject – 'Angela's Ashes'-type poverty. The accoutrements of the Church meanwhile continued to be made of precious metals: gold altar-pieces, silver chalices. And each month, or each week, the priest would visit the hovels and demand his tithe. That was more important than putting food into the mouths of the children. This is not doing God's work. The God of such priests is not God.

"But because we bought into that lie, when we started rejecting the priests and the Church, we also, Rafa, threw out God. Babies and bath-water yet again. Babies, Rafa, and bath-water.

"Now, I think Man has always been materialist. And who can blame him? Squirrels are also materialists, so are foxes. They store food in days of plenty to see them through days of shortage. At a primeval level, materialism is only insurance. And nor is there anything wrong, *per se,* with comfort. The problem with our comfort today is that it's just not very comfortable. Like democracy and happiness, we enjoy (at best) – as you say, Rafa – an ersatz comfort. Usually our comfort is worse than that, it is simply fraudulent. We buy into the fraud (often literally 'buy' into it) that comfort comprises material or physical comfort. Whereas material comfort can only be a *part* of comfort. It's certainly not the *only* comfort.

"You talked about playing 'let's-win-the-lottery'. Well, here too that example holds good. In so many ways we are so similar to the guy who buys a lottery ticket each week, knowing that, if only he won the jackpot, all his problems would all be over. Until the day he does win it. When, a short while later, he discovers he is even more unhappy than he ever has been. Because now he *really* doesn't understand the reason for his unhappiness.

"Science tells us that Nature abhors a vacuum. Well, so does Supernature, whatever it is the generic term for the supernatural. And when we don't have a God in our lives – by which I mean, at least, an acknowledgement that there are metaphysical elements abroad – there is, I think, a tendency to create false gods.

"Gnostic or agnostic, it is, I think, difficult to refute that there is a remarkable spiritual wisdom floating around somewhere in the cosmos. Even Niels Bohr had a horse-shoe on his wall. 'Of course I don't believe in it,' he is reported to have said. 'But I've heard it works whether you believe in it or not!'

"This cosmic wisdom, it's one, I think, into which the enlightened of any age can tap. I think all of us can be enlightened. I think many choose not to be, indeed that *most* choose not to be. Pandora's Box, again. But of the enlightened, I think there are a few supremely enlightened. And it is from these ranks that the spiritual leaders are drawn – the Guru Nanak, for example, or Bodhidharma.

"Is it not incredible, for instance, that in Greek mythology, even before there was Zeus, the Creator God was called Chaos? It's taken several millennia for scientists to catch up with this theory. As I understand it, one of the cornerstones of quantum-physics and – mechanics is the Chaos Theory.

"Acupuncture is another instance. Acupuncture was a therapy which pre-dated the science necessary to appreciate it by several thousand years. This is yet another reason, of course, why we should take time to challenge anything which calls itself 'progress'. All snobbery is harmful. And much snobbery is toxic. None has the propensity for more toxicity, though, *amiga mía,* than chronological snobbery."

"This little exercise of ours, Rafa, I think is one that all thinking people should do for themselves. They need to challenge ancient axioms, examine how truthful they still are, whether their interpretation needs re-assessing, their application redefining. But they don't need simply to discard them as being obsolete. I don't believe in the kind of Bernard Shaw God, the Sistine Chapel God: long beard and flowing white hair. But I do believe that there *is* something divine (however much I may dislike the word) about, say, these seven deadly sins, about the Buddha's Noble Truths, about great swathes of the Tao Te Ching, and much of the Torah and the Qur'an … about the Ten Commandments, even. And perhaps that's what that Commandment meant – is it the First? – about having no other gods. We're today worshiping not even the golden calf, just the gold the calf is made from.

"And that is a false god. And deep within us somewhere we know that. And we also know that worshiping a false god, that is not sufficient to the task of worship. It's profaning not God (not even the real God), but ourselves. Because we worship this false god – or *any* false god – we are dissatisfied. And at some level, as I say, I sense we know that.

"We may worship, for instance, the god of progress. Without even defining what 'progress' is. We cede to progress the same right we so often scoff at with Jehovah: that it works in mysterious ways, that it knows better than we do, that to question it or its efficacy is blasphemous. The computer has, for that reason, been allowed such dominance – and such unmerited dominance. A mixture, rather, of worshiping progress and greed.

"The God of President Bush – another false God – is an almost identical God to that adopted by, say, Britain's Charles I and II or France's Louis XIV: God put him on the throne, therefore he is divinely appointed, therefore he can do no wrong. Or we worship the vicious (and equally false) God of televangelists, those interested only in lining their own pockets, these latterday Elmer Gantrys. They incite worship of a God of hatred. And they impoverish those who follow them – and substantially – not only financially, but also spiritually.

"As do the hate-obsessed mullahs or ayatollahs. There is so little to distinguish between the two of them, the televangelists and the ranting mullahs, that it is frightening. And both condemn the other as preaching violence and hatred whilst they both do exactly the same. Now I don't know either the Bible or the Qur'an well enough to argue whether these mullahs or these preachers are quoting accurately from their holy texts, or whether they indulge in a sort of lawyerese of the soul and choose their quotes extremely selectively. So I'm not going to begin to challenge them at that level.

"This, though, I would say to anyone: If your Holy Book – be it the Adi Granth, the Qur'an, the Bible ... or the Incan Book of Sun Worship (if such exists) – if that text incites you to acts you know are wrong, or inhibits you from doing what you know is right, then ignore the book. Just ignore it. Muhammad never drove a car, the Buddha never flew, Guru Nanak never threw his clothes into a washing-machine, Moses never got ice-cream out of a fridge. For principles to *be* principles, they have to be (as Lao Tsao Tsu would remind us) like water, infinitely malleable, capable of changing shape (even substance) to meet any condition, not afraid to enter any environment, adaptable to a whole range of practical uses. And totally vital for survival.

"The Nuremberg defence of 'we were only obeying orders' is, and properly, derided. And yet we hear the same excuse trotted out time and again in political contexts and in so-called 'religious' ones – I say 'so-called' because I think, at their core, most faiths are forces for considerable good. It has been their manipulation by Man which has turned them into such enormous forces for evil.

"It is no more acceptable to hide homophobia behind the pages of the Old Testament or the Qur'an than it is to flout national and international law by dealing with alleged terrorists by creating a non-state. In both instances, you are allowing the letter of the law to take precedence over the law's spirit. 'We are only obeying orders' is no more an excuse if those orders come from Heaven or from the Pentagon.

"All these false gods today, Rafa, are considered God. Are worshipped as God. That's why I say that the seventh mortal lie today is that God is God. God has never been the God of a venal

Church (or a power-crazed mosque or a self-aggrandising temple or a do-as-we-say-not-as-we-do pagoda). God doesn't need worshiping. God is God, for God's sake. He's not some two-bit TV 'personality'. God doesn't need us to worship God. It is *we* who have the need to worship. It's our need that we worship God, not God's. The problem being, I think it's almost inevitable, as I said, that if we don't worship a benign God we will worship a malevolent one ... or a non-God who, because worshipped, becomes a malevolent God.

"I may not know, Rafa, what God is, but I sure as Hell know what He isn't.

"God isn't hatred, that first of all. Anyone inciting you to hate in the name of God is blaspheming.

"God is not mercenary. Anyone asking for your money to do God's work is not doing God's work.

"God is not knowable. Part of God, of whatever faith, has to remain the mystery of God. Therefore the possibility always exists that God doesn't exist. And therefore God's *enjoinments* might not exist. They can never, in that sense, be knowable. We can *believe* tenets to be divinely inspired, but we cannot – we simply cannot – *know* that they are. Anyone insisting that they *are* known is proving only how very little he, or she, does know God. And anyone claiming moral rectitude for immoral actions because such is the word of God is someone who does not love God, but who hates God.

"God (whatever God you believe in) is a very constructive Being, Force, whatever. In the '*I Ching*' that force is called 'the Creative', in the Bible 'the Creator'. All morality is about insuring the wellbeing of that creation, that construction, and of ensuring such creation and construction continue into the future. Anything which encourages creation is therefore worship, and anything which discourages it desecration; anything which enhances construction is moral; and anything that encourages destruction is immoral.

"The construction of a tank or a warplane is, in fact, an oxymoron. Any construction which is designed for destruction is part of the destruction. It is only semantic callisthenics which allow it to be called a *con*struction. A demolition ball used to knock down slums which will then be replaced by adequate housing is involved in an act of construction. Not, however, if that adequate housing is going to be so expensive that the slum-dwellers can no longer afford it, and will be rendered homeless. How many times has that situation been propagated in the world's capitals, how devastatingly was that scenario enacted during the aftermath of the Boxing Day tsunami?

"The intention has an influence on the event, not least in its consequences to the prosecutor of that event. It also impacts on the consequences to the event's victims. And it is the intention which defines the action as being moral or immoral.

"I said a moment ago, I think a part of God has to be contained within us. And I think, all of us, we all contain a bit of God. And a bit too of the devil, that we all have (as you have said, Rafa) a Higher Self inside of us and a Lower one. And maybe the Chinese are right, and that's yin and yang. And maybe too they are mutually dependent – like pain and pleasure, loneliness and solitude. And maybe when we're hearing messages, or instinct is nudging us, what we're hearing are exhortations from that Higher Self, or the Lower one. The trick is knowing which one is which.

"No God's going to come simply if we wait for Him to show Himself. Returning again to our earlier talk. The tragedy of '... Godot' is not that Godot doesn't show but that Vladimir and Estragon don't go out looking for him. Godot, for God's sake, could be waiting for *them*. On another barren piece of ground. Just around the corner."

"'Jesus was asked,' Rafaél quotes, '"When will the kingdom come?" He replied, "It will not come by waiting for it".'"

"Bible?"

"Gnostic Gospels, Gospel of Thomas."

"Just goes to show! Does it never occur to the two tramps that they might have misheard? We do, you know, us humans, get our wires crossed now and again. Almost the first thing you learn as an assistant director: Don't assume anyone has heard you correctly.

Check. And then re-check. And then check again. Communication is not exactly humanity's forte. In World War Two famously the message went out: 'Send reinforcements, we're going to advance.' It was received as: 'Send three-and-fourpence, we're going to a dance.' These are messages between fellow human-beings, sharing a language, whose unambiguous mutual interest is to understand one another as well as they can. How much greater must be the possibility of misunderstanding between the natural world and the supernatural? Between the human world and the divine?

"We were talking earlier about the subliminal impact that language can transmit. Is it just coincidence, the assonance of 'message' and 'mess'? Wouldn't we better off if we understood the message might *be* a mess? Might be garbled? We might have misheard? How many lives would that one concession save? That one tiny act of humility?"

The bells start summoning the Lyttelton audience back to their seats. The tressed schoolgirl seems to be the solitary member of her party who has left her seat – or maybe the only one returning to it! Polly and Rafa return to their aisle, scramble past slanted knees, resume their seats.

"Even if God is God we should question whether *God* be God. And if God *is* God He would welcome questioning what we are told are His words. Are these messages from God? Or from God's ambassadors? How well have those ambassadors heard God? How well do we hear the ambassadors? Why should the ambassadors be hearing God any better than we do?"

The lights dim. Henry VII is pronounced king. Richard has rudely stamped his way across Bosworth, offering his kingdom for a horse. The previous night he had been visited by Clarence's ghost, by those of Hastings and the princes.

The applause usually of a matinée audience is akin to the tea they tend to drink in the interval: refreshing but somewhat insipid, lacking the oomph of an evening's libation. This applause, though, had been an ovation. The production is a triumph, and we have a need to acknowledge the triumphant. Britain may indeed be lucky to have mothered Shakespeare. But Shakespeare is also lucky to be performed natively by British actors. Whilst such have, on odd occasions, inflicted the most grievous of bodily harms on his text, and whilst the excellent productions of his plays are not exclusive to Albion, in their generality, British actors have an affinity with and a love and understanding of the work which endows each performance with a lustre similar to that burnishing off a great piece of sculpture: it is beauty made tangible.

Heading for home now would be to spend most of the journey sardined with rush-hour commuters. They're in no hurry. They decide to while away the rush-hour happily at the bar.

"Does Richard III have God within him?" asks Rafaél.

"Well, leaving aside for one moment the opinions of the Richard III Society which maintains that Shakespeare's depiction of the king is a complete travesty ..."

"Yes, Polly, leaving that aside."

"Doesn't the fact that he's haunted prove he does? Shakespeare is the dramatist he is partly because he tells us so much about ourselves. Macbeth and Lady Macbeth think they want the crown. When they get it they see it is a hollow ring, and one which has a hollow ring. Sorry. I'm doing a you."

"Just not as well," Rafaél regrets.

"It's too late. The murders have been committed.

"Richard likewise. He gets involved in his own Machiavellian machinations, he starts becoming fascinated by the game, he loses sight of the objectives. He's also a dramatic example of our favourite adage, Rafa, that hurt people hurt people.

"Clearly this process happens to politicians. But doesn't it also happen to all of us? Hasn't that happened in the world today? Isn't that why money is such a God? Consumerism? There's nothing wrong with either. Not of themselves. Not as commodities or as a part of life. There is a lot wrong with both if they start to assume deic proportions.

"Aren't we, so many of us, grappling our way across Bosworth, offering to exchange our kingdom for a horse? And isn't it always too late?

"In ten thousand different ways, are we not all caught up in our own Machiavellian machinations? All blinded by the trees and unable to see a forest? So steeped in our own ambitions, in our hankering for wealth and glory that we are prepared to drown our brother in a vat of Malmsey? Individually, I mean?

"And collectively? What am I talking about? And, of *course*, collectively. And collectively, what's more, is any conurbation you care to designate: nationally, globally, in our city, our street, our company, our profession.

"Today's God, Rafa, is not God. The gods of today, no way are they God. Let's stop worrying about what God is. We'll never know the answer to that. But we can find answers for ourselves as to what God isn't.

"Let's also stop worrying about the next world. Know what? There's not too much we can do about the next world. But there is something we can do about this one. I don't have any existential despair about this life being all there is. Life to me doesn't become meaningless if life starts with birth and ends with death. Nor if the soul starts and ends there. I suspect that even the most avidly atheistic or humanist scientist would confirm that isn't true. DNA links us both to the past and the future, umbilically, inexorably.

"It doesn't condone greed, a lack of life after death. We don't need to be aware of our sins to make the next life more comfortable, but this one.

"Certainly let's strive to be more comfortable. The Puritan and/or Calvinist belief that the enjoyable is somehow sinful is ... well, I don't begin to understand it. 'Course anyone's free to believe anything they choose. Me, I couldn't believe in a god who somehow thought I was closer to him if I slept on a pillow of stones rather than one of down. We're fond of our comfort, us human-beings. And I don't see anything in the least wrong with that. Most animals are as well.

"Where I do think we human-beings need to be careful, though, is (as I've said many times) that our comfort is a first-class one. For comfort to be comfort, in other words, it cannot require the discomfort of others. *Genuine* comfort can't, nor can first-class comfort. How can it? We've *both* said it, Rafa: Knowledge that your comfort has come at the cost of someone else's discomfort, that has to encroach on the comfort you are enjoying. At the very best therefore, that way you can only enjoy a second-class comfort.

"Do we not owe it to ourselves to strive for *real* comfort? For first-class comfort? We most certainly don't need a comfort that ends up making us more uncomfortable than the discomfort we used to have.

"Our world today demands that each of us in the West murders princes in the Tower. Oh, not that we kill them ourselves, of course. Any more than Richard himself killed the princes. We find lackeys to do our dirty work for us. And they do this job so well that we are able to convince ourselves it really isn't us who are doing the killing.

"I wonder how much of that is because, again like Richard, we really don't like ourselves too much. Do we think of ourselves as 'lame, unfinished ...', maybe not on the outside, but on the inside? 'And therefore,' Richard says, 'since I cannot prove to be a lover, I am determined to prove a villain ...' Or a billionaire, or a politician or whatever.

"How unpleasant is it to visit a public restroom that hasn't been flushed? You really don't need to believe in God in order to flush the john. We do it because we want to avoid the next user unpleasantness – and in the hope that previous users will have wanted to avoid us such unpleasantness. Are we seriously prepared to leave a public washroom in better condition than our planet?

"Of course we need God in our lives, even if God is only the acceptance that there is an authority above our own, and above the essentially pragmatic demands of politics – of politics however enlightened. We also need shamans or gurus or yogis – or priests or rabbis or mullahs – those who help us to reach for the

Higher Self within us and to shun our Lower Self. Spiritual sickness is as real a dis-ease as any other kind of ailment. And, just as sometimes we need a doctor, we sometimes need a *spiritual* doctor to help us over a crisis. But, know what, Rafa? Those spiritual doctors, they'll help us best when they stop sermonising at us, and start to listen.

"It seems to me, so very many of the world's problems could start to be sorted out if those who portend to lead us stopped talking so much, and started listening a whole heap harder. Our best oracles are our own auricles.

"And if we started not small-talking but big-talking. Talking about the big stuff, all of us. That which hurts us most. Talk so we stop hurting. So we're not one of those hurt people, like Richard, who hurt people. Know how many princes we'd save that way from being murdered in the Tower? Hundreds of thousands, for sure. Perhaps millions."

"This exercise, *amiga mía,* has been for me most enjoyable."

"For me too, Rafa."

"But do you not think we also need to concentrate on the positive? You mentioned earlier yin and yang. If we have seven deadly sins ..."

"And seven mortal lies."

"As well as ten Commandments, telling us what not to do, ought we not find seven vital ... Well, already this is interesting: there is no opposite of a sin."

"Virtue?"

"Is the nearest I can think of, but is more correctly the antonym of 'vice'. Mayhap one should look for seven lively virtues."

"'*Vital* virtues', maybe better as a term."

"Seven vital virtues?"

"And seven life-affirming truths?"

"Truth is difficult. A bit like what you say of God, Polly, I think Truth is impossible to define except in the negative."

"How about then seven life-affirming ideas?"

"That sounds like something I could drink to."

"Now, there's a coincidence ..."

"I still do like this building, Polly."

"Know what, Rafa? It's even growing on me."

Chapter 19

To begin with, it had all been rather embarrassing. Rafaél is no cook, Polly is scared of being there, Saskja is still shy – particularly of her English –, and Giselle is conscious there is within her a skirmish of emotions which just has to escalate into a full-scale battle. For a time Rafaél had berated himself as a dolt and an idiot. Why had it ever *occurred* to him to have a dinner party? The whole thing was patently absurd. He must be mad.

But on his trip with Polly to Soho's Old Compton Street he had noticed an exotic off-license. There he had found a bottle of pisco. Pisco is Peru's national hooch. Pisco sour is one of the world's great bonhomie-bestowers. If Athualpa had offered Pizarro a pisco sour the Incas might well still have had an empire! Rafaél had mixed some pisco sours.

Polly is consciously drinking moderately. She is, like the other two women, still nursing her second pisco sour. Dinner will be ready in about half-an-hour. The smells wafting in from the kitchen do much to persuade Rafaél that reports of his insanity had been greatly exaggerated. He is recharging everyone's glass, finishing off the jug. He has already opened a bottle of Chilean Chablis. It is now chilling on the dining-table. Which has already been laid. Mayhap this dinner was not such a terrible idea, after all.

He is conscious of a pull towards Giselle. She is a young woman and a vibrant woman, but the allure is not sexual. Not, he suddenly realises, *mostly* sexual. Is that to do with Rodolfo? Is it to do with his own mortality? Or, far more scary, his own dotage? Why has Polly become so coy? And this young woman, Saskja: what's the story there? And what's the story too about the sadness skulking behind those eyes, a footpad in the shadows waiting for the muggable.

Polly had asked her innocently enough what she was doing with her time. She confessed she was doing very little, that she was being *so* lazy it did indeed constitute a sin. There had been a pause at that point. Not a post-gaffe pause, not awkward in that sense. More a pause due to lack of direction, as if the conversation were at some kind of cross-roads dithering whether to go to left or right.

Rafaél at that time jerked his way into the chat by admitting that he and Polly had recently revisited the seven deadly sins. And a recapitulation occurred of what either could remember were the salient points. As he passes amongst them, replenishing glasses, he adds: "And we also defined the seven mortal lies, the lies we need to expose (even if only to ourselves) if mankind is to progress."

Their guests want to know what these are. Between them Polly and Rafaél reiterate them. Those lies are that:

Man is man;
the material is material;
morality is morality;
the happy ending is the happy ending;
democracy is democracy;
self-love is self-love;
and that God is God.

"There is also, I think," says Rafa, "an *eighth* mortal lie: that our so-called 'free economy' is a free economy. That free economy is very much a protectionist economy – of the haves excluding the have-nots. Napoleon said of his enemy, 'England, which the economists who preach freedom of trade consistently quote as a model, is in reality the country of prohibition.' Is a good description of the world's 'free' trade today – free just so long as you are within the club."

"It's a good point," Polly concedes. "Today's capitalists actually despise capitalism. Most so-called 'competition' is entirely fictitious. But it is, Rafa, an *eighth* point."

"I thought I would try just to sneak it in," confesses the Peruvian, with the abashment of a father caught stealing a chip from the garnish of his child's hamburger. "I will not labour the point. Is one which will be rightly exposed immediately there is a commitment to the Truth."

Polly also tells them, soon they will start to discuss the positives that complement these negatives: the seven vital virutes, the seven life-affirming ideas. Giselle reminds them that Tomas Aquinas nominated four '*cardinal* virtues', as he called them. "Prudence," she tells them, "justice, fortitude, and temperance."

Polly laughs at this last, but not too convincingly. They agree that Aquinas's list has value, insight and intelligence. Maybe (or mayhap!), though, they had a need to define these virtues for themselves.

They sit down to eat. They start with ceviche: a marinade of raw fish. Those new to the food are suspicious of it before they start. All very soon, however, find their anxieties stilled. After three or four mouthfuls they declare the dish delicious. Peruvian cooking remains one of the world's best kept secrets. It is quite as individual, quite gastronomically as exciting as any other of the world's great cuisines.

"Saskja and I knew a woman," says Giselle. "Lakshmi. She died a little time before I left Orphalese." Involuntarily tears well up behind her eyes. And behind Saskja's. "She did a similar exercise with the ten Commandments, redefined them for today's world. I thought they were rather apposite.

"The first was: Respect your integrity, your principles."

She couldn't remember them all fluently. Nor could Saskja, but together they cobbled together what was the essence of Lakshmi's revisit to the Commandments.

Two: Respect the integrity and principles of others.

Three: Respect the critics of those principles – but only if those critics themselves have principles.

Four: Respect the time you need to review and, if necessary, adjust those principles.

Five: Respect your past and your future so that your present may be whole.

Six: Respect the physical lives of those around you – and your own.

Seven: Respect the *private* lives of those around you – and your own. Respect their dignity and yours.

Eight: Respect the *material* lives of those around you – and your own.

Nine: Respect your own honesty.

Ten: Respect what are genuinely your own best interests – which, if you *are* genuine, have also to be the best interests of others.

The dirty dishes, Rafa decides, can wait till the morning. They're not about to go anywhere overnight. He'll cope with the whole of the débris then.

As he climbs into bed that night he realises how comfortable he's feeling, how easy (after the first twenty minutes or so) the whole evening had been. He used to feel that way hosting dinner parties with Inma. But the easiness he's feeling now, that (and he knows it) is not driven by nostalgia. It's an easiness all of its own.

Giselle is distinctly *un*easy. And she's uneasy because she realises she too had spent the evening feeling easy. She's used to feeling easy in her own company, and fairly easy in the company of other women, particularly Saskja. (And, she remembers winsomely, even more particularly with Lakshmi.) But she's not accustomed to feeling easy in the company of men. That's not because she doesn't like men: to the contrary, if anything. But men stir waters for her rather than stilling them. Also no bad thing. But not conducive of easiness.

It's also no bad thing, she decides, to *be* stilled once in a while, to feel easy and relaxed. And it's ridiculous, she also decides, that she's now so upset at having felt so easy that she cannot sleep.

She lies on her back, crosses her hands atop her growing baby and gazes vacantly at the Tiffany lampshade on the ceiling. She tries to think of Rodolfo but he keeps melting; she tries not to think of Rafaél but he keeps materialising. She's coiled like a spring because she's so relaxed, and so uneasy because so much at ease.

Polly toasts herself. A rather nice Armagnac, hidden in the wardrobe, kept for special occasions. She did well, honey. It had been a good night and her soul had remained steadfastly with her. Great food, great conversation and … Saskja … Well! … "Dream on, Pol, dream on." A good night, a great night. "Cheers, my dear," she salutes herself. "To the happiness worthy of its pursuit."

Tomorrow, Saskja tells herself, tomorrow she will definitely tell Giselle. Tomorrow. Definitely. She will talk, unburden herself, will start to feel better. Tomorrow. Without fail.

Chapter 20

To the Cockney there is one, rarely voiced, horror about travel to non-London climes: escalator anarchy. Throughout the world-that-isn't-London, those travelling by escalator plonk themselves thereon untidily and randomly wherever their legs come to rest. As important a datum for the tourist to the British capital as that its cars drive on the left, is that so do those wishing to climb the escalator – as opposed, that is, to them who ride it. Who stand, almost rigidly, on the right. Woe betide the ignorant Parisian, Roman, Madrileño – even Mancunian – who seeks to do otherwise. The scowl to which such miscreant will be subjected is as loaded as the rat-tat-tut of a Gatling gun.

The quartet knows this. It has thus now arranged itself on four consecutive corrugated steel steps gliding jerkily past posters for 'Phantom of the Opera', abortion advice and cheap flights to Alicante. Rafaél leads the way: an Eastern potentate, almost, with his caravan of concubines. Giselle follows him, and then Saskja and Polly.

The automatic ticket-collector swallows Rafaél's ticket before, almost immediately, regurgitating it through another slot on its steel top. The jaws of the barrier part in a toothless glare, only to snap sharkly shut again the moment he is through. Even in the station at Oxford Circus there is jostle. The festiveness of the festive season seems not to embrace either those Christmas shopping or those assiduously *not* but who are nevertheless enmeshed within the bag-bestrewn mêlée.

Giselle's left hand seems now permanently to rest on her foetal bulge, her right grips the leather strap of the shoulder-bag which straddles her chest. "So?" she asks. They have reassembled into a group – without even being conscious of having formed a wall around the citadel, which is the pregnant woman. They tend now to cluster thus whenever there's a risk that Giselle could be bumped into. And it is in this unconscious formation that they move towards the exit for Argyll Street. It's not that which would most suit them, but they are not yet within that inner sanctum of the cognoscenti able to negotiate hiccuplessly the arcane catacombs of central London's tube system.

"So?" Polly returns. It's cold. She's secreted about her a small hip flask of dimpled metal, just to keep the chill away. She can feel its shape in her coat pocket, and even its touch invokes a glow of comfort and of ease.

"The first vital virtue?" Giselle asks. "What do you think is the first vital virtue?"

"Love," replies Rafaél baldly, blandly, almost sternly.

"Love, right," agrees Polly.

"Certain. Love," Saskja announces, the auctioneer gavelling the winning bid.

They have arrived at ground level. The last flight of steps was not automated. It is a relatively short flight, but also quite a steep one. Giselle is panting more than she'd like to be. She grips the leather strap yet more tightly, as if thereby securing herself more support.

A surprisingly young man roasts chestnuts in an oil-drum stove. He's lanky but he stoops permanently. His hair, perhaps appropriately, is chestnut brown, but it is oily and spiked, not in deference to fashion, but from a lack of recent shampoo. For no apparent reason he keeps pulling at his ear. His face, like his hair, is also spiked – with a four- or five-day-old stubble. A wind-chafed hand turns the chestnuts over the redly glowing charcoal embers with a big metal spoon. Rafaél can't understand how he's not burning himself.

"Beautiful," exclaims Saskja. They all look at her. "This. Beautiful." She means Oxford Circus. She means the Christmas lights Santaing across the street. She means the tinsel and the sparkle.

"I am appalled," Polly tells her with a ho-ho-ho of mock censure. "This is just awful. Gaudy. Tawdry. ... Las Vegas-sy."

Saskja agrees. "Beautiful," she repeats, "*like* Las Vegas. Like I think Las Vegas will be." Her lips squeeze into a smile she would like to believe were unalloyed. The keen observer would just catch the tang, though, nestling deep within it, of an immutable unhappiness.

Those familiar with the English 'Monopoly' board will know that Bond Street, Regent Street and Oxford Street are the olive green set. There is only a (Monopoly) £20 distinction between them, and none between Oxford and Regent Streets. Such is not quite the case of reality. The business of them all is, of course, selling. They are all olive green whores. Bond Street, though, is the courtesan: a small client list, satin sheets and exotic scents, discretion, elegance – all at a price that few can afford. Regent Street is the call-girl: chic, well-groomed, the regular plaything of the well-heeled and the 'special treat' dalliance of those whose heels are scuffed. Oxford Street is the Soho tart, her boudoir of flaking paint and creaking bed-springs, busiest when the fleet comes in. This, anyway, is the description to which Polly subjects them.

Saskja is still mesmerised. "If tart," she chides, "beautiful tart. 'Irma La Douce' tart."

"The tart with the heart of gold?" snorts Polly.

"Please?" Saskja returns.

"The gold at the heart of this tart," the American continues, "that's the metal. And her gold, that's mostly ours."

"Orphalese, Polly, has no such treasures. This, for me, like Aladdin's cave."

"Is a fair point she makes, *amiga mía*. Also, I think is true, most people here, most people shopping, they are here out of love."

"It's obscene, Rafa. This isn't what Christmas is all about."

"You do not enjoy receiving gifts, my friend?" Rafa asks.

"That is not quite the same thing." Polly tries to chuckle back. Her hand clasps more tightly around the flask.

"But I think, yes, mostly it is. I think all of us, we like to receive. And we all like to give. Is, I think, an act of love. Mayhap it has been distorted."

"May*hap*?" Polly exclaims.

"Okay, my friend, *has* been distorted. Has been distorted, okay,"

Rafa agrees. But it is not a fulsome, nor a full agreement. "Do, though, let us be on our guard, my friend, that once again we do not throw the baby out with the bath-water. Cromwell's Christmases would appear to have been cheerless events. We have a need, Polly, of cheer in our lives. Of joy. Cheer, and joy, they are the accompaniments to love. Love's ladies-in-waiting. Love is mayhap the soup. But love and cheer, these, my friend, are the croutons and the salt."

"That a Spanish expression, Rafa?"

"Oooh!" Giselle suddenly gasps. She stops dead in her tracks. Those passers-by around her glower their displeasure that they are forced to make an instant detour.

"You okay?" Saskja asks unnecessarily. Rafaél has grabbed Giselle's arm just below the elbow, as if to steady a drunk, or guide a blind man.

"Perhaps, what with the baby, you know ... perhaps not the cleverest idea ... the hosts of people, the pushing ..."

"You wish to return?" asks Rafaél.

"To sit down. I wish to sit down. Just to sit down."

"I seem to remember a pub, just off Cavendish Square, a couple of hundred yards ..."

"John Lewis, Polly, I feel certain, it has a cafeteria."

"'Course it will," Polly agrees. "'Course it will. What am I thinking of?"

"You okay?" again Saskja asks, again unnecessarily.

"I feel so stupid," Giselle replies. She's bent forward as far as her bulge will allow her, bent over like a vanquished athlete. She waddles a hobble like a very ancient duck. And she doesn't want to be held by the arm or asked if she's okay or fussed over. She'd just like to be alone and at home, spirited there by the patron djinni of pregnant ex-nuns. In whose direction she aims a muted supplication, not quite as mock as she'd like to believe. She smiles at her own heresy, smiles at what her former abbess would doubtless have called her 'blasphemy'. But she knows it to be no more blasphemy than satire is slander.

Pregnancy in humans has very little to recommend it. One of its very few perks is that, even within a culture becoming daily less courteous, it does sometimes occasion the abdication of seats. Thus, and piecemeal, does the quartet acquire a table which would otherwise have required some time for its taking. The cafeteria is self-service. It affords a luxurious view of Cavendish Square. Saskja goes to buy the drinks.

Polly uses the opportunity to pop to the loo. She is in dire need of some warmth. God bless her dimpled friend.

At the table next to Giselle and Rafaél sits a portly woman, perhaps in her sixties. Her gaze seems to hover above Giselle, and her grin of sympathy and solidarity glides into a stare of oh-God,-wasn't-it-so-lovely?-ness. Her husband, old school, Clark Gable moustache, blue blazer its breast pocket escutcheoned with some unknown badge, clears an admonitory throat. This seems to jolt his wife back to the present. She flicks a quick apology at Giselle and then returns her attention to her lipstick-embossed coffee-cup and to her unlipstick-embossed husband. They start discussing what else to buy Miriam, now they've seen the quite outrageous price of toasters.

Polly returns to the table. Her tummy is considerably less a-flutter than it had been. "What *is* love?" she asks.

Giselle has finally found a position in her chair which, whilst far from being comfortable, at least provides some support to some of her. "Finally," she replies, "love is God. And God finally is also truth. So, finally love is truth."

"God, love, truth:" says Polly, "three in one, huh? And one in three."

"We humans, however," says Rafaél, "we can only imagine such love, such truth. We cannot know it. At best we can only know *of* it. And even that requires enormous imaginative energy. Is like trying to imagine the power of Big Bang.

"Is a good question, though: 'What is love?'. A question we would all benefit from asking ourselves."

Saskja, without any undue reverence to ceremony, plonks down the tray of drinks. She and Giselle are having water, Rafa and Polly coffee. "One thing love not," she says, as she sits down, "love not 'never having to say you are sorry'."

"Love is definitely not that," agrees Polly. "God, that is so craven. Sometimes … sometimes I just cringe at the slogans invented by Hollywood. At so much of Hollywood's output. How much of that output – particularly today's – concerns itself with any kind of truth? How much is even truthful of itself? An act of creation that doesn't at some level seek to be truthful cannot emanate from love. And it therefore has (I think) to be tinged with non-love. Non-love may not be hatred '*per se*', but it incubates the egg from which hatred can hatch. How much television is truthful? Even seeks to be? How many songs, for God's sake?

"It sells *sex*, Hollywood, but how often *love*? And even sex it sells in a dishonest way. Pin-ups with staples through their navels, air-brushed to within an inch of their siliconed lives. Mr Spielberg, asked to defend the historical inaccuracy of one of his war films, returned that neither had Shakespeare been historically accurate. That Mr Spielberg – that, excuse me, Sir Stephen – chose to compare himself with Shakespeare is already significant. But, let us put that to one side. We return to the difference there is between being factual and being truthful. Shakespeare is rarely factual. But he is truthful. And his work has the integrity it has for that reason. There was truth in Sir Stephen's first film, 'Duel'. Also in '1942', even glimpses of truth in 'E.T.' and 'Jaws' and 'Schindler's List'. I'm not trying to suggest, in other words, that a concern for profit does not vanquish truth, and thus love. Nor am I condemning the fact that films make profits. Quite the contrary, in fact. If they didn't, we wouldn't be making *any* films. But when profit becomes the *only* concern, even the primary concern, truth just has to be compromised.

"Frankly, I'm not a huge fan of Sir Alan Parker's work. (Oh, he's certainly directed some fine movies, but I'm not the fan of his opus that I am of, say, Richard Attenborough's.) Sir Alan's flims are certainly within the commercial canon. His sketched cartoons pay witty tribute to the incompatibility of Truth with the profit fixation.

John Boorman's diary, likewise, of his production, 'The Emerald Forest'.

"And when on the rare occasions Hollywood does try to sell love (not Doris Day love, or Sharon Stone love, schmaltz or sex – but the love- of-humanity love) when it does try to sell that what it's actually selling is sentimentality – Frank Capra's 'It's a Wonderful Life', say. And all its various disguises thereafter. Love is most certainly *not* sentimental. Not real love, not true love. And, it seems to me, we do love a major disservice when we pretend that's what it is.

"In fact, love is remarkably *un*sentimental, even pragmatic. Know why it's such a great idea to love your enemies?..." Before waiting for a reply, she steamrollers on, "'Cause that way (a) you get to have less enemies, and (b) 'cause such enemies as you do have have a heap less power over you."

"Is also a (c)," says Rafaél, grimacing at the coffee as if it had just bitten him. He's yet to notice that the cappuccino has left behind a line of its froth on his upper lip. Talking, he senses this, and dabs it away with a paper napkin.

"C?" asks Giselle, her left arm now supporting the small of her back.

"*Claro,*" says Rafaél. "Wilde writes in one of his essays most eloquently about the gift that is gratitude. 'It enhances the joy you have,' he says only far more poetically, 'the joy you have in that which is being appreciated.' Love is very similar. Love is very enabling, very eye-opening. If you love someone, you notice them: the clothes they are wearing, the perfume they've got on; you are aware of a change in mood, are sensitive to their nuance. And you therefore enoy that person more completely. How do we describe someone whom we hate? 'Horrible person! I couldn't even bear to look at him!' You don't listen to someone whom you hate – is probably not even possible to do so. Some*thing* you hate likewise."

"You know the actor, Michael Caine?" asks Polly. The other three wither her a reply. "Sorry. In an interview Sir Michael was quoted as saying, 'Hate is such a powerful emotion. Why would you want to waste it on someone you don't like?'"

"A better actor, then, than a philosopher," suggests the Peruvian. "Is so much, I think, worse than that: Hatred does not deprive the hated, but the hater. Is the ultimate of that expression you have here: of cutting off your nose to spite your face. Is one of the reasons is so tragic, the world's most dominating force today is hatred.

"'What a piece of work is a man,' Shakespeare wrote. 'How express and admirable.' A world ruled by love would understand how express, how admirable is this piece of work called a man. A love-ruled world would treasure that piece of work and nurture it. Would ensure such a piece had everything it needed in order to become the most perfect piece it possibly could. Instead we have a world that destroys that piece, or humiliates it or that suffocates its potential. And by how much would *our* life be improved by recognising the worth of others' lives?

"We have talked, Polly and I, about progress. To us – and please correct me, Polly, if I have misunderstood you – to us a part of the definition of that progress would be this, that unless we *all* progress, we none of us progress. Is that simple. And, until we have a planet whose dynamo is love 'we' *cannot* progress. Is too finally that simple. Is why too love, that has to be the first, and most important vital virtue."

"I think ... I hate being difficult .... I think perhaps," mutters Giselle, "I think I do need to go home." Saskja is about to talk. Giselle anticipates her. "I'm okay, Saskja. It's merely... the throngs ... I was not anticipating – I had not anticipated – the throngs ... It's that I am not easy with the throngs ... Please do not fuss, Rafaél."

They take the Central Line home. As soon as they pass Marble Arch the crowds melt into a trickle of the usual tube-travellers: a teenage Romeo and his pink-haired Juliet, a besuited 'professional' loudly clearing the throat of his displeasure at their amorous displays whilst busying himself reading some sort of closely-typed brief, a couple of fluourescently waistcoated workmen sprawling muddily and munching noisily huge wedges of sandwiches, off-duty schoolchildren with on-duty guardians. Giselle is now easier. And looks easier. The others are easier around her.

Polly and she sit. Saskja and Rafaél stand above them. If they were all seated, conversation would either have to be shouted or abandoned. Saskja is still such an ingénue to London she enjoys the standing, its jiggle and its thrust: Rafaél is of an age that periodically he needs to prove to himself that he can still cope with it.

"In my opinion," says Giselle, "everyone, she would agree that the first vital virtue is love. Even those, Polly, who have no faith in God have faith, is what I am saying, in love. Think that love is a good idea. In fact, *love* the idea of love.

"Even Arthur Blessitt (scarcely one of Cupid's apostles) advertises his meetings as 'A Mission Of Love and Joy' … even those, like Mr Blessitt's colleague, Billy Graham, whose message is a burning hatred, *advocate* love … even the most toxic of Islamic clerics … the most nihilist of philosophers. Probably those who blew up Oklahoma or the Twin Towers would claim they did so out of love. Politicians whatever their hue, and however tyrannical, still talk of love – of philanthropy and humanity. And talk of it, not using the term of course, but nevertheless *as* the first – and most indispensable – vital virtue."

"Is yet another tragedy of today," jiggles Rafaél, "how badly, how shamelessly love is abused. There is so much love in the world – *so* much – that even today's brutality, even today's slide into barbarism cannot destroy it. Look at how human beings respond to emergencies, and then look at how institutions do."

They're at Notting Hill Gate. The labourers have munched their way off the train. A podgy Rastafarian with oddly conservative spectacles wafts in. The doors pfffft closed, and the train lurches off again.

"Is a natural resource, love, apparently unlimited in its abundance. Open your eyes and you will see it, daily, in a thousand acts of kindness happening all around you.

"We don't, though. Open our eyes, I mean. And that is yet another big sadness today. It seems this is part of the human condition. We do notice the bank clerk being sulky, or the bureaucrat being bloody-minded, but we do not notice the woman on the cheese counter smiling at us or the guy at the check-in desk allowing us a few extra pounds on our baggage.

"We don't even open our eyes, apparently, to our own acts of charity. When we perform acts of love, we seem almost to be embarrassed. We shrug off favours done for friends, subscribe to charities anonymously. Not that such troubles me. I really like that anonymity, in fact. It smacks of love indeed. It smacks of a mature love and a wise love – and an unsentimental love. It recognises that the value of giving is *in* the giving, not in the recognition of the gift. I need to work on myself very much more ardently in that regard. I am more guilty than most of expecting an immediate return for love.

"If, as a driver, I do a kindness to another – let him in ahead of me in traffic, as an example – I continue to want to be thanked. And if I don't receive such thanks, I'm likely (according to my mood) to become more or less indignant – and more or less vociferous in my indignation. Is not mature love, that, or wise love. First of all because that makes it *conditional* love and such, whilst not quite an oxymoron, is nevertheless a big compromiser of love. But is not the only reason.

"Is nice to be thanked. Of course is nice to be thanked. And the thanker bestows always a gift on the thankee. (Is this English?) But if I execute this deed (or any deed) in the expectation of being thanked, then I am not acting wisely or maturely. Wisdom and maturity would enjoin me to recognise that the gift of giving is far more the giver's than the givee's. Virtue is its own reward because virtue sets up virtuous spirals.

"When I give way to another driver, such is in my own interests as much as is of the other driver. If all drivers gave way, traffic would flow more smoothly. If enough other motorists also give way, mayhap that driver will in time also start to give way. And thus, as I say, traffic which is now blocked would start to flow. I am ready to bet, *amigas mías*, that most of the traffic jams in the world could be avoided if motorists drove more thoughtfully."

"Or like pedestrians."

"Or, as you say, Polly, like pedestrians. Selfish driving always, *always* leads to traffic congestion. My interests are not protected by selfishness. In fact, so very, very often, selfishness is a powerful enemy of my own best interests. Is that simple."

They have arrived at Shepherd's Bush. Polly continues the analogy of shopping marts as prostitutes. Shepherd's Bush is the street-walker: cigarette dangling from carbuncled mouth; laddered fish-nets and lacquered bouffon; panda, junk-dilated, eyes. Which Polly finds curious or coincidental or something, since a big stamping-ground for (non-allegorical) prostitutes is Mayfair's *Shepherd* Market (with most emphatically no apostrophe!): what is it to do with shepherds and ladies-of-the-night? And what designates the presence or absence of pastoral apostrophes?

In the normal course of events, they would walk home from here. It's not far. But Giselle still feels fragile. It's not, she's now decided, it *was* not anything physical. Some sort of mild panic attack, probably. She still feels wobbly, though. She needs to be home. And alone would be even better. She'll suggest to the others when they get there they go out by themselves. They wait for the 94 bus to Turnham Green. Or the 237. Either. Polly stomps her feet on the ground, trying to bump-start her circulation. They huddle together, a carrier-bagged igloo. Christmas carols blare metallically from the nearby mall. Around them there are more shoppers than non-shoppers. But the overall mood is of grumpiness. There is as much dearth of *joie-de-Noël* as there is of *joie-de-vie*.

A couple of winos reel past, tottering as they do. One has a can of Tennent's 'extra strong' lager clenched purply and defiantly in his fist. He is railing loudly at the injustices of an unjust world. He uses the sides of his soiled double-breasted black overcoat almost as punctuation, like an emu flapping exasperated wings. His friend, not quite arrived yet at a similar apogee of indignation and intoxication, seeks ciderly to placate his ranting friend. They are both headed for

Shepherd's Bush Green. Polly cannot look at them.

A seven-year-old with a shy, missing-tooth grin and a red duffle-coat points a slimey finger at Giselle's midriff and giggles at her elder sister.

Rafa digs in his pockets for his gloves. "One reason why today's brutalisation for so many is as painful as it is," he says, "is because is forcing us – so many of us – to be something which we're not. We are not brutal by nature. But brutalisation is nurturing us into brutalising. When I was at school, those left-handed were still obliged to write with their right. Is that kind of pain."

"Not the greatest analogy, Rafa," suggests Polly. "Most left-handed people are as bright as they are – which is a lot brighter than those of us who are right-handed – because the world forces them to use both sides of their brain a lot more than we Northpaws have to."

"We have talked before of Scott Peck." Rafa pauses in order to pull on his second glove with his teeth. "It was said in one of his obituaries that he could not live by his own standards. I don't know whether this is true. But even if it is, it matters, I think, far less than the obituary writer would have us believe. Ethics, moral standards, these – as I have said before – are goals to which we strive. How many shots at goal are there in a football match? And how many arrive in the net? They are codes of conduct against which we can measure our own behaviour. Often and inevitably we shall fall short of them. Is very much more significant that we strive for them than we succeed. And by placing the emphasis on such success we merely discourage ourselves from even striving. We can allow ourselves to fall short. We can forgive ourselves, we can perhaps recognise that we got closer to our goal this time than the last. The next time, presented with a similar challenge, such might encourage us to greater effort. Ethics are finally there in order that we may become happier with ourselves – and more 'we' than we would be without them.

"The world is not a better place for being populated by those permanently disgruntled because they fail to attain unattainable goals. Is one of the reasons there are so many disgruntled people around today. Worse. Because is not even we who set these unattainable goals for ourselves. Rather are they imposed on us by others. Historically by the Church and the Crown; today industry, bureaucracy, employers and the state, and the pervading ethos around us: globalisation, greed, hatred.

"Dr Peck in one of his books said that it was our responsibility to 'sell the world on love'."

"We talked about this, Rafa, before."

"Not, I think, with Giselle and Saskja. And the point I am here seeking to make, my friend, is also a little different. I do not think Dr Peck was right, that's what I was going to say. Not in this particular case. I *don't* think the world does need 'selling' on love. I think, as I have said just now, there is indeed an abundance of love in this world. I don't think we need to sell the world on love at all. Mayhap we need to be less ashamed of the love we have, less embarrassed by it. That much may be true. And certainly we should not allow religion to continue making its claims that it has a monopoly on love. Mayhap we should be extolling – loudly and insistently – the virtues of love (and of loving) and encouraging one another more in its pursuit. And mayhap too we need to start educating ourselves on how we use the love we have, the love which we crave to give, the love that demands from us that we give it. And, yes, also we need to be wary of the dangers there are in it.

"Gandhi, it should be remembered, preached love. The love he preached eventually saw India regain its independence. And it was certainly mostly hatred which prompted the creation of Pakistan. We do need to ask ourselves, though: Did *ahimsa* – Gandhi's policy of non-violence – did that contribute to that hatred, to that secession and to the million deaths that were thereby caused? We do not get closer to the truth by ignoring evidence inconvenient to our cause. The law may thereby be served, but never justice.

"In my opinion it was not his love, but the *abuse* of Gandhi's love, the abuse of *ahimsa,* which first caused the schism and continues to feed the friction between the two states. At the level of political opportunism, love is very fragile and can very, *very* easily be abused.

"Love, we must always remember, is very hard work. True love. Unsentimental love. Is as demanding a discipline as – yes, Polly, this I have said before – as learning a musical instrument. Love may be beneficial, beneficial mayhap to a degree that is incalculable; love may even be essential and hatred insanely ruinous, but it remains the case that is so much easier to hate than is to love. Demolition (as we also talked about, Polly and I) is an infinitely easier job than construction. How long did it take to build the World Trade Centre? Hiroshima? Coventry? And how long to destroy them? How long does it take to make a film, Polly? And how long for a critic to annihilate it? The act of creation, as I say, is infinitely more difficult, more challenging, more demanding, more time-consuming, needful of more commitment and courage than the act of destruction. It takes nine months to create a human being and one gunshot to destroy him.

"Returning to India ... certainly is true that the Indian sub-continent was robbed by its colonialists. But is also true, its poverty today was not caused by that alone. Nor that it was Westerners alone who robbed the population. But neither will that poverty be eradicated by the invasion of American or multi-national industry. Such is merely economic, as opposed to political, colonialism. Is absolutely certainly not love. Not in any sense. Watch or read any interview with an American 'entrepreneur' there: the attitude is of a Big Mac British Raj. This too is hatred. Contempt is a manifestation of hatred.

"The missionaries of old did not disseminate God's love; they merely propagated the Church's hatred. You do not subjugate those you love, you do not lecture to them; you listen *to* them, you learn *from* them, you realise is the man in the pulpit who is the pupil."

The bus arrives. The 94. They climb aboard, show their tickets to a rather frail-looking woman with extravagant light pink fingernails. She's probably in her late forties, but could be anywhere from thirty-five to sixty-five. Saskja smiles at her. "Happy Christmas," she trills. The driver manages to muster a wan smile of acknowledgement.

"Yeah, merry Christmas," she mumbles back exhaustedly. It could even be sarcastic.

"We need no more teachers in this world," continues Rafaél. "Not anyway in this sense. We all seem to be born teachers. We love imparting our knowledge from a tiny age, love *talking* to people, love *advising* them. Watch even toddlers advising one another. We now have to learn how to *learn*, we have to listen to *how* we listen, we have to study *how* to study. We need no more teachers, but we do need a worldful more pupils. We do not need to sell the world on love, but we have to learn *how* to love. How we make tangible that which is burning within us to be released.

"Already this is happening. That, as Polly would say, is the good news. Love is – albeit terribly, terribly slowly – beginning to reverse a process. Look at today's advertisements. She will tell you, this too we talked about before." Polly manages a ho-hum grin, acknowledging she was indeed about to make that very point. "Look at how many companies are trying to convince us of their ecological commitment, their humanitarian credentials, their sense of global responsibility. And all this is good news. This is great news. Some of the companies may even be doing this. Slowly the message is getting through even to vested interest that it's in fact in the interest of that vested interest that 'vested interest' is understood to be our communal vested interest, rather than a parochial or a personal vested interest ... that methos become wethos. And this tendency should, and needs to be, greatly encouraged.

"A quick look at a company's ledgers would vouchsafe their actual commitment. Let us discover what they are paying to their lowest-paid worker and what to the members of their board, their 'consultants' and advisers, what stock options and 'fringe benefits' are included in the package, their expense accounts. Your company is not working for the good of humanity if is not caring for its own workforce.

"I do not believe mankind will kill itself. And therefore eventually methos *has* to be destroyed. Eventually the option will become clear:

between methos and mankind: one has to destroy the other. There is no alternative.

"Fundamentally I think mankind has more resilience than methos. Just as Truth is more powerful than Untruth. Because finally there is an ethical line in our DNA. Even Hitler and Stalin paid lip-service to benefiting mankind; even caught in a mesh of lies, the politician will respond indignantly to any suggestion he is, or has been, lying.

"Today's liars still insist they are telling the truth. Insist on it. Government reports which are government white-washes nevertheless claim vehemently they are servants of but one master: the truth. The *moral* supremacy of Truth over Untruth or of the individual truth over the lie is never in question; nor is that of love over hatred.

"That methos has to be destroyed is questioned only by those so blinkered that cannot see, or with a death wish – those, for instance, awaiting the Rapture. The question only remains of the most *efficacious* way of destroying methos.

"It *could*, methos, be destroyed *positively*. But only if we learn to listen, if we learn to learn, if we learn ... not to love – that we do know – but how to demonstrate that love, how to manifest it. How to *use* it. It is the glacier of human emotions – eventually, despite its apparent brittleness and despite its exasperating slowness, the single most powerful force. And eventually too, just as glaciers wear away mountains, so love – so '*wethos*' – will wear away methos.

"The positive erosion of methos *could* happen simply by an extension of what I was just now saying: vested interest recognising that its *true* interest is vested in wethos. Indeed its PR campaigns would try to persuade us that such is already what is happening. But is unlikely such is fact. Hatred seems to be also very habit-forming – apparently odium is as addictive as opium! And hatred will not abdicate its stranglehold on the world without a struggle.

"To keep our love intact whilst hatred is wreaking all its viciousness on it, that, my friends, will be an *enormous* challenge. We could cause too many Indias to be divided, too many Biafras and too many Bosnias to be created. It returns us – always, ineluctably – to the same question: Do we have what it takes to do what it takes?"

They climb off the bus. "'The Rajput'," Polly comments of an Indian restaurant opposite. "Know it well. Verity Lambert – God rest her soul – once took me there. She reckoned it was one of the best Indian restaurants in London. Frankly, I didn't agree with the lady on too many things, but in that particular instance she couldn't have been much righter." The others gaze at her blankly. Polly had forgotten the golden rule of name-dropping: the name dropped has to be known to those before whom it is clanging! It behoves those with a predilection for such a hobby to remember that so many of the world's 'stars' twinkle only in their own bathrooms. As if to cover her embarrassment, Polly quickly continues: "So, if love is the first vital virtue, what is the first life-affirming idea?"

"Life," suggests Giselle simply.

"Life?" asks Rafaél.

"Life," Giselle repeats.

"Life is a good idea?" asks Polly. She's now shivering. But she is deriving now some concrete comfort knowing that relief is not too far away.

"Yes," says Giselle simply.

"Life is a good idea?" Polly repeats, presumably for the sake of clarity.

"Yes," Giselle says again, simply again.

"I'll buy that," says Rafa.

"Me too," says Saskja enthusiastically.

"That simple?" asks Polly.

"That simple," affirms Giselle, simply.

"We've talked before, Polly and I, about the odds against life ever having occurred. Is another of those figures so large as to be incomprehensible," says Rafa. "The chances of our winning the lottery anywhere in the world are infinitely greater than was the likelihood of life being created – at least, life as we understand it."

"Since then, Rafa, I found out that a man (named Roger Penrose, I believe) calculated that the probability of life hitting on a universe such as ours is one in $10^{1,010,123}$. Now you're going to ask me what that number means, and I don't know. But the odds are indeed *so* astronomical (sorry, no pun intended!) that they have caused previously agnostic scientists to start believing in some divine force. It's also interesting to note how many of today's quantum physicists are arriving at the conclusion there is indeed a God – albeit a God of a very different kilter than the one, or ones, who have been imagined heretofore."

"With or without God, do such figures, Polly, not make of life a miracle? And are not miracles to be regarded with awe, with respect, with even veneration?"

"Life is a good idea." Polly seems to be rolling the phrase round in her mouth like an expert vintner with a vintage claret.

"If we thought life a good idea, would we not start treating it a bit more carefully?" asks Giselle. "With a bit more respect? Human life, animal life, even plant and mineral life? Plant life, mineral life, animal life – today these are just commodities. As is human labour.

"When I read Kahlil Gibran's 'The Prophet' exhorting us to be grateful to the apple we eat, I thought it was ... well, almost silly. I thought it was funny, to be honest. No, 'derisory', that's the word I search for. I thought it ... derisory. But he has a point. If we thought life a good idea – a really good idea – would we not want the apple too to be as much apple as it could possibly be? Would we not want to ensure that its soil were properly mulched? Would we not start conceding that Nature probably knows more about looking after her own than we do? That she has billions of years more experience than we have? That without Nature's genius today we'd have no apple genetically to modify? Would we not respect therefore all the life around that apple which also helps to make that apple what it is: all the insects and the birds, the other crops, even the bacteria?

"A salmon is not something which tastes good with cream cheese on a bagel. A salmon is a miracle. A salmon has a nose so sensitive that it can detect a single drop of fresh water in eight thousand gallons of brine. How is that not miraculous?"

"Still tastes good with cream cheese, Giselle," murmurs Polly.

"Two hundred other species of life think so as well," Giselle smiles back.

"Particularly on a bagel."

Giselle ignores her. "If we thought life was a good idea, would we not stop killing animals for so-called sport? The unspeakable in hot pursuit, is it not?, of the uneatable. Would we not ensure that animals were slaughtered with kindness and concern? Would we not tender all the creatures on this planet the respect they deserve? Would we not be conscious of the dignity of anything onto which life has been bestowed?

"There were jelly-fish and crabs and insects on this planet aeons before homo was even land-based, let alone being erectus. Bio-diversity is not only necessary, it is beautiful and beguiling ... and fascinating."

"In a time when serious political debate has been abandoned in favour of arguing the merits of two syllogisms," says Rafaél, "I have often thought the most politically radical programmes on television were the wildlife ones. Create a wonder for the natural sciences, for the natural world, and you have to create a respect for life. Those in wonder have to believe that life is a good idea. Create that respect for life and you have to see that 'methos', lunatic thinking that it is, is no respecter of life. Entire species are disappearing – and *not* to feed the human hungry; the human hungry are as hungry as ever – but to assuage the unassuageable greed of the greedy. If life is a good idea, then globalisation isn't – certainly not what we understand by the word 'globalisation' today."

"Life is good idea," says Saskja, almost in triumph. "For me that is first life-affirming idea."

"For me as well," says Giselle, opening the front door, despite herself glowing that it should have been she who had thought of it.

"And me," says Rafa.

"Life is a good idea," mulls Polly, closing the door behind her. "Sure. I'll drink to that."

Chapter 21

Well before the poem was written, on the night before Christmas, visions of sugarplums danced through the heads of even the Scroogest of Ebenezers. As adults we may not care to admit it. But if, as we are often told, there lurks within us always the child there was, at no time does such child make itself more apparent than in the dreams visited us – and visited upon us – on this particular night. This is truly the ghost of Christmas past.

Even the aged, in the Christmas Eve dreams, relive the awe, the wonder, the sheer magic of their infancy's sugarplums. Even the grumpiest of gramps. They do not remember them. They, yes, re-experience them – and vividly: all the sounds, tastes, smells, the tingle in the atmosphere, the tingle in the *bones*, the tinsel and the tassels, the prick of Christmas tree needles, the whiff of its sap, the surprisingly hollow clunk of the glass balls cannoning off each other, the scratchy touch of the thread that holds them ... It is there again tonight, at the foot of their beds, the amorphous stocking or the flaccid pillow-slip – turned, hey! presto!, into a lumpy, bumpy, sharp-cornered treasure-chest, spewing bulimically its Rudolphed goodies. They can see again, and touch again, and rip again (with frantic fingers, now all tiny and awkward thumbs), tear again at Christmas paper and wrestle again with intractable tape – the smell of that paper, that tape, its texture, the promise lurking behind its veils ... there's the red Christmas paper polka-dotted with Dickensian stage-coaches; and there the green Christmas paper with golden 'Merry Christmas'es emblazoned across it; the tin-foil, that's for the tangerines; the blue Christmas paper sprinkled with smiling snowmen. The smell, not of cooking, that comes later ... the indefinable, but unmistakable pre-dawn aroma that choruses Christmas. The aliveness that morning of being alive. Wordsworth's bliss. The thumping of the heart and the duvet cuddles and the all's-right-with-the-worldness. Whilst the whole time the visions of sugarplums are dancing ... dancing ... dancing.

Like a child Polly's been awake for some time. Like a child, almost, waiting for the grown-ups so stir, wanting the fun to begin, wanting the gloriousness of the day to grab her, King Kong to her Fay Wray, and lift her out of all the humdrum dreariness and drabness and irksomeness of it all. Maybe she should have gone with them to church. Where, finally, would have been the harm?

***

Giselle can smell turkey. She closes the garden door with her bottom and starts unbuttoning her coat. The flat is as toasty warm as the outside is crispbreadly icy. She senses the turkey needs basting. She's never before in her life basted a turkey, never roasted one, but the advice was to baste it, so baste it she would. Saskja is still in her room. Saskja and Polly had decided to stay at home, whilst she and Rafaél went to mass. *Went*? Giselle had waddled there.

She's been busy, Saskja. The table's laid. There are the carrots and onions cut up as Rafaél had asked. She herself had prepared another salad. With almonds, this one, courgettes, red cabbage and rocket. Polly is bringing the pudding. Giselle pushes the oven flap and it gently closes by itself.

She pours herself a glass of red wine. "God bless us, everyone," she toasts them all. And suddenly realises she is doing so in earnest. They had made the same toast at midnight, when Saskja had thrust her fingers towards her throat in the gesture that signifies that what is being said is enough to make anyone throw up. Rafaél had been quite firm with her, surprisingly firm, almost Victorian in his stricture. "What finer blessing could there be?" he had asked.

And Saskja, Giselle could see, had felt both humiliated and embarrassed. And then Rafaél had laughed and had quoted Wilde, who had suggested that no man who had a heart could help but snigger at the death of little Nell. Saskja had then laughed as well. But there was a reluctance in that laugh, a chug of manufacture. An impression, and Giselle knew it, had been indelibly etched within her.

Which didn't mean Rafaél hadn't been right. Of course he'd been right. Of course it was the finest blessing you could ask for, the greatest prayer ... Of course it was: "Please God, bless us, everyone."

Again she raises her glass, and again toasts everyone, herself included. "God bless us, everyone." And everyone becomes that: the four of them there would be at lunch ... their friends ... the street ... London ... humanity. She decides again to baste the turkey. Can you over-baste a turkey? she wonders. She decides that's just not possible.

The smell of wine escapes from the glass and wanders gently to meet that of the roasting meat. Maybe there is something madeleine-like in this mix of smells. Suddenly she is as empty as she is full. She hauls out one of the breakfast-bar stools and lugs herself aboard it. She lets her finger trace a circle around the lip of her glass.

It's not that emptiness has seized her. It is that it has joined her fullness. Which is not a completeness. Not today. But, though incomplete, it remains a fullness. And it is not either that the accompanying sadness has usurped the reigning contentment. Rather that it has joined the king on an adjoining throne as a consort – not an identical twin of the king, but a photographic negative of him.

There is an awareness that this is her last childless Christmas. And there is a sadness that it is a parentless one. Tears start taking off their track-suits behind her kitten-grey eyes. She is *six*-years-old again. In Syracuse. It's not that she remembers the event. Just as curmudgeons are with sugarplums, she's *there* again:

She's wrapped under the quilt that always smelled of olives, afraid almost to move. She'd risen once and had unceremoniously been hied back to bed, and woe betide her if she again crawled from it until she was called. Smells are overwhelming her: of almonds toasting in caramel, of goose roasting, of wine being mulled, of cinnamon and nutmeg and chocolate. And coffee. Above all, coffee. The thick, sweet coffee her parents loved. A coffee almost Turkish in its density and sweetness. A coffee all their friends firmly detested.

She hears movement from Saskja's room. The noise zooms her

back to the present. She smiles broadly to herself. She's wished her parents 'Merry Christmas'. She's felt them safe. They know that still she loves them dearly. She takes a good sip from her glass. She bastes the turkey yet again. If it were inedible, the bird, it was certainly not going to be from a want of basting. The baby kicks. Fiercely. She smiles again. Her parents, she somehow feels, have met their grandchild.

***

Polly's soul is nesting. She's lying on her bed, her eyes sometimes open, often closed. She doesn't want her soul to flee. Not today. Well, in fact, not any day (if the truth were known) but particularly not this day. It doesn't even mean much to her, Christmas. But it does to them. Rafaél had already seen her soulless. She'd prefer the women didn't. But she knows they will.

Given that, she'd rather it not be today.

The problem is, the soul she's endowed with, she's not too happy with it. Not at the moment. She's not too happy with her soul most of the time, in fact. Nor has she ever been. Not for as long as she can remember. As a child she'd felt she'd been born to the wrong parents, or there'd been a mix-up at the hospital or something. She once challenged her mother whether she were adopted. Her mother had been appalled by the idea. Outraged. She'd been made to understand that her mother's only return for enduring years of unwelcome sex was her (Polly's) birth and that of her brother. But she'd been told that in words which never evolved into action.

Oh, they'd been good people ... What was she talking about? They *were* good people. Probably very good people – they were just the *wrong* people. Perfect for her brother ... yes, for Peter perfect. But for her ... miscast. Dad (now retired) had been some functionary in a Boston factory and Mom was, like Father Brown, a human dumpling, who enjoyed an antipathy to cooking bordering on the phobic. She was also the self-effacing owner of a soprano voice so resonant she had sung in the local choral society. She should visit. She owed them that. *Really* she should visit again. They'd die and she'd regret not having seen them, not having made the effort. She owed them a visit. She owed herself that visit too.

Peter as a child wanted for nothing. These days likewise. But his these-days-want-for-nothingness, that had been luck. He'd opened a gym just ahead of the fashion. It had gotten itself a name locally and he had been encouraged to expand, not because he wanted to, not even because his wife was pushing him to, but because there were so many investors in line to lend him money – and at ludicrously favourable rates – that it was going with the flow to *accept* the expansion. It wasn't, Polly didn't think, that he wore life like the proverbial loose garment, more that he ran around naked, unashamed – and unimpressed by any of the fig-trees with which he was surrounded.

She, though, had always felt herself not just as naked but several times more so. She felt life was like cling-film wrapped around her – not hiding her nakedness but suffocating it. And cling-film, not under her armpits, but binding her arms; not between her legs, but also chastity-belting them. When in her teens she had realised she was gay, the realisation was a relief. Her constriction and discomfort would now make some sort of sense. But it didn't. No, it *did* – but not for long. The blink of an eye, almost. Her first straight liaison had afforded the same kind of relief, her first long-term girl-friend, when she came out to her parents. Temporary reliefs, all of them: tents for refugees, not the homes of resettlement.

She is perfectly okay with not being okay with the world. There is precious little in today's world she *can* be okay with. Or any right-thinking person can be okay with. But she's not okay with her not being okay with herself. And yet she continues to do things that will make it ever more inevitable that she isn't. Like now. She's appalled with herself right now.

She'd been attracted to Saskja the first time she saw her. "*Claro*," as Rafaél would say. Of course she had been. She was a beautiful young woman, pert and petite, with eyes that sparkled both coquettishness and innocence. You'd have to be blind not to find her attractive. It isn't that, the problem.

The problem is that she's picking up ... something ... not signals, nothing so tangible ... but, what are they? Waves? Subconscious waves, even? And does she only think she's sensing them? She's perfectly prepared to accept that she's imagining the whole thing. She'd indeed *prefer* to be imagining the whole thing. If the whole thing is just her imagining then it poses no – real – threat to a whole bunch of friendships and inter-connected relationships.

But her imaginings as she now lies atop her bed, they're taking another form altogether. She's imagining kissing her for the first time, feeling those silky threads of her hair bouncing on the palms of her hands; she's feeling for the first time her lips brush against hers, feels their tongues touching, insinuating themselves, douching one another.

She's a witness now, as Polly pulls off Saskja's crewneck jersey. She's wearing only a white lace bra beneath it. Her breasts are now rising and falling heavily, aroused, excited. The cleavage plunges to canyon-like depths. She sees the freshness and elasticity of the skin, the navel almost winking at her, enticing her, the flesh melting before it even gets to her mouth. She needs to wait before she sees the breasts themselves. She needs to, yet feels she can't.

She goes to talk. Saskja puts her finger to her, Polly's, lips, stops her. She looks deep into Polly's eyes. "Take me," those eyes tell her. "Do with me anything you want." Lightly, and with one hand, Polly pushes her to the bed.

***

Saskja is feeling new feelings. She's never before considered Sapphic love. She's never discounted it either. It simply has never occurred to her.

For some weeks now she'd felt these strange longings within

herself, Saskja. It had been obvious to her from the first time they'd met that Polly was attracted to her. She'd noticed it and acknowledged it – at least to herself. She'd even (this even more to herself) recognised she'd been quite flattered by it. But the idea that this attraction could ever be reciprocated was so far-fetched that it had no need of being dismissed, it simply lacked the strength to form.

It was nullified before it was.

Extinguished before birth.

Still-born.

Abor … …………

The memory floods into her now.

She can hear Giselle pottering in the kitchen next door. And she wants to go to her, wants to spend some time with her, enjoy her. But she can't. She doesn't deserve to.

***

Rafaél tries not to miss Inma. There's a part of him that even thinks such missing of her would be a betrayal of her: Inma is so ingrained into him now that it is almost impossible, and vain, to distinguish that within him which is *his* and that which he has adopted from her.

He also thinks, missing her would be some kind of abnegation of his responsibility to her. Had he in fact, as he had always assumed he would, pre-deceased her, he would have been anxious that she wreak from this all too short a time on Earth as much experience, as much joy, as much that was special, as much *life* as she possibly could. They'd never talked about it. But he had absorbed enough of her to know that she too would want that for him.

It would be a lot simpler, more clear-cut, if he loved her, Giselle. He wasn't marrying out of love, though. He was marrying for her baby's sake. Possibly on behalf of the family. Bestowing a family name where a family name was due.

Of course that was old-fashioned. He was old-fashioned. He was so old-fashioned, in fact, that he didn't think it old-fashioned to be old-fashioned.

And yet ... and yet ...

No, it wasn't that he loved Giselle. Of course not. Men his age don't fall in love. Not like young men do. The feelings he has for Giselle are not those he'd had for Inma. It's not that they're weaker, they're not even parallel: the comparison would be that between his fondness for chilli con carne and that for raspberry sorbet: the flavours are not comparable. But – just mayhap – they are complementary.

Things are shifting for him. Of that there is no question.

And he knows that because he finds he is missing Inma even more.

Chapter 22

The frost has penetrated the tiny pockmarks in the tarmac – castor sugar sprinkled on a chocolate cake. It crunches underfoot when you tread on it. Both noise and sensation are inexplicably appealing. Almost, indeed, compulsive. Akin to the satisfaction of popping bubble-wrap.

Polly has treated herself to a breakfast of Buck's Fizz. Well, the champagne was now not properly chilled, it was starting to go flat ... it'd be a shame to waste it. At the price it was, a sin, near as dammit. The orange juice was for the vitamins. She feels fortified now. And braced by the cold.

She and Rafaél walk a few steps ahead of Giselle and Saskja, who are holding hands as if they had just escaped from a Jane Austen adaptation for television – like ice dancers, in other words, about to execute some kind of frozen *pas de deux*.

"What a dumb-ass holiday, Boxing Day," suggests Polly.

The back of Rafaél's throat feels very dry. He suspects he might have a cold coming on. Few weeks have passed since he's been in England, though, when he hasn't thought he had a cold coming on. He also hasn't slept very well. Not for any reason that he could fathom – just one of those nights. But it has nevertheless left him feeling both fractious and ... yucky. "The 'boxing' has, I presume," he ventures, "nothing to do with the sport."

"God only knows," Polly returns. "Well, God's British – you knew that, Rafa, right? – so, come to think of it, He probably does know. And He's probably the only one who does. I've heard all kinds of stories about December 26th, about why that's 'Boxing Day': I've heard it was the day landlords brought their tenants 'boxes' of goodies. Traditionally, I think, it was the day of the year when the roles were reversed and the rich served their servants."

"Akin to the Roman Saturnalia?"

"I guess," says Polly with a conviction struggling to be tepid. "I'd lay odds on that serving, Rafa, being fairly token."

"Is a pity. Me, I always thought it was an extremely good idea, that in the Chinese army, for one month a year, all the officers once again became privates. Probably not in today's Chinese army. But years ago I remember hearing that such was the practice. I think the example should be extended to all of us. For one month a year we should all do unpleasant jobs, the ones no-one wants to do. We should draw lots, all of us, and spend some time working nights in factories or sewage farms, as check-out staff in supermarkets or waiters, as train-drivers or road-sweepers ... or traffic wardens! Is my belief, in a short time, such jobs would not be nearly as unpleasant as they are today. I think also we should all experience life on the other side of the fence: doctors should spend time as patients and porters and nurses; journalists should have their private lives probed and publicised; lawyers and judges should do time in jail. And the Nike CEO should work in one of his sweat-shops, and so should the sports stars who advertise Nike's wares, and Mr McDonald's should work in a fast-food outlet ... and mayhap we tea-drinkers should go and pick leaves, and we meat-eaters should work in abattoirs. But this is one of my by-the-bys."

"You think that'd help motorists to think like pedestrians?"

"And, *amiga mía,* vice versa. Yes, I do. I think the best paid, for a month each year, should live the life of the worst paid worker in either their employ or in that of one of their sub-contractors (even of their sub-sub-contractors) – of whichever worker is paid the least. He should experience at first hand the misery on which his so-called happiness depends. I think, as I say, that sportsmen and actors who advertise their wares should be made to do likewise. I think, again in a very short space of time, we would see a *dramatic* improvement in the lot of such workers. I think magically the money would be found that could pay them more than the seventeen cents an hour or sixty-three cents an hour or whatever it is, the shameful sum they are currently paid."

"There's a few 'stars' I could add to the list, ones who could really use some time being a stand-in or extra, one or two directors who should experience life as a gopher."

"Was, I think, Mrs Thatcher (as then she was) who opined that, yes, British Members of Parliament should have jobs outside the Palace of Westminster. That such keeps them grounded in the real world. There are not too many things on which Baroness Thatcher and I are in agreement. But we do agree on this.

"If we are to check the present inexorable decline into political despair, our representatives do have to start *indeed* representing us – and not simply pay lip-service to the notion of representing us. And we, the electorate, have to start being confident that they are representing us; we have to start knowing there are those in power who understand our problems, who may even be able to identify with our problems, who are batting on our side.

"There are, I understand, six hundred or so MPs in Britain. Allow a hundred, say, to be involved in government on a full-time basis: Cabinet, Shadow Cabinet and so on. I think the world of work should then be divided into, say, five hundred lots: postman, customs officer ... oh, fisherman, small shopkeeper, carpenter et cetera. MPs would enter into a giant lottery and, as their second job (the one advocated as necessary by no less a luminary than Baroness Thatcher), the MP should do whatever job he pulls out by lot. And live on the salary such people are paid.

"*Claro*, there are those jobs which involve some skill: airline pilots, for example, brain surgeons – those selfsame carpenters, of course, as well, and electricians. The interests of the skilled, the professional, they too need to be represented. But we do live in the twenty-first century. Overcoming such a hurdle, that cannot be beyond our ken.

"Mayhap there is no chasm between electorate and the elected. But certainly the electorate believes there is one. (Is another manifestation, Polly, of that we talked about in the City: the only reality is the perception of reality.) And if that chasm is to be breached, it cannot (as has been traditionally the case) only be the elector who makes the gesture. The elected need also to come some way to meet those they portend to represent. Else why should the electors not believe that the elected represent only the elite which they, the elected, have now become?

"Like justice, representation not only needs to be done, it needs to be *seen* to be done. Politicians always refer to themselves as 'public servants'. Well, here is a system whereby *demonstrably* they could be serving the public's interests, not theirs: whether theirs be their own personally or 'theirs', the amorphous interest of 'them': the elite, the status quo, the institutions, industry, wealth.

"So many voters are disillusioned with politics today and its process. *So* many. (Yes, you will say, Polly, ''twas ever thus' and I will again say, 'But the consequences, 'twere not ever thus.') And they are disillusioned, not because their interests are disregarded, but because their interests do not seem even to be *known*. Such interests don't even seem to appear on the politicians' radar screen. Well, here is a way to assure voters that, yes, their interests *are* known, that there are those in the representative assembly championing their cause. Is certainly, this idea, very far from being perfect, a long, long way from being a panacea, it certainly will not right all wrongs, but mayhap it will start to right some. Is at least a step in the right sort of direction. And those today, my dear Polly, are steps which are all too rare.

"If we are to have the mediocre governing us (as we do), the lacklustre, the duplicitous, the unimaginative, the lackeys of industry and banks, the crass, then – for God's sake – at least let such mediocrities occasionally supply a voice for the voiceless. Let us see how dedicated are these men and women (in fact and not in proclamation) to the democratic principle."

"You think members of the US Congress, the Senate should do the same?"

"Politicians, Polly, everywhere. Everywhere in the world. One of those politicians who allow companies dispensation from paying minimum wages should be obliged (let us say for only one month a year) to work in such a below-minimum-wage job and should live (with his family) on such wages ... should rather subsist in such capacity.

"It won't happen, of course. Of course it won't happen. The same tired old argument will be brought out of mothballs that the government of the country needs to attract to its cause the country's brightest and their best.

"If globally, my dear friend, we today have the brightest and best working in politics, then the world is in an even worse pickle than I had feared. I think too is very sad that the brightest and the best continue to put their interests before their community's, before humanity's.

"Is simply not good enough that politicians say to us, you *should* vote, you *should* be part of the democratic process. Voters are bored of the choice they've been facing for far too long, between a rock (as I said before) and a hard place. If we do nothing about it, we're not not doing anything: we're enabling a terminal illness, which will not only kill the patient but his carers as well; we are turning a blind eye to all those cattle-trains in station-yards; we're sharpening the axe for our own execution; we're participating in the murder of our children; we are condoning the destruction of our civilisation, and quite possibly our species."

"Health," says Giselle, as the Austen escapers join the flat-mates. "Saskja and I have been talking. The second, we think, vital virtue: health."

"And second life-giving good idea," chirps Saskja, "that *human* life good idea."

They have arrived at the little lake which graces the centre of Ravenscourt Park. This is not one of London's great parks, not Hyde or Regent's, not even Green or St James's. If those are tomes, Ravenscourt Park is a leaflet. But, in its own unpretentious way, it is a very charming leaflet. It boasts a toddlers' play area, a bowling green, a small café ... and a befouled area for 'walking' dogs. And then there is this: the fairy-grotto-like mere at the park's heart. Ducks squawk here and moorhens keep their peace. Shrubs nudge out of rookeries. It's as synthetic as polyester and yet Nature has suckled it herself and has endowed it with much of her unaffected glory and her attitude of letting-the-grass-grow-under-your-feetness.

The ducks appear remarkably ungrateful that, on the day before, they hadn't been eaten. Saskja has brought bread. Before even she has broken it, the mallards are Jarrowing towards her, protesting their hunger. They gobble at the tit-bits greedily.

"It was one of the disgraces of Mr Blair's government, what was done to the British Health Service," says Polly. "In real terms, they did almost nothing to improve the conditions. They just kept redefining the parameters so they could say that 'targets had been met'. Absurd targets. They claimed waiting lists were reduced. Lie. They just created more waiting lists. There had been one waiting list for surgery. They introduced a second: those waiting to be put on the waiting-list for surgery. Thus it was able to massage figures saying how 'well' the government was governing whilst the human misery intensified.

"'Targets': the apogee of political cynicism – and of practical idiocy. They mean nothing. They're all exhortations on liquor advertisements to drink less. No-one's interested in how many operations a surgeon performs. What's relevant is how well he performs them. In history, probably in regard to such 'targets', the world's most successful surgeon was Mengele. This is the level of inanity to which we're being subjected. There are jobs which should not be rushed, where the more is not the merrier, where the cost of fatigue can be death. The rules governing a pilot's working hours are severe. But not those of a president with the capability of global destruction.

"Political cynicism and practical idiocy: two of the major hallmarks, in my opinion, of twenty-first century politics. Along with a duplicity, an obfuscation and distortion as close to direct lying as makes no difference. And, of course, in some cases (most notably when President Bush and Mr Blair took their countries to war), direct and flagrant lying."

"We discussed once the 'sin' that was anger," Rafa tells Giselle and Saskja. They laugh gently. So does Polly.

"I don't think I ever recovered," she confesses, "from Mr Blair allowing McDonald's to sponsor the health section in the Millennium Dome. Which has to be like Henry Ford sponsoring a stud-farm. Or, come to that, a synagogue."

"He was anti-Semite, Ford?" asks Saskja.

"Violently."

"How come we do not know this?"

"Ford's mayhap do not like us to know this."

"And now, honey, you do."

"Health, *amigas mías*, this is not one issue. But very many."

"Yes," agrees Giselle. "Very, very many."

"Please, I am so sorry," says Rafaél. "This, Giselle, this is so very much more your field of expertise than is mine."

"More and more," she starts, "Western medicine is realising that the body is interconnected. With itself, of course. But with the mind too. And the emotions. And, yes, with the spirit. There is a part of the physical allied to the metaphysical.

"Have you ever heard of Dr Siegel?"

"Yeah, we already talked about him," Polly replies, "Rafa and I."

"Well, then you know. 'What is it,' he asks on one of his tapes, 'which tells a cut to staunch itself?' What, in Accident and Emergency, is there that determines that one patient will survive an injury whilst another, whose wound might even appear less serious, will not?"

"We do not know, Giselle," says Polly, "what we do not know." She expounds a little bit more fully.

Giselle resumes. "There is too much arrogance in today's medicine. God only knows what God is – that is no accident of speech. But what God *isn't* is any individual man. Or any individual field of knowledge. It is perfectly acceptable that a doctor reject the concept of God. It is not ... seemly when that same doctor assumes God's mantle."

"I remember an episode of 'M.A.S.H.'," says Polly. "The camp's chaplain is undergoing a crisis of conscience. Its chief surgeon, Hawkeye, is trying to reassure him: 'The doctor sends in the bill,' says

Hawkeye, 'but it's God Who does the healing.'"

"I don't think this surgeon is too typical, Polly."

"No. I don't think he is either."

"Just as we understand ever more clearly the need to treat the whole body – to check diet, exercise, dental hygiene, stress, sanitation – we have also this need when we start diagnosing the Health Service as a whole. Not just here in England, but world-wide.

"In no field of endeavour is it more important that (to use your expression, Rafa) a spirit of 'wethos' exists. Maybe apart from schooling. And yet in none is the spirit of 'methos' more prevalent. If we do not need to examine the spirit of our patient any more than that, already that is very much.

"Doctors know more about illness than insurance companies. Yet we talk (and ever more seriously) of abandoning state run health services. Not only is this a license for insurance companies to print their own money, not only will this inevitably mean that a section of the population will – perforce – be denied treatment, it will also mean that your health care is in the hands of the loss-adjustor more than of your medical practitioner. Your care will be as good as the strength of your doctor to withstand the pressure exerted on him or her by the insurance companies."

"And for every Hawkeye Pierce," says Polly, "there are fifty Frank Burnses." The others look at her blankly. "'M.A.S.H.' again. I guess that means nothing to you, huh?"

"Nothing, Polly, at all, I fear," says Giselle.

"Anyone, then, see Michael Moore's 'Sicko'?"

"Yes, I did," Giselle admits. "It was an exposition of the United States's Health Service."

"An exposé, rather," Polly interjects, "of the United States's *lack* of Health Service. Oh, Mr Moore paints a rather rosier view of the Health Services elsewhere in the world than they are perhaps entitled to. But anyone who champions Stateside medicine as a paradigm for the world really needs to see it. Even if Mr Moore had scoured the entire US to find the subjects for his film, even if the people he filmed were ginormous exceptions ... well, Mr Moore's film contains ... let's call them 'concerns' which I would have thought merited a few moments' consideration.

"You know, I keep hearing about how much he lies, Mr Moore. And yet no-one, when pressed, seems able to identify a specific lie. Ask for specifics and the reply is just generalised bromides. 'Oh, his entire work is so riddled with lies,' remarks of that ilk, 'it's not possible to be specific.' Sure it's possible to be that specific. If Mr Moore is lying, then you have a responsibility to us all to let us know what those lies are. I keep saying it: This generation is going to need to make huge decisions, awesome decisions. In order to make the best decisions, it, of course, needs to know the truth. If Mr Moore is lying we need to know where. Specifically, I mean. And if no specific instances of lying can be cited, then we have to assume he is telling the truth. God, Giselle, I'm so sorry. Please excuse me. Please – I'm so sorry – please go on."

And so, unpursing her not-quite-sulk, Giselle does. "It is probably true," she says, "that throughout history Man has profited – and profiteered – from the misery of others. The insurance companies merely continue a long tradition. The drug companies likewise.

"The extortionate prices those companies charge for their product is, however, yet another element in today's methos that is simply indefensible. (I think, Polly, Mr Moore mentioned this also in his film.) This is not a 'market' force, this is a monopolistic force and a protectionist force. What such companies extort from AIDS victims (particularly in impoverished countries) is, quite simply, a strain on the conscience of all humanity. The way they use their considerable lobbying power on both American political houses is far more deadly than any of the sins you two have talked about. It is as bereft of basic decency as those tobacco companies still insisting cancer is not caused by smoking. And when whistles are blown ...

"Well, when the eminent psychiatrist Peter Bregen wrote his book 'Toxic Psychiatry', his exposure of corrupt practices in his branch of medicine – practices which benefited the pharmaceutical and medical companies at the expense of patients' welfare –, he was vilified both by those industries and by many of his 'colleagues' as being 'un-American'.

"One of the reasons why health care is so expensive is as a consequence of the cost of drugs. This begs a question. Is it the Health Service that we can't afford? (Or Medicare? Or any other state-run medicine?) Or is what we can't afford the metamorphosis from the multi-billion dollar drug industry into a multi-*trillion* dollar one?

"The drug industry's commitment appears to be exclusively to profit. It uses, as I say, its considerable lobby to persuade the Food and Drug Administration to ban many complementary or alternative treatments. It tests its product less these days on animals (to avoid all those pesky protests) and ever more on impoverished 'volunteers' of impoverished nations, in India and elsewhere: where their activities are subject to less intensive scrutiny than elsewhere on the planet. Why should we therefore believe them when they tell us, in their PR handouts and their advertising, that they have only mankind's, and therefore 'our', welfare at their heart?

"Another reason why the Health Service is so stretched is because of a life-style today's economics demand we live. One which is, in a billions of dollars way, beneficial to the commercial interests of ... I can only describe them as 'legalised drug-pushers'. By far the most common reason for patients to consult their doctors in Britain today is 'depression'. And by far the most common 'cure' suggested for that condition is pharmaceutical. And that for the drugs' companies has been a bonanza. They're even allowed to market drugs like Prozac, for example, as non-addictive. Non-addictive?! I've known people who have been addicted to Prozac for years. And who, when they try to withdraw, suffer very similar detox symptoms to those coming off the so-called 'mainline' drugs, like heroin. Or nicotine. There is, I am convinced, a far greater problem socially in the Western world with prescribed drugs than with those which are illegal."

Polly and Rafaél exchange a glance. This is territory they have visited before. Or have they? They decide to hear Giselle out.

"The problem with prescription medicine – particularly tranquillisers, sleeping pills and their like – is, just in numerical terms, a mammoth one. We hear very little discussion about it. Not too many tv shows feature their central, WASP characters popping pills. Mostly, I think, it's one of those things we prefer not to know about because knowing about it is too uncomfortable. And all of this keeps us in the problem. And today's economics *want* us to be in the problem. That's how mad it is.

"How have we created an affluent world here in the West where so many people – tens of millions, if not hundreds of millions – ... that so many people are so desperately unhappy that, unable to change their reality, they have to change their brain? And why, if we have allowed this to happen (as we have), are we not asking ourselves that: '*How* ...,' I mean, '... have we allowed this to happen?'; closely followed by 'What are we going to do about changing it?'

"We all know that a certain amount of stress is good for us. It's also maintained that two glasses of red wine a day is good for the heart. But that does not mean that four glasses of wine are *twice* as good. As far as stress is concerned, most of us working today are drinking not four, but a dozen glasses daily of wine. Two dozen. Is it not time we stopped changing our perception of reality and started changing the reality of our reality?

"If truly we believe that health is the second vital virtue" Giselle continues, "if we truly believe that human life is the second life-affirming good idea then we must start making a concerted effort to work on behalf of both. The implications of good mental and emotional health are ... globally important. How much was the decision to invade Iraq inspired by the President's desire for his father's approval? By Mr Blair's crushing need to be a player on the world stage? What childhood issues has bin Laden not resolved? Or President Castro? Or Colonel Gadaffi? And so on throughout the world, up and down the line.

"I was brought up with the idea that if I thought anything was wrong with the world, the problem was – not with the world – but with me. I was the soldier on the parade-ground. 'Look at Giselle,' my mother was supposed to have said, 'everyone is in step except for her.' And sometimes the censure that's implied is simply not appropriate. Sometimes it *is* the entire parade ground that is out of step. (And, yes, this too is a very real danger contained within democracy, the more dangerous yet by so rarely being voiced.) Sometimes we *are* the lone soldier who is in step. That does happen. A majority in Germany did vote Hitler into power.

"Today too we live in a world where it's entirely possible for us to be the only one marching in step. (Though I am also convinced that, in fact, there are infinitely more people marching in step than you would believe from the media; people who are beginning to see that a spade is that, who are beginning to see the world's kamikaze ethos as what it is: lunacy posturing not only as sanity, but as wisdom.)

"Find any definition anywhere of madness, apply it to the world as we have it today, and see just how snugly it fits. What are the symptoms, let us say, of psychosis? Delusion is one, violence, grandiosity, a can-do-no-wrongness, paranoia ... denial. Which of these are not conditions of the world today? Wherever you are *in* that world? In China or Chile? America or Australia? The Arctic or Zaire?"

"I start to get very cold," says Rafa. "Could we perhaps head for home?"

"Saskja and I, we're off to the movies. Home's the wrong direction for us. Maybe we could get in out of the cold, though. What about, say, a cup of coffee in the little tea-shop back there?"

They adjourn thither.

"But it's also true," Giselle continues, "that the wrongs of the world are not only global wrongs, that there are things wrong with each of us, each one of us. Without, as far as I can tell, exception."

"I know I'm an alcoholic," says Polly. "I can sense you getting uncomfortable. I've already come out to Rafa. I *know* I'm alcoholic, is what I'm saying. No need to be coy."

Giselle acknowledges this. She also appreciates Polly's integrity, but can't think how to express that. "Alcoholism, that certainly is one manifestation," she says, her eyes flicking between Polly's face and the ground. "Comfort eating, *binge* eating, addiction generally, control-freakery, compulsive work. All these are manifestations. But these, to a certain extent, are the easy ones. They are out there. Obvious to all who come in contact with them – usually except for the sufferer himself, but that is a separate problem. An equal problem than these obvious addictions, though, or compulsions (maybe even a greater one) are the manifestations of problems which bleed internally.

"Think of physical wounds. How much easier is it to diagnose and treat the cut you can see. It's there, it's obvious. Internal bleeding, though … that's hard. It may take time before we even know it's happening. Then we have to find out *where* it's happening. Emotionally we're dealing with injuries ten times more hidden than internal bleeding, and a hundred times more difficult to deal with.

"We don't *know* that President Bush's decision to go to war was actually a (probably forlorn) attempt to impress his father. It could have been a reaction to the birth of Jeb. Or Neil. It could have been not being selected for the peewee football team or not getting a date with the prom queen or a thousand other things. The decision – this is the key – was not based on strategy alone (if, indeed, at all), on what was right for the world. Not even for his country. Not even for his contributors, or the oil industry, or his wealthy friends or family. It had as much, if not more, to do with unresolved personal issues – this is the point. And, though I am not a great lover of either President Bush or his policies, he is by no means the only person in power with such problems. Such problems are overwhelmingly more present than absent. How much responsibility for the First World War should be attributed to Kaiser Wilhelm's withered arm? How many of Queen Elizabeth's decisions – the First, I'm talking about – were the result of having had an ogre for a father, a mother who was decapatitated and a half-sister who was very nearly her assassin?

"This personal, undealt-with baggage is quite as responsible for the dangerous place we're in today as any other cause. In fact, I think it *underlies* many of the other causes – probably most of them.

"The world's problems, the world's health problems also, will not be cured by one treatment, one course of anti-biotics or anything. There isn't one cure. (Which is, incidentally, another central problem with penology.) There isn't one pill. And often (so often) the so-called 'cure' leads to more problems than the original complaint – Prozac and Valium being examples, the side-effects of a whole range of proprietary drugs being another.

"The world's problems and health problems are not – this is true – as complicated as they are usually portrayed. But likewise few of them can be tackled, let alone resolved, by one cut of the sword. Most problems are Hydra-like: Cut off one head and two grow in its place. But that does not mean that we need not or should not cut off the first head. Hydra is presently attacking us all. Many it kills: the hungry, those deprived of sanitation or adequate health care. But Hydra will end up killing those too who think they are protected by her. Again, as, I think, exposed in Mr Moore's 'Sicko'. It was also the moderately well-off hardest hit by the latest recession. Even the quality of the wealthiest lives will be hit by methos's lack of ethos. Maybe only eventually. But 'eventually' does eventually arrive. The freedom of the wealthy, that too will then be curbed. It wasn't only the Jews who found Hitler's Germany an unpleasant place in which to live.

"I love this world. I want a future for my child. For my child to have a future worthy of the name Hydra has to be slain – the Hydra of methos. Two, four ... *sixty*-four heads at a time, if needs be. Whatever it takes. Hydra *will* eventually die. If from nothing else then from exhaustion.

"And this is also why we need to be informed by our own set of principles. It's the way we know that we are in step and those around us are out of it. It's anyway one of the reasons why we do: Each of Hydra's heads that we cut off will require of us that we make more ethical and/or moral judgements. Some of them – euthanasia, as just one instance – are extremely difficult ones.

"Where do we start? Well, with the schools, of course. We always need to start with the schools. Many of the more enlightened teachers already know this, those not so enlightened need to learn it. Both enlightened and not yet enlightened teachers need to start insisting they be allowed to impart it: 'Listening', that must be considered as one of the most important of the disciplines taught us. As important, if not more, then reading, writing or 'rithmetic. Reading is taking. *Valuable* taking – sometimes *amazingly* valuable taking –, but still taking. Writing too is often taking. Listening, though, that is giving. The core of wethos is the joy of giving. If civilisation is to progress, we need to teach ourselves how to give. And a major part of that giving is how to listen properly.

"I despair of those who still think that consulting a counsellor or a psychiatrist is a sign of weakness. As Peck often points out, to the contrary, such is a sign already of strength. When people think it weakness it is an indication only of their own weakness. But such people can be dangerous in their weakness. Certainly, as the economy is organised today, it would be fair to contend that we couldn't afford to be paying the amount of counsellors, psychiatrists, psycho-therapists and so on that the world needs. But, know what? We actually wouldn't need that many more. Not if we all knew how to listen – listen properly. Certainly some more, but not the enormous hordes you might imagine.

"If we were taught to listen, we'd be able ourselves to listen one another back to health. Or indeed into health for the first time. I know you, Rafa, don't believe in the concept of original sin. But I think all of us are born with DNA mental and emotional issues. I think we may be born with, indeed conceived with, inherited flaws or weaknesses or maladies. I think we all are. To listen one another back to health is to *love* one another back to health.

"'A problem shared is a problem halved' is an adage which, I'm sure, predates Freud. Probably by centuries if not millennia. And goes to prove that it is important, not only to have common sense, but to apply it. As with much folklore there is a wisdom attached to these few words which belie their brevity and the simplicity of their expression. Other than that it probably underestimates itself. Often a problem shared is a problem not just halved but *eliminated*. The problem is seen to be not a problem at all but a pin-prick. 'Problems,' as another wise friend of mine is fond of saying, 'hate oxygen.'

"I say again, not all the problems in the world are global problems. As many problems, if not more, exist in our individual worlds, and there too are real problems: an abusive parent, perhaps (maybe even two), a chronic or terminal medical condition, bankruptcy, divorce, the death of a loved one ... of a *child*, the collapse of an ambition. All these things happen and have to be dealt with. And these are serious problems. Tremendously serious. They can, as we have seen, have global implications. But we denigrate both those problems and ourselves if we see them only in that context, and fail to recognise that they are serious problems in their own right.

"It also happens that the washing-machine mechanic doesn't turn up at the promised time, or one of the kids is playing up, or your husband didn't appreciate the birthday present you spent days finding for him, or the milk you needed for cooking has turned sour. Not, of themselves, big or significant events, but – another wise piece of folklore – 'from tiny acorns mighty oaks do grow.' An untreated scratch can lead to septicaemia and finally lockjaw; an untreated emotional scratch ... well, the consequences range from a few seconds' sulk to creating Genghis Khan. We cannot possibly tell. I do, however, think it significant that I can think of no tyrant in history who hasn't failed to deal with, let's call them, 'issues'.

"No philosophy in the world, no adage has wreaked more damage on this planet and on humanity than 'Grin and bear it.' We may grin outside, but inside we *cannot* bear it. Inside (untreated) the wound festers and enlarges, festers some more, becomes cancerous ... It needs to be talked about. You spoke (I think) – you, Rafa, and Polly – about there being no reality, there being only the perception of reality. One of the life-threatening lies, no?, that the material is material."

"It's also a lie," says Polly, "that the material is immaterial."

"Whatever the perception, the objective reality remains the same," Giselle continues. "Talking can't do anything about that. The husband remains dead, the house repossessed, the killing fields have been discovered. But talk, and be listened to, and the perception of that reality will not be the same. No, of course, the pain won't magically disappear. But it will change shape. It will just be easier to cope with, that's all; it will make survival more possible and less costly on our health and happiness. And incidentally on the national exchequer."

They are seated in the little café. Polly just 'nips to the loo'. 'Nips' is probably an appropriate word, and not just because it's 'nippy' outside. There is a boy there in round, John Lennonish glasses, wearing a lime-green polo-neck jersey. He's maybe seven and is crashing a large fire engine into, apparently, every table-leg and chair-leg in the place. It is extremely annoying. His parents (presumably) – a pageboy-haired mother of about forty with an imperfect complexion and a coot-headed father maybe ten years older and earnest – pay him such little heed and are so lost in the gaze of the other that Saskja wonders to herself whether both are indeed his parents or whether there is not some tryst here occurring.

"Famously," says Giselle, "Nietzsche claimed that that which does not kill us makes us stronger. But that's far too simple. It contains truth, the maxim, but it is not *the* truth. It is perhaps indicative that the last decade of Nietzsche's life he spent in an insane asylum. Often that which does not kill us still weakens us. It may appear to strengthen us – but that is looking at the outside. Battering rams aimed at castle doors rarely smash through them at their first attempt. Life's blows do crush us – not all of us, but very many. Physically such people may appear to survive, mentally they may appear even to prove the truth of Nietzsche's maxim, but emotionally they have been juggernauted. For experiences to strengthen us we have to soften their impact. And how do we do that? By, yes, talking about them. And it is also by talking about them that we release their strengthening powers." Polly returns from the loo. "Those who have experienced the greatest hardships," Giselle continues, "are not necessarily the strongest members of their species. To be strengthened by experience you have to learn from experience. And to learn you have to be taught. And to be taught you have to listen. And to listen (paradoxically enough) you have to talk.

"Health is not one issue but a life-style full of them. Healthy nutrition, for instance, is vital for so many things. How much so-called 'Attention Deficit Disorder' is down to nothing more than drinking too many fizzy drinks?"

"And yet, back home, Coca-Cola is allowed to, as it's called, 'sponsor' some schools," Polly snorts.

"The correlation between diet and delinquency has been proved over and over again. Yet we prefer to throw young people in jail rather than change their eating habits. And, to be fair, most of such young people – apparently – would also prefer that.

"There was an English chef, Saskja, so appalled by what children were being given to lunch on at school that he devoted a year of his life to improving their diets. This was in an election year, and it was televised, so Mr Blair took the experiment seriously. He even invited the chef to Downing Street to discuss it. And it continued to be taken seriously until the election was won. When the whole idea was simply forgotten. So much for Mr Blair's trifoil priority, 'education, education, education'! Yet *another* example, I should say. You do not – you, Mr Blair, simply *cannot* – successfully educate the malnourished. Even adequately educate them.

"Jamie Oliver was the chef's name. Previously, I must confess, I was not Mr Oliver's greatest fan. In fact, I actively *dis*liked him. But this work was admirable work. Admirable and very important work."

"I wasn't crazy about him either," says Polly, resisting the temptation to grab the fire engine and hurtle it straight into the middle of the lake.

"Where did he encounter most resistance? From the children themselves, of course. Children are notoriously conservative about the food they want to eat. But I do wonder whether that is not compounded by an addiction to the additives in junk food.

"If the government is so picky about drugs, why isn't it also picky about those which go into hamburgers? Or chickens? Why don't we apply the famous 'Just say "no"' adage also to junk food? And is it called 'junk' because it's rubbish? Or because it is 'junk', the synonym for heroin, and equally addictive? You can't say 'no' to a second handful of many brands of potato crisp because there are chemicals inside them which set up a craving. It's not the crisp you want a second helping of, but the chemical. And such conduct is not only countenanced by virtually every government in the world, it is *applauded* by such governments. And it is enthused over by sports stars (presumably paid serious money to avoid them asking awkward questions). The CEOs of such companies are given honours (those that don't buy them!), are invited to dinners at the White House, at Buckingham Palace: They are bringing wealth to the country, they are creating jobs.

"Paying for a few television commercials which encourage us to exercise more, that is not promoting health. That is being *seen* to promote health. That is attaching more importance to the feint than the reality. One thing which Mr Oliver did with the children which certainly made an impact, he showed them the actual ingredients of chicken nuggets. The children were appalled."

"In 'Fast Food Nation'," Polly interjects, "Eric Schlosser describes the abattoirs operated by the hamburger chains. Children should be taken to these too, I think, shown how the animals are treated – shown too how the workforce is treated. Do people who can treat their employees in this fashion, or the animals that they slaughter ... can you really imagine that such people have got the welfare of their clients at heart? Any more than drug companies actually care about their customers? Or insurance companies about theirs? Do they care more about humanity or profit?

"Let me think of another example: If you saw a doctor, say, knock over a pedestrian as he turned his car into his practice, and then saw that doctor simply walk away from the prostrate victim, enter his workplace without a care in the world ... would you then consult that doctor about the pain in your chest? That is precisely the manner in which some of the drugs' companies behave. And yet we make those companies ever richer (ever more obscenely rich) by swallowing in megatons their toxic products – and their even more toxic lies."

"Not to mention the lies of the insurance companies."

"As you say, Polly." A tea-sipping pause ensues. It is a little while before Giselle resumes. "There is, I suppose, something masochistic, almost suicidal about us human beings: the yang to the yin of self-preservation. The dangers of smoking are now very well known. It remains an enormous industry. Motorists know full well that tail-gating is extremely dangerous, and yet continue to do it. There is a sense of immortality endowed certainly on the young, and there is an element in all of us sometimes of sticking our tongues out at the gods, defying them to do their worst. And, yes, health cranks can be, who could deny it?, real bores. So, most of us, we don't eat as healthily as we might, or – probably – as we should. But that does not absolve us from the responsibility of doing our best to ensure that our children do.

"And where should we start doing that? In schools again, of course. And we should be informing our schoolchildren of the need for good nutrition over and over and over again. It's as important to their primary education as the 'times-tables'."

"That and listening, huh?"

"You mock me, Polly?"

"God, no, Giselle. No. Rafa and I, we've also discussed this. It's real important stuff."

"You cannot, I think, discuss it too often or too much," suggests Giselle, with an edge of what could be pique or could be belligerence. "We need to say it over and over again. And yet over again. We've got generations of wrong-thinking to overcome. You think such education is going to happen if, Polly (as you say), Coca-Cola is 'sponsoring' a school? If McDonald's are buying the text-books? If supermarket chains are paying for the sport equipment? And at the same time as we are told we cannot afford to feed our children properly whilst they are at school, how much are we paying out of the school's extremely limited budget to 'upgrade' a Microsoft programme? Which anyway demands upgrading only because the previous one was deficient? Sheriff of Nottingham economics. How much are we paying to incarcerate our young offenders? When often all they need is a salad. Kamikaze economics.

"Of course such education should be meted out by parents – of course it should. Just as a sense of responsibility should, just as social responsibility and self-discipline and self-respect should all be meted out by parents. But that's not going to happen either. Not universally. And, as the economic system of the world is presently organised, it can't happen."

"Yeah, we talked about this too," says Polly.

"We now have a legacy of inadequate parenting. And of those who were parented well, many today are working two jobs, or away from home, or working under permanent undue stress, or on permanent night-shift or ... or ... or and they simply don't have the time or the energy to instil such qualities in their children. It's one of the many smaller traps within the poverty trap."

"And the poverty trap," says Giselle, "each day sucks within its jaws those with more and more money.

"'*In loco parentis*' has to have a wider implication than today it enjoys. It's so easy just to 'tut' at the appalling parenting skills – always of other parents, never of ourselves; it's a lot easier than taking positive responsibility for such charges.

"We have to start seeing *all* children as *our* children. I hear childless couples complain about their taxes. 'Why should we pay?' they ask. 'We don't have children who go to school.' Well, yes, they *do* have such children. Unless, that is, they are so selfish as to believe that the planet's future ends with their own death, they do, of course, have such children."

"And if they *are* that selfish," suggests Rafa, "then we need to listen to why these people are in so much pain."

"Perhaps that too," Giselle agrees. "A lack of education is abusing a child just as much as if we fondle them sexually. Perhaps even more. Because with sexual molestation the child is, at least, aware of the source of his pain, or hers. It is tangible. The abuse of a lack of education is infinitely harder to come to grips with. Victims of sexual abuse often feel guilty because they have been made to feel complicit in their abuse. How much worse for the child abused by a lack of education when often it is inculcated into him that it is he who is responsible for his lack of scholastic prowess or achievement. That it is he or she who is inadequate, not the system which should be eking out the best in him or her.

"Children are children. When there are tugs-of-love between separated parents, councellors remind children of that fact: that they are children. They shouldn't be asked to get involved in such disputes. It's not ... 'appropriate'. Well, it's not 'appropriate' either to ask a child to eke out his, or her, potential. That is our job, us the adults. If a child leaves school as an under-achiever, it is not the child at fault. It is the school. It is usually, in fact, the bureaucracy in charge of that school. It is our fault – the fault of us adults – for allowing that bureaucracy, that system, that school ... for wanting a new car over wanting the world to have a better future.

"It is amazing to me where we see a duty of care and where not, the areas in which we think it is indispensable to 'intervene' and where not, where to apply ourselves. And where not.

"Parents do not even now have absolute rights over their children. Nor should they have. They do not, for instance, have the right to *abuse* their children, to starve them, to abandon them or endanger them or sell them into bondage. No-one is talking either about the 'food police' breaking in at suppertime to check what's on the plate. No-one's even talking about forbidding food – any food. (Well, with the apparent exception of magic mushrooms!) Hamburgers occasionally – even those made by the chains – won't do that much harm, soft drinks in moderation, chocolate bars ... all alright. Not great, of course. But okay. Not okay, though, when they become a staple.

"Feeding children well at school is a vital first step. I salute Mr Oliver for having made the stand he did, for having had the commitment he had. His experiment should be embraced. World-wide.

"Of course the children will bitch and moan and groan. Of *course* they will. Guess what? Children do that. And they're told 'Tough. Deal with it.' Guess what too? That's part of a process called 'growing up'. We don't always get our own way. We do, as humans, have to live with frustration and disappointment. We do have to do things we don't want to do. Coping with that frustration, that too is an important part of education.

"Guess what else? After a remarkably short period of time, the moans and groans, the bitching will stop. Because the strange will start becoming the not-quite-so-strange and the kids too will start realising they are enjoying life more. They will have more energy with which to enjoy life more. And they'll be brighter, more intelligent, more anxious to learn. We'll have a brighter, more intelligent world, in fact. In fact, possibly one bright enough to start addressing the legacy of problems which we are leaving them. The legacy of *titan* problems. It's such a win:win situation we have to ask ourselves why it's not happening. And the answer is very simple. Because we have an economic system based on 'methos', based on greed. Because Coca-Cola and McDonald's appear to be infinitely more interested in their profits than the planet's welfare, and governments are more anxious to stay pally with such multi-nationals than they are to facing up to the duty of care they have to their own citizens.

"If, in school, we taught children how to look after themselves – physically by teaching them about nutrition and exercise, emotionally and spiritually by teaching them how to listen, intellectually by committing ourselves to 'educating' our children and not just schooling them (just these three things!) – the strides forward we would be making to tackle the global crises would be enormous.

"The ripple effect would be felt at every level of society and throughout the globe. The beneficial ripple effect. It would be a far greater commitment to the elimination of global poverty than all the band-aids and comic-aids and sport-aids put together. Also because people who feel good about themselves tend to feel good about the world. And if you feel good about the world, then you will want to protect it. And then too you may have the energy and intellectual capacity to find the means and the methods whereby it *is* protected."

"One of the very, very many problems with globalisation is that is such a misnomer," says Rafaél. He has his hands buried deep within his pockets, his shoulders are hunched against the cold. There is a little, old-fashioned electric fire in the café, but it is a candle in a hurricane. "Is merely a much more subtle form of colonialism or imperialism or whatever else you wish to call it. And because more subtle, much more dangerous. Is, of course, grotesque to talk to a beggar, someone who is starving, about organic food, about five vegetables per day. That beggar, she is grubbing around in litter-bins for any scrap of food, just like feral dogs."

"There's enough food to feed the world, Rafa. I understand there's quite enough arable land that can produce the world's food healthily, without resource to genetically modified crops or barbaric animal husbandry. It doesn't happen because it's conceived such would adversely affect profits."

Giselle pours the rest of the water into her glass. "The British Medical Association –," she says, "the BMA, Saskja, represents all the doctors in Britain – was institutionally opposed (quite heavily opposed) to the creation of the National Health Service. Doctors were worried about how their incomes would be affected. (In a way reminiscent of the worries voiced today by the BMA's American counterpart, the AMA.) Now the BMA is one of the Health Service's most staunch advocates. (Even more so recently, after their substantial pay rises!) Now institutionally it opposes both complementary and alternative medicine. Partially because unscrupulous drug companies use all sorts of incentives to bribe or cajole doctors into prescribing their often over-priced products. It is to be hoped that this too will change.

"Doctors as well need to learn a little humility, to recognise that they too do not know what they do not know. Rodolfo as much as any of them." She slinks a look at Rafaél.

"Oh, I entirely agree," he says.

"A few years ago, Western medicine thought acupuncture and ayurvedic medicine barbarous and useless exercises; homeopathy and osteopathy likewise. Such practices are now seen (by all other than the diehard reactionaries) to have uses and applications in areas where more accepted medical practises have failed. Which are not anyway that 'traditional'. Way before Western medicine was out of its crib, other 'traditional' medicine was being tried. The Arabs were performing surgery in the 9th century. Acupuncture, as we've already said, goes back millennia. Even the leeches thought barbaric in the 20th century are making a comeback! Maggots are being used on some patients who have become inured to conventional anti-biotics."

"This all part of human life being good idea," says Saskja. She appears not to notice the cold. Rafaél does. He shivers. Polly merely talks.

"General Westmoreland –," she says, "he commanded the American forces in Vietnam – opined that death to 'the Oriental' was not the same as death to Americans. Well, that told you all you needed to know about the man, really – a lot about American foreign policy as well. And of course it was lambasted even at the time. Everyone is, of course, entitled to their own perception of life, its importance, its purpose. They do not have the right to impose such beliefs on other people. Particularly not by killing them.

"Suicides have (as also Rafa and I talked about) a perfect right to kill themselves. Some suicides – Jan Palach (for example) or the Buddhist monk who immolated himself to end the Vietnam war – are even quite admirable. But the suicide does not have the right to take others with him – by deliberately staging a road accident, for example, or by detonating a bomb, or by machine-gunning fellow students – or piloting a jumbo jet into a skyscraper.

"In point of fact, I doubt too many would give you an argument on that point. But let's extend it a little: Can we, as a species, assume the rights denied to suicides? Do we have the right to kill the innocent? To exact our revenge on people who had nothing at all to do with an initial atrocity? Is that not the mentality of the Nazis? A storm-trooper gets killed, an entire village is shot in reprisal. We see footage of such crimes today, study these lessons in history, and are (rightly) appalled by them. But apparently we do not learn from them. There is no evidence – at all – (in fact quite to the contrary) that Iraq was involved in September 11th; no evidence – at all – that it housed 'weapons of mass destruction'. Villages have been killed to avenge individuals. Four thousand died on September 11th; half-a-million have been killed in Iraq. Israel lost thirty of its citizens; in revenge it killed thirteen hundred Palestinians. Jews acting like Nazis, how on Earth is that possible?"

"Is a Jewish edict:" Giselle quotes, "'…the Rock of Israel spake to me, He that ruleth over men must be just …'."

" '... ruling in the fear of God'," Rafaél adds.

"I'm very impressed," Giselle admits. And she is.

"Not too much voluntary about Sunday school in my youth," Rafa tells her.

"Nevertheless ..." Giselle eyes him sideways. "Human life is human life. It's that which it is saying: the second life-affirming idea, that human life is a good idea. That's what it's saying. Human life is a good idea. It's that simple. There is no such thing as English life or American life or South American life or Middle-Eastern life. Human life is human life. Period – I think that's what you say, Polly, no?, in America."

"There is an argument," Polly suggest, taking her time, sieving her words, "which maintains that all life is a crap-shoot. Some eggs in the bird's nest have to be eaten because that's how, say, a snake survives. And some snakes have to be eaten because that's how something else survives – a mongoose, say. Human life, according to that argument, cannot abstract itself from the haphazardness of that crap-shoot. We can reduce the odds, but we cannot eliminate them. You think there's any cogency in that argument?"

"Not much," Saskja replies.

"I'm playing devil's advocate here, you understand."

"Life is akin, I think, to what you said about the film-making process:" Rafa returns, "It is hard enough, anyway. We have no need to add to its difficulty. Is human life not haphazard enough anyway? We have, I think, no need to increase ways of making it more so."

"Such argument might be fine," says Saskja, "that life a crap-shoot, if Nature was still boss. But now, in affairs of Man, Man boss. Man wants to be boss. He, anyway, thinks he's boss. Medicine, almost existence of medicine itself, already says, 'We know better than Nature.'"

"No, I don't think so," says Giselle. "There's an element of truth in what you're saying. I certainly know, Saskja, where you're coming from. But much medicine – 'traditionally', anyway, and still in homeopathy and other treatments – uses Nature herself to cure the ills. If there is the stinging nettle, there is the dock leaf. And such certainly would appear to be Nature's way. One of the very many lunacies associated with the world's deforestation is that we're robbing the planet of we know not what. We do not know what we do not know. We could be destroying the shrub that is the cure for cancer."

Polly interjects. "Rafa and I have talked about this as well."

"Oh?" says Giselle.

"And about cancer research," Rafa adds.

"And, yes, about cancer research," Polly agrees.

"Go on," Giselle enjoins them.

"A vast amount of money for cancer research, we said, has been raised by public subscription, Giselle. A vast amount. Are records being kept of the amount raised by public subscription? Who will get the 'profits' when the cure is finally found? Will the money raised by charity be deducted from the cost victims will have to pay for their treatment? Or will the drugs' companies merely be presented with yet another bonanza? We live in a world so psychotically concerned with profit that, sadly, that these are not unreasonable questions to ask. Indeed they are questions to which we should be demanding replies.

"If Ms Klein is to be believed (and why should she not be?), several of the medicines marketed by one Mr Rumsfeld's companies, Gilead, were funded by grants raised originally by American taxes. Including some of the medicines for AIDS. And several treatments for AIDS are (as we've just said) now being sold to AIDS victims at prices those victims cannot afford. Makes you wonder, huh? This too Rafa and I have discussed: Charities simply must become more accountable."

"No argument there," Rafaél insists, with a wistfulness laced with fatigue. "Also no argument, that if human life is a good idea then, *amigas mías*, is a good idea – as Giselle says – for us all. Not just for some of us. Not the winners of the crap-shoot, Polly. Is important equally for Americans and Afghans, for Protestants and Catholics, – and Israelis and Iranians – , for capitalists and socialists, for those in London or Lima, Orphalese or Oslo."

Polly returns "Or Ottawa," she says.

"Or Okinawa," says Rafaél.

"Or Odessa," says Saskja.

"And those of us from Syracuse, what?" asks Giselle. "We do not matter?"

"We have to go," Saskja announces, looking at her watch.

"I know, I know, it's way too early," says Polly anticipating what the other two are going to say. "But, so she says, she *likes* the trailers, likes all the ads."

"Don't get too cold, Polly," Rafa warns her with a smile.

"Nor you," she returns.

Polly and Saskja almost Tigger off together. Rafa smiles at Giselle. And she smiles tiredly back.

"Home?" he suggests. He is still shivering.

They stroll back to their flats in silence. And both secretly wonder as they do so whether that is because they are so easy with each other … or because, actually, they have nothing to say to one another.

Chapter 23

He's not a lover any more, Rodolfo. He's a sex partner. He might as well – almost – be a bridge partner. Or a tennis partner. Like a good game of tennis, the sex is invigorating. And it's certainly not unpleasant or unfulfilling. It's just that it's no longer the poetry it had been.

Rodolfo seems to have become a surgeon too of sex. There is mastery in his technique, an intimate knowledge of his subject, a high degree of mechanical sophistication and appreciation ... but with it, there seems to be an air of almost complacent detachment. The expert who knows he's an expert and who swims effortlessly in the shoals of his own expertise.

There is still sweetness, even honey, in the kisses, still surge in the embrace. They are virtuosos on the instruments that are each other – and that is them together. There is an excellence in performance that circumscribes shock, even surprise. It has a power that has no need of electricity. It's not staid, their coitus, it's not comfortable. And it is a consummation. It's no longer, though, consumption: It doesn't consume them both any longer. It's not spontaneous. It's not urgent. Or devil-may-care. Or fumbling. Or dangerous. Or wanton or craven.

It's all far too perfect.

It's still the day after Christmas; still, in Britain, Boxing Day. He's told Emily he's notes to catch up on, new research papers to read. It's impossible to concentrate at home: the row the kids make all the time. He'd maybe too drop in on his father. Poor old sod. Alone on Christmas.

He'd brought her nice gifts, Giselle, *thoughtful* gifts. *His* gifts, not gifts bought by a secretary or a junior or a flunkey; gifts which showed he cared about her, that he noticed, that he listened to her. He bought her wine-glasses, because she'd complained once about the cheap ones she had; perfume because the bottle he'd bought her in duty-free was now almost empty; a Dory Previn CD to replace the one she'd lent to someone and couldn't for the life of her remember whom. He'd also bought her a dressing-gown because he'd seen it in a shop-window and thought it would suit her; and a bottle of vintage champagne … well, with which to baptise the glasses. He knew she couldn't drink a lot of it – it was just a token, just a gesture. He hoped she'd think that's what counted.

She's now wearing the new dressing-gown – the new 'chemise', he'd rather call it; and he's wearing the old one, whose androgynousness and asexuality were two of the main reasons for the purchase of the new one. He's still in the bedroom, indeed doing some reading. She's in the kitchen, refilling his flute with wine, making herself some mint tea. The Dory Previn album is playing. Giselle feels like she's made contact again with an old friend. She sings along with it – not the whole song, just the odd resonant phrase, a snatch or two of notes she feels she can hit.

Rafaél wonders in from the garden. "I feel so much better …" He is cut short by the sight of his dressing-gowned son, padding in from the bedroom. "Oh God," he says, "I am *so* sorry."

"*Hola, papi,*" returns Rodolfo, as if greeting him at home for breakfast.

"I should have called," Rafaél stammers. "I did not think. Please excuse me. Excuse me, please."

Giselle is saying nothing. She is blushing and she doesn't know why; she is confused and she doesn't know why. And that is compounding her confusion.

"*Il n'y a pas de quoi,*" Rodolfo replies in an accent which would have had most Frenchmen stretching out for earplugs. He is making light of the event, seeking to. He doesn't know what else to do.

"Is unforgiveable," Rafaél insists, but at a mumble. He's five-years-old again, caught – again – stealing money from his mother's purse. "Inexcusable."

"This mine?" Rodolfo asks Giselle of the bubbling glass. She nods that it is. "Won't you join us?" he invites his father.

"I should be going. I should never have come …"

"I'm pouring you a glass. If you don't drink it, it goes flat."

"… Not without ringing. I should be going. Inexcusable. …"

"A toast to Christmas."

"Please, both of you, please forgive me."

"Relax, *papi*. Besides …"

"Besides?"

"It'll give me an opportunity."

"I don't understand. For what?"

"To toast you both properly. With decent wine. Your nuptials, *papi*."

"Scarcely, Rodolfo, the moment."

"Of course it is. Of course, *papi*, it is. Take it." Rafaél demurs. "Take it, for God's sake." Rafa looks to Giselle. She shrugs him back a 'don't-look-at-me' shrug. That shrug also seeks to tell him she doesn't know either what to do, doesn't know how to react. Rafa takes the glass.

"To the bride and groom," Rodolfo announces. No-one present is sure of what it is they are feeling, of what it is they should be, of what it is the others are feeling. At the moment neither Rafa nor Giselle are quite sure whether Rodolfo's toast is in earnest, whether it is sarcastic or whether it is a yashmak to mask a deformity of pain. And neither does Rodolfo know.

They clink glasses. Giselle clinks both with her cup. They smile. But it is a smile squirming at its own coyness. "By the way," Rodolfo adds, "Emily's insisting on coming. She'll take the children to her mum's, but she herself … well, she's adamant. She's not about to miss the wedding, so she says, of her favourite father-in-law."

Giselle is lost for words. And her loss confiscates words from the other two. "That'll be cosy," eventually she says – more than anything to fill a hole. The remark had been spat out, but the expectoration belied the comparative calm with which, if she hadn't received the news, she was now digesting it.

"There's nothing I can do," Rodolfo tells her. "*Nothing, papi,* I can do."

"No," his father mumbles enigmatically. He wants to go to Giselle, to put an arm around her shoulder, reassure her – he doesn't even know what of. He doesn't go to her because it feels to him as if somehow it's not his *place* to. And yet he also knows, *of course* it's his place to. But he doesn't move. And that angers him about himself.

Giselle is likewise angry with *herself*. Because she has a need to be held. Because when she is held the kaleidoscope stops strobing at her, the shapes have some shape, the nebulous becomes a little bit graspable. And she knows she could be held by either man and that she could go to either, but she doesn't want somehow to have resolved some Oedipal joust. She drinks her mint tea, with angry sips, like a bird pecking at an unyielding acorn. And the angry she is at herself becomes the angrier because she knows she need not be angry with herself. And knows too that, yes, she does need to be. And the angry she is with them, that too becomes the angrier because she knows she has no *call* to be angry with them.

Or has she?

Chapter 24

It had been a mistake. They should never have listened to her. Giselle had insisted, the incident in Oxford Street was a one-off, an aberration, no cause for a general alarm. She had thought Saskja wanted to go. And Saskja ... well, she thought because Giselle was making this big thing out of it she should go. Really.

But none of the quartet is fond of crowds. Choosing therefore to see in the New Year at Trafalgar Square is like someone not fond of the sea choosing to celebrate the New Year on a raft cast adrift in the Pacific Ocean. Traditions have changed over the years. Booze, so long the eggs in the omelette of what was New Year's Eve in the metropolis, is now banned. Consequently there is less evidence of ostentatious rowdiness, and a good deal less of kissing total strangers. But today's jostle (for all its boozelessness), and though it seeks to be good-spirited, is often laced with a jabbing-elbows aggression.

They'd stayed to see the New Year in. They didn't know why. They all thought the others expected such of them. They had used much of the evening discussing what should be the third vital virtue. The discussion had been sprinkled even with some acrimony. This had surprised them all. But the acrimony stemmed, not from malice, intellectual or otherwise, but from the fact that none (for their own particular reasons) wanted to be there. At the time none of them was aware of this. And they were all startled by the random flecks of rancour. Which, of course, was the cause of yet further flecks appearing.

Saskja had suggested that they adopt one of Aquinas's 'cardinal virtues': justice. But justice, they had all agreed, was a fantasy – something which, even at its nearest point, is still so distant that it precluded the possibility of being called an aim. Justice, like beauty, is almost exclusively in the eye of the beholder: it is a quality which is entirely subjective, and about which there can only extremely rarely be consensus. Certainly, they had all agreed, it behove Man to work for justice – even more importantly that he work to erode *in*justice. And without any question at all, they further had all agreed, we need to listen very carefully when the word 'justice' is bandied around within the political forum. Too often 'justice' is used as a synonym for vengeance. Justice may be unattainable. Vengeance, though, is very easily attainable – and is almost always self-defeating. Those on whom vengeance has been reaped now see themselves as the victims of violence and they, in their turn, seek vengeance. Hurt people hurt people. It also blinds, vengeance. It is not blind itself, as justice is supposed to be, but it does blind. It's like the deadly sins in that way. We blame the storm-trooper not Hitler. And it can be used to blind: Vested interest often uses it to siphon off anger which should more accurately be targeted at it.

'Equality' was another impossibility. People are not born equally bright or beautiful, equally strong or healthy, to parents who love them to the same degree or who are prepared to make like sacrifices. Therefore even the notions, admirable as they may be, are impossible, those of 'equality of opportunity' or 'equality before the law'. And, ironically, even by considering these impossibilities as goals a credence is ceded them which they most palpably do not deserve. And which renders them yet *more* distant. By striving for equality, in other words, inequality thereby becomes even more unequal.

The practise of law *has* to be a chess game, and lawyers (like chess players) will vary considerably in their ability; one school child may come from a family which encourages homework, and another from one which *dis*courages it. But, hey, who knows? The latter may use the lack of encouragement as a goad and actually out-achieve the child who has been encouraged. We humans are very perverse in our diversity. In human conduct there are very rarely any absolutes. Indeed (so the quartet had asked of one another) are there *any*? Once you have accepted it would have been ethical to have murdered Stalin you open up so very many floodgates.

Giselle had then suggested 'equity'. Equity, she had suggested, is a goal which you could near considerably more than either justice or equality. And, yes, they had all agreed, there is merit in equity's case to be considered the third vital virtue. But in pursuing that discussion further, they had stumbled across that which they all agreed *was* that third vital virtue: imagination. Without imagination there wouldn't exist even the concepts of justice or equality or equity.

They are now walking along a strangely muted Whitehall (mauve on the 'Monopoly' board). Whitehall is the thoroughfare which leads from Trafalgar Square to the Houses of Parliament. In England it is used as a synonym for bureaucracy and many of the bowler-hatted Civil Service adhere like red duct-tape to its boulevarded environs. By day, it has the air about it of the corridor outside the headmaster's study and those who walk along its length tend to do so with that kind of quiet awe and unspoken dread reserved for that august location. At night, like the City, it is almost spookily quiet. The overtime exigencies of globalisation do not touch Her Majesty's civil servants. Even the street lamps seem to be set towards the lower end of a dimmer switch – a child's night-light, maybe, kept burning to keep away the bogeyman. They have a sense, our quartet, that they should somehow be padding through this dormitory in slippers; that they should be Wee-Willy-Winkie-ing their way down the concourse on tip-toes.

"It has a very low worth, these days, imagination," suggests Polly. "I went to a trade fair, oh about three months ago. Film and tv. There were, I'd guess, something like five hundred stands altogether. About two hundred with new cameras, about another hundred for new sound equipment, editing suites, special effects programmes, computerised camera dollies and so on. Know how many stands there were for writers?"

"None?"

"Well, actually one. But you catch my drift. Again, tails wagging dogs. There are good writers in Hollywood, of course there are. Probably as good as ever: the Raymond Chandlers and the William Goldmans. But most of those working today need to be considerably more expert in their pitching than in their writing. It's the persuasiveness of the pitch which determines whether or not a screenplay is made, considerably more than the quality of the literature.

"This goes in tandem with the fact that TV shows – and movies – are being devised now to show off the new technical expertise. The tail wagging the dog all over again. Rather than finding a great script with enormous technical challenges and discovering solutions, the tendency today would seem to be: We now have the capability of creating this special effect or that one. Let's find a story which incorporates those effects. It's like the algebra professor saying: 'Here's the solution. Now let's go find the equation which leads to it.' So much of Hollywood's output today is just a child showing off his fancy new toys.

"In the first 'King Kong', Kong changed size about a zillion times. Know what? No-one gives a damn. It's still by far and away the best version of the story. Maybe because it had a soul. And maybe because the soul of the remakes was robbed from them by a profit fixation. There is no soul in a fixation on profit. And because imaginations are not being stretched, the end products suffer."

"Oh, I agree with you, Polly. As so very often what is happening with films is only a microcosm of what is happening everywhere. Two muscles that we are going to need more than most in the twenty-first century: imagination and conscience, and we're allowing both, in very many cases, just to atrophy. No, that is hyperbole. What is not hyperbole, however, is that we are not encouraging, but discouraging, use of these infinitely precious commodities."

"Conscience is another interesting one," suggests Giselle.

"You know what anamatronics are?" the American asks.

"No," Rafa concedes with mock weariness. "No, Polly, I do not know what are anama ... what you said."

"-tronics. Anamatronics. It's kind of the prosthetics of make-up. They enable you to perform autopsies on living actors, for instance, change the shape of an actor's face and so on. There have been incredible advances in such techniques. And yet we still can't manage to get our actors skeletal. Look at 'Schindler's List' or Polanski's 'The Pianist' – or indeed his version of 'Oliver Twist': characters who would be gaunt, with their rib-cages pronounced, with their eyes contorted by famine, with rickets and lice and hair which would be lank and matted, these are played by actors with bulging cheeks and bouncing hair and who never, ever scratch."

"Is this, though, to do with technical deficiency?" wonders Giselle. "Or is it to do with a perception by the money-men that we, the audience, don't want our reality too real?"

"Mayhap we do not, Giselle. Real reality is often very uncomfortable."

"Don't we then propagate the lie?" Giselle continues to ask. "Aren't we thereby feeding the propaganda machine of the Nazi apologists?"

"Or those," Polly adds, "who minimise the effects of poverty? Doesn't art, for it to *be* art, have to be a quest for the truth – with or without a capital 'T'? And doesn't this lack of make-up, even this apparent lack of striving towards such a make-up, indicate a failure in our duty of care towards art?"

"Or mayhap just Man's predilection for the fairy-story. I think, Polly, you are very hard on your own industry."

"Wasn't it you who urged us all to point our fingers inwards?"

"But with kindness, Polly, and forgiveness."

"Qualities, of course, with which Hollywood abounds! I also find it worrying how paranoid television is as a medium, how much time it takes glorifying itself, and how much time lampooning the other media: books, for instance, fringe theatre. Game shows or quiz shows now regularly include questions about the private lives of pop musicians, about soap actors or characters, as if these were genuine fields of knowledge; sitcom characters debunk reading; an actor working in the theatre, particularly fringe theatre, is (dint of that alone) an object of instant mockery. Even on excellent TV shows, like, say 'Taxi' or 'Friends'. This is not satire, this is self-assurance. And how much potential is being stifled because members of the audience accept such paranoid self-justification as being a justification to themselves that reading is 'difficult' or that fringe theatre is pretentious. And, of course, some reading *is* difficult, and a lot of fringe theatre *is* pretentious. And there would be no harm at all in debunking both. But not as a permanent. And not as an unrelieved permanent.

"There wouldn't be that much wrong with most of TVs formats, with their programmes, other than their unrelieved permanence. We've talked before about how the good intentions of Oprah Winfrey have led to the toxic propagation of violence on our screens, and about how much violence in society those shows have spawned. Why do we not boycott the goods of companies sponsoring such toxicity? Why likewise do we not boycott all sporting events of which Nike is a sponsor? All sporting events indeed 'sponsored' by those whose business dealings are conducted on very unlevel playing-fields?

"We also need to ask ourselves how much are we being spoonfed what it is we should be imagining? Our own code of ethics, for instance? How much is the surrounding methos *dis*couraging us from imagination?"

They are less than two hundred yards from Nelson's Column and yet the raucousness of the Square has exhausted itself by here. If Trafalgar Square is the thunderstorm, two hundred yards along Whitehall there is only the odd droplet of rain. Another quartet weaves along its kerbstones, quite drunk, with helium balloons – the young women wearing only skimpy dresses, their boyfriends flagrantly fondling them; a young hobo and his string-leashed dog sit together, mumbling not-meant-to-be-heard curses; a woman, maybe forty, with frizzy black hair talks earnestly to a much younger man in pressed jeans – an intriguing little tableau. Were these two lovers? Friends? Mother and son? Sister and younger brother? What were they talking about so earnestly? Why was she almost weeping, he so calm? What different scenes would evolve from such a starting-point fed to the imagination of Molière or Steinbeck? Schiller or Miller – Henry Miller or Arthur Miller? Without imagination would we even have clambered from the sea?

They reflect on that. Polly muses, "Even the expression, the 'primordial ooze', even to coin that evocative phrase was an act of imagination." It was she who had (appropriately enough!) *imagined* how tired Giselle would be once the New Year was in. She had therefore parked a lot earlier in a little (and little known) side-street close to St Thomas's hospital. It is maybe a mile away from Trafalgar Square. Giselle had been adamant that her condition was pregnancy: pregnancy, not incapacity. That, *of course*, she could walk a mile. She could walk two miles ... ten.

They are adjacent to the Cenotaph. Rafaél stops for a moment, puts his hand to his heart in silent salute. Polly does likewise. And then so does Giselle. Saskja is curious. She hadn't noticed this obelisk of remembrance. Suddenly she realises its significance. She too bows her head.

"Interesting," says Polly, "now Mr Blair is no longer prime minister, that he feels no need to attend Remembrance Day."

Giselle starts walking again. "I seem to remember the papers saying he was busy with the Middle East peace process."

"Interesting," Polly insists, blowing heat onto her hands, "that such process should debar him from attending Remembrance Day, but not interfere with his public-speaking – a career which gained him, apparently, twelve million pounds last year. Nor from visiting President Obama. How are we not to infer that hob-nobbing with the powerful is of considerably greater importance to him than recognising the sacrifices of his compatriates? Even those for whose deaths he is personally responsible?"

"Consider also this:" suggests Rafaél, "if Mr Blair is chairing a peace conference, the other parties at which would not allow him time to remember those who died in previous conflicts, is it likely there will be a resolution to this one? If Mr Blair's conference is infected with that kind of callousness, its chances of success are extremely remote."

"Now, though," says Saskja, "he has gone, Mr Blair. Mr Bush also.

We move on, no? These men now history."

"The consequences of the two of them are still with us," Rafaél replies. "Sadly. The supervisor of Chernobyl at the time of the accident has also long since gone. The area still remains radio-active. Oh, as individuals, Mr Bush and Mr Blair were very small beer indeed. Rather sad men, even: Mr Bush struck me as one swamped by his sense of inadequacy, and Mr Blair as one floundering frantically in the ocean of his own ego. Little men ... minnows, in fact. Their significance has absolutely nothing to do with them as people, but in what they allowed to be perpetrated in their names: the deification of greed, for instance, the erosion of civil liberties, the dumbing down of the surrounding culture, the complete contempt they allowed to become instilled for honesty or integrity or civilised values ... or for their fellow human beings. They poisoned the well. Is why is so important we continue to talk of them. They are now abbreviations for the legacy of problems which their administrations have bequeathed the world – their administrations and their ministrations.

"Mr Brown was Watson to Mr Blair's Holmes. He, no, cannot be allowed to walk away from his responsibility for the water's pollution today. And we need always to remember that whenever he proposes solutions – because they are solutions to problems he was partially responsible for creating.

"President Obama, however ... Well, I have high hopes for President Obama. I think he is a good man. He is, of course, no ingénue to politics, so probably he has been contaminated. But mayhap not too much. Not yet. Whether he is *allowed* to be a good man, this is a more vexed question. He has powerful enemies, President Obama, very powerful enemies. As they have shown in other parts of the world, those enemies are considerably less committed to the democratic process than they would wish us to believe.

"Even if he *is* allowed to be a good man, it will be for some time yet, that President Obama will be pulling poisoned fish from the water. He cannot not. And he would be right to be cautious too about the speed with which he seeks to act; the speed with which he attempts to redress some kind of balance, both nationally and internationally; the speed with which he tries to remedy all the very, very many ills perpetrated on the world by his predecessor. We have spoken before about the mind-blowing damage inflicted on the former Soviet Union by the ... zealousness of Reagan and Mrs Thatcher in dismantling Soviet communism.

"President Obama has a daunting task. He has to persuade the world to believe in politics again. Is going to be what you Americans, Polly, would call a 'hard sell'. What we need from him – and desperately – is a commitment to some degree of honesty – both from the White House and from the Executive generally. It will require enormous courage on his part."

"And great imagination," Giselle adds. "Returning, I mean, to what we had been talking about. We won't be able to build a brave new world unless we first imagine what that brave new world could look like."

"I completely agree," Rafaél returns. "Where are the blueprints for that brave new world? I have seen blueprints for globalisation. It requires little imagination to see that those blueprints are of a design which would be (and are!) a catastrophe for humanity. We have therefore seen the blueprints for the slums. Where are those for the palace? For the palace we will need to build from the slums' ashes? Where are the blueprints for wethos?"

Not one of them has seen such a blueprint. Rafa continues, "We will need blueprints not only to create a brave new world but even to survive in our cowardly old world. Without those blueprints that cowardly old world could well be the end of the human world. And *is* cowardly, our world, this world we now inhabit. Is a coward who will not look in a mirror, who will not confront reality, who deals with trees because that is easier than the forest. We live in a world, my friends, where is the *twigs* of the trees that are dealt with.

"We need imagination today like a starving man needs food. And know what? We *have* that food. We have vast warehouses chock-a-block with such food. Imagination is a virtue we all are born with in abundance. Sometimes even to our detriment. If we want a loan from a bank manager, a promotion at work, a date with someone we're attracted to, how many variations of those scenes do we imagine, do we play in our heads before the actual event? Virtually all swords are double-edged. The twin edges of imagination are honed to razor sharpness.

"And yet is vital. 'Vital' in the true sense of the word: 'vital' meaning to sustain life. Imagination is also a muscle. It needs exercising. We have more need today of that muscle being exercised than ever before. Schoolchildren should be doing pilates of imagination.

"Play in youth is a preparation, in fun, for what in adult life will be in earnest. This is all obvious. Tiger cubs cuff each other with sheathed claws ... Nature is abundant in such examples. How much play of our children today exerts imagination? There are computer games, which certainly require visual awareness, manual dexterity, co-ordination – and usually a huge amount of killing; there is 'sport' which seeks to teach us how to compete, how to gloat in so-called 'victory' and squirm in so-called 'defeat' and which no longer considers either, in Kipling's famous words, 'two impostors' – which is, of course, precisely what they are; we have television which requires no imagination at all."

They walk past Downing Street. In which are found the residences of the prime minister, the chancellor of the exchequer and the government chief whip. Until very recently tourists and petitioners had been able to walk along its length. Now it is protected like a fortress. Such, we are led to believe, is required – "regrettably!" – by the 'War on Terror'. The more cynical would suggest it also serves to exaggerate the importance of the prime minister. And is required less to protect him than his ego. The indispensable accessory of any wannabe celebrity today is the bodyguard.

"The single biggest revolutionary of the new millennium was J.K. Rowling," Rafa suggests. "She demanded that her readers, young and old, use their imagination. And those readers, clearly, enormously enjoyed doing so."

"Terrible films, though," says Polly. She is beginning to feel both cold and tired. She had deliberately avoided bringing the hip-flask: She was driving.

"I liked them," Saskja tells her defiantly.

"They had the merit, at least," says Rafa, scouring for a middle-ground, "that they didn't dissuade the readers from reading.

"J.K. Rowling *and,* as I said on a previous occasion, the natural scientist, David Attenborough: the two most formidable radicals of the twenty-first century. And their radicalism is so sophisticated that not even vested interest can challenge it. The readers of Ms Rowling's books will – some of them – go on to read Mr Pratchett's work, and – even more radically – Mr Pullman's. And thus along the literary food chain. From the reading of books like Ms Rowling has written, and Mr Pullman, will come the imaginative leaps that will haul us from the chasm into which – at the moment hopelessly – we are sinking.

"Sir David Attenborough in his outstanding television shows, over and over, keeps demonstrating that we need to act now. That it is now we need to deal with pollution, deforestation, climate change; now that the natural world is screaming its echo of the political world, that we need to shift our paradigm from methos to wethos. No, *not* that we need to do so now, but that we needed to yesterday."

"And anyone," suggests Polly, "who encourages reading is today a revolutionary. I saw a doco – a, excuse me, Saskja, documentary – some time back on the tube. It was about the human footprint. It quoted the statistic that there are now more families in the UK with two cars than with two books. God knows how methos has done it, but it has made it smart to be dumb. Not not smart-Alecky. No-one has ever liked a smart Alec. But actually smart to be stupid.

"And that's really scary. Because, as we've said before, we're going to need every brain-cell available to get us out of this mess. It is only a part of the function of books to disseminate information. Their central task is to entertain. But they also serve the function of encouraging thought. And we will not fire imagination without encouraging thought. Television atrophies imagination. Books empower it.

"It's odd sometimes the political bedfellows you meet. I don't, frankly, believe Ms Barbara Bush's much publicised commitment to literacy. Even less when I heard her comments post-Katrina. But let us for the moment give her the benefit of the doubt and *assume* she was sincere. It would be an irony worthy of Shakespeare. For surely a literate generation will be able to see the terms of office of her husband and her son for the epochs they were. Largely because, in a literate society, writers (all of whom are, in effect, historians) will see it as their duty to portray today's administrations as being what in fact they are, and not what they have been spun into being.

"If there is to be a future, we owe it to that future to be honest about our present.

"You don't need imagination to see the present, just a pair of eyes. You don't need imagination either to notice you're in a hole. Again, only a pair of eyes. Where imagination *is* required, though, is to get you out of the hole. We've now shouted ourselves hoarse. No Sir Galahad is going to be galloping by. Or if he does, he's far more interested in rescuing damsels from wicked bluebeards (as who can blame him?) than a ragged, louse-infested us in our hole.

"The paranoid may well see in the lack of nurture given to our children's imagination a conspiracy to keep the status quo intact. I don't agree. But, like you, Rafa, that situation frightens me more. A conspiracy is, as we've said, relatively easy to deal with. You remove the head conspirators and the whole structure collapses. What we have is more dangerous, and infinitely harder to demolish. We are dealing with an ethos – a principle today of no principles. It is that which has caused this situation. And it can only be an ethos – a principle *of* principles – that will change it.

"It's therefore not enough that we create an Einstein or a Gandhi – not even a spiritual Messiah. It's not a Superman we need but the realisation that us together, we are Superman. Us together, we can travel faster than a speeding bullet, can freeze lakes with our breath and douse infernos. And that this cohesive us is the *only* Superman available to us. Maybe it's this, the 'consciousness' that quantum scientists talk about. We have to work towards creating an ethos, we have to replace no principles with principles indeed. This is an act of faith, in the broadest sense of the word, because it is a faith in humanity which touches the whole of humanity. It is also an act which requires imagination. It requires us to imagine that a world dominated by 'I' cannot ever be 'our' world, that 'our' world can only be a world which belongs to us. And that 'my' world is an illusion – possibly the ultimate illusion. If all human sex were masturbatory, how long would our species survive? Even at a molecular level, as Rafa's fond of quoting, co-operation is needed for life to survive."

"Wouldn't those molecular scientists argue that life also requires strife?" wonders Giselle. "Between biotics, say, and anti-biotics? Bodies and anti-bodies? Matter and anti-matter?"

"We've got such strife, Giselle," replies Polly, "and in spades. Each one of us is a permanent battle-ground. We're fighting within ourselves all the time: the higher 'I' against the lower 'I'. Tension likewise, and stress, those are both necessary. And those too we have in abundance. Internally. We absolutely do not need to fabricate more outside of ourselves.

"Hey, it was yourself, not many moons ago, who quoted me back to myself: 'the process of film-making is hard enough ...', all that. We absolutely do not need to create more strife, more tension and stress than is anyway integral to the human condition."

Further down the road, the Houses of Parliament are also these days 'protected'. In an eight-month period during the Second World War, Polly tells them, eleven bombs had fallen on the complex; the power-behind-Mrs-Thatcher's-throne, Airey Neave, had been killed in its car park by a car bomb; it is a building accustomed to the stringencies of real and present danger. Never has it been protected more ostentatiously than it is today. Cynics would have you believe that, far more than to guard our statesmen, these devices are designed to impress us that such statesmen are would-be victims of assassins (and therefore to be revered); that they are important, that they have gravitas, that they are in earnest (and therefore to be respected). That too is all part of today's sleight-of-hand, the spin that spins so fast we become giddy, we stop seeing.

Polly continues, "You also now cannot protest within a mile of the Houses of Parliament. Not without a police permit. So much, huh, for the cradle of democracy!"

"Sounds like Forbidden City," says Saskja.

"So much, also, for the freedom of speech so many Britishers have died for!" suggests Giselle.

"Mr Blair laid waste to more civil liberties than any other statesman in British history, with the possible exception of Henry VIII and Oliver Cromwell. The barbarians have therefore already won. So have the terrorists. They have managed to achieve what Hitler failed to do: cause the possibility in the United Kingdom of a police state.

"There is only one way safely of avoiding a police state:" Polly continues, "you forbid the apparatus that makes a police state possible. ... We've discussed all this before. No point in getting ourselves worked up about it all over again. Louis XIV of France famously once declared, 'L'état, c'est moi.' Mr Blair clearly believed, 'La *loi*, c'est moi.'

"And sadly he ain't alone in that belief," she adds ruefully. They all agree that apparently all the world's leaders (at least that they can think of) now subscribe to this arrant, arrogant, palpable and palpably anti-democratic nonsense.

They start to cross Westminster Bridge. As before, on their river trip, Rafaél can smell coffee, without there being any apparent source of such aroma. The views both sides of the Thames are magnificent. Rafaél thinks Wordsworth wrote a poem describing this view – well, a similar one, one of his time not the twenty-first century, one probably which pre-dated the big fire and thus the reconstruction of Westminster. Polly, now she thinks about it, is sure he's right. Neither can remember a single word, though, from the poem itself. To the east of the bridge is a swathe of rippling jet lacerated with the silver from the moon; and to the west an Amazon of oil coruscated with the constellation of twinkles, which are the reflections of the street lights and the house lights. It is the primordial ooze and the lido of Valhalla cocktailed into one.

The bridge is more crowded than Whitehall had been. And there is more evidence of alcohol's de-restraining effects. A couple of baggy-trousered teenagers, to the great (if wobbly) delight of their half-dozen companions, feel enjoined to re-enact some esoteric pagan ritual by mooning *at* the moon – or, more accurately, the moon's reflection. Closer to the former County Hall another such coterie, this one enswathed in red-and-white scarves, is 'singing' – for some reason known only to themselves – Elgar's 'Land of Hope and Glory'. This to the percussive punctuation of the pshhting which accompanies the liberal opening of lager cans. Taxis trundle self-importantly by, their meters creating small sonic booms as their digits scurry skywards. A couple of policemen edge cautiously and over-casually towards the mooners. Smiles are exchanged, even a nervous laugh. Baggy trousers again encase pimply rumps. The two young policemen are clearly relieved. They hadn't been expecting trouble but, when booze is a factor, you can never be sure what might ensue. 'A policeman's lot is not a happy one/ Happy one.'

The third life-affirming good idea? It has to be liberty, they decide. Has to be. The American Declaration of Independence, what an awe-inspiring document. Yet another of mankind's litany of tragedies is that this document, of so much wisdom and insight and common sense, should have been exposed to so much lawyerese as to debase and sully it.

"Of course," says Rafaél, "freedom, she is a right. But, more – and more important –, is a responsibility. So much freedom today is abused. The freedom of the press, for example. Freedom allows us to unearth secrets of the sex lives of the famous and, without their permission, to publish them. But freedom certainly does not countenance such conduct."

They are walking down the steps that lead to the hospital.

"There's an exhibition on at the British Library," says Polly, "about the fight there was in Britain to acquire its civil rights. I saw a poster for it the other day. It forgot to mention the most important thing of all: we are in danger of losing them. In fact, in grave danger of losing them. Of course Britain should glory in its civil rights. It should see them as a national treasure. More important indeed than its Crown Jewels. They should be seen as a treasure no nation on Earth could afford to lose. We've just passed a monument to millions of men and women who died in their cause."

"It cannot be repeated too often," insists Rafa, "there is no such thing as 'their' human rights. Abuse the right of the individual, you abuse the community. Nothing more need be said beyond that. The Holocaust was not only a crime against the Jews and Slavs and Gypsies, against the homosexuals and the freemasons, it was a crime against the entire of humanity. Because the entire of humanity suffered the loss. Likewise Stalin's gulags or Pol Pot's killing fields or the ongoing violations perpetrated by China today. Guantanemo Bay is a crime against me. Against you. Against all of us, everyone in the world. If today we can kidnap and imprison without trial those denounced as terrorists, then tomorrow we are left only with the hope that the definition of 'terrorism' does not extend to include us.

"Some of the most important words uttered in the Second World War were spoken by the Bishop, I think he was, of Berlin. 'First they came for the socialists,' he said, 'and I did nothing. Then they came for the Jews and I did nothing. Now they are coming for me.' If we say nothing, always it will be us that they come for. Eventually. Why do we so adamantly close our ears to a history as it howls its blood-soaked lessons?

"Jews when (as they should) they protest against the denial by Iran's President Ahmadinejad of the Holocaust also need to protest against President Bush's Patriot Act and the erosion of civil liberties in Britain – or anywhere else. Because essentially they are merely separate twigs off the same branch. They all spit in the face of suffering – and of so much suffering. They should also be supporting those victims of September 11th outraged that President Bush should have used the event to justify his invasion of Iraq, and those victims of the Oklahoma bombing likewise outraged that the atrocity should have been used as a political tool in the debate about capital punishment.

"The liberty that is being snatched from us is the liberty to protect our liberty. That is why is so pernicious. Is stealing from us the foundations on which we can build the ramparts to defend our liberty. I greatly fear that the time is now not far away when lives will be forfeit again in a fight to protect liberty, that those who claim to abide by Voltaire's famous adage are invited by destiny to stand up and be counted. Lives, of course, have already been forfeit. And destiny is already issuing such an invitation. But you need imagination to see the former, and very good ears indeed to hear the latter."

"'Course," says Polly, "no freedom is absolute. We may have the freedom to breathe, but we need the physical constraints of the body to be able to do so."

"Is, of course, true," agrees Rafaél. "But we do not further constrain ourselves from choice – blind ourselves or sever a limb. 'Film-making is a hard enough process, anyway ...', Polly.

"If the body is what coheres the individual life, societal life is today cohered by the law. And, as we have just discussed, each day ever more so. We should be working towards a society cohered by conscience.

"Law is, of course, a restriction of liberty – and, is it coincidentally?, the law's punishment is often the *confiscation* of liberty. Is hugely inefficient. Prison is not a measure of the law's efficiency, but of its *in*efficiency. Prison is not there to deter the law-breaker but to terrorise the law-abider into staying that way. The deterrent effect of prison is eradicated as soon as the cell door closes. If it were successful in combating crime, as I've said before, we wouldn't be building more of them. The principle function of prison, as much as to discourage crime, is to discourage protest.

"A far more sensible way of tackling *crime* is before the event rather than after it. Is just not – to use your words, Polly – very sexy.

"We do have to start realising that, at their very best, the police are about damage limitation. That is not a criticism, is merely a statement of fact. We aim not to start fires or have accidents. Likewise when fire engines and ambulances are on the scene, that goal too has been forfeit.

"And I understand entirely those victims of crime (both crime's direct victims and its indirect ones) being extremely angry that more concern and attention seems to be extended to the perpetrator than the perpetrated. And that is certainly another problem that does need to be addressed ... and, yes, urgently. But anywhere in the world where it has been tried, the idea of longer and more savage sentences, it has been shown that society is not thereby better protected, but worse. As with so much of methos, is not just that so much of it is inhuman, is that so much of it is incredibly – and I use the word advisedly – inefficient.

"Dramatically is a lot more exciting, cop cars whizzing after hot cars than it is counsellors sieving through the onion-like strata of emotional silt. Court rooms house great drama – *great* drama. But they host justice about as often as Quakers fire bazookas.

"This, I think, unearths another fundamental requirement we have for our survival: that is that we have to start finding things sexy we today think of as unsexy. It was sexier to visit the moon, for instance, than feed the poor. And visiting the moon, that was an enormous achievement – a *sexy* achievement. The hungry will remain unfed, though, for as long as we don't think it sexy to feed them. And freedom from hunger, that too is a very important part of freedom.

"And freedom – of course it does – also has to mean freedom from fear. Which – also of course – means providing protection for the vulnerable. And, of course, people have a right to feel safe in their houses, safe on the streets. Is completely possible, for instance, that the Manson 'family' affected the lives of wealthy Californians more than did bin Laden. Crime is frightening. And perpetrating a crime against a person is a violation of his civil liberties – and thus a violation against all of our civil liberties. Certainly.

"But people also have a right to feel safe in their jobs, feel safe that their pension funds are protected, that their life-savings are not just going to suddenly disappear, that they're going to be cared for in their old age ... safe as a child in their homes, and in their schools ... safe that their privacy is not invaded, safe that their dignity is respected ... safe to complain and to protest ...

"I find it ironic too that so many of those politicians who insist (as they pass their Draconian legislation) that citizens have a right to a life without fear also trip over themselves to champion globalisation.

"Globalisation does not, at any level, want a society free of fear. Is something else Polly and I discussed, that far more widespread than the War of Terror is the War of Terrifying. Economically, socially and politically, globalisation *thrives* on fear. For one thing, those who are frightened are more complicit. That's the political upside. Governments don't really care that citizens are unable to visit city centres at night. It suits them that most people don't want to venture forth. There's less chance of them getting together to complain. Almost the first action of any *coup d'état* is to impose a curfew. A self-imposed curfew saves them facing accusations of restricting freedom. In fact, government just *loves* kids like that: the gangs in America's metropolitan areas, the binge drinkers and football hooligans and those here in truculent despair. They create a terror on the streets, and *of* the streets, which gives the executive power to shore up its own power, to confiscate rights which it has taken Man centuries to acquire. And with the consent of the electorate – which (because that electorate is so badly schooled) does not see that the cure is considerably worse than the sickness.

"Oh, those forced to stay at home do complain about these delinquents imposing what is effectively this curfew, or mayhap about the parents of such delinquents. But only very rarely do they complain about the ethos which nurtures that delinquency, the profit-at-any-cost economics, the complicity between government and industry.

"Economically ... Well, the advantages of fear just go on and on ... Fear of robbery helps the sale of security systems and, in the United States, firearms; fear of the future fuels the enormous insurance industry; fear of redundancy keeps people compliant in the workplace, fear of bankruptcy likewise – a useful fear if your aim is that people work against their conscience; it is claimed that fear of imprisonment largely keeps the majority law-abiding; fear of invasion and insurrection allows for enormous percentages of salaries to be diverted into the maintenance and supply of the Armed Forces, and via that again into the bank accounts of the business magnates.

"It amazes me when pundits denounce Orwell's '1984' for being so far from the truth. Everywhere I look I am staggered by how accurate was Mr Orwell's glimpse into what was then the future. CCTVs are ubiquitous, our actions are all monitored and very largely controlled ... Rewriting history becomes a daily event. We even have a name for it. It's called 'spin'. Newspeak is prevalent everywhere we turn. The thought police becomes daily more of a reality with mobile phone calls and emails being monitored and logged. It has to beg the question too: How much are our enemies real enemies, and how much are they invented by our rulers to keep us all in line?

"Fear is endemic to any sentient being, of course. Is an essential tool in the chest which keeps us alive. We are all, every living creature, alert to the dangers of predators and accidents. So much so, indeed, that we have developed a gland, adrenalin, just to deal with it.

"Still today the feeling sometimes we have, just before we sleep, of falling into thin air ... reputable scientists now believe that originated in our simian background, a salient reminder that we were asleep in branches way above the ground, an urge to caution, a simulation and stimulation of fear. And is thought likely that our simian inheritance also causes most of those living in houses to choose their bedrooms to be upstairs – like the branches we slept in as apes. Fear at this kind of instinctual and animalistic level is probably even healthy. There are *plenty* of healthy fears: of fire, for instance, or electricity or disease or speeding cars ... or psychopaths wielding axes!

"But far too often this natural and salutary fear is manipulated by the unscrupulous into a fear which is both unnatural and extremely unhealthy. The fear evident post-war in the streets of Bucharest and Budapest, of Prague and Leningrad was almost tangible. And invidious. Enormously debilitating, enormously unhappy. All-pervasive. Like tobacco smoke. Like smoke too it penetrated everything. And it clung. It clung like a limpet. To everything. It was inhaled and ingested, it was sneezed and sweated. That fear was also tangible in the streets of Madrid and Lisbon. So-called 'communism' (which was, of course, not communism at all) was not by any means the only repressive political system in the world. Not too much Leninism involved in apartheid – except the use of fear as a repressive instrument.

"Much of the world's population today – and far *too* much of it – does not have liberty sufficient to express an adverse political comment without a credible fear of arrest. How many more indictments do we need of the planet's 'morality' (or, more accurately, lack of it) today?

"Hungry, you have no liberty; addicted, you have no liberty; in debt, you have no liberty; denied the right to protest, you have no liberty.

"I can't remember who it was who said, 'Give me liberty or give me death', but if it is a watchword echoed by mankind, we should be preparing Man's obituary.

"Certainly liberty is relative. Of course it is. And, of course, liberty (paradoxically) requires constraints. Perhaps the essence of democracy is that the 'people' (the *demos*) get to choose the constraints on their freedom. But law is an indication of society's weakness, not its strength. It seeks to impose where it cannot persuade. And it behoves us all to remember that.

"And certainly liberty includes the freedom to make mistakes. Hitler *was* voted into power: we need always to remember that. Other mistakes have been made at the polling booth. As a species we have made *enormous* mistakes – perhaps we've been too ambitious for far too much far too soon.

"But freedom also means being able to say, 'Whoa. I've made a mistake. Don't need any longer to go along this path. Not if it's leading to a chasm. *Can* change direction. *Can* make a commitment to carry on living.

"It means we *can* change 'methos' to 'wethos'."

"And here's the car."

"Hallelujah!" sighs Giselle.

"Happy New Year," sighs Saskja.

Chapter 25

Was it irony that Rodolfo had suggested it? Not really. Not unless the whimsy of fate can be described as ironic. No, fate's whimsy was just that: fate's whimsy; and irony was irony. And never the twain shall meet. Right!

There is no irony here, Giselle decides. Really she should concentrate on the words she can hear being said to her. They were, after all, attached to her wedding.

The registry office would brochure itself as neo-Georgian. Mock Sheraton tables inlay their spindly legs into deep-shag carpet. There are flowers a-plenty, neo-Georgian chairs some of whose cushions still remain free of stains. The garden beyond is England at its greenest and willowest – willows weeping not from grief, but joy.

Rodolfo himself – she needs no reminding – had been married in church. But he had attended this little registry office as a witness. He had thought it, as he'd told Giselle, a "pleasing" venue, pretty without being chintzy or cheesy. Would he still be pleased with it now?, she wonders.

She can feel his eyes upon her. She can sense his look: a cheesy, chintzy grin slobbering around his chintzy, cheesy chops. Was he imagining her naked? Was he, rather, *seeing* her naked?

"Repeat after me …" she heard distantly – like the distant bleats of goats on the hill in Orphalese with Lakshmi: a distant bleat on a distant hill in a distant past. Equally distantly she heard herself saying, "I, Giselle …"

She was pretty, Rodolfo's wife, Emily. Not drop-dead gorgeous or anything. But handsome … fresh-faced … Anglo-Saxon. And she was nice, a nice woman. Even a very nice woman. She obviously knew nothing about Giselle's relationship with her husband. Apparently she didn't even sense anything. She'd tried not to be condescending and Giselle had known that and had appreciated it. The class system and xenophobic tradition of Albion, however, are not lightly etched;

they are ingrained deeply: Giselle *was* a foreigner, one who did speak with an accent, and was – after all – but a humble nurse to the Jupiter-like figure of her surgeon husband. Emily had welcomed that nurse to the family, and had assured her in her best Lady Fauntleroy that she was sure they would be firm friends ... firm, yes, friends.

Giselle had of course known that Emily would be nice. She'd never had the slightest doubt about it. She hadn't been prepared therefore for the strength of feeling the introduction had invoked in her: She wanted to slap the very nice Anglo-Saxon straight across the face. She wanted to wrest her Gucci handbag from her hand, empty it of all its American Expressed contents and shove bag, contents, gloves down her cheesy, chintzy, lovely Anglo-Saxon throat. Oh, and the Cartier watch as well. She wanted to see Emily naked. She wanted her as naked before her as now she felt naked before him. Before Rodolfo. Before the congregation – whatever a like assemblage was called in a registry office. Naked as she was before God. As she always was before God. As she was always before all three of her gods. But not naked sexy. She'd never been taken by her God, or her gods. Oh, God – certainly – had entered her, and often. But He had entered her in the way that a sensation intrudes, or a feeling, not as a lover.

She is startled by Rafaél's kiss. He sees her start. "I was told," he says almost apologetically, "I could kiss the bride."

"Of course you can," she dimples back at him, trying to force the smile also to wriggle into her heart. "Of course, o husband of mine, you can."

Chapter 26

Giselle is now almost thirty weeks into her pregnancy. Leaving tube stations, she prefers in her condition to surface via the ramp than the stairs. They have just emerged from Pimlico underground station. They: she and her recent husband, Saskja and Polly. They are these days a stringed quartet, such strings being invisible but, if anything, *more* infrangible for that; not any less harmonic; mostly, indeed, mellifluous.

They are on their way to the Tate Gallery – "the 'Tate Britain' as Blairspeak insisted on re-titling it." The words had been Polly's. They had been uttered whilst the stringed quartet had been sitting in Giselle's flat, drinking coffee before they'd set out. Still Giselle lives there with Saskja; and still her husband, Rafaél, lives above her with Polly. It reads like a scene from a biography of Woody Allen. But, mostly, they are okay with the arrangement. And mostly too, *that* is okay.

"You know," she had said, "in Marc Antony's famous funeral speech he says, well, something like: 'The evil that men do lives after them/ The good is often grinded with their bones…' You know, I'm not too sure how true that is. The evil of Mr Blair's administration is, as we've all said before (and as all right-minded people know), radio-active, that much is true: It will take generations of goodwill to undo it. Sadly, though, I wonder how many historians will bear witness to that fact. So much of *that*, of course, depends on who wins the war between the Truth and the Untruth.

"Perhaps thus it is true that 'the evil that men do lives after them'. Reading their historians, though, you'd be hard put to it to believe it. And that goes also for their architecture. We continue to marvel at the Coliseum, and forget about the mindless extravagance of Nero's golden palace.

"What should be remembered architecturally about Mr Blair's administration is unquestionably the Millennium Dome – an expensive white elephant built to the self-aggrandizement of Mr Blair at the cost of a whole host of genuine benefits to the British community.

"My guess is, though, that there will be a rush of apologists for Mr Blair, who will 'justify' his policies as being 'pragmatic' and 'of the world': Realpolitik. And that art historians will remember not the calamities of the Dome and the inordinate cost of the new Wembley stadium, but the exciting buildings like the 'Gherkin' and the London Wheel and the Tate *Modern*. The Tate Modern, in my opinion, is probably the greatest modern art gallery in the world. To my mind it beats the hell out of anything I've seen in New York or Chicago or Bilbao."

In order to experience such excellence, they had taken the Central Line, the sort of coral red one, which runs (quixotically enough) through the centre of London, almost dividing it between north and south. But during this trip, a concern had started to be voiced about Giselle being able to cope with crossing the Millennium Bridge. Neither bridge, nor Tate Modern – such was the consensus – was about to go away. It would still be there after she'd had the baby. Why didn't they wait till she wasn't carrying so much weight? The consensus also held that the gallery would be full, mostly of tourists. Considerably more than would its sister, Tate Britain. Giselle had tried to point out that January 23rd was scarcely tourist high season. But, so the consensus had decided, there was *never* a low tourist season in London. And Giselle had conceded. They had a need (and she had understood that) to wrap her in cotton-wool and she had a need (which she also understood but rather less well) both that they did so and that she should resent them doing so. They had changed trains at Oxford Circus onto the Victoria (or light blue) Line.

"So often when we ask ourselves," Polly had continued, as they had rattled along in one of its carriages bound for Brixton, "why it is we're today staring into an abyss, we return to the ancient problem of historians opting rather for their own aggrandizement or preferment than to tell the truth.

"The pyramids in Egypt, the ziggurats of Babylon and Mexico, the Forbidden City, when we see these as triumphs for the psychopathic dictators who ordered their construction, we perpetrate the horrors attendant *on* that construction. Certainly they are wonders. Maybe even triumphs, dependant on how you define 'triumph'. But in them are not ingrained the majesty of emperors who were despots, but the possibilities of human endeavour and of a communal striving.

"We were about to go by St Paul's Cathedral. I agree with the son of its architect, Sir Christopher Wren, who's entombed within the cathedral's vault. The son had his father's tombstone inscribed with the words: 'His epitaph is all around him.' And so, of course, it is.

"But so is the epitaph of the many myriads who contributed to that quite lovely edifice: master craftsmen and artists by the score, stone masons, sculptors; artisans and labourers by the thousand – those who quarried the stone in Portland, who transported it to London, who built the ladders, constructed the scaffolding, cooked the food, counted out the wages ... Without any of these, St Paul's Cathedral would just be some elegant lines on a piece of paper. More, because even that would have required the work of tree-fellers, papersmiths, ink manufacturers, quill makers. Without any of these, Sir Christopher's ideas would have been simply that: a few abstract thoughts floating around inside his brain.

"Movie credits are today absurd. Absurd. They mean nothing because they are given to, apparently, everyone. When I got my first credit it was a big moment. I thought I'd arrived. I'd been in the film business for about fifteen years by then. Today those with the most tenuous association with the end product are paid their mention. But, even so, there are far more people *not* mentioned. And there is good reason for that: It's simply not possible. How, on a film, do you mention the woman in the local box office? The usherette there? Those involved in the manufacture and distribution of the ticket which grants you access? Who had been involved in the building of the cinema? What about the army of others who tended to those people? The dentists and the hairdressers, the farmers and the firemen, those who build *their* homes, who transport them to and from work? What thanks is given by a film's producers to any of *them*? And yet without these people's work, there would be no cinema for you to watch their film in.

"As I get older, matter of fact, I have less and less problem with anonymity. And, tell the truth, there's a few movies I've worked on where I'd have preferred *not* to have been associated with it. But let's, at the very least, start acknowledging our interdependence. And, in a curious way, we do that more by a lack of credits, than we do with the abundance we today receive. It smacks, that abundance, of the phony 'have a nice day' society.

"This is exemplified by the thanks tendered to us passengers at the end of a flight by the pilot. That does so very neatly encapsulate the passive aggression of what today is called 'courtesy'. The pilot's reading from a script. His 'thank you's mean precisely nothing. And by their utter vacuousness, the thanks become not indications of gratitude, or even respect, but signs of a sneering contumely: for language, for the intent of verbal communication, for those to whom this vacuity is addressed – and thus, finally, for humanity as a whole. It's interesting how many pilots, in private, refer to passengers as 'human freight'. Certainly most airline companies treat us as if we were such. It all smacks of Captain Bligh caring more about the Admiralty's bread-fruit than for the welfare of his crew."

This soliloquy has escorted them to the ramp of Pimlico station. The consensus is again anxious about Giselle, asking her how she feels, checking she still wants to visit the gallery. She is beginning to get ratty with the concern.

Now the consensus is wondering why in London, where there is never a low tourist season, is there *never* a sign indicating the route from tube stations to the point of interest served by such station. Tourists in London are treated in a manner more akin to an army of occupation than house-guests. It is part of the dichotomy which London exercises in its regard to its bed-and-breakfasters: it loves and drools over their money, but thinks it need do no more to accommodate them than to be there. Cockneys suck in suckers' money like a vacuum-cleaner in overdrive, but they don't want Johnny Foreigner ever to get the idea that he *needs* this grubby lucre. The Londoner takes the money – of course he does – but he handles it with the hoity-toity distaste of a judge at a prestige dog show handling a flea-infested mongrel.

Eventually, after a carousel of searching, they do espy a little arrow directing them towards their destination. They start to walk towards Vauxhall Bridge. The architecture they pass is almost quintessentially London: elegant but austere terraced houses, Regency in style if not all actually of that era, geometrically exact, but perhaps wanting personality or presence or individuality or ... or, yes, soul. There is a want of window-boxes or dazzling woodwork. They exude secrecy, like their owners. Their personalities are kept behind multi-bolted front doors. For public display, the upright and the proper, the adult and responsible. This part of Pimlico is the English stiff upper lip in bricks and mortar.

Given the acrimony attendant on their search for the third vital virtue, the fourth is found quickly and with immediate accord. It is Saskja who suggests it, and then tentatively, nigh on apologetically. "Peace?" she asks.

Truth to tell, in her herself she is still searching for that. Each night she tries not to see the baby she'll now not have; each day she tries not to see Giselle's bulge of life. Each day too she promises herself that today she *will* tell Giselle – today, without fail –, that the burden is too heavy, that she needs to lighten herself by sharing it. And each night, as again the baby's abstract takes physical form, each night she curses herself for not having talked to Giselle. She curses herself as being both gutless and idiotic, as being a waste of the planet's limited resources, a drain on the energy of her friends and family. Tomorrow, though, she *will* tell her. Tomorrow, without fail ...

"Peace," Rafaél muses.

"Peace," Polly 'right on's.

"Is not a bit Miss Worldy?" asks Giselle. "A bit 'I-have-implanted-silicon-into-my-breasts-for-world-peace'?"

"True peace like true love," says Polly, "balks at that kind of schmaltz. It's part, as Rafa would say, of the Untruth. Making something crass out of something beautiful. It's gritty, real peace, and pithy. It's got dirty hands and callouses."

"Peace *is* the fourth vital virtue," says Rafaél. "Virtues will always be distorted or cheapened. Virtue is precious – is genuinely precious. Methos has only contempt for the precious: Pride, as we discussed, is distorted into hubris or vanity.

"President Bush was not the first invader in history claiming to have done so 'for peace'. Hitler claimed peace as his motive for invading the Sűdetenland, even France. But the distortion by the unscrupulous of the special does not diminish the specialness *of* the special. Not finally. It means only that we need to listen with discretion to those invoking the special to support their cause. Because there is rape in the world does not stop sex from being beautiful. Dvořák remains a beautiful composer, even though his music today sounds merely like an agglomeration of advertising jingles.

"We have allowed the valuable to be demeaned, all of us. And, know what? At the sort of advertising jingle level, that's even acceptable. The beautiful is robust enough to withstand abuse. Is similar to the way Truth will always – finally – vanquish Untruth, because (as I have said) the Truth has to include Untruth, whereas Untruth has to *ex*clude Truth. Beauty embraces ugliness, just as ugliness repels beauty.

"That may indeed be just where the divine inexorably enters our life. And, whether divine or not, is the aspect of Truth and beauty which gives us the most hope for the future of humanity. Because if Truth, as it does, finally triumphs over Untruth, so the positive must triumph over the negative – which, by extension, means life has to triumph over death."

"Doesn't death, though, finally always have the last laugh?" asks

Polly.

"Only when we let it," Rafaél replies. "If we see death as defining itself, rather than defining life. Is not the most important and relevant thing about death that without it there is no life? In my opinion, one of the most healthy developments, one of the most positive, in recent years has been that funerals are seen so very much more as a celebration of a life just extinguished, more than woe that death has claimed another victim. Of course there should be sadness at funerals. That's not the same thing. One no longer has access to the love of which that person was the embodiment – except that, of course, one does. One may not be able to touch that embodiment, one may not be able to access specific advice, but one can still be touched by that love. And love, that is just so important to peace. And to life. And to truth.

"The truth is, for instance, that no war was ever won. The Second World War is perhaps unique amongst international conflicts in that it had to be fought. But even that war was not won. Very obviously not won by countries like Hungary and Poland. But not even won by countries like the United Kingdom and the United States. It was simply not lost. And it was a war that simply *could* not be lost: *Humanity* would have been lost with the Allies' loss of that war. And in the history of human conflict, the Second World War is unique in that one side did not lose. In all other conflicts, both sides have lost.

"I repeat, historians do have to accept their share of the blame for this. Of battles like Agincourt or Trafalgar they write words like: 'There were thousands of French casualties, but *only* 900 (or whatever) British slain.' And French historians (and Spanish ones) have written similarly of other battles. What is 'only' about the loss of 900 lives? There were allied casualties of over 40,000 at Blenheim. Churchill (the ancestor of the World War Two Prime Minister) was given a castle to salute this great 'victory', and a dukedom. What was given in compensation to the families of those 40,000?"

"American troops returning from Vietnam," says Polly, "were greeted with leis of silence, and with parades of absence splashed with floats of contempt, and marching bands of embarrassment. President Johnson had an honour guard and a state funeral."

"And is partly the same thing, and partly not," says Rafaél. "There is a problem. States need state funerals. Maybe *we* do. Apart from anything else, is how we define epochs. Is maybe one advantage of constitutional monarchy: that such epochs, thanks to a monarch, are defined outside the political arena. This advantage, of course, gets dissipated when one monarch rules for too long. The world at the end of Victoria's reign was greatly different to that at its beginning. The term 'Victorian' thus is, at best, inexact and sometimes is positively misleading. So we revert to eras defined by prime ministers, almost as if they were presidents. The reign of the present queen comprises likewise not one epoch but several. And the premiership of the dapper, but ill-advised Mr Eden was vastly different from that of the dapper, but equally ill-advised premiership of Mr Blair. And, yes, war crimes were certainly committed by Mr Eden. And no war crime is insignificant. But the scale of deception meted out to the electorate, and the level of civil rights violations in Aden were on a different scale from those crimes and violations perpetrated by Mr Blair. If this is an indication of how everything in the world is escalating, then it is yet more proof, my friends, that we simply have to slow down the rate at which the world is travelling.

"Each earthquake in the world seems to cause yet more devastation and loss of life. Perhaps not surprising as the world's population increases. No-one, not for a second, is suggesting that, in such emergencies, we should not use all our expertise and wealth to mitigate the disaster. Well, except, that is, for President Bush's recent administration. Or those who believe in the late Professor Friedman's social policies.

"But should we not also spend time questioning the wisdom of building on known fault-lines? Should we not stop trying to 'conquer' Nature and start trying to live in harmony – in *peace* – with her? And is not this very much a part of the 'peace' which is the fourth vital virtue? It hurts just as much losing a loved one in a natural disaster as in a man-made one.

"There will always be natural disasters. The universe is a structure of such enormous energy and destructive capability – also *con*structive capability (it itself, it must be worth remembering, was occasioned by a gigantic explosion. I'm not sure what is the significance of that, beyond knowing that it must have significance.) There will always be natural disasters. We simply do not need to create more. 'Film-making is a tough enough process, anyway ...' And we create more when we defy Nature, rather than working with her.

"We know the eastern seaboard of America will one day be devastated by a tsunami. This is no longer tea-leaf reading, this is the best advice of the world's leading seismologists and geologists. Do you see anything being prepared for that disaster, to minimise its impact? It's tomorrow's problem. Tomorrow, apparently, we will have found a way of 'conquering' the tsunami.

"Tens of thousands of people – maybe hundreds of thousands – will therefore be killed. Some may consider their deaths 'unnecessary'. The casualty list will be grotesque ... incalculable. And which scapegoat will then be found to blame for that catastrophe?

"It won't, of course, be anyone's fault: It will be all our faults. Because we're not finding a morality that will ensure that twenty-first technology is used to create a twenty-first century civilisation. Instead we are allowing it to revert us to a thirteenth century *lack* of civilisation – or, if not that precisely, then certainly a thinking, a perception which informed that thirteenth century uncivilisation: a serfdom, in other words, where the overwhelming majority lived their lives in bondage for the greater comfort of the tiny minority.

"The consequences of that, apart from the immorality integral within such a structure, will be the destruction of the world's natural habitats, the extinction of tens of thousands of species ... I *suspect* it will lead to man's extinction, but it *has* to lead to the erosion of anything to do with civilisation. At best it has to undo the moral progress of the last thousand years, at worst it can annihilate millions ... *billions* of years of evolution. By what possible yardstick can this be called 'progress'?"

"Peace," says Giselle, "also has to mean inner peace."

"Oh, yes," says Rafa. "Indeed, the Hebrew word for peace, '*shalom*', not only embraces both meanings but implies that one cannot, as you say, Giselle, have the former without the latter. I suspect likewise so does the Arabic '*sala'am*'."

It is one of London's best kept secrets, how good is the restaurant of Tate Britain, in its basement – presumably where the dungeons had been cloistered when it was the site of the Millbank prison. There is little penitential about its feel today. Polly had been using it from the time she had prepared a film in an office-block just on the other side of the river. Then it had all been pink table-cloths and Nouveau Beaujolais and dumpy, Pearly Queen waitresses; today it is all mineral water and a choice of bread and young waitresses from Eastern Europe. The roam around the gallery had been longer lived than consensus would have wished, but had been curtailed before the anxiety of that consensus had broken Giselle's exasperation point.

They had been early enough at lunch not to have needed to wait for a table. The secret of the restaurant's merit is not quite as secret these days as it used to be!

"If we are not at peace with ourselves," says Giselle, "it will eventually be the world which is at war."

"Is anyone at peace with themselves?" asks Saskja. The other three hear the question as academic. They are not listening enough.

"I think," Giselle replies, "that would depend a lot on how you define 'at peace'." Bread is being proffered them from a basket wielded by a young woman with long blonde hair. She could be Czech. She is very lovely. Saskja takes an instant dislike to her. Giselle has taken a roll. The others do likewise. The Czech waitress is about to leave. Giselle calls her back, takes another two of the basket's rolls. There is a conspiratorial grin shared between her and the waitress.

"The fourth life-affirming idea," says Polly, "can we assume – I mean, as one and two are life, and three is liberty – can we assume that the fourth is the pursuit of happiness?" Her gin-and-tonic arrives. Saskja is also having one. Giselle and Rafaél are sticking to water, albeit of the less healthy, fizzy variety. They both agree, you can sometimes take this healthy living thing ... well, just a little bit *too* far.

"Why not simply 'happiness'?" suggests Rafa. "Its pursuit, its acquisition, its presence, they are all very life-affirming ideas. Those who are happy – truly happy – tend to want others also to be happy. And those who are truly happy also tend to infect others with their happiness."

"Is happiness the same as peace?" asks Giselle, munching through her second roll.

"I think both can and do nurture and support the other," Rafaél returns, watching her demolition of the dough. "Is difficult – not impossible, but difficult – to have one without the other. My understanding of 'happiness', particularly in this context, is that it's a generic term covering a sense of feeling good, starting at contentment and finishing at joy. I think concepts like 'rapture' or 'ecstasy' are outside the purview of 'happiness'. There's nothing wrong with either rapture or ecstasy – provided they are not manufactured – but they are, at best, ephemeral sensations, usually induced by extraordinary stimuli: falling in love, for instance, or fulfilling an ambition. Is not the stuff of quotidian life. Even the chronically depressed can experience euphoria. Is happiness which is lacking from their lives."

"It's sure lacking from mine," Polly confesses. Saskja involuntarily glances at her a flick of empathy which is yearning to be recognised. Again no-one sees it.

"I think, Polly, all that is unusual about that is that you see it and admit it," says Rafaél. He has noticed that Giselle has finished all three of her rolls. He offers her his. She wavers. He coaxes her further with a smile. Graciously she accepts it. "Being at peace with yourself also has to involve being at peace with the fact there is conflict inside you. In fact," he continues, "that would, I think, be my definition of it.

"The peace of the fanatic is the peace of the madman. And the happiness of the zealot is the happiness of the idiot. Once we start 'knowing' we endanger ourselves and others. Life is not only suffering, it is struggle. Civilisation is always struggle: 'The price of liberty is perpetual vigilance': Doesn't that sound like struggle to you? For all creatures, life is a struggle, for all natural things – maybe even for geological phenomena, who knows? There is nothing wrong with life being a struggle. Not '*per se*'. There is much wrong with the struggle today because so much of that struggle today is manmade. Is completely artificial. 'The process of film-making ...', once again.

"This too we have discussed already, my friends, and mayhap adequately. But, again, let us be careful not to throw the baby out with the bath-water. Just as refraining from birching a child does not mean that children do not need boundaries, so eradicating unnecessary struggle should not be construed as wanting all of struggle removed from life. For Man merely to arrive in the twenty-second century is going to involve him in the most titanic struggle. This too I have said before. And it could be – which I have also said before – that the sheer magnitude of that struggle is what is going to create a humanity indeed and not one only in name, a *civilisation* indeed and not one just in name.

"Is going to require a self-discipline which he has *never* exercised, not to this degree. He will have not one ounce of energy to spare. Which is why is so very important that such energy as he does inevitably use he does so sparingly and prudently.

"For us humans – sorry, Giselle – even the act of giving birth is a struggle. Indeed is more of a struggle for us than for virtually any other species. Maybe we should also ponder that when we congratulate ourselves on man's genius! An act of creation is inevitably a struggle, and at every period of its existence, from conception, through gestation to execution and exhibition: Michelangelo painting the Sistine Chapel, a child crayoning a birthday card for her mother, the carpenter fashioning wood, the scientist puzzling over the contrary results of an experiment.

"Principles are a struggle. Finding principles – *your* principles – is a struggle, living by them often a very great struggle. So very often principles seem to be at variance with present needs. So *very* often.

"And – paradoxically yet again – there is no peace in a lack of struggle. Peace comes from knowing ... no, no, we never know, not in that sense ... peace comes from *feeling*, from *sensing* that the struggle embarked on is a good one and a worthwhile one. Decorating a room is a struggle. Decorating a room, there is a part of our brain wishing we were watching football or playing a video game or having a drink in the pub. And we have to fight ourselves – very often – to finish the job. And is, that, one of the reasons why in school is so very much more important to instil self-discipline than to insist on a blind obedience to an imposed discipline. Indeed it should be one of the jobs of schools to encourage their pupils to *question* an imposed discipline. And that too is another element of the essential struggle which is at the core of life.

"Likewise happiness. The happiness I'm talking about is not the opposite of unhappiness, is the opposite of despair. Despair taints everything and saps you of any resistance or energy – 'resistance', 'energy': do those sound like elements in a struggle? Happiness, though, adds lustre to everything, and pep. It fuels determination and purpose. Is very life-enhancing. And is strong enough – the happiness of which I talk – to incorporate unhappiness. You can cry tears of misery and still be happy. The dog can be run over, your best friend can commit suicide, your parents can die – and you will be sad, but you can still, at the core of you, be happy.

"But can we be happy reading about the Holocaust or the napalming of villages in Vietnam? Can we be happy with the images of natural devastation (like the tsunami or Hurricane Katrina) or manmade atrocities like Rwanda or El Salvador? Can we be happy with billions in this world still under-nourished? And even more under-cherished? If, as it is, the ethos of our world is one which demands the compromise of our safety, how can our safety not be compromised? If, as it does, that ethos requires deep unhappiness, how is it not perforce that our happiness is curdled?

"When we are not happy we can have no peace. And when – as you said, Giselle – we have no peace, we will want to fight, however small the fight. Hurt people hurt people. We will want to fight with our partners or our children or our neighbours or our juniors at work, we want to cut people up in traffic or mug them in the street or best them in business or slander them in the press. If we are prime ministers or presidents we may want to invade other people's countries."

"We may also want to invade them," suggests Giselle, "if, as we have said, we have unresolved issues around the fathers absent from our childhood, or if we have a sense of personal inadequacy. The peace inside also means working actively on all the emotional issues and childhood bruises which beset us all."

"Scott Peck in 'Children of the Lie' claims that you will meet more psychopaths at a cocktail party than in a facility for the mentally disturbed," Polly chimes in. The first course has arrived. Giselle and Saskja are having the grilled mackerel; Rafaél and Polly the pâté. The smile from the blonde Czech waitress is enormously expansive. It seems to throw a beam on the entire table. "There's none so sick," Polly continues, "as those who think themselves hale."

"That may be true but it'll, Polly, be another 'hard sell'," the Peruvian suggests.

"You know, Rafa, I'm not too sure any longer that it will. One of the healthiest trends in the world today is the amount of people working on themselves, searching for a new relationship with themselves and their world, often with their own conception of God or the metaphysical, searching for the peace you talk about within themselves. It is remarkable quite how many continue that search despite the sarcasm and the jibes of pundits and comedians and the scorn of those too sick to recognise that *they* are sick. It's not the people working on themselves who are invading Iraq, it's not those searching for a new spirituality flying jumbos into skyscrapers."

Polly sniffs the wine and signals with a nod to the dark-trousered waiter its acceptability. "It is," she continues, "the sick part of us which has brought us to the brink. It will require the healthy part to pull us back. I say that as one of the world's most unhealthy." She raises her glass in a silent toast.

"We will only find real happiness," says Rafaél, "by realising how very unhappy we presently are and addressing it; we will only find peace when we recognise how attractive is the fight to us and addressing that. Let us not mistake the struggle for the fight. Usually we fight because we don't want to struggle. The fight is the precursor of war. Struggle, though, is the requirement of peace. And happiness is the recognition that peace *is* that struggle; the recognition that struggle is the price of peace quite as much as that death is the price of life."

Chapter 27

February 4th is Rafaél's birthday. He thinks some time ago he may well have told Giselle that. But his memory these days is no longer to be trusted. And he certainly doesn't these days *expect* anyone else to remember his birthday. Barely does he do so himself.

But it *is* some kind of benchmark, some kind of ... God knows what. It requires marking ... yes, a bit like a dog marks a favourite tree! He's going to treat himself by purchasing a small painting he's seen in a matchbox gallery in Chiswick. For weeks he's been mulling whether or not to buy it. Now his mind's made up. Yes, he *would* like the work on his walls. It'll look very good in the hall, right next to the mirror. He'll combine it with buying himself a sinful *gâteau* lunch at Patisserie Valerie. Damn the cholesterol. A birthday comes but once a year.

His absence suits Polly. She *has* remembered it's his birthday. She and the other two women are planning a dinner for him. Rodolfo might or might not be coming. They had intended to prepare everything in Giselle's flat. About half-an-hour previously, though, the phone had gone: Rodolfo. He'd be there within the hour. Giselle was abject. She was terribly sorry, but she needed some privacy. Could they maybe give her a couple of hours?

They had told her not to be silly. That, of course, she needed her privacy; that with Rafaél absent there was no problem. They simply took all the ingredients upstairs.

On the basis that there was a dearth in London of Syracusan-Bostonian-Orphalese restaurants, they were going to make him what would have been the *specialité de la maison* had there been one: antipasti, followed by real hamburgers. And for pudding Saskja would try to recreate *tsifalla*.

She stares fixatedly as the chocolate melts very slowly in the pan. She knows she will become Polly's lover – she knows that in the way that she knows she's got two eyes. She doesn't know *how* she knows that; and even less how she feels about it; or how it will feel. Sex with Polly. She cannot even imagine it – any part of it: either the giving or the receiving. And that's alright. That even adds a certain frisson to the anticipation. But it is not alright that she still feels ambivalent about it.

There is electricity in the air. Polly can feel it. It's sexual and it's so obvious it could have neon signs flashing at it. And so charged it could power those signs by itself.

She keeps repeating to herself over and over in her head, Polly, almost like a mantra, "When the gods want to punish us, they answer our prayers ... When the gods want to punish us ..." Her heart it beating hard ... thumping hard ... so hard it's painful. 'This is the stuff that dreams are made on.' "Yeah, and dream on, Polly, dream on." The whole scene is painful. And becoming forced now. Contrived. The casualness, *so* contrived. "How you doing there, kid?" *so, so* contrived. The small talk, the banter and the "pass-the-butter", all of it now contrived, all signifying anything other than what the words actually mean.

Saskja, she notices, has her arms around her midriff. She seems to be fixated by the chocolate melting in the pan. The poor girl – and she can see it – is in some sort of pain, some sort of real pain. Is she mistaking electricity for suffering? She herself, Polly, has been chopping onions. Her eyes are still smarting. She goes to the sink, rinses her hands under the tap, dries her eyes with her wrists, then her hands on a convenient tea-towel. She wanders to the stove – casually – and on to Saskja. "You okay, honey?" she asks her.

Automatonly Saskja tells the melting chocolate, "I had an abortion, Polly."

"Oh, my poor child," Polly responds and, a mother with her daughter, pulls her to her breast to comfort her.

But Saskja doesn't want a mother's hug.

She pulls Polly's face to her and she kisses her. Clumsily. Misshapenly. ... Desperately.

And Polly knows better. She's mature, sensible, caring. She knows this is a child, a child that needs mothering, knows that to have sex with this child now would be taking advantage ... and also knows that none of that – not at this moment – matters a damn.

***

Rodolfo swings through the door like a monkey through the jungle canopy. His movements are lithe, elastic, effortless. He's loosening the tie around his neck as he does so. It's a nice tie: light blue silk, white polka-dots. Elegant. Expensive. She can't afford to buy him a tie like that. He doesn't buy ties for himself. He doesn't have the time. The Christmas presents were all the more valuable for having been bought in time he doesn't have. Emily would have bought the tie.

He pecks her on the cheek. It is a husband's kiss, not a lover's, a 'back from work' kiss, not a kiss of pyrotechnics, a 'Fűr Elise' kiss not an 'Eroica'.

She pours him a drink. Publicly he drinks fine and expensive malt whiskies; privately he's considerably more partial to a '*gin-con-gin*' – gin with ginger ale, lots of ice, any old gin. He splays his jacket onto the couch and lopes effortlessly into the bedroom.

Giselle stays in the middle of the sitting room, on the spot where he had kissed his thank you for the drink. She's thinking. She's wondering.

He, though, is talking. He always talks when he's there. He talks non-stop. He's been talking today since he arrived. Talking non-stop. She used to listen to his talk. She even used to be mesmerised by it. Now it could almost be a record: How bad the traffic is, how impossible to find a place to park, the incompetence of the hospital management, his juniors ... God! his students ... and as for Andrew Bernard ... call himself an anaesthetist? Next thing he'll simply be handing out bullets for patients to bite on ... and on ... and on and on and on ... None of it in the least offensive, some of it funny, some of it even important. But all variations on a theme so often played that the cd is wearing out.

As she feels worn out.

Standing in the sitting room she imagines him undressing. She's not even on his radar-screen at the moment. He has no idea where she is, nor what she's doing. Because the chatter clacks on she presumes he thinks she's still within earshot but she wonders whether that even really matters to him. She lets her arms drop heavily from her shoulders and orang-utans into the bedroom.

He's in bed already. She had known he would be. She'd seen it: him undressing, him springing into bed. He's reading a small sheaf of papers stapled together in the top left-hand corner. Latterly he always comes to bed with a small sheaf of papers stapled together in the top left-hand corner.

"We're not going to have sex," she tells him, searching for detachment and finding only listlessness.

"Really?" This is a genuine question. There is no malice in it, no disappointment or hints at betrayal. His eyes peer at her over his half-moon reading glasses.

"I should have said earlier. I'm sorry."

"Is this because … is it you and my father, this? Or your pregnancy?"

"I don't know."

"Is it us?"

"I don't know."

"Have I done something?" he asks, looping a finger over the arm of his glasses, removing them from his nose and letting them dangle on the finger.

"No," she replies, now finding the detachment she had sought earlier.

"Are you coming to bed?"

"I just said …"

"Not for sex. Not for sex, Giselle. Just for … well, company or something."

"I don't know what I feel," she says, the blandness riding the tumult of her emotions like a dolphin cresting a hurricane's wave.

"I'll just read this," he says, matching her blandness-for-blandness, replacing his glasses. "Mind if I take a little nap afterwards?"

"Are you staying for your father's party?"

"Emily would have wanted to come."

"Of course."

"I thought I'd stay and have a drink with you all."

"Sleep as long as you like. You look tired."

"Thank you." She turns to go. "Giselle." She stops in the doorframe, but doesn't turn around. "Emily, Giselle, would have wanted to come."

"Sleep well," she says. And quietly she closes the bedroom door.

Chapter 28

He'd wanted to do something nice for her. And, no, he never expected effusive thanks for his gifts. Not even, really, any sort of thanks. Chaperoning children through adolescence cures anyone of *that* ambition. But he'd hoped it would make her happy, hoped that he'd see joy in her eyes. Her happiness was becoming daily more important to him. Oh, she was trying to dimple at him, she'd mouthed the appropriate words: "Oh, my!", "How *lovely*", "What a great idea", but in the event, deep in her eyes, was not glee but a morose ennui or a fidgety moroseness, he wasn't sure which. But he does know he's disappointed.

He gazes again at her. Her eyes are now focussed on the stage, on the plush red velvet, tapestried with the Queen's insignia, still sepulchring its mysteries. She is so lovely. Outside and in. He wants to make her happy. Possibly even more than he wants her to be happy.

He pulls himself together. He's her husband, for God's sake. He can't possibly be falling in love with her. That's so *de trop* as almost to seem unseemly! Almost ... well ... perverse. No, damn it, if she wasn't enjoying herself, well, that was tough luck. *He* could. And would. This is a big occasion for him: his first visit to the Royal Opera House, Covent Garden.

The conductor strides into the pit. He is greeted with deferential applause. You know much more about music than we do, that applause tells him, transport us on music's magic carpet. Giselle, he notices, sits forward in her seat. The notes skedaddle off the wall like a trillion different Titanias, all of them zinging their magic, twinkling their fairy-dust, opening the gates to orisons fantastic and infinite – and of infinite beauty.

It had started months ago. He'd seen a poster, Rafaél: The Royal Opera House announcing its spring season. He'd been with Polly. Travelling back, to be specific, from the Tower of London. The name 'Giselle' had leapt out of that poster at him – maybe it had even jetéed out at him. Right there and then he'd detoured to Covent Garden. He'd been determined he would get tickets, thought Giselle would love to see the ballet after which she had been named.

"All Emmas," he had said to Polly, "should read Jane Austen's novel, all Rebeccas Daphne du Maurier's. All Ivans, not just the avuncular variety, should be frog-marched to see 'Uncle Vanya'. It's some kind of debt one has to one's name."

"You're talking to someone, Rafa, who's put on far too many kettles for me to consider the matter frivolous," Polly lamented lugubriously. Nevertheless she had agreed that an evening watching someone else on their toes had the potential of being a great night out.

Giselle had been told she needed a fancy frock. She hadn't been told why. She had been reluctant to spend the small fortune necessary for such a purchase, even though the small fortune was not hers. Particularly as she needed a marquee! One (so she sincerely hoped!) she'd have no further need of in her life. But Rafaél had insisted it was part of her wedding present, had coaxed and had inveigled ... and her frugality had eventually succumbed. Saskja had needed no such coaxing. And she had been in on the secret. Free clothes to Saskja was Armanna from Heaven, and the *ballet* ...

Well ...

She had a musical box at home. She'd had it since she couldn't remember when, from way before she'd met Arkona. A ballerina twirled on its lid. Since she'd had the musical box, she'd always wanted to see a ballet. See one for real, that is. In the ... theatre.

And, if you want to talk about theatres ... well, they don't get much realer, theatres, than the Royal Opera House, Covent Garden: the ROH, as it's known afficionadoly.

It's now the interval. They are standing in the appropriately named 'Crush Bar'. They can see Polly wading, treacly, through the crush of best-bib-and-tuckered humanity. Giselle had not wanted to stay in her seat. Nor does she want the evening to end. She has been transported to delights outside of herself, but to ones also buried deep within her. She's enervated but completely relaxed, stunned but more lucid than she's ever been.

The beauty of a finely produced and exquisitely danced ballet is multi-layered, a benign spiral: one of rhapsody. But the helix of that spiral is not, despite the apparent effeteness of its champions, one that is in the least effete, but very much of the earth, very much (indeed) spit-and-sawdust. Dancers are physically just as fit as any sportsmen, fitter indeed than most. But the 'team spirit' involved in their performances is not devoted to the ephemeral 'high' of winning a game, but to an eternal high of seeking out the precious. This is a quest informed truly by the spirit. And as such, all the dancers on the stage (principals and corps), all their understudies in the wings, all the musicians in the pit ... all their teachers and coaches and wig-makers and wardrobe staff, they are all at some level shamans. They shepherd us to realms outside of all our selves, and to those deep within all our selves. They supply vitamins and protein to our higher 'I's, and wither glances of disaffection at our lower 'I's.

It is an art which is oomphy and bold and hormonal and physical and carnal – and incredibly erotic. And it overflows, perhaps therefore, with the magical and supernatural and divine. Giselle feels herself as close to God as she's ever been. In a distant land of distant sensations, yet a land which has been home to her all her life.

She doesn't go a bundle on the tradition of parents naming their progeny after themselves, else she would have been tempted, should her child prove to be a girl, to call her too Giselle. For the first time in her life she understands the thinking of her parents in the choice of her name. She even condones it.

They drink. They wow – about the dancing, the music, the sets and costumes, about the theatre and the orchestra and the central chandelier. They wow about the whole evening, in fact – how pretty the others look, or handsome. They wow until they have nothing left to wow about. Then their eyes do some more feasting, and their insides (including the insides of their heads and souls) do a bit more jigging and jumping for joy and a bit more reliving of glories just witnessed and a bit more lusciousing of glories yet-to-be-experienced.

In one such pause, Polly says: "The last three vital virtues, they are, right?, faith, hope and charity. I mean, the Christians did get that one right, right?"

The bell rings to resummon them to their seats. "Sounds like good dinner talk," suggests Rafaél, smiling broadly. He takes Giselle's arm to guide her on the steps. She gently slides her hand into his. Neither looks at the other. Neither says a word.

They are now seated in Joe-Allen's. This is no longer the luvvies' ambience which had made its name, but it is still convenient as a meeting-place and an eating-place. Even the odd actor occasionally still visits. They have already ordered.

Into the conversational vacuum (which is them all still mesmerised by the performance) Rafaél tosses: "I agree." The others look at him, wondering whether they have missed out on a segment of conversation, wondering to what he is alluding. "What Polly said in the interval … Faith, hope and charity. I agree that these are the last three vital virtues."

"As well as the three Graces," adds Giselle, her eyes still ballerinaing the spectacle which still pinions her.

"Define faith," says Saskja. "Before I decide if it is one of vital virtues, I have to know what you mean by 'faith'."

"It's very simple," says Giselle gently. "Faith is the belief in the unprovable."

"You know," Polly says, "I think I'd go along with that. For me it's almost easier to define by what it's not. It's not blind, for instance."

"No. Blind faith, this is not a good idea. Was it Abraham ordered by God to kill his son?"

"In my Bible," says Giselle.

"A man told by God to kill his son is either a psychopath," Rafaél suggests, "or worships a psychopath. Blindly to follow an instruction to kill your own son, that is not faith."

"There is so much evil perpetrated today in the name of faith that has nothing to do with faith," says Giselle. "It's probably one of the reasons faith today has such a bad name. It's so simple, if it is a tenet of your quotes 'faith' to do something obviously harmful or hurtful, then – for God's sake (and I used the word advisedly) – change your faith."

"Or change your God," says Rafa. He stills Polly with his eyes not to say that they have talked of this before.

"Or your God," agrees Polly, accepting Rafaél's enjoinment. Saskja has found an unusual appetite. She is attacking the bread as if she'd just returned from the desert after a fast of forty days and forty nights. "I'm fond of quoting Mark Twain," continues Polly, "when he said, 'My country right or wrong is like saying my mother drunk or sober'. Well, if Twain was right, then how even more important should it be that you sieve what is God-inspired or divinely inspired or metaphysical from that which has been venally inspired and which cynically invokes God's name because that is the most effective way to silence opposition.

"It never ceases to amaze me what some people choose to remember from the Bible, and what they don't. Talk about selective hearing. Now, I'm not a great believer in the Holy Text, but I seem to remember talk about it being harder for a rich man to pass into the kingdom of Heaven than for a camel, or something, to pass through the eye of a needle. Yes, I know that's an old chestnut. But it is still a chestnut which deserves its munching.

"Bob Dylan in 'With God On Our Side' ponders whether Judas Iscariot had God on his side. More importantly than that, I can't help feeling, we should be asking of ourselves how closely we emulate Judas. We are surrendering God to Caesar so that God can be crucified. And for thirty pieces of silver. However we define that sum. Or that God.

"And that communal Judasism today also – in an amazing contortion of logic – demands reverence as some kind of moral paragon. (And talking of semantic undertones, how about that similarity: between Judasism and Judaism!)

"There are in England today – you will have seen them – TV programmes where business moguls publicly demean their juniors or those 'pitching' entrepreneurial ideas, or where chefs lacerate their sous-chefs. The intention of them all, of course, is to underscore the propriety of methos … propriety/property: another convenient semantic accident? … to give credence to the fact that selfishness is acceptable, and leads to philanthropy. It also metamorphises these bullies into pundits. Their arrogance becomes something quite astonishing. And not only when they are bullying the defenceless on their own programmes. They somehow consider themselves to be experts – if not soothsayers – on an entire universe of problems. It is incredible to hear them speak. These television 'celebrities' (minor industrialists or not-nearly-as-clever-as-they-like-to-believe entrepreneurs) appear genuinely to believe they walk on water.

"Wealth – as, Rafa, you have said more than once – is only an indication of what has been taken. A person's worth can be measured only by what he gives. We have to find the currency by which that is possible. Clearly that can't be money. We've given money a few thousand years to prove its capability and to say that it has been found wanting is a bit like saying of molten lava that it is somewhat 'wanting' in heat.

"Faith? What has this to do with faith? Well, the faith I have, I have faith that mankind will find that currency. That these self-glorifying bullies and despots will be viewed not with reverence but with the pity they deserve. Even when they give, such people, they give only so that they may take. A public gift is no gift at all. It is an act of self-aggrandisement, a silencer on the muzzle of criticism … or a tax write-off.

"Such people, of course, dominate the media. Not just on-screen. How strange, when we invite nightly into our home such toxic attitudes, we become a society which is poisoned. There are filmmakers – of course there are – who break the mould: Michael Moore, we've talked about, John Pilger, latterly Chris Atkins, a few others. But I get the uncomfortable impression that these are granted their space only as a token to free speech, as something that can be cited as a proof that free speech exists, rather than out of any genuine commitment the media owners have, in fact, to free speech. Such media moguls seem remarkably adept at burying their scruples in China."

"I too have faith," Rafaél admits. "My faith is one in the essential goodness of man. I have said this before, but is fundamental. I believe that Man is born, not with original sin, but with original virtue. Man, in my (admittedly limited) experience, has a far greater propensity, and a far greater capacity, for good than he does for evil. Even those convicted of the most heinous crimes can show an extraordinary compassion.

"This is not to maintain that we are born as angels who then slowly slip further from grace. There are many, and large, genetic predispositions in all of us to all sorts of unpleasantnesses – some of them probably dating back to pre-human, even pre-primate days. For the manyeth time I repeat, one cannot cure a sickness until the sickness is diagnosed. Nor can we expect to control ourselves until we analyse what there is about us which stems from Nature and which from nurture.

"But we also need to diagnose our wellness. And finally wouldn't our emphasis be more healthily applied cheering that wellness? The wonderful that we are? The wonderfulness of us all? All of us as one entity, and all of us as separate entities? 'What a piece of work is a man. How express and admirable.' What excellent words. Wouldn't that be the most sensible application yet of seeing the glass as half-full rather than half-empty? How is it that we apply all the invocations to 'think positively' to every aspect of life bar the human condition? Is this not very contrary of us? And incredibly dangerous? Because thinking the worst of ourselves can, as we all know, become a self-fulfilling prophecy. Is there any area in which this could be more dangerous than when we are dealing with the entire of our species? Should we not stop thinking of the human race *as* a race? As a competition of some sort? As something where there are winners and losers?

"China now claims that no-one in China starves. When a regime suppresses free speech it cannot be surprised if its words are heard with scepticism. But let us for the moment give China the benefit of that doubt, let us suppose that claim to be true. And let us rejoice, therefore, in that achievement and let us applaud it. But that is not – as also I have said before – the end of the problem, my friends. Indeed, in a very real sense, is only the *start* of the problem. And the problems. It may be true that, without bread, Man cannot sustain life, but is also true that 'Man cannot live by bread alone'. The Chinese may have given their citizens life, but they have yet to give the overwhelming majority of them *a* life.

"And when people do not have *a* life, then they are often willing to forfeit life. These are the foot-soldiers for the plethora of al-Qaedas even now gestating, a plethora further swollen when we commit acts like constructing Guantanemo Bay or invading Iraq ... or misappropriating $23 billion there – twenty-three, my friends, *billion* dollars. Simply gone walkabout. Unaccounted for. Lost. How does anyone *lose* twenty-three billion dollars? Even someone as apparently inept as James Baker? How much Medicare does $23 billion buy you? How many new homes for tsunami victims? How many teachers who could help the next generation to find its potential?

"I hear so many extremist groups calling themselves 'the silent majority'. Is a claim made in the United States by the Ku Klux Klan and by the so-called 'Christian' right, by the *Sendero Luminoso* in my country and here by organisations like the National Front and, increasingly and worryingly, by a Christian right similar to, and largely funded by, similar sects in America. I don't believe any of those *are* the silent majority. If they are, it certainly do not square with my experience. I haven't met too many people who want to revert to the days when homosexuality and abortion were illegal, nor who would want schools to eschew Darwin and teach only Genesis, nor who refer to Muhammad as Satan, nor who want ethnic segregation. I don't believe that most people want to hate, as these extremists hate.

But I think they are frightened – and they are right to be frightened – and that such fear is being curdled into hatred."

"I see so many kids today," says Polly, "so angry – and so truculent because so angry. Hope too has been robbed from them. So very many angry people, but particularly the young people. And those kids, they think that by slobbing out, by acts of mindless vandalism or loutishness or by bullying the frail, that they are somehow expressing their disaffection with the status quo. And what (because we school them so badly) they will not see is that, as we have said before, they are the status quo's greatest allies.

"I want to say to those kids, 'Want to know how really to be a thorn in the side of the status quo? Start loving yourself. It is an act of rebellion, an act today of defiance.'

"We also talked before about globalisation's encouragement of fear. Fear's reaction is always reactionary. Always when we are frightened we prefer in such circumstances the devil we know. People today fear for their jobs, fear that their standard of living may be eroded, fear for the schooling (such as it is!) of their children, for the health care (such as it is!), for the drain of needed resources. And, no, these fears are not without foundation. With less foundation are the scapegoats found who can be blamed for this uncertainty: the asylum seekers I talked about, or migrant workers ... illegal immigrants ... drug dealers ... terrorists! And, sadly, there is a measure of truth too in these fears. But the truth is also that it is rarely the people themselves who are to blame for their situation, but an ethos which always seeks to paper over cracks rather than deal with the subsidence. It suits methos very well that we attack illegal immigrants – or Jews ... or whatever. It stops us joining together to attack what is, in fact, our common enemy.

"Sadly, our inability to join together to attack politically is likely to result in groups forming together to attack physically.

"It's interesting to note, as a by-the-by, that Professor Sachs (leastwise, if his book is to be believed) has nothing but scorn for his compatriates and their fears. Not a single word of indictment for all those companies exposed by Naomi Klein's important book, 'No Logo', not one word of rebuke for all the sportspeople and 'personalities' getting rich at the expense of slave labour ... No, let's please not attack anyone with any muscle who might be able to attack back. Let's attack the weak and the vulnerable ... the voiceless. And then let us claim – even better – that it is *they* doing the bullying. This is yet another measure (as if such were needed!) of the contempt globalisation has for real people with real problems.

"It is also, I think, ironic. We have said before that globalisation is only a euphemism for Americanisation. America as a country was founded on the principle that she would not be dictated to. Why does she imagine that other countries are any different? Why don't those Americans propagating globalisation look to their own history and discover from that the likelihood either of its efficacy, or of it being accepted? An imposed discipline, however benign, remains a despotism.

"Principles that become entrenched aren't principles any more. They become dogma. And dogma, almost by definition, becomes the antithesis of the principle from which it was founded. Dogma is like a rock: rigid, unyielding, static, sterile, incapable of being anything other than what it is. And finally really quite brittle. Plants cannot grow on it, animals cannot graze on it, it can sustain no life. Occasionally it has about it a statuesque grandeur. And within it occasionally can be found nuggets of gold. But such usually requires extensive mining. It helps form a landscape, but is not the *sine qua non* of life that water is ... or that principles are.

"The arcane is not the same as the archaic. Or vice versa. Often the archaic is not in the least bit esoteric, it is merely out-of-date. Dogma is *always* out-of-date. Worse than being a faith which is blind, it becomes a faith which does the blinding. It is a bonanza for lawyers, but for humanity it is a mamba and a boa: It both poisons and constricts. It matters not one jot if that dogma is Christian or Islamic, Hindu or Zoroastrianist, political, constitutional, cultural, moral or, even, linguistic: dogma cannot be anything but stagnant, and anything stagnant stinks.

"My faith is so similar to yours, Rafa. I have faith that the world will adopt principles and abjure dogma, that it will encourage not only life but living, that 'getting a life' will not be an exhortation to couch-potatoes but one to us all to allow *everyone* to get a life. The goal of a Buddhist life – at least, so one of its prayers has it – is 'a good and peaceful death', which can then be used as an example to others. And that is a good aim, a worthy aim. There is indeed a whole school of thought which believes the concepts of Heaven and Hell to be your state-of-mind on your death-bed. I tend to think, though, that death is quite capable of looking after itself. And I do not believe that the goal, the end, of life is just life, the fact of being alive. Surely the slogan of the twenty-first century should be: 'Let the end of life be a life'. Would that not be a standard worth marching behind?

"My faith – the faith I learnt from you, my dear Rafa – is twofold. I believe Man is basically born good and that what he needs, rather than the historic whip, is for his good in the future to be carrotted. And I believe Man is good enough to march behind the banner of 'The end of life is *a* life', and that such march will mark the start of a genuine civilisation, rather than the 'spinisation' in which we live today. Let's all work towards a world where our successors ... well, first of all, exist – that is reasonably important ... and who then look back on us today as the Darkest Age Before the Dawn of True Humanity."

The waiter is mincingly camp. He has penetratingly blue eyes, blond, crew-cut hair and a designer stubble of pretty much the same length. He distributes the plates in a curious mix of deference and disdain, in a movement which is a mix of a Playboy-bunny dip and a potter throwing clay onto a wheel.

They eat in silence for a while.

"Such faith," eventually says Saskja, "acceptable as fifth vital virtue." She says it so seriously that the others start laughing. Initially Saskja is perplexed by this reaction. But then, her perplexity not in the least assuaged, she starts to join in the laughter. She feels

Polly's hand on her knee. She resolves not to mind it. And when Polly then squeezes that knee, she too squeezes out a flicker of a smile which she shyly aims sidelong at her. "And fifth life-affirming idea?"

"Do you think," asks Rafa, "we might already have tripped over that?"

"We have?" asks Polly.

"You don't think that the fifth life-affirming idea is mankind's possession, not of original sin, but original virtue?"

"Original virtue?" Polly parrots. She takes a mouthful of haddock, no longer the piping hot it had been when brought to the table.

"Yes," Rafaél confirms.

"Yes," Giselle says. "Original virtue, I think that is a worthy life-affirming idea. I also like 'the end of life is *a* life'."

"Me too," says Saskja. "Know what else I like?"

"What?" asks Rafa.

"Pudding," she replies. "No, I am wrong: puddings."

Chapter 29

Suddenly she had known, Saskja, that this whole liaison, even the attraction behind it, that it was a charade, a fiction. Yet another absurdity. A desperate hope that someone else could love her, that she was to someone – *any*one – loveable. She was no more a lesbian than she was a fish. Oh, she had nothing against lesbians (or fish), but she wasn't one. She hadn't found the intimacy repulsive, just unexciting. There had been no passion, no euphoria, no whoosh.

"Polly," she had said, mid-being-fondled, "I so very sorry." There were tears in her eyes.

And Polly had immediately understood. "Not a problem, hon," she had said to her. But it had been a problem. It still was. As she lies in the remarkably uncrumpled sheets, smoking a cigarette in a manner she is forcing herself to be untroubled, her mind zigzags through the razor-wire of so many problems.

Polly, of course, doesn't know Saskja feels absurd. If asked, she'd probably guess that Saskja feels ... embarrassed, perhaps. Polly also feels absurd. This is a young woman, pretty, universally desired, how could she have been so dumb, so *stupid* as to imagine she could possibly fall for her? A drunk as she was? A tired old harridan as she was? A tired old – let's face it, Polly – has-been?

"You okay?" she asks Saskja. She's now desperate – damn the affair – to hold onto the friendship. It had really only been the friendship she'd ever cared about, it is the friendship that she craves. Saskja's. And Giselle's. Rafaél's too – maybe, especially Rafaél's. The sex? She'd always believed that was a fantasy. She should have kept it as such. Fool that she was. Damn fool that she was. What scares her most now is that the love is also a fantasy. Saskja's love, Rafaél's. It's that which *terrifies* her.

Polly has sealed too many of the alleys in her mind, her soul. She has opted too often to drown pain and not confront it. She's grappling for motives buried now too deep for her to reach them. She doesn't know, but we can, that she too needs to feel not only that she *is* loved, but that she *can* be. "You okay?" she asks Saskja.

"Can you ever forgive me?" Saskja replies.

"Not a problem, hon. Not a problem."

***

A day later. Giselle has asked Rafaél to pop downstairs. When it's convenient. It's nothing urgent. She'd just like to run something by him.

He'd rung the doorbell in the street. She'd buzzed to let him in.

"You lose your key?" she asks casually, as he slides by the stripped pine dining-table in the conservatory.

"No," he replies firmly.

She trips Fonteynly to the kitchen, flicks on the switch of the electric kettle. "You don't need to ring the bell."

"Yes," he says, "I do."

She returns from the kitchen. She hears the earnestness of his tone, and matches it. "No, Rafa, you do not."

He understands. He thinks he understands. No, he does understand. Does he understand? He hopes he understands when he says, "Oh!"

"I haven't told him yet," she says, not able to look him in the eyes, gazing at the black-and-grey rectangles of the carpet. He had understood! "I wanted to know ... wanted to know what you think, Rafa."

"I think this has nothing to do with me."

"I'd like it to."

There is an uncluttered pause between them. Their eyes search the other's for the words that defy articulation. At that level an entire conversation takes place, and all the contents are ingested and *di*gested, but neither would be able to express vocally what has been exchanged. "Oh," Rafaél says, eventually, again.

A shorter pause. Another flow between them outside the purview of the dictionary. Probably for that the more clearly understood.

"I'm not talking about not seeing him," she says.

"No."

"He's the father of my child. I would never deny that. I would never deny *him*. It wouldn't be ... I'm not talking about not seeing him."

"Of course not. Good, I mean. Yes. 'Yes,' I mean, he is – 'yes' – the father of your child."

She weights the words: "So, Rafa, are you."

"No." She's hurt. She doesn't want to be, but she is. This is a rebuff. "I will, of course, do what I can. I will, I hope, be a step-father – I hope a loving and conscientious step-father. The father, though, I can never be."

"You're not an easy person to pay compliments to."

"Excuse me." He slashes, coyly, a flickered grin at her. She wanders back to the kitchen, pours the now boiling water over the two mint-tea-bags she's left in the blue mugs with the yellow insides. From there she trills over her shoulder a budgerigar insouciance. "What would you think about moving in?"

He moves to the kitchen door, leans on its jamb. A rather striking icon, probably Russian, possibly eighteenth century, hangs just below where his arm is resting. "Me?"

"You."

"Move in?"

"We are married, Rafa."

"I'm not sure. Marriage is one thing. Living together, though, that, Giselle, is *big*."

She's going to choose to believe he's joking as a defence. "I know," she says. "God, you really *are* a hard person to pay a compliment to."

"You've thought about this?"

She feels like telling him, No, she hasn't. She just dreamed it up on a whim whilst the kettle was boiling. She chooses not to. "I'm not talking about sleeping together. Not yet, anyway. Well, yes, I am – talking, I mean, about us sleeping together. ..." She has her back to him, is dunking the tea-bags to encourage their infusion. Her voice is very laid-back in timbre, but her body-language is strangulated by tension. "… but not 'sleeping' together. Not sex, Rafa, is what I mean."

"No."

"Not yet. Not …" She points vaguely at her womb.

"Maybe not even after that."

"I'm terrified, Rafa, to look at you."

"That I do understand. Not exactly George Mooney, am I?"

"Oh, you!" And she does turn around. And she does face him. She is laughing gently and the laughter has transformed uncertainty into an innocent brazenness – innocent because undemanding. "You're a good-looking man and you know you are. Even a very good-looking man."

"And the moon, she is made of green cheese."

"Well?"

"Saskja?"

"Good question."

"Good questions usually receive no answers."

"I thought … Well, she will be going home soon. I thought … well, if it was okay with you, of course … I thought, maybe, you could just change places."

"So I'd sleep in Saskja's bed?"

"Perhaps just to begin with. You don't think it's a good idea? Just, Rafa, till … you know … we know a little better. Know each other a little better. I mean, you have no idea what I'm like, how difficult I am to live with. You'd have thought … a nun, well, you'd have thought she'd be used to sharing her home … a nun, you'd have thought, would have picked up some good habits along the way …" She'd made a funny, and she now looks to Rafaél to assess his appreciation of it. But the pun clearly eludes him. She continues her wade through the miasma of uncertainties. "… Not so, I fear, with me. Just ask Saskja. Maybe, before we think about anything else, maybe we should just see … you know, how easily we can put up with one another. *If* we can."

"I'm not easy either. Not to live with."

"Maybe we'd be like double-negatives, cancelling each other out."

"In Spanish they don't cancel each other out."

"London is in England, isn't it? It wasn't, I mean, transported overnight to the Iberian peninsula?"

"Thank you."

"Yes?"

"I can think of not one thing which would give me greater pleasure." And then he allows the tiniest innuendo to smirk in his eye. "Well, perhaps one thing."

She laughs, turns her back on him. Uses the back of the teaspoon to drain the teabag before using the spoon's bowl to remove them from the mugs and slam-dunk them into the sink. "Clooney, by the way."

"Clooney?"

"George Mooney, you said. It's Clooney you're thinking of."

"No, no, Mooney. Sells the vegetables in Shepherd's Bush market. Who's George Clooney?"

"Ah, *that* George Mooney."

"Yes."

"You should have said." She hands him his tea, pecks him lightly on the cheek as she passes him on her way to the sitting room. They have been married for thirty-five years. And, just for the moment, their history's tonnage becomes the age and weight of a hatchling.

Chapter 30

Oh, he blamed himself as well. Of course he did. But Giselle couldn't be absolved from all guilt. There was a copy, for God's sake, of 'Three Men In a Boat' in her flat. The spine had been broken. Presumably therefore she had read it. And presumably therefore she was as aware as he was of the perils attendant on entering the maze at Hampton Court Palace. And yet here they were. With her confinement due in a fortnight or so. Madness. A folly as great as this maze was a folly. Did Cardinal Wolsey really have nothing better to do with his time than spend hours looping from one verdant cul-de-sac to another? Or was that effectively the story of his life? Was that the story of *all* our lives?

On the plus side, though, Giselle seems very relaxed, even bubbly, full of bounce and vigour. It is one of those glorious days of late winter when the bite of the chill finds again its November baby-teeth but whose tartness is sweetened by a robust sun cock-o'-the-walking in a cornflower sky. It is such a splendid day that it is a surprise to them all how few fellow sightseers there are. The car park had been almost embarrassingly empty – like a theatre auditorium where only a dozen tickets have been sold.

Perhaps it's his imagination, but it seems to Rafaél that the Tudor bricks take exception to this slight. As if the tourists' absence were a snub to their beauty or their history or their significance. It also seems to Rafaél that the towers of the façade uncannily resemble cardinals, their brick red like cassocks, their chimneys zucchettoed, their aspect rotund and self-important, even a little bit ridiculous.

"Hope?" he asks. "The sixth vital virtue?"

"The only hope I can cope with right now," says Polly, "is the hope that one day we'll get out of here."

"I think time has gone when we can only hope," suggests Saskja. "I think today hope must be pro-active. I think today hope must not be just passive, just waiting, praying, I think today hope must also be doing."

"My first boyfriend – first *real* boyfriend –," says Giselle, "he was an ex-drug addict, 'in recovery,' as he called it. He said, one of the first things he got back when he got clean was hope. Without hope, he said, tomorrow becomes a matter of indifference. Which means you do nothing to make that tomorrow a better place."

"There used to be a bit of graffiti," Polly chips in, peering as she does so through the hedge, in the forlorn hope of discovering whether or not the parallel aisle might lead towards the exit, "'Due to lack of interest, tomorrow has been cancelled.' Sorry. I thought it was kinda *à propos*."

"I have often thought," Giselle continues, "the world today behaves very much like an addict. I compared it before to a psychotic, but it's even closer to an addict: incredibly selfish, totally irresponsible, arrogant and self-absorbed, prepared to sell all the family's heirlooms to pay for a habit now out of control, self-deceiving, both mendicant and mendacious, absolutely without scruples or principles. Just so long as it gets its fix. I once thought about writing a book, 'My Name's God and I'm an Addict'. It is terrifying how well the analogy holds. The ethos of the world is the ethos of the junkie. We seriously want to bequeath a junkie's ethos to our children?"

"Saskja is also right, though," says Rafaél. "I'm never sure what the word means, 'pro-active'. To me it sounds like sound-byte-speak. Designed to sell yoghurt or car batteries or something. But, *claro*, is past the time when we can sit and hope that those who maintain they care for us actually do. The evidence is now monumental – and I suggest irrefutable – that not only do they not, but also that they do not want to. We are not their concern. *They* are their concern. They, their institutions, their power, their wealth, their perceived kudos – and all of those things as they apply too to their friends."

"Tweedle-dum's chums!"

"Quite, Polly. But, Saskja, I also agree with Giselle. I think the world does seem to behave like an addict out of control. Mayhap we have to organise an intervention. Interventions are sessions organised by those who love the addict when that addict is obliged to confront his problem. Mayhap we who love the world have to oblige it to face up to the problem it has.

"But, mayhap even before that, we have to inculcate it with hope. Mayhap without hope any tomorrow that arrives will be chaotic and shambolic and putrid.

"If today you fail to brush your teeth tomorrow your breath will smell. Soon after your breath will be rank. And your teeth will start to fall out. Your mouth will become a chaos, a shambles ... putrid. For how long has mankind not cleaned its teeth? Perhaps, who knows?, since it started. Mayhap that's the fault in our species which makes our annihilation inevitable. Mayhap," he says pointedly at Polly, "that is the seed mankind contains which will lead to its own destruction. I don't know. We have to 'hope', though, such is not the case.

"And, yes, Saskja, certainly we need to 'do' – but *in* that hope. Else we are 'doing' in the kind of vacuum Nature abhors and Man finds disorientating. We need to speak in the hope we will be heard, we need to protest in the hope that others join us.

"We need to avoid violence, because we hope there is a tomorrow, and a tomorrow heir to a violent today will itself be violent.

"We have to be exigent today about our freedom and our freedoms because without them there is no hope that tomorrow will be better than today.

"We must demand a rigorous commitment to honesty, because else there is no hope that tomorrow's advances will not be ersatz advances and not progress indeed.

"We have to hope that, communally, we have what it takes to do what it takes. You know why? Because finally without hope there is no hope."

"Hallelujah!" Giselle. She has spotted the exit.

They walk hand-in-hand, she and Rafa. They are flanked by Saskja and Polly. The swap has been implemented: Saskja is now living in Rafaél's flat. He is sleeping in Giselle's guest room. Saskja and Polly never allude to their ... whatever it was. But it is Banquo's ghost. And a ghost with voracious needs all of its own. It encroaches everywhere, eats ravenously, quaffs Falstaffly, sprawls ubiquitously, pokes, prods, nudges, nods. Neither has told anyone else about the incident. Which has less to do with respecting the other's privacy than the other's embarrassment or perceived embarrassment – or perhaps their own embarrassment. There is bonhomie in their life together and camaraderie and a lot of laughter. But both are also glad, privately, that Saskja's visit is drawing to a close.

The gardens at Hampton Court may not be formed with the regimental exactitude (in both senses) of Blenheim, they may lack the pomp of Versailles or the orgy of hue that is Monet's garden in Giverny, but there is a majesty to them which is both distinguished and restrained. And which is at variance both with the Machiavellian politicking of Wolsey and the egomaniacal peacocking of Henry VIII. The grass is of a magnificent green – not any fly-by-night green, not any '*nouveau vert*', but a green with its roots deep into the soil of aeons. There are still crocus, gales of snowdrops. Some pioneering daffodils have intrepidded their bonneted heads towards a sun still undecided whether or not to unpack its bags; the first buds are shivering plaintively on branches which seem, Adam-and-Eve like, suddenly to have become aware of their nakedness and, now blushing, are groping feverishly for fig-leaves.

"I vote for individuality," says Giselle. She is making for a bench she has seen, and which is luring her to its lair with all the urbane aplomb of a melodrama villain twirling his moustachios. It's dark green and glossy and, by the standard of bench-painting, exemplarily executed. The synthetic colour, though, merely serves to underscore how pedestrian is man's attempt at colour measured against the richness, the poetry, the profundity which is Nature's. "As the sixth life-affirming idea," she explains as she hurtles for the bench, "I vote for individuality. And for the respect of that individuality. '*Vive la différence*' as a political and moral and economic objective. As their dynamo." With which she plonks herself down heavily – and gratefully – onto the olive-green bench. No goosedown pillow ever felt as good. She plunges into her handbag and removes her sunglasses, then imitates the daffodils by craning her head towards the sun. She bathes in that sun, as if it *were* water. She allows it to splash over her, she allows herself to be doused by it, she elephants in it, hippopotamuses in it. And, again just as if it were water, she feels cleansed by it and refreshed by it. Revitalised by it. To bathe in the sun is both to praise life and to bask in it.

"Look at that lawn," says Rafaél.

"No two blades of grass alike, right?" says Polly. "Excuse me. That is what you were going to say, right?"

Rafaél acknowledges that it was, whilst not being overfond of such interruption. "Nowhere," says Saskja, "in the world. No blade of grass the same, no housefly, no ant ... not even a pebble. Not even, famously, a snowflake."

"And you are seriously telling me you don't find that amazing?" Rafa asks. He sits down next to Giselle. His face too glides towards the sun. The others assume his question to have been rhetorical. In short order so does he himself. "A lawn," he continues, "is only an agglomeration of individual blades. Gardeners don't look after blades of grass, they tend a lawn. And mayhap that's even allegorical. Mayhap that is the weakness of socialism – that it creates gardeners unable to see the blades of grass for the lawn. And mayhap one of the core weaknesses of capitalism is that it expects those blades of grass to nurture themselves. If that allegory has some truth to it, then too the weakness of globalisation is that it has managed to combine the weakest element of both schools of thought. Globalisation protects neither the lawn, nor the individual blades of grass. It doesn't even protect the gardener.

"Generals gloat in their victories whilst soldiers mourn their fallen friends. Laws seek to apply blanket proscriptions to a universe of individual dramas. And, of course, is very often a large part of the lawyer's remit to prove how the generality of a law does not apply to the particular of his brief. And that, of course, is perfectly honourable."

"And then, also of course," says Polly, "other lawyers apply such arguments on behalf of clients who are clearly in breach of the law's intention, but who can wriggle through some kind of slipshod or ambiguous phrasing."

"Is one of the costs of freedom," says Rafaél. "Freedom as a commodity does not come cheap. Freedom – I have said this before –, even before is a right, is a responsibility. Freedom of speech means sometimes we will be offended; freedom from economic servitude means sometimes we will be inconvenienced; freedom to be ourselves means granting everyone else the freedom to be *them*selves."

"I lived once in this apartment block in Kansas," says Polly. "The residents' committee, you couldn't believe it, they'd invented more regulations than there are in San Quentin. The front doors all had to be painted the one colour, there were no plants allowed to adorn the outside of the apartments, no window-boxes – nothing (certainly from the outside) that would stamp any individuality on the place, any character. What most killed me about that was it was these selfsame people who were, to a man, vociferous in their complaints about the Mao suits then being foisted on the Chinese."

"Finally," says Rafa, "there is no humanity without individuality – and no individuality without humanity."

"We all wear uniforms of one sort or another," suggests Giselle, her face still arching towards the sun's rays. "There is even an argument which says that, by insisting *everyone* wear the same clothes, you are in fact encouraging a deeper individuality, rather than suppressing it. That, if inevitably our clothes make an inaccurate statement about us, why not allow them to make a statement about us that is clearly untrue? Nothing could be further from the truth than that we are all the same.

"How often do we in the West – like Polly, your friends of the apartment committee – ..."

"Were no friends of mine."

"How often do we emulate the thinking behind the Mao suits? Many companies today insist that their employees wear a suit and tie," she continues. "That these may be more attractive than Mao suits does not alter the fact that the goal is uniformity, not individuality. Employees – so their employers would argue – are not at such times representing themselves, but the company employing them. Which is a theory that is understandable, possibly even acceptable, provided such is confined to their working hours. It ceases to be acceptable when companies believe (as increasingly they seem to) that they have rights too over their employees' conduct outside of working hours."

"I think," says Saskja, "that it less that we make statements than that we hear them. That we *want* to hear them."

Polly bids her explain. They are now line abreast on the bench, all their faces toasting in the sun, and all their conversation is directed thither as if this were some communal invocation to Ra.

"We see crew-cut we say to ourselves 'skinhead'," says Saskja. "It could be cancer victim. We see Volvo, we see safe, middle-aged, middle-class. It could be car inherited or bought from friend. Appearances, I think, say very much less than we hear from them. There are very many more types of human being in world than makes of car, or fashions of clothes. Appearances, as I say, say very much less than we hear.

"We seem to like to rush to judgement. It should be that, I think, one of seven deadly sins. Much disagreement and dissent stems from it. We do judge books by covers – literally, so I hear tell, as well. And we let ourselves down when we do. Not every man who has spent twenty-seven years in prison is President Mandela. But likewise Mr Mandela was not only remarkable prisoner on Robben Island. And this all part of racism and/or sexism and/or any other –ism you can mention. It part of the need you once talked about, Rafa, with Polly of creating those you can disrespect."

"President Mandela," says Rafaél, "is a remarkable human being. An example in very many ways to us all. Certainly he is a symbol. Even more certainly, though – as you say, Saskja –, he was far from the only remarkable person involved in that struggle. A struggle which is a hope to all of us, because it exemplifies the idea that when the right atmosphere is created, change can be made. Even against insuperable odds. And that change sometimes just *has* to be made. The world is not facing one such situation today, but situations running into their tens, if not their hundreds: from the suppression of women in too many countries, not all of them Islamic, to the treatment of aborigines and indigenous nations, to the illegal occupation of sovereign states by invaders, to child prostitution, to female circumcision, to poisoned water and poisoned food and poisoned airwaves and poisoned values. And on and on."

"And on and on and on and on," says Polly.

"But it also exemplifies the fact," Rafa continues, "that the righting of a fundamental wrong is not the end of the process, but its beginning. What did Churchill say? 'Is not the end, is not even the beginning of the end, but it *is* perhaps the end of the beginning.' The end of apartheid was also the end only of the beginning. Mayhap some of the disappointment could have been allayed if that had been understood from the outset.

"Our age today likewise could be the end of the beginning of Man: could be the end of man cruel, and the beginning of indeed man*kind*.

"If you have travelled some time in the wrong direction, when you turn around, you do not magically start again from the point at which you took the wrong turn. You first of all have to drive back the distance you have erroneously come.

"And when we start on a *new* course we won't immediately get it right. That doesn't mean -- not necessarily – that we need to abandon that course. Examine it, of course. Of course, examine it. Examination is always an essential. But not necessarily abandon it. This is where principles become indispensable. If the principle is right, eventually a way will be found; if a principle is wrong, then the way cannot be found; and if there are no principles we abandon the concept of a destination, so we never leave the roundabout.

"We now have tests for children, from infancy forth. To inculcate into them a competitive spirit from the very outset. As if there weren't enough competition already in this world. Of course there is nothing wrong with testing children. Of course there isn't: *provided* that what is being tested is whether or not some factor of education has been properly absorbed, as opposed to the pupil merely being either a parrot or compliant. There is nothing *right* with 'testing' a child if thereby decisions are made which will affect the rest of that child's future. Nor is there anything right if is to devise Alice-in-Wonderland 'league tables', which studiously ignore all other salient facts.

"Education should only mean one thing: to lead out (from the Latin root which I can't now remember), to draw out of the individual child – yes, Saskja, I still am talking about individuality – his or her potential. That has to mean to reveal to that child the potential within him or her, and to instil into that child an unassailable sense of his or her own worth – to let that child know, unequivocally, that his potential (or hers) is so enormous (as it is) that the struggle (which it is) to release it is worth the lifetime's effort such requires – which it does. I make absolutely no apology for having said that before. I will say it again."

"Over and over."

"And, yes, Polly, over again. Until education has that commitment, it will not be the manufacturer of civilisation but of serfdom. Finally a society cohered by serfdom will collapse. If only because serfdom murders the person who could cure AIDS ... or the plague or smallpox or anthrax. A society will only genuinely cohere if such cohesion is voluntary. And if you feel you need proof of that, just look at some of the families you know.

"There is much wrong with South Africa today. *Very* much wrong with it. That situation was not helped when the then president of the country, Mr Mbeke, denied the AIDS epidemic running riot there. This sort of denial is what we would have expected from the apartheid regime, not from one founded on the principles of forgiveness and truth. But, that aside, virtually everything else wrong with South Africa today was entirely predictable. Including the cynical way in which Friedman's Chicago School (as it is called) hijacked its egalitarian principles and stood them on their head, including too the bitter disappointment of so many of its citizens that the end of apartheid was not the end of subjugation. Because we live in a world of instant coffee, instant global communication, even instant – perish the thought – annihilation, we think too there can be instant solutions to problems, some of which have been millennia in their construction. Mayhap are even inherent in the human condition.

"We talked, Polly and I, about his book. In which President Mandela opines that the thing which most frightens us is our own potential ... Excuse me, Polly. This, I know, you have heard before. ... But we are, I think, less frightened of our own potential than by what we suspect might be the inferiority of my potential compared to yours.

"Throughout history, therefore, we have sought to suppress potential rather than encourage it. And it doesn't matter who is in charge of the educational structure, because that terror remains true to all of us, of whatever class in society, whether we be one of the haves, or the have-nots, or the not-in-a-million-years-will-they-haves. Why do multi-billionaires continue to strive for more money? Those who have demonstrably (certainly in one sense) realised their potential? Because they remain scared that your potential is greater than theirs. Because they need the reassurance given them by their wealth that their 'worth' is greater than yours."

"I think such billionaires would also argue, Rafa, that their choice is not that absolute; that wealth is a fluid substance. It either advances. Or it retreats."

"These are the dictates," Rafa returns, "of the *institution* of wealth. And why have the wealthy allowed such an institution to be created around them? Because is such an easy way they can be considered 'worthy'. And is, at core, for this reason that almost all such multi-billionaires and most multi-*millionaires* would fight tooth-and-nail against another system being devised of economics, of quantum economics ... a system of distributing assets which is not exclusively monetary. Because that would also mean there would exist another measure of worth. I just cannot say it too often: 'a bank balance is a measure only of how much a person has taken; worth is a measure of how much a person gives.' A person is not 'worth' a million pounds or a billion dollars. He has taken a million pounds or a billion dollars. What he is worth is the bedtime story he reads to his daughter, or the tree he plants to help the environment, or the help he tenders a blind man crossing the road.

"By assessing 'worth' in purely mercenary terms we are exacerbating an enormous problem. Most people already feel unworthy. They do not need to feel such unworthiness confirmed. Just as is easier to teach than to learn, to talk than to listen, is so very much easier to demean others than to grant worth to ourselves. Is one of the reasons why sloth is indeed one of the seven deadly sins. We have just allowed sloth for too many centuries, and for too many reasons, to be defined wrongly – which, thinking about it, is yet another manifestation of sloth."

"And yet," says Polly, "lawns are so much lovelier than the sum of all its blades. Not too much individuality, I'm thinking, around parades. .... I'm thinking the state occasions here: the Trooping of the Colour, Diana's funeral. All the pomp around them, all the pageantry and spectacle and colour. All the history. I don't care how much of a pacifist you are, you cannot not be moved by it."

"The corps de ballet," agrees Giselle. "The films of Busby Berkeley."

"Hey, *any* film," Polly protests. "To say of a film that it is a film *by* the director is just a nonsense. Interestingly, one of the best directors, Sidney Lumet, won't have any truck with it. He takes credit as director, sure he does. He *was*, after all, the director. But he won't designate that it is 'a film by ...'. Any film is, and has to be, an amalgam of influences and talents and capabilities. At the very best – and this happens so rarely it is almost a phenomenon when it does –

the director gets to choose those other influences. But the producer, the studio executives, the agents, the stars ... they all have direct input there as well. The director's may be the most important influence, but it is simply not true that his is the *only* one. A film is no more *by* the director, than the moon-landings were 'by' the NASA controller."

"Is it that Man finds something pleasing," asks Rafaél, ignoring these last comments from Polly, "about a group of people working in harmony, or synchronicity, towards a common goal? I agree with you all, there is something splendid – something mayhap stirring – about a parade or a ballet or a great film. And all of which would seem to be at variance with the concept that individuality is a life-affirming idea. And yet is it? Isn't a part of our individuality our commonality and our community? The culture into which we were born or in which we live? And isn't that yet another enormous crime being perpetrated by globalisation that it is demanding the erosion of such cultures? Personally I find it offensive that, wherever in the world, McDonald's is allowed to build its anyway unattractive golden arches without any respect at all for the local architectural conventions or aesthetics.

"I remember the author Bill Bryson regretting in his books the disappearance throughout the United States and Britain of regional differences – differences that added enormous riches to our lives; regretting how much traditional local architecture was being swept away nationally, or internationally, by globally designed shop-fronts, how much local tradition was being lost, even how much folklore. How much greater must the loss be when such cultural extermination is world-wide!

"The arrogant disdain for urban or regional differences – or national ones – cannot be otherwise than indicative of a general disdain this ethos has for the individual and for the concept of individualism. I dread to think that the iconic figure of the new millennium is most accurately Dolly, the cloned sheep. I sense an atmosphere around me where those in power are seeking to make clones of us all."

Polly lays an interrupting hand on Rafa's sleeve. "The trouble today – *the* trouble, like there's only one! – *one* of the troubles today is that unconditional love has so many conditions attached to it. Parents love their children unconditionally, *provided* ...; we love our friends unconditionally, *provided* ... ; companies love their employees unconditionally, *provided* ...; I do wonder whether those who profess to offer unconditional love have bothered to find out what the word 'unconditional' actually means. We are expected to love things unconditionally, absurd things: our country, whatever it might be doing; our religion, whatever it or its ministers might be doing; our company, whatever *it* might be doing; our football team; the whole idea of competition and one-upmanship. We are also supposed to love things which have clearly become a travesty of themselves: democracy, human rights, life, liberty and the pursuit of happiness, free speech. 'Unconditionally' in these circumstances has come to mean 'unquestioningly'. And the only 'unconditional' that is, that is unconditional *hatred*.

"What globalisation seems to be telling the starving is similar. It tells them it loves them 'unconditionally', and will feed them consequently, *provided* that those starving are prepared to give to globalisation their entire commitment, their unquestioning loyalty, their own subjection.

"A medieval king who starved his peasants until they pledged fealty to him in exchange for bread would today, rightly, be considered as a barbarian. How do we make the intellectual leap not to see today's multi-nationals and the 'ethos' they create likewise as barbaric? And the governments complicit in such bondage? And yet such companies ask of us, and expect from us, the regard reserved for saviours and redeemers. So do governments. And in a way typified by the rewriting of history to whitewash the deeds of the Romanovs."

"It was not one thing that brought us to the abyss," says Rafaél. "It will not be one thing that pulls us from it, nor one thing that leads us to a place where a true civilisation can start to evolve. The seven deadly sins all intertwine, the seven fatal lies likewise – and with one another. So do the seven vital virtues, the seven life-affirming ideas. All is one. And so do the lies with the virtues and the ideas with the sins. They also intertwine, the negative with the positive, yin with yang. All is, yes, one. But if we start treating the whole body, we can use such intertwining. It will then indeed become a force for good. Is still, I believe, possible for a benign spiral to be created that will simply wipe out the vicious one in which presently we live. But it will not be for much longer that such *is* possible."

"We owe it to the future to try," says Giselle, her face still firmly in the sun's. Whether consciously or not, she rubs the foetus, folds her hands over it. The other three are still craning at the sun. They do not see this. But they all sense it. Rafaél, though, blinks open one eye … just to make sure!

Chapter 31

There'd been nothing on television. Saskja'd been feeling weary. She'd wanted to read. She'd retired early to bed. She likes the bed. Rafaél had treated himself to a good bed. She wants to know more about alcoholism. She's immersed herself in Catherine Barry's 'The House That Jack Built'. There is a knock at the door. She doesn't bid the knocker enter, but she does look up as the door inches gently ajar.

"Do you mind?" asks Polly's head peeping through the crack.

"No," Saskja replies. Then she decides such is not enough. "Not at all," she adds.

Polly comes in, stands awkwardly at the foot of the bed. "Do you mind?" Polly asks again, pointing to the foot of the bed.

"I do not think it would be good idea ..."

"Just to talk, Saskja." Saskja looks at her searchingly. "Just to talk."

"Please," Saskja invites her. But she pulls the duvet further up her chest.

"It occurs to me ..." says Polly, sitting. Then she gazes long at the floor – apparently at the Mexican rug of lime and orange which adds a touch of fiery tequila to the somewhat austere ale-and-whisky décor of the room. Saskja does nothing to prompt her. Eventually Polly resumes: "It occurs to me, Saskja, that you told me something and I did nothing to respond. Well, of course I did. But it was inappropriate."

"Abortion?"

Polly is taken aback by her directness, then taken aback that she had been. "Yes," she says. "It occurs to me, you were seeking help and I ... As I say, it was inappropriate."

"Took advantage?"

"I've come to apologise."

"No need, Polly."

"You needed help, sympathy, a shoulder ..." The sentence just runs out of puff.

"Polly, please to look at me." Polly does so. "There no need to apologise. If so, maybe me to you. I thought I wanted you. But what I did want, I wanted to be wanted. I felt so horrible, so ugly, so ... unhuman. I wanted, Polly, you to want me."

"You do know, right?, that you're lovely and so completely not unhuman."

"I'm beginning," says Saskja, "to learn. Giselle's boyfriend ... she told you this ... he was addict recovering. He went to Narcotics Anonymous. This she did tell you, no?"

"She did, yes."

"Through him I hear of CODA. CODA is ..."

"Co-dependents Anonymous. I do know. I even went once."

"Then you know. Co-dependent, Polly, someone as I. Someone who has no belief in themselves, except belief given to them by other people." She's making a point. She thinks it is with a scalpel, Polly hears it as a machete. "You helped me, Polly. Helped me very much. That night I saw it was that I wanted: I wanted to be wanted by you. I thought if you wanted me that would tell me I was wantable. Maybe even loveable."

"Don't work, though, do it?"

"No," says Saskja nakedly. "Maybe too this CODA does not work. I know I have to try. It my commitment to hope. You remember, sixth vital virtue?"

"And me? I should try Alcoholics Anonymous? Again, I mean?" suggests Polly, a light trill seeking to warble at the edge of her voice, but finding merely a caw. Saskja allows that caw to settle and then does nothing to fill in the canyon of silence which yawnily springs open.

"Yes, Polly," she says, quietly, deliberately, "you should."

"And, know what?, I know I should. But know what else?"

"You're not going to?"

Polly doesn't want that silence again. She does not want that silence again. She bulldozes on. "No. I'm not going to because, Saskja, I'm a coward. I have a terror, not of being sober, not even – I don't think – of reality. But I do have this fear – this *terror*, Saskja – that, if I strip off all seven veils, underneath there will just be nothing. It won't be that I'm naked, just vapid. I'm less in awe of my potential than terrified there is none."

"I think you would not find that. I think you would be nicely surprised."

"I'm a coward, Saskja, remember? Can't take the risk, my dear. Cannot take the risk."

"I sad for you."

"Hey, *I'm* sad for me. I should have let you talk, Saskja. I'm so sorry. You want to talk now?"

"Now, Polly, thank you, I have talked."

"CODA?"

"There were two women. After the meeting ..."

"You okay?"

"I know I will be."

"That's as okay as it gets."

"Perhaps."

"I don't need to be sad for you?"

Saskja snorts wryly. "No, you do not."

"Just one-way traffic, then?"

"Your choice, Polly."

"Think I'll just pop out for a moment."

"Pub?"

"Pub."

"Also, Polly, your choice."

"Yeah."

"'Night," Saskja says, and returns to her book.

***

There'd been nothing on television. Rafaél'd been feeling weary. He'd wanted to read. He's not wild about this bed. It's Mummy Bear's bed, far too soft. But the book's gritty, an epic love-story: Emily Hanlon's

'Petersburg'. There is a knock at the door. Rafaél looks up. The door stays closed. He gives it a little more time. "Come in," finally he says.

Giselle is a wobbly woman now, at this moment one of undiluted coyness. She's in her night-dress. It's not the one Rodolfo gave her for Christmas. Her hands now permanently grip the base of her distended womb, as if she were trying to balance a pile of twelve dirty dishes, all of them of different sizes; her back is now permanently crescented. Her eyes still glisten with fulfilment, but they are mascara'd now with fatigue. There is about her an element of what Sherpa Tensing must have gone through on the final ascent to Everest's summit: there is a sense of 'Thank God' and '*finally*', there is the anticipation of triumph, but there is also the first intimations of anti-climax – the pre-knowledge of the fact that, once you have got to the pinnacle, there is only one way to travel. Presently those eyes are fixed on toes she can longer see. For some time she says nothing. Neither does he.

"I need to be held," she says.

"So do I," he returns, and pulls the duvet back, inviting her within.

"My bed's more comfortable," she tells him.

"Right." He starts to wriggle up from the bed.

"I need, Rafa, *only* to be held."

"Yes," he says, "I understand."

She looks for a long time into his eyes, and he seeks to open up for her the view as much as he can. "I might also like to be kissed."

"I think I can manage that." He kisses her lightly on the lips. She'd wanted to wait till she was lying down to kiss him throughly. But suddenly she cannot wait. She seizes his head, and cements his lips onto hers.

When finally the kiss ends they say nothing. She takes his hand, with her other she scratches lightly the back of his fingers, and leads him to bed.

Chapter 32

They'd thought about Kew Gardens. But had decided no; if Giselle's waters broke in one of the greenhouses, God only knew how long it would take to get her to hospital. For similar reasons they had discounted the zoo. Saskja had been quite keen on visiting Madame Tussaud's. But Rafaél had said he'd been to too many cocktail parties with wax dummies to want to see more voluntarily; and Polly had said that if she wanted to see lifeless representations of human beings she'd watch a film with Schwarzenegger or Stallone.

They hadn't wanted either to visit Camden Market. Polly had even suggested that to call it a flea market was a slight to fleas. But Giselle reminded them it also contained probably the best ice-cream parlour in London, the Marine Ices. That had been enough to decide the matter.

These days, on the weekend, Camden Town underground station is closed to anyone wanting to depart from the station. So heavy is its human traffic that it can only be used as a point of arrival. Apparently London Transport, despite the substantial cost of its fares, considers itself under no obligation to provide a service adequate to its use.

This is a weekday, so this restriction does not apply. Polly merely makes the point as they jerk up the staccato escalator, its walls adorned with remarkably unseductive advertisements for local eateries and night-clubs.

In days of yore, Polly tells them, this had been the site of a scaffold. Once you know that, you can almost feel it. Before London Transport introduced the weekend wholesale closure, departing passengers had on such days to get to the platforms via a Poe-like and endless spiral staircase. Walking down them, Polly continues, did feel like the drop. It felt too like a plummet, like the helter-skelter to Hades, like the pier into the Styx. There was a smell of compound grime – or was it ectoplasm?; the screech of train brakes – or was it the howling of the hanged?; the clack-clack-clack of a thousand heels on metal rungs – or was it the rattle of keys unlocking the gates of Hell? 'Abandon hope all ye who enter here.'

Hell, yes – they all agree – is the abandonment of hope. How many of the world today have abandoned it? And from how many has hope been confiscated? *Confiscated*? Were they mad? From how many had hope been *robbed*? How many had been consigned to Hell on Earth? Only in order that a tiny handful can have Heaven on Earth? And is that, of itself, not a contradiction? How can there be a Heaven on Earth if that does not embrace us all? If the Garden of Eden excludes anyone, then – a long time before apples are ever eaten – Satan has won. And whilst it is true that without pain there is no pleasure, and that without death there is no life, it is perfectly possible to have wealth without poverty. Indeed, even within today's kamikaze economics, the wealthier the poor the wealthier the super-rich. There is no shortage of riches in this world, not even a shortage of money. The only shortage there is is a shortage of will to distribute these more equitably. They then berate themselves for having repeated themselves!

As they emerge from the station, a small detachment of policemen and -women are 'moving on' a ragged squad of apparent meths drinkers. The faces of the drinkers are florid, with that damson jam puce engendered by the mix of high-octane alcohol and freezing nights sleeping rough. The police are brusque because they can be. And they would argue they have to be. The drinkers yell resistance, vociferously and obscenely. But the resistance is as feeble as their legs. Shivers ripple through Polly's back. She ascribes it to the ghosts of the executed.

They turn to their left. There is an HSBC bank on the corner. Huddled beneath the hole-in-the-wall of which is a beggar, slouched on a flattened-out cardboard box, his black mongrel dog in a desultory slumber between his emaciated legs.

"You remember how, before he came to power, Mr Blair insisted his government would hold no truck with countries lacking in morality?" Polly asks. None of the others was in Britain at the time, so they don't. Polly continues, regardless: "It was a policy which (need I say it?) lasted probably under a month. Certainly under a year.

"A few years later, I saw a documentary on television, exposing the way that the HSBC had … let's say 'withheld' the savings of its Argentinian clients. Know what? I never saw an apology for that documentary, never heard of a libel suit. During Mr Blair's time in office – an office he vowed would be devoted to the morally upright – London's airports became virtually wall-papered with advertisements for HSBC. Arrive at Gatwick, and the whole place seems to be one giant advertisement for the 'world's local bank'. What a great advertisement for England! And for Mr Blair's 'third way': that banks are allowed an entirely different understanding of morality than apply to us humans – even to foreign countries. 'Do as I say, not as I do'. One highway code for commercial vehicles, and another for private ones. God, they seem even to be allowed a different understanding of *legality*."

Discreetly Rafaél drops a few coins in the cigar box nestling with the beggar for that purpose. "Thanks, man," the beggar says. Rafaél returns a small 'you're welcome' smile. They realise they are walking in the wrong direction, and retrace their steps. Again the beggar smiles at Rafaél. Who tries not to feel uncomfortable about that, but doesn't succeed.

"There are those," he says, "who oppose the charity of charities. (And were those, even before we became aware of how much charity money is being misappropriated.) 'Such charity merely propagates a system which creates the misery in the first place,' they maintain. Such people tend, in my experience, to be those who believe that the only way out of the inequity today is violent revolution. They would also argue that the world is anyway so violent today that violence is the only language that is universally understood. And they have a point. I do concede that they have a point.

"They also have, I think, a point when they maintain that those in power would rather, apparently, see the end of the world than the end of *their* world. And that, for the sake of any future at all, we need to eliminate such people before they eliminate the planet.

"But I'm afraid I'm a die-hard liberal. I have hope in mankind. I have hope that Man will understand in the nick of time just what he is doing to himself and to his world.

"Just like their detractors, I do not care for the existence of charities – nor do I care for the way in which so many of these charities are run. And, yes, it completely infuriates me when charitable funds are used further to fatten the already obese. This too I have said many times before. And will do so many times again. As I have also said, that these issues are less important than what the presence of these charities signify: an indication of the goodness of Man striving to express itself in tangible forms. That the greedy are prepared to take advantage of such goodness is yet another indication of how sick the greedy are, how sick is the institution of wealth, how sick is the ethos of methos. The lower 'I's of such people are losing the battle with their higher 'I's. And of course we want to hurt such people. We want to stop them hurting us not only directly but also indirectly – via all the other people these bullies hurt ... or maim ... or kill. If, though, we do start to hurt the bullies back, then likewise it is *our* lower 'I's winning the battle with our higher 'I's.

"Which is why violence is always self-perpetuating.

"Violence is not a bush-fire. By starting another fire elsewhere you do not weaken the power of the first blaze or deprive it of the fuel to continue: You merely have two infernos instead of one. There is only one way to stop violence and that is to stop it. It has to be, for me, a *sine qua non* not even of starting our civilisation, but of retracing our steps to where we took the wrong turn. If we resort to violence we will, in very short measure, be in exactly the same kind of calamity as that in which we now find ourselves. Bad blood between the Montagues and the Capulets always ends with the unnecessary deaths of Romeo and Juliet. Is a play the tragedy of which emanates not from the folly of young love but from the folly of old hatred.

"Is so simple: monetarism, globalisation, these are greed

dependent concepts. Greed is hatred. Violence is also hatred. Whenever one manifestation of hatred exists (in this case, greed), there will always be another: violence, for instance, or bigotry – which is only emotional, as opposed to physical, violence. And is hatred, finally – as, yes, I do know, I have said many times before –, responsible for where we are today."

Giselle says, "I remember reading of a Canadian teacher working in Thailand, obviously a woman of great spiritual commitment. She said, 'I live my faith by surrendering myself to Love.' I thought that was rather beguiling, as a description of faith, I mean."

"Could also be motto of whore," suggests Saskja.

"I'm a whore," Polly confesses. She'd maybe like this news to be received with rather more surprise than it is. "More and more this world requires of us that we become whores. Worse than whores. Sexual whores, what we find disturbing about them is not that they're selling their bodies, but that they're selling their intimacy. Plenty of people sell their bodies and we have no problem with that at all, from the fashion model to the manual labourer.

"I'm guessing when sexual whores sell their intimacy, they can detach their heads, possibly also their souls, from the intimacy they are selling. Us, the non-sexual hookers of this world, we are selling not our intimacy, but our integrity. Our sense of communal responsibility, our wholeness – and a man without principles is a man who is not whole.

"On the ever rarer occasions these days that I get a call to work on a commercial, I don't ask what the product is. I don't ask what the CEO of that company earns, nor what it pays its most menial worker. I don't ask about the conditions of labour, don't question the efficacy or benefit of the product, nor the ethos behind it. And if I did ask such questions I wouldn't be told. And I wouldn't get the job. Or any other – probably in the whole of the film business, least of all on another commercial. At best I would be thought a crank, more likely though I would be designated as a 'Bolshevik', as a 'trouble-maker'. Such questions would be deemed *entirely* outside my remit or my concern.

"And it suits us all for that to be the case. It means that sportsmen don't need to feel guilty 'sponsoring' or endorsing products manufactured effectively by slaves. It means we have no responsibility in the supermarket – where we are, at best, only choosing between two evils.

"It means that lawyers can sleep at night who are employed by tobacco companies to prove that smoking does no harm; or that PR executives can sleep at night who are employed by the NRA to propagate the palpable nonsense that guns do not kill people, that people kill people. It also means those doctors don't need to be troubled by their conscience who prescribe unnecessary and/or harmful medications, or who kowtow to the strictures of insurance companies. It means agents can sell insurance – or exact usurious interest rates, or enforce unjust laws, or manipulate currencies, or ... or ... or. And on and on. We are all hookers, all whores. Far, *far* worse than sexual whores. We are selling ourselves, our souls, our integrity ... we are also selling down the river our civilisation and our humanity."

They are walking over the canal bridge. They stop for a moment to gaze along its muddy length. For all its cityness and murk, for all the battles fought within its lack of depth, it still, the canal, teems with stillness, with a serenity that can be caught more easily than its fish. There is a tourist barge chugging at its mooring. What looks like a class of Spanish school-children, about eleven- or twelve-years-old, is yappingly embarking, their two custodians chihuahuaing Hispanic invocations. In this context even that is peaceful.

"Virtually every religion," Rafa resumes, "(certainly that I know anything about), every political doctrine claims as its basis love. Love, charity, in this context, is the same thing, no? We have to start demanding of those who claim to love that they do *actually* love.

"And I know 'love' was also our first vital virtue. But is *such* a good idea, love, that mayhap it deserves to be both a vital virtue *and* a life-affirming idea. Let us concentrate today on that aspect of love which is the most loving: the act of charity, the act of giving. The act too of *for*giving – yes, this homophone is a coincidence which probably does not occur in every language. But, thinking about it, the same is true, if not quite so evident, in French, Italian and Spanish. Is certainly true that, in whatever tongue, the act of forgiving is also an act of charity – the main beneficiary of which is, as with all charity, ourselves. The act of forgiving, finally, does less to improve the lives of others than it does to improve our own lives.

"No oxymoron in history was greater than a 'holy' war. Is not *possible* to fight for God. Even when Hitler was being fought, the fighting was still godless. World War Two was not fought *for* God, just against the embodiment of evil.

"Is not, I repeat, possible to fight *for* God. Or for Life or for Truth or for Love. However you define God, or however you choose *not* to define God, once you have resorted to fighting, God has disappeared. I'm not talking about the master-puppeteer God, I'm talking about any definition you may care to think of as being the dynamo of the world, the spirit behind humanism quite as much as that of any of the Hindu gods or gods unique to some tribe in the remotest reaches of the Amazon.

"You cannot possibly pretend to love God and hate the so-called 'infidel' or those who are of a different culture to you, or a different colour or gender or sexual orientation ... or, in fact, anyone. You cannot love God and burn witches or heretics, fly jets into skyscrapers, bomb embassies or cities. You cannot *kill* in the name of God. If God is anything – and God *is* something, even if we use God only as an allegory for the impulsion behind life – then God is Truth and Love and Life. Is Satan who is the Untruth and Hatred and Murder. Of course our world is set to destroy itself. We live in a world dominated by hatred and Untruth. Is *therefore* there is violence and mayhem. And worship of the lie.

"Of the holy books that I have waded through – and I don't pretend to have understood any of them clearly – I would say it was impossible to live by all the tenets contained therein. Each of them contains too many paradoxes, too many contradictions. That's alright.

That should be alright. Language is a very inexact form of communication – witness the success of lawyers. Such holy books should be guides, no more, to finding for yourself your own principles.

"When clerics urge us to interpret such words as invocations to hatred, even if their interpretation is correct, God's word has somehow been distorted. Sometimes such misinterpretation is even provoked by pure intentions. But we have no more right to believe their nonsense than someone has for committing mass murder because she doesn't like Monday. Indeed probably even less right than that mass murderer, because we are talking, not about the insanity of an hour, but establishing an institution of permanent insanity.

"More often than not, though, the misinterpretation is not provoked by intentions that are pure. More often than not, is a cynical way to either riches or power. How is it that the televangelists of America are so wealthy? Why do rabbis and mullahs seek political power? Maybe the hatred of such people for our world (or for themselves) is so intense that they do wish to see it destroyed. Are we really so lazy, so indolent, so unconcerned about the future that we're going to let them also destroy us? How is this not the Reverend Jones again? When, as they so often do, politicians also spread their manifestoes of hatred, we do not need to vote for them. And we need to be vociferous when we do not vote for them. Just not going to the polling station is not enough. And when, as they will, they stop us from protesting, then we must protest about our inability to protest. We do have choices. Eventually government cannot survive without complicity.

"Nor can banks.

"'Twas also ever thus that banks and governments were in collusion. Today so much that the latter insist we use the former – indeed use our money to bail out the former. Having said which, there are things we can do even about our banks.

"I find it most hopeful that one of the banks here in the UK is selling itself as being morally responsible. We know Barclays got richer from apartheid, the actions of the HSBC in Argentina were ... well, not their finest hour, the Swiss banks continue to benefit grotesquely from slush funds – even still from the Holocaust! The Co-operative bank, though, is now advertising that it does not, and will not, lend money to repressive regimes. I think it behoves us to respond. To start banking only with those banks who follow the Co-operative bank's lead.

"I was told, for instance, that the Spanish banks charged for handling monies destined for tsunami relief. I have no idea whether or not that is true. The Bank of Santander, though, is seeking global expansion. I would welcome its public assurance that such were indeed *not* the case. Without which assurance, of course, one must assume such statement to be true. In which case, of course, the first billionaire racing driver, Mr Hamilton, has his wealth courtesy of the world's poorest – and from money designed to help those poorest. How is that not Sheriff of Nottingham economics?

"It should be a requirement that banks should make such records available, and that their falsification be a criminal offence. Such is an act quite as anti-social as defrauding the Social Security. If the banks choose to protest about such legislation, we can be left to draw our own conclusions why they are protesting.

"The Co-operative bank now also advertises the fact that it will not lend money to warlords or abusers of human rights. I think we should demand that of all banks. We should all start demanding to know of our banks their record on human rights, of their countenance of torturers and repression (sadly, these days, including our own), of the profits they have made from robbing the world's most vulnerable. How it is that a company supplying torturers is worth $65 million on the Stock Exchange?"

"We do have power. And we do have choices. If the media continue to broadcast their messages of hatred, we can stop watching or listening or buying their newspapers – or reading the free ones.

"At the start of our friendship, Polly and I, we were talking about how very interesting is today that many companies are trying, in their advertising, to prove their green credentials, or prove how philanthropic they are. Soap-powder is being sold today as being in smaller packets so that less carbon is emitted by their transport, energy-saving light-bulbs are being distributed free by one of the power companies, some products now advertise that they are 'fair trading' or that a percentage of profits will go to situations which need help or money. The cynical would say this is all marketing. And only the incredibly naïve would not hear many of such claims with the same scepticism as that, drinking a Martini, you will suddenly be in a hot-air balloon floating over your castle in Spain or that smoking a cigarette will make you irresistible to the other sex. But such scepticism, I think, largely misses the point.

"The point is that *of course* companies are doing this to steal a march on their competitors. But what's considerably more important is that they also think that the way in which to do that is to appeal to the basic goodness in us all, and no longer to that part of all of us which is greed or vanity or lust. And what does that say, finally, about the goodness, the charity – and the *wisdom* – of *us*? That is the point we should draw from this evidence. Even ten years ago (as we also talked about, Polly and I, the first time we met), oil companies were trying to imply that Friends of the Earth and Greenpeace were just latterday beatniks, or politicised tree-huggers, hopelessly and dangerously out of touch with economic and/or ergonomic realities. Those selfsame companies today are vying with one another, trying to convince us that their company is even more environmentally concerned than their competitor or competitors.

"Talk about a quantum shift! What mountains that speaks for mankind's growing wisdom, and for the power contained within an ethos. How far along the journey does that carry us from methos to wethos! Wethos, finally, is only charity. And charity is only giving. Is more blessed to give than to receive because the act of giving is the act of construction. Methos rarely allows us to receive. When we get in methos we are usually taking. Often we are stealing.

"And often the icons we are taught are paragons, they are urging us to steal. Another starting-place for wethos: let us start admiring those admirable indeed and not those whose celebrity is demeaning both to us and to them.

"If mancruel *is* to become man*kind*, and if humanity is to become humane, it must start – not with President Sarkozy's nonsense about making capitalism sexy – but with making giving sexy. And is so easy to make giving sexy.

"The best sex is always the sex when one is giving of oneself most absolutely to one's partner. Its consequence is that one is able to receive so much more. Methos, finally, is masturbatory. Gratifying often, sometimes even necessary, but finally sterile. Wethos is adult sex: incredibly powerful, enormously enabling, that which (finally) makes life possible.

"We need to give till it hurts: our money, our time, our commitment, our love, ourselves. Is *that* which is your worth to me. Is that which is *my* worth to me. Is that our worth as humans and as humanity."

They start to walk again, further along Camden High Street, towards Chalk Farm ... and ice-cream.

"The most expensive press in the world is the giveaway press. Because with it we give away so much of the right of access we have to facts inconvenient to government or industry. Is no more a giveaway than a free sample is a free sample. We pay for it. It comes out of an advertising or marketing budget which forms part of the cost of the goods we buy, whether such be a pound of butter or mascara or life insurance or motor oil. And with this giveaway press, or giveaway broadcasting, we give away control of what we hear to the manufacturers and money-lenders and merchants. Is finally that simple. 'He who pays the piper ...' – is it not this, the expression? – '... calls the tune.'"

"It's the golden rule:" says Polly. "'He who has the gold makes the rules'."

"Witty, of course, and like much real wit, uncomfortably true," says Rafa. "How is this not plutocracy? And how is plutocracy not hatred?"

They are entering the sacred portals of Marine Ices. They are hushed as if entering a cathedral. They come to the altar and drool: the display cabinet, a tutti-frutti *of* tutti-frutti. They decide to have two scoops each, and to relish their eating walking along the canal bank they have so recently passed.

"Is interesting though in the midst of so much hatred how love is just beginning to show through the thorns," says Rafaél, having slurped off enough of the raspberry sorbet summit to avoid it dribbling down the side of the cone. "Is interesting that Professor Chomsky claims he is today being listened to with greater courtesy and attention than he's ever been used to. That, as we just talked about, so many companies are frantically trying to demonstrate their eco-responsibility or their humanitarian concerns.

"Is also interesting that government and industry want to keep more and more secrets from us. Why else would Mr Blair's administration and President Bush's have passed such devastating legislation? I suspect is because they fear exactly what I am talking about: the basic goodness in us all. Governments have controlled us for centuries by appealing to the lower 'I' in all of us. I sense that – albeit very slowly – the higher 'I' in us all, the loftier, brighter, kinder, more committed, more spiritual, more giving part of us is coming to the fore. Mayhap is that which is indeed what the much-anticipated Mayan prediction is all about, that for December 2012, mayhap is that which will prove to be the real dawning of the age of Aquarius. Slowly ... very slowly, but, it seems to me, inexorably ... slowly we are shedding our hatred for ourselves, and finding ourselves worthy. That sense of worthiness will make us much less malleable. Those who know themselves to be worthy won't stand for being abused or short-changed or lied to."

They are passing the Roundhouse. Polly and Rafaél had not passed it again since first they met. They say nothing. But they acknowledge the fact in a silent ice-cream toast to the other.

"We need to stand up and be counted," says Polly. "We need to defy government. It is part of our responsibility to freedom. More and more today, if we are serious in our commitment to democracy, if we are serious in our commitment to the future, more and more we need today to defy government. We need to defy authority. Wherever it appears to come from. Because in today's duplicitous status quo, one thing is almost always for certain: actual authority is never where it seems to be.

"That guy – remember, we were talking about it? – who was thrown out of the Labour Party Conference for heckling? Thrown out and then arrested. The delegates countenanced that violence when they sat in their seats. The conference hall should have emptied. That would have sent a message to Mr Blair, and to all other politicians with his ambitions, that would have resonated throughout his term of office and for some time into the future. I recognise that we all make mistakes, that we all miss the boat on occasions. But their inertia on that occasion increased the electorate's ever increasing cynicism about government's commitment to their welfare, and to concepts like civil liberties and freedom of speech. Those delegates must accept their responsibility for that.

"As Mr Cameron (the leader, Saskja, of Britain's main opposition party) must accept his responsibility for furthering such cynicism. When Mr Blair resigned, Mr Cameron did not censure him, but paid tribute to the outgoing prime minister's 'diligence' and 'integrity'. The whole House of Commons must also accept *its* responsibility. It rose in an unprecedented ovation. This may be good party politics. But it tells the electorate, all these statesmen, they're all in league together, as bad as each other, as corrupt and self-interested as one another ... just warmongers in the wings, war criminals in the making."

"What is the seventh life-affirming idea?" asks Giselle. They walk down the steps by the side of the canal. Giselle's not too sure how clever a plan this is, but resolves she will simply sit on the first bench she comes to. The weather is icy, but it is bracing. Before the trio can gather their thoughts, Giselle prompts them with her own answer:

"For me, it is humanity."

"Humanity is not just another name for charity?" asks Saskja.

"Humanity in both senses is the seventh life-affirming idea," says Giselle. "I think the idea of humankind is a wonderful one. I have never had a problem with that famous Zen conundrum, 'If there is no-one there to hear it, does a tree falling in a forest make a noise?' It seems, that conundrum, to wonder whether events occur only when there is a perception that they occur. It seems to me that whether or not the tree makes a noise is almost irrelevant – except insofar as it may startle a rabbit who then runs into the path of a starving vixen, which then has milk enough to feed her young which would otherwise have died … and so on forever until you get to a butterfly in Brazil causing a hurricane in Beijing, or wherever the theory would have it that the hurricane occurs. The point of the tree falling is that the local eco system requires the tree to fall. Noises aren't made, carbon wasn't created, wildebeest and moose don't migrate in order that these things can be experienced.

"I've heard that, if Man were to vanish from the world tomorrow, in a thousand years there'd be virtually nothing left of his achievements, not a book nor a painting or a note of music. Presumably a few skeletons …"

"And a zillion tons," adds Polly, "of Styrofoam."

"What a tribute to man!" says Giselle. "In a hundred thousand years, bits of the faces on Mount Rushmore may still be recognizable as human shapes, but nothing else. The planet, though, would thrive. And we can hope that another evolutionary trek would start at the same time which would lead, 'Planet of the Apes'-like, to another intelligent species. We have to hope of somewhat greater intelligence than that which we collectively have demonstrated; with an intelligence which is informed by charity – rather than a charity which is informed … well, not really by intelligence but presently by a lack of intelligence. No, that's not true either. We have human beings who are enormously kind, enormously giving and loving … our problem today is that we have created an ethos where humanity's humanity is stifled, where humanity is enjoined to lack humanity. Let's hope that the next evolution is a humanity where the word has only one meaning."

"Hear! hear!" says Polly.

"Was it you, Rafa, who said?: 'The grace of God is not evinced by the beauty of the rose; the grace of God is evinced by the recognition that the rose is beautiful.' I agree with you. What a real tragedy it would be, what an abnegation not only of God and God's grace, but of thought and imagination and beauty and love and life ... what a total contradiction of all that that it would be to have this beautiful, beautiful planet with no-one or nothing on it to recognise how beautiful it is. The Victoria Falls, the Grand Canyon, a stalking tiger, a polar bear playing with her cub, a field of poppies, a butterfly, the Alps in spring, the smell of sweet peas, of grass drying after a downpour – and no-one and nothing to appreciate this lusciousness of beauty.

"You talked, Polly, about the disenchanted young, about the most efficient way they have of radicalising themselves and of irritating the status quo is by loving themselves ... well, part of that process might be for them just to open their eyes. I don't say that in its usual judgemental and school-teacherly way. I say it gently.

"Look.

"Look at all the beauty all around you. Look deeply. Look at all the beauty of those close to you. It's natural, we all of us notice the ugliness every day. How often do we recognise the specialness of people close to us? And how often, in them, do we expect *our* specialness to be recognised? That's just so sad. Multiplied, it becomes a tragedy. How often do we notice the specialness in our streets, our cities, our villages? Even our slums? How much *beauty* is there to be found? I don't excuse slums. I think slums are a scar that wealth has slashed across the face of the poor. But there *is* still beauty there. Great beauty, colossal beauty. Just as there is colossal goodness, a vast amount of humanity in humanity. If we start to see how much beauty there is around us, we will start to see that it is not *their* job to rescue the planet (whoever '*they*' is), it is ours. All of ours. When we start using our eyes, we have to start seeing too that *they* will not do it, so we have to.

"They have only what it takes to take.

"We have to find what it takes *to do* what it takes. We have no choice. If we say there is a future, we have to ensure there is one. What it takes is to give. To give till it hurts. And then some more. Give so much you receive ... everything. Any chance one of you could grab a taxi?"

"You tired?" asks Rafaél.

"Well," says Giselle, "I need to lie down. But I rather think in hospital."

Chapter 33

Even now her breath comes in gasps. It stabs at her lungs, already pierced with a thousand stilettoed wounds. She wants to flick away the sweat tickling between her breasts, rilling from behind her earlobes, but she cannot find the strength. A nurse dries her with a towel, mops her down almost. Giselle pants a smile at her, then lolls her head back to Rafaél, and squeezes his hand. Her eyes are now so heavy. They want to close – woo, there's a twinge again. They so want to close, her eyes, and yet never has she been more awake in her life, nor more anxious to stay awake.

Her baby had been taken from her, just to clean "baby" up, just so Mummy sees a bundle of joy and not a squidge of gore and mucus. She lets go of Rafaél's hand, and, holding the Crown Jewels made of Dresden china, she takes the baby to her breast.

Back in the stone-flagged chapel ... there she had, she thought, felt herself completely holy and wholly complete. ... No, no. She has no need now of a past; no need of a comparison between feelings then and now. This is not akin to anything else. This is not even close to being akin to anything else. All is one. And this is all.

Pregnant she had felt complete. But she now knows, it is the act of separation that is the real act of completion. As in so much in life, another paradox: separation is the key to completion. Rafaél takes the small hand-towel, rubs away the beads of perspiration still forming on her brow. He smiles beatifically at this Madonna and child. She is a Madonna ... and the baby, as all babies, is the Saviour of the world.

The gasps are starting slowly now to ease into breaths. Soon into long breaths. And then she is asleep.

Chapter 34

Runnymede is the site on which, without too much enthusiasm, the English King John (who was in fact Norman) signed the document known as Magna Carta. This was not, as is commonly but erroneously supposed, a people's charter, but a charter which protected the barons. But, for all its feudal intent, it started a process towards safeguarding civil rights. A process which had, with a few hiccups, been jerking along in one direction until the advent of the new millennium.

There is little distinguished about the place of Runnymede. It is a flat stretch of grassland meadow giving onto a frequently fast-moving Thames. A brace of willows weep undramatically into the water. The grass is delicate and springy and of a green struggling in the newish year for lushness. It is a ground for picnics, not for putsches.

They are driving Polly's car, and are en roundabout route to drop Saskja off at Heathrow. The following day they'll be back at the airport waving goodbye to Polly. She feels the need to visit her parents. She may even look for some work whilst she's home. She's no idea when she'll be back. Could be a couple of days, could be a couple of years. It's crazy, she'd told Rafa a few days previously, to keep on his apartment. He's living with Giselle now. She'll be fine. When she gets back, she'll get something sorted out for herself. Please use the car whilst she's away. It's the least she can do, the absolute least. Besides, it'd be good for the car: turn the engine over once in a while.

They say nothing, the five of them, because there is nothing *to* say. Who knows what babies think? But the four adults are solemnly in their own todays. Today, though, cannot be complete without the promise of tomorrow; and all tomorrow can promise, without a respect for the past, is more of history's disrespect for the future. To live in a now stripped of past and future is to seek fulfilment in the quick fix. In which, even during the momentary illusion of happiness, speaks that still, small voice of sanity advising you to "get real", to "stop kidding yourself". For the now to *be* now, there has to be an appreciation of both history and mystery – learning from one to improve the efficacy (and likelihood!) of the other. And, of course, words are often needed to exchange information or opinions. But sometimes the oneness of all just needs to be absorbed. This is one such moment.

Big Bang was equally one such moment, an infinitesimally tiny fraction of a second. But into which all time was encapsulated. Now is an even smaller fragment of time. Even in the time you have thought about now it is gone. And yet now is all the time since Big Bang and all the rest of time until time is no more. All is one.

And – *of course* – it is our responsibility to have the best today we possibly can. But the best today is not a today which ignores tomorrow. I may have the right to allow my tomorrow to look after itself; I do not have that right over *your* tomorrow.

"The history of Britain," says Polly, "has been the history of monarchs and their subjects. That's been the history of most peoples. There've been good monarchs and bad, good subjects and bad. But that has been their story. The people have been 'subjects' because their will and their potential has been 'subjected' – to the caprice of the monarch or to the safety of the realm, whichever. It has still been subjected. The potential of the many has been sacrificed for the potency of a few. It's not for the comfort of the few, not for their benefit – history has proved time and again that not to be the case – merely that they can exercise power. Some control in a world where Man has such little control.

"Surely what history teaches us is that the comfort of us all – the monarchs included – lies in developing the potential of us *all*. The future has to be not one of monarchs and subjects, not of clerics and contumely and crusades, not of nations and wars, not of greed and a neurosis to control, not of them-and-us, not a rapacious, insatiable methos. But a wethos where my highest achievement is the improvement of our lives, where I am no longer working for myself or him or for '*them*', but where we are all working for us."

The baby, Alex, starts a spluttering cough. All four are still parental neophytes and rush to check that they are not involved in a life-threatening drama.

They have come to Runnymede not just as sightseers, but to make a pledge. They have spent some hours in the last few days writing this pledge. It is to Alex. They take turns now to read this pledge, and these pledges, to the baby. Magna Carta was signed on this ground. It is on this ground therefore that they think it appropriate they sign what they have called the 'intima carta' – the intimate charter:

Dear Alex,
Watching you sleeping as we now are doing, we cannot but recognise the enormity of the privilege with which we have been endowed - the űber-privilege. We are the witness to a miracle. There can be no privilege greater in the world than to be witness to a miracle. It saddens us that birth's frequency has perhaps blinded mankind to the miracle that it continues to be, that it will always continue to be. There is no miracle in the world greater than the creation of another life. All man's achievements - the *sum* of man's achievements - are, by comparison with that miracle, mere incidentals.

We spent a lot of time yesterday gazing at your form - a form that is still struggling to define itself as a form: a blob, almost, seeking shape. We don't say this to demean you, quite the contrary. This is all so such a great part of the miracle of birth and of evolution ... the miracle, Alex, of life.

You don't know what your fingers are for.

We spent, all four of us, hours yesterday gazing ... at you, on you ... and within you. Hours. And we saw you, blowing gentle bubbles, concentrating fiercely, eyebrows squished together, staring at your fingers. You were trying to figure out what the Hell they were for. And we wondered how anyone could ever have imagined there were original sin when we're born not even knowing what our fingers are for.

Oh, you've certainly inherited genes which contain devilry; yours are genes (judging by the actions of your forebears) overflowing with the milk of mischief, and curdled abundantly with the whey of selfishness. And you will have inherited genes and traits which you will need to curb, and some that you may even need just to stop. And you will need to curb and to stop them because, ironically, they will be stopping you becoming the most 'you' you can become.

Most of your traits, though, our dearest Alex, you will need to encourage, even those you may be punished for. Naughtiness is not sin. And the world would be a dull place indeed without some naughtiness in it - the pranks and japes, the impishness and impudence.

Real what-is-called 'naughtiness' you will also be punished for. Those who hanker for the Truth are nearly always punished. And real what-is-called 'naughtiness' is not a misdemeanour, not even a peccadillo. Quite the contrary. It is life-affirming and planet-saving. It is heretics who advance faith. Those obedient to tenets they do not challenge cause their 'faith' merely to atrophy. It is bohemians, even anarchists, who develop morality. Progress is never the statement. It is always the question. It is always deciding which is the *right* question.

There are in this world far more sins, and far greater sins, of omission than there are of commission. The complicit have been guilty of infinitely more species-threatening actions than the dissident. The complicit sold human beings into bondage, they buried such slaves alive to escort their emperors to the underworld; the complicit committed acts of genocide, annihilated civilisations, countenanced wholesale rape and looting; the complicit burnt 'heretics' at the stake, made war in the name of peace, killed in the name of their God - killed in the name of peace; the complicit built concentration camps and gulags and extermination camps and killing fields; the complicit are allowing globalisation. The Buddha was a dissident. Christ and Muhammad were dissidents, Copernicus and Galileo, Einstein and Charlie Chaplin; Emily Pankhurst, Mary Stopes, Mary Gaskell, Florence Nightingale, all dissidents. As were Gandhi, Mandela and Martin Luther King. Even Lech Walesa was once a dissident.

We look at you, Alex, and we see the blob that you are: a blob of limitless potential, an amorphous blob just bursting with an amorphous potential, as all that is limitless is amorphous, as all that is holy is amorphous. And when those around you seek to contain you, seek to limit your potential, that, Alex, is the start of the lie.

Magna Carta was a pledge. This, this 'carta' of ours, this charter, this 'intima carta', this too is a pledge, a succession of pledges. Magna Carta was a concession wrested by the over-powerful from the super-powerful. Because there have been dissidents in the world, that charter has come to signify a protection for us all. That protection is now, we recognise, being severely eroded. We pledge that we will strive to reverse that.

We pledge ourselves to strive to expose all the world's liars and their lies. We pledge that we will strive to find ways through the intimate catacombs of deceit that have been created, that we will strive to find ways to expose the lie, the Untruth, the lack of truth, the half-truth, the not-quite the truth, the obfuscation and the lie by omission. We acknowledge that such is one of the most sacred jobs Man can do on Earth.

We pledge that we will strive to alleviate suffering so that you can strive to alleviate suffering; pledge that we shall search for the precious so that you can strive for what you consider to be precious.

We also pledge to you this:

That we will strive to inculcate again into the world the very simple fact that ALL LIFE IS A MIRACLE.

All life, Alex: yours, ours, that of an Ethiopian villager or a Javanese fisherman, of an Amazonian tribesman or a Mississippi gambler. Even that of a misguided economist or a self-glorified rock star! The life of an aardvark is a miracle, so is that of a zebra; of a redwood or a clump of moss ... of the planet Earth itself, Alex, of the moon and the sun and the whole incredible - miraculous - universe.

All life, Alex, is a miracle. And it is right - it may even be incumbent on us - to venerate the miraculous. To adore and worship the miraculous. Even to prostrate ourselves before the miraculous. Perhaps that is the reason why even the most 'primitive' of tribes indulge in some kind of worship. (We encase the word 'primitive' in inverted commas because we are none of us as convinced as our world would seek to convince us that such tribes are anywhere near as 'primitive' as they are designated.)

It is not only *our* life which is miraculous, that which belongs to us, not just the lives of those of our ken or kinship, not just those of our country, our continent - not even those only of our species. Not even just all animal life. All life, Alex. Because finally life is all life.

And we do, yes, have to take life. It's, sadly, the price of admission. As far as we know, there is no way around that. Even taking plant life is taking life. But in taking life we can still venerate it. Maybe a moment's quiet pause before we eat to remind ourselves that others have forfeit their lives in order that we could survive, maybe that (after all) is something appropriate for us to do. Maybe it would help us to remember how fragile all life is; it would maybe encourage us to venerate life, to nurture our wonder, to imbue us again with senses of both humility and humbleness.

A bowl of flowers is beautiful. And it's completely right, it's even essential, that we recognise its beauty. But it's also right that we nurture an awe of the miracle represented by that bowl of flowers. Just like us, those flowers are the product of billions of years of evolution. It is maybe one of the most fundamental reasons why today we are in the parlous situation that we are, because we have forgotten the miracle that is all life. We need to recapture that awe if we are to survive ... if we are to advance towards creating a civilisation in fact. And when we do recapture that awe, and when we recognise the beauty of those flowers, let us also take a moment or two to reflect on the further miracle that we are capable of such awe and recognition. Such indeed may well be the point of life: the search for the precious. And therefore the recognition of the precious when we meet it. And such indeed could also be called the grace of God - even if there is no God in your life beyond the recognition of miracles.

That is our next pledge: to strive for a world where everyone's God is their own God, or their own lack of God. Atheists are just as capable of recognising the miracle of life as the mystic or the shaman. Perhaps even better. Agnosticism, we urge you always to remember, is not a spiritual depth but a spiritual height. There is more truth in an honest scepticism than in an unchallenged faith, more truth too in an acknowledged ignorance than in a feigned cognisance - there may even be more *knowledge* in that ignorance.

Both atheists and agnostics can (for their part) start to realise that, because they may not believe either in religion or in the God as depicted by any religion, such does not preclude them from believing in God. Our Gods - the four of us writing to you - are all entirely different. All of them are also entirely our own. One of us has no 'God'. But even she who is without a 'God' paradoxically is aware of the divine within her. And this is part of this pledge. We pledge further that we will strive with you to find the divine which you contain.

We pledge to you as well that we will strive towards a world where all schools have mirrors, and a world where all schools encourage their pupils (and their staff) to look into those mirrors

- where they, Alex, encourage you to *look* into the mirror. Not to adjust your hair or groan about your zits, but so that you can see you as you really are: a personification of limitless potential. Until you have seen that potential, until you have absorbed the fact that such potential is limitless, you have not looked into the mirror, you have only glanced. And we further pledge that we will be there with you any time you need company whilst you look, any time you need support because the look is scary, any time you need encouragement because it's daunting. And we pledge to be there for you too when, having seen the limitless of your potential, you start also to see those flaws in you which will restrict that limitlessness, which will contain and confine it. We pledge we will be there to help each time you seek to remove motes from your eyes.

Eyes that are less moted, our dearest Alex, can look into mirrors and behold then the whole class with you there, the pupils and the teacher; can behold the whole school, the street it's in, the city. Eyes that are less moted will see the county, country, continent; humanity, the planet and the cosmos. And they can see, Alex - as you will see - the limitless potential of it all. And that their potential is as yours is, is indeed indivisible from yours: if you limit that potential you limit *your* potential. We pledge that we will help you to see all this.

Our next pledge is also to do with looking. We pledge that we will strive to create a world where you can look that world in the eye - the world itself and everyone that's in it. You cannot look someone in the eye if you are stealing from them, or if you have just bought their daughter, or if you are abusing them. If you are a thief or an abuser, if you are benefiting from others' slavery, should you be able to walk tall, you can do so only from bravura.

Such wealth as we today have in the West, our dearest Alex, that is the wealth of the criminal fence: It is wealth dependent on trading stolen goods.

We pledge to strive towards a world which allows you to be

an honest citizen, which does not require you, in order to enjoy a comfortable life, to countenance, even espouse, an economic system which involves theft, torture, kidnap, extortion, mendacity and mendicity. And contempt. For everyone who isn't within your immediate social circle. Contempt for colleagues, for countrymen, for clients; contempt too for law, for morality, for principles - contempt even for fun, for laughter ... the most enormous contempt for love.

We pledge to strive to return laughter to the workplace, to restore dignity to it, and respect. We pledge to work hard to ensure that your hard work is noticed and appreciated; we pledge to work hard so that your hard work is not exclusively *professional* hard work - that you have energy left for the other hard work of your life: raising children, perhaps, or helping in the local hospital or school, painting your pictures or your bedroom, playing soccer or tiddly-winks or the banjo or Banquo.

Unless all men's rights are respected, those he has to life, liberty and the pursuit of happiness, then no man's rights are. There is no such thing, Alex, as *their* civil rights. All civil rights are ours. We pledge to strive that the world you live in understands that, not at an intellectual but at a visceral level; that the world you live in understands that agreements like the Geneva Convention and the United Nations' Charter on Human Rights are not labyrinths within which lawyers can play chess, but unassailable statements about the dignity of Man as it pertains to all of us.

We pledge to strive for a world where your representatives are that: *your* representatives; a world where those representatives are obliged to listen to you and where, if they are found to be lying, it is mandatory that they forfeit their office. We will strive for a world where companies are required to listen to your complaints and to respond to them. We pledge to strive for a world where there is only one set of laws which govern all human conduct, and where in civil suits both sides are allowed only to spend the same amount for their legal advice.

We pledge our devotion to the dream of Martin Luther King and the aspirations of Nelson Mandela and the Mahatma Gandhi (and indeed the speech at the end of Charlie Chaplin's 'The Great Dictator'): That, via a policy of *ahimsa* (of strict non-violence), we create a world where it is not taking but giving which is an indication of worth, where there is prejudice only against the inequitable and intolerance only of intolerance; a world where fights don't become wars and justice is not confused with vengeance.

We pledge our devotion to a world where, if you are hurt, your hurt is acknowledged and attended to before you need to hurt someone back. We pledge our devotion to a world which talks very much less and listens very much more.

We pledge our devotion to an end of conquest and to the start of co-existence and co-operation. When we seek to 'conquer' Nature or space or the elements we abuse them. When we 'dominate' we tyrannise. And tyrants are eventually always overthrown. When we conquer others we do not create vassals but enemies. And when subjects become subjugated we foster, not love, but searing hatred. We pledge our devotion to love.

Perhaps since Man first stood erect, and certainly in the last half century, Man's watchword has been: 'Number one is number one.'

Ironically, it's even probably right. If, that is (as quantum scientists are beginning to believe), *all* is one. If all *is* one, then it is perfectly acceptable to believe that number one is number one, because one is therefore all and therefore the maxim could be interpreted as meaning that 'all is all'. And all *is* all. As all is *one*. And, of course (in that context), *one* must be all. Which, in turn, means unequivocally that when we subjugate the poor in Argentina or Zaire, in London or in Lima, in Orphalese or Syracuse, it is ourselves whom we are mistreating. Abusing and abasing. And demeaning. We are self-harming in a way almost identical to those unfortunates (too often in prison) slashing at their body parts with razors or swallowing sharpened toothbrushes.

As it is applied today, though, that slogan should more properly read: 'Number one *makes* a number one' - 'number ' (the second time) in the sense of more numb, less feeling: Such adoration of the ego has to desensitise us. Such self-aggrandisement is not true love of self. The love of ego, Alex, is not the love of self. Such aggrandisement of self, in fact, however paradoxical, has to make that self a lesser self. It has to. Which is, we suspect, one of the reasons that Eastern philosophies see 'ego' as so dangerous.

The world in which today we live demands we desensitise ourselves. The pain would else be too great to be supportable. You cannot possibly be true to thine own self, you cannot possibly become the most 'you' you could be, you cannot possibly reach your full potential if you desensitise yourself, or allow yourself to be desensitised. It is as impractical, as insane, as do-it-yourself heart surgery.

Maybe slogans of themselves are dangerous. Maybe they encourage the belief that there are universal panaceas to individual ills, sound-byte solutions to complex problems. 'Make Love Not War' was a good slogan, though. And so is: 'Let The End Of Life Be *A* Life'.

And here's another, Alex: even shorter. It could be the banner we unfurl over the Arc de Triomphe which celebrates our new evolution. Or it could be the shroud with which we drape the corpse of civilisation. Three words, Alex, two the same:

'Humanity for humanity.'

It doesn't matter which meaning of humanity you use in which part of the slogan. They all work. They all ... *work*.

Because finally the utter madness of 'Number one is number one', the dementia of methos, is not its callousness (grotesque though that is), not the extreme of its injustice - not even the unspeakable degradation and cruelty and genocide it inevitably trawls in its wake. Its monumental, and cataclysmic, lunacy is that it doesn't even work. It is incredibly inefficient. Because it is founded on hatred it has to breed hatred. And hatred has to trawl violence. Violence will eventually taint the lives even of the überwealthy.

'Wethos', on the other hand, cannot not work. 'Humanity for humanity', Alex, that cannot not work.

We pledge our devotion to 'wethos', we pledge our devotion to 'humanity for humanity'.

Because, Alex, we pledge our devotion to you: to your potential, your protection and your future.

We cannot protect you without protecting us all. Just as there is no such thing as *their* human rights, so there is no such thing as discretionary protection. Either we protect you and mankind and the planet, or we protect the institution of wealth.

We think the choice you will face is stark: civilisation or barbarism, respect or contempt, freedom or bondage, creation and creativity or destruction and destructiveness, the striving for an unreachable Utopia or the settling for an ever more present Hell. The choice, quite possibly, Alex, between life and death.

But it is *we* who think the choice is stark. And we acknowledge that. As we also acknowledge that we do not know what we do not know. Perhaps time will determine that the choice is not so stark. It's important, though, that choice remains open to you.

Will methos give you choice? The evidence seems to be growing (and growing ever more irrefutable) that methos seeks to confiscate choice. Or rather, that it seeks to convince us that a choice of television set is a fair exchange for a choice of government.

We pledge to strive for a world in which, by the time you are old enough to make choices, choice will still be available to you.

'Number one makes a number one', Alex? Or 'Humanity for

humanity'?

Methos or wethos?

Choose wisely. The future of the species depends upon your answer.

We sign this all, with all our love -

It is then that they all sign the intima carta. They seal it within an envelope and put it by Alex in the baby's pram. It's a gesture, and only a gesture, and they all know that. But they all know also that it *is* a gesture, and one not without significance. They are pledges which are that: oaths which honour binds them to honour. Not everything old-fashioned is passé.

Runnymede is grey now, and dank. Just the weather for roast boar and venison and mead. But the rain is holding off. Not, though, for much longer. They scuttle back to the car. Find their way back to the M4.

Windsor Castle eyes them stonily and autocratically as they drive past. The Royal Standard flutters in a swelling breeze.

They park in the short-term carpark. Terminal 2 is, as ever, heaving. Even halfway through March. The Alitalia flight is, they notice, on time. Check-in takes only a few minutes. Rafa and Saskja say their goodbyes. They are very much '*au revoirs*'. Both Polly and Saskja are relieved that their adieux should be so devoid of embarrassment or awkwardness or clutter. That is all now behind them. Before them is a friendship no less close for being geographically so distant.

Polly and Rafaél stay with Alex and the pram. Giselle walks Saskja to the security gate. A tubby little girl in pink dungarees, her light brown ringlets anarchically tangled, collides into them. Her mother slaps her own exasperated thighs, admonishes the girl in German and apologises to the women in a heavily Teutonic English. Then she turns to, and on, her bespectacled husband. Clearly wondering why it was always she who has to watch the child.

"You should have told me," Giselle says. "About the abortion, you should have told me." Saskja blushes. Words will not come. She could easily cry. "It would just have been easier, Saskja. For both of us."

At the gate they hug. Long. Hard.

Giselle pulls her from her breast, looks at her longly, lovingly. "God bless you, Saskja," she says. "And please – Saskja, *please* – remember also Arkona's plea: Please do not forget also to bless yourself."

"God bless us all, Giselle," Saskja returns with an enigmatic smile. "God bless us, everyone."

The End

Or is it?

Would we not be better off if it proved to be

*** **The Beginning** ***